D0009628

Village

BRUCE ELLIOT

AVON
PUBLISHERS OF BARD, CAMELOT, DISCUS AND FLARE BOOKS

VILLAGE is an original publication of Avon Books. This work has never before appeared in book form.

AVON BOOKS
A division of
The Hearst Corporation
959 Eighth Avenue
New York, New York 10019

Published by arrangement with the authors
Library of Congress Catalog Card Number: 80-69987
ISBN: 0-380-79020-3

First Avon Printing, January, 1982

Printed in the U. S. A.

WFH 10 9 8 7 6 5 4 3 2 1

When you're driving into New York City from the west and see the skyline of Manhattan ahead of you across the Hudson River, there's no easy landmark to point out where Greenwich Village is. It's somewhere in that nondescript low area between the skyscrapers of Wall Street and the skyscrapers of midtown.

But the Village doesn't need any landmarks to give it distinction. It's a neighborhood that has remained almost intact while the rest of the city goes on tearing itself down and rebuilding. In contrast to the orderly, numbered cross streets of the city surrounding it, it is a confusion of narrow streets lined with modest brick and brownstone town houses, their Dutch stoops and iron railings leading up to colonial doorways, streets with historic names like Barrow, Bleecker, Horatio, and Perry.

There aren't as many artists living there any more, though that's what gave it its reputation—not since the rents started going up a couple of decades ago. But it still attracts the kind of people who want to live in a place where anything goes and no one cares. And for as long as anyone can remember, that's been the Village's story.

But it's not the whole story. Sometimes, when the streetlights cast a phantasmal glow on the mid-nineteenth-century housefronts—after a winter snowfall, or maybe on an airless summer evening just before a thunderstorm—even with all the parked cars and garbage cans, you might almost expect to hear the clip-clop of a horse and carriage over cobblestones and think yourself back in an earlier time, when other people lived here—

Book I

1845

On a sultry evening in July, the parlor windows of the house on Perry Street were wide open to catch the breeze. By the light of an oil lamp, two women sat across the table from each other, their fingers resting lightly on the back of a saucer that was sliding over the letters painted under dark varnish. They were playing planchette. As if the saucer had life in it, it was pulling their arms from side to side and their bodies were swaying in their chairs as they followed its path over the glossy tabletop, waiting for the arrow marked on the saucer's rim to start spelling out a message.

They were trying to contact the spirit of a girl who had lived generations ago in the ramshackle old mansion across the way. The oldest house in the area, its ghostly presence could be seen through the open windows in the moonlight, set among ancestral trees. It had been built long before the Revolutionary War in the midst of what was then a tobacco plantation.

Back then, the village of Greenwich was only a jumble of huts at the river's edge where Indians, escaped slaves, and ne'er-do-wells lived. But the village had gradually spread, hemming in the mansion, until now with its barns and outbuildings the old house was confined to a single square block across cobblestoned Perry Street.

Miss Ethel Swindon, the older of the two women, was

watching with approval her fragile charge, Mrs. Fanny Endicott, who was taking such delight in communicating with the spirit world, when the saucer beneath their fingers stopped abruptly. Then, as if searching among the alphabet, the arrow painted on its rim began to point out letters.

"M-E-T I-N-D-I-A-N B-Y R-I-V-E-R. F-E-L-L I-N L-O-V-E," Fanny read off breathlessly while the saucer continued its mysterious progress.

Although she was twenty-two, with a baby daughter asleep upstairs and an infant son dead two years before, Fanny Endicott still looked hardly older than a schoolgirl. Her auburn hair was parted in the middle and arranged prettily in curls on either side of her face. She was wearing a flowered calico dress, a crinoline billowing out the skirt under the table. "But how wicked to be in love with an Indian!" she said, her eyes shining.

Miss Swindon reproved her gently. "Don't talk, you'll scare her away." The somberly dressed companion had been hired by Thomas Endicott to look after his ailing wife when they moved up from the city to the village of Greenwich several months before. Fanny needed constant attention because of her neurasthenic spells, but Miss Swindon had no trouble coping with them. She was not intimidated by such behavior, having cared for a variety of invalids before. With her wide knowledge of patent medicines, she had perceived immediately that the best thing for the spells was Dr. Angel's Magic Elixir, a tincture-of-cannabis remedy she herself found ideal for all kinds of female complaints. By this time, there was no doubt in Miss Swindon's mind that she had become quite indispensable to the Endicotts.

Her employer had made it clear that he disapproved of the planchette table as hocus-pocus, but she disagreed. She was convinced that spiritualism would eventually heal the imbalance in her mistress's delicate nature that brought on her spells.

Miss Swindon had introduced planchette to many of her former patients. She believed that encouraging an interest in the spirits prepared them for the imminent death they faced. But she had never been attached to any of them before as she was to Fanny and, unlike them, Fanny was certainly not dying. Her young mistress had the unaffected sweetness of a child and a pure soul, and it was Miss Swindon's observation that as long as that goat of a husband wasn't around, she never had any of her spells at all.

Today he was down in New York getting supplies for his printing shop and would not return until later. Whatever Thomas Endicott thought, she saw no harm in their talking to the spirits. It made Fanny happy if nothing else, and that was the important thing.

"Ask her about her half-breed baby," Fanny was begging. They had talked to this spirit many times before, but like a child with a favorite story she could never hear it often enough.

Tilting back her head in its embroidered prioress cap that emphasized the sharpness of her profile, Miss Swindon called out in an awesome hypnotic voice that Fanny loved, "What happened to your baby, Lavinia?"

A breeze from the open windows made the oil lamp beside them sputter and sent crooked fingers of shadow clutching at family portraits on the walls. Fanny shivered with delicious goose bumps as the saucer beneath their hands spelled out that Lavinia's enraged planter father had his daughter's dark bastard drowned in the Hudson.

"How terrible," Fanny said, but her high color showed that she was more entertained than saddened by the tragedy. "What happened next? Hurry and ask her please!"

In the same resonant voice Miss Swindon asked the long-dead Lavinia to describe her own fate, while Fanny's eyes sparkled.

As they had heard so many times before, Lavinia's father had her Indian lover strung up on the great oak tree still visible in the moonlight behind the mansion across the street, one of its branches blackened by lightning. The unhappy Lavinia had died shortly after of a broken heart and was wandering forever, lost in the other world.

The saucer spelled out "G-O-O-D-B-Y-E" and came to a stop, lifeless beneath their fingers.

"I don't want to stop yet. It's too early," Fanny said petulantly.

Miss Swindon regretted that her charge did not yet have the proper attitude to the spirit world. It was just ghost stories to her. Fanny might be a wife and mother, but she was still so little experienced, how could it be otherwise? "You're not too tired, my pet?" she asked.

"I'm wide awake."

"Just a little longer then," said the older woman indulgently. "Whom shall we contact next, Abigail Adams or Anne Bradstreet?"

But before Fanny had made up her mind, steps were heard on the stoop outside, and the saucer came to life again under their fingers, sliding back and forth from the letter M to the letter A.

"Perhaps we had better stop," said Miss Swindon, knowing full well who it was turning the key in the lock, but she did not take her fingers from the moving saucer.

"No," Fanny cried, as the saucer continued its urgent swooping. "It's spelling M-A-M-A, don't you see?" She was too distracted to pay any attention to the door. "Chester's calling me!" This was her first child who had died of the plague down in New York.

"Hello! I'm home," Tom Endicott called from the hallway and came into the room with his package of printing supplies. Not much older than his wife, he was fair-haired and boyish, but wore a perpetually anxious expression.

Miss Swindon instantly took her hands off the saucer, bringing it to a stop. Whenever he came into the house the mood changed.

"He needs me," Fanny was repeating, ignoring her husband. "Chester needs me."

Miss Swindon stood up, her face impassive as it always was in front of her employer.

"It's my fault," Fanny wailed, clutching the saucer to her breast. "I didn't have enough milk. I never should have given him out to that wet nurse."

Tom dropped his package and ran over to her at the table. "It wasn't your fault, Fanny dear. Chester died of the yellow jack, you know that."

She turned on him, her pretty face contorting. "Don't lie!" Her voice had taken on an ugly edge. She put out her arms rigidly to hold him off as he tried to comfort her. "I know what happened and I won't be talked out of it."

Miss Swindon was already getting a green bottle of the elixir from her reticule.

"But he's dead. The baby needs you now," said Tom, snapping his fingers frantically at Miss Swindon. "Can't you hurry, woman?"

Unruffled, the paid companion poured some water into a glass from a pitcher and measured out a few drops from the bottle.

Fanny was on her feet and pounding the table with her fists

so that the oil lamp rocked. Tom snatched it away just in time and put it on a shelf.

"I won't shut up!" she screamed. "You can't make me."

He took the glass from Miss Swindon, and holding his wife by the arm tried to get her to drink it.

"No!" she cried as she wrenched her arm away, her hand striking him on the face. And then began the terrible litany of obscenity he had grown to dread.

"Come, Fanny," said Miss Swindon firmly, moving Tom aside and catching a flailing hand to hold it like a wounded bird against her bosom. Then she took the glass from Tom and held it out. "Now, drink this."

At Miss Swindon's touch Fanny broke off her screaming. Mouth still open, her dilated eyes seemed to focus on the older woman's commanding face. Without a murmur she let the glass be put to her lips and drank it down.

Immediately she was quiet and looked around in confusion as if she had just awakened. Tom put an arm around her and she leaned against him docilely, his own wife-child again, and he helped her up the stairs.

The crisis was over. Despairing as he was that it had happened again, he was in a fury at Miss Swindon for upsetting his wife with that spiritual nonsense when he had told her not to. He would talk with her first thing in the morning, and this time he was not going to listen to any argument, even if she was the only one around who could handle his wife.

In the privacy of their bedroom, lit softly by a hanging oil lamp, Fanny lay her head against his shoulder. "I'm so sorry, Tommy."

It was the ethereal voice of the girl he had fallen in love with and it moved him so deeply he had to clear his throat before he could speak. "I understand. Why don't you go to sleep now."

He pulled back the counterpane on the four-poster bed and laid her down gently, curls framing her face on the great goose-down pillow. It was always so remarkable how fast the look of frenzy disappeared.

Her eyes were dreamily tracing the intertwined lattice roses on the wallpaper. "I'm such a worry to you, aren't I? I don't know why you put up with me," she said, reaching out for him.

He sat down next to her, pushing aside the billowing crinoline of her skirt, and stroked away the damp hair from her forehead. "Fanny, I wish you wouldn't play planchette. It always upsets you."

She took his hand in hers, holding it close under her chin. "But I keep thinking of little Chester. He was only three months old when we lost him, poor baby." Her lips started to tremble.

With his free hand he touched her cheek, gone so pale. "But it's Veronica who needs you now," he said, reminding her once more of their neglected infant on the floor above with only a nurse girl for a mother.

"Veronica?" she asked as if she hardly remembered. "Oh, yes . . ."

He had hoped that having a second child might erase the memory of their dead son and cure her of the horrible spells. He leaned closer and said, "Why don't you take Veronica out to the park tomorrow?"

Ignoring this, she put a hand on his cheek. "Poor man, it's you who needs looking after."

He brushed away the last of her tears and his heart began to pound, responding to this rare show of concern. "You do care about me, don't you, Fanny?" Through the thin calico of her dress he could feel the softness of her shoulder she had not let him kiss in so long.

Pushing his hand off and looking away, she said in a remote voice, "Mrs. Atkins hasn't been taking good care of you. We've got to find a permanent hired girl."

She was rejecting him as usual. He gave up and fell back hopeless across the foot of the bed.

She raised her head, holding down her crinoline so that she could see him. "Is anything wrong, Tommy?"

He didn't answer and stared at the ceiling.

"Don't be like that." She got up on her knees and leaned over him. "I know I haven't been doing my part, but from now on I mean to see the house is run properly myself."

Seeing her small breasts falling forward against the shirred bodice, he softened, unable to resist pulling her down and giving her a kiss. She giggled and sank against him, letting him stroke the back of her neck. He deliberately went slowly, not to frighten her. When she allowed him to do this he could forgive her anything, but it was rare that she did. These past two years since the baby died he had gotten so little fulfillment.

Everything had been perfect until then. She had let him make love to her with the docility of a good wife. But after

Chester's death she started fighting him off, until he would give up in despair.

Gently, as though it were a game, he maneuvered her over onto her back. Then, leaning on an elbow, he trailed his fingers over her bodice and began to recite her favorite poem. *"I was a child and she was a child, in this kingdom by the sea, and we loved with a love that was more than a love, I and my Annabel Lee."*

She was actually smiling, one finger toying with his hair. Maybe, Tom thought, this time she would let him. Delicately, he started undoing the buttons of her dress, trying not to breathe too loudly. But her smell of innocence was too much for him and he fell on her, taking her lips hungrily.

Instantly she was alive, fighting him off, hissing, "No, no, no," like a trapped animal.

For a moment he was out of his mind, wanting to force her. She belonged to him. He had a right to her. But her voice pierced through the pounding of the blood in his ears. If she started screaming, Miss Swindon and the baby's nurse would hear. He gave up as he always did now and lifted her back onto the pillow. It was difficult to move her because she was holding herself so rigid, her knees locked against him.

Hiding her face in the pillow she said in a faraway voice, "Don't be angry, Tommy, please."

"It's all right," he said, turning down the lamp. "Go to sleep."

TOM WAS TOO AGITATED TO SETTLE DOWN IN HIS STUDY with a book. He took his hat and stepped out into the warm night. The moon had gone behind a cloud and a single gas lamp cast a circle of light on the cobblestones. All was still except for the rasping of insects from the grasses and shrubs around the old mansion across the street and the occasional mooing of cows at Hinkle's dairy in the next block.

He hated it out here in Greenwich. It was as desolate as the upstate town he had run away from. He started walking toward the river, hoping for a breeze from the Atlantic.

He and Fanny lived in a row of attached brick houses that had been built a few years before in the simple Federal style. There were empty lots on either side of the row. Farther along the street more brick houses were going up to the corner. A brook gurgled among piles of building materials before disappearing into a conduit under the street. Houses were being built everywhere in the area now, filling in the last of the empty fields.

But Greenwich was still very much a village on the city's northern fringes, connected by a stagecoach along rut-filled Greenwich Street down to Battery Park at the harbor. Although New York was rapidly expanding north along Broadway—the main road that ran the length of Manhattan Island—the village remained a place apart, almost a rural backwater where people still kept pigs and chickens.

A lonely dog howled at the night sky and was answered by the yipping of foxes somewhere off in the hilly ground and marshes on the outskirts. Tom shivered.

In the sky to the south he could make out the faint glow of the thousand gas lamps in the city. Lower Broadway and the Bowery at this hour, he knew, were thronged with people filling the saloons and theaters and other night resorts. After months of exile up here he resented more than ever having had to leave the city he loved—and all the more because the move had failed to make Fanny better as he had hoped. In fact she was worse—he couldn't deny it any longer. He was at the end of his rope.

Tom Endicott had grown up in Binghamton, a mill and shoe factory town beyond the Catskills, raised by a strict uncle who owned a printshop. It was a barren childhood and at sixteen he had run off, hitching a ride on a wagonload of shoes to Newburgh-on-the-Hudson where the driver got him on the barge transporting the shipment down to New York City.

He found a job as a printer's devil in a large firm on Chambers Street and took a room in the house of a dry goods merchant named Slocum who lived behind Trinity Church. The Slocums were the first real family he had ever known. All the children treated him like a brother, but it was Fanny, the eldest daughter, he became most attached to.

Sitting together in the sunny bay window of the back parlor, he and Fanny often read the latest work of Edgar Allan Poe. Tom always identified her with the ethereal heroine of the poem she loved the most:

> It was many and many a year ago,
> In a kingdom by the sea.
> That a maiden lived, whom you may know
> By the name of Annabel Lee.

Sometimes while her mother was in the kitchen and her younger brothers and sisters played and shouted outside, Fanny seemed so soft and vulnerable beside him that he found himself trembling with desire for her. When she asked him what was wrong he blushed, knowing that someone so completely innocent couldn't even image such things.

Lust had always been a problem for him. Once, in his room over the printshop back in Binghamton when he had been indulging himself with an onanistic fantasy about rescuing a virgin tied to a stake, his uncle had caught him at it and beat him with a cane, warning him he was heading for insanity. After that whenever the urge came over him he tried to resist it, but to his shame he couldn't.

Much as he ached for a woman, the prostitutes waiting on South Street under the bowspirits of the clipper ships at the wharves repelled him. Only a pure woman would satisfy him, and that was only possible within marriage.

At nineteen he decided to ask for Fanny's hand. He was already a pressman by then and his future was secure. But it was with some hesitation that he approached Mr. Slocum, since he earned barely enough to support a wife yet.

Surprisingly, the dry goods merchant made no objection to having him as a son-in-law. He even promised financial assistance as long as he needed it. He could be of further help to him, he said, since he was a member of the Tammany Club, a group of concerned citizens who kept watch over the city government to see that it stayed honest and helped business.

During their engagement, Fanny's willing caresses worked him up to such a pitch he could hardly keep from pulling her to him in a frenzy. But on the wedding night, when he let himself go after holding back for so long, it was as though he was committing some barbarity against her. Afterward, he was ashamed of himself and did his best to comfort her. Still, as a dutiful wife she knew her husband's rights were not to be denied, and from then on did her best to hide her natural distaste for his lovemaking.

After the birth of their first child she didn't have enough milk and had to give the baby out to a wet nurse just as the annual summer epidemic began. When the infant died Fanny was guilt-stricken, though Tom tried to make her understand that it wasn't her fault—or the wet nurse's either. It was the yellow fever, brought in—as everyone believed—by clipper ships from oriental ports. No one gave a thought to the dank wells they got their drinking water from.

Fanny was never the same again. The doctor diagnosed her condition as a severe neurasthenia, and advised that they have another child as soon as possible.

But the birth of Veronica the year before only made it worse. Fanny showed little interest in her second baby and became adamant about keeping Tom off. Most painful of all, her "irrational outbursts," as the doctor called them, began. In a flash she could change from his beloved Annabel Lee to a stranger possessed by a devil. Those soft lips were capable of shouting the most awful things.

She couldn't be left alone any more. But the woman he found to stay with her quit after witnessing an attack. Later, even the hired girl left in tears.

It was her parents, the Slocums, who urged him to put her away. They were afraid no one would marry their younger daughters if there was a question of "severe instability" in the family. But Tom would not hear of an asylum.

The doctor suggested that moving up to Greenwich might be a better solution. The village to the north was set on higher ground and had long been a refuge from the epidemics that regularly struck New York. Away from the city's hubbub and with plenty of fresh air, the doctor saw no reason why Fanny shouldn't get over her fixation about the dead baby and in time become her former self again.

The Slocums had shown themselves almost too eager to help the young couple move out of town by buying the house in Greenwich for them and advancing Tom the money to pay for Fanny's care. In fact, he was beginning to suspect the reason they had been so anxious to marry her off to a poor printer like himself in the first place. She must have had a long history of mental disorder and they had kept it from him.

Since he had brought her up here her parents had all but abandoned her. The mother had only come to see her once, the father never, and her brothers and sisters were forbidden to have any contact with her at all. He doubted that they ever mentioned her name any more.

For a while he tried to hold on to his job at the printing plant down in the city, but coach service was unreliable. Getting there for the night shift was almost impossible, and chancy even during the day since Greenwich Street ran through marshy land along the river and the coach often bogged down in bad weather. He was forced to give up the job, and with additional help from his father-in-law—grudging this time—he made a down payment on a printing shop on Bank Street a few blocks away from his house. But even if he was able to make a living doing jobs on a handpress, he didn't like it as much as working with a crew on the large rotary presses down in New York that turned out books and periodicals.

One of his immediate problems when they came to Greenwich had been to find another companion for Fanny. After asking around, the wife of the German tavern keeper down the street recommended a woman she knew who had cared for invalids before.

Fanny was devoted to Miss Swindon from the start, but Tom had never liked her, feeling her sharp eyes on him whenever he wanted to be alone with his wife—and especially when they went off to bed. She was careful enough to efface herself during the times she wasn't needed by keeping to her room, which was next to theirs on the second floor. But even then he felt her accusatory presence.

Fanny's condition made it impractical for them to have much of a social life. They were invited over by the neighbors at first, but he always went alone, offering the excuse that his wife was ailing. It soon got to be accepted that Fanny did not go out, except for church. "Dear Mrs. Endicott's health" did not permit much visiting, and "what a misery it was for poor Tom."

The moon had come out again. At the end of the street the Hudson gleamed on the incoming salt tide from the Atlantic. The river looked as serene as it must have before the coming of the white man. Just a few miles away to the south, ships and schooners lined the waterfront of New York City, but aside from barges, only steamboats or an occasional sloop bound upriver for Kingston or Albany ever passed here.

Ahead of him, accordion music was coming from a small tavern. It was the Four Winds, where he had heard about Miss Swindon from the tavern keeper's wife. He was not one to frequent the local taverns, although whenever he went down to the city for supplies he liked to stop in for a beer at one of the vast, ornate saloons on Broadway. Now, hearing the cheerful din, he had a yearning to pass some time among ordinary people to get his mind off his troubles.

But as he was about to go in, the swinging doors burst open and four husky Irish seamen hoisted out a sailor whose head lolled down in a drunken stupor. "Into the horseshit with ya, ya limey bastard!" they bellowed, and tossed the sailor onto a pile of manure and straw at the curb.

Clapping each other on the shoulders and soundly pleased with themselves, they pushed their way back inside.

He changed his mind. It wasn't his kind of place. He was about to walk on when his arm was taken by a burly young man with a beard and a lion's mane of hair.

"Don't be alarmed, friend. They're all good lads. Come in and I'll stand you a drink."

The man's eyes were gentle in spite of his rough appearance. Even if some of the patrons were disorderly, Tom didn't want to be alone. He let himself be led inside.

The tavern was crowded and noisy, and he immediately felt better. To his relief, he saw no one he knew. He couldn't bear the usual well-meaning questions, the eyes always looking away out of politeness and embarrassment when he put on a good face about Fanny.

It was a humble place compared to the saloons down in the city, poorly lit by a couple of patent lanterns hanging from the beams. The customers seemed to be mostly fishermen and bargemen from the river who lived with their families in the older wooden houses close by. Seated at one end of the crowded bench along the wall was the accordionist, an old seaman wearing an earring who was playing a rollicking tune called "Blue-Eyed Bonnie."

"Brew for two thirsty bards of the open road, Fritz," Tom's bearded guide called out when they got up to the bar.

It was an odd way to ask for a beer, Tom thought, but Fritz Unger, the big-bellied tavern keeper, seemed to take it in stride and good-naturedly set about filling two steins at the tap before putting them down in front of them. He recognized Tom and greeted him warmly with a handshake.

Tom's companion took out a snuffbox and offered it, and when Tom declined, took a pinch himself. "My name's Whitman," he said. "By trade I'm a scribbler for the *Brooklyn Eagle*, but I write poetry for my soul."

Whitman didn't look like a journalist, in his workman's corduroys and an open-necked shirt under the jacket, but his speech left no doubt that he was an educated man. In fact, Tom was the only one in the tavern in a broadcloth coat.

"Don't let him recite any of his long-winded verse to you, Mr. Endicott," the bartender said in his guttural accent. "It will put you to sleep for sure."

Whitman laughed, his eyes like a friendly lion, and blew the foam from his beer. "Better to put a man to sleep, Unger, than to poison him with your free lunch." He picked up a piece of herring from a dish on the bar and popped it into his mouth.

The tavern keeper shook a fat finger at him and went over to help his stout wife roll in a new keg of beer and lift it up to the bar.

The journalist was delighted to hear that Tom was a printer. "I've been looking for someone to publish a chapbook of my new poems," he said, pulling a sheaf of papers from his jacket. "This is the kind of poetry America needs, Tom." The tawny lion's eyes looked at him, glimmering. "The kind that sings with a big voice."

Tom tried to explain that as much as he liked poetry, it wasn't the sort of thing he printed. He wasn't set up for it yet.

Whitman held the manuscript out to him. "Will you read it anyway? That's all I ask, friend."

In good humor, Tom took it and tucked it away in his pocket. Then, turning to order another round, he got a look at the large painting hanging in the shadows above the bar. A voluptuous nude lay on a buffalo skin with one arm around the head of the beast and the other holding up a smoking six-shooter as if she had shot it herself. She looked real enough to pinch.

Whitman took in his reaction and laughed. "Like it, huh? That rusty-haired chap over there painted it." He pointed to a young fellow with a droopy mustache at the end of the bar sketching away on a pad.

Tom stepped back to get a better look at the painting and the heel of his boot crunched down on the toes of a barmaid coming up behind him.

"Ow! Divil take it!" the girl swore under her breath, plopping down a tray of empty mugs on the counter with a bang. Holding on to the bar, she bent over to rub her foot while he tried to apologize, feeling like an idiot. But she surprised him by breaking out into laughter.

"What are you trying to do to our Molly," Whitman boomed, "trample her to death?"

Tom turned red at the teasing. "I feel terrible—I didn't see her—"

"Pay no mind to that blatherer," the barmaid said, drying her hand on her apron and holding it out to him. "I'm Molly Hanlon, sir. Pleased to meet ya."

She couldn't have been much more than nineteen with a kind of robust good looks that come from health, rather than the pale fragility Tom usually preferred in women. Her lively eyes were blue and her black hair was piled up in curls, with the locks falling haphazardly over her forehead.

As he took the warm, damp hand and gave his name, he flushed again.

She and Whitman laughed. "Whatever brought a gent like yourself in to mix with the likes of us?" she asked, looking him over.

Her familiarity was embarrassing. He was always shy with women, not to mention immigrant working girls. And her teasing him about being a gentleman just because he was wearing his city clothes made it worse. He mumbled something about Mr. Whitman having brought him in.

"Oh, I see, it's like that, is it?" she said with a wink at the journalist as she picked up a full tray of beers.

His blood was pounding as he watched her move off buoyantly among the rough men.

"She's a peach, isn't she?" Whitman said jovially. "Just the kind of woman we need in America." He took a long swallow of his beer in tribute to the barmaid.

Shouts came from the front of the room. The "limey" sailor was staggering back in through the swinging doors, straw sticking to his soiled middy blouse. The four seamen who had thrown him out rushed forward to clap him on the back like an old friend and brought him up to the bar where they ordered him a pitcher of ale.

Tom was feeling completely at home by now and asked Whitman whatever made him come to this out-of-the-way place instead of to one of the big saloons down in the city.

The poet looked around approvingly at the colorful water rats and their rowdy camaraderie, and answered, "You might say, sir, that I come to loaf and invite my soul." Then, seeing Tom didn't know what he was talking about, he laughed. "I mean, I always have a whale of a good time in Greenwich."

Tom shook his head. "If you were forced to live up here like I do, you wouldn't be saying that." He sipped his beer morosely.

"Doesn't sound so bad to me," Whitman said, his lion's eyes taking on a golden hue. "To my way of looking at it, Greenwich is a magic place."

Across the room the old accordionist broke into a polka and two drunken bargemen holding on to each other began kicking up their heels.

"And it's not just half-baked poets like me who say so," Whitman went on. "The Indians thought it was magic up here too." He had done a newspaper story he said, on the Canarsie tribe who once lived around the lower Hudson. Greenwich had been a part of their land and they considered it sacred ground. Medicine men came there to have visions, and they held all kinds of ceremonies, from rainmaking to powwows.

"Oh, come on, Walt, I don't believe a word of it, do you, Mr. Endicott?" the tavern keeper broke in, filling mugs with rich dark beer from the tap and setting them out on the tray for the barmaid.

"I'm not making it up, Fritz," said Whitman, raising his voice over the hullabaloo as the two bargemen polkaed around the room. "The Canarsies had a legend to explain it. They hold that the sun goddess was shot out of the sky once by a magic arrow. Everything went dark, and you know what? She fell right here on Greenwich earth."

"Beggin your pardon, lads." The barmaid with the untameable curls pushed her way between them to pick up the tray, her womanly figure in its tight apron brushing against Tom. Whitman gave her round bottom a pat. She slapped his hand off, hoisted up the tray and, turning around, threw Tom a bold smile as she left that made him uncomfortable. For a moment he could hardly concentrate as Whitman went on with his tale.

". . . Their sun goddess was as juicy as that one," he said, nodding with his mane of hair toward the barmaid. "Naturally, the earth god woke up when she fell into his lap—who wouldn't? I don't believe I have to spell out for you fellows what happened next."

"He fricked her true, is that it, Walt?" said a giant of a young sailor with corn-shuck hair and a freckled face who had come up behind them.

"Billy, my boy!" Whitman exploded, and swept him into a bear hug. "You've said it exactly. It lit her up again and sent her soaring back into the sky." They went into a huddle as the poet bombarded his sailor friend with questions about how the cod fishing had gone off the Banks.

Tom sipped his beer. It was a silly yarn. He knew damn well nobody but an eccentric poet would ever come to Greenwich for a good time, much less any gods out of the sky. Whitman was sociable enough, but he was a queer duck. Look at the way he was carrying on with the freckled-face galoot.

He turned to survey the room and leaned back with his

elbows on the bar, catching occasional glimpses of the busy barmaid laughingly exchanging banter with the rough-talking seamen. It wasn't that she was pretty exactly. She was too fleshy for his tastes.

"She's a good girl, isn't she, Mr. Endicott?" Fritz Unger said behind him as he rinsed out mugs in a wooden tub, and went on to tell him that she had come over from Ireland only three months before. But she was hardly off the boat before she had made the mistake of marrying a fellow countryman who turned out to be a brute and beat her up. She was running away from him when Mrs. Unger met her on the coach coming up from the city and offered her a job. "Such a hard worker, Molly is, and so cheerful," he said, shaking out the mugs. "The tavern is no place for a girl like that, but my wife is here and it's all we can do for her."

When Tom finally paid up and said good-night, he caught one last sight of her across the room, carrying a tray of steins out to the back. It was as if she knew he was looking at her. She turned and smiled directly at him, before pushing through a door marked Beer Garden and disappearing.

It was nearly midnight. Although the village streets were as quiet and deserted as before, he inhaled with pleasure the smells of summer flowers and foliage and sharp river air. He had drunk half a dozen beers, but he was remarkably clear-headed.

It wasn't like Binghamton after all. Though the glow in the sky was mostly gone, he didn't need it to remind him that he was on the edge of the city here. And if he didn't work for a big printing firm any more, there might be advantages in having his own shop. To begin with, he was his own boss.

He bent over to drink at a public pump at the corner, letting the water splash over his face. It tasted so much fresher than the water down in the city.

He couldn't get over the barmaid looking at him like that. Yet for all her sass, she was certainly no loafer—and she didn't let anyone trifle with her either, that was clear enough. He had to hand it to her. She hadn't taken the easy way out. So many girls who went through what she had would have ended up on the streets.

An idea struck him. He had been intending to go down to the immigrant station at the Battery to hire a girl just off the boat. Mrs. Atkins, as Fanny had reminded him, was only filling in since their last hired girl had quit. Was it possible that this barmaid might be interested in the job? He couldn't afford to pay her all that much, but he had no doubt it would be as good as the tavern. Working for a family would be better for her than a public bar. Unger himself said it was no place for an honest girl. He wondered how she would feel about the idea.

As he climbed the stoop, taking out his latchkey, he was whistling "Blue-Eyed Bonnie" under his breath.

Fanny was not asleep yet. She was propped up in the four-poster bed, trying to concentrate on one of the spiritualist tracts Miss Swindon subscribed to.

Whenever she was given the elixir, she had the most extraordinary visions. Tonight had been no exception. After Tom had left, she found herself in a gossamer gown astride a unicorn galloping through a faerie woodland, the mythic creature's muscled flanks beneath her. Higher and higher it leaped, until finally she was thrown off into the air in a soaring arc, landing breathless on a pillow of flowers. She awoke with tears of joy streaming down her cheeks.

This must be the higher state Miss Swindon had been talking about. Her companion said that when her spiritual sense was more developed, she wouldn't need to take the medicine any more. But how was she ever going to bring herself to such serenity without it? If only she could become the wife Tom wanted her to be.

Always it seemed to her that there were forces trying to get hold of her she couldn't beat back. She didn't understand why those words came out of her that hurt her husband so. She didn't know where they came from. They had to be the devil's work.

Yet, sometimes things seemed so unfair. What the world demanded of a woman was too difficult for her. Maybe she should never have been a wife and mother at all. But wasn't that God's will for all women?

She was so tired, so confused. This kind of thinking always led her nowhere. There had to be some way of placating these devils inside her.

When Tom came into the bedroom, she told him that she was sorry about getting a headache earlier and that she was feeling much better now.

He was touched as always that she didn't remember a thing about what had happened. As he took off his trousers and laid them over a chair, he looked tenderly at her. How fragile she seemed in the light muslin nightdress. He was glad he hadn't listened to her family and sent her away. He was perfectly willing to devote his life to taking care of her.

When he got into bed he put his arms around her to protect her with his gentleness. She looked at him so wide-eyed, so vulnerable, he had to kiss her. Her lips trembled and he kissed her again.

And then the undeniable feeling rushed over him—he wanted her, the wife who for two years had been little more than a ghost. As he pulled her against him, she started crying in a pitiful voice, "No, Tommy, no."

But this time he was incapable of stopping. He had been a good husband, considerate, faithful, obeying her commands to desist. It was not that he was a brute, he loved her. He wanted her to know that he loved her more than anyone else in the world. He would prove it to her. He closed his eyes and overrode her protests. "No, no, no!" And as they grew louder, bottled her scream with his mouth as she convulsed around him.

Only when his passion had exploded inside her did he hear her cries. He lifted his head. "My angel," he murmured, looking down at her as she threw her head back and forth on the pillow with her eyes turned up. "What have I done to you? Why are you carrying on like this?"

A door closed in the hall. Miss Swindon's. He swore under his breath and lay back, hating himself. Long after he blew out the lamp, he listened to the whimpering beside him.

TOM ENDICOTT'S PRINTING SHOP ON BANK STREET WAS IN A small two-story brick building originally put up as a bank when a good part of the business of New York City had fled north during one of the epidemics. But the banks that had taken up temporary quarters and given the street its name had returned to the city along with the other temporary inhabitants as soon as it was safe to.

The lower floor had an office at the front with windows on the street and the shop in the back, the upper floor being for storage. Along with the handpress and other equipment, Tom had inherited a capable old man from the former owner who was able to do much of the printing work, giving him time to go out and drum up business. Most of his work until now had been handbills, business and calling cards, wedding programs and funeral announcements, and the like. But he had just gotten a job that was more interesting—an antislavery pamphlet.

His assistant had been pulling a set of galleys and brought them out for him to check over at his desk with the ink still sticky. Slavery in the South was becoming a big issue with tracts pro and con flooding the city, though he hadn't paid much attention because of his concern over Fanny. It was a relief to him that the new girl, Molly Hanlon, was now looking after things in the house. Maybe he could begin to hope that life was going to take a turn for the better.

He started to correct the galleys. He agreed that slavery was objectionable, but he had to be careful about expressing his opinion because the business community was mostly in favor of it. In fact, New York City was making a lot of money off slavery. The bankers loaned the southern planters money at high rates of interest, and the brokers bought the planters' cotton cheap to sell to the mills in New England.

Now that he had got his first job from the abolitionists, he wondered if he shouldn't also go after some printing business from the temperance people. There was even bigger money there. He didn't hold strong views about drink one way or the other. He had once attended a rally at Castle Garden and found it highly entertaining when some reformed drunkards got up and gave their testimony.

If he could do work for both abolition and temperance, he might be able to get a second press. And with two presses and a binding machine he could even do private editions of small books for authors.

He pushed aside the galleys and took out the manuscript that queer duck of a poet Whitman had given him the other night at the Four Winds, suddenly curious about it. He liked poetry. He sometimes read Emerson and Longfellow aloud to Fanny, though not Edgar Poe any more—Poe was too morbid for her condition. But poetry generally had a soothing effect on her.

His first look at Whitman's manuscript confused him. It wasn't like poetry at all, just long rambling lines without rhyme. It was a pity the man didn't know how to write. Tom had liked him, and he was the one who had introduced him to Molly Hanlon, after all.

It was just yesterday that Molly had come to work for them. Fritz Unger, the tavern keeper, hadn't been so happy about him hiring away his barmaid, but the man had been decent about it and left it up to her to decide. She had immediately accepted. She said she was grateful to the Ungers for having taken her in, but there was always the danger that her husband would find out where she was. Working for a family would be safer.

The atmosphere in the house seemed to lift as soon as she arrived. When he let her in at the downstairs kitchen door, a drab shawl over her head and carrying a pitiful bundle of belongings, she might have been any poor immigrant girl just off the boat. But as soon as she threw off the shawl, shook out her black curls and looked around, furrowing her brow in mock disdain, he recognized the impudent serving maid from the Four Winds. "Who ya been allowin to cook for ya in this pretty kitchen, I'd like to know? It's a bit of a mess if ya don't mind my sayin so, but don't worry, I'll set it to rights fast enough."

She wouldn't hear of taking one of the bedrooms on the top floor where the nursery was and where the hired girl had slept before, insisting that she would be perfectly comfortable with a cot set up for her in the pantry. She'd be able to slip out for Mass every morning at five without disturbing anybody. "The kitchen here's the room I mean to make my own anyway," she told him cheerfully, "and I'll hear no more about it."

When she saw the nurse girl trying to induce Veronica to take her first steps on her spindly legs, she declared that she had to get right to work to fatten up the little tyke—as well as her poor mother. "What they need is to have their blood built up and it's my good Irish cookin will do it in no time."

Her enthusiasm was catching and he felt the burden of the past two years lifting from his shoulders. To help her get started he offered to go to the market for her if she would give him a list. He had sometimes done it to help out old Mrs. Atkins, since Fanny had never been able to.

"What do ya need a list for?" she said. She could just as well tell him what she needed and he could remember until he got there, couldn't he?

Now as he sat in the printshop, the poet's manuscript open on the desk in front of him, he admired the artful way she had let him know she couldn't read or write. Even more, he remembered the grace with which she whipped an apron off a hook and wrapped it around her natural uncorseted body so that her breasts lifted as she reached behind to tie it.

A line in the manuscript jumped up at him: "*. . . curves upon her with amorous firm legs, takes his will of her, and holds himself tremulous and tight till he is satisfied . . .*"

To his shame he felt a physical response and shifted in his chair. He wasn't a prig, God knew—behind the barn anything went—but to present this kind of thing to the general public . . . he shuddered to think of his innocent Fanny reading it.

This went beyond erotica—it was smut. Even if a man were fool enough to print such a thing, he would lay himself open to prosecution. In a hidebound little place like Greenwich he'd be run out of town.

The bell over the door jangled. He pushed the poet's manuscript under the abolitionist galleys and straightened up in his chair.

A slight young man with a mustache and long hair came in carrying a portfolio. He introduced himself as Albert Cogswell and asked if he could sell him any artwork.

Peddlers of all kinds were always coming into the shop, though not often dressed as outlandish as this one. Under a broad-brimmed beaver hat his reddish hair fell to his shoulders, and on his feet he wore beaded moccasins. His scrawniness was emphasized by his cinched-up cavalry breeches that looked like they had seen duty in the Indian wars.

Tom said he was sorry, but he didn't use artwork in his printing, and went back to the galleys.

But his visitor was not to be put off and he leaned over the desk. "Come on, man, how can you run a printing business without some illustrations?"

Tom looked up annoyed, and for the first time thought there was something familiar about him. The name Cogswell didn't ring a bell—but that droopy red mustache . . .

"Aren't you the fellow who did that painting at the Four Winds?"

The bizarrely dressed man grinned and said he had to do all kinds of things to make a living.

Feeling a little less put off, Tom said he thought the painting was a fine piece of work.

"You liked it, did you?" Cogswell said, looking pleased. "Then how about me doing a portrait of your wife in oils?" Before Tom could turn him down again, he elaborated, "If not your wife, then your young'uns, your dog, or your mother-in-law—with or without her clothes on. I can paint a flower garden on your dining room wall so real your women will swear they can smell it."

Tom couldn't help smiling and leaned back in his chair. He said he wished he could use Cogswell's talents for something, but he couldn't afford it yet.

"Wouldn't you use illustrations if you had an engraver?" he persisted. "I do engraving too."

"Hold on. I'm not ready to go into anything complicated like that. Besides, the work I'm doing doesn't use any graphics."

"But I could set you all up for it. Look!" He came around the desk and before Tom could stop him he turned over one of the galleys and with a charcoal pencil began to show him what he had in mind. He had already picked up a broken shirt-collar press from a dump somewhere that could be adapted for the printing of engravings, he said, sketching it in quickly with its fat rollers. Next to it he drew in a worktable for engraving the plates, and with a couple of clever strokes added himself with long hair holding an engraving tool. "Wouldn't take up much space and hardly cost anything at all. What do you say?"

Shiftless as he looked, Cogswell sounded like he knew what he was talking about. Engraving demanded a high level of craftsmanship. If the fellow really could do it, it would open up all kinds of possibilities. For one thing the shop would have a better chance of getting jobs from the temperance people. Their pamphlets were always full of illustrations of drunken husbands beating up their wives and children and the like. "The trouble is I'm already over my head getting started here," Tom said cautiously.

The artist hiked himself up on the desk facing him. "You wouldn't have to pay me a red cent for the engraving I do for you, if I could use the setup for my own work too."

"You're being a little generous, aren't you?"

Cogswell glanced at him sideways, sensing his suspicion, then got up and began to pad about on moccasined feet, stopping only to look in at the old man working at the clattering press before turning back. "I'm not trying to put anything over on you," he said. "But can I show you my work first? I think you'll get my drift then."

Tom nodded, watching him as he untied his portfolio and began spreading drawings and watercolors over the desk.

They were picturesque scenes of life along the river. Tom was no judge of art but the rendering of boats and fisherfolk looked as real to him as that nude over the bar. He asked if by any chance he belonged to the Hudson River school of painting that had been written up in the papers.

Cogswell snorted at the idea. "Those guys paint the Hudson like it was still the uninhabited wilderness. I paint it the way it is." He leaned over the desk again so that his scraggly hair fell over his face and, picking up a sketch of the shad-fishing fleet, pointed out some Indians with tooth necklaces in a skiff. "We still got a few Indians around here, I'm glad to say, but it's changing fast. I'm trying to record everything before it goes."

Tom scrutinized another picture showing one of the squatters' towns that dotted the undeveloped land of Manhattan. Cogswell had portrayed every sordid detail, including an urchin peeing in the dirt. "Isn't that that shack town just north of here on the river?" he asked.

"I grant you it's not your Washington Square," said the artist, hiking himself back up on the edge of the desk with a moccasined foot on the rung of Tom's chair, "but it's not a bad place to live."

"You live there?" Tom stared again at the collection of huts improvised out of sod and packing crates and the hulls of boats, with patches of corn and flapping clotheslines between.

"We got Mohawks, Shinnecocks, Delawares, and a lot of half-breeds," he said, "besides plain mavericks like me who want to live our own way." He pointed to a figure with braided hair and a pipe in her mouth crouching on the ground grinding corn. "That's my woman."

Tom was speechless.

"She lets me live my life without any fetters on me, not like one of your dang churchgoing females in a bonnet."

Tom tried to conceive of this man bedding down in his shack with a squaw. "Well, I'll say one thing for it," he managed to get out, "you don't have any rent to pay."

Cogswell jumped to his feet. "It's not rent that's my problem, man. It's vellum and pigments and canvas—they cost an arm and a leg." He gathered up the scattered drawings, shaking them together. "I figure if I could run off a hundred prints of the scenes I do, even peddling them for a few cents apiece, say, I'd come out way ahead of where I am now." He slipped the drawings back into the portfolio and tied it up. "That's why I wanted to set up an engraving process for you. When I'm not helping you, I could use it for my own work—even etchings and lithographs."

"But how would you have time for my work with all that to do?"

Cogswell grinned. "Don't worry, I'll do crackerjack illlustrations for you—whatever you want."

Tom couldn't fail to respond to his obvious sincerity. "Well then, I don't see why we can't give it a try," he said, extending his hand.

After Cogswell was gone, he tried to get back to the proofs of the abolitionist tract, but it was hard to concentrate. An hour before, going into engraving had been the furthest thing from his mind. The press alone would have set him back a fortune. Converting a shirt-collar press was an ingenious idea. Why, if it worked out he could get big jobs, not just this penny-ante stuff he was doing now.

He liked Cogswell and had no doubt he was as good an engraver as he claimed. But it was a pity he dressed so freakishly. No matter how talented he was, the man was going to have trouble convincing important people that he was any kind of an artist looking that way.

He couldn't get over his living in that shack with an Indian woman—lying beside her on buffalo skins. It was unbelievable. He gave up on the proofreading and took out the poetry manuscript he had shoved under the galleys.

O young man passing by,
my hand reaches under your clothes to caress you,
and your hand reaches under my clothes to caress me.

These lines couldn't mean what they seemed to! He gazed out the window, ruminating. A street cleaner was shoveling horse droppings into a wagon, banging the shovel against its wooden side. The poem must be some sort of metaphor for brotherly love, like in the Greeks.

Then he recalled the poet's behavior in the tavern—the way he put his arm around the freckled-faced sailor, their long intimate talk, some of the things he had said. It didn't necessarily prove anything, but all kinds of things did go on in the world, though so far as he knew not up here in Greenwich—in spite of Whitman's tale about some Indian gods coupling here and leaving a restless spirit behind. He went on reading:

Come share my bed
where we shall lie in a naked embrace
all night long.

That didn't leave much to the imagination. Did this fellow really think he could get away with writing about such a thing? Even if it were true, it wasn't something you ought to shout from the rooftops. Whitman must be crazy to expect that even an open-minded man like himself would think of publishing it. Still, one couldn't be sure—it was poetry after all.

He gave up trying to imagine what men could possibly do with each other and took out a sheet of foolscap and folded it over. Dipping his quill into the inkwell, he told the bearded poet from Brooklyn that he would be very surprised if he found any printer at all for the manuscript—it was sure to offend everyone. As a poetry lover himself, he thought he ought to remind him that poetry should concern itself more with the soul than the body. And as a last piece of advice, he suggested that if he wanted to be a poet he should set about learning how to use rhyme and meter.

ON A DRIZZLING, BLUSTERY MORNING THREE MONTHS LATER, Ethel Swindon in a dark rain bonnet and cape was going down Perry Street toward the Four Winds tavern. She held her umbrella in front of her against the gusts, treading carefully so as not to slip on the wet leaves on the slate walk. Stepping around a pile of bricks, she observed with disapproval the new houses going up in the last vacant field between the Endicotts' house and the corner.

She was certainly not going into the tavern. No respectable woman would set foot in such a place. She had no truck with alcohol in any form unless it was labeled "nerve tonic," which she found fortifying.

She was on her way to see her friend Hannah Unger, the wife of the tavern keeper, in the Ungers' rooms above the tavern. She had some questions to ask about the new hired girl, Molly Hanlon, who seemed to be taking over the whole Endicott household to the point where Ethel herself felt in some danger of being eased out of her job.

To start with, she didn't like her looks. Molly Hanlon wasn't the usual lump of an immigrant who knew her place. She had an almost obscenely overdeveloped figure and looked boldly at all of them like she thought of herself as an equal. Worst of all, that gullible young fool of a husband didn't seem to mind. She even caught him smiling whenever the hussy was in the room.

As if that weren't bad enough, he had gotten her angel pregnant again. Sleeping just next door to them, she could hardly avoid hearing his brutal advances. She could not understand why he didn't have the decency to restrain himself when he knew how delicate his wife was, and that another confinement and delivery risked her remaining shreds of sanity, if not her life.

At the corner she struggled to hold on to the umbrella as a gust threatened to carry it off. The day before, after being confined to her room with one of her sick migraines, Ethel Swindon had come down to find Fanny almost hysterical with laughter over some superstitious gibberish about leprechauns the hired girl was telling her. It was plain that she was setting out to win Fanny away from her and take over her position unless she did something right away. She wanted to talk it over with Hannah who had discovered the girl in the first place.

Miss Swindon and Hannah Unger had worked for the same Washington Square family years before, Hannah as cook and Ethel in her first job as paid companion. But when the family moved away, Hannah married Fritz Unger and went to live with him over the tavern. Though Miss Swindon did not approve of taverns, the two women had kept in touch. Whatever one might say about most tavern keepers, the Ungers were a respectable couple who lived a Christian life—and Hannah would do her best to tell her whatever she wanted to know.

If it weren't for the migraines, that hired girl would never have had the chance to get at Fanny. But Miss Swindon had been a victim of the terrible headaches ever since childhood when one misfortune after another had been visited on her. Her irresponsible father had first brought her to live in rural Greenwich in 1822 to escape the yellow jack that had carried off her mother down in New York. The move had ruined any possibility of her growing up in a refined society. Then, in the crash of '37 he lost all the money her mother had left her for a dowry. The young man who was courting her at the time broke off, and without a dowry there had not been another suitor since.

She climbed the wooden outside stairway to Hannah's door, shook some wet leaves off her skirts, and folded her umbrella shut with a snap.

The rosy-cheeked tavern keeper's wife welcomed her friend warmly—she always liked a good gossip. She brought in a pot of coffee and freshly baked plum tarts, and the two women settled down at the bay window overlooking Greenwich Street. Across the way a team of horses was being hitched to the stage for its afternoon run down to the city. The rain would make it a difficult journey through the mud.

"And how is Molly doing?" Hannah asked, arranging her plump figure in a rocker and pouring out the coffee. "Such a good worker she was here. The Endicotts are lucky to have her."

Miss Swindon selected a tart and replied evasively that there didn't seem to be anything the girl wasn't above doing.

Her friend missed the innuendo and beamed. She was so glad her barmaid had found a more suitable place. Fritz always said a tavern, even one as respectable as theirs, was no good for a pretty young woman. "Too many temptations," she said with a significant nod.

Ethel stopped munching for a moment to listen attentively. This might be what she was looking for.

"Ach," Hannah went on, misreading her friend's interest, "it's not the way it was here when I first came over from Koblenz. New York is full of such riffraff nowadays. These immigrants come without any families, no idea they got to work. They think gold is waiting for them to pick up on the street. They don't know what you got to do for it, and so many wicked people around, and nothing to keep them from going bad. You should see how they live in some of those rooming houses over here."

Ethel's nostrils flared over the rim of her coffee cup.

"It's not just girls out on the street any more," Hannah said, lowering her voice, "it's these parents selling their children. Fritz says only nine or ten years old some of them are. Can you believe it?"

Ethel would have liked to know more about such papist abominations, but she had no time to waste and steered the conversation back to the object of her visit. "You're not saying that a girl like Molly Hanlon . . ." She left her implications hovering in the air over the rapidly diminishing plate of plum tarts.

"Oh, my land sakes no! But no thanks to that devil husband of hers. You know what, Ethel? He made her go out on the street to sell her body. The poor child was black and blue, he beat her so. *Ach,* it broke our hearts to hear about it, Fritz and me."

"Do you mean she actually was a prostitute?" This was better than she had hoped for!

"Terrible, it was. That beast made her paint her lips and stand in the doorway, and the only way she could get away from his fists was by going off with a man. But as soon as they were out of sight she gave him her knee, you know where." Hannah's plump body shook as she chuckled. "Another cup of coffee, my dear Ethel?"

But Miss Swindon was already wiping the crumbs of the last tart from her lips and getting up. "I've stayed too long as it is," she said. "Mrs. Endicott will be waking from her sedative and she'll be upset if I'm not there."

The tavern keeper's wife was disappointed at her friend's departing so abruptly. She had looked forward to a long gossip about the old days.

But Ethel Swindon had no time for reminiscing. She was impatient to get to her employer to impart some interesting information.

Tom was in the shop with an apron over his vest and his shirtsleeves rolled up, setting type for a temperance tract. The raw weather had laid up his assistant with rheumatism. He wanted his first temperance job, an essay on the dangers of alcohol for the working-class family, to turn out especially well so that the temperance people would give him more work. In fact, he was so optimistic he had already ordered a second printing press.

He was composing each page with an elaborately designed initial capital letter like a medieval manuscript, while Albert was working on an engraving for it in the back of the shop.

The artist was singing a rowdy chorus of "Oh! Susannah" as he worked at the converted shirt-collar press, inking the stone in the bed with a roller and spinning the handle to press the paper against it.

He made the printing shop lively whenever he was there, the rascal. His ideas were as outlandish as his faded cavalry breeches and his patched green coat. His costume never changed except on cold days when he wrapped a blanket around himself.

When Tom had first told him about Fanny, and her spells, Albert said she didn't sound so crazy to him. Where he lived all the women let off steam like that, and no one called it crazy. Some of them even went into trances and spoke in tongues.

"You can't mess around with our women. They know what they want and they don't let us forget it."

Tom said that they didn't sound civilized to him, but Albert had only laughed. "Send your wife over to live with us. We don't want our women to be civilized, we want them to be natural."

Tom smiled over his singular new friend and dropped a line of type into the bed. He hadn't done much typesetting since working at his uncle's printshop in Binghamton—at his job down in the city he had mostly worked as a pressman. But he quickly got back into the old rhythm, reaching for the type in the font in front of him and laying the letters into a composing form in his other hand. After a while he could follow the text hardly having to pay attention to what he was reading.

The rain drizzling outside did not lessen the happiness he felt. His business was flourishing, Albert was proving to be far more helpful than he expected, and Molly Hanlon's presence in the house had lightened the formerly gloomy atmosphere. Now he looked forward to going home to lunch every day. She always had a bright smile waiting for him as soon as he stepped into the dining room, and even after supper as he sat in his study doing his accounts or reading, it was a comfort to know that she was down in the kitchen humming away as she kneaded dough for the next day's bread.

Albert came over with a proof he had just pulled and slapped it over the type font, breaking his rhythm. "How's this strike you?"

He was exasperated to see that Albert had been working away on one of his river scenes. "Is that what you've been up to all morning? I thought you were doing the illustration for the tract."

"Pleasure before duty is my first rule in life." Albert grinned. "Once I've warmed up, I can knuckle down to 'The Virtuous Maid Led Astray by Demon Rum.' I'll show her with the devil's hand up her skirts. That'll make those pious hypocrites come in their breeches."

Tom snickered nervously. It was impossible to stay mad at Albert, even if he didn't think much of schedules and deadlines.

The bell over the door jangled as Ethel Swindon marched into the shop, unconcerned that her umbrella was leaving a track of water over the floor behind her. She demanded to speak to Tom privately, while casting a sour look at Albert Cogswell.

"Do pardon me, madam," said Albert, nearly genuflecting before her. He rolled his eyes at Tom, picked up his proof, and retreated to the back of the shop letting out a war whoop as if wild Indians were after him.

Miss Swindon made a show of not hearing it and said that ordinarily she would not have considered coming to the shop, but under the circumstances she had no choice.

Suspecting she was up to something, Tom put down his composing form, took off his apron, and led her into the office, closing the door behind them.

When she was seated in the chair beside his desk, she wasted no time getting to the point. "I've just seen my old friend Mrs. Unger, and I've heard the most shocking news about the new housemaid. I thought you ought to be the first to know, sir."

He flushed at her gall. He had an impulse to throw her right out, but everything about Molly interested him, even gossip.

"I'm afraid she's not quite the respectable woman we took her for," she began. "My friend, Mrs. Unger, is so naive, her heart goes out to any stray cat. Well, it seems"—she discreetly lowered her eyes—"that Mrs. Hanlon confessed to her that she had been a woman of the streets." She looked up quickly to catch his reaction. "It's not the kind of thing I could normally bring myself to mention, but with an innocent child in the house—"

He jumped up, ready to show her the door. "That's a damn lie, and why the hell you repeat such a thing . . ."

She kept her seat, imperturbable. "Mrs. Unger doesn't lie."

Leaning toward her with his hands on the desk he spoke carefully. "I'm sure your friend told you what she believed to be the truth. But I'm afraid she got the story wrong. Now if you'll excuse me, I've got to get back to work."

Ethel Swindon rose to her feet, a thin smile on her lips, and adjusted her bonnet and rain cape. "I was only trying to do my duty. After all, she has been doing her best to influence your wife and daughter. If you are unconcerned, I'm sure I don't know why not!"

"Good day," he said, shutting the door on the meddling bitch who, not at all discomposed, marched off into the rain holding her umbrella aloft.

This was too much. He always knew she was jealous of anyone who came near Fanny, but to try to besmirch an innocent young woman! As a paid companion she might think she was indispensable, but he was going to start looking around immediately for someone to replace her. She had just cooked her own goose.

As he sat in the dining room waiting for lunch he repeated to himself that the vicious story was only a fantasy of a jealous old maid. But when Molly Hanlon pushed through the door from the kitchen carrying a steaming serving bowl, her full figure only too evident under the thin housedress, he looked down, feeling a sudden rush of guilt.

"Here's a turnip stew for ya, sir. It was my father's favorite dish back home. I hope ya like it."

He smelled her healthy body as she came over to serve him. What had possessed that Unger woman to spread such a tale? With her bad English she had obviously misunderstood whatever Molly had said to her.

While she ladled out the pungent stew onto his plate, Molly chattered away as usual. "Your wife and I had a sweet time this morning, sir, playin a game of snipsnapsnorum. But we got to laughin so much the cards fell all over the floor." She giggled at the memory and her breasts shook.

Why did she have to wear such skimpy clothes? For an instant he saw her standing in a doorway on lower Broadway with her face painted. He shoved his plate aside, unable to eat.

"Is somethin wrong with it, sir?"

"What were you doing playing cards with my wife in the middle of the morning? Don't you have enough work to keep you busy?"

She put down the serving bowl, turning white as if he had struck her.

But something was taking him over. There was an impudence about her overdeveloped body that *belonged* in a doorway.

"I only went into Mrs. Endicott's room when I was called," she said, now going red in the face. "She asked me to keep her company."

He was trembling. It was not hard to imagine her making lewd suggestions to passing men. "My wife has a companion to look after her."

Her blue eyes darkened with anger. "Miss Swindon was out and your wife was nervous bein alone. I thought I was doin ya a favor sittin with her."

"From now on I wish you would stick to your own duties."

She stared at him, then with a mock curtsy and a sarcastic

"as you wish, sir," she turned and swiveled her hips toward the kitchen door.

Rage boiled up in him. She was walking that way deliberately, like one of those women. He saw it all now. She had been provoking him ever since she got here, pretending it was all cheerfulness and innocence. "Stop!" he shouted, getting up. "Why didn't you tell me the truth?"

She wheeled around at the kitchen door. "What's that?"

He was no longer able to control himself. "I'm talking about your life down in the city."

She set the bowl of turnip stew on the end of the table and walked slowly back, her hands on her hips. "What is it you're tryin to say to me, Mr. Endicott?"

His fists were clenched and his forehead was sweating. "I'm saying," he barked, "that you're not what you pretend to be."

They faced each other like pugilists at a prizefight and she called him a dirty sod.

"Whore," he said, "you're a whore!" The passion for her that he had never faced overcame him. He seized her breasts and thrust her back against the wall, covering her mouth with his.

Just as fast, she gave him a shove, kneeing him hard in his swollen groin. He backed away, bent over, clutching himself. The pain was excruciating.

"Ya won't have any use for the family jewels if ya try that again, I promise ya," she said grimly, an arm still up in front of her heaving breasts. But in spite of her attempted bravado, tears welled from the corners of her eyes.

He staggered into a chair, trying to get his breath.

She walked over and poured him out a cup of tea, shoving it across to him. "Drink it. You'll be all right."

Like an obedient child he drank, not caring that it burned his throat. He set down the empty cup, looking at it miserably. "I shouldn't have done that. I don't know what came over me."

"Who called me that filthy name?" she asked.

He didn't answer her.

"I know. It was that Swindon woman. She hates me."

He turned to her quickly. "I tried not to believe her, but I went crazy when she said that your husband put you on the streets."

"That's right, he did," she said quietly.

Tom looked at her.

". . . but I ran away. I was never a hoor." And then she told him the whole story, adding that she had heard that her husband, Hank Hanlon, was in prison now for knifing a man. "And I hope he rots there," she said, but immediately crossed herself.

Tom was quiet for a moment. "I can guess what you think of me."

"Ya wanted to believe her, didn't ya?"

He put his head in his hands. "May God forgive me, I believed it because I wanted you. Both of us being married, there was no other way unless I could persuade myself it was true." He told her how miserable he had been since Fanny's breakdown, how he had hated having to exile himself up here in Greenwich, and how her cheerfulness and vitality made him love her from the first.

Standing beside him, she ran her hand maternally over his soft, fair hair. "We both have our miseries, don't we?" she said. "I'll confess my heart's been out to ya since I first saw ya."

He turned and put his arms around her hips, pressing his face against her skirts, feeling her vibrant life. It was the first time in two years that he was able to give in to the loneliness and misery he had been forced to hide.

✣✣✣✣✣✣✣

"GREENWICH IS NOT WHAT IT WAS." MISS SWINDON WAS HOLDing forth at the dinner table as the family waited for dessert. "When I first came to live here as a girl," she said, "I didn't have my coughing fits yet. At that time the village still stood on rolling hills and the air was so much better. Oh, yes, they leveled them all down soon after. Why, that proud old house across the street stood on the highest hill of all—would you believe it? But they brought it to its knees, so to speak." She hid her mouth behind her napkin, tittering at her attempted witticism, but quickly recovered herself. "The way building is going on these days around here, it will be no time at all before we're just another part of the city."

It was a Sunday afternoon. Through the dining room windows, the lilacs were budding in the narrow, fenced-in backyard, and the pussywillow bush by the outhouse was already covered with furry catkins. The winter supply of cordwood in the shed along the side fence was almost used up. But the circular patch of rose garden in the middle and the ailanthus trees were still wintry bare.

Tom, in his Sunday-best suit, leaned over and wiped some baby drool off his daughter Veronica's chin. A pinafore over her gingham dress and her hair in long golden curls, she sat in a high chair playing with a drumstick. Molly, who had taken over the care of her from the nurse girl, had fed her earlier in the kitchen, but Tom liked the baby to be at the table with them, always hoping that Fanny would pay her some attention.

"Personally," he answered Miss Swindon, tucking his napkin back into his shirt, "I wish the city had been able to run an avenue right up into the middle of Greenwich. That way it would have brought the business to our side of Manhattan instead of over on Broadway." He looked at his wife whose fragile beauty was enhanced by her impending motherhood. "Fanny, you should see the new mansions over there—and the hotels. I'll hire a buggy one day and we'll go have a look."

"What a good idea," she said, her pale hand stroking the sienna paisley shawl he had bought her from a clipper ship captain just back from the East. "In fact, now that the weather is nice Miss Swindon and I can take a long walk over there."

Her paid companion shook her head with a pursy smile and reminded her that no walking out was possible until after her confinement.

She made a little frown. "I forgot. Of course you're right." But she brightened quickly. "Anyway, it will soon be over and then we'll all go together."

It moved him to see her so happy. These past months during her pregnancy she was so much better. Even in her advanced condition she had joined him at table instead of taking her meals with Miss Swindon in her room as she used to. It seemed that this pregnancy was the right thing after all.

"I disagree with you about the avenue, sir," Miss Swindon said, rummaging in her drawstring reticule for a throat lozenge.

Disagreeing was certainly her specialty. He was still determined to get rid of her and intended to as soon as Fanny recovered from her delivery.

"If they'd cut the avenue through like they wanted, we'd have more of that foreign element coming here than we do already. They'd come straight up from the boats. As it is, we can hardly call this an American town any more."

Molly Hanlon came into the room with a bowl of peach cobbler and Miss Swindon shut up abruptly, patting the napkin to the corners of her mouth and looking from side to side significantly.

Molly caught Tom's eye as she passed behind her and held the bowl for a moment over the woman's head as if she was about to drop it on her, showing what she thought of her blatant anti-Irish innuendos.

Since the day months before when he had lost his head in the dining room, he had controlled his feeling for her, though it had not been easy. He had given it much thought and had come to the conclusion that not only would it be cruel to Fanny, but also wrong to take unfair advantage of a generous-hearted housemaid. He was trying to convince himself that Molly's cheerful presence in the house was enough, but it was torture, as always, to keep his eyes off her as she served up bowls of cobbler at the sideboard, pouring on cream, and setting them around.

With a display of squealing and banging her drumstick little Veronica announced that she too expected some peach cobbler.

"What a little piggie ya are, darlin," Mollie laughed. "I gave ya more than ya could eat in the kitchen, but oh well. . . ." Without asking, she took Tom's spoon and, dipping some cobbler off his dish, went around to stuff the child's mouth, and gave her a loud kiss on the top of her head.

Miss Swindon looked at Tom askance, expecting him to protest such cheek, but his eyes were following the irrepressible hired girl tenderly as she sailed back to the kitchen.

Fanny, who had noticed nothing, said that she found Greenwich a refreshing change after the ruckus of the city. "And I have my dear husband to thank for bringing me here to rest my nerves. We're all so much happier now, aren't we, Veronica lamb?"

The child looked frightened, not used to having her mother speak to her.

Tom beamed at his wife. It was the first time she had ever expressed any gratitude for all the trouble he had gone through for her. She really was so much better. He told her, and he meant it sincerely, that now that she was feeling herself again, he didn't mind in the least giving up their life down in New York.

She didn't seem to understand. "Giving up?"

He tried to read her clear brown eyes that were suddenly fastened on him.

"Whatever did you give up for me?" she said.

With an uneasy smile, he protested that he didn't give up anything that mattered.

"Don't lie to me. You gave up everything you cared about to bring me here." Her voice took on the jagged edge he thought he had heard the last of months before. "And you do blame me, don't deny it."

"But you have gotten better. . . ." He trailed off helplessly. He knew with a hollow feeling it was already too late. His illusion of happiness was collapsing like a tent. Veronica threw down her drumstick and began to snivel.

Fanny pulled herself heavily to her feet to face him, her mouth twisting, uglier than he could have believed. "If I am better, it's only that you haven't come near me," and, gripping her protuberant belly, shrieked out, "because of this!"

He moved quickly around to her and tried to put his hands on her trembling shoulders to calm her, but she shook him off.

"Don't touch me! You don't let me breathe. You think I like being in this condition?" She beat her fists against her belly. "I hate it! I'd like to strangle it as soon as it's born."

When Veronica started to scream, Molly ran in from the kitchen and picked the child up, rocking her automatically as she tried to understand what was happening.

"Quick!" Tom yelled at Miss Swindon, who was fumbling in her cluttered bag for the medicine. But he was too impatient to wait and, grabbing the bag out of her hand, dumped it out on the table. The bottle of elixir rolled straight to Fanny who snatched it away and shattered it against the wall before going at him with her nails.

"Get some more!" he shouted, grappling with his demented wife who was clawing at his face.

"I have no more," Ethel Swindon wailed, watching in anguish as her gentle mistress yanked the tablecloth, dumping the dishes of cobbler, the candlesticks, and the contents of her reticule all over the floor.

"I got some in the kitchen," Molly said, and rushed to get it, the terrified child clinging to her like a monkey.

He tried to hold his wife back as she pounded the table crying out, "Listen to me! Why can't I make anyone listen to me!"

While he struggled with her, Molly brought another bottle to Miss Swindon who, with her usual maddening precision, poured a dollop of water into a glass from a pewter pitcher on the sideboard and measured out the drops. Turning around, in charge of the situation again, she commanded, "Listen to me, Fanny! Chester says to drink this. Do you hear me? Chester!"

With eyes almost rolled up into her head, the demented woman, breast heaving, looked around as if trying to recollect what was happening. Then, in a plaintive voice, she asked,

"My baby?" And allowing Miss Swindon to tip the glass to her lips, she drank the medicine down.

Tom held his breath. As always, the miracle happened. Her attack was over as fast as it had begun. She let him help her out of the room and up the stairs.

Miss Swindon followed behind, triumphant, knowing that her position was no longer in danger. However bewitched the young fool might be by the slattern of a hired girl, he was never going to find anyone else who could get through to his wife at the height of her seizures.

When Tom came downstairs again, he found Molly tucking Veronica into her crib in the kitchen. She asked him how Mrs. Endicott was.

"She's asleep. It's always the same," he said, sinking into a chair at the kitchen table. "God, how she fought me. . . ." For a moment he closed his eyes in utter weariness, then roused himself and asked Molly how she had got the child to sleep so fast.

She sat down across from him. "An old Sligo remedy. A few drops of whiskey in her milk. It always works." She smiled down at the sleeping little girl.

"I don't know what we'd do without you." He put his hand over hers on the table.

But the moment was interrupted by a shriek from upstairs, and Miss Swindon ran down to tell them that Mrs. Endicott had gone into labor.

"Go for the midwife, Tom!" cried Molly, jumping up. "We'll manage here until you get back."

But by the time he returned with the midwife, a son had been born, delivered by the capable Molly who knew all about such things.

As Fanny lay in a half-doze, Molly handed the baby wrapped in a blanket over to him. "Such an easy birth, it was. It just popped out, the darlin."

The midwife said the cannabis drops always made the labor easier.

Tom Endicott looked down at his new son with pity, so sallow and tiny in contrast to his lusty firstborn. But how could it be otherwise with a crazy mother who didn't want it, who didn't want her other child, who hated him? He knew that Molly was watching him, wanting to share her strength with him, but he couldn't bring himself to look at her.

As he had expected, Fanny took no more interest in her newborn son, Claude, than she did in her daughter Veronica. She had never had enough milk for breast-feeding, and this time as before, he arranged for a wet nurse, a relative of the woman Albert Cogswell lived with who had just lost an infant of her own to the croup.

He asked Albert if he thought the wet nurse's husband would mind her moving in with them.

The artist laughed. "You might say she's between husbands just now."

So Phoebe Pagett, a tiny dark woman, came to take care of both children. Beneath her homespun skirt she was barefoot, and her breasts looked full enough to feed a tribe and that was what counted. Her big eyes took in everything. She had hoops at her ears, and her kinky braided hair led him to speculate that there might be more than Indian blood in her veins. Escaped slaves often were given asylum by sympathetic Indians. With the baby at her breast and Veronica piggyback tied in a shawl around her shoulders, she looked like a tiny tree bursting with fruit.

Fanny was slow to get her strength back in the weeks following Claude's birth and the family doctor recommended a convalescence by the sea. Tom had no more illusions that she would ever get really well, but he hoped the sea air would do her good. He took her and Miss Swindon down to the Battery where he saw them off on the little steamer that made daily trips to the Rockaways, a quiet resort on the south shore of Long Island.

He returned home feeling a terrible burden lifted. Moreover, it was the first time he was able to relax around Molly without worrying that someone was looking on.

Phoebe ate dinner early in the kitchen with the babies, and afterward squatted on the floor bathing them in a basin. By the time he got home from work, she was back with them up in the nursery on the third floor.

It was a joy for him to come into the house to find only Molly there. With Fanny and Miss Swindon away, they were free to carry on a lively conversation during his dinner as she brought the dishes in and out. He even had a wild impulse and asked her to sit down and eat with him, but she laughed and blushed, saying it wouldn't be right. So after dinner he took to bringing his evening newspaper down to the kitchen where he pretended to read while she went about cleaning up and baking the next day's bread.

It was a marvel to him that at the end of the day she looked as fresh as when she first brought him his porridge in the morning. Aside from the cooking, she had the whole house to take care of, cleaning and scrubbing and emptying the slops, though with the coming of mild weather she didn't have the ashes to clean out of the fireplaces any more.

Doing the laundry was no work at all, she said, with all the hot water she needed from a tank in the iron cookstove and the miracle of running water right in the kitchen. The pipe and faucet had been installed several years before by the previous owner of the house when the Croton aqueduct started bringing good water down from upstate.

Running water wasn't the only miracle you could buy these days. There were so many new inventions on the market and everyone was clamoring for them. Tom took advantage of Fanny's absence—her nerves would never have stood workmen banging around the house—to have some gas lighting fixtures put in. When he turned on the gas jets in their petal globes, the parlor blazed with light, a wondrous thing after the smoky whale-oil lamps.

One day he came home at noon to find Molly gone and no lunch in sight. Phoebe was sitting on the grass in the sun in the backyard nursing the baby with a great breast shamelessly out, while Veronica scampered around her. He called through the window to ask where Molly was.

"She gone away. The po-lice took her." The dark eyes watched him unblinking.

He scolded her for talking nonsense but she stuck to her story. Two policemen had come to the kitchen door and taken her off with them. Tiny Claude lost the nipple and went red in the face, but she shoved it back into his mouth and he worked away at it happily. "Look like she in plenty'a of trouble."

Tom ran back through the kitchen and up the steps to the street, heading for the police station. But as he slammed the iron gate after him, he saw Molly coming down the street. Without a thought for the neighbors, he ran to her. But she wouldn't answer any of his questions. Her face set, she walked on back to the house and down the kitchen steps. As he followed her inside, she stood by the worktable keeping her back to him, her shawl slipping from her rich dark curls. He turned her gently to face him. Her eyes were full of tears.

"Molly . . . dear, what happened?"

She moved her lips, trying to tell him, but no words came. Then she was crying against his chest.

He let his arms go around her, trying to ignore the scent of her hair, the feel of her trembling body, swearing to her that whatever had happened he would stand by her.

At last she was able to tell him that her husband, Hank Hanlon, had been stabbed to death in a brawl at the jail.

So that was it. How could he ever have imagined she had done anything wrong?

Her head still against his chest, she said, "Sure and I thought I didn't have that man any more, but now that he's gone it's all come back to me what he put me through."

She asked if she might lie down a bit, and he helped her to the little bedroom she had arranged for herself in the pantry, where on the wall above the bed a crucifix hung next to some ears of Indian corn. She lay down and he covered her with her shawl.

"I'll go make some tea," he said, but she held him back.

"Don't leave me now, I'm on a rack of pain."

He understood. In her anguish she wanted him close. Awkwardly he squeezed himself on the narrow bed with her and held her in his arms.

Still shaking, she clung to him. Her skirts had pushed up

and her stockinged leg was soft against him. He was ashamed of himself for his quick desire but hoped that in her distress she wouldn't notice.

Outside, a window banged open on an upper floor of the old mansion across the street and a housemaid called to a knife sharpener who had set up his grindstone on the walk. A wagon-load of lumber, pulled by a team of percherons, creaked and jolted over the cobblestones.

He lay beside her sick with pleasure, kissing her brow tenderly from time to time. From the backyard, little Veronica set up a wail and was comforted by Phoebe crooning to her in an Indian dialect.

If this was all that life ever offered him, he would be grateful.

But the voices in the backyard drew nearer and a door slammed as the little nurse came into the house with the children. Coming to with a start he jumped off the bed, mumbling that he had to get back to the shop, and he slipped out of the room as Molly sat up and stared after him in amazement.

The next day there was an awkwardness between them. She served his meals perfunctorily, avoiding his eyes, and whenever he was in the house she kept herself busy in the kitchen. He was in despair that she thought he had taken advantage of her.

That night as she set his supper before him without a word he couldn't stand it any longer and grabbed her hand. "Please listen. I feel bad about what happened. Forgive me for taking unfair advantage of you."

"Advantage ya call it?" She pulled away her hand with a hard laugh. "Any man in Sligo would have given me some lovin when it was clear I was in need of it. But oh no, not you, Tom Endicott, with your Protestant minginess. Ya torture a girl until she's ready to scream and then ya get up and leave her."

"But you were suffering. . . ."

"I was that. That's when I needed the comfort of ya. Haven't ya ever met a woman with red blood in her veins before?"

"You mean you aren't mad at me because I took advantage of you?"

"Stop sayin ya took advantage of me. I'm mad at ya because ya took *no* advantage of me." She turned in exasperation, looking out at the backyard, which was rapidly getting dark.

"That's what I get for fancyin a man of a different sort than me. Ya never know what crazy ideas they have in their heads."

He finally allowed himself to understand this unpredictable creature. "What would a country boy from Sligo do now?" he asked.

Her blue eyes mocked him. "Well, he wouldn't be sittin there in front of a plate of cold stew, I can tell ya that."

He got up, tossing his napkin back on the table, put an arm around her waist and led her back to her room where they fell on the bed. Before he knew it, her arms and legs were wrapped around him, her whole body shaken by a storm of sobs and gasping. Alarmed that she was having some of kind of fit, he stopped and looked down at her. Her head was flung back on the pillow, her lustrous hair coming undone.

"What's stoppin ya, my love?" she asked, opening her eyes.

"Am I hurting you?"

"Hurtin me? I'm havin the time of my life. Get on with it."

He had only experienced a woman lying passive beneath him before. Not trying to understand her frantic behavior he let himself go—he had held back so long.

Afterward, she leaned over him and, with her curls falling damp against his face, kissed him on the mouth. "So ya are a real man after all, Tom Endicott. It's many a day I been waitin for us to ignite. Now maybe you'll be able to show that poor wife of yours how to enjoy it."

He was scandalized that she should bring Fanny into it. "She would never be able to act like that," he said indignantly.

Molly laughed as she sat astraddle him, in her loose camisole and stockings half fallen down her thighs, pushing her hair back up with one hand. "Oh, I know you men. Ya go to the hoors or the hired girls for a little real lovin."

He simply couldn't keep up with her. "But did you do it with your husband that way?"

"Hanlon? I hated it with him."

"Still, you married him."

"Ah, life isn't always so simple, my pet—ya know that as well as me. When I got off the boat it wasn't all fine ladies waitin there to offer me a position as a housemaid. It wasn't that way at all. Only madams and pimps and the like—the scum of the earth, come to inveigle country girls who had never been ten miles away from the houses they were born in. A fool I was to trust that bastard but I didn't know where to turn, it was all so new. He knew how to worm his way into a girl's confidence, that one did. He bought me a pint right off and even helped me find a room. Greenhorn that I was, scared out of my wits"—she laughed bitterly at the memory—"I married him. But believe me, my darlin, I never once did it with him like I did it with you just now."

He pulled her down to him, nuzzling against this outrageous, adorable woman, letting her carry him away again to perfect bliss.

The following days were his happiest. He spent every night downstairs with her in her little room where she taught him that a woman could take as much pleasure in the act of love as a man. She constantly surprised him, not only with the abandon with which she threw herself into it, but with her adventurousness in exploring every avenue of pleasure.

The one thing that bothered him during this remarkable time was that the little Indian nurse knew what they were up to. Phoebe's dark eyes followed him whenever she saw him going downstairs. One night she actually came in on them kissing—she had come down to the kitchen to refill a sugar-tit, her remedy for quieting restless Veronica—but from the way she nodded encouragement as she backed out of the room giggling, he understood that she approved.

When the letter came announcing Fanny's return from the seashore, he told Molly he was not going to give her up, she had become the center of his life.

"Now listen to me, darlin," she said as she lay in his arms in the little pantry that had become so dear to him, "there's no way we can go on with it in this house. Your poor wife's already half out of her mind with misery and I'm not going to add to it. It would kill her if she found out we was carryin on under her very eyes."

"We could run off!"

"And leave those two little tykes who have only you in the whole blessed world to watch out for em?"

"I don't care." He buried his face in her throat.

She pulled up his chin and made him look at her. "Tom, we got no choice but to face it. What we've had has been a blessed thing. We got to remember that it's more than most people have in their whole lifetime."

She was right, of course. They'd been allowed this little time, but now it was over. He wanted to cry but he couldn't—

there had been a lump in his throat all his life that he couldn't get out, not even now when he was forced to give up the only thing he cared about in the world.

And then they were back. It was worse than he had anticipated. He resented the old invalid routine taking over the house again—Miss Swindon rushing downstairs at all hours to get trays for her mistress and continually complaining about the noise the nurse and the children were making. Even Fanny's pale fragility as she sat in the parlor with a shawl over her knees didn't seem so heartrending any more after Molly's beautiful health.

He had never told Albert about his affair with Molly, believing that a man damaged a woman's good name even by talking to his best friend about her, but now needing sympathy, he confessed to him the whole thing and how wretched he was.

Albert surprised him by calling him a fool for giving Molly up. There was no reason he couldn't keep both his mistress and his wife happy under the same roof. It worked all the time in the shantytown where he lived.

Annoyed at his friend's reaction, he said that it might kill Fanny if she found out about it, and she was bound to find out in such a small house.

Albert told him that women were stronger than he thought. "Of course, there's always the chance that one of them will take a knife to the other and you'll end up worse off than you are now, but you got to take the risk, as I see it. Everything worth having in life is a risk. Look, friend, men are natural bigamists. Especially in your case—you got a sick wife who's no good to you as a woman, where's the harm?"

"But it's immoral!"

"Don't give me that bullshit. If you think morality means a man's got to deny himself what nature means him to have, then you deserve the fix you're in." He turned back to preparing a steel engraving plate for printing, and Tom left the shop disappointed. The solution for Albert's squatters' town would never work for Perry Street.

But as it usually does, nature resolved the situation in a way he couldn't have imagined. One evening toward the end of June after Fanny was in bed, her paid companion had come downstairs in a dark rustle of skirts and announced in her dramatic whisper that scandal was staring them in the face if he didn't do something about Mrs. Hanlon at once.

It seemed that Miss Swindon had the habit of getting up early to have coffee by herself in the dining room, and for the past couple of weeks she had heard Molly being sick every day. "You know as well as I do what that means—she's with a child!" She tried to hide her look of satisfaction by rummaging for a lozenge in her reticule.

He told her to get out, she was talking nonsense. But even as he said it, he was afraid, sickeningly, that it was true. He wondered how he could have overlooked the possibility of Molly getting pregnant. He had been a fool to think that they could get away scot-free. Every pleasure in his life had to be paid for ten times over.

When he heard the door overhead click shut and he knew that the viper was back in her lair he ran downstairs.

The air of the kitchen was yeasty with the smell of bread baking in the oven. Molly was on a stool brushing out her splendid mop of black hair, her voluptuous body in a nightdress. It was the same nightdress with the yellow ribbon run through the collar that she had on the night before Fanny had come back, the last night he had been with her. He felt weak in the knees and leaned against the door.

She saw the state he was in and, without missing a stroke of the brush, asked him what was wrong. She had never looked so beautiful, so healthy, so full of well-being. Maybe it wasn't true. Maybe the old bitch had lied. "What's this I hear about your being sick," he said quietly.

"I'm perfectly well, Tom. There's nothin sick about havin a baby."

"Oh, my God"—he put his hand over his eyes—"what have I done to you?"

She brushed the curls up from the back of her neck recklessly. "Just another case of the poor servant girl tumbled by her master, is it?"

"Don't talk like that. This is serious. Why didn't you tell me?"

"I didn't need to," she said wryly. "That old harpy did it for me. But ya don't have to worry, I'll be leavin before anyone's the wiser. Your family won't be disgraced."

He went over and got down on his knees beside her, taking the brush from her hand and putting it on the table. "Will you shut up? You know that doesn't mean a damn thing to me. It's only you I care about."

She looked at him, her eyes brimming with tears. "Oh, Tom, I'm sorry. It's nature's dirty trick on women, isn't it?"

He held her hand. They were silent. After a while he said, "I'll find some way out of this."

"What can ya do, marry me maybe?" She looked away.

"Why not? I'll divorce Fanny. You're more of a wife to me than she ever was."

She patted his cheek and got up. "Thanks, dear. I know ya mean it, but I'm not helpless like her, as ya well know. Havin a baby's not the end of the world." She opened the oven door and, pulling out the rack, rapped on a plump loaf of soda bread to test it. "Anyway, these things can be taken care of."

"But that's dangerous!"

"Not if ya do it right away, it's not." She set two freshly baked loaves on the windowsill to cool overnight. "There's nothin wrong with it. Even the church doesn't call it a sin before it quickens."

He bent over to her. "I don't want you to do that."

She searched his eyes. "All right, if that's the way ya want it, I won't. Now what do we do?"

"I don't know yet, but I'm not going to let anything happen to you."

They looked at each other without a word. It was painfully clear to both of them that his attempt to sound confident meant nothing.

Ethel Swindon wasted no time in telling Fanny of her discovery, adding that the master knew about it too, though he had not shown much inclination to discharge the girl.

But if Miss Swindon was disappointed in her employer's reaction the night before, she was even more put out by her mistress's failure to show any interest at all. She had hoped that Fanny would insist that he get rid of the girl at once.

Tom spent the next morning in his study trying to do the household accounts, but actually racking his brains for a solution. He even considered the idea of sending Molly off to the shantytown to stay with Albert and his wife for the period of her confinement. They would certainly look after her when he wasn't free himself, but he couldn't imagine his dear girl in one of those shacks among the kind of people who collected there, with immorality all around.

He thought of sending her west and finding her a job with another family to begin a new life, but her condition ruled that out—and besides, the thought of her being so far away depressed him even more.

He had been sitting for a long time with his head in his hands when he felt a soft touch on his shoulder and a sweet voice from the past recited the familiar lines:

> And so all the night-tide, I lie down by the side
> Of my darling—my darling—my life and my bride,
> in the sepulchre there by the sea . . .

Fanny stood beside him, a robe over her trailing nightdress, her old self. "I know what's bothering you, Tommy, and you mustn't worry any more."

He looked up at her, seeing the gentle concern in those light brown eyes. It was an echo of the past.

"She's a wonderful person and I know you love her very much."

She must have fathomed the whole thing somehow.

"We have to do all we can for her. Find her a room where she'll be comfortable. It won't cost much."

He took her pale hand and pressed it to his cheek. "You're so good. . . ." He was unable to go on.

"And you must spend as much time with her as you like and not worry about me. That's how you can make me happy." Her lips barely touched his forehead and she departed as silently as she came.

He understood. His love for Molly was the way out for her. She was releasing him from the physical bond of a marriage that had never been right. He saw at last it had been a spiritual love between them, and now she would always remain his Annabel Lee, the virgin bride he fell in love with.

MOLLY FOUND FOR HERSELF TWO SMALL ROOMS OVER BY THE river. They were in a cul-de-sac where cheap housing had been put up for the immigrants. The place was popularly known as Shamrock Alley and was tucked out of sight just behind St. Luke's Church, which the Endicotts attended. It was nothing like the other village streets with their tidy houses. The first time Molly showed it to Tom, it reminded him of etchings he had seen of the slums of London.

It was another world. Wooden porches ran the length of the rows of connected brick houses, and the two upper floors were reached by outside stairways. The whole thing was like a barracks around a courtyard.

The clamor struck him as soon as they turned into it past a dilapidated tavern on the corner that expelled drunks night and day. Everybody seemed to be living outside for the summer, leaning over the porch railings shouting to one another and lowering pails for provisions or beer. Urchins ran around underfoot, pulling at Tom's coat demanding pennies. He was taken aback when Molly picked one of them up, wiped its nose on her handkerchief, and gave it a kiss before setting it back down.

Her two narrow rooms didn't make him feel any better. The raucous voices from outside were clearly audible. A fat neighbor woman with red hair pushed her way in and introduced herself as Mrs. Brophy. He didn't want his Molly to be here any more than in squatters' town.

"But don't ya see, this is just right for me," she said, sitting on a sagging iron bedstead without a mattress. "It's my world. They'll take me the way I am, and there won't be any trouble about you comin by either. I wouldn't feel right about livin where everyone turned their noses up at me. Ya wouldn't want that, would ya?"

He looked out at the alley dubiously, but she came up to him and pinched his cheek. "You've already been so good to me, ya mustn't be a fussbudget now. I like it here and here's where I'll have my baby."

He couldn't insist, because her mind was obviously made up and he was the one, after all, who had gotten her into the pickle she was in. Trying to hold down his misgivings, he left her there.

When he got home, there was Miss Swindon looking at him with a pursed smile of total comprehension as she pretended to be arranging dahlias on the hall table. She had been waiting for him just to twist the knife. Nobody was going to get away with anything as long as *she* was around.

He saw red. He went right up to her and looked her straight in her beady eyes. "I'm keeping you on for only one reason—my wife needs you. But if you ever open your mouth about Mrs. Hanlon again, you'll be out on the street with no references. And I'll make damn sure that you never get another job in Greenwich."

She gave the flowers a last plump and turned away, tucking stray hairs under her tight hairnet as if his threat meant nothing to her. But he knew she got the point because for once she didn't talk back.

At first he was self-conscious about leaving the house after dinner to go down and see Molly. He felt that his casual remark about going for a walk hung luridly in the air behind him, and not only Miss Swindon and Fanny knew what he was up to, but even Bridget, the new hired woman. A lumpy old thing, he had found her at Castle Garden just off the boat, loaded down with bundles, waiting for a relative who never showed up. She was forever thanking him for having rescued her from the turmoil of the immigration depot.

It didn't get dark until late and all of Shamrock Alley seemed to be in the welcome party every time he came. Feeling overdressed in his checked trousers, single-breasted frock coat and high hat, he negotiated his way past the tavern where beer drinkers in collarless shirts and caps crowded the walk. He didn't look right or left as he stepped through the urchins and women chattering in their loud brogues on the outside wooden stairway. He was sure that everyone was watching him go to her rooms on the top floor. It was only when he pushed aside the curtain she had hung over her open door and felt her loving arms around him that he started breathing again.

But making love here was even better than it had been at home. The rowdy atmosphere of the alley made him feel that he was in a whorehouse. Sometimes as he lay with his writhing and totally unleashed mistress he imagined that he was in bed with one of the women who used to accost him on the waterfront. He didn't get aroused any more at the fantasy of rescuing pale, helpless maidens. It was so different with Molly from what it had been with his passive wife, which once he had thought was normal.

When he was lying quiet beside her again, listening to the women on the porches bantering with the men drinking below, he looked at his darling's happy and perspiring face and was disgusted with his sordid fantasies. But Molly told him things about the life of the alley that fired his imagination—about mothers and daughters who went a-whoring together in the shadows of the Gansevoort Pier, fathers who slept with their own daughters, men who considered themselves married to each other. *Everything* seemed to go on here.

One evening in the fall when they were making love, Molly, beneath him, pushed at him to stop. Out of breath he asked her what was the matter.

"I'm five months along, lovey. Ya must go easy now." She took his hand and ran it over the mound of her belly. It had been getting bigger without him noticing.

In the grip of his lust he had forgotten all about her condition. "Forgive me," he said, abashed at his own selfishness. "I won't do it again, not until after the baby comes."

She laughed and pulled him down to her. "What a funny one ya are. Do ya think we must stop our lovemakin because there's a little one inside sayin, 'Don't press too hard, daddy'? I need ya more than ever now that I'm nearin my term. Ya movin inside me spreads the pleasure around him so he's born happy, and the comfort of it will make the birthin easier."

But he was not reassured. He told her he was afraid that when he got carried away he might hurt her as well as the child.

"If that's what's worryin ya, my pet, there are other ways to do it."

"Just what is it you have in mind?" he laughed, leaning on an elbow.

"I'll show ya." She pushed him over on his back and started to move her lips down his body.

Shocked, he tried to stop her.

"I'm in charge now," she said, and her mouth continued its progress down over him until he was flopping rhythmically beneath her.

He had always thought that such an act degraded a woman. How foolish he had been. The woman he loved was paying the highest tribute to his virility.

When she lay beside him again, she whispered that it was his turn now.

The demand astounded him. He could never do that! No man would.

But she continued to caress his belly and rub herself against him passionately. "Go on, Tom." She took his hand and wiped it between her thighs, bringing it back up so that he couldn't help breathing in her heavy woman-smell. Unexpectedly, a desire to grovel in her like a dog went over him.

As he walked home through the night streets of the village, the only sounds his footsteps on the cobblestones and the steeple bell of St. Luke's tolling eleven, he still tasted her on his lips and felt the chains that had bound him all his life falling away.

SHE GAVE BIRTH WITH THE HELP OF THE NEIGHBOR, MRS. Brophy, on a cold dawn in January, 1847. It was a boy and she named him Patrick.

By the time Tom got there she was sitting up, a shawl over her nightdress, red-faced but happy, the baby at her breast. He couldn't help but contrast this picture of motherhood with the birth of Claude the year before when Fanny had taken so long to recover and had no milk and it had taken weeks of Phoebe's nursing to put color into Claude's sallow cheeks.

When Tom showed surprise at her having named the baby Patrick without consulting him, she said, "Well, we can't call him Thomas Endicott, Jr., now can we? I thought it best to name him after my father who was shot down like a dog by English troopers. So Patrick he shall be."

He was a lusty baby with a patch of hair, black like his mother's. And when she put him into Tom's arms the little blue eyes, which he knew were unable to focus yet, seemed to be looking up at him happily.

Throughout dinner the following Sunday Tom could hardly wait to get away to see Molly and the baby. He had been down to Shamrock Alley every evening since the birth four days before, but this was the first time he would be able to spend time with them during the day.

It was a tender period between them now, even without lovemaking. She had a chance to tell him many things about her life in Ireland he had not heard before. It turned out that at the time her father was shot, she herself was involved with the Fenians who were fighting to throw out the British and she had run off to America to escape arrest.

It was unbearable sitting at the table at home listening to the chitchat between Fanny and Miss Swindon about some bonnet they were trimming. A thin afternoon sun shone on the leftover patches of dirty snow outside in the backyard. He was able to get away only after Bridget brought in the dessert, a watery rennet custard he detested.

But when he had waded through the slush over to Shamrock Alley and was climbing the stairs, he heard sounds of a party.

It was an unpleasant surprise. Instead of finding her alone with the baby, a group of neighbors was with her, stuffing their mouths with smoked oysters and pickled eggs on hunks of bread and washing it all down with beer. Molly in her Sunday best was the center of attention, reclining on the daybed nursing Patrick with a breast exposed before the company as if it were the most natural thing in the world.

The crowded room was suffocatingly hot, reeking of stale clothes and beer. Whatever had possessed her to ask all these people in? They didn't need anybody else around. He wanted her to himself.

"Ah, there ya are, Tom!" She waved him in with her mug of beer. "Ya missed the christenin but you're in time for the party."

A gap-toothed man in an oversized frock coat seized his hand and pumped it vigorously, assuring him that the little tyke would never want for a codfish as long as *he* was around.

When the baby lost the nipple and set up a squall, Molly gave her breast a squeeze to test it. To Tom's mortification, a squirt of milk shot into the air. "Nothin's wrong with it, ya little souse," she said. "Then is it the beer ya want?" She pretended to tip her mug to the tiny mouth as everyone roared.

The infant resumed its busy suckling at the breast and everyone in the room raised mugs in happy salute, joining little Patrick by guzzling down their beer.

Only the blowsy Mrs. Brophy was not too far gone to see how uncomfortable Tom was. She got unsteadily to her feet, brushing crumbs off her lap. "Ah, Molly, I for one have had enough partyin." And raising her voice so no one could miss her meaning, she added, "I'm sure it's time all of us was leavin ya to rest."

They all drained their mugs in a rush and got up to go, letting Tom know by their good wishes and back slapping on their way out that they were well aware of who he was.

"Here, now!" Molly cried. "Ya don't have to go. Tom don't want that, do ya, Tom?"

Mrs. Brophy bent to kiss her on the forehead. "I'll be around to see ya in the mornin, darlin." She also gave Tom a beery kiss and allowed as how proud she was to be the baby's godmother, having stood up at St. Aloysius for the christening. Laughing tipsily, she toddled out after the rest.

"Now why did they have to go, I wonder?" said Molly, looking forlorn, a fallen curl pasted to her sweaty forehead. "Oh, well"—she brightened and raised her mug—"here's to the bashful parents!" She drank it down, smiling at Tom with a mustache of white foam.

He stared in rage out at the sooty snow on the porch railing. Their own private little world had been ruptured, violated. She had tossed it away without a thought for him or what they had together. "What in God's name is all this about?" he asked, when he was able to speak.

She wiped the foam off her mouth with the back of her hand, as Patrick suckled peacefully. "Don't be a sourpuss, darlin. I've had my baby christened. And anyway, what's it to ya?"

"What did you have to do that for?" he demanded.

She colored in quick anger. "I don't want my son growin up to be a bastard, even if you do."

"You didn't give my name at the church!"

She raised the baby to her shoulder and patted its back briskly to burp it. "Don't worry, I didn't give away your dirty little secret. What kind of a Catholic would people think him with a name like Endicott, anyway? Hanlon's a good enough name for any Irishman—and Irish he's goin to be, if I have anything to say about it."

He sat down on one of her wooden chairs, dejected. "Everyone knows Hanlon couldn't have been his father. You weren't with him for months before he died."

She laughed. "What an arse ya are, Tom. Father Doherty knows how hard life is for us poor women down here. It's the innocent mites the good man is thinkin about, God bless him." She yawned and settled the baby down beside her on the bed. "Ah, what difference does it make now anyway?" She snuggled down farther in the pillows. "Ya should have seen the little devil. Ya would have laughed. He peed all over the father's robe as he was bein sprinkled with the holy water."

After that, it seemed to him that Molly threw herself into the life of Shamrock Alley as if he didn't matter so much to her any more. It was a rare visit when neighbors didn't drop in on them without a by-your-leave. Sometimes he found her standing out on the stairs or even down in the alley holding the baby on one hip and laughing with what looked to him like very disreputable characters.

He found his visits more and more depressing. Although there were still those moments when they lay perfectly content in each other's arms in the dark as before, she seemed hardly willing to tear herself away from her social life to be with him.

When he complained, she told him that he was being a sourpuss again, that she was enjoying not being pregnant and having to be so tied down. She didn't have to be afraid of her husband showing up any more, and she was starting to live free out in the world as she had always dreamed.

One day when he arrived after work unexpectedly, she was nowhere to be seen. He paced her narrow rooms, imagining all sorts of calamities, and was on the point of going next door to ask Mrs. Brophy or one of the other neighbors if they knew where she was, when she rushed in with the baby, her blue eyes shining, and announced that she had found herself a job.

"I'm goin to be an independent woman again, Tom. I won't have to take any more money from ya. Aren't ya proud of me? That was my idea in the first place when I came over."

He nearly blew his top when he heard that her job was at another tavern, this one on the waterfront called the Blarney Stone and owned by Mrs. Brophy's son. "Just what are you going to do with the baby while you're there?"

"Take him with me, of course."

"My God! Into a tavern?"

"What are ya talkin about? Them lads were so sweet to him today, he got more attention than your two little ones ever get from their nurse girl and a mother that's too crazy to even look at them."

He held on to the table trying to hold his temper and said that he would not hear of her taking his son to such a place, even if she insisted on working there.

"I'm so glad that I'm not married to ya, Mr. Endicott! Thank God ya don't own me." She took the baby into the other room and slammed the door after her.

The next evening he stayed home. As he sat before the fire in the parlor with Fanny across from him embroidering a tablecloth—Miss Swindon in her room with a convenient migraine—he could hardly hold the newspaper steady, he was so riled up at Molly for defying him. Not only that, but daring to take an infant—his son—into a saloon! Why was she doing it? He had set things up for them perfectly. She didn't need to work.

He had resolved to stay away and let her stew in her own juices for a while. She'd come to her senses fast enough if he wasn't around. In the meantime it wasn't so bad in his own house. Fanny was better since Claude's birth the year before. In fact, ever since the time she had come to him in his study, she hadn't had a single attack.

But as the days passed he felt his pride weakening, and one evening when Fanny asked him out of the blue why he was staying home every night, didn't he have other responsibilities, he could have kissed her with gratitude for making him see how stubborn he was being.

He had been wanting Molly constantly, much as he tried to be interested in the latest chapter of the Dickens novel in the *Herald*. He was more than ready to bury his pride and make up.

By the time he was running up the familiar wooden stairs to her room he couldn't wait to fall on the bed with her and tell her how sorry he was.

Just as he got to her landing, a husky workman came out her door and passed him going down. He had an uneasy feeling, but he told himself not to jump to any conclusions. He had come to make up with her and nothing was going to stand in the way.

But the minute she opened the door to him wearing only a wrapper and with her dark hair loose around her shoulders, he asked her who the man was who just left.

She was staring at him in surprise, as if he were the last person she expected to see. "You here again!" she said as she stood aside to let him in. "Who are ya talkin about? Oh, him. Only deliverin a hod of coal he was." She turned to pick up a pile of wash from the chair he always sat in. "It's been so chilly, I don't want the baby to get the croup. Ya want to see him?"

There was a suggestion of gin in the air. With a sinking feeling, he asked what the man was doing delivering coal at this time of night.

She gave a vague smile, tucking her hair behind her ears, until Patrick set up a howl from the other room and she hurried in to him where he lay in his cradle.

Her bed—the bed they had shared so many times—was all in a tumble. Though he tried to hold back, his sick heart made him blurt out, "You're lying to me. That man wasn't here for coal."

She looked up from the cradle and snapped back, "Who are you to ask me questions about anything? I'm makin my own way now. I haven't seen hide nor hair of ya in days. Ya expect me to sit here all by my lonesome and me a healthy woman, while you're playing lord and master over on Perry Street?"

He felt like the wind had been knocked out of him. "So you did it then. You didn't care after all. . . ."

She stood defiantly in the bedroom doorway, expecting him to come back at her full force, maybe even to hit her, as any man she had known before would have done, which would surely have been followed by reconciliation in bed.

But he would have none of her. He picked up his hat and turned to go.

Frightened by his coldness, this unexpected gesture of finality, she tried once more to provoke him so that things would turn out all right. "Why don't ya look at me? All right, so I did sleep with him! But it was only because I was missin ya so. I thought I was never goin to see ya again. If you're mad at me, Tom, then let me have it, but don't just stand there."

He started to open the door and she was over to him in a minute, trying to throw her arms around him. "Don't go! It's you I want, my darlin. Only you . . ." She clutched at his hand, arm, clothes, but he paid no attention.

As he walked off into the darkness below, she leaned over the porch railing and yelled so that the whole court could hear,

"I want no more of your money, nor does my child, who is a Hanlon and will be raised a Hanlon, not one of you tight-assed Endicotts!"

When he hung up his hat and coat in the hall, tired to his bones, the little Indian nurse was sitting barefoot at the bottom of the stairs in the shadows whispering to the children, who should have been in bed long before, about old Greenwich prison that used to stand by the river, and how all her family used to watch the prisoners being flogged until the blood ran down in pools and they shrieked for mercy. But best of all was when they led out one of the murderers to be hanged. . . . Year-old Claude on her lap and three-year-old Veronica at her feet were staring up at her, spellbound.

In the parlor Fanny and Miss Swindon were playing planchette, the saucer under their fingers swooping over the painted letters on the table between them, and Fanny's eyes were dancing with an unhealthy excitement, red blotches on her cheeks.

He dropped into an armchair in his study and stared into the dead ashes of the fireplace.

But like the phoenix, the flames soon rose again from the ashes. As the weeks passed, he found himself longing to get out in the evening, unable to keep himself distracted by the *Herald*. The pallidly tranquil atmosphere of the house that he had pretended to find bearable got on his nerves. Even Fanny was showing signs of uneasiness the more he stayed around.

It was sex he needed. He had never been so honest as to put it in those terms before, but thinking about his nights in Shamrock Alley showed him that this was it, plain and simple. Of course, there were prostitutes in the city—thousands of them—but whenever he tried to picture one of them in his arms, it was always Molly's face that was there, and he was enraged at her all over again.

But the rage kept turning into desire. He still wanted her. She could whore around as much as she liked but she could damn well be his whore too.

Once more he went back to Shamrock Alley and climbed the wooden stairs. From the landing he heard her laughing inside and he imagined her playing with baby Patrick. But when she opened the door, he saw by the smoky light of the oil lamp the coal man sitting in his chair holding a beer. His house of cards tumbled as he understood all at once how profoundly he loved her.

This time she did not try to explain. She came out, closing the door behind her. "I'm sorry, Tom," she told him, "but ya got to understand that I meant what I said. Ya may not have seen it, but it was comin to an end between us for a long time. I'm not sayin it was no good, but it's over now. I'll always be grateful to ya for helpin me, but we're from two different worlds, you and me."

The blood in his ears was pounding so loud his voice didn't seem to be coming from him, but he had to get her back. "What about Patrick, our baby?"

"*My* baby, Tom. Don't ya see, the world will never let him be ours? Ya comin here all the time would keep him a bastard, and now he's got a chance to grow up respectable—a Hanlon, whose father died before he was born. Ya don't need to worry about us, I make enough at the tavern." She put a soft hand on his arm. "You'll forget in no time." And before he could find anything to say, she slipped back in and shut the door.

Immediately, he had a million things to tell her. He wanted to call after her—no one would ever take care of her as he would . . . he would help her . . . not just money, she would always have him to count on . . . he wanted her to know how much he loved her—he was ready to beg on his knees, but the door with its chinks of yellow light around it was closed against him.

For hours he walked the streets, going through grief, humiliation, and rage, one after the other. He had crawled back to her and she had spit at him. He could see her laughing with the coal man about the spectacle he had made of himself. It made him sick to his stomach.

That night as he lay awake tossing, with Fanny in her nightcap curled up beside him in her drugged sleep, he pictured Molly and the coal man going at it like dogs, with the baby—his own flesh and blood—in the cradle right next to them.

It rankled him that she was getting away with it. The child shouldn't be allowed to grow up with her, Patrick wouldn't have a chance. But what could he do? He couldn't make a public outcry. Even if right was on his side, the courts were out of the question—there would be a scandal.

He had to get the child away from her somehow, kidnap

it if necessary—find an old woman to raise it in the country. She'd never get at it. He'd make her suffer. . . .

He saw the door with its chinks of light closed against him and rolled over, burying his face in the pillow. He couldn't do that. It wasn't the child he was upset about. He only wanted to hurt her because she had thrown him out—and the agony was that he still loved her. How was he going to get along without her?

He'd talk to Albert about it. No. He wouldn't understand—Albert would tell him that no woman was important enough to suffer over, one was as good as another, the same old thing.

He had to find someone who would take him seriously. There was the minister at St. Luke's—you were supposed to turn to your minister in time of trouble. Impossible. He could never go to him—the minister would never understand either. No one could. He'd be locked up.

He was going to bust if he didn't find someone to talk to. The minister wouldn't do, but he couldn't get the bell tower of St. Luke's out of his mind, rising over the roofs and treetops of the village. Although he had never done such a thing in his life or even considered it, he was in such torment that finally he slipped out of bed and got down on his knees on the cold planks of the bedroom floor.

Instead of saying some prayer he knew by rote, he found himself asking for help in his own words. The old lump in his throat that had been there all his life seemed to dissolve, and when he opened his eyes he became aware of the first pale intimations of dawn filtering in around the drapes and the cool freshness of a new day.

He climbed back into bed and pulled the quilts up against the chill. As he drifted off, he imagined—whether it was a dream or not he never knew—that Fanny had hovered over him and put her lips to his forehead.

After breakfast he stepped out, reborn, into a perfect spring morning and filled his lungs with the salt air from the river mixed with the pungency of wood smoke, fresh horse manure smelling like fermented hay, and the riot of lilacs in the garden across the street. At the corner of Bleecker Street he tossed a coin into the hat of an itinerant fiddler with straw hair like a scarecrow, whose music accompanied the clatter of horses and wagons on the thoroughfare.

He still loved Molly—he always would—and it was going to hurt a long time, but he saw clearly the wrong he had done to her. He had lived selfishly and was going to make amends. His higher self was in charge now. He had a great need to find something worthwhile to devote himself to to fill the place where she had been. He didn't know what that was or how it was coming, but he knew in his bones he would find it.

IN THE FOLLOWING DAYS HE KEPT THINKING OF THAT MOMENT on his knees and waited for a sign, for he was sure that his prayer had been received.

At the shop it was clear that Albert guessed something was up, so without going into details he simply admitted that he and Molly were through. Although he couldn't explain it to anyone, he knew that something genuine had happened to him and he didn't want Albert scoffing or calling him crazy.

But from then on Albert never let up, suggesting one woman after another, usually some relative from his wife's extensive family who wouldn't cause him any headaches. Tom fended him off—all that was finished for him. He still had the natural desires every young man was tormented by, but he was convinced that when he found his path it would take care of everything.

One day when the bell over the door tinkled he looked up from his work and in walked the alderman's pretty young wife, Florence Howells, with Otis Skidmore, the bookseller. Mrs. Howells had outraged the women's group at St. Luke's, according to Miss Swindon, by urging them to fight for the right to vote. Otis, who had opened his bookshop recently after a year of wandering around Europe, was rumored to be working for the Underground Railroad, helping slaves escape to Canada.

Some people even said there was a tunnel in his cellar that led to a landing on the river.

When the couple handed him a manuscript they wanted him to print up as a pamphlet for them, he was surprised to discover it was about temperance. He would never connect temperance with people like them. For him, the Temperance Society had always meant his uncle in Binghamton, a fanatical teetotaler who blamed all the evils known to man on drink and the devil.

He spread out on his desk copies of the temperance pamphlets he had already printed up, pointing out to them the various layouts and typography.

Florence Howells, who had removed her bonnet to arrange a bunch of violets fastened to it, shook her head firmly. "Oh, my. No! Those look much too stuffy. They give an entirely wrong impression of what we're all about. We want to shake things up a little." She plucked a wilted violet and tossed it into a brass spittoon. She and Otis had a different idea about what temperance was all about, she told him as she retied the bonnet under her chin, and they wanted their tract to make that quite clear.

The bookseller explained that their object was to attract new blood into the Society and they were banking on their pamphlet to do it. "We hope to get a little controversy going with this thing," he said, slapping the manuscript. "You ought to come to one of our meetings yourself."

Tom told him that even if he wanted to, he wouldn't qualify since he enjoyed a glass of beer now and then.

"So do I!" said Otis enthusiastically, and explained that there were two schools of thought about that in Temperance. His side didn't object to fermented drinks like beer and wine.

"Total abstinence isn't necessary for people like us," Mrs. Howells added. "But some people really need it. We'll never be able to wipe out poverty unless we attack liquor first, because it's liquor, after all, that's keeping those poor wretches down." Embarrassed at her own sanctimoniousness, she smiled. "Besides, we have a very good time in the Society. It's not just fossils there, Mr. Endicott. All the really lively people are joining these days. Our group has started holding street meetings and we go all over the city together. Do come, if you can."

He read over their manuscript when they were gone. It was unusual for a tract, not one mention of the devil or damnation or any tales about country girls in the city led astray by a glass of beer. The gist of it, from what he could make out, was that the liquor interests were making huge profits off the misery of the poor, and it argued for taxing the booze makers out of existence.

A milk wagon clattered by outside, its empty cans banging in counterpoint to the sound of the presses in back.

He was curious about these temperance meetings. He liked both Florence Howells and Otis Skidmore and there was no doubt that they genuinely wanted to help people. He thought of Shamrock Alley and that tavern spilling out its drunks into the street day and night. Those poor wretches down there led such terrible lives. Molly's face rose before him, telling him it was all over, closing the door. He got a grip on himself. He had to do something useful with his life now. Maybe this was it. There was certainly not much else to do in Greenwich.

Albert came out from the back of the shop buttoning his jacket and stopped to look over his shoulder to see what he was reading. With a loud "Oh, shit!" he sent a stream of tobacco juice into the spittoon halfway across the room and left for the day. Albert was getting more commissions than he could handle, painting his opulent nudes in the taverns that were springing up on every corner as the city, swollen with immigrants, expanded northward river to river.

Tom smiled after his unregenerate friend. There were certain things Albert was never going to understand.

On the following Tuesday he joined the crowd at Woolsey Hall on Gansevoort Street. Florence Howells, Otis Skidmore, and other young members of the Society were distributing their pamphlet at the door and welcomed him heartily.

But the program did not get off to a promising start. After the singing of the temperance anthem, some itinerant preacher doing the "devil-and-damnation" circuit thundered that in spite of all the social reformers infiltrating the movement, the real purpose of the Society remained the salvation of souls and the redemption of sinners. From a couple of rows off, Mrs. Howells caught Tom's eye and looked up at the ceiling in exasperation.

Things picked up when Otis bounded up to the stage and said that the movement wasn't going to get anywhere with such fusty attitudes and that it was time they faced the real problem. It was not the drunkards who were guilty. They were only the victims of the liquor manufacturers, backed up by corrupt politicians. Even more important, in his view, it was time the

Society woke up to other important issues, like freeing the slaves and the rights of women.

The scattering of applause from the younger members was nearly overwhelmed by the loud booing from the old guard.

After the usual testimonials from some reformed drunkards, the meeting broke up with heated discussion on all sides. Flossie Howells and Otis and their friends pushed back chairs and joined hands round, singing "Onward Christian Soldiers" lustily. Tom was about to leave when Flossie broke away to take his hand and bring him into the circle.

At first he felt awkward, but the enthusiasm of the singers was infectious, and by the time they dispersed he was feeling so good that he agreed to meet them for a street rally the next night to take their message directly to the people.

With the encouragement of his new friends he threw himself into "the work" as they called it, glad not to have to sit home, miserable and bored with Fanny. It wasn't that he had forgotten Molly, but he was convinced he had found something worthwhile to fill his life with. The only fly in the ointment was his old problem of lust, but he told himself that if he kept busy enough he would conquer it.

One hot summer night he went with Flossie, Otis, and several others to hand out leaflets on Greene Street just beyond Washington Square. It was the heart of New York City's red-light district, just out of sight of the fashionable hotels and restaurants of Broadway. The gaslamps had just been lit, but the street was already in full swing. Men, elegant in their high silk hats, gloves, and walking sticks got out of hansom cabs at the canopied entrances and, as music poured into the street and barkers called out, pushed their way through the swinging doors of dance saloons and bordellos.

Tom did his best to keep his mind on passing out the leaflets, but it was hard not to see the women, dressed in flimsy negligees, fanning themselves in the windows. Through a swinging door he caught glimpses of gaudily done-up women at tables, bells tinkling from their red boots, laughing raucously with men. It reminded him of a picture Fanny had hung opposite their bed in which the flames of hell were licking around just such a scene, while Satan hovered over it all.

A buxom blonde, sitting on the low sill of a window only a few feet away, was fanning her breast that a flamboyant gold satin dress amply revealed. To his discomfort, she caught his eye and winked, even calling out over the noise of the street, "Hey, gents, how about getting rid of the bitch and meeting me inside?"

"Well, I never!" said Flossie, going crimson, and pushed her way across the crowded sidewalk right up to the woman. "Don't be so smart, miss. Can't you see that you're being exploited? You don't have to be here. You could be working at a respectable job."

Heavily painted eyes looked Flossie up and down. "I had a job, sister, working in a cotton mill seventy hours a week for two dollars and a quarter. Go peddle your papers somewhere else." And with that she leaned out and tapped a passing gentleman with her fan. He grabbed it and let her pull him up close for a whispered exchange.

Flossie led her group off dispiritedly down the street through the throngs of men appraising the wares at the windows. "You know, she's got a point," she said when they had turned onto Bleecker Street and were starting home. "We're going to have to offer something more concrete than inspirational ideas to get to people like her."

Discouraged by their lack of success, they didn't stop for buns and coffee at the little bakeshop on Bleecker Street that night as they usually did. But when they broke up, Tom was too disturbed to go directly home, so he dropped by the printshop, thinking he would do some work until he calmed down.

There was a lamp lit in back where Albert was working on his own printmaking as he often did in the evening, but Tom didn't feel like talking. He flopped down at his desk and tried to do some proofreading.

He had never seen a woman looking so debased as that blonde sitting in the window with her painted face and her flesh oozing out of her fancy dress. God, it was degrading how they made you feel.

Albert came out from the back, looking scrawnier than ever in a red woolen undershirt and suspendered trousers. "It's you, is it? I usually have this place to myself at night." He wiped his forehead. "Gad, it's a hot one today. It was sure as hell cooler over by the river this afternoon. What a place to paint."

Tom didn't look up, but the artist was in no hurry to get back to his engraving and sat down on the edge of the desk stroking his drooping mustache reflectively. "You know, there's something about Greenwich that appeals to low-down, unbuttoned sods like me. Can't put my finger on it exactly, but seems to me there's less hassle here than most places I been, in spite of you and your temperance bugs, Tom." Albert grinned, but noticing his hangdog look, asked what was bothering him.

Tom couldn't hold it in any longer. "I thought I'd seen everything," he said, "but tonight we were over on Greene Street and I tell you, it was unbelievable. Do you have any idea what it's like there?"

"You old reprobate. Over at the cathouses, were you? Did you have a good time?"

Tom got up, ready to hit him, but his friend eased him back down. "Hold on, old fella. You know I'm a kidder."

Tom sank back and shut his eyes. "It was horrible, horrible. . . ."

Keeping his arm around his shoulders, Albert said quietly, "It's not so bad, friend. You're just a man like any other. You're horny as hell, is that it?"

He nodded miserably.

"Can't fight nature, Tom. Now that you're finished with Molly and your wife an invalid, a man's got to get his rocks off or he wouldn't be a man. Why don't you let me take you back there? I'll introduce you to some of the girls."

When Tom stared at him the artist nodded. "Sure, I know a lot of them. I've been sketching them for years. They're good girls. They know what a man needs, especially when he hasn't got a woman of his own, like you."

"It may be a joke to you," said Tom, wanting to explain himself, "but I didn't know what to do with myself until I found temperance. It gave some meaning to my life and the people are my friends. If I were to do such a thing . . ."

"Listen to me," Albert said firmly, "this has nothing to do with your work in the temperance. And no one will ever know."

That night Tom went back to Greene Street without Albert taking him there and without any tracts under his arm. And afterward, in spite of his guilt, he told himself it was better to lie with a whore than corrupt another virtuous woman. From then on he went there regularly, and gradually stopped making excuses for it to himself.

1858

TOM ENDICOTT LEFT THE PRINTSHOP EARLY ONE WINTRY EVENing because Miss Swindon had sent word that she was having another of her migraine attacks and was unable to take care of his wife. The task fell to Tom since Fanny couldn't tolerate either of the children for very long, though Veronica and Claude were now old enough to help out. But to his sorrow, their mother's erratic behavior had made them permanently wary of her. In spite of Albert's jibing, it was only his involvement with the Temperance Society that had sustained him these last lonely years.

He hardly looked boyish any more and his clothes were shabby, attesting to the fact that for years he had had no woman who cared enough about him to look after his needs properly. Miss Swindon was always using her headache trick when he was at his busiest. Not only was he needed at the shop, but there was a temperance crusade at Woolsey Hall that night. The presses were tied up running off the program that had to be ready in time for the meeting, as well as with an announcement of a sale of an ice cabinet for preserving perishable food and a zinc-lined bathing tub with a gas water heater attached. The heaters sometimes exploded, but these days, nothing put off the novelty-mad public from buying up all the new household inventions on the market. Tom himself had installed a brick furnace in the cellar that piped warmed air up into the rest of the house.

On his way home from the shop he stopped for a moment to watch some neighborhood boys sledding on the snow-packed street. It was already dark and the gas lamps threw a nostalgic light over the scene, reminding him of bellywopping in the town where he grew up, one of the few pleasant memories he had from his boyhood. Usually he tried not to give in to such sentimental feelings—there was always the danger that he would start longing for Molly again.

He had only run into her once in the intervening years. That was in the autumn of '52 on one of those crystal-clear days in New York when everything stands out sharp and the colors are intense. The air was so fresh it seemed to have blown in straight from the Catskills.

He had gone to the pushcart market down on Hudson Street to help Otis Skidmore who was making a campaign speech. That year Otis was running for the office of alderman on the Temperance ticket, a post vacated by Flossie Howells's husband when he had been elected to the state assembly.

Tom was passing out leaflets while Otis on his soapbox was trying to drum up support from the new voters among the immigrants. Across the street a speaker on Irish independence had collected an enthusiastic crowd with a tirade against the English, but Otis wasn't having much luck. No one in the busy street market was paying any attention to Otis except for some heckling urchins.

Tom was doing his best to shoo them away when he saw her. She was heading back in the direction of Shamrock Alley, which was not far off. With his heart pounding, he pushed his way through a mob of people engaged in busy haggling over a load of fresh fish spread out on the cobblestones.

Until then he had believed that filling up his life with community activities was enough for him. But to his surprise he found himself running after her, everything else forgotten.

As he caught up with her he saw that she had a toddler holding on to her skirt. His first thought was that it must be Patrick, but the child was too small, only two or three. And for an instant he wasn't sure if it was Molly after all, her face was so much fuller and under the shawl her belly was big. But then he realized she must be pregnant.

"Molly!" His voice nearly choked getting out her name.

She turned and her blue eyes looked puzzled under the same

untamable black curls. Then she broke into her broad smile. "Why, Tom, ya haven't changed a bit. You're still pretty enough to turn every girl's head."

He was so nonplussed by her old, sweet naturalness that he dropped his leaflets, and she burst out laughing.

As he fumbled to gather them up, she took one out of his hand and looked at Albert's drawing on the cover of a greedy distiller holding a huge liquor bottle over the open mouths of the poor below.

"Would it be temperance you're in? Ah, Tom, ya never could have been an Irishman."

He couldn't stop coloring like an idiot and looked for something to say. "I see you're married again. I'm so glad."

She laughed with the old heartiness. "Ah, my dear, still the same innocent, ya are. A girl doesn't have to be married to have herself a fine family. I'm not made to stay with one man forever."

He looked down uneasily at the toddler in a neatly patched coat and trousers who stared back suspiciously.

"Timothy," said his mother, giving him a yank, "show Mr. Endicott ya got a tongue in your head."

The urchin only turned to sniffle against her skirt.

"He's nearly four now, would ya believe it? And another bun in the oven." She patted her belly proudly. "Ya must think I'm a lost soul for sure, but I'm happier than I've ever been. I make a good livin at the Blarney Stone and I got no worries."

Nearly suffocating in her presence, he said that he had to get back to Otis but she put a hand on his arm.

"Ah, come home with me first and see Patrick. Such a sturdy little lad. He's a real helper already. I'll say you're an old friend."

But he had mumbled an excuse, saying he would try to come by another time, and watched as she strode away through a drift of brilliant maple leaves on the walk, throwing back her shawl and shaking her black curls loose in the breeze until she turned the corner.

That had been more than five years ago, and for a long while after, it had seemed to him that the life he had so carefully constructed for himself was no more than a makeshift. Nevertheless, that meeting had made it clear to him that it was better they had gone their separate ways. Considering how she wanted to live her life, it could never have worked out—not in a million years.

The boys were shouting in the street around him now as they threw themselves down on their sleds. On a pile of snow against the picket fence of the old mansion across from his house some boys playing king-of-the-hill were pummeling each other with snowballs. For a moment he thought he recognized his twelve-year-old son Claude holding the summit against a barrage of snowballs, until he saw with disappointment it was some other boy.

He sighed as he climbed the stoop and stomped the snow off his boots before going in, preparing himself for whatever might be waiting for him in his gloomy household.

After shedding his coat and scarf in the hall, he looked into the parlor where Claude was playing by himself on the carpet. The boy was so engrossed that he paid no attention to his father. He had constructed a prison yard out of cardboard, complete with a row of scaffolds and nooses made of string with which he was hanging cardboard prisoners one after the other as he made up a story about it to himself.

When Tom interrupted to ask how things had gone for him that day at the boys' academy, Claude looked up with his mother's nervous eyes and mumbled an inaudible reply.

He went up the stairs heavily. He wished he could get closer to his son, especially after his own miserable growing-up with his uncle, but Claude had never responded to his self-conscious overtures. Those eyes bothered him, as if Fanny's trouble might be in him too. The boy had always been frail and still occasionally wet his bed. He needed to get out more, make friends. It wasn't enough for him to help out at the shop on Saturdays as he had been doing lately. Tom resolved to try harder to reach him.

Veronica's door on the second floor was closed as usual. She was fourteen but no more sociable than Claude. She spent most of her time after school in her room writing poems, which she never showed to anybody. He had asked to see them but she always refused.

On the other side of the door Veronica had laid aside her pen and was standing over the hot-air vent in the floor, her eyes dreamy, swaying back and forth as the heat rose under her skirts. Her lips moved as she silently recited a poem. Like her brother, she had no real friends at school and she didn't want any. She knew that if she was very quiet and made herself as plain as possible, she would not be noticed.

* * *

When Tom went into the bedroom, Fanny was sitting in her chair by the window working at her embroidery. He was relieved to see that she was not in the unstable condition Miss Swindon's message had led him to expect. In the last years her attacks had become more frequent again, which left her increasingly listless. Although she was only in her mid-thirties she looked older, her skin transparent and her hair prematurely gray.

As he changed his jacket, something in her quiet pose reminded him of the delicate girl she had once been, and he went over to kiss her cheek.

But she was not sewing. Her hands lay holding her embroidery hoop in her lap, and she stared vacantly out into the night. She scarcely paid attention to him any more.

After Veronica had helped him get her to bed, he sat in his study with the newspaper in front of him. If his children weren't happy it was no wonder, he thought. They didn't have much chance with a mother like that. If only it were possible for him to give them a more normal life.

He let the newspaper drop. He had no interest in the latest Lincoln-Douglas debate, or the fuss over Irish anarchists throwing bombs, or even the slavery issue that filled whole columns.

He could still go to the temperance meeting if he wanted. Fanny was asleep and it wouldn't be any trouble for Veronica to look in on her. But he didn't feel like it—things had been going from bad to worse there too.

Once, in the company of Otis and Flossie, it had been exhilarating to go around together fighting for what they believed in. But tonight he would have to disappoint Otis, even if his friend counted on him more than ever to help shake things up since Flossie had gone with her husband to Albany. And she wasn't the only one of the livelier members who had left. A lot of them had deserted for the antislavery cause and the women's movement—"bloomerism" the papers snidely called it.

The fusty old guard was having it all its own way lately, rampaging against sin. They didn't care about people. They'd stop at nothing to keep the immigrants from moving in and bringing down real estate values. Now that Greenwich had been completely engulfed by the city and with the piers being built along the riverfront, tenements were going up all over the place.

So the fanatics were calling for a crusade against "vice"—which was just another way of attacking the immigrants. Things had come to such a point at the meetings there was even open talk against "pope worshippers," by which of course they meant the Irish. Tom didn't like the way it was going at all.

He shoved back his chair and paced the room from the heavy drapes of the bay window to the portieres closed against the drafts and back again. He and Otis and the others ought to be able to get back at those bigots somehow. He was still young, not yet forty. In fact, he was stronger than he had ever been.

But the way he felt, it was as if his hands were tied. He didn't know what to do—not about temperance, not about his family. Everything was so damned difficult. If only he could make something happen.

If only he could see Molly again. . . .

HE DID SEE HER AGAIN, BUT IN CIRCUMSTANCES HE NEVER would have expected—or wanted.

The following morning, a Saturday, he was sitting at his desk editing a tract that he and Otis hoped would show up the hard-liners at the Society for the bigots they were. Albert Cogswell was off on a trip sketching Indians fishing through the ice up the Hudson, and Claude was at the counter to deal with any customers who came in, when the door flew open with a blast of cold air and a street boy of ten or eleven rushed right up to the desk.

"Are you Mr. Endicott, sir?" the boy asked boldly.

Tom didn't want to interrupt his work and motioned him over to the counter, but the boy held his ground. "No, it's you I come for."

He dropped his pen, his attention riveted. Though he hadn't seen him since he was born, he would have known him anywhere. He was a sturdy lad in trousers belted up with a rope, a patched jacket, and a floppy workman's cap in hand. He had his mother's curly black hair and frank blue eyes. He seemed upset about something.

While Claude gawked from the counter, Tom pushed back his chair and turned fully to Patrick. "I'm Mr. Endicott. What can I do for you?"

"It's my ma, sir," the boy said excitedly. "They wrecked the Blarney Stone last night and took her to jail. She told me often she worked in your house and you'd do anything for her."

Tom asked no questions. He told the astonished Claude to mind the shop and followed after Patrick, who was already setting off in the direction of the Jefferson Market jailhouse.

The snow-packed sidewalks had been spread with ashes, making it possible to move fast. When Tom caught up with him at the corner, he tried to find out what had happened, but all the boy was able to tell him was that "it was the shithead Protestant temperance people who done it." Mrs. Brophy had said they raided a bunch of taverns the night before. "But why arrest my ma? She never done nothin," he said, before breaking into a run as the clock tower of the courthouse came in sight.

At the jailhouse Tom demanded to know from the policeman sitting at a desk behind the wooden barrier that divided the room what they thought they were doing arresting Mrs. Hanlon.

Pulling on his long mustache as he lounged in his chair, the policeman told him that on the orders of some big boys in the Temperance they had raided several taverns on the river on suspicion of harboring anarchists. A fugitive had been found at the Blarney Stone and was shot dead trying to escape. "I'm Irish myself, but these anarchists come here to America and think they can take over. You should have seen the Hanlon woman tryin to scratch our lads' eyes out when we got him. We had no choice but to bring her in."

Tom immediately arranged bail and waited impatiently in front of the barrier for Molly to be released. He hadn't heard about any raid planned by the hard-liners. They must have arranged it in secret. But how had they done it without him or Otis finding out?

"I hope they hurry and let her out. I don't want to lose my job."

He had forgotten all about Patrick, who was sitting on the bench along the wall holding his cap. He went over and sat down beside him and asked what he did.

The boy explained matter-of-factly that he worked a ten-hour day every Saturday and half a day during the week after school helping to put in the new sewer system in Greenwich. "The pipes are goin to dump all the shyte right into the river," he said proudly.

Impressed with his cheerfulness, Tom asked if that wasn't heavy work for a boy his age.

It wasn't so bad, Patrick said, and he was learning a lot. Sometimes they even let him hold the plans for them.

Tom wanted to know how he got the job.

"Tammany got it for me. All I had to do was give em my vote."

"But you're not old enough to vote!"

"I don't know how it works myself, but everybody says it's only Tammany that's ever done a damn thing for us micks."

Tom had heard rumors that the political organization put the names of the dead on the voter rolls, but this was the first time he'd heard they used children as well. He asked him how much he earned.

Patrick said he got a dollar fifty a week and his ma was always telling him she didn't know what they would do without it. "Timothy's not much for workin," he said. His brother who was nine was always getting into scrapes. His ma said it was because he was wild like his dad.

Tom wondered who the father was. Recalling Molly's pregnancy the last time he saw her, he asked if there wasn't another brother too.

The boy said no, only a sister, Sarah, who was six.

Tom questioned him about the man the police had shot at the tavern, suspecting he might have been the father of the other children.

Patrick looked down. "Danny was our best friend in the world. Sarah always sat on his lap when he stayed with us and he kept us laughin all the time with his jokin. I don't know why they shot him." His lip trembled.

Metal clanged somewhere in the back. A policeman opened a door and Molly came out, squinting against the light. Her hair was tangled around her haggard face and the fringe was half torn off her shawl.

"Ma!" Patrick ran over to the rail trying to shake open the wooden gate, but the policeman pushed him back and opened it from the inside to let her out.

Mother and son threw their arms around each other, his head against her breast, until she became aware of Tom standing there. She glared at him. "It's not a vice den I run, and I don't relish spendin my nights in a jail cell—thanks to you and your friends in the Temperance." And pulling Patrick along, she charged out of the precinct house and down the steps to the street, leaving him stupefied.

She couldn't think he had had any part in this. Why, he

would do anything in the world for her. He caught up with her as she stood outside adjusting the shawl over her rumpled hair. "Molly, it wasn't my fault. I swear to God I didn't know anything about it. Let me explain. . . ."

Without answering, she slammed Patrick's cap on his head and hurried off down the street. The boy turned to look back uncertainly at him and then ran after her.

An hour later, when Tom went into Otis Skidmore's bookstore, the bookseller looked up from a heated discussion he was having with several members of their group. "Where have you been, Tom? Have you heard what happened? What are we going to do about these maniacs?"

"I've got to speak to you, Otis," he broke in, not looking at the others.

The bookseller led him into the back and asked what was up.

"You'll have to do without me. I'm finished with the whole goddam thing."

"What are you talking about? We need you. We've all got to stand together now. We've got a fight on our hands."

"Look, can't you see what it's become? It's not antiliquor any more, it's a bunch of bigots against the poor down there in Shamrock Alley who haven't got a hope in hell of getting out of it."

"But you can't blast the whole movement just because of a few crackpots."

Tom shot back that it wasn't just a few, and the proof of its bigotry was that only Irish taverns had been raided. They hadn't touched Unger at the Four Winds, for example. "And in the name of our sacred Society the cops shot a man dead. Can you tell me that that had anything to do with liquor?"

"Well, say that at the meeting tonight! That's just what they need to be told, straight from the shoulder."

"I'm sorry, Otis, I'm through." And he turned and walked out.

When he got back to the printing shop he told Claude that Molly was a former hired girl in the family who had gotten herself into some trouble and he had gone to help. In the silence that followed he could tell from the way his son kept looking at him that his curiosity was far from satisfied. He tried to work for a while but he was too upset and decided to close the shop, sending the help and Claude home. He walked right into the Four Winds and belted down several beers in public for the first time in years.

Although he told himself that he was not responsible for the raid on the Blarney Stone, it nearly drove him out of his mind that Molly believed him to be behind it. He had to make her listen, but with her Irish temper, how could he? And he did feel at fault in a way. He should have known those super-moralists were up to something. Maybe he could have stopped it.

Without a job, she was going to be in desperate need of money. Patrick's dollar and a half wasn't enough. The least he could do was help her out. She couldn't refuse it, if for no other reason than she needed to feed her children.

His first view of Shamrock Alley after ten years nearly brought tears to his eyes. It had hardly changed, except for a woman with a green sash standing at the tavern door collecting money for Irish prisoners. Urchins still shrieked as they played underfoot, while biddies with corncob pipes cackled to each other across the railings of the outside porches.

Upstairs, a little girl with wide eyes and her finger in her mouth opened the door to him. This had to be Sarah, the sister Patrick had mentioned.

"She's sleepin," she said when he asked for her mother.

He walked in. The room was cozier than he remembered it. The shabby furniture was made more cheerful by a bright afghan on the low bed, an embroidered linen tablecloth, and an oval braided rug that covered most of the floor. There was even a small shelf of books and a pipe rack that he thought, with a twinge, might have belonged to the slain fugitive. He glanced down at the wide-eyed child in her neat pinafore, trying to imagine what the father had looked like.

The bedroom door opened, but instead of Molly a boy about nine came out fastening his suspenders. Showing no surprise at seeing Tom, he held his palm right out and asked in a wheedling tone, "Gimme a dime, will ya, mister? I ain't had nothin to eat all day."

"Timothy, ya had cod pie and cabbage, same as we all did," the little girl piped up.

But Tom gave him a coin anyway, and with a whoop the boy grabbed his hat and coat and slammed out the door and down the stairs.

The little girl tittered. "He's runnin with the Dusters now."

The Hudson Dusters, the street gang that snatched purses. What a difference between him and Patrick.

Tom didn't know whether he should wait. He couldn't just sit down and make himself at home until Molly got up, and he didn't want to wake her after what she had been through. He was about to leave, intending to return later, when there was a stamping of boots outside and Patrick came in, his face smudged from work.

For a moment the boy was startled to see him, then he broke into a grin. "I was hopin ya might be comin by, sir." He hung up his cap and coat on a peg by the door, put his lunch pail on a shelf, and went to wash up.

There was an odd contraption over the washstand that Tom hadn't noticed before. Above the basin a barrel had been rigged up, with a pipe extending from the top of it and out through the window. The boy turned on a beer cock at the bottom of the barrel, filling the basin with water.

"We gets our water from the rain," Sarah said. "Pat made it!" She looked proudly at her brother who was bent over scrubbing his ears.

Running water was unknown in any of these old buildings. Everybody had to carry water up from the pump out on the street.

The boy grinned as he dried his neck with a towel. "It's not fixed right yet." He showed Tom through the window how the pipe from the barrel was connected to a rain gutter along the edge of the roof. "When it don't rain it goes dry, but I'm goin to put a tank up there."

It was an impressive thing for a boy of only eleven to have done, and Tom praised him for it.

While Patrick was attacking his mop of hair with a comb, Tom explained that he didn't want to disturb his mother while she was resting, but that he had brought a little money for them. He took out an envelope and added, "Tell your mother that when she needs more to send you over to the shop."

"We don't want your charity!" a voice yelled from the bedroom.

It was Molly. She had been awake, listening to every word. "But it's not charity," he called back, trying to sound reasonable. "I owe it to you for"—he looked at Patrick—"for . . . everything."

"Get your ass out of here!" she bellowed back.

He tried to hand the envelope to Patrick anyway, but the boy refused it. "I think ya better go, sir. Ma hasn't been takin it so good. It's not as though we don't have any money. I'm workin full-time now. I quit school."

On the way downstairs, Tom was racking his brain about what to do, when an old woman lugging up a bucket of water greeted him and he recognized Molly's neighbor, Mrs. Brophy. The red hair was white now and she was shrunken.

"Ah, Mr. Endicott, ya been to see her, bless you. I guess ya heard about it, isn't it a shame?"

He told her how Molly believed he was involved in the raid and had refused to let him help her out.

"I knew it couldn't be you," she said. "But she suffered a grievous loss and is not to be blamed."

He put the envelope into her hand. "Do you think you might get her to see reason? I want to do what I can."

"She's stubborn as a mule, but I'll let ya know." She patted his arm before picking up the pail and carrying it on up the steps.

On his way home, leaning into an icy wind coming off the river, vexed as he was by Molly's refusal to understand, he let himself hope that the old woman would talk her around. The one thing he could do was to send money.

He turned out of the wind onto Perry Street. What a sturdy, nice-looking boy Patrick was, and already taking charge of the family like a man. He wished Claude had some of the same energy, but how could he expect him to be any other way with an invalid for a mother? Patrick had Molly's blood in his veins and that made all the difference.

Was it possible she would never believe he was innocent? He was furious all over again at what the Society had done to her, and was disgusted with himself for having stuck by them for so long.

In spite of Patrick's attempt to keep the family going, life deteriorated in Shamrock Alley. Molly developed arthritis, and gin was finally the only thing that eased her pain.

Timothy was seldom home. He was usually hanging out with his street gang, and when he got nabbed—as sometimes happened—he didn't have much trouble talking the cops into letting him go—they were Irish too. By sixteen he was taller than Patrick and passed for a man. He even boasted about his adventures with women—the Dusters had little mercy on any girl they caught out in the streets in their area at night—and needled his older brother about still being cherry.

It didn't bother Patrick. After all, he had been bringing the family a regular paycheck for years. Since working on the sewer system, he had been getting better jobs through Tammany laying tracks on the city's north-south avenues for the horsecar lines that were replacing the stages.

There was a girl he liked. Her name was Hester. They looked at each other from across the balconies. But he was too busy to waste his time on any girl. He preferred to spend his evenings improving himself by reading the books, mostly on his favorite subject, science, that Danny had left behind.

Molly had given up trying to find work for herself, and got so drunk at the taverns she spent her afternoons in that sometimes she didn't know what she was doing and brought a man back with her. Once Patrick came home to find his sister Sarah crying on the steps outside and in the bedroom a man into his mother's skirts as she lay dead drunk on the bed. Though the man was nearly twice his size, the shame and horror Patrick felt gave him strength to throw him out. Then he sat down at the table and cried, as his mother—whom he could never blame—roused herself to make dinner.

But it didn't take long for drink to ruin her entirely. If Tom had seen her on the street, bloated and tipsy, he wouldn't have recognized her, and soon she became indistinguishable from any number of fat women in shawls laboring through the streets with their bundles.

1864

On a gray winter day, Claude Endicott was walking across the city from Greenwich to take the Broadway stage uptown to Columbia College on Forty-ninth Street. He could have taken the Sixth Avenue horsecar, which was closer to home and the most direct way, but he was in no hurry to get to class and preferred to linger as long as possible on the lively streets of wartime New York. In the four years the Civil War had been going on, the city had become more congested than ever. It was depressing not to be part of the greatest adventure of the century and instead have to devote himself to dreary studies.

He had to wait at Fifth Avenue as a battalion of fresh-faced recruits his own age in new blue uniforms marched by on their way to the parade grounds in Washington Square. Further along, he stopped for a while at the window of an art gallery to admire a painting of the Battle of Bull Run, in which a dying Union soldier with a bloody wound in his chest was passing the flag to a fellow soldier on horseback with his last strength.

At college he was always drifting off during lectures on subjects like Locke's Theory of Social Credit, that he didn't even try to understand. He preferred to dream of being wounded on the battlefield and found unconscious by a southern belle who had him carried back to her plantation by slaves where she nursed him back to health.

He had started going to Columbia two years before when he was sixteen. He hated it and had tried to enlist, lying about his age. But, still being puny at that time and looking far younger than he was, he had been turned down.

It had caused a ruckus at home. His father refused to understand his wanting to go to war and went into his usual tirade—how he had struggled to make his way up from the bottom and if he had ever had an education he would have become more than just a printer, and here he was giving Claude the opportunity of going to college and he was ungrateful.

His classmates at Columbia bored him as much as the lectures. He didn't care about punting on the river, going out to beer cellars, or boasting about chasing after chorus girls. He would rather be alone than waste his time like that.

His sister Veronica said that the two of them were different from other people who were so unimaginative, so predictable, so self-satisfied in their ordinariness, but she could afford to talk that way because she was going to be a poet. He only read books—and dreamed.

As he continued his walk across town, even a pastry shop at Mercer Street didn't let him forget the glorious war he was missing, displaying in its window cookies shaped like soldiers and cakes whipped up out of sugar and cream into martial fantasies of turrets, citadels, and forts with flags and cannons.

Broadway, when he got there, was an exciting bedlam of jostling people and horse-drawn vehicles. New York City was booming with the prosperity the war had brought, its population swelled by people from all parts of the Union come to cash in on the bonanza. Half the men he saw were in uniform and sometimes it almost seemed that as many women were in mourning, which did not in the least reduce the general exhilaration.

He had gotten his draft call earlier in the year after his eighteenth birthday, but though he had pleaded to go, his father wouldn't hear of his dropping out of college and paid the three hundred dollars to buy him out of the army. He tried to point out to his father the injustice of the draft law. Because the poor couldn't afford to buy themselves out, that was exactly why there had been the draft riots the year before and why the city had been brought near to collapse for days by rampaging mobs. But because their neighborhood had been passed by, his father dismissed the whole thing. His father always acted as if Greenwich were some kind of isolated village, when anyone with eyes in his head could see that it was just another part of the city—if more old-fashioned than the rest.

Since he couldn't be a soldier, all he wanted was for the war to be over as soon as possible. After the first few years when everything went wrong for the northern armies, it was clear now that they were going to win, with Sherman heading into Georgia. And just as soon as it was over he was going to quit school and clear out, no matter what his father said.

He caught sight of the Broadway stage dashing through the welter of wagons and horses clogging the street—it was always most crowded here around A. T. Stewart's, the biggest department store in the city—but instead of stopping for passengers, the driver sitting up on top whipped his already frothing team and careered by, deliberately splashing slush on everyone. If his coach hadn't been full and he needed the fares, Claude knew well enough the driver would have raced a competing stage to the stop, creating havoc in the busy street.

But another coach finally came along and pulled over to the curb, the driver so bundled up against the cold only his red nose showed. All the stages were painted up as colorfully as circus wagons with scenes of famous horse races or historic events on their sides. This one had a splendid picture of the great Indian chief Tecumseh handing over his feathered headdress at his surrender at the Battle of Tippecanoe.

All the people waiting pushed forward at once to get on at the back door, but Claude stopped to help a lady having trouble holding her skirts above the muddy curb to cross a pile of horse manure in the gutter onto the step. By the time he got on the stage himself the seven places on each side were filled, and standing on the straw-covered floor holding on to a strap as the coach lurched off, he drifted into a fantasy of his future life in the French Quarter of New Orleans with an octoroon mistress.

He was moving toward the front of the coach to pay when it came to a sudden halt, throwing him across the lap of an elegantly dressed woman. He regained his balance, stammering an apology, but with an air of amusement she murmured it was nothing, as she rearranged her fox-trimmed coat and muff. She had an exotic beauty, with classically high cheekbones, flawless skin, and smoothly coiffed dark hair on top of which was a ridiculous little Parisian hat.

He avoided looking at her, feeling his face hot, but he knew her eyes were on him as he handed a dollar bill up through the slot in the roof to the driver on the seat outside. The fare was five cents so he was chagrined to find, when the change envelope was handed back down, that it contained only forty-five cents. He counted it again to make sure.

Fifty cents was a fortune to let the driver get away with, yet he couldn't bear to make a scene after having fallen all over that elegant woman, and anyway it was practically hopeless to shout up to the driver through that little hole. Of course, all the drivers were perfectly well aware of that and if they wanted to shortchange you there was really nothing you could do about it.

He felt a pull at his sleeve and the elegant passenger spoke. "You really must demand your change. You have it coming."

Wishing that he could sink through the floor, he mumbled that it wasn't worth the trouble.

"But you must," she insisted, and to his amazement she actually stood up and, holding on to his shoulder, called through the slot to the driver to return the fifty cents.

The driver deliberately jerked the reins to make the stage lurch from side to side, throwing the lady back into her seat, and everyone had to hold on for their lives. But when it drew up to the Union Square stop she got right back to her feet, rapping with her umbrella on the roof and insisting that the money be returned.

Everyone was staring as if they were an audience at a play. Claude looked down at the straw on the floor in embarrassment.

To his surprise, the driver handed down the correct change in an envelope. Claude was so pleased he forgot his awkwardness, smiling his thanks to the exotic-looking woman who astonished him again by saying, "Young man, you must be a poet."

He protested bashfully that he wasn't.

"But you do like poetry, don't you?" Her eyes were almost almond-shaped when she smiled.

He assured her that he did.

"Well, then," she said briskly, opening her jet-embroidered bag, "you might like to meet some other poetry-lovers who are friends of mine."

As the coach drew up to the stop at Madison Square—without a lurch for once—she got up to go and handed him her visiting card. "My evenings are Thursdays. If you have nothing better to do, come by at eight." And gathering her skirts in her gloved hand, she stepped over the dirty straw to the back on immaculately booted feet and, easily avoiding the slush at the curb, opened her umbrella and walked off into a lightly falling snow.

Her name, embossed on the card in gold, floral calligraphy, was Mme. Adele Averbach, and she lived on Thompson Street south of Washington Square. He was too excited to go sit in a stultifying lecture hall so he returned home to get his skates, wanting to feel the whip of cold wind on his face as he sped across the ice with his long scarf flying out behind him.

When he came back down the stairs in his heavy sweater, a neighbor girl named Elizabeth Cooper poked her head out of the parlor. Ever since she had been a little girl she found excuses to hang around pestering him. Elizabeth was fifteen now, but to him she was still the brat she had always been. Seeing his skates, she asked if she could go too, but he made an excuse and, slamming the door, ran down the steps to the street.

Over the years the Coopers were the only neighbors the Endicotts had ever gotten involved with. Sensible-looking Mrs. Cooper, far from being put off by Fanny's "vagueness"—as most of the neighbors were—sometimes volunteered to be company for her when Miss Swindon was ailing. Professor Cooper, who taught history at New York University on Washington Square, had been active in the fight against slavery before the war and had tried to interest Tom in the movement. But while Tom sympathized with the cause of abolition, he couldn't bring himself to join any more organizations after his disillusionment with temperance. Nevertheless, he had gone to Cooper Union with the professor to hear an address by Abraham Lincoln who then had been one of the presidential hopefuls of the newly formed Republican Party, which was attracting numbers of liberals.

When the war broke out, Professor Cooper was called to Washington to write for the War Publications Office in the Lincoln administration, and while he was away, his wife, always devoted to causes, organized a group of neighborhood women, including her daughter Elizabeth and Veronica Endicott, to knit wrist warmers, scarves, and gloves for the troops.

The war had brought Tom more business than he could cope with. His printer's devil was drafted and his old assistant was retiring, so he persuaded Albert Cogswell to work with him full-time on the presses. The shantytown that Albert lived in over by the river had been torn down when the piers were being built and he had moved further uptown to another squatters' area in the Central Park.

Albert had discovered photography and built a darkroom for himself in a corner of the shop. He had even constructed a camera from one of Lumière's diagrams. But there was little time for that with so much work coming in—announcements of war charities, drives for winter clothing for the troops, and warnings against "copperheads"—southern sympathizers. They also did folders for the government on how to save on scarce food items like sugar and cooking oil needed for the manufacture of munitions, or what to do in the case of enemy invasion—for a while in 1863, Confederate troops had come as close as Pennsylvania.

That was the year of the draft riots, ignited not only as Claude thought because the poor resented the rich being able to buy themselves out of the army, but also over having to go to war for the liberation of the slaves who would be rivals for their jobs. Thousands of immigrants surged up from the slums, setting fires, pillaging stores, tearing up horsecar tracks, and chopping down telegraph poles. Whole city blocks went up in flames. Molly Hanlon's younger son Timothy was in a mob that was smashing windows and looting—and chasing anyone black they could find on the streets. A Negro was hung from a lamppost across from the Jefferson Market police station, while the cops hid in the basement to save themselves from the mob that tried to break down the door.

Patrick heard the uproar from Shamrock Alley and saw the light in the sky from the flames across the city, but there was nothing he could do to keep his brother out of it. He had worked hard to hold the family together as best he could, but with his mother sodden with drink, Shamrock Alley was no place for his little sister Sarah to grow up in, and when she was twelve he found her a job as maid with a family on St. Luke's Place near the church.

Molly died in the summer of 1864, and Patrick, just past his seventeenth birthday, asked Hester to wait for him and enlisted in the army. By winter he was with General Sherman's forces, poised on the border of Georgia with no Confederate troops left to stop them between there and the sea.

CLAUDE WENT TO MME. AVERBACH'S ON THE NEXT THURSday. It was nearly nine before he got there but he hadn't been able to get away earlier. First there was dinner to get through, which had been delayed because his father came home late from the shop. Then he didn't want the family to see him slipping out in his best clothes and have to explain where he was going, so he had to stay in his room until his mother and Miss Swindon retired and his father was occupied in his study.

Mme. Averbach's town house was much grander than the Endicotts', with tall French windows and slim, fluted columns on either side of the classic doorway supporting a fanlight arc of stained glass.

A servant hung his hat and coat on a rack in the hall already bulging with wraps, and showed him into the crowded drawing room illuminated by the dramatic chiaroscuro of candelabra. It took a moment for his eyes to adjust.

Incense hung in the air like a temple. The guests appeared to be talking animatedly in the shimmering light that threw faces into silhouette, yet the sound in the room was strangely muffled, punctuated now and then by high laughter like the shattering of a glass.

Mme. Averbach, in a green taffeta gown emphasizing her tiny waist, detached herself from a small group and came up to him. Emeralds glittered at her throat and from her lavishly piled hair. She took his hand. "The young man from the omnibus! I'm so glad you came. Do tell me your name again, I want you to meet some of my friends." She waved a gloved hand holding a fan in their direction.

After the introductions—he was too embarrassed to catch any of their names—she said to them, "Didn't I tell you?"

The group studied him curiously while he squirmed.

"You're absolutely right, Adele," said a chubby man in a flamboyant red velvet jacket. "He's the spitting image."

Mme. Averbach turned to him with a ravishing smile. "It's Edgar Allan Poe we're comparing you with." But noticing how uncomfortable he was as the center of attention, she quickly apologized. "How thoughtless I am. I've let our obsession with Poe make me forget you're just in from the cold. Oliver"—she tapped the chubby man with her fan—"why don't you take our new friend over to the fire and see that he gets some refreshment."

"Quoth the raven—at your service, madam," he replied with a mock bow, and to Claude's relief, led him away.

"We'd all die of boredom in New York without her," the chubby man named Oliver said, his little eyes darting around the candlelit room as he sidestepped through the guests. "She's made it almost like Paris here. You know, Poe is all the rage over there." He chattered on about things Claude had never heard about—bohemianism and Baudelaire.

They waited at a crowded buffet where liveried servants were dispensing drinks. "Adele said you were a poet, didn't she? I'm a composer myself. You must show me some of your work. Perhaps I can set it to music."

Claude tried to tell him he was not a poet at all but Oliver dismissed this with a wave of a plump hand. "Anyone who looks as much like the young Poe as you do has to be a poet."

It wasn't only Oliver's red jacket that was odd, but also his dark velvet trousers and big floppy tie. With his fat, red cheeks and impish eyes, he looked the picture of an overgrown schoolboy.

"People say my songs are even better than Stephen Foster's. We're both fugitives from the South, you know. Did you hear that he died of drink at Bellevue Hospital last month?" He handed Claude a glass of a peculiar milky-green liquid.

Claude looked at it uncertainly.

"Don't worry," Oliver said, his little eyes sparkling, "it's only absinthe. Baudelaire couldn't have written a line of *The Flowers of Evil* without it. Some say it drives you mad." He threw back his head theatrically and drained his glass.

Claude took a sip. It had a bitter licorice taste.

"Oh, go ahead. One glass won't destroy your brain."

Claude held his breath and drank it down, and Oliver immediately had their glasses refilled.

As they came up to the roaring fire, the absinthe was beginning to whirl in his head.

"Isn't it a perfect likeness?" Oliver said, pointing out a painting over the mantelpiece.

Claude didn't understand. The picture was of a reclining female nude with a blue satin ribbon around her neck and a turbaned flunky waving an ostrich fan over her—as explicit as anything his father's friend Albert Cogswell painted for barroom walls.

"It's Adele, don't you see?" Oliver tittered. "But then, who bothers to notice a face when the clothes are off?"

Claude stared at it, hardly hearing the chubby man telling him that Edouard Manet had painted it in Paris. Was it possible that his aristocratic hostess, bending toward her guests so graciously across the room, had let herself be painted in the nude? And more unbelievably, was displaying it on her drawing room wall for all the world to see? His face burned from the strange liquor he was not used to.

Oliver was rattling on about how he met Adele in Paris long before she sat for Manet, and what a pity it was that the war had forced both of them—like so many other Americans—to come home, but a good part of her money was invested in the South and all of his own was. "It was hard for her to come back here, when you think of that scandal. But as far as that goes, I'll never be able to show my face in Charleston again. I was involved in quite a juicy little scandal of my own." He looked at Claude expectantly, hoping to be prompted to further revelations about himself.

But Claude, who felt mesmerized by the opulently painted canvas, only asked what had happened to her.

"Her?" Oliver was visibly disappointed but he quickly recovered. "You didn't know about the trial? It made headlines in all the papers—but of course you're too young to remember and I, alas, am not." He told Claude that Mme. Averbach had been forced by her parents into a marriage with a department store tycoon. "You know," he whispered, "Adele is Jewish, but absolutely blue-blood Jewish. She and her husband simply loathed each other from the start, and before the honeymoon was over he took a lover. But I have to hand it to her, so did she."

Mme. Averbach had left her group and was engrossed in conversation with a well-dressed black man who was obviously not a servant. Claude wondered if there was any experience she had not tasted.

Oliver was saying that one summer night at her and her husband's place in Saratoga, Adele was awakened by a noise on the grounds and, taking her little pearl-handled revolver, went to investigate. How could she know it was her husband coming home drunk? There was a spectacular trial and the result was that it was impossible for her to go out in New York society again. "She had to go live in Paris, poor dear."

A group of latecomers entered the room, distracting Oliver from his revelations by their loud talk and hearty laughter. A tall figure in the middle of them was holding forth in a cloud of cigar smoke. It seemed to Claude as if the room had stretched away and the newcomers were at an impossibly remote distance from him. He put a hand against the fireplace to steady himself.

"It's Mina," cried Oliver. "Mina Hunneker!"

The tall figure who had arrived was not a man at all, but a woman wearing a man's suit, her hair pulled back severely and smoking a cigar.

"Come on," Oliver said to Claude whose head was spinning. "You've got to meet her. She's Adele's best friend and the top real estate agent in New York." According to Oliver, she had made a fortune predicting where the city would spread. Although everyone laughed at the idea that the city could possibly expand any further, she was buying up farms at the far end of Manhattan.

Claude was petrified at the prospect of being face to face with such a formidable creature, but Oliver pulled him recklessly after him. He almost tripped over a low divan where three people rapt in conversation looked up, their faces macabre in the firelight.

Surrounded by an audience of male admirers, Mina Hunneker, the tall woman dressed as a man, had planted herself directly in the brilliant light of a candelabrum. "These suffragettes are the bunk," she was declaring in a deep voice. "All that ranting and raving. They're not going to get anywhere that way. They're just rattling their chains."

Her entourage of men laughed and applauded. Oliver danced about trying to get her attention, but she waved him off with her cigar and went on with her diatribe.

"There's no getting at Mina when she's on her soapbox." Oliver leaned closer to Claude. "Don't tell Adele I told you, but they slept together once."

The words settled slowly in Claude's befogged mind and he tried to put them together.

"Just to see what it was like, of course. After all, what can women do with each other?" Oliver tittered again.

Claude didn't understand what he was talking about, but he didn't care. The absinthe had submerged him in deep water and he was being swept along by the current. It was all so different here, so grotesque—and presided over by the lady in the green gown, the magician who had cast this spell. He looked around for her and instead focused woozily on the chalk-white face of a woman with eyes like unblinking nuggets. She seemed to be wearing some kind of nightdress.

Oliver was jumping around from one absurdity to another, but broke off when he saw what Claude was looking at. "That's Tatiana. Ethereal, isn't she? Never utters a word. But what a dancer." He called over to her, "Tatiana angel, your costume is most fetching!"

The chalk-white face gave a grimace that might have been a smile, then quickly composed itself, the nugget eyes as blank as before.

"What's wrong with her eyes?" Claude wanted to know as Oliver propelled him back toward the buffet.

"Oh, that's belladonna and lord knows what else she's taken tonight."

Oliver stepped over the legs of a man who appeared to be asleep, sprawled on cushions on the floor. "But what can you expect? She's supposed to be the granddaughter of the Marquis de Sade."

Claude hardly knew where he was any more. Fragments of conversation came to his ears from people around him, about seances and alchemists and Omar Khayyam. Under hanging braziers of incense, people were lounging on divans and cushions, nibbling sweetmeats set out on brass trays. In one corner, several people were puffing at the serpentine stems of a water pipe, the smoke of the burning hashish bubbling through the water as they inhaled. He had only read about it before in a travel book by Burton who had stolen into Mecca disguised as a Moslem.

"Are you there, Claude?" Oliver's voice seemed to be coming through a tunnel. "It's time we got our seats for the entertainment."

Candelabra were being set about in a semicircle in front of a drape of purple brocade and people were pushing their seats into the center of the room.

Mme. Averbach swam into view talking to the black man, the jewels on her bosom and in her hair flashing in the candlelight. He felt that once he had seen her nakedness, but how was that possible?

Then he was sitting cross-legged on a cushion at the rear of the audience. He looked around for Oliver, but only a stranger sat there, apparently bemused by a servant twirling a dark substance before him on a pin over the flame of a candle. When it had the consistency of taffy, the servant scraped it into a long, carved ivory pipe with a glowing coal in its bowl and handed it to the stranger. The stranger inhaled deeply, then passed the pipe over to Claude.

He took it without question. He was being offered one exotic experience after another, and considering the boredom of his life until now, he saw no reason to resist.

The smoke he inhaled had an odd sweetness totally unlike tobacco. He held it in his lungs, and after exhaling, sucked in a deeper draft that seared his throat like cold fire.

His neighbor took the pipe from him. "That will do for your initiation." The voice was so remote it seemed disembodied.

The guests hushed as Mme. Averbach appeared in front of the candelabra. Raising her arms as if to embrace all of them, she announced that the entertainment would begin with an original ballet entitled "Hymn to Emancipation."

As a harp began to strum ascending arpeggios, the girl with the nugget eyes waltzed onto the stage, her white gown diaphanous in the candlelight. Veils on her wrists floated languidly as she moved her arms. Claude could hardly believe that the wraith had transformed herself into such a shimmering butterfly.

The next moment a black dancer leaped into the light—startlingly naked except for plum-colored tights—and began stalking her erotically. It was Mme. Averbach's black companion.

"Of course I'm all for Emancipation," Oliver, who had

appeared from nowhere, whispered beside him, "but I have to confess that I miss the good old days behind the barn with the slaves."

The girl was pirouetting away from her black pursuer, just eluding his grasp. Then, as if hypnotized, she fluttered on her toes in one spot, helplessly waiting for him.

Claude had never seen anything like it. In the real world it was forbidden. It would end in a lynching.

With the harp rippling to a crescendo, the black man pounced, lifting the haunted girl by the waist. He whirled her around, her head and arms thrown back so that the veils at her wrists brushed the candle flames, until at the music's climax he bent her over in a long kiss on the mouth.

Claude didn't breathe as the glistening black body covered the white body, and amid the bravos and applause that followed Mme. Averbach came forward to embrace them both warmly.

He was so disoriented he couldn't be surprised at anything any more and asked Oliver if the black dancer were Mme. Averbach's lover. He felt his words coming out like beads widely spaced on a necklace.

"Oh, my, no," Oliver said loudly. "Adele is between lovers now. He's Mina's property. She picks him up every night in her carriage after his performance at Purdy's Theater."

"The woman with the cigar?" It was hard to believe.

"Don't be fooled by her male drag. That one is all woman."

Mme. Averbach was announcing a recitation of "Ulalume" by Edgar Allan Poe, who she said had once lived nearby on Thirteenth Street and to whose spirit the evening was dedicated.

All the candelabra were extinguished and for a moment they were in darkness. Then a man appeared holding a single candle that illuminated his face weirdly from below.

Oliver told Claude that the man had been in jail for five years on a charge of sodomy, adding wickedly, "And he's married with six children, to boot!"

Against a series of bell-like notes from the harp, the elocutionist began the verses of the poem in sepulchral tones. A trance fell over the listeners. The candle wavered and shadows hovered like night phantoms. The ghost of the dead poet might have been in the room wailing out its morbid anguish. Claude looked around as arabesques of shadow crept toward him from the walls. The magic of the evening turned to menace. Oliver's hassock was empty. On the other side of him the stranger who had given him the opium pipe looked like Satan. He had to get out before he screamed.

With the demons almost upon him, he scuttled out into the hall where he searched frantically through the mass of coats for his own. He was struggling to get it on when he heard a rustle of skirts and a voice whispering, "Wait, Claude," and Adele Averbach's fan touched his shoulder.

As the mournful cadences rolled on in the drawing room, she said, "Come tomorrow for tea." Then she vanished leaving behind the words "Promise me" hanging in the air with the scent of jasmine.

He stepped out into a bitterly cold clear night. Bells of horse sleighs jingled as they clip-clopped by on the snowy street. The stars overhead cut the night sky like diamonds. He crunched down the steps. His panic was gone and he took great ecstatic breaths of frosty air.

He hardly slept. The next morning at breakfast he couldn't bear to listen to his father's boasting about General Grant's latest victory at Bull Run as if he had been right there himself. What did wars have to do with the important things of life? He felt sorry for his father, who never knew what it was to be young. His mother, who seldom went out of the house, had missed out on life entirely. His sister, Veronica, sitting across from him nibbling her toast absentmindedly as she stared out the window, was forever lost in a dreamworld. None of them had ever been alive like he was.

He could tell Miss Swindon knew something was up, the way her beady eyes watched him as she sipped her insipid camomile tea. She'd drop her teeth if she ever saw anything like the world he had seen the night before.

Just as he pushed back his half-eaten porridge and got up to go, Elizabeth Cooper, who was staying over while her mother was away visiting Professor Cooper in Washington, startled him by asking out of the blue what he thought of Edgar Allan Poe. Did she have some kind of uncanny intuition? But her wide schoolgirl eyes were looking back guileless as ever as she told him she was writing a theme on Poe for school.

With the prospect of tea at Mme. Averbach's that afternoon, going to classes was out of the question and instead, he went to the college library to read up on the legendary poet he was supposed to resemble. In a faded daguerreotype he examined the hypnotic eyes that were reputed to have looked straight into hell and tried to imagine how he would look in the same cape and string necktie.

He even tried to learn a few lines of "Ulalume" by heart, but the rustle of taffeta and the scent of jasmine kept getting in the way so that he finally gave up.

On his way back downtown the streets were so jammed with Christmas shoppers added to the wartime congestion that the horsecar was continually held up. The stores and hotels were festooned with holiday decorations, and as the horsecar passed through Union Square, carolers in front of Delmonico's restaurant were singing "Adeste Fidelis."

When Claude was shown into her drawing room, Mme. Averbach put down her pen and rose from her writing desk. Her mauve watered-silk dress with ruffles falling away at the elbows shimmered in the late afternoon light, a light that gave her skin a soft glow and brought out golden tints in her long auburn curls pinned up at the back of her head. She looked smaller than she had the night before at her salon, more delicate.

"I'm so glad you've come," she said, advancing in a swish of petticoats and extending her hand. "I've been doing my holiday cards, but I have to admit I've been thinking of you all along."

He flushed with bashful pleasure.

Tea was already laid in front of the fire. He started to sit down on a Venetian chair across from her, but his hostess patted the cushion beside her on the sofa and said, "Oh, please, not so far away."

In the fading light, the naked figure in the painting above the fireplace seemed to emerge from the canvas and hover in the air like a presiding goddess, as Mme. Averbach poured the tea. Adding a few drops of crème de menthe before handing him his cup, she asked, "Did you enjoy yourself last evening?"

He told her it had been a revelation to him. "I've always felt like a fish out of water until last night," he confessed.

She laughed as if he had said something witty. "I'm glad you felt at home in our little pond. My friends were all enchanted with you." Her hazel eyes with tiny golden flecks watched him over the edge of her teacup.

He glowed. The enigmatic face in the painting also seemed to be reflecting her approval of him.

"But don't you want to smoke?" She held out to him a small silver box filled with slim paper tubes of tobacco.

He took one eagerly. His father had read aloud at breakfast an editorial in the *Herald* that denounced the cigarette, a recent importation from the Orient, as effete and immoral. To his delight, she also took one herself. Then, after lighting their cigarettes with a taper from the fire she leaned back, her classic profile outlined against the light of the bay window, and exhaled a thin stream of blue smoke into the air.

He had hoped there might be something like this waiting for him in New Orleans, but never dreamed it would fall into his lap right here at home. He wanted to tell her how glad he was to be there but didn't want to sound clumsy. "I like your portrait very much," he said at last, daring to refer to something so intimate, so naked. "I think the composition has classical balance." It was a phrase he remembered from some lecture.

For a moment he thought she might laugh at him, but she appeared to find nothing wrong with it. "I'm glad you like it, but as I see it, it's not just a portrait of me. It's the way a genius of the brush responded to me. It was as fulfilling an experience as love."

No woman had ever spoken so frankly to him. "If you don't mind me saying so, I think Mr. Manet caught your true spirit." He blushed and puffed at his cigarette, not daring to inhale, afraid he might start coughing and make a bigger fool of himself.

"You have such insight!" She leaned toward him almost girlishly. "That's exactly why I have it hanging in my drawing room. I know that some people might not approve, but then don't ordinary people misunderstand everything?"

He was flattered that she didn't include him with ordinary people, and even considered him worthy enough to take an interest in.

"I don't want the world to see me only as a fashion plate," Mme. Averbach said, dismissing her elegant dress with a sweep of her hand. "These clothes falsify what I really am."

He protested that he thought she looked beautiful in them.

She threw him an appreciative glance. "Naturally, I do what I can to make myself presentable, but they're encumbering just the same. Ideally, women should wear simple draperies like the Greeks, garments that move with the body rather than distort and conceal it. I can understand why many men seek out the company of lower-class women who are less bound by fashion and formality."

He was having a hard time following her. Why would any man prefer a lower-class woman to someone as refined as she? His cigarette had gone out and he didn't know where to put it.

"It's such a pleasure talking to you, Claude," she said, tossing her cigarette carelessly into the fire. "Young as you are, you understand me. Some people might think I display the painting out of vanity, but that's not it at all. I do it quite simply to remind men that I am as much of a woman as those in the lower classes they run after. That painting ought to show them." She laughed and poured more tea.

He tried to laugh with her but he was becoming uncomfortable.

She handed him back his cup. "It was only when I woke up to the fact that the morality society expects a woman of my class to follow was artificial and stifling that I was able to throw it off." She pressed his hand. "I wonder if you understand what I'm talking about?"

He was confused. "I'm not sure I've ever thought about such things, Mme. Averbach."

"Adele," she corrected. "And it's high time you did." Leaning closer she said softly, "In that painting I am as God made me. Doesn't it please you?"

"Yes," he said uncertainly, "as I've already told you—"

Her eyes gleamed with yellow glints in the gathering twilight. "Then why don't you kiss me?"

His confidence shattered. He had never been with a woman before in his life and he was scared to death. He stumbled off the sofa onto his knees, groping for her hand in boyish clumsiness. "I would do anything in the world for you, Mme Averbach, but it's all so new—"

She stopped his words with a hand on his lips. Bending forward, she embraced him tenderly, her breasts beneath the silk pressed against his cheek. "You're inexperienced, you mean? My sweet boy, I wouldn't adore you if you were any other way. But you mustn't think I'm making any demands on you. We've only just met. You'll come to my Thursdays and I'll play the piano for you at tea. Do you like Chopin?"

He was comforted by the warmth of her bosom. Her jasmine scent was intoxicating. His arms slipped around her and he looked up to find her waiting lips. . . .

Afterward, as they lay in the glow of firelight, he let his fingers run over the flawless body of the odalisque who had stepped out of a painting and made him a man.

The following Thursday he was accepted at Adele's as her protégé and treated as a regular. Oliver bustled around presenting him as the young dauphin. Mina Hunneker and the elocutionist invited him to take part in a tableau they were arranging as a birthday surprise for Adele. And he shared another pipe with the opium smoker. This time no feeling of menace disturbed his euphoria, as a guest pianist played impromptus by Schubert while a cageful of canaries was released into the room to fly about singing.

In bed that night Adele held his face between her hands looking deep into his eyes and said, "You must be careful of opium, my darling. The others are experienced and able to handle it, but it can so easily take you into a world where I can't follow. Believe me, I've seen it happen before."

Holding her close, he scoffed at the notion that anything was ever going to come between them, but the whole next day he resisted using the new inlaid ivory pipe the opium smoker had given him.

He visited her every afternoon at teatime, all the while letting his family believe he was still attending his classes at Columbia. When he left his house in the morning, he spent the day with her friends, often drowsing away the hours with the opium pipe until time to see her.

On Christmas Eve his father was visibly annoyed when he excused himself from the family circle around the candlelit Christmas tree—the Coopers were over, the professor having come up from Washington for the holidays—and went to Mina Hunneker's flat on Twenty-third Street to rehearse the tableau.

And shortly after the new year of 1865, in Mme. Averbach's drawing room he wore a white robe as the central figure in a series of living pictures entitled, "The Assumption of Edgar Allan Poe into Heaven." Oliver, Mina, and the others in purple portrayed the Olympians of the arts waiting to receive him at the portals. Adele watched from a throne chair and said afterward that she felt the poet himself had been in the room.

At the end of the evening they decked him in garlands and led him upstairs, the dancer with the chalk-white face strewing rose petals before him, while the elocutionist recited, "*O moon of my delight that knows no wane. . . .*"

As the procession entered the flower-filled bedroom, Adele was lying naked on her bed of white satin, the blue ribbon from the painting around her neck, in the identical pose.

Leaving the lovers in each other's arms, the group serenaded them from outside the closed door with the Bridal Chorus from *Lohengrin* before departing.

As February passed and the unusually warm days of March started thawing the piles of dirty snow that made the narrow streets of Greenwich almost impassable, Claude lay in his room on the evenings when he was not at Adele's and sank into the delicious half-sleep the opium smoke induced. No longer was he a victim of the mundane world that had so bored him and driven him into empty fantasies. He didn't need fantasies any more. Reality was in Adele's encompassing arms, and that was superior to anything the world had to offer.

In April, Perry Street was again filled with the scent of lilacs from the garden of the old mansion across from the Endicotts'. The mansion was finally being demolished to make way for new houses, and sledgehammers were smashing down the inner walls, and timbers were flying out of the upper windows. A team of horses strained against their harness to pull down the sagging outbuildings.

One afternoon Adele canceled their rendezvous because her dressmaker was coming, but Claude couldn't keep himself from going over anyway for the joy of seeing her lovely body being fitted with silks and satins. As he climbed the stoop to her front door, he anticipated her mock distress at his barging unannounced into her feminine world, and then her impatience at having to stand still until the dressmaker unpinned her so that she could throw herself into his arms.

When the street door was opened, he rushed past the servant who tried to stop him and reached the top of the stairs before it came to him that there had been a man's hat and cane on the table below. As he hesitated, Adele came out of her bedroom tying the sash of the Japanese robe she always wore at their trysts, and demanded to know why he was there.

"Didn't I tell you not to come here until this evening?" she said coldly. Her body's musk came through the jasmine scent.

He could only stare at her.

Then taking pity on his evident shock and confusion, she said in a kindlier voice, "You know, my dear, neither of us ever made promises."

* * *

Downstairs, as the servant closed the door after him, his only thought was his opium pipe, to blot it all out. But at the bottom of the steps in front of the house Oliver rushed up holding a copy of the *Herald* with the banner headline, "Lee Surrenders."

"It's over! Oh, lordie, Grant's done it! I'm a Southerner myself, and if they cut my tongue out I don't care, but"—and his voice shook—"this is the happiest day of my life."

Claude looked at him dumbly.

The chubby man immediately understood what had happened. "My dear boy, it's dreadful for you I know, but it had to come sooner or later. We all knew it would." He put an arm around his shoulders. "We've all been through it with her and you have to be grateful for what you get. There's a law of nature—I had to learn it myself the hard way—the strong devour the weak, and she's stronger than any of us."

Claude walked away, hardly aware of the people pouring into the streets, the noise in the air as the city went into a frenzy of jubilation. Hysterical newsboys were yelling out the headlines, and their extras were grabbed up. Strangers were swigging from bottles and passing them from hand to hand. In front of a French restaurant an accordionist was playing while the waitresses were dancing with the passersby. On Washington Square even the rich had come out of their mansions along with the servants to join the festivities.

He moved like a phantom through the dense crowds at Jefferson Market where soldiers were kissing every girl in sight and whirling them around. From every church in the city, bells were ringing out the universal joy that peace had come at last. But his pipe was the only thing that mattered to him.

When he got home finally and shut the door, the house was empty. Even his mother was out. The rooms were still and joyless in contrast to the frantic activity of the streets. It suited him that way. In his room on the third floor he fumbled with his opium paraphernalia that he kept in the drawer of the bedside table and soon was sucking in searing lungfuls of smoke. But the oblivion he wanted did not come. His head throbbed from the roar of cannon going off in the harbor and the shriek of ships' whistles in the river, the popping of firecrackers and people shouting in the street below—and everywhere the infernal clanging of the bells. He put the pipe away and lay staring up at the ceiling.

* * *

That evening when the family came home after having attended a thanksgiving service at St. Luke's, Tom Endicott glanced through his mail, which he had overlooked in the excitement, and found a letter from Columbia College informing him that his son had been dropped from the rolls, not having attended lectures since December or taken any exams.

He was at his wit's end over his good-for-nothing son. He took a lamp and stormed upstairs where he found Claude lying in the dark in total inertia.

What in God's name was the boy always lying around for? It smelled terrible in his room—as if the furnace were leaking fumes through the register. But the furnace wasn't on. Putting the lamp down on the desk, he banged up the window to let in some fresh air. Claude didn't even bother to turn his head to look at him, putting his arm over his eyes against the lamplight.

"I suppose it was too much to expect you to be here to go to church with us on this tremendous occasion," Tom said sharply. "But to actually drop out of college without a word to me! Is that what I bought you out of the Army for? Boys without a fraction of your privileges have been dying like flies for four years while you've done exactly nothing."

Claude didn't answer.

"Don't you have anything to say to me?" He was trying to control his temper.

His son still didn't look at him, only mumbling, "I know I'm a failure, you don't have to tell me."

"Don't get sarcastic with me, you damn sniveler! I never made you do anything you didn't want to do!" The spoiled weakling just lay there, arm over his face, as if his own father meant nothing to him. The piled-up frustrations of years overwhelmed Tom. "I've worked my life away for the lot of you—you, your mother, and your sister. All I wanted was what every other man wants, a reasonable family life—and what did I get?" He was stomping around the room, clutching his head and shouting. ". . . a family of misfits! Your mother has just sat there and made a fool out of me for twenty years!"

Claude put down his arm and glared. "Don't you say a word about her!" He didn't care what his father said about him—he was used to it—but to talk about his mother like that when it was clear to everyone that she was the victim. They were all his victims. He was overcome with the injustice of it all and got up on an elbow, yelling, "You're nothing but a cold fish! You've never cared about any of us. If I'm a failure as a son, what kind of a father do you think you've been?"

Tom was stunned and sank down on the stool in front of the desk. Claude had never raised his voice to him before. He had scarcely done more than mumble.

To Claude, his father suddenly looked prematurely old and beaten, the lamplight etching the lines into his face. He threw himself back on the pillow, more miserable than ever. "I'm sorry I said that."

But his son's unexpected denunciation had knocked the wind out of Tom. "You told me you didn't want to go to college," he said. "I shouldn't have pushed it." Then he added wistfully, "God knows, I always wanted us to be friends, with your mother ill and Veronica off in her own world."

It was the first time Claude had ever seen the loneliness in his father, and it made him feel that this was someone he could talk to after all. "I quit school because of a woman, pa," he said, and the story of Adele and how she had thrown him over came out in a rush. "I don't know how I'll ever get over it."

Father and son were both quiet. Outside, the noise of the victory celebration had died down. In the distance a fireworks display was bursting into floral fantasies in the sky.

Finally it was Tom who broke the silence. "You'll find a way to live with it. I did."

Claude raised his head and looked at his father.

Tom nodded. "That's right, the same thing happened to me once. I know how you feel." Relieved at being able to talk about something he had kept to himself for so long, he told about Molly and his illegitimate son, Patrick, in Shamrock Alley, as Claude sat up cross-legged listening intently.

Claude said when he had finished, "He was the boy who ran into the printshop that day, wasn't he? I've never forgotten."

"That was him. I've heard he's just back from the war. Wounded in the leg at Savannah by a sniper the day Sherman reached the sea."

"Have you seen him?"

"No. I'd like to, but I'm afraid he wouldn't want anything to do with me."

How incredible, Claude thought, a brother he didn't even know about. This man in front of him, his father, was not as ordinary as he had always thought. "I could go see him, couldn't I?"

Tom considered it. "I suppose so." Then his face lit up. "Why, that would be fine!"

They sat talking for a while longer until the hall clock struck eleven, when Tom picked up the lamp and left.

BUT THROUGH THE ENDLESS HOURS OF THE NIGHT THE IMAGE OF Adele returned to torment Claude, and in the morning, hopeless, he saw no reason to get up to face the world without her. The singing of birds and the brilliant sun coming through the drapes only seemed to mock him.

In the kitchen Veronica was preparing a breakfast tray for her brother, having heard the loud voices the night before and knowing how he was always crushed after one of their father's onslaughts.

When Elizabeth Cooper dashed in from next door—she had come to sit with Mrs. Endicott because Miss Swindon was indisposed—she volunteered to take the tray up to Claude. She had on her school uniform—middy blouse with white sailor collar and navy-blue pleated skirt.

Outside his room, with her heart fluttering, Elizabeth took a deep breath, gave the door a tap, and went in with a bright "Good morning." Her sleeping prince, who had never paid the slightest attention to her, was lying there with the quilts pulled up to his nose, and from the look on his pale face, utterly out of sorts. She set down the tray and hurried to open the drapes, hoping the beautiful spring day might cheer him up. But his eyes only squinched up against the sunlight and she heard the low but unmistakable sound of a fart from under the bedclothes.

Ignoring the vulgarity, she set to work plumping up his pillows, letting him know that she was not going to be put off that easily. He scowled at being forced to sit up and was not mollified when she poured out a cup of steaming coffee and handed it to him.

"You might feel better if you drank it," she said as she sat down on a chair and gazed in admiration at the truculent youth with sleep-matted hair who was staring ahead gloomily. "Go on, drink it."

He took a sip with a grimace and immediately spit it back, nearly upsetting the cup. "What are you trying to do, scald me?"

Thrilled by the long-lashed eyes in the pale face finally noticing her, she leaned over briskly to put a napkin in the saucer where he had slopped his coffee over. "You oughtn't to be such an old grouch, you know. The war's over, it's spring, and if you looked outside you'd see that the whole world is happy."

"Who cares?" he said, still frowning but sipping his coffee more cautiously.

Satisfied at having gotten a response out of him, she sat back. "What's the matter with you today?"

He took another look at her, annoyed at her schoolgirl curiosity. "I wish you'd go away. There's nothing the matter."

She was not about to retreat, she was enjoying it too much. She crossed her arms. "Of course something's the matter. You've been acting queerly since just before Christmas."

He looked at her in alarm, nearly spilling his coffee again. "Have you been spying on me?"

"I have not! It's perfectly obvious that something's been going on. You've been putting on your best clothes every day, you've let your hair grow awfully long—*why*, I don't know—and you've been going around with your head in the clouds." She reached back to straighten the collar of her middy blouse, outlining her young breasts.

He was almost embarrassed to notice she was not the pesky child any more. Her hair that had always been in pigtails was now tied back attractively, and her green eyes were clearly beautiful. He turned away. "Well, that's all over."

She took his cup abruptly and poured him more coffee, in despair that anyone would ever take her seriously. "I know you think I'm still a child. But I'm sixteen now and I'm getting pretty sick of looking on at other people's lives, wishing I had one of my own."

"Oh, yeah?" he said, turning back to her. "What would you say if I told you I'd been having an affair with an older woman?"

It was the most extraordinary thing anybody had ever said to the young girl. She didn't know what to think, it was so exciting. "That never occurred to me, I must say. I thought of something else. . . ."

"Well, it's no damn fun," he said, leaning forward, his elbows on his knees. "I shouldn't have told you that, I guess, but you may as well know what a horse's ass I am." And he told her how Adele had used him. When he was finished, he closed his eyes against the pain of it all.

In a state of confusion, Elizabeth went to the window and looked down with relief on the ordinary street scene where housewives were buying vegetables from a pushcart peddler, the half-demolished mansion quiet because of the holiday for the end of the war. "How awful for you," she said at last, keeping her back to him to hide her burning face.

"Are you shocked?" He was afraid he had gone too far. She wasn't quite the brash kid he had taken her for.

She turned around quickly. "Certainly not! I've heard much more scandalous things than that." Still unable to look at him, she picked up the breakfast tray. She had to get out of there. She was aware that she had spent over a half an hour in his room alone with him. "I wish there was something I could do to help you, but . . ."

He raised himself on an elbow. "Don't go, I need somebody to talk to."

"I'm afraid I can't right now," she said, "I have to get down to your mother." But at the door she added, "Maybe we could meet in Abingdon Square this afternoon, if you like." And amazed at her own daring, she dashed downstairs.

When she had gone, he opened the bedside table drawer, fitted together the sections of his inlaid ivory pipe, and lit the candle to soften the resin.

While Elizabeth sat reading to Mrs. Endicott, she got over her shock and became used to the idea of Claude being part of a world of depravity. How right it was that the young man she adored had done something so wickedly romantic and, most wonderful of all, who could ever have imagined that he would take her into his confidence?

By the time she was sitting with him under the flowering elms in the park at the end of Bleecker Street, she was proud of him for being someone who wasn't afraid of life and actually did things.

She asked him about all the details, unable to hear enough about the lurid candlelit atmosphere of the artistic soirees. "Opium!" she cried when he told her about the drugs some of the people used there. "How decadent! Did you try it?"

Flushing, he denied that he had.

"What a pity, I wouldn't have been able to resist." She looked dissatisfied at the commonplace mothers and children in the park around them. "Oh, but I do envy you," she said. "All my life I've wanted to know artists and writers and people like that. I'd give anything for even a glimpse of Tatiana and that colored dancer."

"Well, it's all over for me now. I'll never go back there again." He posed moodily, imagining the picture of Poe.

"You're thinking about her again, aren't you? There are other women in the world, you know."

"You don't know what she was like," he said. "She was more than beautiful. Every man who ever met her fell in love with her. She's like Circe turning men into pigs." He was overcome with self-pity.

"Well, you've got to forget her," she said in a practical tone. "Get back to your studies and make something of yourself. Someday she'll be sorry for what she did when she sees how famous you are."

He told her it was too late for that, unfortunately. He had been thrown out of Columbia.

She considered a moment. "Then get a job in a bookstore. You like books, don't you? And you'd meet all kinds of people."

"I could never do that," he said. "I can't talk to people. They make me nervous."

"But what about at the salon?"

"They were different."

Reflecting more seriously, she said, "I know how hard it's been for you and Veronica growing up, your mother ailing and all. Of course, it's a far more romantic atmosphere than my house. I love mama and papa, but we're so conventional. If only you got along better with your father, it might be easier for you."

"What a coincidence you should say that," he said, more impressed than ever with the understanding of this girl who had always been a child to him until today. "My father came up to my room last night. He was in a snit about me getting thrown out of school, but the strangest thing happened. He told me that years ago he had an affair with another woman too, and would you believe it, he said I have an illegitimate brother living down on Shamrock Alley."

"A brother! And illegitimate—that's even better. I'd give anything to have an illegitimate brother. It's part of being an artist."

"I haven't got used to the idea myself," he said almost cheerfully.

"Why don't you go see him? Aren't you dying to know what he's like? Maybe he's an anarchist."

"He's Catholic, I know that for sure."

"All the better. Mme. Averbach was a Jewess, like in Ivanhoe." She sat back, sighing with the wonder of his revelations. "I think you should write a novel about it all. Everyone would want to read it."

Her enthusiasm made him smile.

"Don't laugh," she said, her bold green eyes chiding him. "It's the perfect way to get over a tragic love affair, and when you meet your brother it will open up a whole new world to you."

"Will you help me write it down?" he asked. His life was beginning to seem less tragic to him already.

"Of course I will. I don't have your imagination but you can dictate it to me. I always won prizes for my penmanship."

She might still be a schoolgirl, he thought, but she was very sensible.

When he got home, Veronica was in the parlor covering a lampshade, busy with parchment and scissors, spectacles perched on the end of her nose. In her prim, starched dress and hair pulled back in a bun she already had the look of a spinster, though she was only twenty-one. Since finishing her studies at the Greenwich Academy for Young Ladies, she had taken over the work of running the house.

Though it had been some time since they had had a real talk, Claude sat down and asked her what she thought about Elizabeth's suggestion that he get a bookstore job and live a more normal life.

"I used to think I wanted to be like other people too," she said, snipping off a length of brown ribbon, "but the more I've worked on my poems, the more I've come to see what a blessing it is to be different."

That sounded like sour grapes, he said. Deep down, didn't she really want a normal life too, maybe to get married some day? Hadn't she ever been in love?

She fitted the ribbon around the lampshade. "Of course I expect to fall in love, but when I do, it will be in my own way and my own time. I'm not in the least worried about it." Having tied a big bow, she patted it with satisfaction and gathered up her materials.

Annoyed at her complacency, he thought she needed a jolt and told her about their illegitimate brother, Patrick.

"That has nothing to do with me," she said firmly, and walked past him down to the kitchen.

His sister was like a creature under a rock, refusing to come out into the light. Well, he certainly wasn't going back to that himself. He had wasted too much time already.

He spent most of the next few days with Elizabeth. They walked around the reservoir at Forty-second Street and rode the ferryboat across the Hudson to Luna Park in Weehawken and sat in Abingdon Square, the tiny yellow flowers of the elms falling on them like powder, while she read to him from Hawthorne's short stories.

She was forever asking him to describe for her again the Thursday evenings at Adele's, and he was beginning to feel proud that he had been part of such an exotic world. The only thing he didn't tell her about was his opium habit. Whenever the pain of Adele came over him, and it was not quite so sharp any more, he took a pipe in his room. By the time his supply of opium was finished, he wouldn't need it again and planned to give it up.

In the middle of reading a story called "The Prophetic Portrait," in which a beautiful couple got married and went off to Europe on their honeymoon, Elizabeth put down the book and asked why the two of them shouldn't get married too. He was so taken aback he laughed, never having considered such a thing—and besides they were too young.

But when she pointed out that they were a perfect match because she understood what he had gone through, he saw it might not be such a bad idea. Wasn't her healthy optimism the best antidote to Adele? Besides, what else did he have to do?

Their life together would be dedicated to the arts, she said. He would be a writer, and although she hadn't settled yet on just which one of the arts she intended to pursue, she was so interested in all of them, she too would be an artist of some kind.

At the Endicott dinner table that night she announced that she and Claude were planning on getting engaged as soon as she finished school in June. Tom couldn't have been more pleased, once he got over his surprise at how quickly his son seemed to have recovered from his broken heart, and he got out a bottle of hock he had been saving for a special occasion.

The next day, feeling better all around, Claude went to Shamrock Alley to look for his half brother Patrick. He had always avoided the area because the immigrant toughs who lived over there beat up any outsider they caught in their territory.

The tavern at the corner was packed with regular patrons and returning soldiers still celebrating four days after the end of the war. The tavern keeper pointed out to him the Hanlon staircase. In front of it, Patrick's younger brother, Timothy, a hulking youth with an incipient red mustache, was pitching pennies with some other teenage roughnecks, blocking the way.

As Claude walked toward the stairs, conspicuous in his college jacket and tie, he felt them looking him over, and one of them even spat into the dirt. They didn't move, forcing him to go around them clumsily. When he got to the third floor landing and knocked at the door, Timothy, who had followed him up, leaned against the porch rail within earshot, chewing on a toothpick.

Patrick was lying down when he heard the knock, resting his leg that had taken a bullet in the battle of Savannah. As he got up with a grimace of pain and limped to the door, he pulled up the suspenders of his army trousers over a collarless flannel shirt. He was not tall but he had a sturdy frame, with the broad face, dark wild hair, and the blue eyes of his mother.

His leg throbbing, he was hardly cheered up to see the pale, effete-looking young man in fancy clothes standing in the doorway. But when Claude introduced himself, he was shaken. He held the Endicotts directly responsible for destroying his mother. Through her last hellish days she had railed against Tom Endicott and it had become clear to him that his father was not the dead Mike Hanlon after all.

"You might not remember," Claude said, attempting to bridge the awkwardness between them, "but we saw each other once in my father's printshop."

"I remember, all right," Patrick muttered.

"You do?" Claude said, pleased. "I couldn't figure out what was going on."

"That was the blackest day in my mother's life."

This wasn't the way it was supposed to go. Claude tried to find something right to say to this thickset, bristling stranger who was nothing like the brother he had imagined. "I'm so sorry about what happened to your mother. I never knew about it until the other night."

"A fat lot of good sorry does." A twinge in his leg made Patrick grab onto the doorjamb.

Claude saw at once the pain he was in. "Look here, you shouldn't be on your feet. Let me help you to a chair."

Patrick stood his ground and said through teeth gritted against the pain, "Was it your father sent ya down here?"

"Oh, no, he didn't. Not really. I came because I wanted to. He had nothing to do with it. I mean, he is concerned about you, of course," said Claude, feeling himself getting into even more of a mix-up. "Look, can't I come in and talk for a minute?"

"We got nothin to talk about." Patrick stepped back to close the door.

Claude tried to hold it open and pleaded, "I've had a hard time too. Won't you even give me a chance?"

Patrick boiled over and yelled, "If you don't get outta here, I won't be answerable for what I might do!"

"But we're half brothers!"

"As far as I'm concerned, there's not a drop of the same blood in us." Patrick shut the door and limped back to the table. He was shaking, his feelings in a turmoil.

In his anger against the Endicotts he had never given a thought to this brother his own age. Why did he have to come around now? He didn't want to know him. He didn't want to know any of them, not after what happened to his mother.

He certainly didn't need their help. He may have started out digging sewers, but just as soon as his leg healed, Tammany had a job waiting for him as foreman of a crew extending tracks for the horsecars into the northern reaches of the city. He had a future in public transportation. While he was away at the war, he had thought of ideas for putting tracks in the air and even below the ground that could revolutionize city transit. And he was going to marry Hester—a good Irish girl who loved him—and raise a family, and he would go a lot further than that sad-eyed nincompoop of an Endicott who had the nerve to suggest that there could ever be any brotherly feeling between them.

Outside on the porch, Claude stood for a moment dazed by what had happened. Timothy, who was leaning against the rail with his toothpick in his mouth, watched him and, when Claude finally started down the stairs, followed behind. When they reached the bottom, Timothy gave a signal and his gang grabbed Claude and pulled him into an alleyway where Timothy began to beat him with his big fists. Several people in the court saw what was going on and ran over, shouting.

Patrick came out on the porch to see what the racket was about. He heard someone below crying, "Stop, Tim!" and forgetting his leg, the young veteran vaulted down the stairs holding on to the rail.

His brother was stomping and kicking Claude Endicott, who lay writhing in the dirt. He pulled Timothy off and smashed him hard against the brick wall. Then, with a neighbor's help he got Claude to his feet and they half-carried him out to the street, laying him nearly unconscious on top of a pile of old clothes in a ragpicker's wagon.

At the Endicotts' house it was Elizabeth Cooper who answered the door. She stifled a cry, seeing Claude bloody and battered, and helped Patrick get him up to his room. Veronica went for the doctor while she set about washing the wounds and getting some whiskey down him.

When Patrick got home he found his brother Timothy on the couch, holding his head as if in agony. Their sister Sarah, who at fifteen was married and expecting a child, was laying on cold compresses and trying to comfort him.

"Get up, ya blitherin shit!" Patrick shouted and limped over to pull his whimpering hulk of a brother to his feet. He grabbed a cap and jacket from a peg and thrust them at him. "I shouldn't be doin it, but I'm goin to give ya a chance to save your worthless skin."

With Sarah wailing and wringing her hands, he pushed Timothy out the door. At the corner of Greenwich Street he flagged down a hansom cab and took his brother straight down to the Battery where he signed him on a freighter leaving that night for Liverpool. Patrick did not heave a sigh of relief until the lights of the ship disappeared out in the harbor.

* * *

Although Claude spent a fairly peaceful night, with Elizabeth never leaving his side, he did not fully come to and the next day he started heavy sweats and periods of unconscious raving. The doctor suspected there might be neurological damage as well as a concussion. Claude's heart had always been weak and the doctor said it would be a while before they would know the extent of his internal injuries.

When Patrick came to the door at noon to find out how Claude was, Elizabeth asked him in and took him upstairs. For a moment Claude recognized him and smiled weakly, and Patrick tried to tell him what a skunk he felt like for the way he had treated him the day before. As soon as he was well, Patrick said, he wanted him to meet Hester, the girl he was going to marry.

Elizabeth went down to the door with Patrick afterward and thanked him for what he had done. All the way home he thought hard about the remarkable girl with the green eyes who was ministering to her beloved like an angel.

In the early hours of the following morning Claude went into convulsions. In his delirium, with his arms flailing, he pulled out the drawer of the bedside table, upsetting the contents onto the floor.

Before the doctor could get there, he died, with Elizabeth, Tom, and Veronica looking on helplessly. At a cry from behind them, they turned to see Fanny standing in the doorway in her nightdress, her hair wild and tears streaming down her face.

Afterward, the doctor discovered the sections of the ivory pipe and the brown lump of resin on the floor by the bed and asked Tom about it, but Tom said that he had never seen it before. The doctor sniffed it, tasted a bit of the resin. After a pause he said that internal injuries might not have been the only cause of Claude's death. It appeared he had been an opium addict, and with his weak heart, had died of heart failure from being deprived of the drug.

Bells were tolling everywhere on April 16, 1865, the day after President Lincoln's assassination at Ford's Theater, as a small party of mourners walked behind a cart carrying a casket through empty streets to St. Luke's Church. Claude Endicott was buried in the churchyard in the presence of his family and the Coopers, while the shocked city grieved for the Great Emancipator.

1870

FACED WITH THE HEADY POSSIBILITIES OF THE POSTWAR BOOM, the city had soon put aside its grief. Tom Endicott's printing business also shared in the general euphoria. Even without temperance jobs, the presses were kept humming. There were circulars for the opening of Macy's department store, announcements for the first production of *Aida* at the Academy of Music, broadsides against Boss Tweed, the unscrupulous head of Tammany who was bilking the city of millions, and all kinds of other printing jobs. But Tom no longer took much interest in it and left the bulk of the work to his employees.

For a while it was all he could do to cope with Fanny. In the months following Claude's death her behavior became more erratic than ever.

Though the poor woman had never paid much attention to her son while he was alive, his death seemed to affect her deeply. The cannabis elixir wasn't effective in controlling her outbursts any more, and in fact produced visions that made her crazier. Even with Veronica's help, Miss Swindon could hardly handle her and had to move into her bedroom to be with her every minute, while Tom slept on the sofa in the study.

One day Fanny broke away from her companion and ran up to Claude's old room where she started to fling his things out the window onto the street, shrieking that he needed them in heaven. The time had finally come when Tom had to face the fact that he couldn't keep his wife at home any longer. He found a private asylum for her uptown overlooking the Hudson where she would be well cared for.

On the day the attendants from the home came, Miss Swindon went berserk trying to keep them from taking Fanny away from her, and fought a pitched battle in the downstairs hall, shouting that Tom was the cause of all her mistress's troubles, fathering an Irish bastard to drive his legitimate son to addiction and his wife out of her wits with shame.

Tom didn't even have his friend Albert around any more to keep his spirits up. The squatters' settlement Albert had been living in in the Central Park area had been pulled down to make way for the city's new museum of art and he had gone with his wife to live with her people, a tribe of clam-digging Indians on the eastern tip of Long Island.

Elizabeth Cooper, who always made the house livelier with her banging in and out, had also gone. She was away at Vassar, the country's first college for women, which had just opened.

Although Veronica was still at home, doing most of the housework and cooking herself now, she was not much company. Father and daughter never had much to say to each other.

With so little to do with himself except for visits to Fanny at the sanitarium, Tom often wished that he could have some contact with his natural son Patrick. At the time of Claude's accident he had been impressed all over again with the extraordinary young man. They had spoken briefly a couple of times, though it had been awkward between them. Tom had tried to make it clear that he would like Patrick to continue visiting them, but after Claude died he never came back.

He couldn't blame Patrick for still resenting him. What kind of a father had he been, after all? The way he had treated him seemed more inexcusable than ever. Why hadn't he insisted on seeing his son all those years, no matter what Molly or the world thought about it?

He got news of him now and then through old Mrs. Brophy. Patrick had left his job laying horsecar tracks and had gone to work helping to build the first elevated line in the city down the length of Greenwich Street. From his front stoop Tom could see the girders of the structure that already blocked the view of the river. Property values along the path of the elevated were plummeting and people were moving out. And it was bound to get worse when the trains were rattling overhead, hauled by steam locomotives belching God only knew how much smoke over the area.

Mrs. Brophy had kept him informed when Patrick got married after the war to his girl Hester and they moved to a small flat farther away below Houston Street. But Hester had one miscarriage after another, her health declined, and in the first summer of the seventies he heard that she had died after another stillbirth, of childbed fever.

Under the circumstances Tom didn't see any reason he shouldn't go to see Patrick, but as it turned out he didn't have to.

The end of summer was always the most melancholy season for Tom. That had been when the bold-eyed servant girl came to work in the house, and for a brief time his life had been transformed. One evening when an orange moon hung over the row of houses across the street where the old mansion had stood, there was a knock at the door. He seldom got callers in the evening. When the Coopers came over, they never bothered to knock.

A young man with his cap in his hand and a black armband on his sleeve was standing there. Patrick.

"It's only a moment I need of your time, Mr. Endicott, and then I'll be on my way," he said with more than a trace of his mother's brogue. He was leaving New York in the morning and had something to get off his chest.

He was as stocky as ever, with the broad, open face Tom remembered so well, but his hair was tousled and he looked like he hadn't slept.

Tom stepped back and invited him in.

"I expect you're surprised to see me after so long." The young man looked uncomfortable in his workingman's clothes in the hall where the woodwork had been polished for a generation to a dark gloss.

"Yes," said Tom, who was more than surprised, "but come in, come in."

With a hand on his back he guided Patrick into the parlor, trying to think of something more to say. He had thought Patrick never wanted to have anything more to do with him, yet here he was. He offered him a chair.

"I'll stand if ya don't mind." He ran a hand over his square unshaven jaw, seemingly as unsure as Tom about how to begin.

"I should have told ya years ago, Mr. Endicott. I never even told my wife, I felt so bad about it."

Unable to make any sense out of this, Tom said how sorry he was to hear about his wife's death. The words sounded stiff, all wrong, but Patrick didn't seem to notice. Twisting his cap as he stood there, he said he was leaving New York because he had made a mess of everything. He had been bad for his wife—not to mention his brother Timothy—and what he had done to Tom was shameful. "I'd like to straighten it out with ya before I go."

"Shameful?" said Tom, trying again to get him to sit down, but the robust, curly-haired young man who looked so much like Molly and yet so different ignored it and kept on talking about that brother of his.

Timothy was the one who had done it, Patrick was saying—he had been with the Dusters. "When Tim heard me yellin at Claude, he got the wrong idea. I never meant it that way, Mr. Endicott. Your boy only wanted to be friends."

What was he talking about Claude for? The accident had happened so long ago. Tom tried to follow as Patrick went on, saying that he only put Timothy on the boat out of respect for his mother's memory.

"It wasn't right, I know, and now Hester's gone and all. . . ."

There was a certain catch in his voice and he put a hand over his eyes for a moment. ". . . I hardly knew him . . . refused to know him, I mean . . . it was as though I killed him myself."

Tom had made little sense out of the rambling, incoherent words, but now he understood. That thug of a brother had been the one to give Claude the fatal beating, and it was on Patrick's conscience that he had put his brother on a boat to save his skin.

Patrick put on his cap. "I'll take myself out of here now and I promise you'll never see nor hear of me any more."

Tom watched helpless as this lost son, who had reappeared out of the night, started to leave. He had let the world take Molly from him—was he going to let it happen again? He sprang to the door in time to get his son by the arm, pull him back to a chair and make him sit down. "Now just be quiet and let me say something for a change." He stood over him and told him that Claude didn't die from that beating. Claude had had a weak heart and there were other complications that he wouldn't go into. "And about you putting your brother on that boat, the Molly Hanlon I knew would have said you did right, and I'm not saying no."

Patrick looked confused. "Ya mean ya don't hold it against me?"

"You brought Claude back here, didn't you? I'll never forget that."

Patrick was silent.

Tom walked to the window, his back to the young man. The moon was higher now, and brighter. "Claude is dead and all that's over. What I feel bad about," he said, "is that all those years you were growing up I neglected you." There it was out in the open. He hadn't expected ever to have the chance to say it to this boy whom he had made a bastard. But now that he had started, he wanted to tell him the whole story of his love for Molly, and he did, without apology and not sparing himself. "When your mother let me know that she didn't want anything more to do with me," he finished, still gazing at the moon, "I used that as an excuse to stay away." The room was still, except for the crackling of the fire.

"But ya gave us money. . . ." Patrick said at last.

"Those measly sums?" Tom turned around. "Maybe it's too late, but I'd like to make it up to you. I've got some money put by. . . ."

Looking down at his callused hands, Patrick said he didn't need anything.

Tom came over and took the chair across from him. He sighed. "I wish I'd done something when there was time. With you going away I won't have the chance. I'm getting old I guess."

Patrick started to protest but Tom shook his head. "I may be only fifty but it's been a long while since I've had much to live for. My daughter doesn't need me and my wife is in an asylum. I need a friend. No"—he corrected himself—"I mean I need a son." He looked straight at Patrick. "If it's not too late."

"Ya shouldn't ought to say that." Patrick's eyes were round and his forehead creased. "I been feelin so bad. . . ." he said, and started to blubber like a baby.

Tom was upset too. He had never seen a grown man behave like this. He fumbled with a bottle of whiskey, poured out a shot and handed it over.

Patrick looked up from his misery, tears rolling unashamedly down his broad, innocent face, and gulped it down.

"All right?" said Tom.

Patrick gave a last snuffle and rubbed the back of his sleeve across his face. He grinned through his tears. "Ya really set me off, but I wasn't expectin ya to take it like that."

Tom poked up the fire and after a while they started feeling easier with each other. Patrick confessed that his marriage had never worked out very well. His wife had been a saint in every way, she never complained, but somehow she always made him feel like a brute. It was like there was no fight in her.

Tom thought what an irony that this boy's marriage sounded so similar to his own. But Patrick was still young—there was still time for things to go better for him. He vowed to help him however he could.

It was his sister Sarah, Patrick was saying, who had been the real solace to him since Hester died. She had two little ones now, with another on the way. Her husband, Bill Yates, was in the same work gang as him on the elevated. "Ya can see the el from here," he said. "Isn't it a fine sight?"

In no time he was holding forth loudly about his work as if he hadn't just been bawling his eyes out. "And that's only the beginning." His hands gripped his thighs enthusiastically and he described a tunnel that was being built downtown for an experimental underground train. "There's the real future for municipal transportation. Can't ya see it?" He spread out his brawny arms. "The whole city crisscrossed with tunnels carryin passengers and freight in every direction, and our streets fit to walk in again." He gave a sheepish grin. "Ah, but I'm bein carried away. Hester used to say, 'Pat, ya only live for them tracks and tunnels.'" His eyes misted over.

Alarmed at the threat of another waterfall, Tom tried to divert him by asking him about his ambitions. Patrick said his dream was to become a construction engineer on the el, but that would depend on his getting taken on as an apprentice by the engineers. He had no education, but on practical matters he could show them a thing or two if they would just give him a chance.

"Then you won't be going west after all?" Tom was starting to get an idea.

Patrick frowned. "Well, I'm not so sure. You're makin me feel different about things."

"Look here, I know a couple of engineers on your elevated," said Tom. "It happens they attend my church. Maybe I could introduce you to them on Sunday."

"Go to your church with ya, ya mean?"

The way he said it made it clear that going into a Protestant church was unthinkable. Tom amended his offer. "I could talk to them about you, if you like."

"Would it be possible, sir?"

Over another drink Patrick told him that he was giving up the flat and taking a room closer to the work site. Sarah had asked him to move in with them, but it would be too crowded and he wouldn't be able to study his engineering books.

"Why don't you move in here with Veronica and me?" The words were out before Tom had even thought of it.

Patrick's jaw dropped. "Here?"

"Why not? There's plenty of room and Veronica's a good cook."

Patrick said he couldn't think of doing such a thing. "It would mess up your life. What would ya tell people?"

"I've a right to take in boarders, don't I?" Then a thunderbolt hit him. "Why don't I adopt you?" It was so perfect, he wondered how he hadn't thought of it before.

"Adopt me? But I'm a Hanlon—and a Catholic!"

"What's to stop you from becoming an Endicott and a Protestant?"

"Protestant? But that means eternal damnation."

Tom was not going to let a little thing like that stand in the way now that he saw what to do. "We take all the sacraments at my church too. You could go to Mass there every Sunday the same as you do now."

Patrick scratched his head. "I'm not the one for goin to Mass every Sunday, I can tell ya."

"Well then, I don't see that it'll be a problem, one way or the other."

By the time they said good-night Patrick had agreed to come over the following Sunday and they would talk about it more.

Tom couldn't wait to get things started and rushed off the next day to consult his lawyer about the legal procedures necessary for adoption.

But on Sunday when Patrick was back again and they sat in the study with a decanter of port on the table between them, Tom didn't like the look of things. Patrick, in high collar and Sunday-best suit too tight for his stocky frame, was fiddling with his glass as if embarrassed to look at him.

"I've given your offer much thought, Mr. Endicott," he

finally began, "and I do want to thank ya for it. It's not that I'm a religious man exactly. As I told ya, it's not every Sunday that I go to Mass, but my mother was born in the church, and me, and everyone I know as well, so I don't see how it would be right. . . ."

Tom told him that he wouldn't have to give up his faith if he didn't feel right about it. He could come live with them anyway.

But Patrick was still adamant. He said he wouldn't feel easy about it, in this kind of place away from his own people. . . . He broke off at the sound of rustling skirts and lively whistling in the hall.

A girl, whose softly piled hair reflected the russet tints of the chrysanthemums she was carrying in her arms, appeared in the doorway. Her green eyes widened when she saw Patrick. It was Elizabeth Cooper, back from Europe a week before.

After graduating from Vassar, she had gone abroad as traveling companion to an elderly widow. The galleries, the cathedrals, even a flirtatious interlude in Paris—she had loved it all. But with the clouds gathering for a war between France and Germany, the old lady got nervous and they had come home. Though back with her parents only a few days, Elizabeth had perceived Tom's loneliness and was already doing her best to cheer him up.

She dropped the flowers into a vase on a side table and came in. "You're Mr. Hanlon, aren't you?" she said to Patrick. "It's marvelous to see you again."

Her remarkable eyes had stayed with him all these years without his knowing it. And she remembered him too. Overcome, he could barely mumble a reply.

But she could see they were having a serious talk, she said, and was not going to interrupt them. Before they could stop her, she started for the door at a girlish skip, but got in trouble with her skirts. Turning around to give her bustle a mock slap of disapproval, she threw them a delightful smile and disappeared.

It was such a breath of fresh air to have her back again, Tom said, observing Patrick's high color.

"It's next door that Miss Cooper lives, if I'm not mistaken?"

"Yes," Tom said, playing his hand for all it was worth, "but sometimes she's here more than there—not that I mind."

Patrick studied the ruby liquid in his glass. "It's true I was christened Hanlon in the church, but then Hanlon is not my father's name when ya think about it, so Hanlon's not really my name... so maybe my religion's not my religion ...can we look at it that way?" He cocked his curly head roguishly.

PATRICK'S ARRIVAL IN THE HOUSE WAS UNDERSTANDABLY difficult for Veronica. Although her father had never paid any more attention to his reticent daughter than she had to him, he might have anticipated her lack of enthusiasm when he told her out of the blue that Patrick was to come live with them. She was not scandalized—she had known of his existence for years—but she was not happy about being forced to share the house with a semi-immigrant from the slums.

Her worst fears were confirmed when the loudmouthed stranger in workman's clothes showed up with a battered carpetbag and stomped up the stairs after Tom to settle in. She couldn't understand her father's sudden interest in him.

Patrick, for his part, found this prim, twenty-six-year-old girl with spectacles and a sheaf of poetry manuscript under her arm almost as ridiculous as she found him crude. That first evening, when he came down to sit with Tom in the parlor wearing only his long-sleeved underwear under his suspenders as he was used to doing at home, she picked up her cat and walked out in a huff.

Tom was embarrassed that anything should go wrong so soon. He apologized to Patrick, explaining that she had the high-strung nerves of her mother and that until she got used to him, it might be better if he kept his shirt on downstairs.

Things did not improve at breakfast. Uncomfortable sitting with Tom and Veronica in the dining room, Patrick waxed enthusiastic about the technology of the new flush toilet upstairs. Where he came from, chamber pots and privies were still the order of the day.

Veronica was so outraged that she forgot her usual restraint and spoke up. "People do not discuss such things at table, Mr. Hanlon."

Patrick, who had been trying his best to hide how clumsy he felt in her presence, shot back before he could check himself, "Ya mean ya don't have calls of nature like the rest of us, miss?"

Veronica turned crimson and looked to her father, expecting him to reprimand this vulgarity.

Instead, he reprimanded her. "Patrick is not a Hanlon any more, Veronica. He's an Endicott now," he said quietly, reminding her of the fact of the adoption.

She dropped her napkin and got to her feet. "You've taken leave of your senses, papa. You can't make him a substitute for Claude, no matter how hard you try." And she ran out of the room.

Things got even more strained when the Coopers came to Sunday dinner to meet Patrick. Everyone except for Veronica was happy for him, but even with a natural physical grace, he had not had time to learn their table manners. He tied his napkin around his neck and swilled his soup noisily, while Veronica looked mortified.

Seeing the awkwardness of the situation, Professor Cooper asked him about his work on the elevated.

Swiping his napkin across his mouth, Patrick said that thanks to Mr. Endicott—immediately blushing and correcting it to "my father"—he had been taken into the engineering office as an apprentice. "We're goin to be puttin up elevated railroads all over New York City," he said, planting his elbows on the table and leaning forward. "Ya know what that means, sir? It's goin to bring the city right into Greenwich."

"But I thought we were trying to keep the city out," said Veronica acidly.

"Maybe we thought we could keep the city out," Tom said, taking Patrick's side again, "but this is 1870 and we can't turn our backs on progress."

To everyone's relief, the hired girl walked in with a baked ham on a platter. But when Patrick heard her addressed as

Kathleen he pulled on her apron string and asked wasn't she Big Jim O'Hara's daughter who lived in Shamrock Alley? The girl stammered in confusion and hurried back to the kitchen.

Made aware by the silence of his blunder in being too familiar with the help, Patrick started explaining how Big Jim had taken him to the Tammany Club and gotten him his first job.

Veronica whispered to Mrs. Cooper beside her, "He'll be asking the girl to sit down with us next."

Elizabeth frowned to hide her amusement. Veronica was being impossible, of course, but even if Patrick was as beautiful as the Adam in the Sistine Chapel, he did lack a certain finesse, devouring his food like a bear and scattering bits and pieces around him on the tablecloth. Claude was still her model of what a man should be and she intended to devote herself to a life in the arts and fulfill both their dreams.

She could understand how lonely Mr. Endicott had been, but she wondered if he might have been a bit precipitous in giving a home to this uncouth young man. Still, there was something about him. . . .

Professor Cooper said that maybe Tammany getting Patrick a job was not a bad thing, but Bill Tweed had driven every honest civic leader out of the organization.

Patrick disagreed hotly. "Mr. Tweed may not be to everyone's likin," he said through a mouthful of food. "But ya got to admit it was a bunch of crooks he threw out, even if they was posin as 'honest civic leaders' as ya call them." He mashed up the remains of his peas and potatoes. "When my wife was failin, it was Tweed's boys sent a basket of food around, and how would I ever have got my job when no one else would hire a mick? They're all crooks anyway, so if they want me to vote for them, why the hell not?" With his knife and fork he stuffed his mouth.

Veronica had had enough. "But it's the moral issue we're concerned with here, Mr. Hanlon."

He swallowed his food with a gulp and glared at her. "You can talk, Miss Endicott, raised in this house from the time you were born. My mother never sat at this table, she scrubbed the floors. Shyte on your high-and-mighty moral issues!" He shoved back his plate and banged out of the room.

"Oh, dear," said Mrs. Cooper, "we have no right to act superior. But don't worry, Tom"—she put a hand on his—"he'll get over it. He needs time to get used to us all."

Elizabeth excused herself and followed after him up the stairs. She had never seen anyone behave like that, but he was the product of a proletarian background, and Veronica was driving him to the wall. They had all been rude making him feel that they were ganging up against him. She wanted to apologize.

She found him at a window in the parlor, looking surprisingly sleek in his new worsted coat and checked trousers, glaring out onto the quiet street where only a few carriages were parked at the curb, their horses munching oats out of nose bags.

"That was a pretty little scene you just pulled, Mr. Endicott."

He turned around with blazing eyes, but seeing her, faced the window again and said in despair, "I'm not an Endicott and I never will be. I don't fit here. It's too hard for a dumb ox like me."

"You were just boasting about how hard your life was in the slums, or did I misunderstand you?"

Keeping his back to her, he muttered, "Oh, shut up about what ya know nothin of, ya fancy bitch."

She was hardly intimidated. "Is your vocabulary so limited that all you can use is obscenity?"

He turned around to see her flushed cheeks and the green fire of her eyes, and broke into a grin. "Ya sure you're not a mick yourself? Ya got the sass of one."

She was not letting him off so easy. With her hands on her hips she gave it back to him. "Poor downtrodden slum kid—and illegitimate to boot. That's your big excuse for everything, isn't it?"

He burst out laughing. "I'm sorry I called ya that. I did something wicked in there, didn't I? I knocked them on their asses."

She couldn't help laughing with him. "Yes, you did, but they'll get over it."

He told her that he had no education, how could Tom Endicott have thought he would fit in here?

"I've had plenty of education and European travel and I can't do anything. You can build elevated railroads."

"Still, it's manners that makes all the difference in this world."

"If that's all you're worried about, I could teach you. It's nothing you couldn't pick up in a minute—that is, if you don't mind a woman showing you." Her eyes gleamed at him playfully.

"Where do we begin?" he said, rubbing his hands.

"Well, I suggest that you come back to the table with me and we have dessert. But for mercy's sake, don't tie the napkin around your neck, even if it is the best way to keep the chocolate sauce off your tie."

At the elevated construction site, Patrick was the first Irishman to work in the engineering office. If the engineers were a little prejudiced at first, as the months passed they discovered how useful he was. Having started at the bottom, he had a practical knowledge that none of them had, combined with a natural aptitude for technical matters.

One day when he had been there nearly a year, his sister's husband, Bill Yates, who was still on one of the gangs, caught him outside the office and invited him down to the house. Sarah had received a letter from Timothy, who was living in Ireland.

This was as good a reason as any to get together with his sister again. Since he had moved up to live with his father, their occasional meetings had been awkward. But after six years he was surprisingly interested in getting news of the brother he had banished.

The Yateses lived on Greenwich Street on the second floor of a house sold by its original owner because of the elevated going up outside the windows.

Sarah was nursing her baby when he came in. She looked worn out after having had three children so young. His usual bluster failed to overcome her shyness, and seeing the candle burning before a religious picture on the wall, he became more aware of the gulf that had opened up between them. A momentary nostalgia came over him as he remembered the Latin chanting of the priest.

It was a relief to smell stew coming from the kitchen and have something familiar to talk about.

"Ya don't want any of that, Paddy," she said, when he asked for a taste of it.

"What do ya mean I don't? I haven't had Sligo stew in I don't know how long."

They all felt easier as she put steaming bowls of kidney, potatoes, and leeks before them. When he tucked his napkin into his shirtfront the way Elizabeth had taught him, Sarah tittered. He quickly retied it around his neck and, feeling his old self again, made a show of lapping the stew up with gusto.

Her two toddlers stared at him openmouthed as if he were

a stranger, but after he finished eating he got down on his hands and knees and played with them. They squealed and crawled all over him while Sarah fluttered around protesting that he was dirtying his handsome trousers on the floor.

When the children were tucked into a big iron bed in the corner, he collapsed into an armchair and read Timothy's letter aloud. Their brother was living in Cork, working for a ship's chandler, and had married a local girl. He wrote that there wasn't much money in Ireland, but he liked it better than in America because you didn't see any signs like "No Irish Need Apply." "I got into mischief over there because I was ashamed of being Irish. Paddy putting me on that boat was the best thing that ever happened to me."

Afterward, over tots of whiskey, Bill said, "It's a cryin shame Tim had to leave the country. He could have been workin on the elevated like us."

Patrick said there wasn't that much work back then and, feeling uncomfortable, changed the subject by telling them about the girl next door to the Endicotts he was keeping company with. While Bill refilled their glasses, his sister asked which church the girl attended.

"Ya may as well know right now, Sarah, she's not a Catholic."

"Oh," she said, and got up to clear the table keeping her face averted.

Since she was upset, he thought he might as well let her in on the whole story and get it over with, and he told her that he wasn't a Catholic any more either.

As she turned at the door in disbelief, he said, "Ya don't have to take it that way. My real father wasn't a Catholic. It's not the same as with you and Tim, is it?"

"Is that how ya see it?" she said stiffly, and went into the kitchen.

Although she pressed a packet of gooseberry tarts on him when he left and said she was ever so glad things were going well for him, he couldn't help noticing that his sister did not urge him to come again soon.

Elizabeth Cooper was strolling down Bleecker Street on the arm of her fiancé. It was a Sunday afternoon in spring and velocipedes were going by, some of them even pedaled by women showing bright stockings below their shortened cycling skirts. She had given up her original idea of their spending the afternoon at the new Metropolitan Museum of Art because Pat had made such a face about it. But even if he didn't share her artistic interests, she was happy. Being together was all that mattered. In fact, it was just their differences that were going to be the strength of their marriage. She admired the unique qualities he brought from his ethnic background, so colorful compared to her own. And once they were married she would tactfully introduce him to the arts, the same as she had taught him table manners. Although still his expansive self, he already behaved well enough socially even for hypercritical Veronica.

She waved to two friends passing in a pony cart, wanting to show him off in his beautiful pearl-gray suit with velvet trim around the lapels and a dapper bowler hat.

After their wedding in June they were going to live in the Endicott house. Tom had insisted on moving up to the top floor with Veronica where he would have another bathroom put in. She couldn't wait to fill those old-fashioned rooms with some solid ornamental furnishings that reflected her own tastes. And Patrick was planning to install the newest plumbing and heating devices.

After stopping to buy a penny bag of peanuts from a vendor, they started talking about their forthcoming wedding in her parents' garden.

"Is it the real thing when ya marry that way?" Patrick teased, cracking a whole handful of peanuts at once. "No one I know ever got married outside a church."

She gave a little frown. "Maybe you shouldn't have given up your faith. Tom wouldn't care if you went back to it, I'm sure." She had always adored the idea of Catholicism, she said. It was so aesthetic. The cathedrals in Europe were the most inspiring structures she had ever seen. "We don't have anything like them here."

"I don't know, St. Aloysius is as fine an edifice as I'd ever want to see," he said, picking out the shells and tossing them right and left. But she mustn't think the church was all so beautiful as it seemed, he told her. It was the money from the pockets of the poor that built those cathedrals she was so fond of. He popped the peanuts into his mouth. There was a lot of malarkey in it too. Plenty of people went to confession on Sunday and sinned the rest of the week, knowing they could get away with it.

But as they passed Our Lady of Pompeii on the next corner, it didn't escape her that he crossed himself automatically.

The night before the wedding Patrick sat up with his father, drinking whiskey in the parlor. His fellow engineers on the elevated had given him the bottle as a wedding present. His old work crew had tried to get him to spend the evening with them, but although he had never heard of a bridegroom not going out with the boys, he felt it was the right thing to come home since Tom had done so much for him.

With all the goodwill in the world, it was always hard to keep a conversation going with his father. Even after two years there was still a certain strain being alone together. Patrick was trying, without much success, to keep things a little lively by talking on his favorite subject. "I got the idea myself for a subway a long time ago, and here these bloody limeys have beat me to it," he said, referring to the London underground that had just opened. But it was his opinion that New York was going to have special problems when it built one of its own, because Manhattan island was solid granite. "I haven't worked that one out yet," he added with a grin.

"What about smoke in the tunnels?" Tom asked. He had been reading the articles about it in the *Herald* in order to be able to keep up with his technically minded son who had so impressed the chief engineer with his abilities once he was given the chance. "They say that smoke from the locomotives almost asphyxiates the passengers over there in London."

"I'd solve that one fast enough with a system of ventilation." And Patrick enthusiastically went into the technical details of air shafts.

The clock on the mantelpiece struck nine and Tom couldn't keep from yawning with weariness after the excitement of the wedding preparations that day. It was the ultimate satisfaction to him that his newfound son who had come up from nothing and already made such a good show of himself was marrying the perfect girl—a girl almost more of a daughter to him than his own.

Patrick sensed the evening coming to an end and, hoping to forestall it, suggested another drink. "I shouldn't feel so antsy I guess. If I was out with the lads they'd be gettin me drunk and maybe even tryin to get me to one of them hoorhouses over on Greene Street."

Tom blanched at mention of the street he continued to patronize in secret.

Mistaking his expression for disapproval, Patrick reassured him with a laugh that he wouldn't have gone with them anyway, and reached for his glass to refill it.

But Tom put his hand over it and got to his feet, saying he wanted to be up to the mark for the big day.

When his father had gone upstairs after a handshake and formal congratulations that made them both uncomfortable, Patrick thought how different Tom was from the kind of men he had grown up with. He knew that behind the stiffness his father had a deeper affection for him than any of the lads who were always putting an arm around his shoulders, but he could never show it. There was so much yet about this new life he had to get used to, even after all this time. He wished he could run over next door to see Elizabeth as he would have any other night—Veronica was over there with her—but this was the one night that wasn't allowed.

He suddenly drooped and started to pour himself a drink, then thought better of it. Being alone in this genteel atmosphere was too much for him and he slipped outside and headed for Shamrock Alley to find his friends.

Albert Cogswell said afterward that the light in the garden on the day of the wedding was ideal for picture taking. At Elizabeth's suggestion, Tom had asked him to do the wedding photographs and he had traveled in from Long Island especially for it. In a rented cutaway he looked almost civilized, his jungle of hair and beard tamed by brilliantine and a barber's comb.

Instead of setting up his tripod in the parlor and taking the usual formal groupings, Cogswell surprised everyone by trying out an idea of his own, made possible by the new dry-plate process. He took his tripod and camera out into the garden, and though several of the guests objected to the mechanical intrusion on such an occasion, he set it up in various places during the ceremony and the reception that followed, wherever he thought he might get an interesting picture.

Whenever he called "Stop!" everyone was to hold still until the image had registered on the plate. Elizabeth loved it. How original to think of photographing a wedding while it was going on!

He focused his apparatus first on the latticework bower erected in one corner of the garden where the ceremony was to take place. The rambler roses that had just burst into bloom trailed over it and a papier-mâché cupid was perched on top.

He got a picture of the bridegroom waiting in front of the bower with old Reverend Hendryks, whose round steel-rimmed glasses clearly reflected the tripod and camera. Patrick, handsome in his wedding suit, was staring so curiously at the gadget pointed at him he might have been about to step forward to take it apart and see how it worked.

Albert turned his tripod around to snap a radiant Elizabeth on the arm of her father in the rear doorway. She was wearing her grandmother's veil and wedding dress—an Empire gown of startling simplicity, the skirt falling free to the floor from the high-waisted bosom—and carrying a bouquet of sweetheart roses, lilies of the valley, and violets. Partially visible behind her was Veronica, her maid of honor, looking like she wanted to die in the elaborately curled hairdo and velveteen dress with flounces and bustle Elizabeth had chosen for her.

With his camera focused on the wedding party under the bower again, Albert called "Stop!" throughout the ceremony as well, making it a series of charming tableaux. After the bridal embrace, he got Patrick sweeping Veronica into a bear hug with a big kiss, saying, "Ah, Veronica, you're a real sister to me now," as she blushed furiously, delighted.

While the guests were being served fruit punch and sponge cake from the buffet, Albert wickedly got a picture of Sarah Yates dipping into an automatic curtsy, having come unexpectedly on a former employer. Afterward, Elizabeth tore it up before anyone could see it and chided Albert for taking it.

The Yateses were ill at ease. It was the first time they had gone to a wedding without their children, or seen a wedding party without children running about underfoot and the men getting soused, but this was the strange way the Protestants did it. Bill had a fiver ready, but no one ever passed the basket around like at a regular wedding.

In the middle of the reception, while the camera was focused on the bridal couple receiving congratulations, a flamboyant young colored woman dressed in the height of Parisian chic made an entrance, and with a cry of "Elizabeth, honey!" tripped over to embrace the new bride. When Albert yelled "Stop!" the woman turned to the camera, hiding Elizabeth completely.

A moment later, with a loud "Where did you find him? He's delicious!" she threw her gloved arms around a thunderstruck Patrick and kissed him on the lips, holding it for Albert to get the most sensational picture of the day.

It wasn't until the newlyweds were on the day coach bound for their honeymoon in Saratoga that Patrick finally had time to ask about her.

"I told you, Pat, that was Winifred Beaufort. I knew her in Paris."

When he kept silent, she continued, "Can you imagine, she was a slave until she was fifteen!" Winifred's owner had been a cotton merchant in Louisiana, she told him, who raised her as a servant for his daughters. She was with the family in Paris where her owner was doing business when Emancipation came, so she ran off and got herself a job singing in a music hall—she had spoken bayou French from childhood and had no trouble with the language. "That's where I met her," Elizabeth added. "Isn't she extraordinary?"

"Ya didn't go to a music hall! That isn't respectable."

"But of course I did. We saw each other all the time. She was the only American I knew there except for old Mrs. Saltonstall, the woman I worked for." Elizabeth didn't mention to her new husband that a young man named Jean-Paul who was in love with her had been the one to introduce them backstage.

"Maybe I'm old-fashioned, but I don't feel easy with them."

"You will, when you get to know her. She's so much fun." She snuggled against him. "In Paris it's the most ordinary thing. You even have ex-slave owners mixing with ex-slaves socially. Of course, they would never mix with them here."

"Well, I don't like it," he said, looking out at the Hudson River already shadowed in purple as the setting sun lit the peaks of the Catskills orange.

She rubbed her cheek against his shoulder and looked up at him adoringly. "Oh, but things are changing, Pat. Anyway, Winifred's different." She planted a kiss on his set jaw.

He had to give in to his saucy little bride with her ridiculous ideas. The passengers around them smiled knowingly as he took her in his arms and kissed her.

Winifred Beaufort had come back from Europe on the chance of a job in a music hall on Fourteenth Street. An American theatrical agent working in Paris had given her a letter of introduction to Will Kennedy, the impresario, after hearing her sing one night in a little café. With her sultry voice and European style, the agent told her, she was exactly what Kennedy was looking for.

She had not intended to return to America—she was completely at home in France. In her seven years there she hadn't done so badly, in her own eyes, though her ambitions were far from fulfilled. She regularly sang in the chorus of musical reviews. She even got to perform alone sometimes in café concerts, developing her repertoire of songs for the day she would be a star. But from what the agent said, it sounded like she might get ahead faster in New York and she decided to take a chance on it.

Her only memories of America were from when she had been a slave. Back then, even a free black person on the streets of New York could be kidnapped and sold into slavery in the Deep South again. But since that time, Negroes had been declared citizens and given the vote, and she had heard show business was receptive to entertainers of her race.

For her interview with Kennedy she had put on a figured

green shantung dress from Paris with a mauve cape and matching sun parasol, which was smarter than anything even the best-dressed women wore at the Broadway Central Hotel where she was staying. But as she approached the theater she was somewhat dismayed by the grubbiness of the marquee and the rundown look of the whole block, with brownstones converted into businesses and rooming houses and many of the lower floors into saloons.

Even the finest New York buildings looked measly to her after the elegance of Paris, but she reassured herself that under the magic light of evening with carriages drawing up to discharge well-dressed patrons, it could be a very different matter.

There was no way for her to know, nor for the agent in Paris, who had been away a few years himself, that the neighborhood had undergone a rapid deterioration as the city continued its frantic push north. When the agent had last seen New York, Fourteenth Street had still been very much in the center of things, but that was before Delmonico's restaurant had moved uptown to Twenty-third Street, before the fashionable residences on Union Square were turned into business establishments, and when the Academy of Music was still the only opera house in town.

Will Kennedy was not one of the leading impresarios of the city, the agent had said, but he could give her the start she needed. She held on to the thought for reassurance as she picked her way through the ropes and props of backstage, and finally sat in his bare office that daylight hardly reached and even with a gaslamp on it was gloomy. Kennedy lounged in a swivel chair with an unlit cigar stub in his mouth, polka-dot suspenders over his striped shirt, a bowler hat tipped back on his bald head, appraising her as if she were on the auction block again.

He barely glanced at her letter of introduction. "What's your speciality, kid?" he growled in a New York street accent. "Gospel, rag, or minstrel?"

Holding her indignation in check, she said haughtily that she sang French music hall songs and, exaggerating slightly, since there was no one within three thousand miles to contradict her, told him her last job was as the star of a musical review on the Champs Elysée.

When he looked dubious, she got up and with a flamboyant strut that waggled her bustle, went over to a battered upright piano. Laying her parasol on top of it, she sat down, and with improvised flourishes on the keyboard sang a ditty called "La

Demoiselle du Regiment" that had been on everybody's lips when she left Paris. As she did the chorus, she turned to him and put in lots of "ooh-la-la's," which she knew were irresistible to Americans.

She was in the middle of the verse that always brought down the house, where with rolling eyes the mademoiselle describes the succession of soldiers in her arms, when the impresario bawled out that he had heard enough. "That kind of stuff don't go over here. Can you pick a banjo?"

She spun around on the stool and glared. "What do you think I am, anyway?"

He smirked as he shifted the cigar stub between his lips. "Where do you think you are, anyway? I got a job for you as a banjo picker. You get to sing a chorus or two even." He leaned back with his hands clasped behind his head and ogled the brown bombshell. The customers would eat her up. He could see her already—breasts and bottom bursting out of skimpy rags with a cotton-field backdrop, singing a little jig tune as a chorus of fieldhands did a buck-and-wing around her.

With his checked trouser legs spread wide, she couldn't fail to see that he was deliberately flaunting his excitement. The theater managers she had dealt with in Paris had also expected her to come across. If they were smoother, with the inevitable hand-kissing a lady was supposed to fall for, they were still pigs at bottom. But they never began *this* crudely.

"You wouldn't recognize a special talent like mine if it were shoved down your throat, Mr. Kennedy," she said, pulling on her gloves. She tilted her chin defiantly so that the gaslight caught the sheen of her hair dressed in a mass of braids pulled back into a chignon.

Kennedy had a hand on his thigh. "Take my advice, kid, it's not very often a colored girl gets a chance. Most of our tootsies are in blackface. I'm doing you a favor offering you anything at all." He got up, tugging at his pants to make himself comfortable, and came around to put a hand on her shoulder. "You know why I'm willing to take a chance on you, Winnie? It's because you do have something special." He tickled her ear, making a pendant earring glitter.

She shook him off and got up from the piano stool, aware that her Junoesque proportions were driving him crazy. As she picked up her parasol and gathered her skirts, she told him in her most refined accents that he didn't have as much in his trousers as he thought, and if he expected her to get down on her knees and worship that, he had another guess coming. She turned on her heel and walked out.

"If you change your mind, I always got a job for a looker like you," he yelled after her, and came out to watch her from the stage as she swept up the aisle to the lobby, her skirts held to one side emphasizing her magnificent behind.

Blinking against the bright sunlight on the street, she was seething over that pipsqueak impresario. He couldn't run a flea circus. The agent in Paris had sold her a bill of goods and she had fallen for it. No one who knew her back in France would believe she had been such a sucker.

As she walked toward her hotel, it hit her what a mess she was in. She didn't have a dime to her name, not to mention paying her hotel bill. But by the time she got to the hustle of Broadway, things didn't seem so bad. With her voice and looks and a Paris wardrobe in her trunk, nobody was going to keep *her* down.

WHEN THE HONEYMOONERS RETURNED FROM SARATOGA, they expected to have the house mostly to themselves, since in the meantime Tom had moved up to the top floor with Veronica.

But to their surprise and consternation a dinner party had already been arranged for them, cooked by Veronica with Mrs. Cooper's help. The two families joined them at table without being invited, eager to hear about the honeymoon and their plans for the future. Not wanting to hurt anyone's feelings, the couple did their best to look pleased.

After dinner the families followed them upstairs to the parlor, chattering even more animatedly over coffee as their eyes drank in the lovers. The lovers on the other hand had been dreaming of nothing else, since taking the train back that morning, but of having an intimate supper together and stealing off afterward to their room.

The Coopers gazed at their ripe daughter and virile son-in-law in wonder. They were reminded that twenty years before, in their fumbling attempts at passion, they had had a glimmer of what was possible. But it had quickly died out and they had been distracted by their many liberal causes. They had scarcely thought about it since—until tonight.

For Tom, it was bittersweet to see the children united with

the blessings of the whole world. Patrick's merry blue eyes evoked Molly's and the memory of a love that could never be.

Even Veronica felt a peculiar glow she couldn't account for. It was her first experience of people radiating fulfilled sensuality and it thrilled her. Her goose bumps she attributed to her new fondness for her thickset, curly-haired half brother who was so happy with his lovely bride.

When the newlyweds finally got to their bedroom, which Veronica had redecorated for them as a surprise, Elizabeth closed her eyes at the horror of the exquisite floral-bouquet wallpaper having been painted over white, stark as a monk's cell. And even more awful, the heavy maroon tapestry drapes with the cluster-ball velvet fringe had been replaced with gossamer curtains that made her feel exposed to the world. Something had to be done at once, but how could she ever change it all back without hurting her hypersensitive sister-in-law?

When the lamp was out and they were in bed, the feelings that they had been holding back all evening were not there. They lay listening to Tom's footsteps coming downstairs to the bathroom outside their door, the cataract as he pulled the chain, the endless gurgle as the water trickled into the tank again, and his steps back up to his room, followed by Veronica's mouselike tiptoeing down and her frantic jerking on the chain since the tank had not yet refilled. Patrick muttered that he would make sure the new bathroom was installed up there the next day, even if he had to do every bit of the plumbing himself.

No sooner had Veronica retreated back upstairs, than Tom began to cough directly above them, the springs of his bed creaking as he turned over.

Patrick sat up, whispering that he wished they were back in the hotel by the lake where they could have a little peace.

Elizabeth, who was just as upset, still dwelling on the hideous evening, said she couldn't understand how her parents could have been so insensitive, inviting themselves over like that. Her mother had sounded positively asinine chattering on and on about her own honeymoon at Long Branch, which she had hardly ever mentioned before.

"Yeah, and did ya see how Tom looked at me misty-eyed all evenin? It made me feel queer all over, knowin he was thinkin of my mother. Damn them all!" In a fury he grabbed his pillow and flung it across the room.

She cautioned him to be quiet, but he was already out of bed, pacing the floor in his nightshirt on bare feet. "What the hell do they think they're doin? We're not a pair of freaks on show like Tom Thumb and Lavinia Bumpus. I'd like to wipe out the lot of them."

"Please don't, Pat. They're going to hear," she pleaded. But he ignored her, snarling that they were going to move out of this assembly hall. When she didn't answer, he stopped. She was crying softly into the pillow, trying to muffle it.

In a moment he was beside her, sorry for his outburst. He had never seen her cry before. All the women he had known cried, but Elizabeth never. It rent his heart. It was terrible. He took his quivering bride in his arms and kissed her face all over, begging her to forgive him. "I'm the most goddamnedest sinner in the world, my darlin."

"Oh, Pat, I do love you so!" She threw her arms around him.

He reached for her breasts instinctively, bending down to kiss them. Passion postponed was back again, and they scrambled to the exercise of their love.

As the days passed they kept waiting for the well-meaning but suffocating devotion of their families to wear itself out, but their relations seemed even more determined in their efforts to please. Veronica begged Elizabeth to be allowed to go on cooking for them. It was the one thing she had to offer, she said. So Elizabeth had to put off trying out on Patrick the special little dishes she had learned in France.

Mrs. Cooper expected her daughter, as a young matron, to participate in the many humane causes she herself was involved in. Elizabeth had looked forward to devoting herself to making a home for her new husband, but her mother shrewdly played on her social conscience, which she knew to be as well developed as her own.

"It would be nice if we were free to devote all our time to our personal lives, dear," her mother said brightly, "but I'm afraid the world's many injustices won't allow us to be so selfish. Don't tell me you can bear to stand by while thousands of horses in this city are being beaten and worked to death every day. And as for the immigrants and their hellish slums . . ."

Elizabeth couldn't close her eyes to cruelty to animals, or immigrants, or the plight of women, or children in factories, so she found herself giving up her free time and sometimes not getting back home until after Patrick did.

Tom's oversolicitude was even harder to take. When he was sitting with his son in the parlor after dinner each night, the minute Elizabeth came up from the kitchen after trying to help Veronica he made a point of jumping up and leaving them to themselves, making them uncomfortable knowing he was going to sit alone upstairs in his room.

When Pat came home from work with only one thing on his mind, to get upstairs and break in on Elizabeth's nap for a few moments of bliss before dinner, Tom inevitably jumped out of his easy chair and buttonholed him about one fool thing or another, while he had to stand there and pretend to be interested, not wanting to hurt his old man's feelings.

When they woke up and, in that sleepy morning softness, wanted to hold each other more than ever, there was always that knock on the door and Veronica whisked in with the breakfast tray and poured out their coffee, her eyes shining in unconscious response to the odor of intimacy that filled the closed room.

One day when Patrick came home for lunch, as he often did, and their embrace at the door turned their knees to rubber, Elizabeth put a finger to her lips— Veronica could be heard humming away in the dining room below as she set the table— and they tiptoed giggling up to the bedroom.

With the door shut, Pat said with a bashful grin that much as he wanted to, it wouldn't be proper in the middle of the day, but without a word she nestled against him letting her hands clutch him greedily to her.

As they lay disheveled and dreamy, ignoring Veronica's calls that lunch was getting cold, he idly traced her breasts with a finger, and said, "It's good I'm not a Catholic any more, ain't it? I always used to say if it weren't for the church I'd fuck all the day long."

She pushed him away. "You mean you don't think the Episcopal rite is as sacred as the Roman?" she said as sternly as she could manage. "I wonder if you're taking your new faith seriously."

Then, seeing his hangdog look, she laughed and kissed him. "But you're right about one thing, dearest. In our church we don't insist that lovemaking just be for procreation. A husband and wife are allowed to"—she blushed—"you know what I mean . . . whenever they want."

"Ya darlin little slut." He grinned, and with a growl he pulled her over on to him.

In this marriage he had discovered the joy of sex for the first time. Though he had been married to Hester for nearly five years, she always lay under him like a stone, virtuously permitting him the exercise of his marital rights, so Elizabeth's natural response was a revelation.

In no time she was pregnant. And though they were happy about it, in one way it made matters worse—both their families became, if anything, more suffocating with their attention. It was even harder to find time to be alone. The irony was that now Elizabeth wanted her husband more than ever. Pregnancy only seemed to increase her randy appetite, though it took her a while to convince Patrick, after his sad experience with Hester, that satisfying it would not lead to a miscarriage.

Tom and even staid Professor Cooper, who was not a garrulous man, talked about nothing else but the coming grandchild. Veronica began to knit little garments endlessly, only dropping her knitting needles to run down and get Elizabeth hot milk, which she hated. Mrs. Cooper, heretofore a sensible woman, put aside her causes and went on a grandma binge, bringing back layettes, baby blankets, and an avalanche of toys. She even dragged Elizabeth off to lectures on child care.

Matters reached a head one night when Patrick came home from work to find Tom in the parlor entertaining his old friend Albert Cogswell, who had just moved back to a rooming house in the neighborhood after the death of his wife.

Tom started to get up, insisting that his son come in and have a whiskey with them. But Patrick was ready for him. Nothing was going to stop him this time from rushing straight up to Elizabeth. Holding his ground in the doorway, he firmly declined his father's invitation, and to make it quite clear that he meant what he said, shut the door on them.

Congratulating himself, he came into the bedroom only to find Elizabeth sitting with Winifred Beaufort, deep in conversation. He was exasperated. "Is it too much to ask to be alone with ya even for a minute?" he snapped out, ripping at his collar.

Winifred, who knew a family crisis when she saw one, hastily gathered up her things and rustled across the room to the door, tossing over her shoulder, "I was never here."

"Don't be upset," Elizabeth said, jumping to unfasten her husband's collar. She was sorry that he had come in on Winifred, whom he couldn't accept being in the house. She was usually gone by the time he came home, but they had been so deep in talk about the problems Winifred was having, she had forgotten how late it was.

For several months Winifred had been making the rounds of theaters, vaudeville houses, and even dance saloons all over the city, and had finally been forced to admit that no one wanted to hire a negro entertainer no matter how much talent she had. Having only worked in Paris where the race situation was better, she had been completely misled about the way things were in America. "The only thing they want a colored girl for here is hustling or housework, and I'll be damned if I do either," she had been saying just before Pat broke in. She bemoaned that the only thing left for her to do was to crawl back to that two-bit entrepreneur Will Kennedy, and take whatever degrading part he offered her.

Patrick was carrying on as Elizabeth worked on his collar studs. "Either you and me move out of this house right now or I'm goin to become a mass murderer." He turned his head so she could get at the recalcitrant button. "We'd have more privacy in a boardin house than we have here."

She agreed, with a sigh, that the situation had become intolerable.

"This whole neighborhood is givin me a pain in the ass. I'm goin to be workin farther uptown soon. What's to stop us from movin out of here and into one of them fine apartment houses they're puttin up on West End Avenue? They got hydraulic elevators that carry ya up to the tenth floor and gas cookstoves in the kitchen and runnin hot water besides. A couple of the fellas I work with live there. How about it? We'll let Tom have his house back."

"It's true," she said, looking out the window at the row of Federal-style houses across the street, "some families are moving away. They say Greenwich isn't the same any more." She knew that if Pat had the power he wouldn't hesitate for a minute to tear down all those handsome houses and put up one of those godawful West End Avenue monstrosities. She turned back to him and started unbuttoning his shirt. "Oh, Pat, things are bad, I know. Maybe we will have to move, but do we have to think about it before the baby comes? I really can't bear the thought."

He took off his shirt, wadded it up and threw it into the corner, putting his hands lightly on her waist. "Sure we'll stay, for a while. But honest now, does that flashy friend of yours have to be around here all the time?"

She unbuttoned the top of his long johns, feeling sure of herself again. "I wish you'd try to like Winifred a little. She's having such a hard time. Things haven't worked out for her here, and don't forget she was a slave until the war. Once they even kept her locked up in the house."

"That's not such a bad idea." His eyes were merry as her fingers toyed with the hair on his chest. "I'd like to keep you locked up too—just for me." He scooped her up into his arms as she kicked in mock protest.

"Not again today!" She giggled.

"Shut up, ya want them to hear? Ya can bet they're all listenin at the door."

"All right, you lecherous beast, but be careful of the baby," she murmured as he carried her to the bed.

Will Kennedy was mounting a musical revue called *Carry Me Back to Old Virginny*. It was to be full of nostalgia for the old South that the Union armies had not long before destroyed. This suited the current mood in the North, which was already tiring of the postwar period when idealistic young people had flocked south to help the newly freed slaves, setting up schools and health programs. It was already apparent the government was not about to break up the plantations and give land to the Negroes. The K.K.K. was riding in the night to force them back into working in the cotton, and all the financial interests in the North tacitly approved.

Winifred was so broke she had to take a job in Kennedy's show. If she had the cash, she told Elizabeth, she would take the first boat back to France. But beaten down by months of doors being slammed in her face, she numbed herself to what she was being asked to do in rehearsal.

She was the only real Negro in a blackface chorus line of happy darkies. With a red kerchief knotted around her head and a ragged skirt that showed glimpses of red-and-white-stockinged leg, she went mechanically through the shimmy steps Kennedy had worked out for them.

But in the middle of the first night's performance she woke up to what she was doing. The chorus, rolling their eyes, was letting more leg show to keep the drunken customers tossing small change as they sang about "Waitin on the levee for the white boys to come" and "Oh, oh, oh, we'll show em how to love."

She couldn't take it another minute. She tore off her kerchief and, to the whistles and jeers of the audience, ran off the stage.

Will Kennedy found her wiping off her makeup in the dressing room in a fury. She turned on him like a wounded panther and let him have it as she got into her street clothes. How dare he think she could go along with his filthy myth of happy slave times? It was an obscenity! She knew what it was like to work in the cotton, and stand up on the auction block to be leered at and pawed over by those swine, and be the target of every white man's lust in the house where she was raised.

He was knocked on his ear. He had never seen such a gorgeous woman in his life. He couldn't bear to see her walk out on him again. As she headed for the door he grabbed her and shook her hard to make her listen. "Okay, okay. I'll give you a solo."

It wasn't one of her French songs—he wouldn't go that far—but it wasn't all that bad considering this was West Fourteenth Street. She sang about an octoroon from Guadeloupe, daughter of a white planter and a slave mother, who became the toast of Paris.

On the first night the drunks quieted down and some of them even applauded. Will was dazzled. By the second night she felt her old confidence back and threw in a chorus in French. Will said he'd allow it if she'd do a little sashaying and high-stepping across the stage, so she did, and it brought down the house every night.

Stage-door johnnies who hung around after the show to pick up the girls, she ignored. But one night a bouquet with a note in French was delivered to her backstage. *"May a little band of painters pay homage to a beautiful chanteuse and toast her in champagne?"*

She was as delighted to meet the group of young Americans just back from studying art in Paris as they were to come upon her in provincial New York. All of them talking away a mile a minute, they took her off to an impromptu party at their studio building on Tenth Street, where they kept her singing her entire repertoire of French café songs until dawn.

As soon as she was able to pay her bill, she moved out of

the hotel into a boardinghouse her new artist friends recommended. It was full of show people, and turned out to be at the other end of Perry Street from the Endicotts.

For months, Patrick Endicott announced to everyone he met that it was going to be a boy. In June when Elizabeth gave birth to a girl, he put his arms around his wife as she lay exhausted but shining and told her that it didn't make any difference—he was the happiest man in the world. But she saw almost at once that he didn't take much interest in the baby girl.

It was as if the infant, whom they named Alice, understood her father's disappointment from the start. But her grandfather Tom adored her, and it was to him, later on when she was old enough to begin talking, that she reached out her little arms and addressed her first word, "Papa."

It got on Pat's nerves to see the two of them cooing at each other. Occasionally he tried to pick Alice up himself, but she always cried. It was bad enough that his old man was a pain in the neck, now he was taking his child away from him.

Elizabeth was usually busy with the baby when he got home, so there were no more private moments before dinner and he had to put up with his father's unrelenting attentions more than ever.

One night before dinner while waiting for Elizabeth to finish nursing the baby upstairs, he was relieved because Tom hadn't shown up yet and he was able to read the *Herald* in peace for once. He was deep into a story about a small tribe of Indians in California called the Medoc that had been resisting being taken off its land and shipped to a reservation in Oklahoma. The U.S. Army was throwing everything it had at them with not much success. Just when he was getting into the details of the latest battle, in which a dozen braves were holding off a battalion of soldiers, the front door opened and Tom came in, visibly upset about something.

It seemed that Albert Cogswell's room, which was in the tough area by the river, had been ransacked and his drawings messed up. It was over a roughneck tavern called the Galway Bay, and Tom had warned him against moving in there, but Albert didn't understand that parts of the village had changed since he had lived here before. Tom had spent the afternoon helping him move his belongings into the unused storage loft over the printshop, which would do temporarily as a place to stay.

"The kind of people coming into the village these days . . ." Tom sank into an armchair and pulled out a handkerchief to wipe his forehead. "It's just not like it used to be."

There it was again, Patrick thought, turning a page of the newspaper impatiently. Like all long-time Greenwich residents, his father felt an automatic superiority over newcomers. That was the "American Ward" attitude, pure and simple. Nobody else had a right to be here. They thought they owned the place. "The micks are takin over, is that what ya mean, Tom?"

"Who knows who those people are? It just isn't safe over there any more. They're even calling it Murderers Row."

Ever since he got married, Patrick had been holding back his irritation against his father, but this was too much to take. "That sounds like anti-mick talk to me, however ya slice it," he said, looking at Tom over the paper. "The lads at the Galway aren't a bad bunch. I stop in there for a beer myself sometimes."

Tom heard his son's resentment and backed off. "Don't get me wrong, I'm not saying they had anything to do with it."

Patrick raised his voice. "If ya really want to get a knife in your back I'll tell ya where to go. Go up to Hell's Kitchen where the wops are, that's where. I'll tell ya one thing, Tom," he said, shaking a finger at the older man, "those lads are worth every bit as much as any of your almighty snobs who act like they came over on the *Mayflower*." He slapped his paper down. "Oh, they make ya feel like shyte around here, they do."

Hearing him shouting below, Elizabeth handed the baby

over to the hired girl. The infant set up a shriek, adding to the commotion, but Elizabeth rushed downstairs, buttoning her bodice. For months Pat had been threatening to tell his father off. She had begged him not to. It would be too awful. But as she came into the room she knew from his red face and Tom's pale one that the worst had happened.

"For heaven's sake, you two, what's going on down here," she said, trying to make light of it. "Please, not before dinner. Veronica's been slaving all afternoon on a gateau amandine."

"Fuck your gateau!" Patrick yelled, swatting the folded paper against the chair as he jumped to his feet. "I'm sick of all this talk against the micks around here. No one says what they mean and ya never get a moment alone with your wife." Alice was screaming louder than ever upstairs. "What the hell's that kid squawking for? Didn't ya feed it?" He went to the window and, his back to them, gripped the frame on both sides with his fists.

Elizabeth and her father-in-law looked away in embarrassment.

"He wasn't attacking the Irish," she said at last, "were you, Tom?"

Tom, who was in shock at discovering the extent of his son's hostility toward him, mumbled that he certainly hadn't meant to.

"There, Pat, you see?" she said brightly. "And don't worry about Alice. It's natural for her to cry. She's a baby. I think what we all need is a good dinner." She went over to him and took his arm.

But the significance of the outburst did not escape Tom. How could he have missed seeing before this how much he had been in the way?

He waited until the meal was over and Veronica was out in the kitchen getting the dessert. Then, looking at both his children as casually as he could, he said that in all the fuss over Albert's getting robbed he had forgotten to tell them the main thing. He would be moving out soon. He was going to share the loft over the printshop with Albert.

The young couple's eyes met guiltily like children discovered in a shameful secret. This was not lost on him, though he went on briskly. He and Albert were about to embark on a new project, something they had both been talking about for years. Until now he had been too busy building up the business to start on it. They were going to put out portfolios of lithographs of Albert's river sketches.

At least that much of the story Albert already knew about, he thought ruefully—he wondered what his old friend would think about their sharing the place together. "It'll be a lot more convenient if I'm living over there too. We'll fix it up and be as snug as two bugs in a rug."

Patrick was overcome with remorse. "Tom, I didn't mean nothin of what I said."

"I know you didn't, son. I've enjoyed sharing the house with you, but it's time I made a change."

Elizabeth went around to embrace him. "You mustn't go, Tom. Why—whatever would we do without you?" She had tears in her eyes.

"Now, now, my mind is made up. Anyway, I'll just be a few blocks away." He patted her gently.

Patrick reached over impulsively and took his father's hand. "I don't know how ya ever put up with a son of a bitch like me. I'm the one who should be leavin around here."

The kitchen door was pushed open and a beaming Veronica came in carrying the cake which she put down on the table, dowsed with brandy, and set aflame.

That night when Tom went up to his room on the third floor he wondered how he was going to bear leaving this house where he had been so content as part of Patrick's little family. But what really hurt was having seen how quickly and with what obvious relief his children had accepted his clearing out.

TOM ENDICOTT'S PRINTING SHOP HAD BECOME WELL KNOWN for the quality of its work. He and Albert often went directly to the clipper ships to choose the best papers brought back from the Far East. This attention to detail paid off—from all parts of the city people brought in special jobs.

One winter day, a conservatively dressed gentleman of about thirty came in with a short story to be printed up in a small edition as a gift to family and friends. He had written it himself. His address was one of the grand old houses on Washington Square still occupied by some of the city's more patrician families, at a time when the newer rich were building mansions up Fifth Avenue as far as Central Park.

This was something Tom knew would interest Elizabeth and Veronica when he saw them next. Going to Sunday dinner at the house on Perry Street had become a regular thing since he had moved out a year and a half before. His particular joy was little Alice, a golden-haired angel of two, who still called him Papa.

Everything had turned out better than anyone could have expected. The Coopers no longer found the young couple such a novelty and let them alone—even Veronica gave up monopolizing the kitchen. At last Patrick and Elizabeth were living their own life.

When Tom went over that Sunday, the house was in its usual happy turmoil. Alice dropped her doll and ran for him to pick her up, while the family bulldog Cicero barked excitedly. Smells of goose and mince pie came up from the kitchen. Patrick shouted hello from the study—he was on the floor repairing the sewing machine with the parts strewn all around.

In front of the blazing fire, Elizabeth and Veronica patted a place for Tom between them on the sofa. His granddaughter climbed onto his lap and played with a wooden printing block he brought her, as he told them about his well-dressed customer from Washington Square and the story he was printing up for him. It was called "The Passionate Pilgrim" and was so fancily written he was having a devil of a time proofreading it.

"Henry James!" Veronica cried when he told her the writer's name, and begged him to let her see a copy of the story. Not only had she heard of him but she already knew several of his stories from magazines—she considered him the most talented young writer in America. Though it was uncharacteristic of her, she talked a blue streak about him all through dinner and kept begging Tom for every detail of their meeting.

A few days later when James came back to the shop to pick up the copies of his story, he surprised Tom by mentioning Veronica's poetry. Apparently in the intervening week she had sent him several of her poems, though she had never let anyone else see them before—certainly not her family. James said he found her style remarkable. In fact he went on about it in such a complicated fashion that Tom could hardly follow. The one thing that was clear to him was that this was the first man who had ever expressed the slightest interest in his daughter. Even without having met her, he seemed enthralled.

When the writer asked him to convey his high esteem to such a talented poetess, Tom took the bull by the horns and invited him to join the family for dinner on Sunday. His daughter was an admirer of his work and would take great pleasure in hearing the words from him directly.

James had a kind of New England formality about him and it was hard to imagine him in the simple environment of Perry Street, but then Veronica had much the same kind of reserve herself. She had never shown the least interest in getting a husband and at thirty-one she seemed perfectly content to settle for spinsterhood, but there was nothing to lose by bringing them together.

Elizabeth was just as pleased as Tom was when he told her

James was coming. She agreed he had done exactly the right thing by inviting him. But Veronica was aghast at the prospect of meeting the writer face to face. He was already a sacred figure to her. What if he should comment on her poems in front of everyone? At the most she had hoped for a note. She wished she had never done such a foolish thing as send the poems to him. He would feel obliged to pretend that he liked them.

Elizabeth pointed out to her sister-in-law that James wouldn't have accepted the invitation if he didn't like her poetry. There was nothing for her to worry about. She would invite her parents over to join them—they would be suitable dinner companions for a literary guest. She would see to it that the conversation stayed on agreeable topics, and Veronica wasn't to worry that Patrick would talk about public transportation. She knew how to handle him.

When Elizabeth explained the situation to her husband that night, he agreed good-heartedly that it was Veronica's show and he wouldn't put his clumsy foot into it. He would only open his mouth to ask for the butter. Besides, what did he have to say to "artist types" anyway? They gave him a pain.

As she kissed him, she ruefully thought how true this was. Though once she had hopes of bringing him around, since their marriage he had obstinately refused to be interested in anything to do with the arts.

This was not to be an ordinary family Sunday dinner. It was Veronica's first and only chance. Overriding her sister-in-law's complaints that she was making far too much of the whole thing, Elizabeth marched her off to A. T. Stewart's and got her to buy a new dress.

On Sunday, all were in a festive mood—except for Veronica, who was laying out the silverware on the damask cloth in a state of near panic. The floors and woodwork had been oiled, the rugs beaten, and Alice and Cicero banished to Albert Cogswell's care for the afternoon.

As Elizabeth rushed about with her mother and the hired girl to finish last minute preparations in the kitchen, the men were drinking hot buttered rum upstairs while waiting for the guest to arrive.

Leaning on the mantelpiece Professor Cooper was joshing Patrick about Bill Tweed, the Tammany boss. The politician had finally been caught with his hand in the till. "Even with your admiration for the rascal, you have to admit ten years is still letting him off easy."

Tweed was an old bone between them and Patrick grinned. "How can I argue with a college professor? I'm too busy puttin up elevateds to worry about the crooks catchin the crooks."

His father-in-law clapped him on the back. "Just promise you won't put an elevated up Perry Street."

"Okay, if ya promise me you'll get Albany to let us build our subway."

"Isn't that up to the voters?"

"What's the good?" said Patrick. "The railroad big shots buy off any governor ya put in office."

Before James arrived, Elizabeth and Mrs. Cooper saw to it that Veronica came up with them to join the men and they were determined not to let her escape back to the kitchen. The hired girl knew what was to be done, and if there were any problems Elizabeth would see to them herself. She wanted Veronica to have the maximum opportunity to become acquainted with this writer she admired so much.

How well Veronica looked this afternoon. The wedding photographs had shown Elizabeth what a mistake she had made overdressing her as her bridesmaid in that elaborate velveteen gown with the flounces. The simple mauve crepe de chine she had chosen for her this time was far more becoming. Her hair was simply pulled back from a center part into a loose bun at the nape of her neck. She decided her sister-in-law had a look of classical refinement—even an ethereal quality like her poor mother.

She saw how right she had been to insist Veronica look her best when a few minutes later Henry James arrived dressed in the best English tailoring, and bowed over Veronica's hand as if he were about to kiss it. "Miss Endicott, this is indeed an honor. . . ."

He had pale patrician features and his colorless hair was too precisely parted, but Veronica's flush of pleasure showed that she found him to her liking.

Patrick winked across at his wife, but she sent him a look reminding him of his promise to behave himself.

James bowed just as stuffily over Mrs. Cooper's hand and then Elizabeth's own, when Tom presented him. Patrick and Professor Cooper were distinctly put off by his brief handshake and murmur of civilities, instead of the hand-pumping and effusive greetings they were use to.

Elizabeth was about to offer him a hot toddy when the bell for dinner rang. The hired girl had gotten it wrong—she had been instucted to wait half an hour before calling them down. But under the circumstances, Elizabeth was just as glad. Considering how formidable the guest appeared to be, it might be easier to get things going over the meal.

She had planned a perfect dinner for someone from the high-toned world of Washington Square—canvasback duck stuffed with oysters. Old Mrs. Saltonstall had told her often on their trip to Europe that it was a favorite of the best society.

At the dining room table, when James pulled out Veronica's chair for her in a courtly manner, her sister-in-law's timid smile as she looked up at him made her almost pretty. He took the chair beside her, laid his napkin across his lap instead of tucking it into his shirt, and leaned toward Elizabeth with a thin smile. "I was just telling Miss Endicott how unusual your centerpiece is," he said, referring to the arrangement of gourds and pinecones on a carved alabaster pedestal she had brought back from Italy.

The hired girl started ladling around the terrapin soup—without splashing, for once. Elizabeth had put her into starched cap and apron especially for the occasion.

Pouring out the hock, Tom said to James that he hoped his family and friends liked the booklet he had printed for him.

The author sipped the wine, reflected, then pronounced it first-rate, before replying, "It was an excellent job you did, Mr. Endicott. You know, I'm getting some very creditable reactions. The curator of special editions of the New York Society Library has asked for five copies for the collection." He looked immensely satisfied with himself.

He was conceited as well as pretentious, Elizabeth thought, but she was pleased that Veronica seemed to be drinking in every affected syllable. She smiled across at her handsome husband who was being good as gold, not even slurping his soup as he ordinarily did.

"Are you by any chance of English origin, Mr. James?" Mrs. Cooper asked, impressed by his meticulous way of speaking.

"I've been asked that before," he said. "Actually I was born right here in New York in the same house I still live in with my family, but I've gone with them to London frequently since I was a child. The day after tomorrow, in fact, I'm departing again on the *Britannia* for an indefinite stay."

"I do so wish we could afford it. I'd like to study the effectiveness of their child labor laws," Elizabeth's mother said. "My daughter was in London six years ago."

The kitchen door opened and the girl brought in a brace of canvasback ducks on a platter with glazed carrots, cranberries, and oyster shells filled with whipped potatoes.

"Bravo!" said James as they all exclaimed over it.

Patrick was bored out of his mind by the stuffed-shirt guest and was only too happy to devote himself to the carving.

"I would be interested in hearing your impressions of London, Mrs. Endicott," James said, turning to Elizabeth when they settled down to the main course.

His formal courtesy was not without its charm, she thought, and told him about seeing Queen Victoria in her barouche on The Mall, but her greatest thrill had been the Gothic art at the British Museum.

"How extraordinary that you should say that," said the author. "Very few Americans give a hoot about the Middle Ages. They're all obsessed with the Renaissance. Why can't any of them even begin to understand the subtleties and complexities of European civilization?"

"How true," cried Veronica, who until now had been too awed to say a word.

James turned to her and asked if she had observed this herself.

She flushed. "I've never been to Europe," she said, "but it's always seemed to me that those very subtleties and complexities you speak of must make life so much richer there." She looked surprised at having spoken out. She was not used to speaking her private thoughts at all.

James gave her a lofty smile. "As a poet, your concerns are hardly those of most Americans, I'd say."

She returned his smile shyly.

"I've read your verse with great pleasure, Miss Endicott. You are a lyricist of some power and originality."

"Oh, please. . . ."

"I warn you though, your odd rhymes won't be a simple matter for publishers to accept. And using dashes instead of punctuation—definitely unconventional, but splendid."

"You mustn't, Mr. James . . . I'm embarrassed." She gave a flustered look around, as if half-expecting them to be laughing at her.

James patted his lips with his napkin, enjoying the effect

his words were having on her. "Very well. No more about poetry just now. But I won't be put off, I insist on a talk with you privately after dinner."

As Veronica squirmed with pleasure, Elizabeth exchanged a conspiratorial look with Tom who was following the little scene as avidly as she was. Things were going exactly as they wished.

Professor Cooper, unaware that anything was going on, asked James what he thought of Disraeli's new bill giving the vote to factory workers in England.

"For heaven's sake, Papa!" Elizabeth said, ready to strangle him. "No politics, please." She turned quickly to the author. "Tell us how you found London the last time you were there."

"It's still the most livable city in the world," he said, as he deftly sliced bits of meat from a wing with knife and fork. "The only thing I disapprove of is that ghastly means of public locomotion they have installed underground. I made the mistake of taking a ride on it."

To her horror, Patrick's forkful of mashed carrots and duck stopped halfway to his mouth. "Did I hear ya say, Mr. James, that ya took a ride on the London subway?" He was alert and quivering like a pointer on the scent.

James seemed to look for the first time at her husky, black-haired young husband at the head of the table. "Why yes, I did! My brother insisted on it. But I confess I didn't like it much. I got off at the first stop."

Patrick was tensed, as if ready to leap into the air. "It was the smoke drove ya out, I bet."

Oh, dear God no, Elizabeth prayed.

"Why, indeed it was the smoke," said James. "It was abominable."

"Electric locomotives will cure that. We're workin on them here."

Veronica was mutely appealing to Elizabeth who broke in. "I'm sure Mr. James doesn't want to hear about subways, Pat dear." She gave him a hard look.

He grinned back. "It wasn't me brought up the subject, now was it, darlin?" He winked and bent his head dutifully to stuff his mouth with oysters and mashed potatoes.

But James was not ready to let it go. "Are you somehow involved with subterranean railways, Mr. Endicott?"

Pat looked at his wife, begging for permission.

"Personally, who wants to ride in a hole in the ground,"

said Tom, looking around brightly, but no one paid any attention to him.

To Elizabeth's annoyance, James persisted. "Do you intend to build one of them here?"

This Patrick could not be expected to let go by. "I wish we could, but the boys in Albany won't let us."

Elizabeth tried again to rescue the situation. "Well, no one may agree with me, but I for one have no interest in—"

James overrode her as if she weren't there. "Why won't they let you build it?"

"Can't be done, they say. It's solid granite down there."

"Granite? That must be a real obstacle."

Elizabeth looked so disapproving that Patrick couldn't ignore it and said, "Darlin, I'll just answer the gentleman's one question, okay?" And without waiting for her permission was off and running. "There's nothin to it. It's the shipworm gave me the idea, see?" And he was into the story she knew every word of, as James leaned on an elbow, engrossed—or pretending to be, the pompous ass.

She was in despair. Why did her husband have to look so attractive, his generous features alive with energy, his curly hair already mussed, jabbing his fork into the air to illustrate how he would get through the granite as easily as the shipworm bored through wood. There was no stopping him now. Her heart went out to Veronica who was sitting frozen as the afternoon collapsed around her.

Once again they had to hear about that silly worm with the digging shell in its nose and how it passed the wood pulp back through its body, mixing it with the lime in its gut—she saw Veronica cringe at the vulgar anatomical reference in front of her literary idol—to pave the walls of its tunnel behind it.

". . . so what's to stop us from doin the same thing? We got a team of men with chisels and pickaxes, followed by masons cementin it up, see, and we got ourselves a subway tunnel." He looked around proudly like a retriever dropping the quarry at its master's feet, wagging its tail, waiting to be petted.

She could kill him. She saw how Veronica sat lifeless in front of her untouched dinner. They were not going to stay here another minute listening to him blabber on. She rang the bell sharply for the girl. It might not be the usual thing, but they would take dessert upstairs with the coffee where she would make sure Pat didn't get near James.

But this failed miserably. The change of plan threw the

maid into a tizzy. She couldn't cope with serving the chocolate mousse in the parlor, and Elizabeth had no choice but to go into the kitchen to show the stupid girl how to do it. She had to help her prepare the goblets of mousse with whipped cream, and the coffee things. Then, taking the silver ewer herself, rushed upstairs, leaving the girl to bring up the tray.

But of course it was too late. By this time Patrick had James pinned to the fireplace. "Don't ya see? It's not just passengers we'll carry, but freight as well. No more of them delivery vans cloggin the streets."

And poor Veronica standing beside the Coopers and Tom in her mauve dress, forlorn as a discarded violet. In a pique, Elizabeth poured out the coffee. What on earth was making him carry on like this? She had never seen him go on for so long—and with an "artist type" he had scorned a short while before.

With one eye on her impossible husband and his victim, she handed cups around to her parents and father-in-law. Veronica shook her head miserably.

So long as Pat got the slightest encouragement he always went on propounding his schemes. But why was James pretending to be so interested? It didn't make any sense. He could see perfectly well she was serving the coffee, but he never looked away from Pat for a moment. He had nothing in common with her practical-minded husband. He was a snob.

She handed around cream and sugar. He was hanging onto Pat's every word as if it were Emerson lecturing on transcendentalism. He was even egging him on with idiotic questions. Answering him, Pat's voice had the Irish lilt it always had when he was carried away, as he emphasized his points forcefully with his square hands.

She stood sipping her coffee, intrigued. James was laughing much too appreciatively. Why, he was flattering Pat to death!

Could it be?

She had heard about such things. Winifred had even pointed it out in Paris. But here in Greenwich? In her own parlor? The possibility enchanted her. She had always been amazed at how her husband had the ability to charm even the sourest old prunes, but this was something different. Why, poor Mr. James looked ready to get down on his elegant knees and lick his boots—or whatever they did.

To think that all that stuffy pretension hid a shocking secret. How hard it must be for him to put on such an act all the time.

And dear Patrick, carrying on as if it was municipal transportation that so fascinated his listener. Wait till she told him, the innocent. But on second thought, she wasn't sure she would. He might not be up to such "subtleties and complexities." She nearly giggled.

A door closed behind her. Her parents and Tom were still chatting, but Veronica had slipped out.

Veronica was shaking as she locked herself in her room. If she had stayed there another minute she would have started shrieking. She was ready to die of shame.

After a while Patrick came up, begging her to open the door, trying to explain through the crack that it was his blathering tongue ran away with him.

Through the door she told him stiffly that it didn't matter, it wasn't his fault and please go away. But when an hour later Elizabeth came up, Veronica let her in and wept on her neck. "Can you ever forgive me for what I did?"

"I should never have put you through it," Elizabeth said. "We're all miserable. Pat feels totally responsible."

Veronica broke away and sat down on the bed. "He could have gotten away from Patrick if he'd wanted to," she said bitterly. "I thought he wanted to talk to me about my poetry. You heard him say so yourself, didn't you? But he didn't look at me once." She put a hand to her mouth to stifle her emotion that was threatening to get the better of her again.

Elizabeth sat down at the end of the bed. "You mustn't blame Mr. James altogether for acting that way. He's a more complicated man than we knew."

"Don't excuse him," Veronica said with a spark of anger. "There's no excuse for such rudeness. I just can't believe he's the same man who writes those beautiful stories . . . that one about the old maid . . . with her widowed father. . . ." A sob escaped her before she choked it off.

"My dear," Elizabeth said gently, "great art has nothing to do with being kind."

She blew her nose. "You're right, of course. I am naive. The man's a perfect boor."

"I think he may have a sensitive side."

"Was it sensitive of him to make me feel so worthless I had to run out of the room like a dog?"

"Naturally, you don't understand," said Elizabeth. "I didn't either. I thought it was all Pat's fault too, taking him over like he did. But then I started watching what was really going on. . . ." She told the story to her unworldly sister-in-law without mincing words, trying to keep her voice as level as she could, considering how bizarre the whole thing was. "So you see, it was really nobody's fault. We were defeated before we began—but I hope it won't make you despise him the more."

Veronica was quiet for a little. Finally she said, "How naive I am. I thought things like that only existed in classical mythology." She started looking almost cheerful at once and gave a wan smile. "Isn't it funny, dear sister, you did your best to snare him for me, but it was Patrick who snared him."

Elizabeth, giving her a kiss good-night, said that Patrick knew nothing about such things and she thought it best that they not tell him.

The lamp in Veronica's room at the top of the house was not turned down that night until she had written a letter:

Dear Mr. James,

I do hope you'll forgive my sudden departure after dinner, but I'm occasionally struck by a migraine. I want you to know how much I admire you and your work. Although I doubt that we will meet again, I believe deeply that the greatest bonds are spiritual, and that is more than enough for me.

I wish you a bon voyage and all good fortune. I know the brilliant literary milieu of London will make a place for you.

I remain

Yours respectfully,
V. Endicott.

At the time of the dinner for Henry James, Elizabeth was already pregnant, and she gave birth to her second child, a boy, on July 4, 1876—two weeks early—while the rest of the family was off to the Centennial celebration in Washington Square.

When the stupendous fireworks display over the Hudson was over that night and Patrick came home to find he had a son, he let out a whoop of joy. He couldn't have been born on a better day if they had ordered it! "And a fine christenin at St. Aloysius's my boy is goin to have," he said, kissing Elizabeth soundly on the cheek.

It had been such an easy delivery that she was already sitting up in bed with her hair brushed and falling in soft waves around her shoulders. She reminded him that he no longer attended St. Aloysius's but she would have no objection to having the baptism there if he wanted it.

He grinned. "A slip of the tongue, darlin. St. Luke's it will be, and just as fine too."

They named the baby Thomas John after the two grandfathers. But from the start he was Jack—Pat's all-American boy, robust and happy—and the whole family revolved around him.

WINIFRED BEAUFORT HAD GONE ON WORKING FOR WILL KENnedy in his down-at-the-heels music hall on Fourteenth Street. Her songs had earned her a small measure of success in the several years she had been there, but as the city's entertainment center continued to move northward, the audience was dwindling.

Will Kennedy adored her. He had made that clear from the start. But whenever he tried to get serious, she kept him at bay with a barrage of smart talk, letting him know as delicately as she could that she was not interested. She liked him—he had given her a job when no one else would—but it was impossible for her to take him seriously. His sights were not set high enough for her. Much as she tried to make him listen, he stubbornly refused to understand that theater could ever be anything more than his cheap revues catering to the lowest tastes. Though she was glad for the meal ticket, she was still waiting for the break that would put her before an audience who appreciated the full expression of her talent.

Her young painter friends from Tenth Street still came to see her devotedly, and it was in their company that she felt most at home. After the show, they often took her down to a tavern across from Jefferson Market on Sixth Avenue called Gridley's, where they bought her suppers of chowder and fried chicken. She was sometimes the only woman there. Except for those who didn't give a fig for their reputations, women didn't set foot in taverns. But she was not about to be held down by New York's provincial definition of a woman's place, which was a far cry from the freedom she had known in France. Among her artist friends—their conversation laced with French—she was able to relax and forget for a few hours how unsatisfactorily things had worked out for her in New York.

Joe Gridley, the proprietor, liked the lively young painters who made his tavern a gathering place, and he let them hang their canvases on the walls. Artist cafés were popular in Paris, but in New York they were almost unknown. The tavern even began to attract a few blue-bloods from Fifth Avenue, glad to escape the stifling formality of New York society.

But the elegantly dressed young black woman in the midst of it all made Gridley uncomfortable. He was uneasy about what some of his customers thought about her flamboyant presence, though no one had objected so far.

Her friends were always urging her to sing for them, even in the tavern. In Europe a singer often performed spontaneously in a restaurant or café when asked—at Gridley's where there was only some occasional drunken bawling around the piano, she resisted.

But one night, when she had been reminiscing about singing in a café on the Left Bank, she surprised them by going to the piano. Every sound in the room stopped as she made her way between the tables, a dark queen in a magenta gown, her hair pulled up in a tight psyche knot fastened with a rope of pearls. Sweeping up her skirts on one arm, she arranged herself on the bench. Then as her fingers rippled over the keys in a gay waltz tune, she began to sing in her throaty voice a song about the Paris streets.

When she finished, the patrons went wild, some of them even standing up on their chairs and cheering. After a few more songs she returned to her friends in triumph. A group of young swells in evening clothes even sent over a bottle of the wretched house wine.

Gridley's reservations about her evaporated. He had never been abroad but he knew good business when he saw it. Why not try to reproduce a little of the atmosphere of Gay Paree in New York since it seemed to meet with such favor? Amidst the laughter and toasts of her friends he proposed to Winifred that she come to work for him. He couldn't pay her much to start, he told her, but if she brought in business—and by her reception tonight it looked a good possibility—he would be able to give her a real salary.

Of course, she would have to adapt her performance to local custom—not so much shaking her shoulders, no showing the ankle, and tone down that ooh-la-la business. He was all for good clean fun but he didn't want to get the reputation of one of those places on Greene Street.

Winifred was exultant. It was exactly what she had been waiting for. She calculated the possibility of finding herself broke again if it didn't work out, but of course it couldn't fail. Look at the effect she had had on the audience tonight!

Her friends were just as excited as she was. They immediately began planning her new career as "New York's only genuine continental chanteuse." They bestowed on her an exotic pedigree. She would be, as in her solo at Will Kennedy's music hall, Guadeloupe-born, the daughter of a French planter and a beautiful Creole mother.

"Win! What's got you up so early?" Will Kennedy threw down his racing form and swung his high-laced shoes off the desk to pull up a chair for her close to him. "Have some coffee." He poured from a pot on a kerosene burner into a battered crockery mug and pushed it across to her. Even in a fawn-colored walking dress and cape which subdued her naturally extravagant proportions, Winifred Beaufort was dazzling. Her perfume made him squirm in his pants.

Waving the coffee away as she pulled off her gloves, she swept over to the grimy window and tried to think of how to start. She had anticipated this little scene for a long time, but now that it had come she couldn't stand Will Kennedy being so nice. He had taken her in when every other door in New York was slammed in her face.

"Okay, let's have it," he said, puzzled that she was not already tearing into him about something. Her gripes were continual—drunks in the audience, the pianist who didn't keep up with her, the girls chattering backstage during her number.

She still didn't speak, digging the tip of her closed parasol into a crack of the floor planks.

"I know," he said, "I bet you want another raise."

She shook her head, making her spangled earrings glitter.

Her silence was worrying him. He wanted somehow to goad her into her usual sass. They had a routine between them. It was all he ever got from her, but it was something. "Don't tell me you're finally going to come across?"

"No." The look of mock impatience that always signaled her usual comeback was not there.

"Is it the costume again? If you'd lose five pounds you'd stop splitting the seams." He could almost feel his hands running over her, though whenever he actually tried she pushed him away.

Still without looking at him she said quietly, "I'm quitting, Will."

He sat back down, puffing up a cloud of smoke from his cigar. "So you got an offer from the Garden? Tell me another."

With her figure outlined against the window, unattainable as Cleopatra, she told him about Gridley's offer.

"Who you kidding?" he said when she had finished. He tried to detect a glimmer of the usual mockery with which she fended him off, but the eyes looking back at him under long sweeping lashes were serious. He tossed his cigar into a spittoon and shuffled through a mess of papers on his desk, pulling out some sheets covered with his wild scrawl. "Here it is, my new revue. I want you for the lead."

She didn't listen. "I'm going to sing what I want the way I want. It will be like the Left Bank."

So it wasn't a bigger part in the show she was after. He began to panic. "This is New York, remember, honey? Nobody will go for that here."

"How do you know? You think the only thing anybody is interested in is Blackbirds."

He took a swig of her cold coffee and wiped his mouth with the back of his hand. "You're forgetting one thing. There's no audience down there. The only place to go in this town is Twenty-third Street. That's where the money is."

"Big uptown spenders? That's not what I'm interested in. You've never understood anything about me. I'm a chanteuse. I need an intimate atmosphere." What had made her think she ought to feel the least twinge of guilt about leaving the show? He was making it quite clear that he didn't give a damn about losing her.

"And you think down at Gridley's saloon you're going to find this special audience?"

"I've already got an audience."

"Your little handful of nellie-boys? Don't make me laugh." He took another cigar out of his vest pocket and, with maddening coolness, clipped the end off and ran a wet tongue over it to keep the leaf sealed.

He was deliberately trying to get her goat. She walked up to the desk and, with a hand on her hip, glared at him. "You don't know the least thing about art, Will Kennedy."

Lighting his cigar, he blew out puffs of smoke. "I don't need to. There's no money in it."

"Some people think about other things than money."

"Well, Gridley better think about it. He's sure as hell going to lose his shirt if he puts you on. This isn't Paris. A colored girl can't set herself up as a solo act in a tavern. Not in New York she can't."

"Oh, all that's been worked out. I'm being presented as a Creole from the islands. I'll have a French accent."

"Creole from the islands?" He gave her a horselaugh. "You got any idea what those Greenwich rednecks will think about that?"

"That I'm an uppity nigger you mean?" Her eyes flashed.

"I didn't say that."

"Well, you're right." She jerked a thumb at her elegant bosom where inset garnets winked from under the cape. "But this here is one smart uppity nigger, and I know when a good thing comes my way."

"You'd be better off staying with me."

She sat down on the edge of the desk and began to pull on her gloves. "Sorry, but I'm not wasting any more time wiggling my ass at a bunch of two-bit drunks who come in to sleep it off."

He came around and put a hand on her shoulder. "Ah, Win, at least take a look at the script I worked out for you."

"It's too late." She got up, adjusting her cape and gathering her skirts. "Can't you get it through your head it's been a dead end for me here?"

He stared at her, his neck swelling as he went red. "Then go on, you crazy bitch!" he hollered. "You think you're too good for me but I'm the one who took you in off the streets. Somebody's going to bring you down off that high horse one day, and when it happens don't expect to cry on my shoulder. I wash my hands of you for good."

"That's okay by me," she sang out, going through the door. "Thanks for the charity." Her heels echoed mockingly down the corridor.

By the time he decided to go after her and beg her to stay,

the outer door slammed. He swore and kicked his boot hard against the desk, spilling coffee over the script.

Winifred was an immediate success. Within a few weeks Gridley was persuaded by her devoted following to rename the tavern "Café de Paris." Business doubled and he was able to give her a decent wage.

Elizabeth kept begging Patrick to take her there, but he wouldn't hear of it. He wasn't interested in anything that had to do with Winifred Beaufort, and a tavern—no matter what fancy name they called it—was no place for his wife.

Furious at his obstinacy, she set about wheedling her parents into taking her. The Coopers, although they were fond of Winifred, were almost as dubious as their son-in-law about going into such a place. But Elizabeth insisted that cafés like this were perfectly respectable in Europe for women as well as men. If her parents claimed to have liberal views, it was their duty to help break down the social restrictions in New York.

As usual, they couldn't resist their determined daughter whom they had brought up, after all, to have a mind of her own. Professor Cooper asked Patrick if he would mind them taking Elizabeth just this once to see her friend perform. Patrick muttered, as he tinkered with a model train for his infant son, that if they wanted to waste their time that way, it was their business.

Elizabeth was enchanted with the place as she and her parents sat over coffee at one of the small crowded tables. Gridley had done little to change it from the simple neighborhood tavern with sawdust on the floor it had always been, except to move the piano to a more prominent spot. But with the artists' canvases on the wall and the animated crowd under the gaslights, it was transformed. Besides Elizabeth and her mother, a few other well-dressed women were present. She had to pinch herself to believe she was in sedate Greenwich, where nothing ever went on.

In a red satin gown and egret feathers in her hair Winifred came out and seated herself at the piano under a hanging lamp that bathed her in a warm pool of light. She introduced each song that she sang in French by telling the story in an exaggerated French accent that made Elizabeth laugh. When she finished her songs, she acknowledged the enthusiastic reception with deep curtsies like a diva.

Then, as if she had just seen Elizabeth and her parents for the first time—even though they were sitting practically in front of her and she had been throwing them looks throughout the program—she held out her arms to them dramatically. "*Mes chers amis*, but how *délicieux* that you have come to see my little show!" She sat down with them and, putting on a deep southern accent, whispered not to give her away or everyone would walk out. They all laughed, and Professor Cooper ordered a bottle of imported wine.

THE LEAVES WERE BEGINNING TO TURN YELLOW AND RED when a telegram came for Tom at the printshop. It was from the Bloomingdale Sanitarium.

Leaving Albert to help with the printing of handbills announcing an opening sale at the rebuilt Jefferson Market, Tom took an elevated train up to the gloomy red brick pile by the Hudson that he had grown to hate.

There he was told his wife was dying. He had been expecting it. On his visits over the years he had watched her deteriorate physically as well as mentally.

At first she had appeared almost herself when he and Veronica had gone to see her. They had sat on the veranda of the sanitarium and walked through the grounds above the river. Then, it had seemed to him almost a pleasant retreat. It stood in open countryside beyond the city. But New York's inexorable northern march had leveled the hills and laid out streets, until almost at a gallop, buildings filled in the fields right up to the asylum grounds.

Both Fanny's parents had died shortly after she was put into the sanitarium, and unexpectedly she was left a share of the inheritance along with her brothers and sisters, none of whom had ever had anything to do with her. The money had been helpful. Invested in railroad bonds, the income had paid for her care that got more expensive as her condition worsened.

Though the doctors kept telling Tom not to lose hope that his wife might recover, he knew better. After a while, the times when she was able to recognize him became rarer. Eventually, she was confined—with the other incurables—to a ward, wearing only a gray smock, listless, no longer caring he was there.

The last few years it had become dreadful. In addition to her advanced dementia, she developed consumption, and soon became hardly more than a skeleton wracked with coughs.

Tom was at the asylum gates before it occurred to him that he had not let Veronica know about the telegram. It was probably just as well. Lately, she seemed increasingly shaken after each visit to her mother. Though Patrick and Elizabeth were unaware of it, he knew how his daughter felt living off the crumbs of other people's happiness. It was better to spare her this last agonizing confrontation.

Fanny had been moved from the ward to the hospital wing some months earlier. Even before he went into the room, painted a bleak institutional green, the rancid smell hit him. He was nauseated as always, and then guilty over it.

He could hardly bear to look at her. What had that creature in the bed to do with him? Under the sheet she was shrunken to the size of a child, the only evidence of life a harsh breathing in and out of the maw that had once been her mouth. Her eyes were closed, the thin blue-veined skin of the lids like a newborn, featherless bird.

"Fanny," he whispered, taking a chair by the bed. It was obscene to apply that name to this wasted being who had no resemblance whatever to the delicate girl he had once hungered for.

She didn't move or open her eyes. Only that hideous hawking in of air through the open mouth.

"Can you hear me?" he tried again in a voice totally false. The truth was he felt nothing.

She seemed unaware of him as he sat there, when unexpectedly there was a stirring under the sheet and a talon of a hand emerged clutching a paper. So she was still conscious after all! Though he hated himself, he was sorry—he wanted to be done with it at last. Gingerly, he slipped the scrap of paper away and the hand fell like a puppet with the strings broken.

This past year, since she had become unable to speak, she had scratched notes to him several times. Just a few shaky words, almost illegible, pitiful pleas to take her home. Only once had she said something else. She had asked how Elizabeth was, which made him think briefly that, incredible as it seemed, she might actually be getting better. But the next time he came she didn't even know him, screaming hysterically when he tried to talk to her, until it had ended in a coughing fit.

Putting on his spectacles, he saw that her writing was more legible this time. Instead of a plea to get her out of here, the words "MY WILL" were printed at the top. Under it was written "My money to Veronica" with "Promise" at the bottom heavily underlined. It was the Slocum inheritance she must be referring to, the money from her parents.

When he looked up, he was alarmed to see her head turned toward him, the eyes open, huge and unblinking, waiting. They were darker than they had ever been, full of an intensity that belied the shrunken frame.

"But dear, this isn't necessary," he said automatically. "You're going to get well and come home."

Her head almost lifted off the pillow in her effort to get words out, but it was too much for her and she fell back in a fit of coughing. When he started to pour her some water from the bed stand, her bony fingers clutched his wrist, holding him back and forcing him to look at her.

"Yes . . . all right. . . ." he nearly shouted, in a panic not to be touched. "I'll give her the money."

The fierce eyes watched him for a moment and then dropped shut again. The coughing had stopped, but sputum trickled from her open mouth. The breathing, always noisy, changed into a gurgle.

He ran out in the hall to find a nurse, but by the time he got back the terrible breathing had stopped forever.

On the elevated going home, as he stared out the window hardly seeing the solidly built-up new blocks of the city; his only feeling was relief that he would never have to go back to that awful place again. No matter how tranquil his life had been these last years, she had always been in the background like an apparition, and hanging over his head, the monthly visit.

The girl he had loved so long ago had nothing to do with that poor wretch he had taken leave of with a final kiss on the cold brow. He tried to remember the strange, delicate girl who had once nestled against him in a sunny bay window as they read together their poem, the poem that was her:

> For the moon never beams without bringing me dreams
> Of the beautiful Annabel Lee.
> And the stars never rise but I feel the bright eyes . . .

He shuddered, still seeing those huge vulture eyes fixed on him with their unmistakable message of hatred and accusation. In his fist was the crumpled note with the words "MY WILL," and he remembered his promise.

When he told Veronica about the will, she broke down in tears all over again. It was proof, she told him, that her mother had never forgotten her. Even in the asylum and ill as she was, she must have known how inconvenient it had become for her, living in the house with Patrick and Elizabeth and their growing family, where there was less and less privacy. And now the bequest would allow her to live out her life as an independent woman.

She made plans to settle in a cottage in Sands Point on Long Island where she had friends from school, a pair of unmarried sisters, and she began going through her things, filling trunks and boxes.

AFTER WINIFRED'S INITIAL SUCCESS AT THE CAFÉ DE Paris, things took an unexpected turn. Though her following remained faithful to her, there was some local muttering that a colored woman had stepped out of her place and set herself up as if she were as good as white. Unpleasant things began to happen. One evening when she was singing, there were catcalls from some louts at the bar. Gridley had them thrown out and Winifred laughed it off, dismissing it as jealousy.

But next morning the word "nigger" was chalked on the door of the café. Then a few nights later a brick crashed through a window during her performance. The audience began to stay away.

Distressed, she offered to quit, but Gridley would not hear of it. When he complained about it to the police, demanding better protection, they told him that some of the workers on the new elevated line being put up there on the avenue were hanging around the neighborhood after work hours. They suggested that he hire a bouncer.

For a while there was no more trouble—and then it happened. One night after the café had closed, Winifred left with two of her painter friends. As they passed the alley behind the building, a gang of hoodlums jumped them. Before she knew it, both her friends were knocked out, and she was not only badly beaten but dragged into an unused carriage house and raped by the whole gang.

The next morning a boy brought Elizabeth the news. She left the baby with the hired girl and nearly ran the two blocks down the street to the boardinghouse where Winifred lived. She found her in bed, bruised and suffering, her lips almost too swollen to talk.

Elizabeth was so distraught, that she was late in getting back for Jack's noon feeding. The hired girl had taken Alice with her while she did the marketing, leaving Patrick, who was through with lunch, holding fretting baby Jack with all the helplessness of a young father. "Where ya been?" he asked, when Elizabeth came in. "He wants to eat."

She put a towel over her shoulder and took the baby as she told Pat what happened.

"It's too bad," he said, "but she asked for it, didn't she? Anyway, I got to get back to the job." He grabbed his hat and was gone.

She stared after him in disbelief at his callousness, until Jack set up a wail and she gave him the breast.

In the days that followed she spent most of her time with Winifred, coming home only to nurse the baby. She could not forgive Patrick for his attitude. Using her preoccupation with Winifred as an excuse, she slept in the spare room and hardly exchanged a word with him.

Patrick was working on the new elevated line near Jefferson Market, supervising the construction of a station up over the avenue with iron stairways leading down to the sidewalks. Gridley's was just across the street, boarded up now. He was furious every time he looked at it, thinking of Winifred Beaufort, who he was convinced had caused all this trouble between him and Elizabeth.

He didn't understand why his wife was carrying on like she was, acting like it was his fault. It was a damn shame what had happened, but why did that woman have to push her way in where she wasn't wanted? She had asked for it. Every time he looked across at Gridley's, he wanted to tear down the building with his bare hands.

A week later when he passed the tavern on his way home to lunch, several young laborers were huddled around the poster that once had announced Winifred's nightly appearance. A big fellow was scrawling something on it with a hunk of charcoal as the other two sniggered.

He recognized them. They were on one of his work gangs, though he didn't know them personally. He had seen them lately at the Hell Hole bar where he liked to stop in for a beer after work.

All his boys were hard drinkers and he sometimes had to send them home to sleep it off. A week before, this trio had shown up in the morning with bottles in their pockets and already three sheets to the wind. He didn't like the way they took it when he told them to go home and come back when they were sober, joking that if he let them stay they'd build the el wobbly. Though it was nothing he could put his finger on, they were not the kind of good-hearted lads he liked to have a beer with.

There was something queer about the way they were carrying on now in front of Winifred Beaufort's poster. He stopped and casually asked the biggest of them, who was called Smitty, if he had ever gone to see her sing.

"Not exactly," Smitty cracked, as his pals went on sniggering.

"Ya know her then?"

Smitty said, "Well, ya might call it that." They all laughed again.

"She's a real tomato, huh?"

"Not bad for a jig, wouldn't ya say so, lads?" And they broke into howls of dirty laughter.

He got a look at what Smitty had scrawled across the poster: "Nigger bitch got it good."

The rest of the day he couldn't get the trio out of his mind. The morning they had come in drunk was the morning after the rape. It might be a coincidence, then again it might not. But even if he told the police, he knew they wouldn't do anything—not over the rape of a colored woman. Besides, he had no proof.

He wanted to talk to his wife about it that evening but she was away at Winifred's, and after a lonely dinner with Veronica he went to the Hell Hole, waiting in the shadows at the far end of the bar for some of the gang to show up.

He was about to give up and leave, when Smitty and one of his sidekicks came in and began washing down whiskeys with beer. About midnight the sidekick, very drunk, staggered out, but Smitty stayed on. He was the size of an ox and apparently unaffected by the amount he was drinking.

It was nearly two in the morning by the time Smitty left. Patrick followed not far behind through the dark streets near the riverfront, a slicing wind blowing dead leaves into drifts. When Smitty stepped into a cul-de-sac to take a leak, Patrick waited until he was through, then challenged him, "I'm goin to beat the shit out of ya, Smitty."

Smitty whipped around as if he might be about to draw a knife, but seeing it was Patrick, relaxed and grinned. "Oh, it's you, Mr. Endicott! Ya scared the bejesus out of me. I thought it was the wops from Hell's Kitchen."

"I know what ya did to that woman," Patrick said, moving toward him.

Smitty sized up his stocky but much shorter opponent. "Ya had too much to drink, Mr. Endicott. I wouldn't want to have to hurt ya."

Patrick let fly with a jab that caught him on the chin. Smitty flinched, and then with a smirk moved in, clearly expecting his size and weight to finish Patrick off in a jiffy. But Patrick had a rage in him that no size was a match for, reveling in the satisfaction of pure vengeance as his fists smashed repeatedly against muscle and bone.

He left the hooligan in a heap in the alley, and as he walked away he felt pure exhilaration. He was ready to reclaim his wife again.

When he got home, Elizabeth was waiting up for him, nearly out of her mind with worry. But when she saw his bruised fists and disheveled clothes she was furious. "I don't believe it," she cried, smelling the liquor on his breath. "You're just a mick after all, drinking and fighting and staying out all night! What about your children? What a disgusting father they have. I wish I'd never married you."

He didn't answer. He went up to the bedroom and stripped to his long johns. Only after he had doused his head in the washbasin did he turn to her, his black curls dripping. "I thought ya cared for your friend Winifred."

"What has that got to do with it?" she asked, facing him, rosy with indignation.

"I got one of them bastards, that's what."

She went dead quiet as he told her what had happened. Afterward, she pressed herself against him, begging him to forgive her, and he took her soft body to him.

* * *

Gridley had decided not to reopen the café for the present because of continuing threats. In any case, Winifred was in no state to go back to work. For weeks she kept to her room, long after her bruises healed. It was not that she lacked friends. The boardinghouse she lived in was full of theater folk, a sympathetic breed. The painters from Tenth Street even took up a collection.

Elizabeth still spent as much time as she could with her. She understood the tremendous shock her friend had suffered. That Winifred had fallen into despair was natural, but that it should last so long was frightening. It was as if the most vital person she knew had stopped wanting to live.

Elizabeth begged her to let her contact Will Kennedy. He was devoted to her. He had a right to know. She might even go back to work for him.

But Winifred was adamant. Under no circumstances was he ever to hear what had happened. She was not going to crawl back to him on her hands and knees. So Elizabeth had to promise not to tell him.

Since the attack Winifred had missed one menstrual period, which the doctor ascribed to shock, but after missing a second, it was discovered that she was pregnant. She collapsed all over again.

"I don't want it!" she wailed to Elizabeth. "Not like that! I'll kill myself first!"

When she calmed down, Elizabeth suggested the possibility of having a medical intervention. Although it wasn't talked about openly, abortion wasn't illegal, even if lately certain organizations had started to campaign against it. But abortionists still advertised freely. Curiously, they all had French names, Mme. this and Mme. that. Elizabeth had seen their ads in the back of *Demorest's Ladies Magazine* describing their services euphemistically as "correcting menstrual irregularities."

With Winifred's approval she chose a Mme. Restelle because of her address nearby on Fifth Avenue, and went to see her. As she paid the cabman she could tell from his look that he thought she was going for the notorious procedure herself.

From the outside, the address appeared to be a fine town house among other palatial establishments lining the avenue where the city's wealthiest lived. A butler admitted her, just as if she were a rich young matron making a social call, and led her through the ornate foyer to a reception room.

When a rear door opened and a woman came in, she caught a glimpse of a brightly lit hospital corridor beyond, with white-aproned nurses going about their duties.

Mme. Restelle, despite her exotic name, was stout and capable looking and introduced herself without a trace of French accent as they sat down at her desk. If she was not French, it was with French directness that she stated her price right off, three hundred dollars.

Hoping she had come to the right place, Elizabeth told her the story of the gang rape.

Mme. Restelle shook her head in disbelief and agreed that an abortion was absolutely justified, advising that for safety's sake it be performed as soon as possible. She got out a leather-bound record book and, taking up a pen, asked who the victim was.

Elizabeth hesitated.

"You don't have to worry," said Mme. Restelle. "I wouldn't be in this profession long if I weren't discreet. Many of my clients are from the best social circles."

Satisfied, Elizabeth gave her Winifred's name.

"But wasn't she the one who was singing down in . . . ? I think she had a perfect right." The woman dipped her pen briskly into the inkwell. "I'm putting her down as Mrs. W. Smith."

Elizabeth arranged to bring Winifred the next day, but when she was walking back to the hack stand where the steaming horses were stamping hooves metallically against the cobblestones, she asked herself where they were going to find the three hundred dollars.

Winifred didn't have a penny. Pat might be able to borrow it, but after what he had done already she couldn't ask him for so large a sum. Though she handled the family finances, she kicked herself for not having her own bank account.

Her father couldn't help. He was away at the University of Virginia as a visiting professor for a term. Winifred's friends would do anything for her, but they were all poor as church mice.

Will Kennedy. He was the one to go to. Of course there was that promise Winifred had got out of her never to contact him. But what was breaking her word against Winifred's entire future happiness?

That evening, cloaking herself in a mohair pelerine with the hood up, she went to the music hall and asked for him at the box office. But the ticket seller said the show was already on and the boss was entertaining a party in his box, she would have to come back the next day.

Without hesitating she bought a ticket and, brushing aside the astonished usher, marched straight into the box at the rear of the orchestra interrupting Will Kennedy, who with a group of cigar-smoking sharpies was watching the show. Onstage, to the thumping of a razzle-dazzle band, chorus girls in blackface were kicking up their legs as aroused patrons threw coins. The girls were encouraging the pandemonium by raising their skirts to slip the money inside their rolled-down striped stockings while barmaids were rushing about with drinks for the thirsty audience.

Will recognized immediately that something was wrong and took her out into the corridor.

"Serves her right for running out on me!" he shouted when he heard what had happened, but he was ashen-faced as he grabbed her arm and rushed out to get a cab.

If Winifred's outbursts had alarmed the other boarders on numerous occasions, Will's roaring at her as he charged into her room entertained them greatly.

"You crazy, know-it-all bitch, didn't I tell you it wouldn't work?" Then, seeing her on the bed in a faded wrapper so changed, her brilliant eyes hopeless, he fell to his knees beside her and scolded her tenderly as he stroked her hair. "Why didn't you let me know, Win? Did you really think I didn't care?"

As Elizabeth stepped back into the hall, Winifred was sobbing in his arms.

It was Will who accompanied Winifred to Mme. Restelle's the next day, and when she was well again, took her to stay with him in his rooms behind the theater.

The following week, appearing totally restored, she visited Elizabeth wearing a smart robin's-egg blue street costume with a fox fur piece and muff. Will was closing the music hall, she said, and they were opening a gambling club on West Twenty-fourth Street in the Tenderloin. She was going to be the hostess.

"But won't the police cause trouble?" Elizabeth wanted to

know, observing the flashy beaded fringe on her friend's cape and the touch of paint on her cheeks.

There was nothing to worry about, Winifred said. Will had already fixed it up. They were going to rake in more than enough to pay off the cops.

When Elizabeth asked about her singing, her answer was just as smooth. "Green stuff is all I care about now, honey. If you got it, nobody can touch you—even if you're colored."

Her cynicism gave Elizabeth a turn, but considering the ordeal she had gone through, how could it be otherwise? She had always been sassy, and anyway she was as beautiful as ever and with all the old spirit back again.

Elizabeth said she would give anything to see her as gambling queen, and Winifred said, Why not? She'd get Will to sneak her in for a look some night and Patrick would never have to know. They howled and it was like old times.

Her friend was truly a phenomenon, Elizabeth thought when she had gone, leaving a scent of frangipani flowers in the air. Of course, the face paint and the gaudy trimmings were excessive, but ostentation was acceptable in that world, as she knew well enough from Paris where all the most elegant women in the professions painted. She did so want Winifred to have a little happiness after her hard life.

The one thing she regretted was that Winifred seemed to be giving up her singing altogether.

Elizabeth had never been happier with Patrick, their marriage having weathered its first serious crisis. But Winifred's audacious way of life was a reminder to her that she had never wanted to limit herself to being just a wife and mother. There were aspects of living she meant to explore, even if Pat was unwilling to follow. Having her own ideas and keeping a part of herself separate from him only made her feel more of a woman, and indeed, their lovemaking was more satisfying than ever.

She and Patrick were both relieved, though they didn't admit it to each other openly, that Veronica was going to move to a home of her own on Long Island. Her trunks were called for, and on the morning she left they all said good-bye at the cab in front of the house. As Elizabeth hugged her she promised they would be out to visit her on the following weekend.

It was only after lunch when she went up to air out the empty room that she found the note stuck in the bureau mirror.

As she stood in front of the open windows letting in the brisk March air and the trills of early robins from the backyard below, she read Veronica's message—she had sailed at noon on the *Franconia* for England where she was going to make her home, "because it's the ideal place for an old maid like me who writes poetry. . . . You have both been kind to put up with me for so long. . . ."

Tom came over for dinner that night. They were all in a state of shock around the table as they discussed it, wondering if there wasn't something they could have done. Elizabeth blamed herself for not paying more attention to her lately, having been so preoccupied with Winifred. Patrick remembered that when he had offered to make any needed repairs at her new home on Long Island, she had been evasive. In fact, she had refused to allow any of them even to see the cottage.

Tom mentioned how taken she had been with the young writer, Mr. James, who had also gone to England to live. Was it possible the poor girl was still smitten with him, Elizabeth speculated, and had run off to throw herself at him? "I do hope not. I know for a fact that he never answered her letter. How awful it would be."

Tom thought that whether or not that were the case, it was probably better that Veronica go off to find a life for herself at last, now that she had independent means. "Fanny and I were so wrong for each other, our children didn't have much chance," he said gloomily over his coffee.

The hired girl brought in Alice and the baby to say good-night, Cicero at her heels, and as Patrick held baby Jack in the air, Alice called out "Papa" and climbed into grandpa's lap.

as she stood in front of the open window was setting in the [illegible] [illegible] and the [illegible] early robins [illegible] the back yard below the road [illegible] she had stood at [illegible] of the [illegible] and [illegible] she was going to make her [illegible] [illegible] the [illegible] for an old maid like me who [illegible] [illegible] and [illegible] up with me for so long.

[illegible] came over for dinner that night. They were all in a state of shock around the table as they discussed it, wondering if there wasn't something they could have done. [illegible] [illegible] for not paying more attention to her feelings, [illegible] been [illegible] with [illegible] and when he had offered to make any needed repairs at the new home [illegible] the island, she had been evasive—in fact, she had refused to allow any of them even to see the cottage.

[illegible] [illegible] how taken she had been with [illegible] [illegible] who had [illegible] to England [illegible] was [illegible] the poor girl was still smitten with him [illegible] [illegible] he never answered her letters [illegible] would [illegible]

[illegible] that whether or not this was [illegible] it was probably better [illegible] go on [illegible] at last now that she had independent means [illegible] [illegible] [illegible] [illegible]

[illegible] [illegible] and the [illegible] to [illegible] [illegible]

1886

In June, Alice Endicott had her thirteenth birthday party, the first family celebration after the period of mourning for Elizabeth's mother, who had died the year before. The portieres between the parlor, with its green brocade walls, and the plum-papered study were thrown back and the room was festive with crepe paper strung from the chandeliers, just converted from gas to electricity.

Six of Alice's girlfriends were invited over. They were playing charades, taking turns acting out book titles for the others to guess, while Elizabeth sat with the mothers, chatting over punch and birthday cake in a row of chairs along one wall. Before the bay window looking out on the sunny backyard, the hired girl was at a buffet table serving the cake and a large bowl of fruit punch.

At the other end of the room Patrick was on his hands and knees with nine-year-old Jack astride him in an Indian headdress, whooping and kicking for his horse to buck harder. At thirty-nine, Pat was a little paunchy but his curly black hair was as thick as ever. Through the war whoops and the girls' laughter and clapping at each other's antics, he was managing to hold forth to Professor Cooper about the horsecars on tracks that were at last replacing the old stages that had survived on Broadway long after the other avenues.

"Just ya wait until they're electrified," he said, pausing to wipe the sweat from his forehead. "We've got an electric engine in the works already."

"Personally," said his father-in-law, "I'm still partial to the horse."

"Giddy-up!" Jack yelled, bored with his lazy steed.

"In fifty years there won't be a horse left on the street," Patrick said, bucking lackadaisically. "I predict—"

"Hey, Paddy!" yelled a drunken voice. "What in hell's goin on here?"

He looked around to see Bill Yates, his sister Sarah's husband, who had barged in through the parlor door without even taking off his cap. Bill had never been to the house before, though he and Sarah had been invited for dinner a number of times—they always had an excuse to get out of it. He must have belted down a few to get up his nerve. His face was red and his eyes blazed with Dutch courage.

"What is it then, Bill?" Pat said, getting to his feet as Jack slid off unwillingly.

"It's them wops I'm talkin about," Yates started in loudly. He was a foreman of a work gang on the el.

"Ah, don't get so riled up now." Patrick took his brother-in-law's arm and tried to lead him out to the hall, but Yates shook him off.

"Those bastards are tryin to make trouble on the job and I'm not takin it any more."

The girls in their paper birthday hats had stopped in the middle of acting out *Rebecca of Sunnybrook Farm* and the mothers sat with their cups suspended in the air as they stared.

In a white pinafore and ruffled pantaloons, Alice came up behind her father and pulled his sleeve, whispering furiously to get him out of there. She had always been ashamed of her Irish relatives, and now stamped her foot and shook her long curls, vexed that her party was being ruined.

Patrick, pleased at his highfalutin daughter's display of low-class Irish temper, devilishly pulled her around and held her in front of him. "Ya remember your Uncle Bill, don't ya? He's here to wish ya a happy birthday, aren't ya, Bill?"

The girl burst out, "But he wasn't invited!"

"That's enough, young lady," said Elizabeth, coming up and taking her away. "Go get Mr. Yates a piece of cake."

Ignoring his sister-in-law, Yates lurched over to look up at the electrified chandelier. "So it's incandescent bulbs ya got, Paddy? Gettin too fancy for your relations?"

"Come on now, Bill, we can talk better outside." Patrick tried to move in on him but he slipped away, having spied the punch bowl.

"Ain't ya goin to offer your brother-in-law a cup of cheer to toast the little birthday girl?"

"It's not the kind of punch ya go for, Bill."

But Yates was already ladling himself a glassful. As Alice and everyone else held their breath, he threw back his head and gulped down the punch. Then, with a terrible face, he spewed it out into the room. Pulling out his handkerchief he hawked and spat into it. "What kind of pizen is this to give a man?" he bellowed, staggering toward the row of flabbergasted matrons.

As little Jack laughed and jumped up and down, Patrick gripped Yates in an iron hand and marched him past the livid Alice and her saucer-eyed girlfriends, out the door. "Off we go, Bill. We'll talk it all over at the Hell Hole where we can get ya some real stuff."

Once outside on the bright street, Yates recovered enough to remember what he came for. Forcing Patrick to stop, he poked a finger into his chest for emphasis and blasted the Italian immigrants who were pouring into the village. "Them wops don't know nothin about workin steel, Paddy. All they're good for is donkey work."

A small neighbor girl was staring up at Bill with her mouth open. Patrick swung her into the air over his head as she squealed with delight. Then, putting her down, he led Yates off toward the tavern.

Although he did his best to keep them headed in a straight line down the sidewalk, his brother-in-law kept yanking him from side to side, making them both look drunk. Several women stopped sweeping their steps to watch curiously. Tongues would wag. Elizabeth would be amused when he told her.

"So what was I sayin?" said Yates. "Oh, yeah. Them wops said why shouldn't they do the weldin too. I tried to get it through their heads that weldin takes experience they don't have. I told them real nice, but get this"—he stopped and dug his finger into Patrick's chest again, blocking the sidewalk and forcing a woman with a market basket to step into the gutter to go around them—"one of them pulled a knife on me! That's right, Pat, pulled a knife on me! It was that Benny Alfano who never give us a bit of trouble before."

Patrick got him moving again and guided him across Hudson Street as Yates went on with his harangue. "I hustled him right off the job and told him if he ever showed his face around there again I'd wipe the floor with him—personal. But I'm not kiddin, if those other dagos hadn't pulled him off, I'd be pushin up the daisies now. Ya got to do somethin, Paddy. We can't go on workin with them."

Patrick steered him out of the way of an iceman balancing a chunk of ice on his shoulder with a pair of huge tongs. In the wagon at the curb his partner was making ice fly, chipping away with a pick at great blocks of it that had been stored from the winter in sawdust in a cellar.

Patrick put on his most soothing tone. "Aren't ya forgettin, Bill, twenty years ago they talked the same way about us micks? Remember those signs 'No Irish Need Apply'?"

Yates spat into the gutter. "And what's happened to Tammany, I'd like to know? Once they helped us keep the niggers out and now they're bringing these greaseballs in special."

Patrick explained patiently that with the city growing so fast there was enough work for them all. The Italians, whatever he might think of them, were good workers.

But Yates was not interested. "Don't kid yourself, Paddy, they're animals. Ya see how they look at our women? They don't have no morals."

They were outside the Hell Hole at last. Patrick stopped and turned to him. "Listen, Bill, they're Catholics the same as you. And now, goddam it, there's not enough micks to do the work and if you or any of the other lads don't like it, ya can damn well quit. We're goin to get this elevated built." Then, seeing Bill's bewildered red eyes, he put a hand on his shoulder. "I got my job to do, the same as you. Ya see that, don't ya?"

Yates scratched his head under his cap. "Okay, Paddy, if ya say so, we'll give it another try."

"Atta boy. Let's have a drink on it." He started into the bar.

"Wait a minute," said Bill, holding him back. "What are we goin in here for? Sarah's heart is breakin that ya don't come around any more. Come on and have a whiskey with us."

It was true enough, Patrick thought, he hadn't been by to see his sister in months. Alice's party could wait a while longer.

Yates had sobered up a little by the time they set off down Greenwich Street in the shadow of the el. A train rattled by deafeningly overhead, and they stepped into a doorway to avoid the coal cinders and sparks raining down from the locomotive.

"That's why we got to electrify," Patrick yelled over the din as they brushed off their shoulders.

The smell of cooked cabbage hit him as soon as Bill opened the door to the flat. With five children still at home, the rooms were as crowded with bedsteads as ever.

His sister was already fattening into middle age. "Patrick! I didn't know you was comin. The place is not to rights." Her fingers picked at a spot on her apron. She was self-conscious in the presence of this well-dressed brother from another world.

"Ah, Sarah, it's not a stranger I am. With family ya don't have to make a fuss." But the children looked at him as if he really were a stranger. Tinted engravings of Jesus, Mary, and all the saints stared at him from every wall reprovingly.

"What are ya waitin for, woman?" Yates cried, pulling Patrick over to sit with him at the table. "Get your brother a drink."

She brought in a pitcher of beer and mugs for them and was about to sit down when Yates said, "Get Paddy some of that corned beef ya fixed for supper, why don't ya?"

Patrick tried to protest that he wasn't hungry and not to go to any trouble.

"You're an Irishman, ain't ya? A real Irishman is always ready for corn beef and cabbage."

As his sister set heaping plates in front of them, Patrick wanted to feel the way he used to about the food of his childhood, but it didn't taste the same as he remembered, and it was only by swilling the beer Bill kept pouring out for him that he managed to get any down.

The children quickly got used to him and were running all over the place, screaming and jumping up and down on the beds. When Yates yelled at Sarah to shut them up, she doled out bowls of molasses pudding for them.

"She's got more than me!" a boy whined. He was wearing a raveled turtleneck sweater as though it were winter.

"I have not!" screamed a pretty little girl, putting her arms around her bowl. She had blue eyes that reminded Patrick of his mother.

"It ain't fair," the boy wailed.

"Just shut up now, Colin," Bill shouted, "or you'll get the back of my hand." He stood up and drained his mug. "Paddy's throwin a big birthday party today for that daughter of his, Sarah," he said thickly and made his way over to flop down on one of the beds. "Ya ought to see how fancy it is up there. Electric light they got now." He started to snore almost immediately.

Sarah sat down in her husband's chair and watched Patrick eat. He forced one last bite of cabbage down, embarrassed he had not invited them to the party. "Ya understand, Sarah, Alice just had some friends in."

Sarah gave a little smile, partly awkward and partly wanting to make him feel better. "We couldn't have come anyway, Pat, none of us. Bill had to work, and I got to keep poppin into the Jews down the street on Saturday to tend their cookin. Ya know, they ain't allowed to lift a finger on their Sabbath day."

The children were playing on the floor now, building a house with odd scraps of wood.

"Ya got a good heart, Sarah," Patrick said.

She looked at him with moist eyes. "Bill tells me how good ya are with the men on the job. I'm glad it's turned out so well for ya, Pat."

When he got up to go she gave him a holy medal, saying Timothy had sent it and she knew he'd like him to have it.

That night, with his arms around Elizabeth in their ornately carved walnut bed, the balmy air billowing out the muslin curtains, he told her about the visit. "I felt like a stranger with my own sister, can ya believe it? I don't belong there any more. And over here, my daughter's ashamed of me. Where do I belong, do ya think?"

She yawned and told him that Alice was at her most sensitive, overcritical age. All children went through it and it would pass. She knew how hard it had been for him to go from one world to another, she said, but what a good job he had made of it. "I'm so proud of you," she murmured sleepily.

As he pulled her close and turned down the bed lamp, he whispered in her ear that he couldn't have done it without her.

On the other side of Greenwich, in the Italian section near Washington Square, Benno Alfano and his wife were also awake. He had been fired that day by Bill Yates. Their children were asleep in another bed in the tenement room whose windows looked out on the elevated tracks where they curved from Sixth Avenue onto Third Street.

"What's the matter?" his wife asked, for Benno had turned to the wall instead of to her as he always did.

His voice muffled in the pillow, he said he couldn't think about anything but losing his job.

She made him turn back and pulled his head against her breast. "We'll get along," she said.

But he wouldn't be comforted. He raised his head, tears wet on his cheeks. "I only showed him my knife. I wanted him to know I make it myself, I know about steel. But my English no good. He don't give me a chance." He got more excited. "Why the hell can't we do the welding too? We got families just like them."

"Shhh," his wife whispered, "it's okay." She ran her hand down his back.

"It's not okay! We already late on the rent."

She kissed the tears from his eyes and told him to go see her brother Tony in the morning. He had a vegetable stand on Bleecker Street and was doing fine. Even if they didn't get along so well together, maybe he could help Benno out, rent a pushcart, something like that. "What you want to work with steel for anyway? It's dangerous. You just get hurt." She caressed him under the covers.

Responding, he leaned over her, slipping a callused hand into her nightdress to cup a breast, but she cautioned him to be quiet about it. "Mario's not a child any more. He's a man already like you, Benno. I saw."

A screeching of iron wheels on tracks came from outside, rattling the window frames, as an elevated train made the turn onto Third Street. The beam of the steam engine's light flashed across the room and for a moment they saw their thirteen-year-old son Mario's curly head as he lay asleep between his younger brother and sister.

THAT FALL WHEN PATRICK WAS WORKING ON AN EXPERImental project to electrify a section of track on the el, he took his son to see it. Jack loved to go with his father to his job. He knew all the men and took a keen interest in everything that was going on.

He was in his Sunday best, a navy-blue sailor suit with short pants and a round boater on his head with red midshipman ribbons hanging down behind. Just past his tenth birthday, he was a sturdy boy, the image of his father.

Up on the platform near a group of Irish workmen eating their lunch, Patrick was explaining to him how the generator would send electricity through the third rail to power the train. A prototype engine was expected to be delivered any day now, though it was still in the experimental stage.

Jack, who caught on to such technicalities as quickly as they were explained to him, asked if there wasn't any danger of the iron wheels grounding the electricity and shorting the whole thing.

"Better watch out, boss," one of the workmen yelled over, "if ya tell the lad too much, he'll be takin over your job and you'll be back with us on the gang."

"That's okay with me," Patrick said, putting a proud hand on his son's shoulder. "I'll step aside for him anytime."

An engineer came out of the construction office at the end of the platform and called over to him. There was a problem with the blueprints and they wanted to consult with him about it.

"Will ya look after my boy, Mike? They can't get along without me for a minute."

Jack ran over to the workman and exchanged some mock punches with him, giggling.

Inside the office it was Patrick as usual who found the mistake that was causing the other engineers the trouble. They kidded him about being too smart for them, but on his way out he heard two of them arranging to go rowing with their families in Central Park the next Sunday.

It was always like that. No matter how well they liked him on the job, friendship ended at quitting time. In the first years he had been too busy catching up to notice, but eventually he got the message that these men were never going to forget the difference in his background and theirs.

When he came out, Jack wasn't where he had left him. Mike said he was down the platform.

To his dismay, his son was sitting in the middle of a group of swarthy workmen who were sharing their lunch with him. One of them was playing a mouth organ and they were all laughing as Jack buried his face in a big sandwich stuffed with meatballs. The sauce was all over his chin and sailor suit.

Acting unconcerned, Patrick sauntered over and reminded his son that it was time to go home. The boy was still munching the sandwich as Pat led him away and the men waved goodbye. But as soon as they were on the stairway going down to the street, he pulled the greasy mess out of Jack's hand and, ignoring the howl of protest, threw it on a pile of trash.

On the way home, the boy was in a stew and wouldn't talk to him, until a sudden downpour caught them and they had to run for it. By the time they got to the door, they were both soaked through and laughing together.

The boy was shivering as he excitedly told Elizabeth about the trip to the work site. She made him take off his wet clothes and wrapped him in a blanket, scolding Patrick, then poured them some hot chocolate in the kitchen.

That night Jack developed a high fever and within twenty-four hours was dead of diphtheria.

In her first shock Elizabeth could only think it was the drenching that had brought it on. Patrick, still not believing it had happened, ranted about the "dirty wop food." But the doctor told them diphtheria needed at least two days to incubate, so both their ideas were wrong.

Patrick's joy in living disappeared overnight. He went about the house like a sleepwalker. Elizabeth hardly had time to mourn, she was so concerned over the change in her husband. He no longer touched her and he barely spoke to anyone. As much as she tried to interest him in life again, he returned home from work each day to sit dully waiting for dinner, not even looking at the newspaper or his engineering manuals. She wished he could find a way to express the grief bottled up in him, go out and get drunk even—anything to bring him back to life.

After a short period of wild sobbing over her dead brother, Alice recovered and threw herself into music lessons, announcing she was going to become a concert pianist. But the atmosphere in the house remained so gloomy that she spent most of her time after school at her grandfather's place over the printing shop or practicing piano at her music conservatory.

Not long after the funeral, Professor Cooper took a leave of absence from New York University to join a Quaker group out west, trying to do something to stop the illegal, senseless slaughter of the Indians. It was a painful decision to leave his only daughter and her family, but he was so depressed after the death of his wife—and then Jack—that he wanted a complete change. Before leaving, he turned his house over to a realtor to rent for him.

Patrick, who ordinarily would have scoffed at his father-in-law's idealistic scheme to save some Indians, was too submerged in his misery to take any notice. Only when the house next door was put up for rent did he shake himself out of his lethargy briefly and show some anxiety that Italians might move in—already they were spreading up along Bleecker Street from the area south of Washington Square. Elizabeth started to hope that his mutterings against them meant he was coming back to himself, but it was soon evident that not much had changed.

Patrick was relieved when a couple named Ashmore moved in next door—until he got a good look at them.

Fleming Ashmore was a painter just returned from several years in Paris. He was tall and lean with a Vandyke beard and sported an odd costume of smock and beret. The first weeks, having gotten permission from Professor Cooper, he busied himself cutting out the walls on the top floor and putting in a skylight—creating a studio, so he said, like the one he had in Paris.

His wife, Corinne, who set herself up to do Parisian dressmaking for the women in the neighborhood, turned out to be French. She had garish orange hair piled on her head, and her buxom shape was stuffed into overbright dresses with too many ruffles and bows. For a woman well past thirty she had a girlishly flirtatious laugh and manner that got on Patrick's nerves. He had heard what they said about French women, and when he saw her with a cigarette drooping from her lip one day as she was pinning up a dress on Elizabeth, he knew it was all true.

Desperately unhappy herself about her dead child and her grief-stricken husband, Elizabeth welcomed the arrival of the colorful pair next door. It had been months since Patrick had taken any interest in her and at least it was a distraction.

She didn't mind that so many of the old families were moving to better neighborhoods uptown. She liked the immigrants coming in with their European ways, and the trickle of artists like the Ashmores attracted by the low rents. Even the genteel shabbiness that was settling over the Village she found artistic, giving it the air of an old quarter.

One of the few things that gave her any respite at all during this lonely period was her friendship with Winifred Beaufort. Over the years since Winifred had moved away, they had seen each other less often, attributing this to the different directions their lives had taken. But the truth was that the rape had opened the eyes of both women to a problem they had been unwilling to face before. New York just wasn't an easy place for a colored person and a white person to be friends in.

When they used to meet at Elizabeth's house or in public, there were forever little unpleasantnesses both pretended not to see—unfriendly neighbors, whistles and remarks from men, rude treatment by waitresses, hansoms passing them by.

Winifred, though as flamboyant as ever after her recovery, became more cautious going about by herself. On the occasions they did get together, it was Elizabeth who usually went up to Winifred's rooms over the gambling club in the lively entertainment area behind Madison Square Garden. Of course, Patrick never knew anything about these visits—he would have been stupefied to hear that his wife sometimes alighted from a cab in front of a gambling hall where sports made indecent proposals as she passed by. But she found these little escapades a welcome antidote to her domestic life and enjoyed keeping them secret.

Once inside Winifred's upholstered boudoir, both women could forget that any color problem existed. Winifred regaled her with stories of life in the gambling casino, how she paid off the police, how she enlisted prostitutes into the club to keep the customers spending, and how afterward the girls took the johns out to hansom cabs where they tipped the driver to shut his eyes to what was going on in back.

Elizabeth, who until Jack's death had found monogamy blissful, was both fascinated and shocked by her friend's casual love life. She found it hard to believe Winifred's claim that Will Kennedy didn't mind her carrying on whenever the mood struck her. There had been a railroad magnate, once even a cabinet member, and always there were men she just liked the looks of.

Since Patrick's depression set in, Winifred's company meant more to her than it ever had and she found herself visiting her more often.

One afternoon in June, still dressed in mourning, she mounted the familiar carpeted steps on West Twenty-fourth Street. It had been seven months that she had been a wife in name only, and as they settled themselves on a pair of blue velvet sofas facing each other in the cozy little boudoir with its scents of talcum and rosewater, she was grateful for Winifred's diverting gossip. Diamond Jim Brady, it seemed, had been into the club that week and dropped a cool fifteen hundred dollars without batting an eye.

In her mid-thirties, Winifred was remarkably handsome. Uncorseted in an embroidered Japanese kimono, she was heavier than she used to be, which she did her best to camouflage by wearing what looked like all her jewelry, including a diamantine choker more usual in a ballroom than a bedroom. "You should have seen the women flocking around him," she said as she reached for a box of Turkish cigarettes, the wide sleeve of the kimono falling away from her plump brown arm.

Elizabeth accepted a cigarette, a thing she never dare do anywhere else.

Winifred scratched a phosphorous match across a claw leg of the sofa and they both lit up.

For Elizabeth, this was the world of the living again. She leaned back and crossed her legs under her black voile skirts, puffing smoke into the air. She was cheered simply by the idea of what her neighbors on Perry Street would think if they saw her, a proper Greenwich matron, with a cigarette between her lips in a boudoir above a notorious gambling establishment.

Everything about the intimate room was designed for its impact on men. Even the quilted yellow satin walls were chosen to set off Winifred's chocolate beauty.

Elizabeth asked if Diamond Jim Brady resembled his pictures in the newspapers.

Winifred took the cozy off the teapot and started pouring. "He's got a gut and a big red nose like Santa Claus. If he didn't have money, nobody would look at him. But you ought to feast your eyes on my *new* gentleman friend."

She laughed. "Not another new gentleman! What does this one do?"

"What doesn't he do!" Winifred stretched luxuriantly against the back of the sofa, her cigarette in the air. "He's a piano player. Plays rag like you never heard—and honey, he's darker than I am. I didn't think I'd ever meet a colored man again who could stand up against Rafer."

"I never heard about any Rafer." Elizabeth was enjoying herself. This was exactly what she had come for.

"Didn't I ever tell you about him?" Winifred kicked off her embroidered slippers with French heels and put her feet up on the cushions, giving a glimpse of green silk chemise under the kimono. "I was only thirteen. He was a field hand, the most beautiful man I ever saw. We had three months of it, until that white family took me off to Paris. It nearly broke my heart."

"Your whole life's been so exciting, Winnie."

Her friend caught the wan note in her voice. "I can make it sound good when I want to. Things no better for you, huh?"

She confessed that nothing had changed. "I'm just going to have to wait until Patrick wakes up, but"—she sighed heavily—"I'm beginning to doubt he ever will."

Winifred refilled her cup. "Honey, when are you going to do right by yourself like I been telling you? If one man don't do it for you, get another."

There she went again. That was her one solution for everything—a love affair. Elizabeth sat back to wait out the sermon.

"You wouldn't have any trouble. You've aged a lot better than I have. Sure, I get plenty of attention. But it's the way

I fix myself up. A complexion like yours doesn't come out of a jar, and that hair and figure aren't a bit changed from the first time we met."

She didn't react.

"Why is it," Winifred said, putting the back of her fist to her forehead in exasperation, "when you're trying to help somebody, you want to kill them if they don't listen?"

Elizabeth came over and sat beside her. "I'm sorry, Winnie. I know you're trying to help, but I really can't see another man as the solution."

"There are other possibilities," Winifred said brightly.

"A new hobby?"

"You might call it that."

"Thanks, but making birch-bark playing cards wouldn't take my mind off my troubles."

Winifred looked at her coolly, exhaling. "I'm not talking about that."

A momentary quiver passed over her. Winifred's world always went slightly beyond her imagination. That was what attracted her. "Well, what are you talking about?"

Winifred examined the high buff of her nails. "How about a woman?"

"What?"

"If you're not getting any romancing from your man, a woman might be just the thing—while you're waiting."

Elizabeth laughed uncontrollably at the utter absurdity.

Winifred stretched out her arms along the top of the divan like an orchid with trembling tendrils. "I find a woman is sometimes just right when men are getting me down."

Elizabeth stared. A musk was in the air that made it hard for her to sit still.

"We all need a change from time to time. Usually a man fills the bill, but once in a while it's a woman."

"Like those women at the Café Select?"

Winifred gave a raucous laugh. "You're all mixed up. Those weren't women. They were men."

"I've read about women with women of course, but this is the first time . . ." Her cigarette had gone out.

"Well, there's always a first time, isn't there?" Winifred struck a match, but instead of lighting Elizabeth's cigarette with it, she leaned forward and kissed her on the mouth.

She had been kissed by women all her life—friends pecking her quickly on the cheek—but that a woman could kiss another woman as passionately as a man . . . the scent of frangipani nearly made her swoon. She jumped up and started arranging her hair in front of a gilt-framed mirror with a garland of snowdrops incised around it. Her face was burning.

Winifred blew out the match and brushed ashes from her lap. "I guess I scared hell out of you, didn't I?" She laughed.

"Certainly not!" Elizabeth said, furious that her voice was shaking. "It will give me a lot to think about."

Winifred got up, retying the sash of her kimono, and went over to sit down at her vanity table. "Well, let me know sometime what the verdict is." She removed her choker, dropped it into a jewel box, and started creaming her throat, watching Elizabeth's confusion in the mirror.

Elizabeth couldn't keep herself from chattering on inanely. "I accept all behavior as natural, of course. It's the principle of my life. I can't stand puritans. I'm entirely open to the unconventional, but . . ."

". . . but you're a woman who needs a man?" Winifred started rubbing a rosy tint into her brown cheeks, getting ready for her evening stint at the club downstairs. "I agree with you completely, honey. That's what I been telling you for a long time."

All the way home in the hansom she fidgeted. Of course, Winifred would always be dear to her, but living in the demimonde as she did, she couldn't be expected to understand that if you really loved a man, you wanted to be faithful to him. It didn't have anything to do with Winnie, but it was just that with all her frustrations over the months she was ready to scream.

At home she tried to settle down with *Salomé* by Oscar Wilde, which she had been reading. She was up to the scene where Salomé was performing a lurid dance, holding the severed head of John the Baptist by the hair. When the dusky princess kissed the dead mouth, which might have amused her two hours before, now it made her uncomfortable, as if those frangipani lips were stifling her. She got herself a glass of sherry, but she was so agitated it didn't calm her.

At her wit's end, she slammed the book shut and hurried around to the printing shop. Watching Tom and Albert doing the technically exacting work of making their lithographs always soothed her. Although it was after five, Patrick wouldn't be home for two hours since he had deliberately taken to working late, and she had already prepared a cold supper for him. She didn't have to worry about Alice, who had taken to practicing the piano at her music school for hours every day.

In the months since her estrangement from Patrick, she and Tom had drawn closer together. They had long talks. They read each other letters they got from Veronica in England. He even encouraged her to participate in making the prints, where her artistic eye could be useful.

When she got to the shop, the two helpers had already left for the day. She went past the printing presses to the back where the engraving and lithography was done.

But Tom wasn't there. Albert Cogswell was working by himself, his gray hair falling around his bearded face as he lay a sheet of paper over a flat lithography stone on the worktable. When he told her that Tom was at the Brooklyn docks picking up a shipment of rice paper from Shanghai, she turned to go.

"Wait a minute, Lizzie," Albert said.

She winced at the nickname.

"I'm about to pull this proof. I want to see what you think of it."

The lithographs Albert and Tom had been turning out were selling regularly to art collectors. Currently they were working on a portfolio of prints entitled "The Legend of Greenwich Village," a Canarsie Indian tale. The rough sketches for it were tacked up on the wall. Elizabeth had helped them write the text for the story that was to be inserted in the folder.

Albert noted her flushed cheeks as she waited impatiently while he aligned the paper with the crossmarks on the corners of the stone. This had to be done exactly so that each successive color printed over it would fall in the right place.

He knew that he had never fit her conception of what an artist should be—he was too homegrown and folksy in his style of life. She would have preferred that he paint impressionist landscapes as they did in Paris. "Did I ever tell you how they invented this process?" he said as he ran the hand roller over the paper. "This fella sat down on a stone one day where a farmer had just painted his acreage markings, and when he stood up it was printed on the seat of his britches." He peeled off the wet print and held it up to her.

For no reason at all the lithograph struck her as ridiculous. What looked like a hairy hermit with a bare behind was in the act of mounting a naked Pocahontas sprawled on the ground. She broke into a peal of laughter that ended in a hiccough.

What was wrong with her, he wondered? The picture was exactly what he had intended, the earth god waking up after the sun goddess was shot out of the sky by an arrow. Elizabeth Endicott wasn't the kind of woman to be shocked by the subject, no matter how ladylike she acted.

"I'm sorry, Albert," she said, holding a handkerchief over her mouth to control herself. "I don't know what's wrong with me. I think you caught it exactly."

"No," he said, studying the background. "The Jersey shore is all wrong."

"Jersey shore?" This seemed even more hilarious. Tears were streaming from her eyes.

He started wiping the picture off the stone with a turpentine rag.

"No!" she cried. "You mustn't."

"Oh, it's not you. That one was just for practice," he said, cleaning his hands off and smiling. "You must have had a merry time of it today."

"It hasn't been that at all," she said, getting hold of herself, but she began to titter again at the thought of the hairy earth god.

"Well, something's got into you. Look here, I'm knocking off." He put on his jacket, pulling his gray locks out of the collar. "Can I give you a cup of coffee? Maybe that will calm you down."

"I feel a perfect fool," she said. But it struck her as funny all over again, the way he took the stairs two at a time ahead of her to open the door—and he was sixty-six years old!

In the loft overhead that he shared with Tom, he offered her a chair and went to get the coffeepot from the stove.

The place was primitively furnished with a table, two plain wooden bedsteads, Albert's watercolors tacked to the walls, and the iron stove that served both for heat and cooking. Every time she thought of the litho of the bare-bottomed hermit and Pocahontas she could barely hold back her giggles. When Albert poured a dollop of liquor from a medicine bottle into her coffee, saying that the Shinnecocks brewed it from wild cranberries, she screamed with laughter again.

Something was eating her. He couldn't be sure what it was but he had a good idea. "You sure caught the laughing bug," he said, sitting across from her on the stool with a glass of the red liquor in his hand. "Are things that hunky-dory?" His warm eyes were twinkling.

She burst into tears at once, covering her face with her handkerchief as she wept.

He waited until she was finished without taking his kindly eyes off her.

"I've never done that in my life before—at least not in public," she said at last, embarrassed. She wiped her eyes.

"There's nothing wrong with crying."

She had never talked openly with him. They had never even been alone together before, but she began to tell him how much Patrick was suffering over little Jack's death. "I'm so concerned. He's miserable and I don't know what to do."

"Seems to me with him treating you that way, you must be awful mad at him."

She nearly snapped out a denial, then she thought about it. Actually, she told him, though she hadn't admitted it to herself before, she *was* mad at Pat—mad as hell.

He said that the women he knew were more in touch with their feelings and acted more natural with their men. "They let everything out right off—if you get what I mean."

"But they're from a different background," she protested. "Women in my world have to act the way we do. Men wouldn't want us otherwise." She was filled with gratitude to him for making her see this.

"Not me," he said. "I've never gone after that kind of proper-acting woman. Too much bullshit to get through."

His using the obscenity so naturally in front of her, as if he were talking to another man, pleased her. She considered using it herself casually in her next gossip with Winifred—and reddened at the thought of what had happened that afternoon.

"But to be open with you, Lizzie," Albert was saying, "I've never believed that you were near as high-and-mighty as you act."

"Why, Albert! I've never been high-and-mighty. Women who act that way bore me out of my mind."

"Oh, yes you are. You walk around in your fancy duds talking that Vassar College accent, but you don't fool me. I know the woman you are underneath."

They both laughed.

This homespun philosopher, she thought, knew more about women than dear Tom ever did. He obviously had a lot more experience. Maybe she had been pouring out her troubles to the wrong person all this time. "You're making me feel so much better," she said, holding out her cup for more coffee.

"That's because you're real, like me. You've got too much marrow in your bones, Lizzie, for anything to keep you down for long." He chuckled and splashed some more cranberry liquor into her cup without even a gesture toward the coffeepot.

"Don't call me that awful name, please. I'm not one of your squaws."

He roared. "You're wearing a lot of flossy clothes instead of a blanket, but they can come off just as fast."

She turned scarlet. "Don't be vulgar."

"You'll go crazy without love, Elizabeth. You're a woman who needs it"—his voice sank to a growl—"and I love doing it."

She gave a faint laugh. "But you're Tom's friend . . . my father-in-law's . . . it's absurd."

"You think I can't cut the mustard just because I've got myself a belly now?" He raised a shaggy eyebrow.

"I didn't say that. . . ." Her voice was husky and she was having trouble breathing. The vigorous man sitting so close with his legs spread was someone who had never lived by any rules. He was an artist who had painted his pictures in the wild, lived with his women in the wild—women who were not bound by convention as she was. He had taken them in shacks, had run them down in the fields, in the woods. . . .

She got no further. He pulled her up by the hand, put his arm around her, and kissed her.

She walked home past the playground where, on the warm June evening, children were still squealing on the slides and swings, the hurdy-gurdy carousel, and the pony ride. Street sweepers were singing as they raked their twig brooms over the cobblestones.

She was inordinately pleased with herself. With all the talk these days about women's rights, it was high time she had an affair. She had been a dutiful wife long enough, sitting by while her husband moped his life away.

True, there had been that incident in Paris with Jean-Paul, but that was long before her marriage and didn't count. Albert was a dear for going along with her. He was a little rustic on the surface—she would never tolerate that "Lizzie," but she certainly understood how all those women had fallen for him. If it weren't for Patrick . . . who knows, she might even consider continuing it. It was so French, after all, not to have to be in love with your seducer.

Seducer. The word thrilled her.

She looked around at the passersby, the women with their children in the playground, most of them middle-class wives smug in their stereotyped "virtue." Wouldn't their eyes pop if they knew that half an hour before she had been lying with a strange man in a bachelor's studio!

Turning on to Perry Street, she realized with a guilty start that she had been humming all the way.

At the breakfast table next day, sitting across from Patrick, she glanced at herself in the wall mirror behind him to see if it showed, then looked at him to see if he had noticed anything. But as usual, she didn't exist for him. He sat eating his porridge and reading his newspaper as he had done for months.

Albert had pointed out that she was angry and had a right to be. Well, she was, she was furious. Where were Pat's instincts? How could he not sense the fulfilled womanhood radiating from her every pore this morning? If she had hoped the incident with Albert would provoke him into a reaction—anything—it had failed dismally. She was so annoyed that she was on the verge of announcing what had happened and damn the consequences, when he folded his newspaper and left the room.

He was unreachable in his self-pity and she was sick of it. If he thought she was going to sit around passively waiting for him to wake up, he had another guess coming. She was not going to deny herself any longer.

That afternoon she did her hair in a softer style, recklessly sprayed on her Worth perfume, and changed from her ordinary black mourning dress into a purple sheath under black lace. As she set off for the printshop, she knew that she had never looked better.

But everything had changed. The shop was a beehive of activity—the helpers noisily running off handbills on the presses, and in the back, Tom and Albert, two old men fussing over another litho in the series, the sun goddess soaring back into the sky, her raiments rekindled.

When she left the shop again, if she had had any idea that an affair with Albert would solve the problem, it was apparent to her how impossible it was.

She had to fill up her life somehow and decided to throw herself into social work, helping immigrant mothers at a settlement house on Barrow Street.

There was a ghastly infant mortality rate among the poor and she lectured them on proper infant diet and health care, advising the Irish mothers not to put whiskey into the baby bottles with the milk and the Italian mothers not to give them wine. She also advised them not to leave their babies locked up in their tenement rooms alone when they went out but to take turns looking after each other's children, and not to overswaddle them but to allow them freedom of movement.

As she had hoped, this outside activity helped. Although she was supposed to be the teacher, she was touched by the outpouring of maternal concern these women showed her, their solicitude about her life, asking her to tell about her husband and children.

When she said she only had one child, a daughter, they scolded her loudly. The Italian women wagged their fingers at her and said she was young and healthy. She ought to be having many more *bambini* for her husband.

"*Figlio,*" they shouted, "you must give your husband a *figlio*."

A teenage Irish mother who was nursing her baby, laughed and said that the word was "son" in American.

"Yes, yes," said the others, "you need a son!"

Moved by the concern of these simple women, she broke down in tears. Immediately they surged around her to comfort her. "Why is the pretty lady crying? She is so young, she have such a good life."

Unable to control herself, she sobbed out that her son had died. She was inundated with caresses and exclamations of sympathy.

"You must have a new son. That take care of everything."

She confessed that her husband didn't want her any more, he missed Jack so much.

"But it's the wife who has to do it," they said. "You're the strong one. Man thinks he's strong one when he's acting like a big shot to his friends, but he just a child to us. Don't be such a grand lady. Where does it get you?"

"I don't understand. What can I do?" she asked.

"It's easy, *signora*. Us women always on top, no matter what the men think. They dumb. They slaves to that little bird in their trousers. All we got to do is make it sing and they crawl after us on their bellies, don't forget it."

Up-to-date as she was, she felt herself blushing.

A small, fat dark-eyed woman pushed up to her. "Tonight

in bed, don't wait for him to come to you. Go to him. You make him feel good there where he likes it. Take his little bird in your hand, kiss it, make it a rooster again. The cock crows, your husband wake up and see you again. Make you a son—you see."

Impulsively, she put her arms around the little woman and pressed her cheek against hers. No one had ever talked to her so frankly or made so much sense.

All the women laughed and nodded at each other in approval. The Irish teenage mother was giggling so hysterically she had to put her baby down on the table to keep from dropping it.

In no time, Patrick was in love with her all over again. But she had already missed her period and knew she was pregnant by Albert. She was aghast at first, then in the euphoria pregnancy always brought her, it came to her that there was no reason not to pass the child off as Patrick's. When the time came, the child would be "premature," and he would love it in any case and never question its paternity.

She waited a few weeks before telling him. As she had expected he was supremely happy, convinced that another son was on the way.

FOURTEEN-YEAR-OLD ALICE BEGAN NEGLECTING HER PIANO TO hang around the studio of Fleming Ashmore and his Parisian wife next door. Elizabeth was amused that her snippy daughter, who had always been indifferent to boys, had developed her first crush on the debonair painter—and a married man at that! She would end up with a broken heart, no doubt—and no doubt recover just as fast, but it would be a good introduction to the world of art to which she herself had always been so attracted.

For his part, Ashmore, who painted in the style of Renoir, was charmed by Alice's pubescent sparkle and asked her if she would like to pose for him—with her mother as chaperone of course. Overjoyed, she rushed to beg for permission.

Elizabeth was gratified that Ashmore was taking an interest in her difficult child whose airs had always got on Patrick's nerves. When he sketched his conception of Alice in a summer dress holding a parasol in a French garden—still an adorable child but with just a hint of approaching womanhood—she looked at her daughter with new eyes. Evidently she didn't appear to the rest of the world the way she did at home.

When she told Patrick about it, he wasn't keen on the idea at all. He didn't like the looks of that fancy pants of a neighbor, he said, or that redheaded floozy of a wife of his, either.

"But he's a real artist, and it will be so good for Alice. She's been so pouty lately and this could be the best remedy. I know you don't think much of it, but do remember, it's all right for a girl to be interested in art."

"She ought to be out with her school chums," said Patrick. "Sittin up there with a middle-aged man, I don't like it."

"She won't be alone, I've told you that. I'll be there. I admire his work tremendously and it will be an experience for me too. Please, Pat."

Her pregnancy just beginning to show, his wife at thirty-eight had never looked so lovely to him and he was more passionately drawn to her than ever. With all his misgivings, he was too happy about his coming son to say no to anything she wanted.

Elizabeth was nearly as excited as Alice when they were in the studio and Ashmore began the portrait. She loved the smell of turpentine, and the stacks of canvases, and the couch with the worn oriental rug covering it, and the paint-spattered easel set up under the skylight. She had to admit that Alice was a perfect Renoir child with her lambent eyes and awkward grace as she posed on the platform in a light frock and parasol.

For a few weeks she sat with them every afternoon from three to five. But Ashmore was such a perfectionist he was forever wiping out in a moment what he had been working on for days. As her pregnancy developed it became harder for her to sit up, and she began to long for an afternoon nap. Winter was approaching and it was chilly in the studio, even with the potbellied stove. No amount of heat could warm up that barn of a place with the drafty skylight. Even in her mittens and shawl her bones still ached, and it seemed like the portrait would never get done.

Ashmore's wife, Corinne, who broke off her dressmaking to look in on them regularly, bringing tea and cookies, saw her discomfort and suggested, to her relief, that it wasn't necessary for her to come every afternoon. She herself would always be around and make sure her husband did not get so wrapped up in his work that he forgot to give Alice regular rest breaks.

Ashmore seduced Alice the first day Elizabeth was not there. It was done expertly, while his wife kept judiciously out of sight downstairs, presumably finishing up a rush order.

He put down his brush and went over to arrange his young model's dress, saying he was dissatisfied with the pose, tilting her chin, putting a hand lightly on her waist and another at her back to turn her gently into a "more paintable stance."

She was transported by the sensitive hands of this magnificent being she was infatuated with.

Later, as he lay next to her on the couch in the studio, his long johns unbuttoned and a hand resting on one of her ripening breasts, he asked her if he had made her happy.

"Oh, yes!" she sighed, overwhelmed. "But what about Corinne? I like her so much, I don't want to hurt her."

"Don't worry about that, cupcake. She knows I'm an artist." He ran a finger under her petticoat along her inner thigh.

"But what if she should catch us?" she asked, trembling from the exploration of his fingers.

"Corinne and I are above the bourgeois conventions," he whispered as he drew her to him again.

As soon as she was back in her pose with the parasol, Corinne came in with wine for them both, and seeing Alice blush, made a point of going over to kiss her tenderly, saying, "It's all right, dear child."

The next day Ashmore told her he no longer saw her as the Renoir child in a garden of innocence. If she would let him, he wanted to start the painting all over again, this time portraying her as "Diana Fleeing the Storm." He put her into a diaphanous shift, draping it to reveal one of her newly formed breasts as if the wind had blown it aside as she ran.

Gently taking her hand away from her breast, which she had covered in modesty, he assured her that when the painting was finished and her mother saw how beautiful his new conception was, she would approve completely.

The painting progressed like a dream. He declared he had never had such an inspiring model to work from and he felt renewed in his art. It was going to be his masterpiece.

The running pose was difficult to hold, even for a healthy young girl, and Ashmore often had to put down his palette to massage her limbs on the couch, which led inevitably to lovemaking.

Even Corinne was caught up in the excitement of Ashmore's artistic enterprise as she discreetly slipped in with little snacks of bread, wine, and cheese.

Alice often stayed to have supper with them after the posing session. Corinne liked the effect of this sweet girl on her temperamental husband. No matter how hard he had worked, he always revived when his foot touched that of his young model under the table.

On the day the painting was finished, the three of them went to celebrate at a little restaurant Fleming Ashmore knew on Washington Square. It was a frosty night in February as they set off, walking through the narrow Village streets until they came out at busy Sixth Avenue where new electric streetlights made everything like day.

Under the elevated a chestnut vendor in a shabby greatcoat left over from the Civil War was stamping his feet to keep warm. The pan of chestnuts roasting over the charcoal sent billows of pungent smoke toward them. Fleming held Alice's arm tightly against his side as they plunged into the clattering traffic, dodging hooves and wagons and avoiding the heaps of manure. She felt as though she was almost one of the grown-up ladies with their escorts in the passing hansom cabs.

When they were nearly across the avenue, a stallion pulling a wagonload of firewood was practically on top of them before the driver reined the beast up just in time. It reared with a powerful snorting of confusion, great gusts of steam coming from its nostrils as it tossed its mane, nearly upsetting the cart.

"Keep your fuckin eyes open, why don't ya, mister!" the driver shouted.

Alice fell back against Fleming who laughed and held her close.

As they walked on toward Washington Square, he told her that artists were moving into this neighborhood and not just those like himself back from abroad, but from all over America. "I first heard about Greenwich Village in Paris from an extraordinary woman who used to live right near here. Averbach her name was. She was my first patron. We were very good friends."

"Very, *very* good friends," Corinne interjected with a laugh.

He ignored her. "She told me that when she lived here years ago, this section below the square was called the French Quarter. That was before the Italians started moving in."

The restaurant he took them to was on the south side of the square and was called Le Chat Noir. The silhouette of a big black cat was painted on the door. It was a noisy little place with red-checkered tablecloths and candles stuck in wine bottles. After they had squeezed into a table, Corinne went off to the ladies' room and returned with her orange hair fluffed out and her lips painted orange to match. She lit a cigarette and passed one to her husband.

Alice was astonished at her transformation. She was like something out of a picture in a magazine of Parisian life in the artists' quarter. Other women were fixed up in the same extreme manner. The place had a raffish atmosphere totally unlike the restaurants she had been to with her parents. It resounded with talk and laughter as the patrons refilled their glasses from earthenware jugs of wine, and great steaming platters of spaghetti held high in the air by waiters were being delivered to the tables.

The owner, a fat woman with eyebrows plucked to a thin line and scarlet cupid's bow lips, stopped by to greet Fleming and Corinne. She kissed them soundly on both cheeks and they all chattered away in French.

"Enchanted, mademoiselle," she said when Alice was introduced. "She's charming, Ashmore."

"Isn't she? She's my Diana Fleeing the Storm." He looked at his model fondly, thrilling her to her toes.

When the owner had moved off to greet other customers, Fleming told Alice that she rented out rooms upstairs to artists and writers.

"She's in their beds as much as she's making them up," Corinne added with a dirty laugh.

A large man with a beard came up to their table. As he kissed Alice's hand, Fleming introduced him as a sculptor named Augustus Saint-Gaudens. In a loud voice that rode over the uproar around them, the sculptor invited them all to his studio to see a new bronze he was finishing, an Artemis ten feet high that had been commissioned for the top of the new Madison Square Garden.

Fleming said what a coincidence, he had just finished painting a Diana himself, and here she was. He took Alice's hand.

The sculptor turned and appraised her with a professional eye. "She's a little underage, isn't she, Ashmore?" he said with friendly malice and a wink at her.

When he was gone Fleming told her confidentially that Saint-Gavdeus had a certain talent but he had been getting so many public commissions, he was selling it down the river.

"And don't be fooled, cupcake, by that hand-kissing or his name. He came over on the boat from Dublin."

The waiter appeared and Corinne ordered a meal of snails, onion soup, and frog's legs—everything typically French. And when a bottle of champagne arrived and Ashmore popped the cork, Alice was floating on air.

The next day she arrived breathless at the studio on the stroke of three and found Fleming with a new canvas on the easel, sketching in a cornucopia of fruits, with a still life of a mandolin, persimmons, and late apples set up before him. He waved her out of his way with the brush. "Your painting is finished," he said. "I've got a commission now to do a mural for Carnegie Hall."

"Yes," she said, "but what about me?"

He looked at her, puzzled. "But I told you, the painting's done," he said and went back to his work.

She stood there for a moment. But when he paid no more attention to her, she turned and ran down the stairs.

Corinne, who was on her knees in the parlor pinning material to a dress form, called her in just before she got to the front door. With pins in her mouth and barely glancing at her in the doorway, she said, not unkindly, "It's not much fun now, I know, *chérie*, but you're young, you'll soon get over it. They all do." Then, seeing Alice's stricken face, she explained, "You were the painting to him, don't you see? He always makes love with his models. It makes the work so much better. He's that kind of man, *chérie*, you know it yourself." Realizing that the girl was too stunned to hear, she stuck the pins in a cushion, got up, and went over to take both her hands. "It may sound cruel now, but nothing is forever in life. You had a sweet moment, didn't you?"

To avoid the childish, uncomprehending eyes, she turned back to her work. "I don't care what anyone thinks, I approve of it. It keeps him young and makes him a better lover for me."

In the next few days Elizabeth, who was very pregnant, noticed that Alice had stopped going next door to pose and seemed in a worse sulk than usual. She asked if the painting was finished, but Alice was evasive.

When she went next door to see for herself, Fleming said he was still completing the background and thought it bad luck to let anyone see it until it was finished.

But Alice's sulk continued, which had her mother mystified.

Patrick irritated his wife with his gleeful I-told-you-so attitude. "Ya see, it's what I said all the time. Those artists you're so crazy about didn't do her a bit of good. Now admit it," he said, kissing the tip of her nose and patting her big belly.

Elizabeth had grown so large nothing fit her any more and a few days later, when Corinne was over measuring her for a new robe, the dressmaker said, "Poor little Alice, I hope she's feeling better by now. It's so hard when these things come to an end."

The innuendo made her think, and later, when her daughter came home, she asked her about it and Alice sobbed out the whole dreadful story.

The next morning Elizabeth waited until she saw Corinne go out to the market with her string bag, and then puffed her way up the three flights of stairs to Ashmore's studio. She passed right by the astonished artist at his easel without looking at him, and pulled the cloth off a large painting leaning against the wall.

It was even worse than she expected. Instead of the Renoir child in a garden she had been imagining all these months, her daughter was painted with a bare breast like a prostitute, and little else hidden by the gauzy shift. It was plain to see what had happened. She threatened him with a lawsuit if he didn't destroy it.

"Don't worry," he said. "It's much too precious to share with the world. I'm keeping it for my private collection."

She was breathing so hard from the effort of climbing the stairs as well as from pure rage, that he brought her over a chair, but she pushed it away. "You're not worthy to be called an artist."

"Don't be a hypocrite, Mrs. Endicott. I see through you. You play conventional on the surface, but you urge everyone around you to live dangerously so you can enjoy it through them."

She got her breath and yelled. "You had no right to hurt her!"

He turned back to his easel. "You know as well as I do that she wasn't hurt in the slightest. Sure, she's young, but she's tasted life and she's going to be the better for it." He picked up his palette and brush and started painting the dew on a perfect apple, as if dismissing her.

She faced the bitter truth that great art did not necessarily come out of noble souls. Even if she wanted to punish him, she knew he was immune from any moral consideration beyond the necessity of his painting. She turned to go.

As she got to the door, he said after her quietly, "I admire you, you know."

She half-turned and saw his cool artist eyes appraising her. "You're very unusual. It's not many women who are tough enough to take that."

That evening after dinner while Patrick massaged her back with witch hazel as he did every night now in her final months, she told him that she had seen the painting and was thoroughly disappointed. It looked nothing like Alice. "You were right," she said. "I shouldn't have encouraged her to do it. It was a waste of time."

"Ah, who gives a hoot about it, anyway? It's all over, so let's forget it." He pressed his thumbs into the flesh of her lower back where he knew she needed it most, and she groaned with bliss.

She persuaded him to let Alice spend a few weeks with a girlfriend on the Jersey shore, even though it meant interrupting the school year, using as an excuse that the child's moodiness was just too much for her to put up with in her condition.

The day after Alice left, while Patrick was at work, she made a call on the family lawyer. Since her father had given her power of attorney, she instructed the lawyer to notify the Ashmores that their lease was being terminated because the property was up for sale. They were to vacate the premises by the end of the month.

Crocuses were already coming up in March of '88, when New York was hit by a blizzard, preventing even the hired girl from coming in. The city was at a standstill, paralyzed by the worst snowstorm anyone could ever remember.

Patrick was terrified that night when Elizabeth went into labor a month early, though she did her best to calm him down knowing perfectly well it was on time and nothing was wrong.

There was a telephone in the house—Patrick had had it installed, he claimed, for "transit emergencies" and it was the first one on the block. But now with the biggest emergency of all, he couldn't get through to the midwife at St. Vincent's Hospital. Though he cranked away for central, it was no use—

the lines were already down. So without any real idea of how severe the storm had become, he plunged out into it and fought his way in the dark toward the hospital through mountainous drifts.

He was no sooner gone than the electric light went out. Between contractions, Elizabeth managed to get a lamp lit, and with the storm beating at the windows, gave birth by herself to a girl.

It was hours before Patrick made it home, nearly berserk having been away so long. But she was all right. She had completely dealt with the whole mess herself, and the baby, wrapped in one of his flannel shirts, was in her arms.

With the snow melting off him in pools, he got on his knees beside the bed, holding his wife's hand to his heart and sobbing. As she ran her fingers through his hair she saw that it had gone gray that very night.

Although he had wanted a son so badly, it was love at first sight between him and this tiny girl with wisps of reddish hair. They named her Polly.

And amid all the fuss after the birth of the baby, Elizabeth paid little attention to the Ashmores' moving out. But when Alice came back from New Jersey—her old self again, though with a wistful look in her formerly innocent eyes—Elizabeth thanked God for having had the power to get rid of them.

A year and a half later when Elizabeth was pregnant again, her father-in-law came by for supper with some startling news. Albert Cogswell had run into Fleming Ashmore, and Ashmore had invited him to a show he was having at the gallery in A. T. Stewart's on Broadway. The major work was the portrait he had done of Alice, entitled "Diana Fleeing the Storm." Albert had gone to see it, and, though he didn't care for that studio type of painting, thought it was the best thing Ashmore had ever done.

Elizabeth was appalled, but Alice, who hadn't mentioned Ashmore's name once since coming home, went on eating as though the news meant nothing to her.

Elizabeth begged Pat not to go see it. It wasn't worth all the fuss. But it griped him that Ashmore had put a picture of their daughter on public view without asking for his permission. He would not be put off from going no matter what she said, and the next day she accompanied him to the exhibition, hoping for the best.

They had no trouble finding the painting. It could not have been more prominently displayed. It was hanging on the wall opposite the gallery entrance and a crowd was around it. When Pat saw that it was Alice almost in the altogether, he roared out, "Why, that son of a bitch!"

As everyone turned to stare he broke away from Elizabeth and charged through the crowd determined to pull the picture down off the wall and smash the canvas and its elaborate gold-leaf frame to smithereens. The onlookers watched dumbstruck as guards stopped him just in time and hustled him off, with Elizabeth following along behind wretchedly, clutching his bowler hat which she had rescued from the floor.

Hauled before the immaculately suited director, Patrick wrenched himself free from the guards and demanded that the picture be removed at once.

The director reviled him icily for having dared to lay his hand on such a masterwork. Didn't he know it had already been purchased by the Smithsonian Institution? Emboldened by the presence of the guards, the director added that if he ever showed his face around there again, he'd have him thrown into jail.

When finally they were allowed to leave—Elizabeth doing her best to get Pat out the door—he kept shouting that he would cut Ashmore's balls off.

The next day the telephone rang. When Patrick heard Elizabeth exclaim indignantly into the mouthpiece, "What are you talking about!" he grabbed the receiver.

It was the gallery director again. He had communicated with Mr. Ashmore, he said, and the artist wanted Mr. Endicott to know that up to this point he had not revealed the identity of his celebrated Diana. But if Mr. Endicott were to make any more trouble, the newspapers would learn quickly enough who she was.

Patrick went straight to his lawyer who eventually made him see that, much as he had moral right on his side, his legal rights were less clear. Moreover, a court trial would certainly be more humiliating for the family than the painting's brief exposure at A. T. Stewart's, before being consigned to the obscurity of the Smithsonian. Unfortunate as the whole thing was, the elderly lawyer thought it best to drop the matter.

1891

ALICE WAS AT THE PIANO PLAYING ARIAS FROM *LA TRAVIATA*. It was an April morning. The front windows were thrown open and a breeze was riffling the pages of her music.

At seventeen she had long recovered from her adolescent anguish. A quiet girl, her coloring was more delicate than her mother's and she had light gray eyes like no one else in the family. She was as ethereal as a ballerina in her clinging pleated skirt and shirtwaist blouse with high collar that emphasized the graceful way she held her head aloft.

As she followed the score, she saw herself in the doomed heroine of the opera who also had lost her lover. Only the mistiest image remained to her of Ashmore himself, and if she had ever dreamed of anyone to replace him, it was more an opera prince in plumed hat and tunic than a figure like the tall, urbane artist.

From the street came the cries of children playing and the occasional clatter of a horse pulling a wagon. Embellishing the florid themes of the opera on the piano keys, she hardly heard the cry of a vegetable vendor outside, "Baby carrots, new peas, strawberries, and bright red cher-reez!"

When she began playing her favorite theme, Alfredo's love song to Violetta, to her surprise a glorious tenor voice floated in through the window singing the "A Quell' Amor." Without missing a note, she accompanied it to the end of the song where it soared through the final phrase with barely a wobble and managed to take the last note an octave higher, holding it long after the piano chords faded away.

She jumped up and ran to the window. But it was not a prince declaring his love for her. It was a street boy she saw by a vegetable wagon who called out in a coarse New York street accent, "Hey, miss, ya wanna buy some strawberries?"

For a second she was disappointed, but when he flashed her a smile with beautiful white teeth, she heard the pure Italian syllables of the song again and he was transformed.

He repeated his question, and she nodded shyly and went out to him. While he filled a horn of newspaper with strawberries from a basket, she asked him where he was studying singing.

He furrowed his young brow. "Me study? Who needs to study? I'm Italian. We're the people of Verdi and Bellini."

His look was so intense she dropped her eyes. Every bit of the wagon was crudely but brightly painted over with all the fruits and vegetables of the four seasons. She asked him who had done that.

He told her he had painted it himself.

"But you're so talented!" she exclaimed.

"Why not? I'm from the people of Michelangelo and Leonardo."

They both laughed.

He handed her the crisply folded paper of strawberries, but when she reached into the pocket of her skirt she discovered she had no money with her. She blushed, saying she would go get some.

"Never mind," he said. "I'll be by this way tomorrow. You pay me then."

His name was Mario Alfano, and she invited him to come over and sing on his afternoon off while she accompanied him on the piano.

Elizabeth, who was up in the nursery with three-year-old Polly and her new baby son, Eugene, was taken aback when she heard the tenor voice reverberating through the house. Coming downstairs, she was even more surprised to see her ordinarily standoffish daughter playing the piano for the swarthy boy who sold produce to the neighborhood and who was singing at the top of his lungs.

After he left, Alice couldn't stop talking about how gifted he was and how she couldn't wait to see him again.

Although her mother agreed with her that he was beautiful and talented, she reminded her of how her father felt about Italians and thought it might be better not to bring him back to the house just yet.

The baby started to cry and Elizabeth went up to diaper him, leaving Alice looking after her, dismayed.

The long-awaited second son, Eugene, had arrived the year before. And with all the medical assistance in the world this time, the birth had been so difficult it nearly killed Elizabeth.

Despite Patrick's often-announced wish for a son, he did not take particular interest in Eugene, having already given his heart to little Polly, a pixy-faced child who did not resemble him in the slightest.

But for Elizabeth it was different. Eugene was the first baby she felt special about. Though she couldn't have explained it, it was as if he needed her more than any of her other children had, this child who had come when she was past forty.

Alice and Mario were quickly in love. He took her to a café in Little Italy where they ate spumoni and listened to singing waiters mangling their favorite arias. She took him to the Metropolitan Opera House where from the top balcony they heard *La Traviata* with Emma Calvé and Jean de Reszke.

"They weren't so bad, even if they weren't Italian," Mario conceded, entwining his fingers in hers as they walked out under the dazzling lights of the marquee and started down the avenue for the Village, too full of the music to take the trolley.

"The Italians are so marvelous," Alice said. "Why don't I have any exotic blood in my family?"

He reminded her that her father's side was Irish.

"Oh, that's not the same thing at all," she pouted. "It's so low-class."

"Boy, are you stuck up. You think Italians aren't low-class? Maybe I'm too low-class for you?"

She reassured him with a kiss on the cheek. Excited, he looked around before pulling her into the shadows of a store entrance where he hugged her tight against him, but she pushed away giggling and skipped off down the street with him in hot pursuit.

* * *

One day, after they had been to the San Gennaro street fair, celebrating the patron saint of the Italian neighborhood, he took her to his family's for dinner.

The Alfanos had long since moved from the room by the elevated into a tenement over on Carmine Street. Benno, Mario's father, who had been fired from his construction job on the el, was now in the vegetable business with his brother-in-law, and Mario worked for them. There were several more children and an old aunt living in the crowded railroad flat.

Alice sat in the midst of the noisy family and loved it. Two tables had been pushed together and were loaded with platters of Italian food and a big bottle of red wine. On one wall was a tapestry depicting the sunset over the Bay of Naples, and across from it bunches of blown-glass grapes hung on each side of a painted statue of the Virgin. Over the fireplace were framed oval photographs of the grandparents in Italy. The grandfather with a big walrus mustache and the grandmother in black with a cameo brooch were both staring into the camera glassy-eyed from the phosphorous flash.

The whole family made a fuss over Alice, refilling her wineglass and teasing her with sly allusions about her being Mario's girl. But the mother, carrying plates back and forth from the kitchen, watched her narrowly.

"Such beautiful hair she got," shouted the old, deaf aunt sitting next to her. "Her people from the North? Milano?"

Mario tried to correct her. "No, aunty, her name's Endicott. En-di-cott."

The old lady was impervious. "What kind of name is that? She go to St. Anthony's or Our Lady of Pompeii?"

The younger children snickered. Mrs. Alfano set a dish of cornmeal with tomato sauce and cheese before the toothless old woman to shut her up.

"Is no problem," Mr. Alfano said. "Father Pellegrino give her instruction in no time. She be good Catholic girl for Mario."

Alice was about to object that she had no intention of converting and was not planning to marry anyone, when she caught Mario's velvety eyes on her from across the table. She got his message not to let them upset her, they would be alone soon, and never mind what they were saying now.

The next evening after dinner, she carefully introduced the subject of the San Gennaro street fair to her parents. It was like a carnival, she told them. The whole street was blocked off and there was music and dancing and food, and it was only a short walk away. It was amazing that none of them had ever been there before. She thought they would enjoy it too.

Elizabeth looked up from a letter she was writing to Veronica, took off her glasses, and tried to catch her eye.

Patrick muttered from behind his newspaper that he had to deal with them on the job and that was enough for him.

"But they're such warm people, papa, so spontaneous, so beautiful."

He lowered his paper and looked at her grumpily. "Ya don't work with them. They stink of garlic, and if ya try to tell them anything, they pull a knife on ya. They been here for years and don't even try to speak English right." He went back to his paper again.

"How can you say that?" she cried. "You talk as if they're low-class, but they're the people of Michelangelo and Verdi."

"I don't know about those billy goats, but the ones I know spread disease." Turning a page of the paper, it crinkled and he slapped it flat.

"Alice. . . ." Elizabeth warned.

But she was not going to stop. "Why don't you ever listen to me! You've never been interested in anything I like. At least try to understand. Do you have to be such a bigot?"

"Young lady, you shut your mouth!" said Elizabeth sharply.

Her mother had never spoken to her that way before. She was mortified and ran from the room.

Elizabeth sighed, put down her pen and letter folder, and, saying she would be right back, went up after her. On the second floor landing, before going on up to Alice's room, she cocked her ear at the half-open nursery door to make sure the baby hadn't been awakened. Eugene was so sensitive to noise since he was weaned.

She found her daughter lying across the bed with her head in her arms. Shutting the door behind her, Elizabeth said, "I'm sorry I spoke that way, but why in heaven's name did you have to bring that up? You know how he feels."

Alice turned to her with wet eyes. "But why is he so stubborn? His mother was an immigrant too, wasn't she?"

Elizabeth pointed out that she had not always spoken so well of her Irish relatives.

"It's not the same thing at all. Mario's family is different—they have such a rich culture. I can't wait for you to meet them and see how they live."

"I'm sure they do, and I want to meet them," she said, turning to go. "But there's plenty of time."

"You don't understand," Alice said quietly. "I want to marry him."

Elizabeth took her hand off the door and came back to sit down on the bed, thinking hard. She had been expecting it, but not so soon. "That will be difficult, dear. I'm afraid your father would never agree to it."

Alice looked at her, bewildered. "Not you too, mama. . . ."

"Of course not." She pressed Alice's hand. "He's a lovely boy, and I'm for you all the way."

"I knew you would be." Her daughter gave her a hug, then looked grave. "But how am I going to bring papa around? He won't give him a chance."

Elizabeth decided quickly. "If you love each other, there's no reason you should wait for that. I know your father. He'll only agree to it when he has no choice."

"You mean we should go ahead and plan the wedding, and you'll get him there?"

"No," she said. "I mean you'll have to elope."

Alice didn't understand. How could she get married without her parents? Who would make the wedding?

"The Alfanos will have to, I suppose. I don't think we have any choice in this case."

Alice thought for a moment. "No, I suppose not." Then she looked up wistfully. "But at least you'll be there."

Elizabeth gazed fondly at her firstborn and stroked her hair. "Darling, it will break my heart, but I couldn't come without Patrick. I'll work on him though, and once you're married, I promise you it will be all right."

As she started down the stairs, she was vaguely uneasy that she might have been precipitous, but the more she thought about it, the more confident she felt that she had done the right thing, telling her to go ahead with the wedding without them. And what's more, for Patrick the marriage could be a blessing in disguise. Once he accepted it, he would have overcome the irrational prejudice against the Italians he had harbored ever since Jack's death.

Alice began taking instruction in the afternoon at Our Lady of Pompeii. The wedding date was set and the banns were posted.

One afternoon when Mario picked her up at the church, they

walked to Hudson Square Park and sat in a secluded corner in the cool green shadows of old chestnut trees. They were out of sight of the boating pond and the busy promenade where ladies with parasols pushed spindly perambulators past benches full of immigrant mothers in shawls with children playing around them.

Mario was steaming because his cousin had gotten into trouble the night before. He and his friends had fought off an Irish gang who had come over to Carmine Street to break windows. The cops had picked his cousin up and his aunt had to go to the precinct house to get him out.

"Them cops talked fresh to my aunt," he said bitterly. "They hate us. They act like we don't have no right to live here too. Who the hell they think they are? No music, no art—they live like animals."

She tried to calm him down. She said that not all the Irish were like that. Her father was half-Irish after all, and she had Irish relatives. She didn't know them very well but they were respectable people.

He grinned and, saying he was sorry, kissed her hand. He could hardly wait for the wedding to show her how much he loved her.

She scuffed the toe of her kid boot in the gravel. "We're not children any more, Mario. We're going to be married, aren't we? Why should we wait?" She laid a hand tentatively on his thigh.

His brow furrowed and he looked severe. "Don't talk like that. We're not man and wife in the eyes of God until the sacrament."

She withdrew her hand at once. "I didn't mean that, you naughty boy."

He looked at her curiously. "What did you mean then?"

"This," she said, and without bothering to look around to see if anyone was watching, she put her arms around him and gave him a long kiss, and as his tongue slipped into her mouth, she took his hand and moved it over one of her breasts.

On the day she was received into the church, they were married in a side chapel of Our Lady of Pompeii, attended by the Alfano family and a single representative of the Endicotts, the bride's grandfather, Tom. And when the happy, noisy party got back from the church, there was a blue banner over the door of the railroad flat across the hall that was to be the newlyweds' home, with the words in gold "Buona Fortuna."

Tom brought Elizabeth news of the wedding, although his old legs were not up to climbing the five flights to the Alfanos' for the celebration afterward. But a couple of days later while Patrick was away at work, Alice visited her and told her all about it. She was ecstatically happy, she said, and longing for her parents to come see her new home.

Elizabeth waited for Patrick to relent, but days passed and her obdurate husband showed not a sign of dropping his ridiculous pride and accepting the marriage as a fact.

One night when she came back downstairs after putting the babies to bed to find him blithely whistling away as he glued together some broken toy of Polly's as if his older daughter didn't exist, she had had enough. Instead of delicately pussyfooting around the subject, she brought the whole thing out into the open. After two weeks he had no excuse any more not to give his blessing to his own daughter and her new husband, she said.

Instantly, he scowled. "I'm tellin ya for the last time, Elizabeth, I'm not goin to see her and I don't want her settin foot in this house."

She was seething. She had taken his feelings into account and had even missed her daughter's wedding. She was sick of being reasonable. "What you're doing is vile. She's your daughter!"

"What kind of daughter, I'd like to know? She was always ashamed of me. And now look what she's done, disgraced us all by marryin into wops, no better than niggers."

"Shut your filthy mouth! They're as good as you are!"

"Oh, are they? Now you listen to me." He caught her arm by the sleeve and wrenched her up close so that drops of saliva spewed into her face. "I want ya to swear to me that ya won't go there."

He had never laid hands on her before. "I'll cut my tongue out first," she said. Breaking free, her arm flung out, slamming him across the chest. She staggered back against the side table, causing a Dresden figurine to shatter to the floor. "I hate you," she shrieked.

His face drained of color. He stood there with his arms held stiffly, as if her words had turned him to stone. Starting to gasp for air, he groped around for something to hang on to.

For a moment she didn't understand. Then she saw that something was terribly wrong and went to him. She got his arm around her neck and helped him to a chair. "Darling, be calm. I'll call a doctor. Just be quiet. Only a moment." Her cheek felt the cold beads of sweat on his brow.

"Swear to me," he gasped. "Swear ya won't go. . . ." His hand clung to hers like iron.

"Of course I swear," she said.

He had suffered a mild heart attack. The doctor explained that it was not so unusual, even for a man only in his mid-forties and in such good physical condition. There was no special cause for worry. It was merely a warning. He mustn't think he could go on forever swinging from the girders of the elevated and jumping across from track to track like a monkey.

He recovered quickly, but continued to act as if Alice didn't exist. While he got a kick out of baby Eugene, who was taking his first steps, it was three-year-old Polly who remained the apple of his eye. She was his girl as Alice had never been. He would bounce her on his knee while she screamed in ecstasy.

Unhappy as she was over the situation, Elizabeth didn't bring up Alice's name again. She kept her promise never to go to Carmine Street, though she didn't see any reason why she shouldn't meet her daughter on the outside.

Alice told her how happy she was with Mario, but as the weeks passed she started complaining that the reality of living in such close confines with his family was not so pleasant. All the Alfanos ran in and out of their little flat whenever they felt like it, and Mario didn't see anything wrong with it—he thought that was the way it was supposed to be.

Elizabeth was sympathetic and told her about her own experience when she first got married, with Tom and Veronica in the house and her parents right next door and never a moment of privacy.

If she had her piano, Alice said, it would be more bearable. But in any case there was no time for music because her mother-in-law expected her to spend most of the day with her, learning how to become a good Italian wife. It was as if Mrs. Alfano was a drill sergeant who saw it as her duty to her son to train this ignoramus of a daughter-in-law, not only in the kitchen but haggling in the markets too—besides going to Mass every day with the other women. At such close range, the world of the Alfanos didn't seem so colorful to her any more, with all of them talking at the top of their voices.

Elizabeth said lamely that it was sure to work out eventually. The important thing was that she and Mario had each other, even if things were a bit difficult just now. But Alice's face showed that these optimistic words didn't mean much, and though Elizabeth wanted to offer something more practical, she didn't have any ideas.

It wasn't until her daughter told her she was pregnant that she saw the way to help.

Her father had settled permanently in California and his house next door was still being rented—at present an elderly couple was living there. But why shouldn't Mario and Alice take it over? That would solve everything—a better street, a backyard, plenty of room for a growing family, and blocks away from the Alfanos.

Alice loved the idea, but reminded her bleakly about Pat's opposition.

"But don't you see, your baby is the answer to that!" said Elizabeth, unwilling to admit any obstacle. "Your father can't resist babies."

"Oh, mama, do you really think so?" she said with the same trusting look that had once made her so vulnerably appealing to Ashmore.

But as the months passed, Alice grew more hopeless. She had entered marriage anticipating her life with Mario would be carefree and full of music, not this reality of being heavy with child in a five-flight walk-up next door to a domineering mother-in-law. Elizabeth remained helpless in the face of her daughter's unhappiness and waited impatiently for the baby to be born so that Alice could move with Mario into the Coopers' house where everything would be all right again.

She asked her son-in-law to send for her as soon as Alice went into labor. But in the spring, when Alice began a difficult delivery in the Carmine Street flat, Mario was so distraught he forgot all about letting her know. Mrs. Alfano did not bother, because she considered Elizabeth to be an unnatural mother for not having put on—or even attended—her own daughter's wedding. But when it was clear that Alice's life was in danger and the priest had been sent for, she told her husband Benno to go telephone her.

Fright made Benno's usually broken English almost incomprehensible over the wire, but Elizabeth understood.

She didn't feel any obligation to keep her word to Patrick in such an emergency. Trying her best to keep the panic out of her voice, she begged him to go with her. He turned pale, but shook his head without a word, nor did he try to stop her as she hurried out.

By the time she came into the humid little bedroom with its single window facing the wall of the next-door tenement, the midwife had been working all day. The woman's sleeves were rolled up to the elbow and she kept pushing her hair back from her forehead. In a flood of Italian and graphic gestures she made Elizabeth understand that Alice was built too narrow, and after so many hours of labor was worn out and not trying any more.

Elizabeth bent over her semiconscious daughter and, laying a hand on her cheek, said, "I'm here, darling. Try again."

Alice opened her eyes and saw her mother. As another contraction came over her, she started to scream.

Elizabeth shoved a towel between her teeth. "Bite on this," she said, and as the contraction got more severe, she ordered, "Push from underneath. Push into it. Push!"

In a gush of blood and fluid, a tiny dark-haired baby slipped into her hands.

It was a boy, and as it started squalling, Alice faded away before her mother's eyes.

Mario, who had been waiting just outside, rushed in and threw himself across his young wife's bloated and discolored body in a fit of loud sobbing, as the priest intoned the final blessing and slipped a rosary into her hand.

Elizabeth handed the infant to a broken and lamenting Mrs. Alfano, wiped her arms on her petticoat, and quietly left.

She walked down the dark stairs of the tenement that reeked of cooking and came out into a bright, noisy street with kids yelling at stickball, pushcart peddlers shouting their wares, women screaming from window to window where lines of laundry crisscrossed the street. Only a few people took any notice of the American woman with the drained, expressionless face walking away.

Two days later a funeral Mass was held at Our Lady of Pompeii. A casket covered with flowers was set up in front of the altar on black velvet. The cavernous church was nearly empty except for a scattering of old women mumbling the responses and the loudly mourning Alfano family in the front pews.

In the back, Elizabeth sat with Tom. The old man wept quietly for his beloved granddaughter, but Elizabeth was dry-eyed. Her grief was masked by self-loathing. Some words Fleming Ashmore had once said were torturing her, that she was the kind of person who pushed others to take chances while taking none herself. It was true. Her daughter had had real qualms about marrying against her father's wishes and she was the one who had made her do it, dividing father and daughter. Now Alice, her child, lay in her wedding dress inside that pink-satin-lined box, her eyes closed forever, her face a painted mask. How could she, a supposedly mature woman, have ever thought that she knew better than anyone else what they should do with their lives. She didn't know anything.

My daughter, my daughter.

It was the choir that brought the first tears to her eyes, the high sweet innocence of the boys' voices. With the tinkle of the sanctus bell and the censer sending out clouds of incense, Elizabeth wept freely as the priest intoned the Latin Mass, more awesome because she could not understand. This alien rite taking place before a gilt and jewel-encrusted altar bespoke to her of ages of women accepting their losses as the will of God.

With a veil drawn over her face, she and Tom followed the funeral procession in a hansom cab a short distance behind the rented carriages of the Alfanos and the hearse, ornate as an ebony jewel box and pulled by horses in funerary trappings. The procession went across the city to the East River and over the bridge to Long Island, where beyond the tree-shaded streets and modest frame houses lay St. Mary's graveyard.

There, amid a jumble of statuary and baroque mausoleums, they watched the group at the graveside, Tom leaning on her arm with a cane. They did not attempt to go up to Mario, whose sobs set his tiny newborn son wailing in his grandmother Alfano's arms. She was rocking the infant quiet with the sureness of the women of her race who knew how to raise men.

When the casket was finally lowered, Elizabeth closed her eyes and said a prayer. Alice's child was in loving hands. She didn't know how yet, but she would find a way to stay in her grandson's life and watch him grow, even if Pat never came around.

•

PATRICK REMAINED UNALTERABLY OPPOSED TO GOING TO SEE his grandson, Dominic, but Elizabeth did not keep from him her own regular visits.

If Pat showed his disapproval at home, it was no easier for her on Carmine Street where Mrs. Alfano treated her like an interloper. One day when Mario was there and saw how his mother was acting, the Alfanos had a fight over it in front of her. Even though it was in Italian, Elizabeth knew what it was about—she made out her name and the gist of it with no trouble. What kind of a mother was this anyway, Mrs. Alfano wanted to know, never having come to see her own daughter? Mario defended her, insisting she had a right to visit her grandchild.

Several weeks after Alice's death, Patrick was going over a report on the feasibility of a subway system for New York that he was devoting much of his time to these days, while Elizabeth was getting lunch ready downstairs. An organ grinder came down the street singing a Neopolitan air as he cranked out a rackety accompaniment.

She was humming along with the music in the kitchen when she heard Patrick yelling out the window so the whole block could hear, "Take that thing out of here, will ya? Don't ya understand English?"

It made her sick. He wasn't getting over it, he was getting worse. And there wasn't a thing she could do about it.

She called him down to lunch, but he didn't come. "Patrick!" she called again from the foot of the stairs.

Still nothing.

His heart. He was so robust, she was always forgetting. She ran upstairs.

He was in his chair, his head in his hands and crying.

She knelt and embraced him. "Won't you go with me to see the baby, dear? It would make everything all right."

Without taking his hands away from his face, his big frame still heaving, he shook his head again and again.

Patrick began going over to his sister's more frequently, sometimes taking Polly with him. He didn't feel awkward there any more—the grief he had gone through returned him to his own. It was a solace to be reminded of his boyhood when he and Sarah and Timothy had all lived together with their mother in Shamrock Alley, until the raid on the tavern ended everything for her—for all of them.

Sarah's rooms were homey, with sagging furniture and an old afghan of his mother's on the sofa where the horsehair was bursting out of the upholstery. He felt at home with the souvenirs of family outings to Coney Island, dusty palm fronds from Palm Sundays of other years, lace curtains and antimacassars that Sarah crocheted endlessly, and a rubber plant grown leggy reaching for the light above the elevated tracks out the window. Though he wouldn't have given up the electric light in his own house for anything, the gas lamps at the Yateses', if not the candles and kerosene lamps of his childhood, shed a glow of an earlier time.

Most of Sarah's children were grown and away. He seldom saw any of them when he was there except for the youngest, a boy named Dennis who was Polly's age, and the two teenagers who were in and out. Occasionally one of the married daughters stopped by with her own children.

He and Sarah were easy with each other again. It didn't matter what they talked about—or if they talked at all. She was to make no fuss over him, he told her each time he came, but just the same she was in and out of the kitchen—her lifelong habit—on her swollen legs, fixing him Irish coffee and bringing treats like the raisin pudding his mother used to make for them. She was younger than Elizabeth, although she looked much older. But it was just her shabby, unreproachful presence that comforted him.

It was a relief to get away from Perry Street where he was continually reminded of what had happened, and especially of the grandson he had never seen. He couldn't bring himself to talk to Elizabeth about it—he didn't know why, maybe out of some kind of Irish stubbornness—but kept the pain inside.

One evening as he was leaving with his brother-in-law to have a beer before going home to supper, they heard a commotion on the next block. Around the corner they found themselves in the middle of a noisy brawl in front of St. Aloysius's Church.

He saw immediately what was going on. Some Italian roughnecks had come over to beat up on the Irish. It was nasty. Yells splitting the air, the lot of them were bashing one another with fists, sticks, chains, anything they could get hold of, and stomping and kicking whoever fell. A rock went wild and hit a horse hitched to a delivery wagon by the curb. The beast lurched off at a gallop, bottles of seltzer tumbling from the wagon and smashing on the cobblestones behind.

"Jesus, Mary, and Joseph, there's my boy!" Bill cried, pointing at two young hooligans going at it. He and Patrick waded in to separate them.

"Scrap, will ya? And after ya promised your ma?" Bill said, dragging off his redheaded son who was cursing him and trying to get free.

Patrick hung on to the other boy, who was shouting that he was going to kill that son of a bitch. For a skinny kid, he was a tough little number.

It was only when a priest came out of the church that the melee broke up. The gang scattered in all directions, except for the two boys Bill and Patrick were holding on to.

"What are them Italians doin over here, Bill?" the priest called out, coming down the steps of the church.

"Damned if I know, Father, but don't worry, we got it under control," said Bill, getting a better grip on his son who was momentarily chastened by the cleric's appearance.

"Better get that Italian out of the neighborhood," the priest said to Patrick. "Our lads will make mincemeat out of him if they catch him." He turned and went back into the church.

Bill gave his son a cuff on the head and pushed him down the street, kicking him as they went.

Muttering away to himself, the Italian kid tucked in his torn shirt and dusted his trousers off with his cap as Patrick led him off. A group of Irish lads loafing under a lamppost opposite a candy store eyed them narrowly as they passed, and the boy stuck closer to Patrick. Without his gang around he wasn't so cocksure. But he had a filthy mouth on him just the same, cussing out the "dirty micks" coming over to his block to break the windows and turn over pushcarts. And just when his gang had begun to give them a taste of their own medicine, he whined, they were stopped. "But don't think, mister, we won't be back. We're goin to leave those bastards with their heads shoved up their fat asses."

Patrick was reminded of his young rascal of a brother, Timothy, who once hung around these same streets. This dark little punk didn't look anything like Timothy, but he was every bit as tough with the same infernal chip on his shoulder.

"What's the point of all that bellyachin, I'd like to know?" he said, softening a little. "Those lads have it no better than you."

"The hell they don't!" The kid took in his good clothes. "But you wouldn't know anything about it," he said with a sneer.

"Oh, wouldn't I now?" Patrick's eyes twinkled. "Are things that hard for ya then?"

The boy studied him for a moment in the light of a streetlamp as they waited for a wagon to pass. "Mister, you don't know the half of it." He told him about the day labor he did, unloading freight wagons in the wholesale market.

"You're a little small for that kind of work, seems to me."

That wasn't the problem, he said. There was no money in it. But he had a plan. He stopped and fished a wrinkled cigarette out of his shirt. Striking a match on the brick wall of a building, he lit it up and took a drag. "I'm going into the Black Hand."

"Are ya now? That's got a reputation for bein a bunch of crooks, don't it?"

"Lemme tell you something, mister," said the boy. "They take care of you when nobody else gives a damn. They got their eye on me. They're going to call me one of these days."

Patrick was about to ask what sort of jobs he thought he'd have to do for them, when the boy stopped in front of a tenement.

"Here's where I turn off. You didn't have to walk me all the way, you know." He flashed an unexpectedly winning smile, skipped up the steps, and was gone.

He was in Little Italy. He hadn't meant to come this far. At a table on the sidewalk in front of a restaurant, a man and woman sat eating spaghetti. They stared at him as he started back for home.

He had avoided the area for years but he had been so caught up in the lad's blarney, he hadn't paid any attention to where they were heading. Into the Black Hand he was going, was he? He certainly had a lot of spunk in him, the little devil.

The sign on the corner read Carmine Street. He caught his breath. How many times had Elizabeth begged him to come here . . . where his daughter had lived . . . the grandson he didn't know. . . .

He started to cross the street and go on, then changed his mind. With heart pounding, he turned and walked down Carmine Street to the end, before going home.

That night as they were getting ready for bed, he asked Elizabeth for the first time about their grandson Dominic.

She had been waiting for this for three years. Watching him in the mirror as she brushed out her hair, she told him that Mario had remarried a young widow with several children of her own who was good to Dominic. The little boy was talking a mile a minute now and had started asking her about grandpa when she took him out to the park for the afternoon to play with Polly and Eugene. She cautiously suggested he come with her one day. But he got into bed and turned away without saying anything.

The next evening when he came home from work, Polly and Eugene jumped up from the rug in the parlor where they had been playing blocks and ran to him calling "Papa!" He took them both in a bear hug and kissed them loudly. Then he saw the little boy with brown velvet eyes staring up at him from the middle of the rug.

He stooped over and picked him up and held him out in front of him. "And what might your name be, little man?"

"Dommie."

"Dommie is it? That's a fine name."

Elizabeth walked in from the hall just in time to see them.

After that, Mario often brought the child and left him for the day before going off to work at the family vegetable store. Sometimes Patrick walked the little boy back to Carmine Street, and even managed to exchange a few polite, if awkward, words with the Alfanos.

On a night in February Elizabeth was leafing through a copy of *The Yellow Book*, an arts magazine that Veronica had sent her from England. Her graying hair was upswept softly and she was wearing a high-necked, rose-colored dress in the long, slim style made fashionable by the illustrator, Charles Dana Gibson. Although it was cold out, it was stifling in the parlor. Besides the hot air pouring in from the central heating registers, Patrick had installed a gas log in the fireplace. She would have preferred a wood fire, but he was so happy with his "improvements," she couldn't say anything.

Beyond the portieres in the study, he was tinkering with wires and batteries, improvising a bell system to connect the children's room on the second floor with the kitchen. He had some idea that it would save her steps in calling them down to meals. Dominic was staying over for the night and the three children were playing upstairs until it was time for bed.

In the magazine on her lap, she studied a drawing by Aubrey Beardsley with its elegant peacock design. Then, as she toyed with a gold pin at her throat—a scarab that Mme. Averbach had once given Claude—she looked around critically at her own fashionably cluttered sitting room.

She had chosen the carved horsehair furniture herself, the velvet draperies festooning the windows, and the dark Flemish landscapes in their rococo frames. She had always been complimented on her displays of coral and old porcelain, as well as the Belgian rug with the millefleur pattern, rescued from her father's house next door when it was sold. She felt now there was something wrong with it all, though she couldn't put her finger on it exactly.

How glaring the light from the chandelier, which had been converted from gas, and the bare electric bulbs in ornamental brackets on the walls! Worst of all, the dust catchers around the ormolu clock on the mantelpiece—birchbark and pinecones and seashells from family vacations at the Jersey shore and in the Adirondacks!

She had always believed in the axiom "simplicity of design results from vacuity of thought." Well, the room couldn't be in better taste—she knew that. But after seeing these Beardsley drawings, it all looked a hodgepodge. And she was tired of it. It lacked a theme, a motif that would better express her own aesthetic sensibility, the way she felt now.

What if she were to sweep away the accumulation of twenty-five years and redecorate? But how?

She was about to ask Pat what he thought of the idea when the clock chimed eight and she lay aside the magazine to go up and put the children to bed.

In the back bedroom on the second floor where the children slept, Polly, who was eight, was initiating a new game. She, her brother Eugene, and Dommie were sitting in a circle on the floor with their pants pulled down as she had ordered.

Playing "doctor," she reached out a hand for Eugene's peepee and said, "What have we here? I'm afraid we're going to have to operate." With two fingers she scissored away at it.

She told six-year-old Eugene that it was his turn to be doctor and stick his finger in her poopoo to make it well.

He said he wouldn't.

She insisted.

He pummeled the floor with his hands and feet. "I don't want to!"

She turned to the already sniveling four-year-old Dominic. "You do it then, Dommie. You be doctor." She grabbed his hand, which he made into a fist, and tried to pull a finger loose.

"I don't wanna," he said, starting to bawl.

"Okay, you little crybaby, you asked for it." She grabbed

a floppy-armed Topsy doll. "I'm going to have to give you an enema and it won't be any fun."

Elizabeth came to the half-open door just as Polly pulled Dominic over her lap and started pressing the arm of the rag doll between the bare little cheeks of his bottom. It tickled and he started to giggle.

Smiling, Elizabeth stepped back out of sight so as not to make them self-conscious. Pretending to be just coming up the stairs, she called out that it was time to get ready for bed.

When she came downstairs again, Patrick told her that Tom had called on the telephone and was on his way over with some news. He had sounded very lively. They both agreed that it must be about the sale of the printshop.

Tom was nearly eighty and still lived in the loft over the shop, although Albert Cogswell had left a few months before to go stay with one of his children who ran a saloon in San Francisco. The printing business had long since fallen off to a trickle of old customers, and Patrick and Elizabeth had been trying to get Tom to sell out and move back in with them, but he had always refused, saying he would have nothing to do with himself if he gave up the business. As much as he enjoyed his grandchildren, he said he didn't want to be in the the way—and besides, he was used to taking care of himself.

But since Albert had left, he was feeling differently about it. It was harder than he thought to manage by himself. He had put the shop up for sale at last and agreed to come live with them when it was sold.

A few days before, he had gotten a couple of offers for it and had asked their adivce. One offer was from a real estate developer who wanted to demolish the building to put up a seven-story apartment house on the site. The other was from a young printer who had the ambition of publishing books on the side. The real estate developer was offering cash, while the printer could only afford to pay it out over a number of years.

When Tom had come over to discuss which offer he ought to accept, Elizabeth and Patrick had gotten into one of their classic wrangles.

Naturally, she had plumped right off for the young printer.

Pat said it was Tom's decision, not hers, then went on to argue that the shop had been erected in 1818 and ought to be torn down along with a lot of the other old eyesores in the neighborhood.

She was furious. The young publisher was just what Greenwich needed, in her view. She liked it that the Village was being passed by while the rest of the city was in a frenzy of rebuilding. Why not keep it just as it was with its old houses and quiet streets?

He had come back at her, dismissing this as sentimental hogwash. Money was the only consideration. That printer with his harebrained schemes sounded like a poor risk to him.

It had gone on like that, and by the time Tom left he had been so upset by their bickering, that he said he wasn't going to sell after all and he was damned if he was going to come back to live with them!

That had been a few days before, and as they waited for him now they promised each other that they were going to keep their opinions to themselves, no matter which offer he had decided to accept. The important thing was that he was retiring at last—long past the age when he should have—and moving back home where he belonged.

Tom came right in without ringing the bell, even forgetting to stamp the slush off his boots on the doormat. Though arthritic and getting feeble, he was chuckling away to himself as Patrick helped him off with his coat.

When he was settled in a chair by the fire with his cane beside him, Patrick assured him that they would be happy whichever offer he had accepted. Elizabeth sat at his feet on a Moroccan hassock and said they were thoroughly ashamed of themselves for the way they had acted.

"Well, before you two start spatting again," he said with twinkling eyes, "let me tell you what I came about. I've made up my mind I'm going to live with Veronica."

"Holy Mother!" said Patrick.

"In England?" said Elizabeth, repressing a smile.

They exchanged a look. The old man couldn't make it by himself over to New Jersey, much less across the Atlantic.

Tom chuckled. "I thought that would surprise you two." He had it all worked out, it seemed. Veronica was alone and he was alone. She had a nice little house by the seaside. She had been after him for years to come over, and now they would be able to take care of each other. He would be no trouble to anyone that way.

"But, Tom," said Elizabeth, taking his hand, "whoever said you'd be any trouble? You belong with us."

He ignored this. "I'll be off just as soon as I straighten out my papers. I've never seen the world and Veronica will show me London town. I should have made this trip years ago."

"What about selling the shop?" said Patrick.

"Oh, yes, I suppose I will have to do something about that, won't I?" He looked uncertain, as if he had forgotten all about it.

"What I think we need is some coffee," said Elizabeth brightly, jumping up.

But the old man shook his head and gripped his cane, preparing to get to his feet. "No time for that, I'm afraid. I've got to pack."

"Aw, don't go yet," said Patrick, moving his chair closer. "If it's London you're goin to, maybe you'll get yourself a limey wife."

She watched them as Pat went on gently humoring his father who said he was already thinking about a trip with Veronica to Constantinople—and maybe even Samarkand.

Poor dear, imagining he was going anywhere at all. But those place names! How thrilling it would be to travel again. She fingered the gold scarab at her throat, remembering London and Paris and Rome. She had hardly been farther than Saratoga since.

Her eyes dropped to the Moroccan hassock with its gold-stenciled design of minarets in the red leather. All at once she understood what was wrong with the room. It was the image of stodgy married life. It lacked any sort of mystery, romance, or adventure—all the things that that hassock stood for and she believed in.

She would redesign the whole room around it. She saw the windows filled with plants. It would be like an oasis—not just those ferns in their wicker planters, but hanging baskets of ivy and spiky palmettos in pots to filter the sunlight. And at night paisley drapes that would enclose the room like a seraglio, the eyes of peacock feathers gleaming in nacreous vases, a Turkish carpet with all the arabesques of the East, and fringed lampshades suspended from the ceiling, casting a rosy light over everything. Patrick would do all the rewiring. She couldn't wait to get started.

"I take it you're pleased about what I'm going to do, Elizabeth," said Tom, misinterpreting her smile.

She had forgotten all about him. Ashamed of herself, she

went over and kissed his cheek. "I think it's wonderful, Tom. Now you really must stay and let me make some coffee."

He considered. "Maybe I'll just do that. I can start my packing in the morning." He settled back in his chair, hardly able to keep his eyes open.

She was thoughtful as she went downstairs to make the coffee. Redecorating the parlor would have to wait. There was something more important to do first—the children had to be moved to the top floor so that a room could be made ready for a tired old man.

1900

TOM ENDICOTT WAS RESTING ON A LOUNGE CHAIR IN THE backyard. It was not cold but his granddaughter Polly had put a shawl around his shoulders, and when he asked for it, covered his legs with a robe. It was May, and the ailanthus trees were in bloom. He had a letter in his hand that Polly had already read to him. It was from Veronica. Tom had never gone to England after all. Elizabeth and Patrick had taken him in to live with them, and shortly afterward he had become an invalid.

Now, with his eyes closed, the thin sun warm on his brow, he was remembering the days when he first lived here on Perry Street with Fanny, and little Veronica and Claude played in this same yard.

The slamming of the front door roused him. The family, except for Polly, had been to a ground-breaking ceremony at the Battery for the subway that was about to be built. The start of the subway construction was a personal triumph for his son Patrick, and Tom couldn't have been prouder himself.

He heard Elizabeth telling the boys to set up a picnic table. That would be Eugene and his best friend, Toby, from down the block, along with his great-grandchild Dominic, a chubby boy of seven. He perked up as the boys charged out the back door and started to put together some sawhorses and boards for a table, the three of them chattering about the ships they had seen in the harbor and how much cake and ice cream they were going to eat.

Polly was lying on her bed writing in her notebook when her father came upstairs to change his clothes. She was wearing a pinafore and leggings, and the spectacles on her pug nose gave her freckled face an owlish look. She was twelve and, at the moment, dedicating her life to poetry.

Just when she was searching for the perfect rhyme to end her "Ode to Spring," her father walked right in without knocking, fumbling with his cuff links.

"How's my little monkey?" he said, smacking her on the bottom and sitting down beside her. He had pulled off his jacket, and his shirt, stretched across his big chest, was wet in the armpits and along the suspenders.

"Oh, papa, don't call me that," she said in despair, slipping her notebook under the pillow. "And I've told you to knock. I'm not a child any more." But she had to smile when she saw her helpless father holding out his starched cuffs for her to undo. She jumped to her knees and, giving him a kiss on the cheek, bent over the cuff links.

"I'm sorry ya had to miss all the fun, monkey," he said, beaming at his impish-looking daughter. "Was grandpa any trouble?"

With her tongue between her teeth in concentration, she slipped the mother-of-pearl cuff links out of his shirt cuffs. "I've been so busy I forgot all about him."

"Better not spend all your time writin that stuff. You'll never get a boy to pop the question."

She leaned against him as she began to work on his collar studs. "I don't care. I'm going to be a poet like Aunt Veronica."

"Your aunt would have chucked all that nonsense fast enough if any man had ever given her the time of day."

She wrinkled her nose. "That's not true. A lot of girls decide not to get married." Deep down she was convinced no one would ever want to marry her. She was too homely. She didn't take after her beautiful mother or handsome, black-Irish father. But like Trilby, the heroine of her favorite novel, one day she would discover a world of artists and writers where there would be a place for odd girls like her.

Down in the backyard the boys were squabbling as they cranked away at an ice cream freezer.

"Lemme do it too!" Dominic's voice whined.

"It's Toby's turn now," yelled Eugene.

"That's no fair." The smaller boy began to cry.

Patrick called down to them through the window, "Let Dommie take a turn, boys."

"He just did, pa," Eugene said, and started giggling at something his inseparable friend, Toby, was telling him.

Patrick took a long breath of the spring air, pungent with the aroma of the ailanthus blossoms that were shedding over everything. Polly's window overlooked all the backyards of the block, each with its sagging board fence. The foliage was sparse because the houses and trees blocked most of the sun, but here and there was the yellow explosion of a forsythia bush, and daffodils and tulips glinted among the scraggly patches of grass.

It was one of the best days of his life, the culmination of years spent fighting for the subway, working on commissions, submitting plans to recalcitrant legislators, getting preliminary bids from contractors.

He came down to the yard, slipping on an old striped flannel jacket over his shirt. "Ya should have been there, Tom," he said, interrupting his father, who was trying to tell the boys from his lounge chair how to get the top off the ice cream freezer.

"Oh, there you are, Patrick!" The old man waved his letter at him. "Where have you been all day? I've just heard from Veronica."

It always upset him to see how daft his father had become. At breakfast the old man could talk of nothing but the groundbreaking, and now it was as though he had never heard of it. And that damn letter—it had come a week ago, yet he went on making a fuss over it every day as if it had just arrived.

Patrick bent down to tuck the robe under the old man's feeble legs. "Veronica, is it? How is she this time?"

"What would you say if I told you I was thinking of making a trip over there to see her?"

Elizabeth, who had come out with a layer cake, looked away. She couldn't bear to listen to any more of that babbling. But it was not just her father-in-law. Truthfully, this change of life she was going through had made the whole day a nightmare. She didn't feel like putting up with anyone, not the way she felt.

While Tom rambled on about how he was going to treat

Veronica to a sight-seeing trip all around England, she took a rag and flicked the soot from the two iron filigree garden chairs drawn up to the table on one side and from the old wooden bench on the other. How dirty the city had become, and all this construction making it even dirtier and more unlivable. She told Eugene and Toby to stop squabbling over the ice cream and bring out two dining room chairs for her and Pat—and at once!

Patrick lined up seven plates in front of him as if dividing the cake were an engineering problem to be solved, and called out to Polly to come down. "It was a grand occasion, Tom," he said, deftly slicing the cake across. "The mayor was there, and the governor, and all the big railroad boys—the lot of them standing around actin like it was their idea all the time."

Polly had come down, slipped in at the bench beside Toby, and was looking up at her father adoringly with her bespectacled eyes.

Elizabeth had never seen her husband looking more glorious. At fifty-three he was still dashing, and more than ever today, basking in self-satisfaction. It was unfair, just when she was feeling so rotten, so unattractive, so old. The boys were making so much noise kicking each other under the table while Eugene served up the ice cream that she could hardly hear herself think.

"Twenty-five years ago when I started pushin for a subway, those bastards wouldn't have none of it." Patrick flourished his spatula like a sword against the infidel.

"Pat, the children want their cake," she snapped. She never wanted to hear another word about that subway again. The first thing that morning, instead of asking her how she felt, he had started right in about it. He hadn't shut up since. Not once had he complimented her on her hair, dressed in the fashion of a Roman matron. A heat flush came over her and she felt as if she were strapped to the track and suffocating in a subway tunnel. She gripped the edge of the table. Her corset was soaked through with sweat and he didn't care.

". . . but once we got those electric engines," Pat was saying, "they couldn't hold out against us." He plopped a piece of cake onto a plate and handed it to Dominic to take to his grandpa. "Of course, they're still not lettin me do it the way I want. We ought to tunnel down through the granite, but this surface diggin method will work, even if it makes a mess of the streets for a while."

"For heaven's sake, Tom doesn't want to hear about that," said Elizabeth.

"Oh, yes I do," said the old man, taking the plate from Dominic and putting an arm around the boy.

"Honestly," she said, holding a hand to her throbbing temple.

Patrick paused in mid-sentence to ask, "Is anything wrong, darlin?"

"Nothing at all." She forced herself to taste the ice cream Eugene had passed to her.

He missed the sarcasm and gave her a happy little grin. "The only thing I'm sorry about is we're goin to have to detour it around Greenwich. All these damn crooked little streets. Not one big avenue for us to dig under."

"I don't think we need a subway through here," Elizabeth said, reviving somewhat from the ice cream. "We like our neighborhood just the way it is."

"We're goin to have to put one through here one day. If they won't tunnel down the way I want them to, then we'll just have to cut an avenue right through. It would only mean tearin down a few old houses."

"Patrick, have you taken leave of your senses? That would mean destroying the heart of the Village!"

He slurped his ice cream and said that things had been going downhill around there for years, and it might be just the ticket to bring business back and get things moving again.

She wiped ice cream from Dominic's chin. "I'll tell you one thing, people would never stand for it. There'd be a revolution."

Polly, who had just put a second piece of cake on her plate, peered at her father through her spectacles. "Do you really think they might put an avenue through down here, papa? How spiffy!"

On the other side of her, Toby reached over and took a big bite of her cake while she was turned away, rolling his eyes at Eugene.

When she turned back and saw the small piece left on her plate, Eugene giggled out of control at what his hero had done.

"That will do, Eugene," Elizabeth said as her freckle-faced daughter looked indignant. For the first time, she was struck by how much Polly resembled Albert Cogswell. She had always had his coloring, but because of how close father and daughter were, Elizabeth seldom thought of her not being his blood child, the same as Eugene was. She was such an earnest little thing with her plans to be a painter one day, a poet the next. Since being infected with the Trilby craze, she had talked of nothing else but living a bohemian life in a garret. But how plain she was. Things were not going to be easy for her.

"Grandpa," said Dominic.

A plate clattered to the ground behind them.

Tom's head had fallen forward. For a moment they thought he had dropped off to sleep clutching his daughter's letter, with the ailanthus blossoms falling across him like snow.

Book II

1909

On a late winter afternoon when only a few patches of dirty snow remained in the gutters, Polly Endicott got off a double-decker motorbus at the corner of Fifth Avenue and Eighth Street with a portfolio under her arm. She was returning from her art school uptown. A block below, the sun glinted off the triumphal arch that put a classical finale to the sweep of Fifth Avenue.

She hurried down Eighth Street because she was meeting a friend at a teashop and was late. They were going to see *The Great Train Robbery* at the Bioscope.

Even if Polly had been pretty it would have been hard to tell, for she was wearing the utilitarian garb of young Village women who considered themselves emancipated—a severe coat and long skirt of dark oatmeal hopsacking, with brown stockings showing at the ankles. Her thick reddish hair was cut short under a wide-brimmed felt hat.

Many of the houses along the street had skylights, for their attic rooms had been turned into studios for artists. She liked this part of the Village better than where she lived on Perry Street over by the river. She'd been trying to talk her parents into taking off the high stoop of the family house and moving the front door down to street level as these houses had done. Although her father wasn't opposed, her mother had put her foot down. She said their house was beautiful just as it was, even if some people no longer appreciated its old-fashioned Dutch stoop.

Her mother had a lot of ideas about the Village and had tried to form a Village Preservation Society to keep the streets exactly as they were, but luckily nobody was listening. To Polly's mortification, she had even tried to get Eugene and her to go around and get signatures on petitions against a proposed avenue that would cut through the Village. Her father had said that, like all her mother's other causes, this one would fade away too. But much as they loved her, her ideas were sometimes difficult to put up with.

She crossed the street to turn down MacDougal, dodging between a horse-drawn delivery wagon and a motor taxi that blared its claxon at her. She passed an alley where the stables were being converted into more artist's studios. When she was a child, Greenwich Village had been an ordinary place, but during the past few years it had been changing. New people were moving here to pursue the arts—or pretend to—while living it up in the heart of the city that was too busy growing taller to interfere. The change had suited her entirely. If men were paying no attention to her, she was making a very satisfactory life for herself with her painting classes at the Art Students League and being caught up in the exciting ferment of ideas all around her.

On Washington Square, with its bare sycamore trees and black iron railings, several motorcars and a horse and carriage were parked in front of the elegant old brick houses. Blocking off the far side of the square were the gray, unaesthetic buildings of New York University. She preferred Judson Church on the south side with its golden Florentine bell tower, designed by Stanford White, who had shot his rival over a Ziegfeld girl several years before.

Below the square she plunged into the turmoil of the Italian slum where a lot of teashops and cafés had opened up, catering to the new people moving into the neighborhood. Everyone was walking in the street as casually as on the sidewalks. Some teenage boys on a stoop jeered at her because of her short hair and glasses. What oafs, she thought, to be so set against the revolutionary changes going on all around them! There were more emancipated women with bobbed hair like her every day.

She skipped down a short flight of steps into a teashop called

The Pirate's Den. It was a popular hangout because it was just below the Liberal Club, where all the most advanced people went to discuss the latest radical ideas. She had been there the night before to hear the anarchist Emma Goldman.

Her girlfriend Helene, who worked as a life model at the Art Students League, was waiting for her at a corner table. Polly was vexed to see that she had a man with her. Helene was always making plans for them to get together, but with her face and figure men never let her alone, much less letting her spend time with girlfriends.

Polly herself didn't have any such luck. She hated to have to sit with Helene and one of her pickups while they flirted. No matter how much she tried to hide it, she always felt left out.

In despair, she sometimes felt the only man in the world who could really like her was her own father. They had always adored each other. She wasn't so close any more to Eugene who was going to Columbia and had no time for anybody but his girlfriends. And Dominic they hardly saw since he had gone to work in the Alfano family restaurant.

She would have turned around and walked right out of the teashop if her friend hadn't seen her already and waved her over. Putting on a bright face, she sailed up to the table and, to hide her awkwardness, loudly scolded Helene for not coming with her to hear Emma Goldman the night before. The young man barely gave her a look, too busy entwining his fingers in Helene's curls. He had the kind of insipidly handsome face she abhorred. Helene was always telling her the details of her affairs, and she would hear all about the ecstasies of this one tomorrow.

Taking the young man's hand out of her hair, Helene wanted to know if Emma Goldman had mentioned Free Love. Polly shook her head and, leaning her portfolio against the leg of the table, imitated Goldman's Russian accent and incendiary style—she was good at mimicry. "Women, there is only one word on our banner." She paused for dramatic effect. "Revolution!"

Helene laughed, but the young man stared as if she were crazy.

"Much as I adore Emma," Polly said, sitting down and loathing him, "I was sorry she didn't come out in support of scientific sexuality."

Helene turned to her boyfriend with a giggle. "Polly is our high priestess of Free Love."

"Emma is the high priestess," Polly shot back at her. "The rest of us are only vestal virgins, even if you're trying to make it otherwise, Helene." She took a dim look at the insipid young man.

Helene clapped her hands and even the young man laughed.

She sat back, pleased with herself. She might not have a man, but she was at least clever enough to get everyone's attention when she wanted to by being a clown, if not by her art.

She had given up on poetry. When she was eighteen, she had had a booklet of her poems printed up herself, called *Quintessence*. Nothing had happened, and, except for a few copies given away, it was still stacked in her room. Though she had thrown herself into her painting since, she was beginning to suspect that enthusiasm and willpower were not enough to make up for lack of talent. But growing up in the Village, and with her handsome mother talking as if art were the only goal in life, there seemed nothing else to do—especially since men remained distressingly indifferent to her, except as a pal.

The waitress set an order of milk toast in front of Helene. Bland though it was, it was a favorite at the teashops. Helene began to feed the young man with a spoon, to their mutual absorption and Polly's disgust.

She swore to herself that if Helene subjected her to this once more, she would never go anywhere with her again. She looked around the teashop. She didn't know anybody there and hated them all. And those posters of avant-garde Paris art shows on the walls! She didn't see any point to the distorted figures with three eyes and two noses.

"Goldman has to push for revolution, she's too ugly for love." A skinny boy with long hair at the next table was talking to her.

"I beg your pardon?" she said, dismissing him.

He pulled his chair around to face her. "No one would ever want to make love to that battle-ax."

"Men adore her," she said snippily, pretending to be studying the menu card through her thick glasses. "If you had the soul of an artist, you'd see how beautiful she was."

He laughed cynically, and pulled his chair closer to her. "I am an artist, and an artist sees with his eyes. Let the bourgeoisie keep their little souls." His protuberant Adam's apple wobbled unpleasantly.

"Don't be horrid. Everyone has a soul," she said. He was wearing a heavy sweater and a ridiculous velveteen jacket with what looked like a red firecracker embroidered on the breast pocket.

"Okay, I got a soul if you say so," he said, grinning and waving his strong artistic hands, "so long as it doesn't get in the way while I'm painting."

He made her feel as if she was being looked at by a man for the first time. It was an odd sensation, like a bird being hypnotized by a snake.

Helene interrupted to ask what time the picture show was starting.

While she and Helene were discussing it, the young man leaned over and got into her portfolio and took out one of her paintings. It was a simple study of Central Park. She blushed scarlet and tried to snatch it away from him, but he held it out of reach.

"Wait a minute. It's not so bad, for Impressionism. . . ."

"Give it back please!"

". . . but the trouble is, it makes New York look like Paris."

"Give it back!"

"Impressionism is no good for skyscrapers and ash cans," he said flatly, slipping the canvas back into her portfolio. "It pretties things up too much."

She moved the portfolio where he couldn't get at it again. "But the purpose of art is to make things beautiful."

"Bunk! It's to show things the way they are."

She was flustered. She didn't agree at all with what he was saying. "What about the Old Masters? They didn't emphasize the seamy side of life."

"And there was no Industrial Revolution back then, either."

"Well, I don't want to paint factories."

"You don't understand very much," he said, resting a leg on a chair, revealing long underwear under the pants cuff. "You ought to see my work. It'll put you on the right track."

She asked him where it was on show.

He laughed and said the galleries were all as old-fashioned as she was, but his studio was just down the street. She could take a look at his work now if she wanted to. He stood up, waiting for her to come with him.

She hesitated.

He said matter-of-factly that it wouldn't take more than a few minutes.

She looked back at Helene who was snuggling with the insipid young man and appeared to have forgotten all about her.

She got up and followed him.

"Hey, what about the Bioscope?" Helene called after her.

"I'll be right back," she said. "Watch my portfolio."

The young man took her hand and led her up the steps, pulling her along after him through the crowd on the street.

She had been to artists' studios many times before with other students from the League. This studio turned out to be a shabby room over a machine shop with a screech of lathes audible from below through the splintery floor. It was cold, and he poked up the coal fire in the potbellied stove. The room didn't have much more than a cot and an easel, but it was not the meager furnishings that held her attention. The walls exploded with huge canvases of slaughterhouse scenes, lurid with slabs of raw meat and pools of blood. It was sickening.

With his foot up on the cot and a hand on his hip, he smiled and asked her what she thought.

"Well," she said, trying not to betray her nausea, "you must have read The Jungle." The muckraking novel about the Chicago stockyards had been discussed at the Liberal Club.

"I don't get my inspiration from books, I paint from life. That's what your work lacks—real life."

She looked around at the starkness of the room, the unmade bed, the violence on the walls. What was she doing here? If this was real life, it frightened her. "I think you're trying too hard to shock," she said, moving toward the door.

"Wait!" He skipped over to grab her hand and pull her back. "I want you to see these." He made her sit down beside him on the cot and pulled out some small canvases stacked underneath.

His arrogance was unpleasant. She really wanted to get out of there, but he was forcing her to look at more of his work. She didn't like it much, certainly not these grim scenes of street life under the elevated—a saloon with drunks, streetwalkers, a policewagon hauling away derelicts.

"You don't think these are shocking, do you?" he asked her teasing.

She was annoyed at his sitting so close, but she made herself concentrate on the canvases. His bold brushwork and harsh colors had a certain power. She didn't know what she thought of it. She was on the side of the masses as much as he was, but it looked to her like he was deliberately exploiting their misery in his work. She wished his knee were not against hers.

While she was holding out a painting of an all-night diner, he took her glasses off and kissed her. She made a little struggle to get up but he held her fast. For a moment she was in a panic, but as he kissed her again she told herself that this was life. She talked Free Love and liberation, but Helene was living it. It was time she gathered up her courage and exposed herself to it. She could always stop before he went further then she wanted him to.

His kisses got more insistent and his tongue went into her mouth. It was disgusting, but she closed her eyes and tried to let herself submit. Then she felt his hand beginning to unbutton her coat. "Don't do that," she said.

"But I want to."

She closed her eyes again, telling herself she was plenty old enough, far older than Helene had been. It was different than in her mother's generation. Girls today were giving themselves to men of their own free will. Indeed, to prove that they were advanced, they were supposed to. She thought of Emma Goldman.

When he uncovered her breasts she was embarrassed and tried to hide them. "They're so small," she said in a shaky voice.

"I like them," he whispered, leaning over to kiss them.

She tried not to feel what was happening down there. He was the first man who had shown any real interest in her, and she could always stop him when she wanted to.

But when he laid her on the bed and forced her legs apart, everything was suddenly wrong. His breath was harsh in her ear. She tried to get him off. He was a stranger who didn't care anything about her. It was not the way it was supposed to be. This was hideous, like those slaughterhouse carcasses spread-eagled from hooks staring with lidless eyes from the walls.

"Please don't!" she cried, and when he paid no attention, she screamed, "No!" But he didn't stop and her scream was lost in the noise of the machines from the floor below.

When it was over he raised himself and looked down at her

crying in the pillow. "Damn it! Why didn't you tell me you were a virgin?"

"I tried to. . . ."

"But you talked so big back there."

"What am I supposed to do?" she cried, furious and ashamed. "Everyone thinks because I was born in the Village I invented Free Love. Anyway, I didn't know it was going to be like this."

He sat on the edge of the cot, buttoning up. "What was wrong with it? Nobody's ever complained before. Maybe there's something wrong with you. You must be frigid." He leaned over and tried to wipe her tears with an end of the dirty sheet. "Gee, I wish you wouldn't cry, but you got me so hot, damn it, I couldn't stop."

She shoved him away and made him turn around while she limped over to the water tap and washed hastily, straightening her rumpled clothes.

He went on apologizing, sounding much younger than before. "I really am sorry. I couldn't help it, but you should have told me."

"You don't have to say that any more," she snapped, her face blotchy. "You got what you wanted, didn't you?" She yanked on her coat and walked painfully out, down the iron steps, past the open door of the machine shop where workmen looked up at her from behind their goggles, and onto the street.

When she got home the family was at dinner in the dining room below, and she was able to sneak up to her room without being heard. She was still in pain and prayed she wouldn't have to call the family doctor. He was so old-fashioned. It would be horrible.

She was in a panic and there was no one she could talk to about it. She would die before confessing to her perfect mother how she had bungled it. Eugene would only pity her. He was already an expert with girls—he and his friend Toby spent all their free time chasing after them. If only she could put her head against her father's chest and cry her eyes out.

She wondered if what that bastard painter had said was right. Something had to be the matter with her. All the girls she knew who bragged about their conquests had never reported anything like what she had gone through, not even the first time. From what they said, it was divine all the way, not painful and odious.

When she was calmer, she took down her Havelock Ellis from the shelf beside Freud and Oscar Wilde, and looked up the section on Disturbances of Female Sexuality. She was positive she had found what was wrong with her when she read an exact description of it, Vaginismus, defined as "painful penetration." The case study, a Miss L.B., had never been able to engage in satisfactory sexual congress with anyone without experiencing acute pain. She had gone the rounds of doctors and psychiatrists, but no cure had ever been found for her disorder.

Polly didn't call the doctor, and a few days after the bleeding and pain stopped she felt no different than before it had happened. She took a grim satisfaction in the fact that she was no longer a virgin, but she knew it was only a technicality, because even if by a miracle another man were ever to pay attention to her, sex would never work.

She had held to the principle that sexual fulfillment must be the basic requirement of any liberated woman's life, but to tell the truth she was relieved she would never have to go through the hideous act again.

As much as she wanted to push out of her mind the thought of the boy who had seduced her, she couldn't forget what he had said. It was as if he had turned a powerful searchlight on all her pretensions. He had revealed to her that she was a fraud. She had to face the fact that she was never going to be an artist—any more than she had been a poet. Her work at the League was a pale echo of Impressionism—the style of a genteel age, it now seemed to her, that had lost its energy. Her only talent was to follow her art teacher's instructions. She had no ideas of her own. It was clear that real art took a boldness and daring she lacked, the same as love did.

The word "frigid" might not be technically correct, but it was right nonetheless. "Love goddess" indeed! She was sick of the act she had been putting on with her friends, talking a fast line and implying she was as physically liberated as they were. Just because she had grown up in Greenwich Village, she had assumed she was supposed to be something she was not capable of nor destined for.

Her father, who had always ridiculed her attempts at art, understood her better than her perfect mother who had pushed it down her throat. But much as she needed him now, she didn't feel so free with him any more. His strength, which she had always seen as her haven against the world, repelled her. She couldn't say why.

In the days to come, her classes at the League became increasingly meaningless, and one day she tore up all her drawings and canvases. On the way home she threw them into a trash bin on Madison Square and never went back. Helene and her other girlfriends called to find out what was wrong, but she put them off with excuses about having to take care of her invalid mother. It was such a preposterous fib, her mother being the last person in the world who could ever be described as an invalid, that she fell on her bed after she hung up the receiver and had to stuff a pillow into her mouth to hold down her fit of giggling until, unaccountably, she dissolved into tears.

Having quit the League and her Village activities, she was in a quandary about what to do with herself, when one day she saw an article in her mother's *Atlantic Monthly* about young women who were taking jobs in business offices and even living on their own for the first time away from their families—"bachelor girls," they were called.

Although she would have scorned such a life before, now it seemed to her just the solution—a world where girls did not have to prove themselves in bed or in the art studio. She liked the idea of herself settled in her own midtown apartment and making her own money. That was a kind of liberation she had never thought of before. Going to an office and working at a typewriter didn't sound half bad. And however conventional the business world might be, she would be spared any further test of her sexuality. Nor would she be forced into ridiculous exhibitions of artistic creativity she had no talent for. Her ears burned as she remembered again the ridicule of her pallid little study of trees in Central Park. That bastard. Well, he had taught her a good lesson. She supposed she ought to be grateful to him.

Whatever the magazine article said, it was highly unusual for unmarried children, especially girls, to move away from their families. Her father, she knew, would be miserable when she moved out, he depended on her so, but she was sure she would be able to talk him around. He never refused her anything.

The next Monday she went to an employment agency on

Forty-second Street and, because of her high marks in mathematics in school, immediately got a job as a clerk in an insurance company on Lexington Avenue. They told her that once she started working she could attend free evening classes in typewriting, which would qualify her for one of their better-paid secretarial positions. Exhilarated by getting a job right off, she set out to find a place to live.

"YOUR FRIEND LIKES HIS MUSIC LOUD, DOESN'T HE? THAT IS, if you call that music." The rather serious young Barnard girl sitting beside Eugene Endicott on the couch raised exasperated eyes to the ceiling as the ragtime piano jangled from the Victrola horn.

"But it's Scott Joplin," Eugene said. "He plays the hottest piano since Paderewski."

The girl, whose name was Clare Marshall, looked at him impatiently. "Now whoever told you that?"

She could have been pretty, Eugene thought, if it weren't for the severity of her expression. "Well as a matter of fact," he shrugged good-naturedly, "Toby said so."

"I thought so." She gave him a condescending look. "I was pretty sure it was your friend's idea."

Across the living room, Toby Harris in a flashy striped blazer and bow tie was showing off, dancing with Clare's cousin Effie, a busty blonde who couldn't stop giggling at his antics. In contrast to Clare's tight braids pinned in a coil at the back of her head, Effie's plump little body was swathed in a dress of chiffon veils and her crown of golden curls was held with a sequined band across the forehead.

It was Toby who had found the girls. He had met Effie outside the biology lab on the Columbia campus. She wasn't a student like Clare. She was only in town for a few days from Cincinnati staying with her cousin at the Barnard dorm, which was across from the Columbia campus. The girls from Barnard often took classes at Columbia and Effie was waiting for Clare to come out of her biology lab. When Toby asked Effie for a date—he never wasted time—she said she'd love to but she'd have to bring her cousin along. After all, Effie was staying with her.

Toby had sized Clare up as a cold fish as soon as he met her—she was a sociology major, for God's sake—but the winsome little blonde from Cincinnati had lit a fire inside him and he asked Eugene, as his best buddy, to come along and take care of the bookworm.

Toby and Eugene had brought the girls down to the Village from Barnard to see a play by writer named O'Neill or O'Hara or something like that, that was being performed in a cellar on Cornelia Street. It had been Eugene's idea, he had heard it was scandalous. But it didn't turn out to be scandalous in the way they had hoped. It was full of heavy silences, and at the end of the first act when the family in the play discovered the mother was a morphine addict, Toby had stood up and pronounced it "putrid." Effie had giggled, but Clare, who was taking a course in abnormal psychology, wanted to stay and thought Toby a perfect boor. But he carried on until the audience yelled for them to leave so the play could continue.

It was only nine o'clock when they got out to the street and Clare wanted to go home and study, but Effie insisted they couldn't refuse Toby's invitation to go to his parents' apartment nearby to dance. He had all the latest Victrola records, and his parents were out for the evening, which made it even better. Eugene, who had hopes that he might loosen Clare up to stay once she had a little wine in her, finally got her to agree by promising to see them back to the dorm before curfew.

But as he sat with her on the couch watching Toby impudently tickling the little blond in the ribs while dancing—Toby always said the easiest way to weaken a girl's resistance was to get her laughing—Eugene was beginning to doubt that he was going to get anywhere with Clare at all.

Ordinarily he didn't mind going along as the partner for the obligatory girlfriend of the girl Toby was hot after, he usually enjoyed himself anyway. This one, though, didn't want to dance—and she had hardly taken a sip of her wine.

"Well, I find his taste in music not only low level," she was saying, "but his behavior in the theater was inexcusable. You may find it amusing, but to me it was simply juvenile."

Eugene was taken aback. No one ever said anything against Toby. Everyone liked him. In his first semester at Columbia his friend had already made the sculling crew, was a promising welterweight on the intercollegiate boxing team, and was being unofficially rushed by every fraternity on campus, though rushing wasn't supposed to begin until the start of the second term.

Effie was screaming with laughter as Toby, dancing so close his knee was going between her legs, quick-stepped her around a library table. Things always worked out like that for Toby, girls loved him from the start. Eugene wished he had that automatic effect on the opposite sex. He dropped his arm casually around the back of the couch and moved a little closer to Clare. Toby always said let them feel the heat of your body, it drives them wild. But Clare went right on talking.

". . . of course it doesn't take much to impress my cousin, she's so boy-crazy." The record ended, and she called out that they ought to be going because of the curfew.

But Effie only pooh-poohed her. "Don't be crazy, Clare. The party's just getting started."

"You betcha, honey," Toby said, winding up the Victrola.

"I'm sorry, it's too late," Clare said, starting to get up. "It'll take us an hour to get home."

Effie pouted. "Oh, dry up, Clare. You know perfectly well the girls leave a window open downstairs. You showed it to me yourself."

Toby slipped another record out of an album, put it on the Victrola, and dropped the needle into the groove. As the quavery strains of a tango began, he caught up the willing girl, and holding her tight with his cheek pressed against hers, swept her away in a long glide, before halting abruptly and taking off in reverse direction.

"Who does he think he is, the Sheik of Araby?" Clare said to Eugene and turned away from the dancers to look around impatiently at the expensive new varnished oak furniture.

Since the time Toby had lived around the corner from the Endicotts on Perry Street, his father had made a lot of money and his family had moved into a modern French flat on the west side of Washington Square. They were on the seventh floor of an elevator building with a living room three times the size of the Endicott's parlor, and with big windows that looked out over the treetops of the Square.

"What does his family do?" Clare asked, suggesting that the spanking-new grandeur must imply something illicit.

Eugene said that Toby's father was a lawyer for J.P. Morgan. "Toby's going to be a lawyer too. He's taking pre-law at Columbia."

"He looks more like Phys. Ed. to me." Toby was bending the giggling Effie almost to the floor in an exaggerated back bend over one arm while passing his other hand over his slicked down hair like an apache dancer in a moving picture show.

"Look here," Eugene said, thoroughly piqued at her continual sniping at his friend, "why are you so down on Toby?"

"Did I say I was down on him? I just don't like show-offs." She turned to Eugene. "I'm really surprised that you two are so chummy."

"Why shouldn't we be? We've known each other since we were kids."

"But you don't look like you have anything in common." She held a forefinger to her chin as she studied him. "It's obvious you're an introvert."

Eugene laughed. "I'm a what?"

"It's nothing bad. It only means you don't throw your wares in everybody's face. Personally, I prefer introverts."

"If you'd stop analyzing everything," Eugene said, feeling flattered, "maybe I could get you to dance."

She smiled for the first time. "That's my problem. People always say I have a tendency to be overintellectual. I really ought to enjoy myself more. But why do men expect a girl to stop using her mind when they go out?"

For a moment they looked at each other openly, when they became aware that the tango was over and the needle was turning around scratchily in the groove.

"Where are they?" Clare said, with the edge back in her voice.

Eugene looked around. The dancers had disappeared. He settled back with a grin. "I guess they went out for a walk." He took her hand, but she pulled it away.

"Listen!" She was on the edge of the couch again. "What's that?"

"What's what?" said Eugene, who heard perfectly well the sound of Effie's muffled giggles coming from another room.

Clare was on her feet, heading for it.

"Hey, come back here!" He ran after her. Damn Toby. Why did he have to get so carried away that he forgot to shut the door? As he caught up to Clare, she was standing speechless in the doorway of a bedroom.

It couldn't have been worse. On the bed Effie and Toby were a bouncing tangle of arms and legs.

Clare began to scream. The heap on the bed collapsed.

"Oh, for mercy's sake, stop that!" Effie cried, raising up on one elbow, not in the least embarrassed. But Clare had fallen apart and finally Effie had to get up to quiet her. Smoothing down her dress, she led her cousin toward their wraps in the foyer.

Toby stumbled out into the hall after them, holding up his pants. "Hey, aren't you coming back?" he called.

"I've got to get her home," Effie said disgustedly as she got her cousin into her coat.

"But what about us?"

Effie was pushing Clare out the door. "I'm sorry, Toby, what can I do? I guess you'll just have to come to Cincinnati."

"What about tomorrow?"

"I'm leaving in the morning," she said, and they were gone.

Still holding his pants, Toby yelled down the stairwell after them. "To hell with both of you, do you hear me?"

Eugene, who was thinking of the neighbors, maneuvered his outraged friend back into the apartment and shut the door.

Toby got another bottle of wine and started swigging it down."Boy, did she leave me hanging off a cliff. Did you ever see such a hot piece, Gene? I'd almost go to Cincinnati for that. If it wasn't for that fourteen-carat gold-plated virgin of a cousin, I'd have made it. I got to apologize for setting you up with her."

Eugene said he really thought he ought to go see them home.

"Forget 'em. They're not worth it." Toby finished the bottle and said he was still so hanker he had to go to the Turkish bath and sweat it off.

Eugene had never been to a Turkish bath before, and he was astonished to discover that Toby knew all about it. His friend was always astonishing him.

They spent an hour sitting in the steam on the wooden benches among other towel-wrapped figures who had been out on the town, drops of water falling on them from the tiles of the domed ceiling. When their names were called he followed Toby through the tiled and vaulted hall to the row of massage cubicles resounding with the slaps of masseurs pounding the flesh of their clients.

Then he was lying on his stomach on a marble table in a tiled cubicle next to Toby's, a thin partition between them, while a middle-aged Swede kneaded his muscles. Lulled by the steamy air, the echoing noises of clogs on tiles, the banging of pails, the continuous dribbling of water, his thoughts kept going back to Clare Marshall getting so hysterical. He had never seen a girl go completely to pieces like that—and just when they were starting to talk. It was a pity. She was the only girl he had ever met who had anything interesting to say.

What a crazy pal he had, not even closing the door, but Toby was so uncomplicated about everything. That's why girls liked him so much.

But with Eugene it wasn't so simple. He wasn't any good at meeting girls himself. It was Toby who got him dates and he depended on his friend's antics to keep things going. It had always been that way. It was Toby who got him into that pickle when he was fifteen and the girl's irate father had come to the house after dinner to demand that Mr. Endicott punish Eugene for trying to seduce his daughter.

As if it had been his fault! The girl had asked him in after their date, saying her parents were asleep upstairs. They had been petting and his hand was up her skirt when the lights went on and her father stood there in his bathrobe.

He had really expected to get it when his father ordered him into the study and closed the door. He hadn't denied anything when he was pressed, but he finally admitted, without looking up from the rug, that Toby had already lost his virginity—and besides, Toby had already had the girl. And he had taken the precaution, on Toby's advice, of bringing along a "French letter."

To his surprise his father had said, "Well, no harm was done," and Eugene looked up to see him grinning proudly. After his father made a transparent show of warning him to be more careful in the future, he had actually given him a cigar. They were a lot closer to each other than they had ever been before.

From the next cubicle he heard Toby's laugh as he kidded with his masseur. Toby was so easy with all kinds of people. Eugene wouldn't have been able to think of anything to say to the old Swede who was pounding the back of his thighs painfully.

His father might have been happier with a son like Toby. Eugene always felt uncomfortable when his father walked in on him and his mother having one of their long talks about books and things. But Gene had always been as bored as his mother was by his father's endless talk about elevated trains and subways. His father was just as bored when his mother had carried on about his winning the American Legion contest for a patriotic essay the year before. Ironically, his subject had been his father's rise to engineer from an immigrant background.

Toby was giving loud yelps on the other side of the wall as he was being pummeled. His own masseur's fingers were working into his calves and down to his feet.

After the pickle over the girl, it was Toby who had found the solution to the problem of his virginity. He arranged a date for him with a woman he knew who was being kept in the Village by her ex-boss from uptown. She was always free in the afternoon and told Toby she liked nothing better than inexperienced young men.

The masseur flipped him over on his back. To his shame, he had an erection. He shouldn't have been thinking of that woman. But the old Swede appeared not to notice anything—after all they were both men—and went on working on his scalp.

The girls put out for Toby most of the time, though Eugene usually failed to get his dates to come across—like tonight. But it didn't upset him all that much when that happened, not like it did Toby.

The masseur worked down his chest to his abdomen, an arm accidentally brushing against his erection, making him tremble. He kept his eyes shut, unable to resist the feeling that flooded him while the masseur worked over his stomach and thighs, his arm brushing against his erection with every stroke up and down. He wanted to tell him to stop, but the man didn't seem to notice what he was doing and it was too embarrassing to say anything. At that moment in the next cubicle he heard Toby give a joyful yelp that ended in a long groan. To his mortification, Eugene couldn't help himself—he came off.

But as if nothing at all had happened, the old Swede with a big soapy sponge washed him from head to toe on both sides and doused him with a bucket of warm water. Then he slapped his rump in a businesslike manner, saying, "That's it, buddy," and, helping him get up—he was still shaking—wrapped him in a sheet and showed him to a dormitory down the hall.

He and Toby lay on cots in the rest lounge, swathed like mummies.

"Boy, there's nothing like a massage to finish off with when the canaries have let you down, is there?" Toby, his eyes shut, hands crossed under his head like a pasha, was smiling.

Eugene was in a panic. "You mean," he said, trying to sound natural, "that always happens?"

"What?" Toby looked over. "Oh, that!" He grinned. "Sure, if they see you need it they help you out. Why not?"

But even if what Toby said was true, Eugene still felt funny about it and he was glad to put it out of his mind in the excitement of rush week that was about to start.

All through high school he and Toby had looked forward to joining a college fraternity together, but on the night they were invited to a smoker at Sigma Chi—the most prestigious fraternity on campus and the one Toby wanted most to pledge—Eugene felt suffocated by the over-heartiness of the fraternity men, and when Toby, who took to it like a duck to water, did his imitation of a woman wriggling out of her corset that everyone howled at, he felt unaccountably nauseated. Later, when they were taken with a group of other freshmen to a lounge upstairs and invited to pledge, Toby was the first to accept, but Eugene said he wanted to think it over.

He had avoided Toby's puzzled look, and on the way home when his friend slung an arm around his shoulders and asked him why the hell had he done that, he found an excuse to move away and look in a bookshop window. He mumbled something about his grades, knowing Toby knew as well as he did that he had a strong B average. Unlike Toby, he enjoyed his studies, even thrived on them.

Toby quickly said that didn't make any sense. If it was grades he was worried about, hadn't he heard the frat kept a file of term papers and even copies of exams?

His father was the reason, he improvised weakly. He didn't want to put him to the extra expense of the initiation fee and the cost of living in the frat house. Maybe he'd be able to join next year.

None of it made any sense. You didn't get rushed after the

first year and they both knew it, but Toby didn't say anything more about it, retreating into a hurt silence.

Eugene went home wondering if he was losing his mind.

EUGENE WAS SLUMPED IN HIS CHAIR IN THE LOW LIBRARY READing room, Milton's *Paradise Lost* open, unread, before him. It was early May and from the high, many-paned windows shafts of sunlight caught floating motes in the air. Around him students were preparing for end of term, consulting piles of research materials and writing papers at the long tables lit by hanging green-shaded electric bulbs as others picked up books at the check-out desk, bending over to whisper a few words to friends as they passed.

Lulled by the echoing hall, he was thinking of the semester since Toby went into the fraternity and their lives had gone in such different directions. He had got to the stage of marveling that he had followed his instincts not to join the frat, even though at the time he had not been at all sure he was doing the right thing.

Though he enjoyed his classes and a world of serious thinking was opening up to him—the history of the English novel, the dialectics of Hegel—after Toby moved into the frat house he had keenly felt the loss of his easygoing friend. It had been a surprise to discover how much he depended on Toby to fill up his life.

Going home every night had seemed so dismal in those early weeks of the semester. His sister Polly had moved out, and after years of squabbling about one issue or another, his parents were hardly talking to each other. His mother, who had always been his confidante and ally, was obsessed with her campaign to prevent Seventh Avenue from being extended through the Village, and his father was just as determined to get it slashed through so that his precious subway could be put in under it.

He and Toby had planned to see each other often, but either fraternity activities prevented Toby from showing up, or—as he explained on the phone—being a pledge meant he had to be at the beck and call of the brothers at all times of the day and night.

Actually they had only gotten together once, and after six weeks of not seeing each other, both had been self-conscious as they sat in the noisy student hangout just off campus at 115th Street and Broadway. Sipping their beers, they had tried to pretend that everything was the same. Toby covered the awkwardness by telling him all about his life in the marble-columned fraternity house overlooking the flats of Harlem—the hazing, the beer-guzzling smokers with girls sneaked into the rooms afterward. Toby's social life was so active—not to mention his sports practice—that he hadn't been able to give as much time to his studies as he ought to, but the fraternity was arranging for the tutoring he needed to keep up the required C average.

Eugene couldn't talk about his own life because he knew it was nothing Toby would be interested in—his discovery of philosophy and literature and the great minds of the past. Once he caught his friend looking around as if hoping for some distraction, and when they left the bar they promised to get together more often, but Eugene hadn't talked to him since.

Now, drowsing in the hum of the cavernous reading room, he slid down in his chair to rest his head against the back with his legs stretched out in front of him under the oak table.

To fill up some of the free time he no longer spent running around with Toby and Toby's girlfriends, he had gone to some meetings of the college literary society. Because of his growing interest in English Lit, he expected to have something in common with the society's members, but they turned out to be a bunch of affected snobs who made him feel stupid with their talk about things he had never heard of, like the Imagists and Futurism.

It was in the middle of March, when he had just walked out

on a literary meeting in disgust, that Toby had passed him with a couple of fraternity brothers. Toby was so busy talking away, he appeared not to see him, but a moment later as Eugene pushed through the glass doors of McManus Hall on his way to a philosophy class, he caught the reflection of Toby's group going around the corner and at that moment he saw his old friend turn and look back at him.

He remembered that look. Something about it had troubled him. Was Toby as satisfied with fraternity life as he made out? Maybe he missed hanging around with Eugene too. As long as they had known each other, they had never really talked seriously. Toby didn't like to be serious about anything. But he didn't have to be. He always had everything, or at least that's the way it seemed.

He wanted to ask if everything was all right, but it would sound crazy. Besides, he couldn't just go and ring the bell of the frat house.

His sister Polly had known Toby as long as he had and he wondered what she would think. He hadn't seen her much since she had moved uptown to take a job in an office. She was living in a boardinghouse for young working women in the east forties.

But when he telephoned her, the atmosphere had been all wrong for any personal talk. The phone at her boardinghouse was in the hall and he could hear girls calling to each other, doors banging, mules clattering as they ran through the halls. One girl was even yelling at her to get off the phone, she was expecting a call.

He hardly had a chance to open his mouth anyway, his sister was so busy talking nonstop about her new job in an export-import house and how busy she was with evening classes in shorthand and all the men she was going out with. As a matter of fact, she said, she was getting ready to go out to see the opening of the new George M. Cohan musical at the New Amsterdam Theater. Had he read the reviews? They were raves! She was sorry she couldn't talk any more, she had to run.

He had been depressed when he hung up. He and his sister had nothing in common any more. Just like Toby, she had thrown herself into a frantic social whirl that seemed to leave no room for outsiders.

But Toby's look reflected in the glass stayed with him and one day he got up the nerve to ring the bell of the porticoed fraternity house.

There was so much noise going on inside that nobody heard the bell and he finally opened the door himself and walked into bedlam. A row of pledges were bent over with their pants down submitting to the thwack of paddles from bellowing upper classmen. Toby was not among them. In a side lounge he found one of the members reading the sports pages, and asked if Toby was around.

The fellow squinted up at him over the top of the paper. "You want him for something?"

Eugene said he was a friend.

"He really pulled a fast one. He's in Cincinnati. He sent us a telegram—he eloped with some girl he knew out there."

Eugene had been pretty sure he knew who the girl was, and a phone call to Toby's mother had confirmed it. It was that plump little blonde with the interminable giggle he had run off with, throwing up at one stroke college, fraternity, and all the athletic triumphs everyone expected of him.

Eugene pulled over *Paradise Lost* and propped the book on his stomach against the library table in front of him. The whole situation was clear to him now. Toby had never been cut out for college. It had only been an excuse for more social life and he certainly would have flunked out in short order anyway—he must have known that. Marrying Effie was exactly the right thing for him to do.

How could he ever have felt Toby was such a superior being all those years? He had been fun to run around with—Eugene had learned a lot from him—but he was just an ordinary guy. Why shouldn't he marry an ordinary girl?

He was thinking about how Toby's elopement had put the finishing touches to a whole period in his own life, when he became aware that a girl sitting across from him was trying to get his attention.

"Would you mind moving your legs?" she said crossly. "My shins are black and blue."

As he straightened up with an apology, he thought there was something familiar about her. She had gone back to taking notes from a thick volume of charts, graphs, and statistics—the kind of thing he never could make head nor tail of. It was the girl Toby had got for him on the double date with Effie. Clare Marshall, the cousin. The same serious face with braids wound around the top of her head like a crown in the soft light. He didn't remember she had looked so good.

She must have felt his eyes on her because a moment later she looked up. Then she recognized him and smiled. He didn't remember that she had smiled at all the night they were out together.

A little later they were sitting over lemonade in the student cafeteria with Gothic windows looking out on a baseball diamond where a team was practicing. The dark paneling of the walls was decorated with crossed school pennants and plaques celebrating athletic victories and framed photographs of the winning teams going back to the middle of the nineteenth century.

"That's exactly how I always felt about Effie!" Clare said when he told her of his change of attitude about Toby. "I've never told anyone, I was ashamed to, but can you believe it, I was envious of her ever since we were little girls. She was always the popular one—boys swarmed around her. That's why I got so upset when I caught her with Toby. I was awful, wasn't I?" She blushed charmingly. "As you say, he's got all the good looks in the world, just like Effie. But she doesn't have a brain in her head either. They really deserve each other."

They laughed.

"They're just perfect specimens meant for breeding," Eugene said, and was delighted at her reaction to his risqué remark. Beyond her, on the ball field out the window, a batter hit a pop fly and one of the outfielders leaped up, catching it in his glove.

Clare was pleased to hear he had refused to go into the fraternity. He was simply not the type, she said. She hadn't even considered a sorority herself. She was majoring in sociology and minoring in psychology, and she felt just as he did that the most exciting thing in the world was the intellectual adventure of higher education.

Eugene agreed with her completely. "I had plenty of running around in high school. It seemed fun at the time, but looking back on it, it was just a lot of meaningless promiscuity." He had never used the word before, but it rolled off his tongue easily. With this bright, approving girl across from him he had once scorned as too intellectual when he was under Toby's shadow, he felt able to talk about anything. He wasn't sure the three times he had slept with girls actually qualified him as promiscuous, but he had never felt so much a man before. Her hands were so small, and her fragile shoulders under the polka-dot blouse made her look like she needed protecting.

A trace of the old seriousness settled over her face. "Dr. Bieer, my psychology professor, has interesting ideas about that. He says that sexuality is only justified in the context of a responsible relationship." She went on as if quoting a recent lecture. "Giving in to one's random impulses is the cause of all the unhappiness in the world."

"Well, I'm not sure it's the same for a man as for a woman," Eugene said uneasily, avoiding her eyes. Behind her on the ball field a player hit a home run and as he trotted around the diamond, the basemen patted him on the behind in congratulations. Eugene jumped to his feet and suggested they go down to Riverside Park and walk along the Hudson. "Do you have time?"

"Let's!" Clare picked up her books and hugged them to her. "We'll play hookey!"

They were inseparable for the final weeks of the semester. As they walked around campus holding hands, everybody smiled at them. Eugene loved the feeling of having a girl of his own.

He was always wanting to smooch with her but he was just as glad she held him firmly in check. Whenever he went too far, she explained to him that she had her sexual needs too, but she was willing to wait. Still, she always kissed him passionately when they said good-night on the steps of her dorm.

On the last night of the term, sitting in the visiting lounge under the strict eye of the housemother, Clare said she would be seeing the newlyweds when she went home to Cincinnati and asked if he had anything for her to tell Toby. Toby had found a job out there selling automobiles and he and Effie were living in an apartment near her parents' house.

Eugene said to tell him "best of luck" and they both laughed and agreed once more how ridiculous it was to get married so young and give up your education.

Clare regretted she had committed herself months before to do settlement-house work in Akron with slum children for the summer.

Eugene said he didn't know how he was going to get through the long hot months without her.

"Why don't you come with me and get a job too?"

"To Akron? Where would I live?"

"If we got married, there wouldn't be any problem."

"Married?" He was thrown off guard at the enormity of the idea. He hadn't envisioned marriage for years, not until he was grown up, in a profession, settled in life at some distant time. Besides, it was against the rules for undergraduates to marry.

But Clare firmly rejected the idea that there would be any difficulty with the college authorities—she would see to that. And they would find a room for themselves nearby when they got back in the fall.

Under the disapproving eye of the housemother, they sealed their engagement with an awkward kiss.

DOESN'T ANYBODY BUT ME CARE AT ALL ABOUT THOSE LOVELY streets, Elizabeth Endicott asked herself on that day in September, 1911, which ever afterward she considered to be either the worst or the best day of her life. She was driving back home from City Hall in the family's Franklin, turning from MacDougal Street onto Fourth through the Greenwich Village she loved, which was now to have a hideous swath cut down through its middle so that an extension of Seventh Avenue and, ultimately, Patrick's subway, could come through. It was going to necessitate tearing down hundreds of the wonderful old Federal and Italianate houses that were becoming more unique and precious with every year, as the mad building craze continued. New York insisted on obliterating its past to make way for "business" and "progress," words she had always hated. They were the enemies of everything she valued—tradition, beauty, charm.

For years she had been fighting against the cut-through, trying to alert other Villagers to the danger to their community, but the forces she had rallied had been so pitifully inadequate. No men at all. Not all of them were as blindly obstinate as her husband, but saving an old neighborhood was considered somehow a feminine cause, something unworthy of even the most intelligent man.

Even the artists whom she had counted on most to rally to her side had shown no interest. They were willing to take advantage of what the Village offered—studios they could rent for a song, the freedom to live as they chose—but they couldn't see that they had to fight to preserve it, for themselves if not for posterity.

"Elizabeth Endicott's Suffragettes," her little group of civic-minded ladies was maliciously dubbed in the newspapers. Any woman who tried to do anything at all was labeled suffragette nowadays.

Houses in the path of the new avenue were already being condemned and boarded up, and wreckers were starting to demolish them—why, they even planned to slice buildings in half! She and her handful of supporters had gone down to City Hall to picket the office of the mayor, the one man who still had the power to stop the whole thing.

They had started at eight in the morning when the streets in the Foley Square area were full of people on their way to work and could see them holding their placards, "SAVE GREENWICH VILLAGE," "DON'T RIP THE HEART OUT OF THE VILLAGE." But the workers had only stopped to jeer—and not just the men, either. "Suffragette" had been hurled at them repeatedly like an obscenity.

When finally they had been allowed in to leave a deposition, Elizabeth had thought they just might have a chance, but it had not been the mayor they saw. It was a minor assistant, and he hadn't even bothered to hide his complete lack of interest and had looked at them like hysterical females.

She turned onto Sixth Avenue, honking at a dog that ambled across the street unconcerned.

The whole thing had been a fiasco. Her last card had failed. She wanted to cry as she drove past Washington Place and Waverly Place that now lay in shadow, even on this brilliantly sunny September afternoon, because of the elevated that Patrick had helped to put up in the name of "progress," turning a once-pleasant avenue into a near slum. The people passing by, including an artist who had set up his easel to paint the busy scene under the el, were totally unconcerned that the city's vaunted new motorized bulldozers were about to move in to carve out the heart of their neighborhood.

The car skidded off the unused trolley tracks still embedded in the cobblestones, and a horse pulling a delivery wagon shied, and all around her was the squealing of brakes, klaxons blaring, and the yelling of wagon drivers reining in their teams.

She wanted to cry at the injustice of it all. If Patrick had lost, he would be bawling his head off—he could always cry so easily when he was hurt like a child. It was in his blood to cry like that, get all his pain out of his system at once and then bounce back newborn, ready to leap back into life with the same blind energy. She had wept only a few times in her life and it had been so long ago, she didn't know how any more.

At Ninth Street across from Jefferson Market and the Courthouse, she passed an ice cream parlor that years before had been Gridley's bar where Winifred Beaufort had sung for that brief time. How she wished she could talk to Winifred who had been the only person in her life she could reveal her innermost self to. But Will Kennedy had been arrested in a vice cleanup and sent to prison the year before. His gambling casino had been completely wrecked in the raid. Winifred had rescued what she could and had gone back to New Orleans, the place she had left years before as a slave. She was going to open a school for colored children while she waited for Will's eventual parole.

Reluctantly Elizabeth turned off in the direction of Perry Street. She never wanted to go home these days. Her home had become a place where she was treated as a stranger by her husband and had been deserted by her children. For the life of her, she couldn't remember what she had ever thought she had in common with any of them.

She was so distracted that she had to slam on the brakes and blast the klaxon to keep from running down some children playing ring-a-levio in the middle of the street. Shifting into third, the car bucked, and she drove on swearing under her breath at the difficulties of life—even driving, which normally she was a whiz at. Driving was something that gave her a feeling of being in complete control, of being obeyed by a powerful machine.

Her daughter Polly had been the first of her children to disappoint her. She had thrown up her art studies for no reason at all and taken it into her head to play at being a "bachelor girl" and work in an office.

She hated offices. She had been in so many these past two years, trying to cajole those hardheads into doing something about the extension. As she drove past St. Vincent's Hospital where the avenue was to begin cutting through to the south, she had the wild notion of chaining herself with her small band of supporters wrist to wrist in front of the boarded-up old brewery that was soon to go.

She could imagine the conventional reaction of her daughter, who sided with her father on everything. Why, Polly's real father, Albert Cogswell, had been an artist! It distressed her most that Polly had turned out to be such an ordinary person. How she hated the ordinary.

Even more crushing was her son Eugene's unexpected marriage to an ordinary girl he had met at Columbia. She hadn't liked Clare Marshall from the first time she set eyes on her. Such an opinionated priss, who was leading her son around by the nose.

Eugene had it in him to be a writer—she had always hoped for it—but now he was talking about becoming a technical editor when he finished college, because Clare—how she loathed the name—had convinced him it paid so well. She had done her best to raise her children with high ideals, but what could she do? Always there had been her husband's philistine influence to counteract her every effort.

Since she had begun fighting to save the Village, it had become clear to her that she had never had anything in common with Patrick. They lived in the same house, the world considered them man and wife, but they had long ceased sharing the same bed. Though they hardly said a word to each other any more except when other people were around, there was mockery implicit in his every look. His subway meant more to him than she ever had.

When she turned onto their block he was waiting for her on the stoop, cocky in his victory. He had had the same look on his face when she left the house that morning. With his insufferable knowledge of the way men ran things, he had known that she didn't have a chance at City Hall.

Their grandson, Dominic, was on the steps with him, and Polly, her papa's darling with Albert Cogswell's homely pug nose and freckles—she was over for dinner.

She felt their eyes on her as she parked the automobile at the curb and turned off the motor. Well, they weren't going to get the best of her. Before getting out she took off her motoring veil that held her ostrich-plume hat in place and tucked up straying gray hairs.

She drew herself to her full height as she walked toward them. At sixty, she knew herself to be a handsome woman.

She was heavier than she had been but she bore her weight like a Juno. Without looking at either her husband or her daughter, she walked up the steps to kiss her grandson, who at nineteen had a round face and glasses. He had none of the delicate features of his long-dead mother or his handsome, gregarious father, Mario. He was going to a restaurant academy in Italy for a year and would stay with a relative. "Dominic dear, you must be so excited about the trip."

Without showing much enthusiasm, he said he guessed so.

"So ya managed to get yourself back in time after all, Elizabeth," said her husband. "Your grandson has to be at a celebration for him at the restaurant." Patrick was wearing a ridiculous striped shirt over his beer belly that clashed with his checkered trousers.

"We thought you wouldn't get here in time, mother," Polly said. "Dommie's got to go." As usual, she was echoing her father—even to the point of implying that what her mother had been away trying to do was of no importance. Leaning against the rail in an affected pose she must have seen in a magazine illustration, Polly was wearing a dress with a dipping hemline far too outré for her plain face and mousy red hair that had grown out again.

"Wait a minute before ya rush off, Dom," Patrick said, getting to his feet with a lightness that belied that he was in his mid-sixties, "I've got a little treat for ya."

As she heard him opening the roll-topped desk in his study, she tried to maintain a grandmotherly interest in the only son of her dead daughter, but much as she tried to keep a conversation going, Dominic hardly ever had anything to say. Even sailing tomorrow on the *Vulcania*, something she would have given her eye teeth for, seemed no more important to him than going down to Canal Street. He didn't have a single opinion of his own, or a passion for doing anything except what his father wanted him to. It was Mario who had enrolled him in the cooking school in Italy, foreseeing for his taciturn son a future as a chef in the family restaurant. She was relieved when Patrick returned, presenting him with a brand new hundred-dollar bill and she could escape to the kitchen to start supper.

As she opened the door of the icebox and started taking out some cold cuts—she wasn't up to fixing more than a cold supper tonight—she heard Patrick on the steps outside, going on about how he was expecting Dom to fix him a first-class ravioli dinner—as if he knew what that was—just as soon as the boy got back to the States.

She was well aware that Patrick thought she'd got what she asked for. Who was she to try to influence the mayor against a scheme that everyone knew to be the best thing for the Village since he himself had put up the Greenwich Street el back in the seventies? She hated that kind of thing. She hated him for winning. She knew her husband well enough to know that he wasn't about to let her suffer her defeat quietly. He was just crass enough to find a way of rubbing it in.

And he did, that night at the table.

His sister Sarah had also dropped in for dinner, as she was apt to do without an invitation, to read them one of brother Timothy's letters from Ireland. Sarah's husband, Bill Yates, had been killed in a subway accident and Patrick was forever going on about how they must do all they could for the poor woman since times had been so hard for her, with never a thought for what his own wife was going through! Sarah, still in black long after the year's mourning period, brought over every one of Timothy's long, boring letters, even though he had ceased to exist for any of them except as a dull echo. The young hoodlum Patrick had put on the boat so long ago was no longer recognizable in the bigot who condemned everything with the strictest interpretation of church dogma.

Patrick, who had appeared to be giving his rapt attention to Sarah's laborious reading of the letter, an especially gloomy one, suddenly turned on Elizabeth and asked what his honor the mayor had had to say that afternoon.

She was caught off guard and blurted out the flimsy lie that her meeting with the mayor had been postponed because of an emergency City Council meeting.

"City Council meeting, was it?" He looked at Polly with a twinkle and sat back complacently in his chair. "As ya may have heard, Sarah," he said, grinning, "my wife's been wagin a heroic battle all on her own against the forces of capitalist exploitation who are out to wreck our precious Village by cuttin Seventh Avenue through."

Sister Sarah, who was well aware of the conflict between husband and wife, gave an embarrassed giggle.

Clutching her hands so tightly under the table the tendons stood out, Elizabeth said in a strange voice that the Village was perfectly livable the way it was.

Patrick was still enjoying himself too hugely to let her off the hook. "Well, your daughter didn't find it so livable down here any more. She had to move uptown. Isn't that so, Pol?"

"Oh, really, papa," Polly said, pretending to scold him.

Elizabeth's hands were numb. "A beautiful neighborhood is not improved by slashing a highway through it."

"But haven't ya been tellin us all for years about them avenues they cut through Paris, and I thought that was supposed to be the most beautiful place ya ever been in."

Elizabeth took a quick breath. "This isn't Paris. It's the Seventh Avenue Improvement Association, for God's sake."

"Ah, Elizabeth," Sarah piped up, "the Improvement Association has our best interests at heart, I believe. They're still carousin on the streets when I go to early Mass."

"You're right there, Sarah," said Patrick. "Greenwich Village is not what it used to be, not by a long shot." While his wife had her head in the clouds, he said, trying to save a few old houses nobody gave a damn about, she had failed to see that things were falling down around their ears. He went on nailing down his argument until she was at the point of exploding, when to her great relief, Sarah's policeman son Dennis stopped in off his beat.

Her youngest nephew had a blarney tongue and natural good spirits that made him irresistible to everyone. As he came into the room, he took off his regulation hat from his swiped-back sandy hair with a flourish and bent over to kiss her, his favorite aunt, before going over to his mother whom he had come to take home.

The way he looked in his uniform always made her heart lighter, though she was not only his aunt, but nearly forty years older than he.

"What's this you're saying about the Village not bein safe then, Uncle Pat?" Dennis asked, reaching for a toothpick to diddle between his teeth. He was sprawled in a chair, his legs stretched out in front of him to rest his feet.

"You're an officer of the force, lad, ya know what I'm talkin about." Patrick turned to him, sure of another supporter in his ranks. "It's all these artist types my wife is so crazy about who've seen fit to come and set themselves up in the neighborhood as if they owned the place. Ya can't walk down into Sheridan Square in even the brightest daylight without them floozies who claim to be artist models givin ya the wink and lettin ya know what their real profession is fast enough, not to mention all them fairy boys mincin by. It's a disgrace to decent women and children, having to put up with that. When Seventh Avenue and the new subway spur is put through, we'll get some more respectable folk down here again."

"That's utterly ridiculous," she said, avoiding looking at him. What a prig he was, stuffy, hypocritical. Why had she put up with his shanty Irish morality all these years? Turning back to her nephew she said, "My husband would like this neighborhood to be as dull as any other in the city. It's just the people who are out of the ordinary who give it its wonderful flavor, don't you see?"

Dennis laughed. "These queer characters we got around here sure give it a flavor all right, Aunt Elizabeth." His eyes twinkled back at her. He liked her. Patrick's eyes had once looked at her like that, bold, mischievous, ready for anything. Flushed, she turned away to Sarah to ask her if she wanted any more coffee.

Patrick was disappointed at Dennis's lack of support and growled that this element they liked so much was actually dangerous.

Sensing her nephew's approval at the high color in her cheeks, Elizabeth said, "Because people are out of the ordinary doesn't mean they're dangerous."

Ignoring her, Patrick snapped at his nephew, "If ya kept your blue eyes open when ya was walkin your beat, Dennis, ya wouldn't talk like that."

"Don't get hot under the collar, Uncle Paddy," Dennis said, unbuttoning his blue policeman's coat and hooking his thumbs in under his suspenders. "Aunt Elizabeth isn't so far off at that. I can tell ya for a fact there's less crime here than there is in a lot of the other precincts. Hell's Kitchen for one, and them chinks is always cuttin each other up down on Pell Street."

"Praise God for the finest," Sarah exclaimed apropos of nothing, her eyes beaming at her last-born whom she saw as single-handedly saving them all from being murdered.

Elizabeth smiled at him gratefully before turning to Patrick. "There, you see?"

Polly banged down her coffee cup. "Well, I for one think you're absolutely right, papa. I know the artists in Paris may have been different in your day, mother, but these people who call themselves artists here are just out to take advantage any way they can."

Elizabeth couldn't believe her ears. "Have your months of

living uptown whacking away at a typing machine made you lose all your senses? You're being irrational . . . and stupid!"

Polly sat speechless, turning red.

"What the hell are ya sayin to her?" Patrick said. "Pol, your mother didn't mean it."

Elizabeth knew she had gone too far. "I'm only saying that artists are perfectly good citizens and have as much right here as we do."

Polly pushed back her chair without looking at anyone. "If you'll excuse me, I've got to get back to my stupid uptown life." She hurried out of the dining room and up to the front hall.

"Ah, come on back, Pol." Patrick was already on his feet. Going up the stairs after her, he said loudly enough for them all to hear, "She's just all bothered up because she hasn't got anywhere with her crazy scheme, that's all. . . ."

Even Dennis could find nothing to say to cut the deadly silence in the dining room as the three of them sat listening to Patrick pleading vainly with his daughter at the front door.

When she had gone and Patrick came back glowering, the young policeman made a feeble joke about needing to get his mother back early through the dangerous streets, and took her home.

The moment they were alone, Patrick turned on Elizabeth, furious. "What ever possessed ya? I wouldn't talk to a dog like that, much less my own daughter."

Elizabeth was stacking the dinner plates in a clatter. "You're always worrying about that precious daughter of yours."

"I never thought I'd be sayin it, but you're a cold mother," he said.

She elbowed past him with a pile of plates. "Well, I can't bother to understand her little quirks. I've got my own problems."

He was on her heels. "Ya don't understand her because she's nothin like you are—there it is, pure and simple. Thank God, she takes after me."

Elizabeth had had all she could take. She stopped at the kitchen door in a blind rage and the words flew out. "What do you mean, 'takes after you'! She's not your daughter at all. Her father was an artist!"

Patrick stopped dead. "What's that ya said?"

In confusion, she set the dishes down before she dropped them. She couldn't believe she had let those words out. It was unthinkable. He couldn't have heard it. "I'm not making sense any more," she stammered, feeling herself on the verge of a precipice. "You've got me so upset."

She felt him behind her, staring dumbfounded.

"Why are you paying any attention to me anyway?" Her voice was wobbling, out of control as she held a plate under the water tap, ignoring the leftover cold cuts falling into the sink. "You and Polly and everyone ganging up on me so . . . the day's been hellish . . . and not a speck of understanding from any of you . . . how can I be expected to be—"

He wrenched her around, the dish clattering from her hand into the sink. "What is that you was sayin', then?"

She put a hand on her forehead, she was going to faint. "How do I know? Don't expect me to make any sense. It was just gibberish. I never should have gone through that awful dinner." Blindly, she tried to pull away. "My head is splitting, I'm going up to bed."

But his fists held her. "Pol is my daughter! She's mine! Isn't she? Isn't she?"

She was crying now, as her words tumbled out helter-skelter. "I didn't mean anything by it. Of course she's yours. She's more your daughter than mine. She adores you. For mercy's sake, let me go."

"Who's the father then? Tell me before all the blood pours from my heart. Tell me before I fall dead at your feet." He slapped her hard.

She shrieked, "All right, then!"

He let go of her and she dropped into a chair.

"Who, then?" His voice was suddenly remote, almost like a child's.

Choking on the words, she told the story of Albert Cogswell, the secret she had planned to take with her to the grave. She tried to explain that Albert had never known about Polly, that it had been just that one time and only because she had been so frightened, so tormented by her grief over little Jack's death. But everything she said came out wrong, completely wrong. As long as she had been the only one who knew it, she had felt she was justified, because at the time it had seemed the means of bringing Patrick back to her. But now in the open, revealed, it only sounded hideous and tawdry, and as it was dragged out of her, she knew her life was over.

"So that's the truth of it," he said afterward, and without saying anything else, turned and walked upstairs to his room.

For a few moments she was too dazed to move. Then the enormity of what had happened struck her. She jumped up and rushed after him.

He had closed his door. Her first fear was that he had suffered a heart attack and it flashed into her mind that she would have to hurl herself against the door. But when she turned the knob, it opened.

He was sitting on the bed staring out the window into the gathering darkness.

She stood in the doorway. "I'll go away," she said. "Polly will never know."

When he didn't answer, she thought sickeningly that that was what he wanted, but after a while he said quietly, "Ya don't have to do that."

She moved toward him around the bed, wondering if she were going to throw herself down at his feet and beg for forgiveness, but she surprised herself instead by sitting down beside him—she didn't know why.

They had not shared the same bed in five years. Not once in all that time had he tried to touch her. Not once had she wanted to touch him. But now he did. He reached out and pulled her roughly against him.

She let herself go, let herself submit totally to a dark, demonic part of him she did not know. He threw himself at her like a young man, so violent he might have been about to punish her for the hurt she had done him, even beat her to death. She didn't care. But when his teeth bit at her lips and his fingers gripped her nipples painfully, taking her over selfishly, not caring that he was hurting her, she started fighting back selfishly too, letting go the feelings she had been bottling up.

They took each other out of instinct alone, this man and this woman who had not understood or liked each other for so long. But this coupling had nothing to do with liking or understanding.

Whether it was hatred that made Patrick start it, she never knew, because when it was over—though it had been so ruthless between them, so swift, so incomprehensible for two people whose passion had ended—they had come together on a level that was primordial rather than romantic. It was too much to analyze, as she had all the other crises of her life.

Afterward, he didn't say anything, nor did she. He did not stay with her, but went downstairs to his study where he sat alone in the darkness. And in the cold hours just before dawn when he came upstairs again, it was not to his own room he returned, it was to hers, the room they had shared when love still bound them.

Though they never spoke again about what she had revealed to him and Polly was never told, in the coming days, in the years that remained to them, he slept with her and made love to her until the day he died.

POLLY WAS STANDING WITH A GIRLFRIEND, GLADYS, ON Bleecker Street in the falling snow, as their dates, two out-of-town businessmen named Will and Clarence whom Polly had met in her office, were struggling to start their stalled motorcar. The boys, both in evening clothes and driving cloaks, their patent leather pumps soaked through in the snow, were taking turns cranking the car, with no luck. They had all been out to dinner at the Astor Hotel and when they had heard from Gladys that Polly had grown up in Greenwich Village, they had insisted on coming down to see the wicked life among the artists.

Finally, Gladys, clutching her thin evening coat around her, screamed at them to give up on the car, she was frozen stiff. It occurred to Polly that they were only a few blocks from her parents' house, but she wouldn't dream of letting her mother meet these out-of-town salesmen. Her mother would see them as loud and superficial, everything she couldn't abide—and they were. Instead, Polly guided them toward Sheridan Square where she remembered a little café from the old days. Each man shielded his date from the snow with his cape, using the weather as an excuse to get in some cuddling. There was nothing wrong with Clarence, Polly's date, except that he was bland, simple-minded, pleasant, and smiled too much. It might make him a top salesman of ladies' lingerie, but he was a carbon copy of all the men she'd been going out with the past four years since she had moved uptown.

She was sick of all of them. They didn't have an idea in their heads except getting their hands on her, when the time came for petting at the end of the evening. She could usually keep them from going further than she wanted them to. Occasionally she let them go all the way, but she always regretted it—it was as hideous as the first time.

It gave her a peculiar sensation to be walking through the streets of the Village again. Once she thought she was going to have a brilliant arts career and had talked so glibly about "liberation." That girl was dead as a doornail. But, she thought ruefully as Clarence's arm tucked her tighter against him, who was the girl who had replaced her?

"Where are all the sex fiends I've been hearing about?" Gladys's young man Will asked as they trudged through the falling snow along the deserted street.

"Is that what you're interested in?" Polly snapped. "Then what did you bring me down here for?" She was cold and these guys were even more banal than usual. And as far as that nitwit Gladys went . . .

Just ahead of them was the wasteland where the streets had been torn out to make way for the Seventh Avenue extension. Some houses were half demolished. The snow had settled over the standing walls and the rubble, and in the pale light of the street lamps the eerie desolation seemed to stretch into infinity.

"Hey, we got here too late!" Polly's young man laughed. "Why didn't you tell us they were tearing the place down?"

Polly, who was surprised herself at the extent of the demolition, suggested that they look for a place to warm up closer by. Gladys spotted the glow of a crackling fire through the window of a cellar teashop called The Teaspoon, and they all trooped down the steps and inside.

It was a snug little place after the snow—checkered tablecloths and candles stuck in wine bottles and, tacked to the wall, caricatures of the regulars. There were only a few customers in the place. Two men bent over a chessboard in one corner and a gaunt man with long hair and paint-spattered corduroys was making a charcoal sketch of a starved-looking girl with big eyes. At another table some students were arguing loudly over the latest issue of a small radical monthly called *The Masses*, which was being passed around.

As they rubbed their hands in front of the fire, Will and Clarence joked about coming all the way from Pittsburgh to wicked Greenwich Village only to end up in a teashop. Still vexed, Polly said under her breath that teashops were very much the place to go to see the real Villagers.

When they sat down, a bored young waitress in gypsy kerchief and hoop earrings explained that they did not serve wine. The men tried to cajole her with a fiver into going out and getting them a bottle—this was the Village, wasn't it?

"Sorry, messieurs," said a plump woman with orange-dyed hair coming up to the table, "we don't serve wine here, but if you go around the corner there's the Paddock bar." Rouged lips matching her garish hair emphasized the ravages of what must once have been an attractive face, and the multicolored gypsy skirt was not flattering to her dumpy figure. But penciled brows emphasized intelligent lidded eyes that saw everything.

Gladys squealed that she was mad about the place, it was so picturesque—and besides, it was much too cold to go outdoors again. They ordered coffee with whipped cream.

The proprietress suggested that they might want to have their portraits sketched and snapped her fingers at the artist with the gaunt face, who immediately left off drawing the waiflike model to bring over samples of his work. Gladys and the boys exclaimed over the portraits he spread out on the table, as Polly groaned inwardly at being taken for a tourist like the others.

"You ever see a better likeness of Teddy Roosevelt?" Clarence asked Polly.

She cracked that it looked more like Abraham Lincoln to her.

Ignoring her, the artist explained he could do a likeness of each of them in just five minutes and they could pay him anything they wanted.

As he began to sketch Gladys and the boys watched, fascinated by his quick, skillful strokes, Polly gazed wearily into the fire, wishing she were anywhere else.

The proprietress with the orange hair came over, flopped down on the bench beside her, and lit up a cigarette. "You're not exactly having the time of your life, are you?" Under eyebrows plucked to a hard, thin line, her eyes with drooping lids were ageless, giving her a look of immeasurable sadness that her brisk manner denied.

Polly gave a bitter laugh and the woman laughed with her as the others carried on inanely about the sketching. Polly said she was exactly right.

The woman raised an eyebrow in the direction of her friends. "But they look like charming boys."

Now they were exclaiming over the artist's sketch of Gladys, which flattered her shamelessly.

"They bore me to death. I'm absolutely disgusted with myself for always getting into situations like this."

The woman flicked her cigarette ash on the sawdust floor. "Why do you do it, then?"

"I don't know any more," Polly said. "I'm not sure I ever knew."

"How old are you—twenty-two, twenty-three? You sound like you don't expect any more surprises in life."

Polly looked at Gladys and the salesmen. "With them, there aren't any surprises."

"Hey, Madame Pompadour, get your beautiful behind over here!" A swarthy giant of a man with a bushy mustache leaned out from the kitchen over the serving counter and roared in a thick accent. "The slop is ready for the bourgeois pigs."

The proprietress got up and, throwing her cigarette into the fire, said to Polly, "Why don't you tell them to go to hell then?"

The woman was extraordinary. She had grasped in a flash her whole stagnant situation. As Polly sipped her coffee, she mused that there must have been people like her in the Village all the years she had lived down here, but she had been too self-absorbed to notice.

She gave only perfunctory attention to the sketch Gladys showed her—she was watching the proprietress and the giant of a cook in the kitchen. She must be at least twenty years older than him but it was easy to see from the way he gave her a little pinch or a pat every time she went by that there was something special between them.

"Hey, you trying to clip us?" Clarence had raised his voice.

"Not at all, sir," the artist said, unruffled, "but twenty-five cents is not even in the realm of payment."

Clarence slipped his change purse back into his pocket. "Well, it's all you're going to get from me. You think what you're doing is work? Why don't you get a real job if you want to make some money."

"Don't be such a cheapskate," Polly said, opening her handbag. "I'll give him something."

"Don't you do it, Polly!" Clarence said, reaching over and snapping her bag shut. "It's not the money, it's the principle of the thing. This guy thinks just because we're from out of town he can take us for suckers."

"I assure you, sir," said the artist, "you're wrong on that count. . . ."

Hearing the commotion, the great bear of a cook came up and grabbed Clarence by the collar. "Bourgeois pig! Pay up or get out!"

"Take your hands off me or I'll call the cops!" Clarence said in a voice not quite so bullying as before.

Gladys screamed and reached for her boyfriend's arm.

"Call them, pigs!" the cook roared. "They know Zoran. We'll see what happens." He pointed to the door. "Out!"

"Maybe we ought to get out of this dump," said Will.

"You're damn tootin'," Clarence said, straightening his coat. "Come on, Polly, we're going."

She hung back.

"Polly, what's wrong with you?" cried Gladys, grabbing up her things. "They're out to scalp us!"

Polly, who had been watching the scene unfold with increasing detachment, heard herself saying, "Go on ahead. I'm staying awhile." Her riled-up companions argued with her, but she wouldn't budge. Finally, dumbfounded at her behavior, they left.

The cook banged the door on them, muttering "Bourgeois pigs," then headed back to the kitchen. As he passed Polly, who had gotten to her feet intending to go after them, he looked at her with blazing eyes and told her to sit down.

"But I have to . . ."

"No arguments!" he roared and disappeared into the back.

The orange-haired proprietress poured out two cognacs. She had already brought Polly another coffee when the others had gone, telling her to wait until she had a minute to get off her feet.

"I thought you didn't serve liquor," said Polly, who still couldn't get over having told her friends to go to hell, just like that.

"I don't sell it but I can offer it to anyone I like. I'm sorry if my cook was a little rough with your boyfriend but some of the hooligans in the neighborhood try to cause trouble and it's good to have a strong man around, if you understand me." The heavily shaded eyes looked fondly in the direction of the bear of a cook who was rolling out pie dough in the kitchen singing in a falsetto voice, "Corinska is my little dove." When he saw her looking at him, he threw her a kiss.

"Are you Corinska?" Polly asked.

"That's his Hungarian embroidery. Actually, my name is Corinne."

When Polly introduced herself, Corinne asked if her family lived on Perry Street.

"You know them?"

"I used to." The proprietress told her that she and her ex-husband, Fleming Ashmore, had lived next door to her at the time she was born.

Strangely, it did not surprise her. Feeling no barriers between them, Polly told her how out of place she had felt growing up in the Village and how she had gone to try an uptown life, but it was the same story there, she simply didn't fit in. And, moreover, she couldn't get anywhere in her jobs because she was a woman.

The proprietress nodded. "The only solution for a woman who has to work is to start her own business." She had faced the problem too, when her husband divorced her. Ashmore had dropped her when he became a success and started chasing after the society women he painted. "That one in the kitchen was having trouble with his wife, and my husband left me, so we clicked. *Eh, Voilà!*"

Polly said she would leave her job in an instant if she had an inkling of what to do with herself.

"You could work here while you're making up your mind about it. I need someone to help out."

Polly looked around the cheerful little restaurant with the fire blazing cosily. Being a waitress was nothing she had ever remotely considered, but she suddenly liked the idea. The trouble was, she didn't want to move back with her family.

"There's a free room upstairs," Corinne said, as if reading her mind. "You could live there and you'll have your meals here with me. Zoran will wait on you hand and foot, but you'll have to put up with his roaming hands."

She moved in, and Corinne dressed her in a gypsy tearoom costume like her own with a purple bandanna, hoop earrings, and a lot of beads. The customers were entertaining, and soon she knew them all by their first names. They expected her to live through their creative agonies and the complications of their love affairs with them, and sometimes stake them to a meal or even loan them a little money that they swore they would pay back, but both knew they never would because people who lived for dreams couldn't be bothered with details like that. Whenever they got too much for her and she got snippy, Corinne reminded her to be glad they weren't running a lunch wagon in Schenectady.

Zoran was always there in the kitchen if she needed him. He seemed never to sleep except for five-minute naps when business was slow, lying flat on his back on the counter with his hands folded across his big chest, snoring loudly. Then, when she called in an order, he leaped to his feet and returned to the stove, sometimes even finishing a sentence he had been in the middle of when he had dropped off. She couldn't help noticing that at least once whenever she was on duty, he disappeared for fifteen minutes upstairs to Corinne's apartment and returned more energetic than ever.

While he was gone, she had to fill in in the kitchen, preparing the omelets and sandwiches and salads that most people ordered. But she had always hated to cook, and was glad when he returned, bellowing at her to get away from his stove.

He never failed to pinch her behind whenever she came into the kitchen, but she soon got used to it. As if it were a fly landing on her nose, she simply brushed it away and went on with her work. Corinne told her it was just his nature. "What do you expect, *chérie*, he's a lot younger than me, he's got energy to burn."

It was not the job she could see her perfect mother approving of, and she put off going up to Perry Street for a week.

Before she could tell her father about her new job, he started in railing against her mother who was out trying to drum up support for her latest cause, some Village zoning law. He warned Polly not to mention Eugene when her mother came in. Her brother was a sore point ever since they had gone up to dinner at Eugene and Clare's little apartment near Columbia. They were both about to graduate and Elizabeth had learned, to her fury, that instead of becoming a writer as she wanted him to do, Eugene was going to take a job so that Clare could go on to graduate school.

"It was a tug-of-war, Pol," said Patrick, "and Eugene in the middle not able to open his mouth." And he went on about how her mother was not as young as she had been, and less reasonable than ever. She hadn't even kissed Eugene when they left and hadn't stopped talking since about how that opinionated daughter-in-law had made their son into a lapdog and a mollycoddle.

"I got nothin against that girl myself, she's Gene's choice after all—though it's true I prefer a lustier woman, like your mother."

Polly had never been so acutely aware that her father was getting old, and her mother, when she came in, didn't give her any chance to speak either, hardly bothering to say hello, in her wrath over the latest news about the Seventh Avenue Improvement Association. After having made such big promises about beautifying the new avenue, it had absconded with the funds appropriated for the project even before the avenue was put in. "Nobody paid the slightest attention when I warned that the whole thing was a disaster. Boulevards of Paris, indeed!" she said, flashing a look of scorn at Patrick.

Then he complained that it was wrong of her to hold it against him. If he had got his deep-bore method through, they wouldn't have had to tear down a single house to put in the subway. "But they wouldn't listen to me, either," he said. "Did I ever tell ya, Pol, about the shipworm?"

Even when Polly was finally able to break in and tell them about her new job, they showed little interest. "You'd both love Corinne. She's so generous. She gives out free soup to patrons who are down on their luck, 'starving artists' stew' she calls it. And the most amazing thing is, she was once our neighbor."

Her mother came to life. "Really? What did you say her name was?"

"Corinne Ashmore."

Her father's face turned deep red.

"I thought she and that husband of hers had left town long ago," her mother said icily.

"She's not married to him any more."

She couldn't understand her parents' reaction, and when her mother was out of the room she asked her father about it.

"I think ya better ask your friend, Mrs. Ashmore, that question," he answered evasively, and she couldn't get anything else out of him.

"Yes, I was heartless," Corinne said after she had told Polly the story of Alice and Fleming Ashmore. "When he cast your sister off so brutally, I should have been kind to the poor child. That I will always regret. But that my encouraging them in their love affair was immoral or degenerate or any other of those meaningless words conventional people use, that I deny. Of course, I understand your mother's point of view. But I believe it is never wrong for a girl to begin her erotic education during her most impressionable years, before she hardens against it."

"You're so right!" Polly said. It was exciting enough to hear the story of her dead sister who had only been a faded portrait in the family album, but it was thrilling to hear the exact cause of her own sexual problem. "Oh, I do wish something like that had happened to me at that age."

The older woman looked at her curiously. "Why do you say that?"

"Things might have turned out so differently. . . ." The anguish in her face must have been all too evident.

"Tell me," Corinne commanded.

And with relief and for the first time to anyone, Polly told about her experience with the young man over the machine shop, and how ever since, it had been just as painful and humiliating, and she was afraid love was not in the cards for her because of her vaginismus.

"What nonsense are you talking?"

Polly gave her the clinical description.

"I don't think that's your problem." Corinne lit a fresh cigarette with the stub of the old one and inhaled as if it were a life-giving breath. "That's all terminology made up by men. Men think women's behavior is a terrible complication. We're not so complicated."

"But I know what I feel! It's excruciating and painful."

"Yes, *chérie*, I don't doubt it, but I know—"

Zoran, the cook with the walrus mustache, came up with a glass and reached for the bottle of cognac between them on the table. "Now what, my dove? What are you two little birds twittering about?" He pulled up a chair intending to sit down between them.

"Merde alors!" Corinne's eyes blazed. "Can't you see we're talking here? Bugger off!"

With a flamboyant bow, the big cook tripped off ridiculously on his toes, waving the bottle. When a bearded youth who had been dozing with his head in his arms looked up bleary-eyed to see what was going on, Zoran roared, "What you looking at, bourgeois pig?" and plunked the cognac bottle on his table and sat down across from him.

Corinne, who had watched her lover's performance with pleasure, turned back to Polly. "It's a pity you've never known a man like that who knows how to be gentle with a woman. You've got to choose the men who are right for you."

Polly took a dubious look at the ferocious Hungarian. "But how will I ever know?"

They had long talks about her predicament on drizzling Village afternoons when a drowsiness was in the air in the nearly empty tearoom. Her perfect mother had never said a word to her on this subject and she had never dared bring it up, and now ten years too late she was beginning to learn the ABC's of it. Although she didn't see any solution, she began to feel less desolate about her life.

Meanwhile she was meeting new people. A little acting company that performed in a loft nearby often came in after rehearsing, and one day the director asked her if she'd like to help them out. Soon, her free time was taken up with painting sets, and pasting up announcements of their shows all over the Village, and even playing a few bit roles.

EUGENE AND CLARE GRADUATED IN JUNE, 1912. THE JOINT ceremony for both Barnard and Columbia was held on the steps of the library overlooking the Common where the guests were seated on folding chairs, the ladies holding parasols against the morning sun.

Clare's parents had come by train from Cincinnati. Seated nearby with Patrick and Polly was Elizabeth in a wide-brimmed straw hat trimmed with damask roses. Though pretending to be in a festive mood, Elizabeth was annoyed because her daughter-in-law, whom she knew to be nowhere near the intellectual equal of her son, was awarded a degree *summa cum laude*.

Clare was going on for a master's degree, while Eugene had a job as a copywriter with an advertising agency, arranged for him by his father-in-law, who was a college chum of the agency's president. It was agreed by everyone except Elizabeth that, given his literary bent, this would be an ideal job for him, and at the same time he'd be getting in on the ground floor of a booming new profession.

But though the job turned out to be easy for Eugene and his superiors liked him, it didn't interest him very much, and with Clare off to the library all the time, he found himself bored with nothing to do in the evenings.

One night when he'd gone down to the Village to have

dinner with his parents, he and his mother got to talking about his writing again. Since he had so much free time on his hands, she suggested why didn't he try to write a magazine article on his Uncle Claude and Mme. Averbach's circle back in the sixties. He was enthusiastic.

"What do you want to do that for?" Clare asked when he told her about it over breakfast the next morning. "They like you so much at the agency. Why, if you put all your energies into it, you'd rise to the top in no time. Remember how everyone loved your copy for the Arrow shirt ad in *Metropolitan Magazine?* I wish you'd talked it over with me, Gene. There was no need to go to your mother."

"But don't you see," he said, wanting her to understand, "it was really my idea. I've been thinking of free-lance writing for a long time. It was just that talking to mother reminded me of it."

"But why write about your uncle? Do you think anyone would be interested?"

"I'm interested. He was a colorful character. When you think about it, he was in at the start of the whole bohemian thing down there."

She shook her head as she spread some toast with raspberry jam. "Honestly, you do sound just like your mother. Why not write about somebody who's really doing something with his life—Jack London, for example?"

"Everybody's writing about him. But Claude was in my family. I can get all kinds of background from my mother."

"I'm sure she'll have lots to tell," Clare said, popping a piece of toast into her mouth.

He ignored her sarcasm. "Before he died, my uncle told her everything about his affair with Mme. Averbach. And I'll be able to work on it while you're studying."

His punctual young wife got up and began gathering up the dishes—her first class was in half an hour. "You should have told me before I started that you resented my going on to graduate school."

"Don't be silly. You know I'm glad you're going. This will keep me out of mischief nights, that's all."

"Well, I don't want to fight about it." She went over to kiss him. "You have been understanding about my education. And I suppose it is important for a man to have a hobby."

He began his project immediately. While Clare was off with her books, he started going down to the Village to record what his mother remembered and do research. Even though the local library on St. Luke's Place was in some turmoil, with part of the building having been sliced off because it was in the path of the new avenue, he found scrapbooks of clippings in the archives from the middle of the previous century.

Walking around the streets where he had grown up and that had been his uncle's milieu so long before, he was struck by the numbers of odd-looking people who now lived in the area. In an attempt to look artistic, men sported all kinds of costumes, with beards, capes, berets, and alligator-headed walking sticks in abundance. One young man he saw even went around dressed in an Elizabethan court jester's outfit with a lute over his shoulder.

Their girlfriends were just as bizarre. They shadowed their eyes exotically with kohl, and their hair was shorter than the men's. Some of them painted their lips like prostitutes and wore fringed Spanish shawls with tight skirts showing their ankles. From his mother's descriptions, he could imagine these same women in other costumes at Mme. Averbach's salon, embodying the fantasies of Poe.

He located the house Mme. Averbach had lived in south of Washington Square. It was taken over by several Italian families and the ground floor had been converted into a live-poultry market filled with crates of squawking chickens awaiting their turn at the chopping block, the vat of boiling water, and the feather plucker. Even though the paint on the window frames and cornices was flaking, the battered door was still flanked by elegant colonettes, and the fanlight window over the entranceway, though cracked, proclaimed an earlier grandeur, as did the tall French windows on the parlor floor, even though they were now hung with laundry. He tried to imagine the morbid young man who looked so much like Poe first taking to the opium pipe here.

But though his interest in the research continued, as he absorbed the atmosphere of the old Village a disturbing presence began to make itself felt. At first he couldn't put his finger on just what it was. It was as if digging up the old foundations of the demolished streets where the avenue was going through had exposed to the glare of the streetlamps a certain kind of inhabitant that until now had been invisible.

He had heard such people joked about, but they had never impinged on his world before. They were almost indistinguishable from everyone else, yet now that he was aware, he wondered how he could have missed them. They seemed to be everywhere, on every street, lurking in every shadow. They had the stark fascination of something every fiber of his being was repelled by but he couldn't keep from looking at, no matter how hard he tried. And yet it was those outcast eyes looking back at him that made him so uneasy. Why were they looking at him?

He found himself loitering on his way back to the uptown el station on Fourteenth Street, falling into a slower step as if waiting for something to happen, he didn't know what. And then one night he stopped himself just in time from going into one of their bars.

He went home in a sweat of self-disgust, sick over his morbid curiosity about such things. Clare was already asleep when he got home. Without even waking her, he threw himself on her, forgetting his usual precaution in his need to empty himself of the images that throbbed in his head.

He was through before his wife was fully awake. She was frightened and bewildered by his irrational behavior. He felt dirty as he mumbled something about not being able to control himself when he saw how beautiful she was, sleeping there. She looked at him uncertainly—she had never gotten such a compliment from him. But his agitation was too visible to deny and she pulled his head awkwardly to her breast and said what an impetuous boy he was.

But six weeks later when there was no doubt that she was pregnant, she was furious that he hadn't withdrawn early, the method they had always followed. She didn't want a child now. She wanted her degree first.

But Eugene, though outwardly shamefaced, was pleased. It was a confirmation of the manliness he had begun to doubt. He had awakened from a nightmare and was grateful that he would be kept busy in the future by the needs of a growing family.

In spite of the disruption of pregnancy, Clare went on with her studies, determined to get as much credit as she could before she was forced to take a maternity leave. But Eugene, much as he wanted to settle down to writing his article—he had all the notes he needed—was drawn back against his will to the night streets of Greenwich Village. No longer fooling himself with any illusion that he was gathering material, he stayed out later and later roaming the streets, his eyes covertly seeking out this strange brotherhood. But when anyone met his eyes, he quickly looked away. They had chosen a life that cut them off from all respectable society. He would never do that.

One night, as though he had been waiting for something to happen, a young man very much like himself—without any of the obvious signs like red tie, wristwatch, too dandyish clothes—passed him from behind on Greenwich Avenue and then looked back with expectant eyes before stopping at a drugstore window ahead of him and pretending to be studying a display of liniments. Hardly able to breathe, Eugene stopped at a shop window farther on and saw in the glass the man's reflection walking slowly past him, before stopping at the next window and again looking back.

At the last window before the elevated stairs where Eugene was pretending to be interested in a collection of men's hats, the young man came up beside him and said without looking at him, "Would you care for a sherry? My place is just around the corner."

Eugene turned away and fled up the grimy iron staircase, dropping a nickel in the turnstile with a shaking hand, not breathing until he was on the train, the doors shut, roaring northward through the night.

When he got home, as he had done before he threw himself on Clare, who again took his desperation for passion. But before he found his release, he froze, realizing he was imagining the young man in his arms. Sickened, he turned away and began to smash the pillow with his fists, his breath hissing through clenched teeth.

"Stop it, Gene!" Clare cried. "What are you doing?"

He fell into the pillow, his voice muffled. "It's got nothing to do with you."

He was ashamed to tell her what was wrong, he said, it was unspeakable. But Clare persisted, reminding him that she had studied psychology and that all problems, no matter how dreadful they seemed, could be solved.

"But it's contemptible! I hate myself!"

"What on earth have you done?"

He said he hadn't done anything. It was what was in his mind.

Clare was obviously relieved. If he hadn't done anything, she said, there was nothing wrong. What was in his mind was only imagination. He could tell her. She was his wife. She would understand.

Finally he sat up on the edge of the bed and told her—

revolted at the way it must sound to her—what had been going on, and that he was afraid he was like them.

"I knew this whole writing project was absurd!" she burst out, but immediately controlled herself and moved over to sit beside him, taking his hand and making him look at her. "I realize you've been under a strain, Gene, and I blame myself. I've been too busy with school to give you the attention you need. I don't think it's so terrible. It's normal for a man to go through a crisis when he's going to become a father. You're taking on a great responsibility, and those morbid people your mother suggested you write about, it's led you in the wrong direction."

His voice was barely audible. "Please don't talk about my mother. She's not to blame for this."

"Of course she isn't." His young wife put her arms around him. "I am. What you need is all the love I can give you. That will drive those silly thoughts out of your mind."

He looked around at her abjectly. "You mean you don't want to leave me?"

"Of course not, you dunce! You've done nothing to be ashamed of and you never will."

Later, when they lay in bed listening to the clop of the milkman's horse and wagon in the street below and the clinking of the bottles as he dropped them into the wooden boxes at the front door, she suggested to him that if he was still concerned he might talk it over with Dr. Bieler, her psychology professor and graduate advisor, who would convince him that he had blown this thing up out of all proportion.

But while Eugene was relieved at how she had taken it, he knew she wasn't facing up to how serious it was. Bringing it out in the open had made it more real to him, and although he did not go back to the Village all the next week, neither could he bring himself to touch his wife.

The following Friday was his twenty-fourth birthday and Clare made a point of staying home from her classes and fixing a special dinner. He had been uneasy from the moment he opened his eyes that morning and she greeted him with a tender birthday kiss.

All day at work he dreaded the evening to come. They ate by candlelight with champagne afterward, but though she made a show of easy banter, he knew her eyes were watching him.

Later, she changed into a new nightdress—it was peach

colored with ruffles and he never forgot it—and smiled at him from the bed, her hair carefully tumbled about her on the pillow.

He was beyond sorrow as he got into bed, switched the light off and mumbling good-night, turned away from her. He lay there listening to the ticking of the clock, wondering how long she would wait.

"I've tried, Gene," she said snapping on the light at last, "but I really don't think it's all my fault." When he didn't answer, she let him have it. Not only had she given him plenty of time to pull himself together, but he hadn't even tried. He hadn't gone to see Dr. Bieler when she'd made a special appointment for him, and for days he had treated her like she was not even there, knowing the pressure she was under, wanting to do everything she could to help. He hadn't given her a chance. Not once had he reached out.

When he still didn't respond, she went out of control. She didn't know him any more. Where was she supposed to fit into all this? Was he doing it just to defy her? And just when she needed him most to take over while she was having his baby. What kind of a man was he? The baby needed a father who was a real man, not a pansy.

When he still kept his back to her, she yelled, "Well, I'm fed up. I'm going home to Cincinnati if you don't want me."

"Why don't you?" he said quietly, not caring. He had known it was coming. He had listened to everything and it had made no impression. His marriage was dead to him. He wanted it to be over.

She stopped and caught her breath. "I didn't mean that. I don't want to leave." She was waiting, wanting him to take it back. But he didn't—it was too late. "You really want me to go then?" He had never seen her so close to tears before.

Sitting up, he told her that maybe while she was waiting for the baby it would be the best thing. In a few months she wouldn't be able to climb the four flights of stairs anyway, and it wasn't a bad idea for her to be with her mother during this time. It would be better all around. Once the baby came and she was ready to come home, he'd have a larger apartment waiting and he would give up the writing project and do whatever she wanted.

"All right," she said in a small voice as she sat on the stool of her vanity table, looking at him through eyes full of tears, her hair in disarray around her thin shoulders in the ruffled peach peignoir. "When you're ready for me you can find me out in Cincinnati with my mother." She smiled at him bravely, but it was evident to both of them that her studies in modern psychology had not given her all the answers.

EUGENE GAVE UP THE LITTLE APARTMENT NEAR COLUMBIA AND moved back in with his family as soon as Clare left. He explained to his parents that it was Clare's decision to have the baby at her mother's, but the more reasons he gave to explain her departure, the less credible it sounded even to him.

His father raised his predictable objections that his grandchild was going to be born so far away and what were these newfangled ideas that a wife had to be separated from her husband just because she was having a baby? But his mother, who had listened in tactful silence, gave his father one of her looks and said she thought it a perfectly wise thing to do under the circumstances and refrained from making any other comments at all.

With his mother there to talk it over with and to encourage him whenever he ran out of steam, he finally was able to start writing the article about Mme. Averbach and his Uncle Claude. As the piece took shape, he began to feel an identification with his long-dead relative who had been just as confused about life as he was. He even started to let his hair grow like Claude's in an old daguerreotype and wore a flowing tie which, considering some of the odd outfits to be seen on the streets of the Village, attracted no attention. It was a mark against him at the advertising agency but he didn't care. He disliked the job and knew his days there were numbered.

He felt that his temporary separation from Clare was exactly the right thing. Their correspondence was frequent and friendly. Clare told him she too thought it was for the best. From a distance she had gained perspective on herself and saw that her overinvolvement in her education had become obsessive, which in itself would be reason enough to make him feel neglected. Although she was looking forward to motherhood—her mother was fixing up an extra bedroom as a nursery—she couldn't wait until the baby was old enough to travel and she could come back to him and the three of them would all be together to begin a new life and make a real marriage.

As he worked into the late hours in his old room on the third floor, he had never been more sure of his love for her. Although he had made an appointment to see her psychology professor right after she left, when he started working on the article he felt his problems evaporating and he canceled it. Putting everything he had into his writing was exactly what he needed. Even this period of celibacy was a necessary factor in his development as a writer, so that all his energies could flow into it. He no longer had any curiosity at all in exploring the depravity of the Village streets. He wondered how he ever could have cared about it.

When his article was finished his mother found it entirely accurate and insisted he show it to his old English advisor at Columbia. The professor thought the piece had real merit and passed it along to the editor of *The Masses*, whom he knew from Harvard. Speechless, Eugene read the note that came shortly after from Max Eastman, accepting the piece which, he wrote, would fit perfectly into the issue they were putting together at the moment.

He had heard of *The Masses*—it had something to do with the Liberal Club and political protest—but he had never seen a copy. All he knew was that its circulation was small. His mother said that wasn't the point—it represented the avant-garde in the world of ideas and the arts, and it was a greater tribute to him than if it had been taken by the *Saturday Evening Post*.

He went to their offices on Charles Street, met Eastman, and readily agreed to some minor changes in grammar and construction.

It was his sister Polly who was the first to see the article in print. At that time she had a walk-on in a play called *Hobohemia* written by a member of the company named Sinclair Lewis. The director was a volunteer proofreader in his spare time on *The Masses's* totally-unpaid staff and he had brought her a set of the galleys. She rushed right over and read it aloud from beginning to end to the family at the dinner table. Eugene listened in awe to what he had created. It sounded completely professional.

After the magazine came out, he didn't know what he expected to happen, but when no one mentioned his piece, as if that particular issue of the magazine had dropped into the sea without a ripple, his mother said he mustn't expect immediate acclaim and the best thing to do was begin another article at once. Why not try a piece on Henry James? His late aunt Veronica had practically had a love affair with him once.

But her advice was no consolation. He felt like a failure. He didn't want to write anything else. He didn't even want Clare to come back. His job at the advertising agency became more meaningless than ever as he sat at his desk trying to think up a reason anyone in his right mind would want to drink Dr. Dooley's sarsaparilla.

The next day, along with the usual fat letter from Clare, his mother handed him a stiff, gold-trimmed envelope. Inside was a note.

> Dear Eugene Endicott,
>
> Max brought me the latest issue of *The Masses* and I read your wonderful piece. You make the period come alive for me. I had no idea there was anyone in the Village like Mme. Averbach then. By coincidence I have a few people in myself on Thursday evenings. Won't you stop by this Thursday? I'd love to meet you.
>
> Respectfully,
> Mabel Dodge.

His mother knew all about Mrs. Dodge, whose evenings were mentioned in gossip columns. She was a wealthy woman from Buffalo who lived on lower Fifth Avenue across from the Brevoort Hotel and entertained not only people from the arts and literary worlds, but political radicals and high society. Her lover was reputed to be the hotheaded radical writer, John Reed.

The invitation was like a trumpet announcing a change in his destiny. If Mrs. Dodge thought it a coincidence that her evening was the same as Mme. Averbach's, to Eugene it seemed not at all surprising. In his new identification with the romance of his uncle's short life, he saw it as natural that he should find his own Mme. Averbach.

When he left the house on that first Thursday evening in early September, his mother gazed after him mistily as if he were indeed the reincarnation of Claude and he were setting out to continue the life of the romantic young man who had died too soon.

And when he entered the drawing room and saw the hundred twinkling candles in the great chandelier with brightly enameled birds perched all over it, it was as if he were stepping back into that salon in 1864. Even if it was really 1914 and the guests were in modern clothes, it made no difference.

A discussion of some sort had just broken up and chairs were being pushed back against the wall. People were arguing about a silk workers' strike in Paterson, New Jersey—a man even jumped onto a table and started haranguing everyone to get out on the picket lines and show some solidarity. Servants were maneuvering through the guests with trays full of champagne and a glass was put in Eugene's hand.

For a while, he was cornered by a woman with bitten fingernails who talked of nothing but the war that had just broken out in Europe and told him that unless he agitated against it, he would be prime cannon fodder.

It was his editor, Max Eastman, who rescued him, telling him he must meet his hostess. Eastman was bald with steel-rimmed glasses, but he could as well have been Claude's chubby guide in outrageous red velvet jacket back at Madame Averbach's. Mabel Dodge was called The Sphinx, he said, leading him over to her. She had incredible intuition, he would see for himself.

And then they were before her. She was a majestic woman, big-boned in flowing draperies, but it was her eyes Eugene saw. Though they were small and shrewd, they were painted like an Egyptian queen's, extended with black lines and shadowed with purple and green.

"Here's a riddle for The Sphinx," Eastman said, pushing him forward into the center of the group surrounding her.

"Don't tell me—it's Eugene Endicott," she said in a straightforward midwestern accent that lacked the cultivated tone he had expected.

"Mabel, you amaze me," said Eastman. "How did you know that?"

"I know many things about him." She turned on Eugene an expression which, even more than her exotic eyes, made him understand why she was called The Sphinx. Running a finger around the line of his jaw, she said, "I knew from the way he wrote that he had to be beautiful."

He had never been called beautiful. He would never think of himself that way—if the word could be applied to a man at all. People like Toby were beautiful, people with classical features and athletic bodies.

Mrs. Dodge said she wanted him all to herself and sent Eastman over to cheer up "that little waif in the corner. Her name's Fanny House . . . or Hearse . . . something like that. She writes sentimental little stories. Dreadful."

The other people who had been standing around her turned away to talk among themselves, leaving him alone with her.

As her eyes that the cosmetic paint seemed to enlarge into hypnotic moons encouraged him, he told her about how he had come to write the article.

She couldn't help feeling a certain kinship with that Averbach woman, she said, though of course she herself was no beauty. When he protested, she said she wasn't ruling herself out by any means. She had her work to do too—providing the right setting for stimulating people to exchange ideas in. That's what her get-togethers were for, to create an Athens on the Hudson.

Others competing for her attention pushed up and she had to relinquish him though not before she gave him orders to circulate and meet all her special people.

And meet them he did, though he couldn't forget her and kept looking around to catch sight of her—not a steel butterfly like Mme. Averbach, but there was steel in her and mystery too, as Eastman said, behind her robust personality.

He was introduced to John Sloan, the leader of the notorious Ashcan school of painting, and the novelist Theodore Dreiser, who told him to apply the seat of his pants to the seat of his chair and not to worry about a highfalutin prose style like Henry James but just to tell his story straight out.

Big Bill Haywood, the founder of the International Workers

of the World, was pointed out to him across the room, a giant of a man with an eye patch. Eugene found it hard to believe that such a harmless-looking man flirting with the girls around him was actually the labor organizer the newspapers said was destroying everything America stood for.

People were discussing things that weren't mentioned in polite company—birth control, for one. Margaret Sanger, who was always being arrested for dispensing information on the subject, was talking to everyone about a woman's right to control her own body. Others were praising to the skies the modern French paintings at the Armory Show that even after a year was still being ridiculed in the press, and loudly condemning the munitions makers who were out "to drag us into that dirty war over there for their own profit."

He met Sinclair Lewis, the author of the play his sister Polly was in. Lewis, a pockmarked young man who was called "Red" because of his shock of fiery hair, told him that Mrs. Dodge had lived ten years in Italy where she had entertained Europe's aristocrats and bohemians at her villa in Florence. When Eugene asked about her husband, he said, "Oh, she devoured him long ago. See that tousle-haired young fellow she's with? That's the current one, Jack Reed. He directed the pageant they put on in Madison Square Garden to raise money for the Paterson strike."

And then Mrs. Dodge was back to ask more questions about his writing. He told her about the Henry James piece he was working on and, stimulated by her luminous attention, became excited about it for the first time.

When John Reed broke in to take her away—Eugene could see that he was a little dynamo of a man—she turned back, for the moment ignoring her lover completely to give Eugene her full attention, and declared that she wanted him at all her Thursdays from now on.

On the way home he thought how foolishly he had babbled to a woman who knew the greatest writers of her time, but he felt she didn't mind and understood exactly what he really meant to say—and she had called him beautiful.

He went again on the following Thursday and on the Thursday after. She had already become the most important person in his life. In the evenings, while he worked on his James piece, his mother and father downstairs reading under their fringed lamps, he looked out over the moonlit ailanthus trees in the backyard thinking about Mabel Dodge, just as Claude must have thought about Adele Averbach fifty years before—the pressure of her hand each time she greeted him, the way she always found a few minutes for him no matter how besieged she was by her illustrious company, the interest she always took in the progress of his work, her eyes that the theatrical makeup made luminous. She was the kind of woman he should have married. He understood now that it was an older woman he needed, just as Claude had.

One glorious autumn night, full of the sudden possibilities of his life, he left off his writing and walked over to the Hudson, wanting the freshness of the river air, the solitude of the deserted waterfront. Along the river the covered piers were outlined with silver by the late September moon. He walked out onto an open pier and gazed across the water at the lights of a ferryboat crossing to the Lackawanna ferry slip on the Jersey side and, farther up the river, Luna Park with its roller coaster and Ferris wheel, lit up like a faerie land. He smelled the salt air of the Atlantic coming in with the tide from beyond the distant lights of the Wall Street skyscrapers.

The headlight of a little tugboat putt-putting in to the pier to tie up for the night swept across the water and the weathered planks. It was the perfect touch to turn the night into a seascape by Albert Ryder. A seaman threw a hawser onto the pier, then jumped across and looped it around the bulkhead. Eugene lost all interest in the seascape by Ryder.

"Looks like we're in for a cold snap," the man said, taking his pipe out of his pocket and hunkering down on the pier.

Eugene went weak in the knees, mumbled something, and walked back to shore as quickly as he could.

The lit windows of a diner across the street from the pier was a beacon in a night suddenly turned ominous. But the strong black coffee he ordered did not steady him. There was only one person he could think of who would hold back the night.

He gave the waitress a nickel to use the wall telephone, cranked for the operator who seemed never to come on, and when finally he had given the number, it rang for a long time before the voice of the butler answered.

Mrs. Dodge was with guests at dinner, he reported. If the caller left his name, he would give it to her later. But Eugene wouldn't be put off and said it was an emergency.

"What is it, Eugene?" In spite of her slight irritation at having to leave her guests, when she heard the panic in his voice she agreed he might come by to see her later on—her company would be gone by eleven-thirty.

He lost count of the number of cups of coffee he drank in the noisy cafeteria on Sheridan Square waiting for the time to pass. Simply her telling him he could see her was enough to hang on to. The cafeteria was an awful place, but it was crowded and anonymous and that was what he wanted. The light bulbs hanging from the molded tin ceiling glared over the greasy marble tables and the floor covered with sawdust and leftover bits of food. Occasionally, local characters stopped to pester him to buy a poem written on a napkin for a cup of coffee or ask for a handout. But his eyes did not veer from the hands of the clock on the wall.

When he arrived, Mrs. Dodge was still not free. As he was led across the foyer past the open doors of the drawing room, the guests in their formal evening clothes looked up curiously.

It was after twelve before she came into the library in a trailing organdy gown, apologizing for the delay.

Without waiting for her to arrange herself on the gilt settee and turn on him her witch's eyes that always made him feel whole, exhilarated, he started spilling out his writing plans, realizing that he had told it all to her before, but not able to stop. Over and over he repeated that she was his inspiration, his goddess.

Mrs. Dodge, who listened as always with exquisite patience and tact as though it were all new to her, protested that he was giving her far too much credit, that he was a very talented young man who would make his own mark quite as well without her encouragement.

No, he insisted. Without her nothing would be possible. She was the only woman in his life who mattered.

"But what about your wife?" she reminded him. "Max told me you were married."

That had nothing to do with it, he said, jumping up out of the delicate period chair he was sitting in and going to look down at the crowded sidewalk cafe of the Brevoort Hotel across the street. His wife didn't appreciate the literary experience. He had left her and was never going back to her.

He turned around to her face Mrs. Dodge. Since writing the piece about his uncle and Mme. Averbach, he said, he seemed to be reliving his uncle's life. The first time he walked into her drawing room he felt himself to be Claude.

"But don't carry it too far, Eugene. I'm not Mme. Averbach."

"I know you're not free—but that doesn't matter. I mean . . . don't you see that I worship you. I love you!" The words were the exact expression of his feeling, though he hadn't known he was going to say them. He was shaking with excitement.

Mrs. Dodge straightened up and, as if throwing off the dazzling mantle he had conferred on her, said plainly, "Come over here and sit down with me, Eugene."

Apprehensive, he did as he was told. As he sat beside her on the settee, she seemed to grow larger and fill up the whole room.

"I'm perfectly willing to offer you the spiritual stimulation you need, but as to the physical, you don't love me that way at all, and I hope you're not confusing them."

"But I'm not! I mean I do need you, in every way. You're the only one who can help me."

"Yes, of course," she said, "and I want to help you the best I can."

The flicker of uncertainty disappeared. "I knew you'd feel that way." He reached for her hand, but she gently withdrew it.

"I hope we'll always be friends, Eugene, but I'm going to speak frankly even if I risk losing your friendship."

He started to object but she told him to pay attention. "I don't think anything I say will really surprise you, though you may be shocked to hear it put into words. I've known a lot of young men like you, though not many of them so talented. You see, you don't want me in the way you imagine—and I don't think you want any woman."

He began to stammer. What was she saying? It was a lie, but she grabbed his hand and held it tightly.

"Listen to me, Eugene, I know these things in my bones." And she told him there was nothing wrong with him, that people tormented themselves over such things unnecessarily, and the world was cruel about it. But there were many paths of love, and he had been trying to deny his. "Haven't your dreams been telling you what you really want?" she asked.

Panicking, he looked around for escape, but she held on to his hand and lifted his chin to force him to look into her eyes, the sphinx that spoke only the truth. "I'm right, aren't I?"

When he refused to answer, refused almost to listen to her—his mind rejecting the words—she told him that if he was going to develop as a writer or even just as a man, he had to accept all sides of himself. Of course it was tough. He was going to have to fight the whole world, but there was nothing wrong with what he felt, and he was making himself sick over it.

He clenched his teeth, waiting for her to finish. Why was she going on this way, tearing apart the last shreds of his dignity?

"And remember, it's not just men who feel these things, women do too. I've had some beautiful experiences with women myself."

He looked up, trying to connect her with what he had seen on the streets, those eyes, everywhere—he was revolted. And she was talking about it as if it was a great adventure in self-exploration—as if it were noble!

"You have to have the courage of your own way. There really are no rules in love, no matter what the world says." She laughed and her voice became more flat and midwestern. "I'll tell you this though, you're lucky to be living here in New York and not in Buffalo where I grew up."

He sprang to his feet. "You're all wrong!" he shouted, hating her, and stumbled his way to the door, down the hall past the startled eyes of the butler and out the front door into the night.

In the first cold days of October, the hot-air furnace Patrick had installed back in the nineties gave out and he had steam heat put in.

One day when Eugene was alone in the house, the plumber called him down to the basement to hold a pipe while he fitted a difficult connection. Afterward, sitting down on an old mattress, they shared coffee from the plumber's thermos bottle. When Eugene handed back his cup and got up to go, the plumber pulled him down and they fell back together on the mattress.

Eugene went down to the basement every day after that, until the afternoon his father came downstairs unexpectedly to see how the job was going, and caught them.

Without saying good-bye to anyone, Eugene ran off and enlisted in the Canadian Ambulance Corps. Before the troopship left for France he wrote to his wife that he had come to a decision for a divorce and explained why, wishing a good life for her and the child.

He wrote one more letter, to his sister.

POLLY WAS JUST ABOUT TO OPEN THE ENVELOPE WITH THE MONtreal postmark when there was a crash from the back of the teashop. As if things weren't bad enough already since Corinne had left, she ran back to the kitchen to find pancake batter all over the floor and the new kitchen boy trying to shovel it up with a spatula.

She pushed him aside, snapping that he could do it better with his toes, and started cleaning it up herself, as the boy stood by apologizing. He didn't know the first thing about working in a kitchen, though when she hired him he swore that he had been a short-order cook back home. She mopped the floor, furious at herself for being so gullible.

He had practically begged her for the job. New to the city, just in from Des Moines, his name was Larry Mathews and he claimed to be nineteen, though he looked a lot younger—a wholesome, cornfed kid, a little too anxious to please. He had come to New York to become a painter, he said, and showed her some pen-and-ink sketches. She had even considered the possibility of training him as her cook.

Well, that little illusion was knocked for a loop.

She had never wanted to take over running the teashop. She had liked things the way they were, with Corinne in charge and the mad Hungarian keeping the kitchen humming—if that was the word for it—leaving her plenty of time for her theater group which had become more important to her. At the time Corinne left she was offered a real part, not the usual walk-on for a change, and she had to turn it down.

It didn't matter that Zoran and Corinne, one as temperamental as the other, brawled in front of the customers. They always made it up and for a while went around twittering like lovebirds. It was only when he began to stay away from the Teaspoon after their fights that things had gotten bad. There was another woman. Corinne had always known about her, she told Polly. She lived somewhere over in New Jersey, but as long as he only spent an occasional night there, it was of no concern to her. She had laughed at Polly's look and said there was plenty of Zoran for both of them, plenty for a dozen women in fact.

But his visits to New Jersey got more frequent as the summer heat drove the two of them crazy in the airless little cellar teashop. As the "coffee breaks" up in Corinne's room got rarer, the fights got worse. Several times Polly woke up to the two of them yelling at each other in the middle of the night. Corinne swore at him in French, while he let loose a string of Hungarian expletives before stalking out, declaring he was never coming back to such an exploiter of the working classes. She was a bloodsucking capitalist.

Polly, feeling sorry for Corinne, who was showing the strain, got up her nerve and told him one day in the kitchen that he wasn't being fair. He turned on her and called her a bourgeois pig and what did she know about life, and then had roared out, so everyone in the restaurant could hear, that all any woman wanted was his cock, half the world would crawl on their bellies for it. And then his great laughter filled the teashop.

He began staying away for days at a time and Polly couldn't help asking Corinne how they were going to manage with him gone so much. But her employer, whose orange frizz of hair was tied back with a ribbon as she dripped oil into the egg yolks she was beating for mayonnaise, told her he'd be back, *chérie*, he always came back.

And he did, right in the middle of the noon rush, wearing a fitted velvet jacket with a brocade vest and bowler, looking like a Levantine confidence man. Putting on his apron over everything, he shoved Corinne aside and, with a wink, said he'd been away on monkey business.

Finally his visits upstairs stopped altogether and he was

hardly ever at the teashop. Corinne still carried on as if nothing was wrong, saying he was a selfish oaf but he needed her as much as she needed him. But Polly saw her go up to the street now and then to look for him. She even took the ferry over to New Jersey one day, saying she had paid him a month in advance and wasn't going to let him steal from her.

To Polly's surprise, she found him and brought him back. He stayed for a time, grudgingly, and the fights went on. Every customer was "bourgeois pig" to him. But the visits upstairs were not resumed. Even with all her face paint on, the dark circles under Corinne's eyes could not be hidden.

One day after one of their fights he threw his chef's apron on the floor, shut off all the burners on the range, and said, "I take this shit no more!"

Corinne refused to give him a cent if he walked out on her without notice. They carried on in front of everybody until he pushed her out of his way, took a handful of bills from the cash drawer and started out. She followed after him screaming "*Cochon!*" and that she was calling the police. It had been the worst ever. She clawed at his face, he grabbed at her red frizzy hair and, hideously, it came off in his hand, leaving her like a plucked chicken with only some thin gray hair, the paint she covered her face with ending abruptly at the hairline.

Even Zoran was stupefied and tried to put the wig back on her head, but she got it away from him and started beating him with it, beginning to cry. He pushed her into Polly's arms. "I good cook. I good man," he said, "but she want slave." And he walked out for the last time.

After that, Polly watched helplessly as the Frenchwoman let herself go, not bothering to wear her corset, giving up on the face paint, haggard. She spent most of the time in her room, and every morning there was an empty cognac bottle thrown out in the trash. Polly had to manage as best she could with a succession of temporary cooks, because Corinne still had a glimmer of hope that Zoran might come back.

It was the news of the outbreak of war in Europe and German troops crossing into France that rallied her. She bought a new red wig, made herself a stylish traveling suit on her old dress form, and with pins in her mouth told Polly she was going home to take care of her old mother and sister in Armentières. Until the war was over, Polly was to run the shop for her and send her money every month.

The last thing Corinne said on that crisp October day before they hugged good-bye at the gangplank was for Polly to remember what she had told her about thinking of her own pleasure with men, and not to worry about her at all. In France, a woman of her age was not considered garbage, like she was in this lousy country. As the French liner full of anxious Europeans returning home pulled away from the dock, she waved confidently from the rail, looking years younger in an extravagant cartwheel hat with a saucy feather, ready to defy all the armies of the night.

After she finished cleaning up the spilled pancake batter, Polly sent the apologetic young kitchen helper out to wait on tables and took over the cooking herself.

She closed the shop early that evening because she was too exhausted to go on. If she were going to open up for the breakfast crowd she had to get some rest. She was just about to turn out the lamp beside her bed when she remembered Eugene's letter and got it out of the pocket of her dress.

She was relieved he had written, because he had run off so unexpectedly the week before. All the note he had left behind said was that he was enlisting in one of those ambulance units and going to the war.

It had made no sense at all—not that she'd had much time to think about it. Just when things seemed to be going so well with him after having broken into print. He had given up the advertising job he hated and was devoting all his time to his writing.

She had never seen her father so upset over anything. What's more, he refused to talk about it, even to her.

The letter from Montreal began innocuously enough. He was writing to her, he said, because she was the best one to explain to their mother about it. But when she read what her father had had to witness in the basement, she was so aghast she could barely read on as her brother tried to explain. The only possible explanation was that he had gone berserk. Actually saying he had known for some time about it, but hadn't been able to admit it to himself! Why, he was nothing at all like those people. She saw them in the teashop all the time. She knew them in her acting group. They could be fun to listen to sometimes, the way they carried on—hilarious even—but they were freaks! Eugene was nothing like that. He was her brother. Besides, he was married and he was about to be a father. It had to be some kind of temporary aberration, something he would get over.

But how could he have done it to them? Their parents were so old now—her heart ached for her father. No wonder he hadn't mentioned Eugene once since he ran off. With his heart condition this might kill him. And Eugene expecting her to tell their mother, as if it was just some schoolboy prank!

She snapped off the lamp and tried to settle down, but sleep was impossible. Pederast, nancy-boy, fairy . . . the words they called them went on mocking her through the long hours till dawn.

As she flicked impatiently at the bric-a-brac on the mantelpiece with a feather duster, Elizabeth repeated for the hundreth time in the last week, "Whatever made him go off to that horrible war without even a word?"

Patrick, who was sitting in his chair doing absolutely nothing, muttered, as he had been doing all week, that it was the best thing he could have done.

She turned around to face him, tossing the duster aside. "Will you stop saying that? He's your only son!" But she couldn't get another word out of him and, exasperated, went upstairs looking for more work to do.

Polly arrived, glad to find her father alone. She hadn't opened the tearoom that morning and had sent young Larry Mathews off to the Metropolitan Museum for the day. "How awful for you, papa," she said, leaning over to put her arms around him protectively when she saw how bewildered and old he looked hunched over in his chair. She told him about the letter.

He looked away and said it wasn't fit for a girl like herself to hear such things, let alone to have such a brother.

It was better she did know, she told him. She didn't want him to have the burden of this horrible thing all to himself. She asked him to stay downstairs while she went up to talk to her mother.

"What do you mean he sent you a letter?" Elizabeth snapped. "Why on earth hasn't he written to me? I'm his mother. Not a word, not a single word. What's happened to him?"

"I'm trying to tell you, mother, if you'll give me a chance."

Elizabeth stopped, hearing the authority in her daughter's

voice. Until this minute, she had never thought of her as a grown woman. She listened as Polly told her the gist of the letter, not saying a word when she finished.

"It's some kind of rebellion against papa," Polly said, "some horrible insanity. It's heartless."

Elizabeth didn't hear her. She sat with her hands folded. "The poor boy," she said at last, almost to herself.

"How can you say such a thing?" At that moment Polly loathed her. "What he did was vile, absolutely vile. If I weren't—"

The postman's whistle interrupted them, and Elizabeth, coming alive, hurried down to intercept the mail. "Maybe he's written me," she called over her shoulder. "I do hope so. . . ."

When Polly followed her downstairs, Elizabeth was standing with a letter in her hand calling Patrick to come hear. Polly's first thought was that Eugene must have written to her mother after all and the foolish woman meant to subject her father to it, in spite of what he'd already gone through.

But it was not from Eugene. It was from Cincinnati. Clare's baby had been born. "It's a boy," said Elizabeth, her eyes blinking away the possibility of tears, "and she's named him Seth." She forced a brave smile. "Oh, if only Eugene had stayed long enough to hear this."

As Polly took her father's arm—he was trembling—she was furious that her mother was taking her usual unrealistic attitude, as if that miserable baby's arrival at such a time was anything to celebrate.

THE SPRING DAY IN 1916 WAS COLD, RAW EVEN, BUT AS PATRICK strolled back from Sheridan Square in his formal clothes, the crisp air invigorated him and he filled his lungs with it. That morning, he and other pioneers of city transit had been honored at the ceremony to inaugurate the opening of the new IRT subway station in the Village. After being presented with the Knickerbocker Medal for public service, they sat back in their top hats and tails on the dais, tolerating with amusement the self-congratulatory speeches of younger engineers who addressed the gathering as if the old-timers had never existed and the subway had been their idea all the time.

Patrick was seventy. He had officially retired five years before, but that hadn't kept him away from the subway construction site on Seventh Avenue during that time. It was his baby after all, and they needed a man of his experience around, even if they weren't always smart enough to take his advice. He had had the idea of a New York subway before any of them were dirty thoughts in their daddy's mind. It might have taken them a while to get around to it, but finally he had gotten some recognition.

"Oh, Patrick, you were the handsomest-looking man on the platform," said a buxom neighbor lady with a hat like a galleon under full sail, as he turned off the square, "but don't tell

Elizabeth I said so." She had the look in her eye that made him know she meant it.

He certainly wouldn't tell his wife, Elizabeth couldn't abide the woman. "Ah, ya mustn't turn my head now, Carlotta. A fine-lookin woman like yourself is in danger if ya give me such ideas." He was sure he detected a trace of a blush in her cheek.

He felt the appreciative glances of everyone he passed as he continued his walk up Fourth Street. He knew he made a fine figure of a man in his formal tails rented for the occasion. The striped pants were his own, and the spats—cleaned up—looked as new as ever, though he had bought them for Tom's funeral sixteen years before.

With his walking stick he nudged an old dog snoozing in the middle of the sidewalk. The dog waddled out of his way, staring after him reproachfully with its one good eye.

Patrick had the girth suitable to his dignity. Elizabeth had to let out his pants, but there still wasn't an ounce of fat on him. Even with his beer belly, he was as solid as he had been when he first went to work for the elevated. He saw how skittish she still got every time he looked at her. He was randier at his age than other men at thirty.

He knew she had been truly happy for him today. They'd had their little tiffs over the years—with her crackpot ideas about wanting to keep the neighborhood old-fashioned. He could see tears in her eyes when he was called "one of the visionaries of municipal transportation" and the mayor presented him with the medal. After the ribbon-cutting ceremony at the subway entrance, and after he had come back up from the subway platform where the official party had welcomed the first train through the new station, Elizabeth told him to forget all their differences over the subway, she was so proud of him, and she had sent him off to Jack Delaney's Bar with several of his old colleagues who had been honored with him. There, between toasts, they had recalled the old days when they were putting up those first els, trying to make practical sense out of the muddled blueprints, and finally doing it their own way.

Neighbors and friends kept stopping to wish him well. With the new subway, the neighborhood was sure to revive, they all said, and they had him to thank for it. He went on, feeling like he had never retired at all.

It had been a good life, a few vicissitudes along the way—they came to every man—but all in all he hadn't done so bad for a lad from Shamrock Alley who was born without a pot to piss in, ya might say. He had worked at the profession he wanted, and succeeded at it—not every man could say that. He was married to a superior woman. And his children? Well, they took ya up and they took ya down, but who said it was supposed to be any other way? On this superb April day, all the pain was gone, and he thought back pleasurably to the time he took little Jack to visit the elevated when they were putting it up on Sixth Avenue. Now there was a smart one for ya, smarter when he was ten than some of those younger engineers who had been shooting off their mouths today. And snippy little Alice at her birthday party when Bill Yates came in drunk that time, the divil. And Polly, the little monkey, with her freckles and red hair, crawling all over him.

He turned onto Perry Street. That was some cock-and-bull story about old Albert Elizabeth had told him when she was peeved at him that time. He gave a lamppost a whack with his walking stick. Oh, he'd put all that behind him years ago. He supposed every man felt a little uncomfortable about his children once in a while. Except for baby Seth, his one child who was a complete pleasure to think about. His grandchild, he meant. He shook his head at his absentmindedness. It must be those whiskeys he had at the bar with the boys.

He and Elizabeth had gone out to Cincinnati to see their grandchild the previous fall. Seth had taken to his grandpa right off. Patrick smiled broadly at the recollection of how the little pisser had climbed right up on his lap as soon as they met. By the end of the two-week visit, Seth was already saying his first word—Grandpa. And now he and Elizabeth were going out there again next month, and the mother was going to let them bring the little lad back for a visit here. Seth had inherited his own Irish eyes and curly black hair, his one child—grandchild—who had come out as Irish as he.

"Hey, Pat, you all right?" someone said touching his arm.

"Perfectly fine, Bill." Patrick was so preoccupied, that for a moment he thought it was his sister Sarah's husband, but Bill Yates was long dead. "Oh, it's you, is it, Ben?" he said, recognizing his doctor's boy. "I was off on a cloud, ya might say. It's been a big day for me, I guess ya know."

He straightened up and walked on slowly. His legs seemed a little mixed up. He remembered how he used to visit his sister Sarah with her kids under the el on Greenwich Street, and then he thought about Shamrock Alley. The alley was gone now, torn down, and a big red brick office building covering over the whole area.

He thought about his mother then, always laughing no matter how hard life was, so fine and healthy and happy he remembered her, until that day they shot Danny Halloran dead at the tavern and took her off to jail.

He was in front of his house, his own hand on the railing while he caught his breath, looking down the steps to the kitchen where once his mother had worked as the housemaid. He was thinking of his mother, and Timothy and Sarah and Shamrock Alley all of a jumble together, when the pains struck him and his strong thick fingers that had never failed him before slipped from the black iron railing and clutched at his heart.

It was the biggest moment of Polly's life at her little theater group, finally to get a chance at her first real part after all those walk-ons—and in the most significant play the Players had ever done.

They were meeting at the Liberal Club bookshop as they always did for rehearsals, sitting on their coats on the floor among the bookshelves. The dregs of cold coffee in innumerable cups testified to the hours they had been arguing over the play since early that morning.

Polly had arrived late, after attending her father's subway opening. She was penciling in the names of the actors on a slate board to make herself useful to the director as he chose them for the roles, not expecting anything for herself, when out of the blue he handed a script over to her. It took her a moment before it sank in that he meant for her to read for the supporting role of the companion to a spoiled rich girl traveling on a freighter. The companion comes upon the girl at the moment she is being raped by a stoker in the hold and tries to rescue her.

The director had already chosen the rich girl, a dazzling newcomer to the group with chestnut hair and expressive eyes like wells named Edna St. Vincent Millay, who had just come down from Maine after winning a national poetry contest.

He explained to Polly the significance of her part. She, the traveling companion, was the symbol of Puritanism struggling with the elemental sexuality of the stoker over the soul of America, the rich bitch.

It was a magnificent new O'Neill play, shocking in its realism—so different from the vapid theater of Broadway she despised, with its farces and costume melodramas. The dialogue of the play was so frank, it might even get them raided by the police.

The director wanted her to read the climactic scene where she interrupts the rape, but as she waited for her cue, trying not to squint without her glasses and shaking with nervous excitement, the phone jangled outside in the hall. The man who ran the bookshop broke in to say it was an urgent call for her.

She could have screamed with vexation. As she went to the phone, the director was already asking another actress to read the part.

By the time she got home, her father had been carried upstairs and was lying in the center of the great Victorian bed. He was ashen as he fought for breath, his barrel chest heaving under the sheet. The doctor had told them that after such a massive coronary attack, he wasn't really conscious any more even if his eyes were open, and it was only a matter of time. There was nothing more for him to do.

But his eyes looked so natural, a little perplexed as if he couldn't understand what was happening to him. He might not be conscious, but his body refused to give up.

The doctor had gone outside in the hall where a neighbor had fixed him coffee. To Polly's annoyance, her mother, kneeling beside the bed as she patted her husband's sweaty forehead with a towel, was trying to get him to talk, as if she thought she could actually jolt him out of his coma.

"What is it, Patrick?" she kept calling to him. "Tell me, what are you trying to say?"

Her mother interpreted his pitiful gasping as an attempt to speak. He was making a grueling effort as he fought for breath, but it was certainly not to speak, didn't she see that? Her mother couldn't seem to get it through her head that Patrick couldn't even hear her.

"He's not trying to say anything," Polly hissed at her. "Leave him in peace, can't you?"

"Be quiet!" her mother snapped back at her without looking around. "I know my own husband. He's trying to tell me something." She was guarding him like a tigress. She leaned closer to the dying man, her ear almost at his lips. "You want something, Patrick, I know it. . . ."

"Back off, mother, let him breathe." Polly came around the bed to make her give him room, but her mother blocked her with an arm of iron.

"I understand, Pat!" She lifted her head, her face lighting up almost demonically. "It's a priest you want. That's it, a priest!"

"What are you saying?" Polly was filled with rage against her mother. Her father hadn't said a word.

"Call St. Aloysius's!" her mother commanded.

"He doesn't want a priest!" Polly screamed, forgetting where she was.

"Are you going or do I have to go myself?"

Polly stood firm.

"Damn you!" Her mother pulled herself up and rushed out of the room.

Polly stared after her in disbelief. She heard the footsteps clattering downstairs and the cranking of the telephone. At the one moment her mother should be most calm, most clear-headed, she had lost her mind.

She dropped beside her father and took one of his hands. "Don't worry, papa," she said, forgetting in her turn that he couldn't hear her. "I won't let her force that on you. I won't let her do anything you don't want." Helplessly, she had to watch the dying man struggle for breath as he tried to suck air into lungs already filling with water. Why must he fight so hard to the very end?

But even dying he was beautiful. Her father had always been beautiful, of course, the only one who had ever cared for her. She remembered how he used to break in on her with his irresistible grin while she was writing her silly schoolgirl poems, holding his arms out like a big helpless baby for her to remove his cuff links. Her helpless papa. And now there was nothing she could do to help him—nothing anyone could do. And the final, precious minutes were racing—

Footsteps entered the room behind her. At the same time, her father's eyes, so wide and confused before, seemed calmer.

A priest was in the room.

Standing beside her mother, she was forced to witness as last rites were given and her father's fingers gratefully curled around a rosary before he closed his eyes.

She felt betrayed, as if he had kept this secret from her deliberately, as if she had never known who he was. On his deathbed he had shown himself to be a stranger.

LARRY MATHEWS WAS WHISTLING AS HE SET THE CHAIRS BACK on the floor from the tables in the teashop. Polly was upstairs in her apartment getting dolled up for a midnight bash he was taking her to—or rather, she was taking him to. Her little theater group was invited to the studio of the artist John Sloan, who was giving the party. John Sloan was practically as famous as Toulouse-Lautrec!

Larry had already cleaned up the teashop kitchen, and before he hung up his apron he sprinkled fresh-smelling sawdust on the newly mopped floors to keep them dry with everyone tracking in slush from the winter streets.

He rolled down his sleeves over the tattoos on his arms. He had gotten tattooed when he was thirteen and had run away from the orphanage in Des Moines for a couple of days. He didn't know what he wanted to do with his life back then, but that was before he found the Toulouse-Lautrec book in the library.

In his two years in New York he had become Polly's assistant at the Teaspoon. Not only that, but he had a swell place to live upstairs and was starting to paint in oils. If only Polly would take him seriously. But she went on treating him like a kid brother. He might be only eighteen, but he thought he looked a lot older. Growing up in an orphanage made anyone mature pretty fast. The truth was that he was crazy about her and had been ever since he first saw her.

He gave a last look around at the spanking-clean teashop and put on his jacket. Tonight, at this party, he'd find some way to make her see that he was the right man for her.

The trouble was that every time she took him to one of those Village places he got more tongue-tied than ever. Everyone seemed to know everything there was to know about the arts and made him feel like a hick. What he really wanted was just to be alone with her and hold her hand and tell her how he felt about life. She wanted to know all about him and she was always telling him all about herself and she was the first and only person who had ever been interested in him, but he could never make himself open his mouth.

He went upstairs to change into his suit. He had bought it secondhand over on the Lower East Side. It was double-breasted with a pencil stripe and made him look older.

When he first came to New York he was prepared for everyone to be suspicious and unfriendly, but when he had walked in off the street to ask for a job, Polly had hired him without question. And then when she found out he didn't know anything about cooking, instead of throwing him out, she had started teaching him the ins and outs of the job. She had even encouraged him to break out the walls of the apartment she had gotten him—it had belonged to the former owner of the teashop—to make a real painter's studio out of it, while she stayed on in her smaller quarters next door. Why, she had actually believed him when he said his ambition was to be a fine artist and had taken him off to Gertrude Vanderbilt Whitney's little gallery-museum on Eighth Street, which featured American artists, to hear John Sloan talk. He was glad to be her escort even if he knew she only asked him because she didn't have anyone to go with. She was always taking him places—or had, until her father's death. She had really taken that hard.

Tonight was the first time she'd wanted to go out since then, and he was determined to make the most of it. He had always been such a strong kid, and with those tattoos people tended to dismiss him as a knucklehead. But if he got a chance to open up tonight, he'd talk to her about Toulouse-Lautrec, and how he was a hunchback cripple who found a world for himself among the whores of Paris, and even when the whole world looked down on him, the whores had sympathy. And about when he was sixteen and got out of the orphanage, he had come straight to Greenwich Village because it sounded like the kind of place a kid without a family would fit into.

It was hard for him to make friends here, but he had found Polly. Even if he couldn't talk to her, he knew that she understood him. That was why she told him everything about her life.

He was fascinated. Her family was nothing like what he had imagined family life to be, since he never had one. Her father sounded like everything you could want in a father. But even growing up in a family, he knew she was just as lonely as he was inside, especially since her father's death.

On his deathbed her father had asked for a priest. It had been a surprise to them all, Polly said. She had never thought of him as a Catholic, though they all were Catholic on his mother's side of the family. But the way Polly explained it, it was his way of joining his mother again in the afterlife.

It had been an awful shock to Mr. Endicott about Polly's brother. She was always blaming Eugene for their father's going downhill, and she resented her mother for taking Eugene's side. Polly knew a lot about Freudian psychology and said it was her mother's possessiveness that had turned Eugene that way. Larry wasn't so sure about it. In the orphanage a lot of the boys used to climb into each other's beds at night and nobody thought much about it, if the matron didn't catch you.

Every time Polly went to see her mother she came back fuming. According to her, Mrs. Endicott only had two subjects. She talked as if her zoning law that had just gone through—to save the Village from being torn down for factories and warehouses—was a greater blessing than the discovery of fire, and Polly couldn't make her see it was the avenue cut-through she hated that had raised the value of Village real estate and had got her precious law passed.

But what got Polly's goat the most was her mother's other subject—"poor Eugene at the front." It was unfair, Polly complained after every visit to her mother, that he was getting away with that hero stuff after what he had done.

As he pulled on his trousers, Larry could hear the water from her bathtub gurgling down the big pipe in the corner of his room, and he imagined her standing in front of her steamed-up oval mirror dusting herself with lilac talcum. He buttoned his fly and swore under his breath as a button popped off.

He couldn't get over it that she didn't think of herself as

good-looking. She was twenty-nine, it was true, but she didn't look any older than he did. She was always making cracks about her freckled face and pug nose and how she was no threat to any woman. One of her psychology ideas was that her problem with men came from being too close to her father, but he didn't see anything wrong with missing someone if you loved them. Anyway, if she would only let him, he would show her that she had no problems and that she looked as good as any woman around.

She was always comparing herself to Edna Millay, the star in her acting group. Polly saw her as everything she wasn't. Millay had won a prize for her poetry, wrote plays that were actually being put on, and she had all the men she could handle. She even used a man's name, Vincent, just like George Sand, and wore pants to make herself stand out.

It was "Vincent" Millay, in fact who had gotten the acting group invited to John Sloan's studio party tonight. Sloan was painting her portrait, and Polly was sure they were having an affair. Larry wasn't looking forward to the party much, but he had never been inside the studio of such a famous artist.

But he didn't get to see Sloan's studio that night. When he and Polly got there, a note on the door said to meet at the arch in Washington Square. Sloan had drawn a clever squiggle at the bottom, a caricature of himself astride the arch waving a wine bottle in the air.

Polly said did he think they were Eskimos? It did seem crazy on such a cold night in February to hold a party outdoors—they weren't dressed for it—but they went anyway.

When they got to the arch with its two cold granite statues of George Washington grimly guarding the entrance to the park, no one was in sight, but they heard the sounds of a party coming from somewhere. A voice called Polly's name, and looking up, they saw the party was going on on top of the arch. It turned out that there was a service door in the side of the arch which Sloan had discovered but nobody had ever paid attention to before.

They groped their way up inside the stone staircase, giggling together like children exploring a haunted house, while Larry lit matches along the way. Coming out on the granite roof enclosed by a balustrade, they found about a hundred people packed into an area smaller than a tennis court, whooping it up in the frosty night. Bottles of wine were being passed around, and the atmosphere was hilarious as people burrowed under heaps of blankets to keep warm. A bonfire was going in one corner and a crowd around it was toasting marshmallows and singing to a mandolin.

He recognized John Sloan, a tall bearded man in tweeds, who was holding on to a flagpole on the front balustrade and energetically leading the singers by the bonfire in an English song about "knocking the Kaiser on his heinie."

It was even colder up here in the wind, and Polly, saying she was about to freeze her fanny off, pulled him along and found a place for them in a pile of blankets and bodies, and before he knew what was happening, she was snuggling up against him to get warm. He stopped giggling fast enough when he found himself under a rug holding the girl he was crazy about in his arms.

But when she felt how aroused he was, she pushed him off. "Oh, Larry, you're the limit!" she scolded, and told him to behave himself and listen to the singing.

He had never touched her before. He felt like walking around the balustrade, balancing high over the park. He was actually with her under a bearskin rug, looking up at the tiny frosty stars and sliver of moon, listening to the crackle of the fire and the occasional backfire of a passing automobile. It seemed a long way off where John Sloan was leading the singers to the strumming of the mandolin and some wild figures cavorted in the firelight.

He was in bliss as she told him how much fun it was to have him working with her in the teashop, and how it was too bad he hadn't known the Frenchwoman who had it before her, who still owned it really, and what an exciting life Corinne now had, running a hospitality center for the troops in Paris. She wondered if she ought to send Corinne's address to her brother so that he could look her up, but she sighed and said she guessed she wouldn't. She even let him hold her hand.

It was perfect, until some man she knew crawled up under the blankets on the other side. She took her hand out of his, turning completely away and ignoring him. There was nothing to do but to wait for her to finish talking to the man and come back.

Polly was feeling perfectly peaceful with Larry, when a large head emerged from the blanket near her shoulder and fleshy lips in a deep growl against her ear said, "Hello, hunky-punky."

Two enormous eyes over a bush of a mustache were grinning

at her. It was Corinne's Hungarian madman, Zoran. His shaggy head and the bearskin rug gave the impression that a furry animal was spread out over her breathing its hot breath into her face, and a great animal tongue were about to lap her enthusiastically.

She had turned away from Larry and started to raise herself, asking him what he was doing there, but with a big soft hand he shoved her back down. "I'm here on monkey business, what else?" he said, and gave a rumble of a laugh.

Surprisingly, it had seemed perfectly natural in that unnatural setting to have him turn up like that. She tried to make him be serious to find out what he had been doing since they last saw each other two years before, but all he said was, "A little of this, a little of that. You know us Hungarian gypsies, we steal a chicken, do some horse trading, and carry off the little daughters." He pinched her cheek.

She had to laugh.

"I don't make you cry?" He was hovering over her, his old outrageous self, making her feel like a child. He began to nip at her earlobe.

A sheet painted with a skull and crossbones was run up the flagpole at the balustrade and John Sloan started calling for everyone's attention.

"Stop it, won't you!" She couldn't help laughing as Zoran nuzzled up to her. "I want to listen."

"What are you afraid of me for? I bet you're still a virgin, am I right?" His dark whiskers smiled over her.

Aware that Larry was watching them, she tried to extricate herself. "That's none of your business."

"You are," he said, "and I know it and you've been waiting for Zoran to wake you up, haven't you, little princess?"

With the skull and crossbones fluttering in the icy breeze in full view of the Rhinelander mansion and the sweep of lower Fifth Avenue, John Sloan was shouting that they would never support the filthy war going on in Europe, even if the rest of the country was stupid enough to get into it, and therefore he was proclaiming Greenwich Village as an independent republic. "Do you hear that, world?" he shouted out over the empty square with its black iron railings and skeletal branches of the trees. "The glorious republic of Greenwich Village says No to war!"

Everybody cheered, and Vincent Millay, the beautiful chestnut-haired poetess of the theater group, ran up and hugged him, and then with an arm around his shoulders, recited in a throaty voice, "*We are the music makers, we are the dreamers of dreams*..."

Polly had never been so comfortable in a man's arms before—bear hug, rather. For a moment the thought of him and Corinne crossed her mind, and she was vaguely aware that Larry had slipped off into the darkness, but then Zoran kissed her.

She hadn't known that a man could be so soft, so playful. But my God, what was he doing with his hands! He was being scandalous. "Stop!" she squealed. "You're awful!"

"You don't like it?"

"But there are people..."

"Shut up," he growled in her ear. "Nobody care. I make you woman."

She looked into the sad, gentle eyes and understood.

"Don't worry," he said, "I wait until you ready," and when he knew she was, he whispered, "You've got hands, Polatchinka, help me."

The sounds of the cavorting crowd, the fire, the recitation, even an awareness of where she was, faded, so overcome was she by her own feelings of pleasure. All that remained were the stars in the night, and the man breathing beside her.

Larry had never seen her so happy. It tore him apart. In the days that followed, she told him everything, going over it again and again. It wasn't cruel, it was the natural overflowing of a woman who had thrown off fetters that had always bound her.

He was forced to hear all about the crazy Hungarian, how he had been a revolutionary in his native country before escaping to America, how he lived from doing odd jobs—he was a wizard at fixing all kinds of broken gadgets—how full of surprises he was.

One of his little surprises turned out to be a wife and children. He announced to Polly one day that he had to go to his son's wedding in New Jersey. For a while she was ready to break off with him, but he only laughed and called her a goose, and when she thought it over and realized that, much as she adored him, she wasn't in love with him that way, she decided she was being silly not to be grateful for what she had—after all she was close to thirty.

The whole situation at the teashop became so painful to

Larry—most of all when he heard the heavy-footed Slav bounding up the stairs to her room at night—that when America entered the war in April 1917 and he got his draft call, he was glad to go.

1918

FOLLOWING THE ARMISTICE IN NOVEMBER, THE WHOLE COUNTRY clamored to bring the boys home by Christmas. Not all the troops got home in time, but on a late Friday afternoon in mid-December aboard the U.S.S. *Grover Cleveland,* being pulled into a berth at the foot of West Thirty-fourth Street, were a thousand lucky doughboys who did make it.

An escorting fireboat sent long spouts of water into the air, the tugs tooted, and a brass band on the pier played "Stars and Stripes Forever." Streamers of confetti were falling from the ship over the welcoming crowd, and children perched on shoulders and waving tiny flags grabbed in the air for it.

Polly Endicott in a stylish hat trimmed in red fox and a matching neckpiece waited beside her mother, trying not to feel goose-pimply, and steeling herself against all the emotional hoopla. It was so obvious how they concocted this kind of atmosphere—anyone who knew anything at all about the theater could see that. It had nothing to do with how she felt about her brother, whom she had by no means forgiven.

Since he had been gone, she had tried her best not to think about him at all, though her mother always managed to bring his name up at least once whenever they saw each other. When America got into the war he had transferred into the American Expeditionary Forces, and had spent most of his time pinned down in the trenches on the Marne. Once, on leave, he had run into Corinne Ashmore at the hospitality center for Allied troops in Paris. Poor Corinne, on a visit to her family later, had been killed in a bombardment.

It was ironic that the only one of her friends who had been killed in the war was a woman. Every one of the boys she knew who had gone to fight had come home—her cousin Dennis Yates, and Lieutenant Larry Mathews—who had written her already from back home in Iowa—and now Eugene.

She tried not to look up at the hundreds of wildly yelling soldiers jammed at the ship's rails as the hawsers were dropped around the moorings and the gangways were pushed into place. She didn't want to pick him out. She was only here because her mother had begged her to come. It was pure sentimentality, and now she realized what a fool she had been to give in.

She wished she had gone instead with Zoran to see some of his Hungarian friends in Brooklyn—there was always food and music and turbulent political argument. He had come by to get her, and when she told him she couldn't go, they had had a terrible fight. That meant she wouldn't see him for a week. It was the same story as with Corinne—he disappeared over to New Jersey until he got bored with whoever was consoling him there. The Slavic lunacy that made him irresistible to everyone also made him the last man any woman could ever count on. Meanwhile, she had learned that other men besides him could find her attractive, as she fox-trotted with soldiers and sailors at the Red Cross social center on Times Square.

She could even have gone this evening to MacDougal Street and helped paint sets for the next production of the acting company she worked with. The Provincetown Players was attracting a few uptown critics down to the Village with experimental productions of Village playwrights. She was still running the Teaspoon, but it was really only her acting that meant anything to her. Although most of her parts were small, for a whole wonderful month she had been understudy for *Anna Christie* and had prayed the lead actress would fall through a trap door and break her neck so she could go on, but it never happened.

On the pier the band broke into "Over There" as the troops began marching off the ship, shouldering their packs. The cadre tried to form them up into ranks in the big shed below, but the crowd pressed forward and turned it all into confusion, anxious to reclaim their returning heroes.

"There he is!" Her mother gripped Polly's arm, waving her umbrella at the farther gangway.

"Mother, you don't have to . . ." She tried to feel some irritation, but her heart was pounding as her mother pulled her along, jostling her way through the milling crowd in the vast shed. For a week her mother had talked of nothing else but Eugene's homecoming.

"He's a man now, look at him!" Elizabeth said loudly, using her umbrella and her elbows to get through the people who stood between her and her son.

Polly saw him standing in the midst of a raggedly formed platoon in his campaign hat and puttees, and kicked herself for having come.

She would never forgive him, never.

Eugene was miserable as the other soldiers who had nothing to be ashamed of were welcomed back into the bosom of their families with joyous shouts. He was hoping against hope that neither his mother nor Polly would come. If only all this happy homecoming hoopla would get over with, they could be loaded onto the waiting trucks and taken over to the camp in New Jersey where in a few days they would be officially discharged.

He would only call his mother once he was out of the army and settled in a furnished room somewhere. They'd meet in a quiet place where things could be talked out unemotionally. She had alluded to nothing in her letters, but he knew she knew, and he dreaded the awkwardness between them.

He didn't want to see his sister at all. She had made it all too clear how she felt about him—she had never written a line. His mother tried to give the impression in her letters that Polly was so busy with her many activities she hardly saw her herself, but it was transparent. Polly had always sided with their father in everything. The one thing he was glad about, though he was ashamed to admit it, was that he would never have to face his father again. The whole time he had been off to the war, no matter what the dangers he had faced, what had happened on that day in the cellar and what his family thought about it was never entirely out of his mind. He prayed that they wouldn't show up.

A soldier named Hymie Liebman standing nearby was burned up that it had to be a Friday night the ship got in, so his family couldn't come over from Brooklyn to meet him.

They were Orthodox, and Friday sundown being the start of the Sabbath, they weren't allowed to carry money, not even the nickel for the subway.

But he was so excited about being back home in New York, he could hardly stand still. His bright eyes darted around everywhere, taking in all the emotional reunions in the noisy, echoing shed. He was watching the scene as Elizabeth, a handsome old woman in an English-worsted coat, and Polly, whom he took to be the fiancée, came up to Eugene. The fox skins around that doll's neck his furrier father wouldn't turn his nose up at.

While the band segued into "Glory, Glory Hallelujah," Elizabeth held her son at arm's length for a moment. Then she pressed him close with her eyes closed.

Stepping back and dabbing at her eyes with a lace handkerchief from her sleeve, she turned to Polly. "He's home, dear," she said.

Eugene and Polly faced each other. Polly was determined not to let anything show and held a stiff artificial smile on her face as she greeted him. Eugene, embarrassed, reached out a hand, but she couldn't go on with this ridiculous formal charade and her face broke. She threw her arms around him, tears slipping down her cheeks as she bit her lip.

"It's all right, Pol." He patted her back gratefully.

"Bless you for coming home to us, Gene," she said, looking up at him at last, and kissed him on the cheek.

It was the most undemonstrative welcome Hymie Liebman had ever seen. This fellow was just back from hell with poison gas and crab lice and Big Bertha blowing everybody to bits around him, and they acted like he was coming home from a Boy Scout jamboree. His own family when he saw them would go hysterical. They'd have to hold his mother up,to keep her from collapsing, and his sisters wouldn't stop crying as they held on to his sleeves, and even his strict old father would blubber like a baby, hugging him again and again.

If the women didn't show much, the fellow was even worse. Didn't he have any balls? Any girl deserved a better welcome than that. Hymie tilted back his campaign hat, trotted over, and moved Eugene aside. "Buddy, if she were my girl, this is how I'd do it." And, sweeping her into a big hug, he gave her a kiss she wouldn't forget so soon.

The three Endicotts stared at him as if he were a wild Indian.

Then, to his pleasure, they all came to life and laughed, explaining to him that the "sweethearts" were brother and sister. Hymie, who wasn't the least embarrassed, winked at Polly and said he hoped she'd excuse him, but he'd been away so long he couldn't help himself, and a knockout like her shouldn't be left within reach of a doughboy who hadn't seen an American girl or a bagel in a year.

Pleased with himself, he went back to his knapsack, but he couldn't take his eyes off the little shiksa with her light hair and turned-up nose like a dolly, and when the troops started getting into the trucks for the camp in New Jersey, he ran over and asked for her address.

✢✢✢✢✢✢✢

LIFE HAD SEEMED DULL TO ELIZABETH ENDICOTT SINCE HER husband's death, in spite of her volunteer war activities. She felt her spirits reviving when Eugene came home and the two of them started having their wonderful talks again. There was so much to catch up on, and Christmas was the perfect time for it, with the house redolent with the smell of pine from the tree in the front room—the first tree in years. They had got out the boxes of the exquisite Victorian ornaments from her childhood stored on the third floor, all still intact except for the Venetian glass angel that shattered in Eugene's hand.

It was so long since they had been together. She was glad that she had thrown out Patrick's old gas log after his death, so they could sit before a real fire of spruce, sipping eggnogs. They talked about many things—Polly, who was so sophisticated now with her odd Hungarian—Dominic, still under his father's thumb at the family restaurant—and always Eugene's writing, though he didn't show much enthusiasm when she spoke of his getting back to the Henry James piece. They went on talking in the kitchen as she rolled out dough for pumpkin pie. She brought him up a breakfast tray and then sat on his bed for hours.

They had their own little world again, though she was careful not to bring up anything she thought might be even mildly upsetting, after what he had gone through in the war. She didn't dwell on his father's decline after Eugene had gone off so precipitously, ending in the heart attack the night of the opening of the new subway when she was the only one who knew what his incoherent syllables meant—that he wanted a priest. It had made his death less painful to her that at the end he had acknowledged the faith he had seemed to be indifferent to for so long.

She described for her son, instead, his father's triumph on the dais when he was given recognition at last as a pioneer of the city's subway system, and most of all, his pleasure in seeing his grandson—the son Eugene didn't know—on their trip to Cincinnati, shortly before. Perhaps she shouldn't have mentioned to Eugene so soon how much Seth resembled him and how the serious little boy had climbed into his grandfather's lap and how they adored each other. But she was so anxious to have Eugene reconciled with his wife and child again that her grandmotherly bumbling could be excused. She should have known it was premature when he had hardly looked at the Kodak snapshots she showed him at the boat. Why, he still had the mud of the trenches on his boots!

For Eugene, it was all perfect, his homecoming. He hadn't expected it to be so easy. But why did his mother have to keep bringing up Clare and the baby? She had never alluded to them in her letters, and she knew he had asked Clare for a divorce.

On the long boat trip back to the States over the wintry North Atlantic, leaning on the rail at night with a cigarette, he had thought about what he was coming back to. While he was at the front, he was able to hide this thing in himself that he didn't understand, especially since his one attempt to give in to it had ended in the horror of his father's discovery. Not that it wasn't always at the back of his mind, but the penalties outweighed the temptations. Soldiers were court-martialed for it, and once he had seen a soldier beaten almost to death behind the barracks.

Going off to the war had been a solution for his predicament, but it was only a temporary one. Still, he hoped that he could avoid any open discussion with his mother about it.

It was while they were trimming the tree, her son on the ladder tying on the Viennese crystal pendants and she sitting by the fire pulling apart tinsel into strands, that she felt it was the right moment to talk about what was on her mind. After all, she wanted to help him get back into civilian life, and it was her belief that what had driven him off to the war would never have happened if Clare hadn't gone out to her mother to have the baby. Clare and he wouldn't have to expect too much of each other at first but, given his impulsive nature, he needed the security of being back with his wife and son.

She started chattering gaily about her own trip to Cincinnati a few months before and about how Seth was already making up little stories though he was only four and how well Clare looked, and then asked casually had he thought about going out there for a visit before settling down to his writing? It wouldn't commit him to anything.

He turned around on the ladder and, in a shaking voice unlike anything she had ever heard from him, told her to mind her own business. And when she said she didn't mean to tell him what to do at all, he accused her of pushing Seth and his wife on him from the first minute. Then, less unkindly, he said, "I know Seth is my kid, mother, but I'm not ready to be his father yet, don't you see? Clare and I are getting divorced and I don't want to argue about it."

She bit her lip, trying not to show her hurt. Of course it was the war making him talk like that. The newspapers were full of advice about returning soldiers needing to be handled with care after what they had gone through, but until now Gene had seemed so much like his old self. She had spoken too quickly again.

She told him that he had misunderstood her. She knew what a strain the war had been on him and he just needed time to get over it. He didn't have to do anything he didn't want to.

But his mother's excessive sympathy only made him angrier. He felt that his feelings were being swept under the rug. Simply in order to go on breathing he had to disperse the miasma of unreality smothering him. He got down from the ladder, went over to sit next to her, and took the tinsel out of her hands. Keeping his voice under control, he said, "Look, there's something we're not talking about and I think it's time we did."

"Oh, all that fuss about what happened in the basement," she said, knowing instantly what he was referring to. "What does that have to do with anything?" What a pity, she thought, that he had run off to war because of that, but the whole thing had been blown up out of all proportion. It was just unfortunate that his father had gone downstairs at that moment. After all, Eugene took after her and was an imaginative person. Pat had been limited in so many ways. She had learned to live with him but it was never easy, even though she had loved him, she supposed. "Do you have to torment yourself over it, dear?" she said. "It only happened once and that was a long time ago."

He was in despair. She could only see it as an escapade, not the result of something that had been burning inside him for years, driving him wild—and still was. He threw the tinsel into the fire and said harshly. "If it doesn't bother you, the rest of the world doesn't take it so lightly. There are laws against it. And look what happened—my father went to his grave because of it."

When she insisted it was heart trouble, he wouldn't let her off the hook. This thing in him, he said, was wrecking everybody's life, not just his own. "Look what I did to Clare, and what kind of life is my son facing, with a father like me? God, what if he's inherited it!" He put a fist to his forehead. "It's horrible," he said. "The world hates me for it, my own father hated me, and I hate myself worst of all."

This Elizabeth couldn't allow—not her son. "Stop that, Eugene!" she said, putting a hand on his arm as if to transmit the steel of her ancestors whose morality was based on the dignity of every man as an individual. "In the first place, your father did not hate you. I'll admit he couldn't understand, any more than I really can, but I saw from the way he looked at your son who is the image of you, that it was you he loved in him."

"Don't talk sentimental gibberish! It must have broken his heart all over again to be reminded that he had a nance for a son."

There was no doubt that she was shocked by the word. In itself it meant nothing to her, but the way he spat it out brought home to her better than all his talk the depths of his bitterness and despair.

She was at a loss how to help him. The single idea she clung to was that he had to get back to his writing. He was a fine writer—his published article had proved it to the world. But for four years he had been cut off from it. Without an outlet, his fertile imagination had somehow created this morbid phantasmagoria he couldn't deal with.

The next day she did not bring him his breakfast in bed, and when he came down to the kitchen for coffee, she told him that she had been doing a lot of thinking and it had finally come to her that what he needed most was a special place of his own to work in, and she had the solution. She was going to call in workmen immediately to convert the ground floor of the house into a separate apartment for him. She'd be just upstairs if he felt like seeing her. That way he could get right down to work on the Henry James piece he had never finished.

She was so full of hope this morning, his indomitable mother. In spite of not understanding the first thing about it, she had come up with one of her "sensible" solutions that was supposed to take care of everything—even arranging it so that she would be there, as if there was anything that she could do.

But he too had done some thinking in the night. Bringing that word out into the open, applying it to himself for the first time, even if it was repulsive, had made a change in him. He was as baffled as ever how to live with it, but he felt able to take the first step.

He told her as carefully as he could that the Henry James piece belonged to an earlier period of his life. He had lacked experience of his own to write about then.

As he talked, he was thinking about how to tell her that he had to find a place of his own, but she counted so much on not losing him—why, she looked twenty years younger as she sat there, full of her plans for him, for the two of them together. But he'd never find out who he was if he stayed here. The very walls of this old house he had grown up in watched him, made him feel guilty.

There were no guides ahead, no books of instruction. All he had ever seen were a few ambiguous items in the papers about arrests and scandals. He had never found anyone to explain anything—the way Mabel Dodge had talked was up in the clouds. A part of him wanted the safety of wife and child, the comfort of mother, but that would only be running away.

When he told her that he had to move out because he needed more privacy for his work, she bravely said she understood—but how old she looked to him then.

As her son went on about his plans to find some kind of part-time job, behind Elizabeth's show of encouragement she was thinking that what he needed the privacy for was more than just writing, and she was afraid.

POLLY'S ON-AGAIN OFF-AGAIN AFFAIR WITH ZORAN HAD TAUGHT her a lot, but he had never been the right man for her. With Hymie Liebman it was different. From the moment of his flamboyant embrace at the troopship, she was head over heels. When he took her phone number she only waited for his call. She expected it the next weekend after he had a few days with his family, but it turned out even better—he phoned her from Penn Station the minute he got in from the army separation center three days later, and came down to see her before catching the el home to Flatbush.

He was the same energetic little guy she remembered, but with his discharge in his pocket he had thrown over the last pretense of conforming to military regulations. He was still in uniform—he had nothing else to wear until he got home—but he was hatless, and his hair already growing out was falling over his brow as if declaring its own freedom. He had left off the belt of his scratchy Army overcoat and it hung in a decidedly unmilitary manner. Even the puttees around his shins were laced up crookedly.

Right off, he picked up his knapsack and dumped it out onto one of the tables. Fishing around, he came up with a bottle of perfume he said he got for her in Paris. She reminded him he hadn't known her until three days ago and it must be for his mother.

He told her his mother wouldn't know perfume from chicken soup, and besides, he had a cuckoo clock for her. "Take it," he said, handing her the perfume, his eyes bright on her.

She took his gift.

At thirty, Polly felt like a late starter to have fallen in love for the first time. But she looked ten years younger than her age and she saw no reason, since Hymie was only twenty-three, not to let him go on thinking that she was Eugene's little sister.

When he came by the next evening, with a bouquet of long-stemmed roses for her, the slovenly doughboy of the previous day had vanished. He was dazzling in newly purchased splendor he must have gone into hock for—an expensive blue pin-striped suit and snap-brim fedora. With his sleek hair parted on one side as he thrust a bunch of violets into her hand, he had the flashy look she once despised in the men she went out with, but was just right for this dark alert young man from Brooklyn.

He asked her where she would like to go that night, the sky was the limit. Without thinking, she said dancing at the Peacock Court of the Plaza. Some buyer from out of town had taken her there during her secretary days and she couldn't think of anywhere else that sounded fancy enough, considering how he was dressed.

Hymie laughed and said he had just spent his last two bits on the flowers. "Will you take a rain check on the Plaza and settle for the Staten Island ferry instead?"

It was freezing on the deck crossing New York harbor, but from the shelter of a warm-air vent they watched the skyscrapers of lower Manhattan vanishing into the fog. In a cocoon of white mist they listened to the plash of water against the hull, the warning blasts of the ferry's horn, and the answering toots of passing boats alternating with the eerie chiming of buoys.

Hymie was full of plans for his future in real estate. Before the war, he had worked for an uncle who had a realty office in Brooklyn, but his sights were set on Manhattan. There were two or three neighborhoods a clever real estate man could make a buck in and, though no one else had caught on yet, Greenwich Village was the best of the lot. As the city had grown, the

Village had been overlooked, but it was clear to him that there was a fortune to be made there.

"But it's got such a bad name," Polly said, and told him about an article in the *Saturday Evening Post* that called it "a nest of freaks and perverts."

Hymie was undaunted. "Let 'em say it. I can sell that. It's free publicity." He leaned an arm against the rim of the ventilator. "The war's over, people are ready for a good time again. They'll flock down to ogle the freaks and perverts. Come here, you little pervert." He gave her a hug.

The old-fogey thinking of the real estate companies, he went on enthusiastically, was dead as a doornail. They still thought people only wanted to live like the stuffy rich on their Park Avenues and Riverside Drives. "But this is a new age, Polly. It's veterans like me—young people like us—who are going to lead the way. We're throwing all the old ideas out the window." And he picked her up and whirled her around.

She envied him, she said, when he let her get her breath. He was moving so fast, the way he talked—and she was stagnating. "I've been stuck at that teashop—" She stopped herself just in time from saying, ". . . for six years," and giving her age away. He made her feel a million years older than him.

"What do you do it for?"

"I don't really know." For a long time, she told him, she had to stay there because Corinne Ashmore had left her in charge. After the news of Corinne's death, when she had taken over the lease, she had thought about giving it up and going on the professional stage. "But I don't have that much experience and"—she couldn't tell him that you didn't start a theatrical career at thirty—"and besides, I don't think my face is right for Broadway."

"What are you talking about? You're gorgeous. Why don't you sell that teashop you hate so much and give it a try?"

"What's there to sell? It's not like I owned the building. Only some old tables and chairs and an iron cookstove."

"You've got a going business, a regular clientele, a reputation. It's worth a bundle."

They were so busy talking about so many things that when the boat got to Staten Island they didn't get off, and when it got back to Manhattan again, they didn't get off either. They rode back and forth until dawn broke over the skyline, dispersing the last wisps of fog.

As they walked up lower Broadway through the canyons

of the empty financial district, the windows of the towers reflecting the red streaks of the sunrise, Hymie made up a song for them.

"We were so jolly, we were so merry,
"We rode all night back and forth on the ferry."

At the end of the last century, waves of immigrants had poured into the country expecting the gold that was fabled to be picked up on the streets. Many of these arrivals came from other places than those who had come earlier. They were swarthier people—Mediterranean, Semitic, with unpronounceable names. But instead of finding gold, they were packed into tenement slums and blocked on all sides by an entrenched society that was determined to hold the barriers against them. Yet their children went off to the war just like the scrubbed sons of the "real Americans"—and went through the same nightmare.

The war that blew up their buddies also blew to smithereens the old barriers that kept the immigrants down, and those who came back were lean and hungry, no longer willing to accept crumbs while others got the pie.

One of the hungriest was Hymie Liebman. He had been waiting his whole twenty-three years for his chance, and after the Armistice he shot out into the postwar world like a cannonball.

Hymie was the first Jew to be hired by the Darby and White Real Estate Agency on Eighth Street that specialized in Village properties. He wouldn't have gotten the job if they had known he was Jewish. But after having the door slammed in his face too many times because, in the euphemistic language of the employment agencies and want ads, he wasn't "clean cut," he got smart and gave his name as Henry Lambert.

"If I'd caught them looking too hard at my shnozz, I was ready to tell them I had a French grandmother in the woodpile," he told Polly jubilantly, "but they swallowed Henry Lambert hook, line, and sinker."

Using a fake name didn't bother him one bit if it would get him a foot in the door. When they heard his ideas, they'd soon see he was worth triple the peanuts they were going to pay him.

In the opinion of Darby and White, the Village was a near slum and they had little interest in keeping it from deteriorating further. No one wanted to buy old houses anyway which, unlike the Endicotts' house, were mostly either dilapidated, had inadequate plumbing and wiring, or were teeming with boarders, insect and human. There were plenty of impoverished artists and their camp followers flocking to the Village for cheap rooms and studios. But even if the agency did a brisk business renting to them, rents were so low that the commissions were, as Hymie quickly learned, pitiful.

Still, it was clear as day to him that real estate in the Village was ready to take off in a whole new direction. The old gentility was out of date. He'd show them how to sell the bohemian angle, instead of pretending that it didn't exist, and people with money would come because it was fun to live there. Now was just the time for Darby and White to invest in some of those crumbling old buildings off Fifth Avenue that had turned into rooming houses and renovate them. All they'd have to do is rip out the old plumbing and makeshift wiring and cut away the low-class brownstone stoops, and fix them up as elegant one-family residences again.

But when he laid his plans out on the table, the old boys failed to share his enthusiasm. They had the goyish idea, he told Polly, that doing business with caution and dignity—the way they always had—was more important than trying something new and going after the big money. It was going to take him a while to get through to them. They weren't used to a live wire like him.

But time was just the thing they didn't have if they were going to capitalize on the opportunity he was showing them. If Darby and White didn't do it, somebody else would.

If he could only lay his hands on a little capital—a couple of thousand, say—he'd tell them to go blow and do it himself.

He found himself a couple of ramshackle rooms at the corner of Christopher Street and Greenwich Avenue above a bar popularly known as the Working Girls' Home—why, nobody knew, because it attracted a hard-drinking crowd.

The first time he took Polly to show her his place, as soon as he closed the door, they fell onto the bed. For a second she remembered a shabby cot in a loft above a machine shop and a frosty night on top of the Washington Square arch, but this time she was in love.

Hymie pulled her over on top of him and breathed, "My own shiksa, come to your Jew boy."

As excited as she was, she was taken aback.

"Say it, tell it to me with your goyish lips."

She tried to turn away her face but he forced it back.

"Say 'my own Jew boy.'"

She felt herself tightening in the old way and, despairing, she saw herself losing him. But he kept insisting and, feeling a profound shame, she managed to choke out the words, "My own Jew boy." The words set her on fire and she opened to him. And soon, locked in his arms, she was crying out uncontrollably and repeatedly, "My own Jew boy!" answering his sobbing, "My own shiksa."

Afterward, lying on an elbow, she studied his wiry body, wondering at his circumcision.

"You look like something out of the Fourth of July," he said, running a finger over her uptilted freckled little nose. "You're the most beautiful thing I've ever seen."

She raised an eyebrow. "With these little titties?" She giggled as she sank down against him.

"You're nuts," he said. "I don't go for big Jewish boobs." And he lovingly fondled her nymphet breasts.

She was due back at the Teaspoon and it put her in a rage. As she wrenched on her clothes, she told him she wished she could douse it with gasoline and set a match to it once and for all. She hated the place.

"If you got rid of that damn albatross like I told you, you could do what you want for a change."

"How could I?" she said impatiently. "Who'd buy it?"

"Didn't I tell you I could sell it for you?" he said, lying back with his hands behind his head, watching her. "I'm a real estate genius, even if Darby and White don't know it." He laughed.

As she put a foot on a chair and pulled up her skirt to roll down a garter, his eyes feasted on the display of white thigh above the stocking top. "Why don't you let me try? It'd be fun and you'll be free to become a star in the moving pictures. You're a lot cuter than Lillian Gish."

She blew him a wry kiss. "It takes a while to become a star, fool, and I don't much want to move back with my mother while I'm waiting."

"No problem. Move in here with me—this place could use a woman's touch." He waved an arm around the bare room with unpacked boxes stacked on the linoleum floor. "We'll live off my salary until you make it."

"And then we'll take the teashop money," she said, buckling the strap of a shoe, "and go on a spree."

"We'll blow it on the Peacock Court!" Then he sat bolt upright. "Wait a minute!" He threw off the sheet and jumped out of bed, naked. "Why didn't I think of it before? There's the cash I need!" Dancing around the room, he told her that now he could buy one of those run-down houses on Tenth Street and fix it up. "I don't need those old fots at the agency. We'll be on easy street."

When Polly saw the plausibility of the scheme, even with no head for business, she was so caught up in the prospect of doing what she wanted that she grabbed the key to the teashop out of her pocketbook and, brandishing it in the air, ran to the window to throw it as far away as she could.

"Are you nuts?" he said, leaping to grab it out of her hand. "How am I going to sell it without that?"

She tried to tell Hymie about Zoran so there would be no secrets between them, but he stopped her with a kiss. "Great idea! Then I'll tell you all the details about the mam'selles I had in France, okay?"

She protested that he was not taking her seriously, treating her as if she were a little girl, but she was greatly relieved.

But the problem remained, what to do about Zoran. She knew there was no reason to feel guilty—he himself disappeared all the time to beds in Jersey and elsewhere—but it was not going to be easy to tell him it was all over between them. Impossible as he was, he could be such an angel.

She hadn't seen him since he had walked out in a rage the day of her brother's homecoming. But sure enough, one day he waltzed into the teashop all hearts and flowers again. With a big wet kiss, he said, "Hello, beautiful." His large eyes looked at her like a St. Bernard. "How's my little Polatchinka?"

Wishing he didn't have to make it so damn hard for her, she said she had something to talk to him about. He paid no attention but tried to drag her upstairs, entertaining all the customers. It was like getting untangled from an octopus, but she managed to get him out the front door and around the corner to Chumley's bar where they could sit in a quiet booth.

She couldn't bear to think of him being out of her life, but it wasn't right to Hymie to go on with him.

"Did my little pancake miss me? What a pile of shit Zoran is. I promise I never walk out on you again."

He was making it even harder for her. She said she didn't mind his walking out—he had a perfect right to. They had agreed always to leave each other free, and that's what she wanted to talk to him about.

He snuggled up. She was so edible, he said, and he began to nibble her ear.

She pushed him away. "Will you stop it! I'm trying to talk to you." And she got up to sit across the table from him.

Keeping his hands that were exploring under the table from going up her skirt, she told him about Hymie and her plan to sell the teashop and move in with him, and that though she was sick at having to do this to him, she had to break it off.

When he appeared not to have heard and went on trying to get at her under the table, she asked if he was listening. She was only sorry she wouldn't be seeing him, because she did think of him as one of her best friends.

"Why we don't meet any more? I miss you if I don't see you." He managed to wiggle his great body under the table and appeared up on the chair next to her, snapping his fingers at the waiter for champagne for the bride.

When it arrived, he told the waiter to put it on Polly's account and called him a bourgeois pig for good measure. Touching his glass to hers, he said he hoped she was going to be very happy and, putting on a fierce face, added that if the new boyfriend was not good to her, he'd tear him limb from limb.

Then, putting his cheek against hers, he murmured, "How about we do it too from time to time?" looking up at her with his big sad eyes.

He had done every number in his book, but he was such a transparent clown. She put her arms around him. He gave his rumble of a laugh and let her rock him in her arms.

POLLY HAD SCRUBBED HER FACE WITH SOAP AND WATER SO that her freckles showed and her snub nose was shiny. She looked with approval at her teenage-looking reflection in the mirror. Not that she could stand her gamine face any more than she ever had, but at least now it was going to be good for something. She had an audition that afternoon at the New Amsterdam Theater on Forty-second Street to try out for the part of the kid sister in a play called *Lilac Time*.

She was through with the teashop. Hymie had sold it for her to a woman who claimed to be a Hungarian countess, but who Zoran said was as much Hungarian as he was Filipino and it took a pure-blooded Magyar to smell a fake.

She was living with Hymie now and, with his encouragement, was going after parts in Broadway plays. He didn't see any future for her in the semi-amateur experimental theater company in the Village she had been fooling around with, and she agreed with him.

Since she felt at least ten years behind her real age anyway, and looked it too, it was simply being more realistic for her to try out for character juvenile roles—older actresses with her kind of looks were always cast in them. Before Hymie, she had done nothing with her life that meant anything, except for her affair with Zoran, which had been the merest beginning. She was only starting to do now what other people would have done ten years before.

Hymie had used the money from the sale of the teashop to buy up one of the old rooming houses off Fifth Avenue and he was in the process of turning it back into the handsome town house it once had been. He said he would be able to buy two more of the old wrecks on the block with what he would make from the sale of it. It would be a start. He still had his job at the real estate agency, but he was going into business for himself as soon as the deal paid off. She had already typed up the prospectus for him to show buyers. He had swiped a list of gilt-edged customers from the files at Darby and White's. He didn't feel any loyalty to those racist bastards.

She tied her hair back with a big bow like a schoolgirl and, just to be sure, powdered over again a kiss mark on the side of her neck.

Hymie was a powerhouse in every way, never wasting a minute. He always brought home a briefcase full of papers to study from the office. After losing a year to the Army, he said he had a lot of catching up to do if he was going to be a millionaire by the time he was twenty-five.

And when he wasn't working, he was always ready for a lark, like going over to Hoboken for steamed clams, or sneaking into the Ziegfeld Follies at intermission. Once, at midnight, they even took off their shoes and stockings and splashed in the august fountain in front of the Plaza Hotel.

He was as intense about his appearance as he was about work and play. When they were out, he looked like a brilliantine ad, the pants of his pin-striped suit pressed to knife-sharp creases and his pointed black shoes polished like mirrors. He was such a bundle of energy, women couldn't keep their eyes off him.

She teased him about the goo-goo eyes Edna St. Vincent Millay had for him. The vamp of the Provincetown Players had become even more successful as a poet than as a playwright, and her appetite for men had not decreased either. Whenever they ran into "Vincent," she always bantered with Hymie about the possibility of him selling her house for her. It was reputed to be the narrowest house in the Village—just nine feet wide. He would make some comeback, that they both found hilarious, about not having come across any midgets to buy it yet, or people who liked to live sideways. He was just as ready as Zoran to jump at every calculating woman's bait.

But he teased Polly back, saying that with her irresistible freckles and cute little nose, she didn't have to worry about competition from any high-powered man-eaters—and besides, what about her and Larry Mathews?

Her former assistant was back in New York painting in a studio over by the river and was always asking her advice about his girl problems. He wasn't as bashful with girls any more—though still the strong silent type—and was making up for lost time. But as Hymie well knew, she and Larry were like brother and sister.

Her mother adored Hymie, of course. She could never hide her attraction for young men and basked in his flattery that she looked like Lillian Russell.

But whenever Polly asked him about his own parents, he was evasive and said, what did she want to meet them for, they lived way out in Flatbush.

It was clear that he didn't want to talk about them, so she let it drop. She suspected he was not on very good terms with them since they hadn't come to meet him at the troopship. Maybe he was ashamed of them—they probably spoke with an accent and lived in a tenement. It must be that—that they were old-fashioned. He was so fanatic about being up-to-date about everything.

She struck a pose in front of the mirror with her hands on her hips and a grin on her face, as if she had just made a wisecrack to big sister. She might be over thirty, but no one was ever going to know it. She was a perfect character juvenile, and this was her big chance.

Just as she was putting on her coat to head uptown to the audition her stomach went into a spasm and she ran to the sink and began throwing up.

When it didn't stop, she went to the doctor who confirmed that she was pregnant.

She waited until the following evening. She and Hymie had already made plans to go to a new speakeasy on Eighth Street, but now a raucous atmosphere was the last thing she wanted. She cajoled him into taking her back on the Staten Island ferry, using the unlikely ploy that it was their eleventh-month anniversary.

Was she crazy, he said? It was November, and cold out there. But she said it wasn't *that* cold. She was feeling sentimental, and it was exactly what she was in the mood for.

"Since when are you so schmaltzy?"

"There are a lot of things about me you don't know."

But standing against the rail at the back of the boat watching the wake, the nostalgic mood she was hoping for didn't materialize. He kidded her that the eye shadow she had put on to hide the ravages of a sleepless night made her look like Theda Bara.

She held off until they were out in the middle of the harbor and were reminiscing over their first date on the same ferry. She had an idea, she said offhandedly as he lit her cigarette. Wouldn't it be fun if they got married?

Married? What had gotten into her? He already had enough problems without that.

She looked out over the white-roiling wake to the Statue of Liberty whose raised arm had been closed to the public because it couldn't hold the weight of sight-seers trudging up to the torch. She tried to keep her tone light. "You're going to make all those buckets of money and I want to be sure I get my share."

But he didn't laugh as she hoped. Why change anything, he said? Weren't things just fine the way it was?

"Of course, it's fine. I just want to, that's all."

He fixed his dark, intense eyes on her, then puffing fast on his cigarette, turned away toward the lights of Ellis Island where his parents had landed a quarter of a century before, just in time for him to be born in America. He ground the cigarette out on the deck and lit another. "You're serious about this, aren't you?"

"Well, wouldn't it be fun?" she said, sensing it was not going right. "We could play house for a while, and if we get tired of it, we could get a divorce—everybody's doing it."

But the more anxious she showed herself, the more remote he became, until exasperated, she dropped the last of her pretense. "Well, what's wrong with it? I thought we were supposed to be crazy about each other. Don't tell me you have a wife too!"

He was still looking off over the dark water, smoking restlessly. "If that were the problem, it wouldn't be a problem. I don't know if I can make you understand." He turned back to her and after a moment said, "It's my family."

"What do they have to do with anything!" He hadn't even let her meet them. How could he be so sure they wouldn't like her?

It wasn't that, he said. It was that his family still believed in the old traditions. "I may have a business haircut and drink bathtub gin and even eat bacon and eggs with you every Sunday morning Pol, but a part of me has still got invisible earlocks flapping."

"What in hell are you talking about?"

He explained that his parents were Orthodox, and if he married her, they'd go into mourning for him as if he were dead and grieve for the rest of their lives.

She said if they cared about him so much, why hadn't they come to the troopship to meet him. When he explained that that was because it was Friday night, she said she had never heard of anything so cockeyed.

It probably didn't make sense to anyone else, he said, but his religion was five thousand years old, and after what they had gone through to keep it, they weren't going to drop their customs just because they seemed out-of-date.

She wanted to grab him and shake him hard and tell him she didn't care about all that, he had to marry her, she was pregnant. But something held her back. He was far more complicated than she imagined—almost alien. Much as she hated to admit it at this moment, maybe it was this unknown part of him that had always attracted her the most.

"So you see, Pol," he said, putting his arm around her, his fast-talking self again, "it just wouldn't be the right thing for us. We're okay the way we are, aren't we? We love each other."

Defeated, she wound her scarf around her neck against the chill and said that of course it was all right as they were.

He was as eager as she was to pull back from the abyss that had opened before them, and he sang his corny song about being very jolly and very merry and riding all night back and forth on the ferry.

But they didn't stay all night on the ferry this time. They went back to the Village to the new speakeasy he wanted to go to on Eighth Street where she drank too much gin, and when they came home and he tried to make love to her, she told him she wasn't feeling well, her period was coming on early.

It wasn't hard getting the name of someone. A woman she knew who ran a weaving shop across the street had used the man a number of times already and took her to the ordinary apartment house out in Queens. As she lay waiting on the makeshift operating table, the man, who claimed to be a doctor, said there was nothing to worry about, she'd be as good as new in no time. But two hours later she was still bleeding when he said she had to get out of there. Her friend helped her to the cab and she went to her mother's to rest up for a few days.

Every time Zoran had made love to her, he slipped on a "safe," but Hymie never had. She had been too embarrassed to say anything, but why the hell hadn't she? *She* was the one who had to spread her legs on the kitchen table to be mangled by the abortionist. It was her own damn fault playing the innocent twenty-year-old when she was thirty. If Hymie was irresponsible, she couldn't afford to be.

Before going back to her lover, she turned around the gold birthstone ring her father had given her so that it looked like a wedding band and went to the Margaret Sanger Clinic to be fitted for a diaphragm.

With the diaphragm in her purse, she followed an impulse and stopped off at a hairdressing salon to have her hair bobbed and marcelled. Everybody had been talking about this new hairstyle since the rotogravure pictures in the papers of French women at the Armistice celebration in Paris. Still it was an extreme thing to do, but she didn't want any trace left of that pug-nosed, freckle-face little daddy's girl. Her old act revolted her. Hymie would have to take her as she was.

But prepared for the worst, she got a surprise when it was over. With her hair short, she looked even younger than before.

On New Year's Eve—it was 1920—as she and Hymie toasted their first year together with champagne cocktails, he said they hadn't seen anything yet. The new decade was going to be a roller coaster ride like nobody had seen before and the two of them were going to take it all the way to hell and back together.

How adorably innocent he was, how maternal she felt. My love, she thought, as she looked into his eyes and they touched champagne glasses, I'm crazy about you and can't live without you, but I won't fly off into the blue any more. You can have your dreams and I'll be there for you all the way, but I'm looking after myself from now on.

"ADDIO MI BELLA NAPOLI..." BEYOND THE KITCHEN DOORS OUT in the restaurant where the engagement party was taking place, his father began singing in his still-glorious tenor voice. Dominic Alfano stopped whipping cream to listen to the song that always made him homesick for the Naples of his ancestors. Even if he had been raised by Italians, as an Italian, it was the Italian half of him that sometimes seemed to be more the orphan.

But now everything was going to be all right—he was getting married. But with all the relatives and friends gathered to celebrate the engagement, he wasn't sorry to escape out to the kitchen. *Nonna* Alfano, his grandmother, loved his Zuppa Inglese and had asked him as a special favor to make one at the last minute, although that morning he had already baked anise and pignole cookies, and a spumoni with six flavors of ice cream was in the icebox.

"*...Addio mi bella Napoli...*" The boisterous company was silent as his father's voice soared above accordion and violin accompanying him. Even the children had stopped running around among the tables.

In his year in Italy studying cooking Dominic had gone down to Naples, even taken the little train around the slopes of Mt. Vesuvius and the vaporetto out to Capri—he had seen it all. But listening to the sobs in his father's bel canto voice it was not the Naples he had seen that he longed for now, but some lost paradise.

In Turin he had met a girl he wanted to marry, a blonde girl of the north, like the pictures of his mother who had died at his birth. But his father had discouraged it, and made him see that it was better that he marry an American.

When he got home, he had been too busy helping build up the restaurant to even think of marriage. But once it was doing well, his father said what was he waiting for, he was nearly twenty-seven years old.

He added a few drops of Strega just before the cream was completely whipped, and when it stood in peaks, he got down from the cooling rack the large pan holding the cake of egg batter and candied fruits, and soaked the cake with rum before swirling the whipped cream over the top.

He liked being the cook—the kitchen was the place he was at his best—but when the family had first started the restaurant, he resented having to work there after school and on weekends because it had cut him off from his mother's family, the Endicotts, especially his wonderful grandmother Elizabeth. She and Polly and Eugene were at his engagement party today, even if *Nonna* didn't want them to be invited, but his father had shut her up. *Nonna* was always talking against them.

The restaurant was called the Bocce because of the *bocce* court in the back room with the hard dirt floor where neighborhood men bowled with steel balls as others sat at tables beside the low rail, drinking and eating and commenting on the game until their turn to play. The Bocce had attracted from the start a regular clientele of neighborhood people, so the Alfanos didn't have to depend on outsiders who didn't know good Italian food from bad. They didn't need liquor to make a go of it. They served the best food anywhere, in the Bolognese style that combined butter and olive oil and homemade wine.

The *bocce* court made a picnic atmosphere where families came to spend hours at long tables as if they were eating beneath the vines behind a farmhouse in the old country. His father had painted every inch of the walls with sunflowers and olive and lemon trees like a garden, and on the ceilings, cupids among the clouds. They had made it even more festive for the party today with crepe paper rosettes and streamers and silver cutouts of Punchinello and Colombina.

As a final touch, he sprinkled over the whipped cream a

handful of crushed pistachio nuts and chopped candied cherries and put a fringe of paper around the pan. With one foot he pushed his way through the swinging door into the dining room and, resting the tray on his shoulder, stood behind a pillar painted with a prancing satyr and waited for the music to finish.

Still pouring out the endless verses of the old song, his roly-poly father was standing behind the head table, gesturing with his pudgy arms and dabbing a red handkerchief from time to time to the sweat on his bald head. His father had sung at parties ever since he could remember—he loved to be with people so much, how could he help but be the center of attention? It was almost as if his father were the one getting engaged to Rosalie.

His fiancée was gazing up entranced from her chair, listening to the song with her full lips parted. In a beaded pink dress with lace around the neck, she had the air of a Titian madonna he had seen in the Turin cathedral, and with the same hint of a blush on her face. *Che bella*. It was only in Italian—the language he had learned from his *Nonna* before he knew English—that he could describe her, his *promessa sposa*. She was just out of the convent school of St. Joseph on Sixth Avenue, educated by nuns the same as in Italy. Her father was a wholesale butcher, and the restaurant got its meat from him.

Rosalie was younger than he was and they hardly knew each other, but she would be a good wife. He had so little experience with women, but of course, if he needed any advice, his father would always be there for him.

She was going to work in the restaurant with the family and *Nonna* would train her. His Italian grandmother, though she was nearly eighty, still supervised making the red wine they served, even though it had become illegal since Prohibition. But there was nothing to worry about. They weren't a speakeasy and the cops knew it. How could you eat Italian food without wine?

A lot of the other restaurants in the Village had turned into speakeasies and were packed with uptowners coming down for bootleg liquor. When that happened, it was the end of a place as a restaurant, his father said. His father didn't want to have anything to do with liquor or the bootleggers who supplied it. When they came around talking tough, he threw them out—he wasn't afraid of anybody.

But even with the talk of bootleggers forcing restaurants to turn into speaks, it wasn't all bad—not the way Dominic saw it. A lot of people in the neighborhood who didn't have a chance before were going around these days with money falling out of their pockets, and some of them were already parking their fancy automobiles under the fire escapes and laundry.

"*. . . Addio mi bella Napoli . . .*" His father was into the final refrain. Among all the Mediterranean faces, his three Endicott relatives stood out. His grandmother Elizabeth, in a big hat swathed in veils and a lavender suit, was sitting imposingly between Eugene and Polly at a table on the side. It was hard to believe that she was almost as old as *La Nonna,* who was wrinkled and bent over and always in black.

He was glad the Endicotts didn't understand Italian because of the things *Nonna* always muttered about them . . . Elizabeth a widow and dressed like that, for example. When he defended Polly's short hair because she was an actress, the old woman said it was the next thing to being a *puttana*.

He didn't care what she said. He loved his grandmother Elizabeth, and Polly had always been nice to him. It was harder to talk to Eugene, but then Eugene was a college graduate and a writer, and he himself had such a stupid tongue. His *Nonna* didn't have a good word to say about Eugene either—he had left his wife and gotten a divorce. There was no good in any of the Endicotts and she was always warning him that he had to watch out for their bad blood in his veins.

The song ended. His father was triumphantly wiping the sweat from his bald head as everyone stamped and applauded, shouting for an encore, but he saw Dominic waiting with the cake pan. "Hey, Dominic, where you been? You come over here and sit down by your sweetheart where you belong. What you runnin away for?"

His father trotted over and, as everyone laughed, took the cake, flourishing it in the air with one hand and with the other pushing Dominic over to the chair beside the girl he was going to marry.

Dominic wasn't able to look at her with all the people watching, but he was dizzy from the scent of her long dark hair. Even her skin smelled as fragrant as orange blossoms. For a moment he had a faded memory of the delicate blonde girl in Italy he had broken off with, but he put it out of his mind. Was this vivid creature really going to share his bed? How could he wait the months till June? Now that they were engaged, he hoped that they wouldn't have a chaperone every time they were together.

The violin and accordion began a peppy *danza* and his father, his cheeks flushed with wine, called out to him, "Hey, Dom and Rosalie, what you waiting for?" Everyone started clapping in time to the music, urging them to take to the floor. But Dominic didn't want to fall on his face in front of them all and make a fool of himself with Rosalie—he never could dance, he couldn't follow the beat—so he made a comic show of hiding his head under his arms.

The room roared. His nimble father gulped down a glassful of wine and wiped his hands on his rotund belly. "If he don't want to, Rosalie, I guess we got no choice!" He held his hand out to the blushing girl and danced her off in a tarantella.

Everyone joked about what a perfect couple they made, calling out to Dominic that if he didn't watch out, his old man was going to carry off his bride. His grandmother Alfano, having drunk too much, hollered that that was the kind of girl her son should have married in the first place and, turning to Dominic as she kept time with her old gnarled hands, said that with Endicott blood in him, no wonder he couldn't dance like a real Italian.

"Ah, grandma, you're crazy," he said as he clapped to the music.

His father, in spite of his weight, was as light on his feet as a boy, and after dancing Rosalie recklessly around the room, he delivered her back to the table, a flush of excitement on her cheeks and the tight armpits of her pink satin dress wet. As she sat down, she glanced at Dominic, then looked away embarrassed—she was still so shy with him. That was the way a virgin should be, his father had said, like a sleeping princess, and it was up to the husband to awaken her.

The musicians were playing a medley from *La Traviata,* and everybody joined in singing the drinking song. But when the "*A Quell' Amor*" began, his father's voice took over and he turned to sing it especially to Dominic and Rosalie. But he wasn't singing for them. It was as if the music had carried him away, as if he were thinking of something else, long past—and listening, Dominic felt a stab of the old longing in his chest. Before the reprise, his father turned away and moved across the room to stand in front of grandmother Elizabeth. His hand on his heart, he sang to her alone Verdi's affirmation of an impossible love, his grandmother Elizabeth's eyes never leaving his.

Dominic didn't know what the memory was that bound

them. What had happened before he was born had never been spoken about, but he knew that what he was homesick for was a world that had disappeared before he was born.

His father was taking the final note an octave higher, as he never did ordinarily, and when it faded away, his grandmother Elizabeth waited a moment in the silence that followed as if controlling her feelings, then raised her wineglass to him in a gesture of thanks.

Then, everything happened so fast he was never clear about it afterward. Everybody in the Bocce that night told different versions of it to the police. His father came back to the table in an exalted mood and, smiling broadly before them, banged a fork against his glass for attention. "My dear company," he said, "join me in a toast to the good fortune of my son and the beautiful girl who is to be his bride. . . ."

He had never looked so happy, his father, so full of love, when the front door of the restaurant was kicked open and three men with guns, the turtlenecks of their sweaters pulled up over their noses and the brims of their hats down to their eyes, stood in the doorway and opened fire.

His father's body fell across the table in front of him and, as the place went into pandemonium around him, Dominic stared at the blood spattered onto the bosom of Rosalie's pink dress.

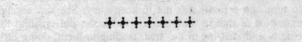

In the years following her husband's death, Elizabeth Endicott fell into the habit of spending Sunday mornings in bed reading the *Times*. On a wet Sunday in the spring of 1921 she was propped up on pillows wearing a rose-colored bed jacket, her still-ample gray hair in a net, the paper in sections around her. Beside her on a chair was her breakfast tray—the shells of a soft-boiled egg, the crumbs of a corn muffin, an empty orange juice glass. She was going to be seventy-three her next birthday, but she felt better than she had twenty years before.

Getting cold on the bedside table was a pot of coffee. Eugene always came by for coffee around nine, but it was well after that and he hadn't shown up yet.

She examined a photograph in the women's pages of the modernized interior of a house in the neighborhood with stark white walls, low, block-shaped furniture, and cubist pictures in metallic frames. It looked like an icehouse. She couldn't imagine living in such a place.

There were always stories about Greenwich Village in the papers stressing its oddity. Hymie Liebman, of course, would be highly pleased with the piece. In the past year he had been quite successful cashing in on the growing reputation of the Village, since he had left the real estate office to set up on his own. He was doing so well with those renovated houses on Tenth Street. Thank God he was rescuing them from decay.

Polly was spending most of her time these days doing his secretarial work, but he was such a charmer, who could blame her? Elizabeth would have been more pleased if they had gotten married, but Polly insisted that marriage was the last thing she cared about—it was the twentieth century, after all. To her daughter, anyone who still remembered Queen Victoria was a fossil.

She poured herself a cold cup of coffee. She wouldn't wait for Eugene.

She still had her activities during the week—the easiest way to turn into a fossil was not to keep busy. She saw enough examples of that in the volunteer work she did, visiting the elderly and shut-ins in the area, reading to them, doing little chores, trying to keep their spirits up. But it was an uphill struggle, and she was getting tired of it. Why, she had never been sick a day in her life! She saw no reason for anyone to sit around all the time like a vegetable.

She got up and went to the window to see if Eugene was coming. He was living such an interesting life now and knew so many of the arts people in the Village. He made his living working as a bartender nights at 86 Barrow, a charming little restaurant, and during the day he helped put out a literary magazine that had published one of his stories.

The magazine, *The Little Review,* was run by two of the most formidably intellectual women she had ever met, Margaret Anderson and Jane Heap, who shared a bizarre little apartment on Fourteenth Street where they edited the magazine and rented a room to Eugene on the floor above. Their living room had gold wallpaper and a sofa suspended from the ceiling by chains. They were publishing James Joyce's unreadable novel, *Ulysses,* in installments and causing a scandal. Every other issue was impounded by the post office, and they had gotten into so much hot water over it, they were talking about moving to Paris.

Eugene made her laugh so much, telling her about the unusual people who came into the bar where he worked. She wished there wasn't always a squint of worry about his eyes, a nervousness he was at great pains to hide from the world, but that she always detected. Thank God he was finally going out to see his son—Seth was already seven years old. His ex-wife, Clare, was going to marry again—Eugene's boyhood chum Toby Harris of all people!—and they had invited him out to the wedding. Toby Harris was also divorced with children, and had an automobile dealership out there.

Eugene had read her Clare's letter which said she ought to have married Toby in the first place. What an absurd idea that was! Clare claimed she had always been attracted to Toby, though she hadn't realized it, and went on to say she and Eugene were much too alike ever to have made a go of it.

The very idea! Clare had never understood the first thing about her son—their interests were far too different. That was what had been wrong from the start.

Clare said she was convinced that Toby would be a good father to Seth, who already adored him, and Toby had added a postscript to the letter seconding the invitation to the wedding.

Going out to meet his son at last was just what Elizabeth had hoped for Eugene. He needed to have his son in his life. It would make up for all the unhappiness he had gone through.

Out the window, Perry Street was deserted in the wet. It had changed so little through the years, except for the parked automobiles. The old houses were still the same. A horse and wagon came along and stopped to deliver milk. The delivery boy, a dark-haired young man, ran up the steps of the house across the street and as he came back to his wagon, happened to glance up at her. Her heart contracted as she remembered Mario. It had been a year since that ghastly night at the Alfanos' restaurant. Suddenly weary, she went back to bed.

Dominic's world had fallen apart—it had always centered around his father. But they had gone ahead with the wedding at St. Joseph's in June, though under the circumstances the ceremony had seemed to her more like a memorial service than a wedding.

After that, Dominic had wanted to close down the restaurant and take a job as a cook somewhere else, but his grandmother Alfano and his wife kept after him arguing that what had happened to Mario was not only God's will but also the mob's, and told him he just couldn't walk out on a good business with Rosalie pregnant. It wasn't as if selling liquor was a sin, everyone knew that—and the only thing to do was follow the way all the Village restaurants were going.

Elizabeth had to agree that Prohibition was a foolish law, but she wasn't so sure that Dominic didn't have the right idea about getting out of the place, considering the painful associations it must have for him now. Still, the two women were too strong for him and he submitted. The restaurant reopened as a speakeasy. It was clear that the vacuum in the boy's life left by the death of Mario was going to be filled by his new wife. Elizabeth had spent so many nights aching over the monstrous killing of Mario. It would haunt her forever.

The doorbell rang. Eugene must have forgotten his key. She got up, put on a robe, and slipped off her hairnet. They would talk over what he was writing, all stream-of-consciousness prose she couldn't make head or tail of, and he would distract her from that awful memory.

But it wasn't Eugene at the door. It was her nephew Dennis Yates in civilian clothes. He was a lieutenant on the police force now, but he still dropped by to visit her. He had married only after the death of his mother, and she thought at first that he must be coming to thank her for some gift she had sent his little boy, Timothy.

But it wasn't about the gift, she managed to gather that much, and he was having difficulty telling what it was about. In spite of her foreboding, it took some probing to get out of him that Eugene had been arrested the night before, and considerable reassurance on her part that he could tell her all about it and he mustn't be concerned that she wouldn't understand.

"You know about Eugene, Aunt Elizabeth?"

"I think I do," she said, trying to keep her voice under control. "Now tell me, please."

It was worse than she expected. It turned out that Eugene had been arrested several times over the past year—always terribly drunk and in situations that Dennis couldn't bring himself to describe to a lady. Until the night before, he had always been able to get him off. Once, the judge had been a personal friend and he asked him as a favor at night court to dismiss the case. Another time, he got the arresting officers to let him go before booking him. But about this arrest he couldn't do anything. They were having a crackdown on vice in the Village—all this publicity about it in the papers, orders from higher up—and the only thing to do was to hire a lawyer who would pay off the judge and the arresting officers. That was the way it worked.

"How much will it cost?" she asked without flinching.

"It will be two hundred dollars, I'm afraid. I could chip in twenty—that's all I got on me."

"I've got it." She went over to Patrick's old rolltop desk where she kept money for emergencies. She asked him if that would clear Eugene of all this terrible business.

Dennis said that he would definitely be let off that afternoon, but he couldn't promise her there wouldn't be more trouble in the future. Even if Eugene kept out of trouble, in every vice case from now on he'd be an automatic suspect and be picked up. "Why does he do it? Doesn't he have any self-respect?" Dennis's good-natured face screwed up in disgust. "He couldn't have had a better mother than you. If you ask me, he'd be better off if you put him away."

Elizabeth said she was grateful for all he had done, but for the first time she was annoyed with Dennis and his limited police mentality.

While she waited for Eugene's telephone call, she was sick at the thought of the humiliation it must be for her son. Now she knew why he had seemed drawn and nervous. Why hadn't she done something? She blamed herself for not guessing that he was suffering. She was going to insist he bring it all out in the open.

But when his call didn't come by five o'clock, she went to his room on Fourteenth Street.

It was twilight when she got there. She knocked, but there was no answer. One of the women who lived on the floor below was coming out of her apartment and told her that he was home, she had seen him come in earlier.

She had a stab of fear and rapped louder, calling his name. Eventually there was a sound and the door opened. In the glare of the hall bulb he looked terrible, his face unshaven and bruised, with a black eye.

"What did you bail me out for?"

She said nothing but pushed past him and turned on the lamp. The Murphy bed with its tumble of bedding nearly filled the room. She quickly straightened it and pushed it back up into its niche in the wall. Then she went to fill the pot at the washbasin for coffee.

He was still standing haggard by the door, watching her. "You can stop playing the understanding mother. I'm not going to apologize."

"I'm not asking you to." He was in no state to listen to anything. Lighting his makeshift kerosene burner and setting the pot on, she clutched at the one idea that would help give him back some self-respect—the trip he was going to make out to Cincinnati to see his son Seth. He *was* a father, after all. Being reunited with his child might save him. She would have to look for a way to introduce the subject.

It was when he told her she shouldn't have come, he was going to go away, that she saw her chance. "Of course you're going," she said brightly. "You're going to Cincinnati." He might even make his train reservation sooner. She could do it for him.

"I couldn't look that kid in the eye."

"You'll feel different after you get some rest. And you'll see Toby Harris again. Clare wants to see you too, and she says Seth has been talking of nothing else."

Eugene said to stop pushing him, he was never going to let the kid see him. He was just going to get on a bus and keep moving. There was no place he could live, the way it was.

"But you can't go 'no place.'" She didn't spring the plan that had begun to form in her mind until she had scrambled him some eggs and gotten a few bites down him. It was impossible for him to go on with his life in the same way. He'd get into even worse trouble than he was already in—Dennis had made that quite clear. But was there any point in bringing up such brutal facts? As casually as she could, she said that if he wasn't ready to visit his son just now, might not Paris be a solution? "It made a big difference in my life once, maybe it can do the same for you. You'd get away from all this unpleasantness, and it would be a good place to go on with your writing."

She was heartened to see a spark of hope in his eyes, but immediately the resentful look returned. He said that he had no money, and if she was going to offer to pay his way, to forget it. He was past thirty and he had messed up his own life beyond repair and no kindly old mother was going to rescue him.

His using the world 'old' gave her a momentary start, but she covered it with a determined smile. "You could live for very little over there now, from what they tell me, and it won't be any sacrifice for me to advance it to you." When he still remained adamant, she reminded him that so many creative people were going to Paris since the war. He had told her himself that Jane Heap and Margaret Anderson were thinking of transferring *The Little Review* there.

"I'm finished with all that. What good is it?" he said, looking out at the lit skylights and back windows of the studios across the way. A violinist was practicing double stops, and a typewriter was clacking away.

There were times when only brutality worked, and she laid it on the line. "I don't think you have much choice. Dennis tells me that just because he got you off this time doesn't mean you won't be picked up every time they're looking for someone."

She saw that this hadn't occurred to him, and he collapsed into a chair under the weight of his predicament. He said that even if the law kept punishing him for the way he was, he was stuck with it.

It didn't look good to her at all. He was so defeated by his wretchedness, he couldn't do a single thing to save himself. As they sat on in the drab little hall bedroom where the pages of a forgotten manuscript lay forlornly around the Remington typewriter, she saw a way to get him to the boat. "Would you mind if an old lady went with you on a voyage of nostalgia?"

He didn't look up and she went on rapidly, "Not to be your keeper—don't think that. I mean for a few weeks of sightseeing while you get set up, before I come home."

His posture in the chair had not changed but she knew he was listening. "I know what a joke it's been in the family, my talking about Paris, but I've wanted to go back for so long. But your father never would, and now I've got my chance."

Her son, who had been keeping his battered face turned away from her, raised his head and met her eyes. Elizabeth turned the house over to Polly, and she and Eugene sailed for Le Havre a week later on the *Ville de Bordeaux*.

POLLY WAS IN A SNIT AS SHE CAME DOWN THE STAIRS OF THE Sixth Avenue elevated a few blocks from Hymie's office. It was a sunny day but there was always a seedy, leftover-midnight feeling under the el, and it didn't help her mood any. The audition she was coming from was supposed to have been at nine, but it had turned out to be one of those cattle calls where everyone showed up, and the producers hadn't gotten around to her until nearly eleven. Her knitted Nile-green suit and cloche hat she had bought especially for the "young aunt" part, only to be told even before she opened her mouth that she wasn't the right type! She was fed up—too old to be an ingenue, wrong for leading lady, too young for character woman. What the hell was she supposed to do while she waited?

A big open touring car pulled away from the curb and belched exhaust in her face. An elevated train roaring by overhead covered her with soot. And her father had predicted that electrifying the trains would end the dirt problem—the poor innocent!

She was ready to call it quits on the acting. Since Hymie had gotten rid of the Teaspoon for her and she had started making the rounds, she had had exactly four acting jobs, two of them walk-ons, another as an extra in a D. W. Griffith one-reeler shot out in Astoria, and another demonstrating potato peelers at Woolworth's.

When she had left the apartment that morning, Hymie, with his usual optimism, swore she would knock them dead and promised to keep the decks clear for a celebration lunch—he was going to lock the office door to the world and catch up on paperwork. She needed that lunch and a couple of drinks, even if there was nothing to celebrate.

Hymie's storefront office was between a laundry and a tattoo parlor. It wasn't much, but it was a toehold. The couple of houses he had fixed up and sold had brought in enough capital for him to speculate on several other modest properties. Real estate in the Village was booming, but he was facing a lot of competition from other small-potatoes operators like himself, and even from some of the big boys who were moving in. He was way over his head in debt, but he didn't care, he said—that was the way business worked now. She didn't understand all the details, but it astonished her the way he operated—the outrageous way he conned his clients, his indifference to living in the red.

He had finally managed to pay her back the money from the sale of the teashop and had invested it for her in the stock market. She saved him the price of a secretary by doing his office work for him. It filled in some of the time she had on her hands from all the roles she wasn't getting.

She wondered why her own ambitions never seemed to come to anything. Hymie believed in what he was doing, maybe it was as simple as that. And even if he believed in what she was trying to do too, she had to admit she herself had never been more than lukewarm about the theater. But it didn't make her any the less furious when she was turned down and treated so shabbily, like today. It was a pick-me-up to know Hymie was waiting for her. What would she do without him?

But when she got to his office, he wasn't waiting for her with the consolation she needed. He was holed up with a customer after all, giving him his spiel about a listing on Charles Street.

She leaned against her desk in exasperation, waiting for him to finish. But he was too busy spinning a fantasy about the property being a perfect example of the Greek Revival style of the 1860s to even give her a glance. She knew the house he was talking about—it sagged so much, that the floors were sloping. She cleared her throat several times trying to get his attention, but he was in the middle of dispelling the client's doubts about the racial tensions in the neighborhood between the Irish and the Italians.

"Take my word for it, the papers are making a mountain out of a molehill. With the values going up the way they are down here, the locals are selling out as fast as they can. A year from now you won't be able to touch a house like this at double the price." And, knowing full well that she was waiting there, he had the nerve to suggest to the customer walking right over and taking a look at it.

Her heart sank—there went the afternoon.

Her hopes revived when the client still expressed doubts about the neighborhood. But that bastard Hymie wouldn't give up and insisted the house was just around the block and it wouldn't take more than twenty minutes to look at it.

What about her? Was she supposed to go and have a hamburger at a lunchwagon by her lonesome? Not caring what the client thought, she went over and planted herself in front of Hymie's desk so that he couldn't miss her and reminded him point-blank that they had a luncheon date and she was dying of starvation.

Hymie was speechless, possibly for the first time in his life. But he recovered fast and jumped up to put an arm around her: "Pol, why didn't you let me know you were here?" he said with a feigned innocence that made her puke. "You know how I am when I'm hot about a property." He gave an angelic smile and, turning to the client, smoothly introduced her as the famous painter, Pauline Endicott.

What in hell was he doing? Did he take the client for an idiot? But to her surprise the man looked at her with fascination, and said that he and his wife were both interested in art.

She was about to disillusion him in no uncertain terms, but Hymie was already going on, inventing an instant career for her, with reputation, shows, and rave reviews, and the man was asking her about her gallery.

Damn him for getting her into this. She wasn't going to play along with the silly charade another minute. She told the man she had quit her gallery and had given up painting. Let Hymie deal with that one! She gave him a wicked look.

Hymie was undaunted. He laughed and asked her how many times she had threatened to do just that, but her collectors would never stand for it. And then he told an even bigger whopper to the gullible client—that her studio was in the same block as the house he wanted to show him. And moreover she wasn't the only artist who lived around there—there were at least a dozen other well-known painters and writers in the radius of a few blocks. "Isn't that right, Pol?" He returned her wicked look.

"Yes," she said, beginning to enjoy the contest, "and every goddam one of them is eating lunch now except me."

The client seemed only more entertained by her display of "artistic temperament," and before he left, Hymie had talked him into bringing his wife to see the house on Charles Street the next day.

Hymie was jubilant when he came back from showing him out. "Did you ever see such a quick turnabout in your life? I didn't have a hope in hell of selling that guy until I said you were a painter. He was drooling over it."

Polly had to smile at her irrepressible lover. "When he finds out I don't have a studio on Charles Street, or anywhere else, he'll sue you for misrepresentation."

"The hell he will," he yelled, washing up in the little room in back that was already cluttered with cartons of papers and books and the cot he kept for catnaps. "He'll probably screw his wife tonight thinking of you."

They went to lunch at one of their favorite places, Minetta Tavern on MacDougal Street in the middle of the nightlife area south of Washington Square.

As she sipped some bootleg gin and ate lasagna, her failed audition didn't seem so important any more. Hymie was so full of beans at his prank, he kept hopping up all through lunch to feed nickels into the player piano that had a new set of Dixieland rolls. She was completely restored by the time dessert came, when he remembered to tell her he had found a tenant for her mother's house.

Her mother had been putting off her return from France from month to month, and had finally decided to stay on for a year. She had written that Polly was to move into the house or rent it, as she liked.

"There's this sugar daddy from uptown," Hymie said, "who's willing to pay two hundred dollars a month to keep his pussycat in style and out of sight."

Polly said did he want to turn her family home into a bordello. But she had to admit she loved the idea of a tycoon drawing up to the curb in a big black car for a tryst with his girlfriend in her parents' Victorian bed.

Hymie had his eye on a party of uptowners at a nearby table. All kinds of people were coming down to the Village, attracted by the stories in the *Mirror* about the lurid goings-on.

"Pol," he said, doodling with his Waterman on the paper tablecloth, "if you'd only set yourself up as an artist in one of those studios in Washington Mews and I could put up a grandstand and sell tickets, we'd clean up."

Polly, who was eating her zabaglione from a tall glass with a long spoon, said that if she could afford one of those fancy studios on the Mews, she'd be a Vanderbilt and wouldn't need to sell tickets to anyone.

He printed on the tablecloth paper in bold letters, LIVE WITH THE ARTISTS IN GREENWICH VILLAGE. "How does that strike you as a slogan?"

"*Sleep* with the artists might be better," she said, licking off her spoon.

But he was already scratching out his motto. "That's no good. They won't buy that."

"Sleeping with artists? Why not?"

"Nah, show them what's really going on and you'd scare hell out of them." He indicated the tableful of uptowners. "Look at them, they're crapping in their pants that one of those long-haired characters at the bar will come over and try to cadge a dime. It's a fantasy I'm selling down here, don't you see? A picturebook story." He was studying her, his mind racing a mile a minute. "It's got to be clean, all-American—like you."

She said she was bored to tears with him thinking of her that way, and why didn't he give up that image of her once and for all?

But he didn't answer her. He was having a new brainstorm. "If we had a studio . . ." he said, still looking hard at her. "We could have used the teashop . . . good location. Too bad we let it go."

"What are you talking about?"

"Come on." He pushed back his chair. And without letting her finish her dessert, he raced her off to Perry Street.

"Get rid of the doodads, throw some Spanishy *shmattas* over the furniture, put a few Dada paintings on the walls, and with an easel, we've got our artist's studio."

They were in her mother's parlor. The house had been closed up for months and there were dust covers over the furniture.

"But what about the sugar daddy and his girlfriend?" she asked him.

"Forget it." He was walking around the room snapping his fingers as he described his plan to her. "The way it will work is, I'll tell the client I'm stopping in to see an artist friend—a really classy Village dame—and they're welcome to come by with me for a drink, if they don't mind the bohemian atmosphere." He stopped. "Mind it? What am I saying! They'll trample me down to get here and I'll be able to sell them the Brooklyn Bridge."

Polly threw herself on her mother's old horsehair sofa and put her feet over the arm. "Mother would die!" She screamed with laughter. "I'll be in a smock, painting a three-eyed woman, and I'll get Zoran to lie around on the floor sniffing cocaine. Or I'll dig out the old gypsy outfit from the Teaspoon and do interpretive dancing to *The Rites of Spring*."

"With a tit hanging out like Isadora Duncan?" He snickered, then shook his head. "We don't want to scare them off with too much of that Romany Marie shit. Artists are weird, but underneath, just plain folks—that's the angle we got to play. Have a few kids running around, maybe. You can borrow some from those dago relatives of yours."

Polly cracked that the one thing she couldn't stand was a kike who thought he was better than dagos.

They got to work packing away her mother's fussy knick-knacks from the mantelpiece and the tabletops.

She didn't know how Hymie's scheme would work out, but the irony of it enchanted her. She had never been able to be the real artist her mother expected—even the theater had fizzled. But to play a fake one, and in her mother's house, what divine revenge!

ROSALIE ALFANO WAS SITTING BEHIND THE CASH REGISTER. Her first child Stefano was not even a year old and she was already heavily pregnant again. Her ankles were so swollen, she could hardly walk.

She watched her stolid husband showing a party to a table across the room. Dominic didn't know how to joke with the customers like Mario, his late father, did, but most of the people who patronized the Bocce cared about only one thing now—booze—Canadian Club or Seagram's Seven brought in over the border from Canada, or rum and scotch from some ship anchored beyond the three-mile limit, and they were willing to pay for it.

Old Angelina, the grandmother, had got Dominic to cut out the fancy food he used to spend so much time on. That wasn't where the profit was any more, but for a while he had been too thickheaded to see it. Spaghetti and meat balls with a little tomato sauce would satisfy the uptown customers—when they wanted any food at all—she told him, and the neighborhood people would come anyway for Angelina's wine and to sit around the *bocce* court in back.

The Bocce had been a speakeasy for a year and a half, and if it weren't for having to pay off the mob and the police, the Alfanos would have been on easy street. The restaurant was dominated by a magnificent new mahogany bar with cut-glass mirrors and Chinese vases. The curtains at the front windows were never opened, even on sunny days, and the front door had a peekhole so the customers could be screened.

Rosalie self-consciously straightened her blouse so her breasts would look good. One of the men in the party across the room had his eye on her. She was glad she was sitting down and he couldn't see her belly. She used to think she was pretty, but she hadn't had much attention from men since her marriage. It seemed to her that she had been pregnant and unattractive the whole time.

The man was still ogling her. Even if he was an old goat, she was pleased. The women with him at least weren't bad looking and were smartly dressed.

Filippo, the waiter, who was a cousin of Dominic's, brought over a fifty-dollar bill and started telling her how the local ward boss had left it on the table without waiting for change, when Dominic came up to tell him to get back to work. Not a word or a look at her, as if she weren't even there. It wasn't much different when they were upstairs together in the apartment. Even when the old woman wasn't there babbling away about how they should do this and how they should do that, he had nothing to say to her. He carried around his father's death like a sack. He still took it so hard that he didn't even want her to mention his name. She sometimes wondered if that life-loving man who had taken her breath away dancing her around the room could actually have been his father. What a dummox she had been, thinking the son would be like him.

She couldn't even get Dominic to show any interest in the baby. Whenever he had any free time at all, he never relaxed with his family. He just wanted to keep busy, going over his accounts or finding things to do in the restaurant. Even at dinner he stayed just long enough to get the food down. How could you live like that?

She was no more to him than the cash register in front of her. When the lights went out in their bedroom, he turned to her without a word and went through the act as if he were emptying himself of something dirty. She had no other experience of it, being a good Catholic girl taught by the sisters, but from her girlfriends who were married she knew there was more to it than that. Their husbands were passionate, whispered beautiful words in their ears, wanted them to be passionate too. But when she started to let herself go, Dominic always lost interest immediately and turned away. What kind of life was it? She wasn't even twenty-two, with a husband who acted like a lump, and the old woman, Angelina, always on her back about something no matter how hard she worked.

Sitting at the cash register night after night, it was as if she were behind a glass wall with the customers getting drunker and noisier and the man she was chained to for life gloomily taking the orders and writing out the checks, and without an ounce of pleasure in his bones.

Her eyes met those of the bouncer sitting on his stool beside the front door. Luciano his name was—such a beautiful name when she whispered it to herself while she was out in the hall lavatory, the only place she could be herself. Dominic hated him, of course. Luciano they had been forced to hire, he was the mob's arm. He kept an eye on things to be sure the Alfanos weren't cheating and made sure another mob didn't try to muscle in. Every night he took the mob's cut with him when the black Packard came to pick him up. Even Angelina upstairs, who saw dealing with the mob as only business, didn't have a good word to say about Luciano.

But every time he looked at Rosalie behind the cash register teasingly with his gray eyes—so unusual in a swarthy face—she felt herself go weak. They never spoke. Dominic had forbidden her to say a word to him. But though she didn't tell any of her girlfriends, and there was nothing to tell the priest at confession, Luciano kept her hope alive. He made her feel she wasn't totally defeated yet.

She risked another look at the bouncer, but he had gotten off his stool and was sizing up some new arrivals through the peekhole in the door—there was always the chance that even if the cops had been paid off, there could be a raid.

A party of two couples came in. To her annoyance, she saw that one of the women was Polly Endicott, her husband's relative. Dominic went over to greet her, a smile on his face for once. Rosalie hardly ever saw him come alive like that—and that woman had the nerve to kiss him on the cheek.

As usual, Polly was dressed fit to kill in a coral print dress, showing no bosom and with the waistline around her hips—it must have cost a fortune. She was all painted up with plucked and penciled eyebrows, and her bobbed hair looked suspiciously blonde. She was with her real estate boyfriend and made a big show of introducing him and the other couple to Dominic. There were several empty tables, but to Rosalie's disgust, Dominic had to seat them at the one nearest to the cash register.

Polly recognized her and flashed a phony smile, but Rosalie pretended not to see. She knew the Endicotts hated her and she hated them back. She always found it hard to believe that Dominic was related to them in any way.

Why was he playing up to her like that, snapping his fingers for Filippo and telling him to give them anything they wanted. Polly waved a cigarette holder and said in her affected way he was a perfect angel. It made Rosalie's stomach turn.

When she got the chance, she asked Dominic what were they doing there. Polly hadn't been around since Stefano was christened. He told her to stop glaring at them—Polly and her boyfriend were just showing some people the Village.

Rosalie wasn't glaring, she was just taking in that long string of jade beads she would have given her eyeteeth for, but that hair was bleached to a frazzle—and who did Polly Endicott think she was kidding with all that paint on, she still looked every minute of thirty-five. And she went on waving that cigarette holder and swinging those beads as she prattled away about her "studio" and her "painting." She had a nerve, she was no more a painter than an actress.

Her cigar-smoking boyfriend was laying it on just as thick, leaning forward to tell the suckers that Polly wasn't the only artist there, and as Polly made a show of waving to some friends at another table, he said it was a cinch to be part of the "arts world" once you lived down here. It was all a lot of hooey, but the suckers seemed to be eating it up, rubbernecking around as if the Bocce was a sideshow.

While the boyfriend went on blabbing about what a kick he got out of living in the Village, Polly pulled Dominic over and stopped guzzling her highball long enough to ask him, "Remember, Dommie, when we used to play upstairs with Eugene? No, of course you don't, you were too little." And she screamed with laughter as if someone were goosing her.

What nerve, acting as if he had ever been one of the family to her. But her gullible husband said sure he remembered and laughed along, forgetting the Endicotts had dropped him like a hot potato years before, although she reminded him often enough.

The final straw for Rosalie was when they asked for the check and he told them it was on the house, like a bigshot.

She kept quiet until after closing when she was in the kitchen with him counting the cash drawer and he told her Polly had moved back to his grandmother Endicott's house on Perry Street and had asked them for dinner.

"Over my dead body!" she said, putting a rubber band around a bundle of tens. "I wouldn't cross the street to see her. They think we're dirty wops."

"What are you talking about, Rosalie? I told you how we grew up together. She's my family. You'll see."

"What I see is she's a stuck-up bitch and you're some kind of chump to fall for it."

He tied up the bag holding the day's cut for the mob. The bouncer was outside at the bar waiting for it. "Why are you always carrying on about her? You and my *Nonna,* the both of you nagging at me. It's all on my shoulders. You're just jealous of her, that's all."

She slammed down the lid of the cash box. "What's on your shoulders? If you were the man your father was . . ."

He put down the bag, slowly, his usually expressionless face going dark. "I told you before, never mention him. You're not good enough to kiss his ass."

He had never spoken to her like that, but she knew she had gone too far. "I didn't mean nothing," she hedged, picking up the pencil and turning back to the account book. "Putting on her hoity-toity airs, she just got me mad, that's all."

But when she went upstairs where the old woman was looking after the baby, Rosalie still heard the edge of menace in her husband's voice, the rough language he had used—and she liked it.

PLAYING THE FAKE ARTIST FOR HYMIE'S CLIENTS STIMULATED Polly's imagination as trying to be a real artist never had. Hymie had told her to borrow some paintings from her friends to hang on the walls of her "studio," but when she got out the old easel from her art school days and bought some new tubes of paint, she couldn't resist dabbling at a canvas. Without having an instructor looking over her shoulder or classmates around more talented than she was, she was able to relax and enjoy herself, turning out one canvas after another—clever imitations of Utrillo and Klee and Kandinsky. Her mother's Beardsley drawings in their old bamboo frames were banished to a closet, and she hung her own unframed canvases up on the walls recklessly.

To launch the scheme, Hymie had brought around a married couple he was trying to interest in renting a house—the man did something on Wall Street. After trying on one outfit after another to receive them in, Polly finally decided on a nubby tweed skirt and batik blouse that she thought gave her the eccentric, arty look of a Gertrude Stein, the American expatriate who had discovered Picasso and wrote hilarious nonsense like "Toasted Susie is my ice cream."

With a smock on and what Hymie called a *shmatta* on her head, she was busy painting at her easel when he arrived with the clients, presumably just happening by for a drink. Without putting down her palette, she asked them to find someplace to sit, the light was too perfect for her to stop just then. Aware of the effect she was making, she went back to working on a still life of apples set up in front of her. She dabbled briefly at the canvas, where she had already turned the round shapes of the apples into a cluster of rectangles, juxtaposing their insides, outsides, and backsides. She felt she was giving a brilliant demonstration of cubism that even a simpleton could understand.

Then she stepped back from the canvas with an emphatic "There!" Turning to the couple she cleaned the paint from her hands with a turpentine rag and said that a lot of people didn't consider that to be art, but they didn't know what they were talking about. The wife hurried to agree that most people still thought Maxfield Parrish's *Saturday Evening Post* covers were the ultimate in art, but not her.

While Hymie was pouring them all chianti, Polly flopped down on a hassock, pulling off her kerchief and shaking out her short cap of sandy hair, as she went on talking about her life as a painter. Hymie was giving her looks of admiration for her performance of a free soul glorying in the creative atmosphere of the Village. And by the time they left, the husband and wife were already condemning Victorian morality, trying to sound like real Villagers.

When Hymie came back after putting them in a taxi, he and Polly were so elated at the way it had gone—the couple was going to rent the house—they picked up brushes and painted funny faces all over Polly's cubist apples, before falling on her mother's sofa and making love.

After that he brought prospective clients by frequently when he thought it would help to clinch a deal. When it looked like cubism was beyond the clients, she dashed off a painting of Raoul Dufy sailboats on the Riviera or a Montmartre street scene, and she chattered about the harmless colorful characters in the neighborhood. She sensed how titillated they were by the flicker of sin around the edges, prepared as they were by all the tabloid stories of daughters running away to live with depraved poets.

With the studio visits a success, she started getting new ideas, and when Hymie showed up one evening with an elderly businessman, they found a sketch class in progress. A nude model was posed against the drapes as some "artists" sat round on the floor drawing her. Polly had gotten Larry Mathews's current girlfriend, a plump voice student named Stella, to play "model," and the "artists" had come along for the free wine.

She hadn't let Hymie know what she was planning and he was clearly bowled over. Playing the role to the hilt, she put down her sketch pad to make the client comfortable on the sofa with some wine and then called a rest period for the "model." Larry's plump girlfriend slipped into a kimono and—as she and Polly had agreed—perched herself on an arm of the sofa, and it went like a dream. The delighted businessman heard the "real-life" story of an artist's model who was actually an opera singer, financing her voice lessons by posing.

After it was over and the man was gone, they sat around finishing up the wine. Hymie said the nude-model idea was pure genius and wanted her to hold a sketch class every time after that. But she had another inspiration, and the next time he brought a client over she had set up a studio group show of some of her friends' paintings, and with all the artists present they were celebrating the "opening." She even talked the client into buying one of Larry Mathews's canvases—an Iowa cornfield with menacing storm clouds hanging over—promoting him as the best undiscovered young painter in America.

After that Larry said she ought to open an art gallery herself. There wasn't a single serious commercial gallery in the Village, they were all uptown, and even those bastards didn't know art from baloney and he couldn't get a foot in the door.

She worried about Larry. He painted compulsively for days at a stretch, hardly eating. But as furiously as he painted, he couldn't express everything that was in him, either on canvas or in words. His moody, pent-up energy made women want to take care of him, as much as sleep with him. Stella Banks, the voice student-model, was one of a long series of girlfriends since the old days when he moped after Polly at the teashop. His women alway started out thinking that he would fall in love with them back, but inevitably he threw them out and went on another binge of painting.

Only one of Polly's ideas for impressing Hymie's clients went wrong, and that one turned out to be such a farce they never stopped laughing about it. Hymie was playing a wealthy widow client from Los Angeles on his line, and Polly got Zoran to come over rigged out in white robes like Kahlil Gibran, the mystical poet. Zoran was the perfect holy man, his roguish eyes under his wild hair flattering the widow shamelessly. With his big frame lounging in a wicker throne chair, he discoursed on the Secrets of the East as he cracked sunflower seeds with his teeth, scattering the shells around him. Even if he forgot himself sometimes and denounced all followers of mystics as "bourgeois pigs," the widow from L.A. was not put off in the least. She immediately became his disciple and invited him to come to her hotel to give her "lessons in enlightenment."

Never one to resist any of life's possibilities, he let her take him off to Los Angeles where she promised to build him a temple to preach in. "What can I do, Polatchinka. There's more money in this line than being a two-bit gigolo," he said, pinching Polly's cheek.

Her next improvisation was more successful. Things were set up for another sketch class. While they waited for Hymie and the client, Stella Banks, wearing her kimono ready to model, was fooling around at the old upright piano, singing bits from Broadway shows. It was the first time anyone had heard her sing anything other than opera, and instead of the sketch class, Polly persuaded her to stay at the piano.

When Hymie got there with the client, Polly put a finger to her lips at the door and brought them in. The client was as impressed as everyone else by Stella's torchy impersonation of Fanny Brice in the *Follies*. It turned out he knew a booking agent, took Stella's name, and shortly after, she temporarily put aside her plans for an opera career and was singing at a piano over the bar in a cellar club on Waverly Place.

When Polly and Hymie went to hear her in the smoky bar patronized by a bevy of young men, she was taking her torch singing more seriously. Her heavy figure draped in folds of loose chiffon, she sang "Can't Help Lovin' That Man" with tears in her eyes. Polly knew they were genuine, for Larry Mathews was already being mothered by someone else.

One afternoon on their way home from Hymie's office, they ran into Vincent Millay, the poet from Polly's Provincetown Theater days. Not only was she more famous than ever, but she looked better than she ever had in a lavish sealskin coat and elegant fur hat. But she had the same old glitter in her eye when she looked at Hymie.

She was on her way to a cocktail party at the Brevoort and invited them to come along. They had dinner reservations and were on their way home to change, but when the poet said what a pity, the party was being given by a friend of hers who was also in real estate, Dave Lauterbach, Hymie nearly wet his pants. The Lauterbach Corporation had put up many of the skyscrapers in the city in the past decade. He had to go, wild horses couldn't have kept him from the chance to meet the czar of New York real estate, but Polly wasn't about to walk into any room with Vincent Millay and feel like an ugly duckling again. She told him to run along and have a good time and she'd soak in the tub until he got back to take her to dinner.

But long after time for dinner he still hadn't come back. She called the Lauterbach suite at the Brevoort, but whoever answered the phone couldn't hear her because of the noise, and besides was too drunk to get through to. When she tried again later on, she was told by the hotel desk that the party was over.

She made herself a drink to keep her spirits up and ate some crackers and cheese while she waited. It was nearly midnight when it occurred to her that he might have stopped by his office on the way home and, as he sometimes did, lost all track of time. She walked over, hoping to find him there.

His storefront office first appeared to be dark, but the streetlight lit up the interior well enough for her to make out the sealskin coat thrown across his desk, and then she saw the dim light shining from the back room where the daybed was.

He came home an hour later jubilant about his meeting with the building tycoon. "He liked me, Pol. He wants me to come up to his office next week and talk to him, can you believe it?" He threw himself on his back across the bed. "What wouldn't I give to get even the crumbs from the Lauterbach Corporation."

She smelled the heavy lilac perfume on him. "Did you go out with him to dinner?"

He sat up and snapped his fingers. "Holy Moses, our dinner date! Sweetheart, will you ever forgive me? I guess it just went to my head, meeting him."

She asked him again if Lauterbach had taken him to dinner.

"Me? Are you kidding?" He leaned on an elbow with his head in his hand. "I got stuck with Vincent. You were right about her, she is a man-eater. It took me all this time to shake her, for pete's sake!"

"Was she a good lay?" She tried not to let the jealousy that was tearing her apart show. Though neither of them had slept with anybody else since they met, they had never made a contract not to. She hated herself for her eyes filling with tears.

"Honey," he said, going up to her on his hands and knees on the bed and trying to kiss her, "I didn't sleep with her. I told you I don't go for her."

"You mean for the past four hours you've been sitting playing Parcheesi?" Her voice came out shrill.

"That's right. I mean, not Parcheesi, but I told her I had work to do at the office and she insisted on coming back with me. We sat drinking gin we copped from the party."

"In the back room?"

"We couldn't drink in front of the window, could we?"

"Was that all?"

"We made up poems."

"For hours?"

"Well, she started telling me about her favorite romantic places in the city, so I told her my ferryboat poem, 'We were jolly, we were merry,' remember? Oh, I guess I shouldn't have told her, but she was reciting poems about her love affairs and . . ."

She tried not to hear his equation of their love affair with Vincent's one-night stands. He was answering her doubts so innocently, it made her feel like a grand inquisitor. "You really didn't sleep with her, did you?"

He took her in his arms. "I didn't even kiss her when I left her at her hotel." And he went on gently explaining that nothing had happened and apologized for telling their poem, but Vincent was a professional poet after all, and it wasn't like telling the poem to just anybody—she even wrote it down in her notebook.

When he was sleeping beside her, his leg over hers, Polly decided that even if he had made love with Vincent—and she would never know for sure—it could only have been a totally naive mixture of business and pleasure. She knew that meeting the construction tycoon had meant far more to him than any casual adventure. And she suspected that Vincent had cooked her goose with Hymie once and for all. She smoothed the hair over her peacefully sleeping lover's forehead. If she had sworn once to look out for herself, she saw now that she had to take care of him too.

He was especially considerate the next day, doing his best to hold back from talking continually about his meeting with Lauterbach, though it was clear he was having a hard time. He was taking her out to dinner that night—this time, he said, even the Marines couldn't stop him.

And when she went up to her hairdresser's in the afternoon, he insisted on going with her. While her hair was being bleached a shade lighter, he slipped off, saying he had to pick up a surprise for her at the jeweler's. Daydreaming under the dryer, she dared to hope he had gotten over his traditional ideas at last and was getting her an engagement ring.

After a candlelight dinner, he took her to the little club on Waverly Place where Stella Banks was singing her torch songs. They drank some dubious champagne and laughed a lot over a note the waiter delivered to Hymie from an unidentified customer on the dark side of the bar that read, "Get rid of the bitch and meet me outside."

When Stella began her husky interpretation of "Can't Help Lovin' That Man of Mine," Hymie reached for Polly's hand, and with that easy giving-in to sentimentality that was so much like her father and so alien to her mother, he said, "I'm on my way, Pol, but I couldn't have got to first base without you." He reached into his pocket. "I'm a shmuck for not telling you often enough how much I love you. I've never said that to anyone else, will you believe me?" His eyes as bright on her as the first time he spotted her at the troopship, he put something into her hand.

But it was not a ring. It was a string of pearls.

Much as the episode with Vincent had shaken her, Polly couldn't deny the meeting with Lauterbach turned out to be the opportunity Hymie was waiting for. The real estate tycoon not only liked him but was in agreement with his idea that Greenwich Village was prime residential property, and was already planning to put up several modern apartment buildings there. He gave Hymie the job of buying up properties for the building sites. To make up a large enough parcel of land for each of the apartment houses, Lauterbach needed someone to negotiate with dozens of small holders and clear the titles.

If some people thought these big apartments were out of place in the Village, Hymie repeated Lauterbach's argument that this was the only way to preserve the historic neighborhood because it would bring in a better class of people. So even if they had to tear down a few of the original houses to clear the sites, it was necessary to sacrifice them to save the rest. Lauterbach wasn't forcing out the Irish and Italian poor. The money he was paying for their run-down properties gave them the chance to escape to newer neighborhoods in Queens or Brooklyn, which they considered more "American," anyway.

House sales and rentals became less important to Hymie as he began devoting most of his time to Lauterbach's business. The staged art sessions weren't needed much any more, and Hymie often didn't get home for dinner because of conferences at the corporation's Madison Avenue headquarters. Frequently, Lauterbach invited him on to dinner at his Park Avenue apartment afterwards. Over brandy and cigars, Lauterbach liked to tell how at first he had not been able to rent an apartment on Park Avenue, and had only licked the Park Avenue Associations anit-Semitic restrictions by buying a parcel of land through a front and building his own apartment house there. He had even had a tougher battle to get himself his estate out on the North Shore—years of litigation cracking restrictive zoning laws in the face of the whole pack of snobbish blue bloods. Now he was fighting the country club and the private schools.

Polly was soaking in the tub when Hymie came home to say that they were invited out to Oyster Bay for the weekend. She asked if Lauterbach had really invited her. She had only spoken to the man on the phone, and as far as she knew he thought of her as Hymie's secretary.

"Well, not exactly," he said, sitting on the rim of the tub and soaping her back, "but aren't we a couple?"

"Couldn't you have said I was coming?"

He hedged. "I didn't think of it. I just assumed . . ."

She stood up, dripping, and wrapped a big towel around herself. "You mean you're willing to take the chance that Lauterbach will accept me as your weekend companion, no questions asked?" She wanted to hear him say, What was she talking about, he wouldn't go anyplace without her and if she wouldn't come with him he wasn't going, even to the private retreat of his millionaire patron.

But he didn't. To her dismay, he said, as he rubbed her with the towel, that maybe she was right. He'd be talking business most of the time anyway and it would bore her to death. Next time, he'd make sure Lauterbach invited her personally.

But she saw he was relieved that she wasn't going—she was a complication he wasn't ready to deal with.

She went with him to Bloomingdale's to find suitable clothes for a country weekend. As he tried on tennis whites, she thought that for someone who came from immigrants and had never worn such things, he looked like he was born to them. She picked out a monogrammed weekend bag for him and when he left the house in his blazer, red tie and panama hat, he looked like a young lawyer just out of Yale.

He was away most weekends after that. She never went with him, but he told her about the lavish grounds and the pool, horseback riding with the family, and when the weather was warm enough, swims at the private beach on the sound. It was clear that Lauterbach had taken him under his wing, even talking about sending him down to Washington to work on getting government contracts.

It was almost a relief to her when he still brought prospective clients around for a drink occasionally. Though mostly occupied with Lauterbach Corporation business, he continued to handle a few neighborhood listings and, if he had time, tried to find buyers.

The night he brought Miriam by, Polly was thinking how good it felt to be performing her role of Village artist again. Even her cubist apples were fun to paint. It wasn't just a student exercise any more. Having done the same subject over and over, she was starting to do something original with it, and didn't want to break off as she usually did.

Miriam had been presented as one of the clients and, watching from a chair just behind her, she commented—with Smith College diction—that Polly's signature was in every brushstroke, and that no woman painter had grasped cubism as well as she had.

Ordinarily the clients watched in awed silence. Something in this girl's smooth manner made her suspect she was making fun of her. Polly painted in the folds of the cloth the way she had seen them handled in a Braque painting, but she got so self-conscious with the girl watching her from behind that she put down her palette and brush and started cleaning up, saying the light wasn't good enough any longer.

Hymie had taken the other clients in the group he had brought that night to the front windows and was pointing out some of the architectural features of the buildings across the street. She wanted him to come back and take this high-class bitch off her hands.

"I'm sure that visiting any studio less thai Monet's must be very boring for you," she said, sitting down on the hassock and giving the young woman the once-over. She was definitely not the usual client. Even when they had money, they never had her kind of taste. That was a Chanel suit she was wearing, and her crisply marcelled hair was Antoine of the Ritz. She couldn't be more than twenty-five.

"Why, no," the girl said, appraising her as candidly. "I'm delighted to be here. And Mr. Liebman is so persuasive." She looked over at him and laughed, as if there was something funny about it.

Polly was nonplussed. "You make it sound like you and Mr. Liebman are very good friends."

The girl laughed even harder and said she had to confess that she wasn't a client and was in on the whole thing. She was Miriam Lauterbach, the daughter of the builder, and when Hymie was out at their house in Oyster Bay, he had intrigued her with his talk about the phony studio visits that his assistant set up. "I do hope you don't mind. You mustn't blame Hymie for my crashing this way. I insisted he bring me and made him swear not to tell. I do think your performance is just marvelous, Miss Endicott. I only wish I had a talent for something. But I'm afraid I have none. I'm just an ex-art history major who will have to settle for being a housewife."

So this was the "little" Lauterbach daughter Hymie had mentioned. From the way he talked, Polly had assumed she was about ten. All those croquet matches on the lawn, the tennis, the night swimming at the private beach! And here she was, the picture of marriageability—cultivated, feminine in a way that made Polly feel gawky and boyish, really twenty-five when Polly felt every minute of her thirty-five. And worst of all—and here Polly remembered bitterly the night on the ferryboat when Hymie had refused to marry her—she was Jewish.

Polly looked across the room where Hymie was standing with the clients, and as if feeling her fathomless despair, he looked back at her quickly, guiltily, though he tried to cover it up with an affectionate wink. So that was what the wink that always had made her feel good meant. And then he gave the knife a final twist—he winked at Miriam too.

It looked to her like Lauterbach had picked his son-in-law. Miriam would be the perfect wife for a young tycoon. And there was no doubt about it, with Lauterbach behind him, Hymie would get to the top.

* * *

Poor Hymie was in a quandary when he returned from seeing Miriam and the clients into their cabs. His boss's strong-willed daughter had been a problem for him from the start, and not only because Lauterbach kept pushing them together. She always did exactly as she pleased. Like this evening. She wasn't supposed to have told Polly who she really was—that had been the condition on which he had agreed to bring her. She was a royal pain in the ass, but he couldn't afford to offend her.

He kicked himself for having allowed her to believe Polly was only his assistant. But it wasn't in his best interests to let any of the Lauterbach family know the real state of things—he couldn't be sure how Dave Lauterbach would take it that he had a *shiksa* mistress in the Village.

Of course, neither had he discussed Miriam with Polly, not that he was the least bit involved with her or had anything to hide—they were never more than weekend tennis partners. But now that Polly had seen her, he knew it was going to be hard to convince her there wasn't anything between them.

It was clear that he was in trouble when Polly didn't look up from her drink as he came back into the house. "You're not sore, are you, Pol?" he began, wondering how he was ever going to prove his innocence. "She made me let her come. She's just a spoiled kid who gets everything she wants."

"That's obvious," said Polly in a voice that made him feel charged, tried, and convicted. "Why didn't you tell me about her before?"

"I did. I told you about Lauterbach's kids."

"The 'little daughter'? You made me think she had braces on her teeth and pigtails!"

"Well, you saw her, she acts like a kid just out of high school."

"Smith College," she corrected him acidly.

"Yeah," he said, trying to make her see he was on her side, "private schools, riding lessons since she was three, daddy gives her everything—she's spoiled rotten."

Everything's wrong with her, Polly thought, but she's Jewish and that makes everything perfect. She would never say that, but she had to say something. "Does Mr. Lauterbach tuck you two into bed at night?" She heard the bitchiness in her voice and knew it was only making her uglier.

"Wait a minute, Pol. I always sleep in the guest room."

"Then maybe she creeps down the hall when the lights are out? Or is a Smith girl too high-and-mighty?"

He asked her why she was doing this, and to cut it out. And they had an ugly scene—the first real fight they ever had—and it ended with him going back to his own place to sleep.

After he went off, hurt and perplexed, she was sick at the way she had acted. He could sound so innocent, like with Vincent, maybe it was true that he saw that calculating husband-hunter as a kind of kid sister and didn't really take her seriously.

But nothing was right after that, even though he made a special point for her sake of turning down most of Lauterbach's invitations out to the North Shore to show her that their relationship was strictly business. As the weeks passed, though he never mentioned her, she felt Miriam between them, poisoning her every minute. Still, there was nothing she could do about it without wrecking his chances—it was inconceivable that she insist he break off with Lauterbach. What she and Hymie had together was built on air, on the dreams of youth, on romance. Lauterbach was offering him a substantial life, something he could build on. She saw that he was not happy either, much as he put on his bright face. She began to feel she was in the way of the inevitable.

Still, she hung on, not knowing what else to do, until the day in June when the cablegram arrived from Eugene.

Their mother had had a stroke in Paris and he wanted her to come. She was almost relieved. It was as if she had been waiting for something to set her in motion.

The cable came on a Friday and, since it was the beginning of the summer rush, she was lucky to be able to book passage on a transatlantic ship sailing Monday. Without calling Hymie, she went to get out her valise and there, stacked in the back of the closet, was her book of poems, *Quintessence*, that she had had printed years before. Her hopes for it had been such a dismal failure that she had never read it since. But now she opened it at random, and the poems seemed prophetically to speak to her present situation. Forgetting her packing, she sat down and read the volume through. She had thought she had become a different person altogether—knowing the answers, without illusions—but this heartbroken voice from the depths of the past was immediately recognizable as hers. It was as if at the threshold, she had written the book of her life.

She knew she ought to start getting her things together, packing, but instead, with the minutes ticking away, she sat on in the studio, dreading what was awaiting her in Paris—

and, most of all, knowing what the separation would mean for her and Hymie.

Darkness settled in, the book still in her lap.

It was after eight when he came in, flipping on the light switches, and not even questioning why she was sitting there in the dark, he announced he had gotten a huge commission check and they were going to Provincetown for the weekend to celebrate.

"Right now?" she asked, unable not to respond to his ebullient energy, and wondering about telling him about the cable and her booking passage for Monday.

"Why not? I got a car outside. We'll be there by morning. How does a swim before breakfast sound to you?"

As if he were on top of the world again, he hugged her tight and told her everything was going to be different now. She couldn't tell him about the cablegram then either. She even forgot about it herself as she let herself be carried away by his enthusiasm.

He had borrowed a Stutz Bearcat, and with their valises strapped on back, they sped up the old Boston Post Road in the warm night, singing and laughing. Then out along the winding Cape Cod road, roaring through sleeping villages, and as dawn broke, they came out into a world of sand dunes and cranberry bogs along the bay, with gulls wheeling high over the sea, and filled their lungs with the salt air.

They turned a bend and ahead of them in the morning sun lay the isolated little fishing village strung along for a mile on the furthest curve of the Cape, with its piers and clusters of fish sheds. Fishing boats had already returned with the night's catch, and the Portuguese fishermen who made up most of the town's inhabitants were unloading it and tossing worthless bait fish to circles of flapping, caterwauling gulls. They passed the pier where the Provincetown Players had started in an old shed before moving down to New York and were about to open another summer season with a repertory of gloomy O'Neill plays that the critics from New York would make the long trek up to report on.

Narrow Commercial Street was slippery with cobblestones and the tracks of the little trolley that ran all the way out to the public beach on the ocean where the lighthouse of the neat white Coast Guard station warned vessels away from the point. Hymie was immediately full of a plan to buy up all the fishermen's shacks along the waterfront and fix them up as studios for summer rentals. Only a few artists were coming up so far, but he saw its possibilities.

Polly laughed. "Let's not tell anybody about it. It's perfect just the way it is."

"You're right." He grinned. "No more real estate while we're here. I'm going to devote myself to that button nose and those freckles."

If the cablegram existed at all, Polly thought, it was fiction. This was reality.

Just beyond the village, hidden away from the road by dunes tufted with beach grass, they found the cottage he had rented, hardly more than a shack of weathered boards with fishnet curtains at the windows. And beyond a tangle of bayberries, a wide beach leading down to the sea.

With the waves breaking on the white sand, even after the all-night drive they were too excited to be tired and got out their bathing suits. Hymie snatched away her old itchy wool suit and handed her a box with a Lord and Taylor label.

It was a tank suit of black jersey. "I'll be thrown into jail!" she gasped.

"Scared?" he teased. Already into his belted trunks and white top, he watched appreciatively as she wiggled into the brief, form-fitting bathing suit.

They spread a blanket in the dunes, and with the pearls he had given her around her neck, she paraded like a mannequin for him, until he tackled her down and they made love under the open sky.

Still naked, they lay drowsy in the morning sun, miles from the city, on the blanket among the dunes, and Polly saw the boat on Monday sailing off without her and she didn't care. The cable from Paris was unreal.

Hymie was tickling her belly with the strand of pearls as he told her that this was the turning point for them. The hard times were over and there would be all the money they could dream of from now on.

Silly man, talking about money now. She lay with her eyes closed in the warm sun. Her pores were open and she drank in his voice like a faraway lullaby.

There was something he wanted to ask her about, he said. It wasn't anything he was going to do, he just wondered what she'd think about the possibility.

She heard the raucous cry of a gull high overhead somewhere, but she didn't open her eyes.

She knew, he went on, that he would always love her, didn't she? It would never be this way with anyone else. When he was with her, it was always perfect.

Beach grass was scratching her and she swiped it away, but the wind kept blowing it back.

He told her that Lauterbach was very pleased with his work, and saw no reason why he shouldn't go right to the top in the corporation. "...and he even has the crazy notion that he wouldn't mind at all having me for a son-in-law." He gave a nervous little laugh.

Wide awake, she raised herself on her elbows, opening her eyes. He was a vague blur in the white glare of the sun. "He wants you to marry her, is that what you're saying?"

He kept his eyes on the pearls he was running over her thighs. "He didn't say it in so many words, but essentially those were his terms."

She pulled her leg away and started brushing off sand. "What are you telling me this for?"

"Don't get upset. I was only asking what you thought of the idea. It wouldn't mean any difference with us. Miriam's nice enough. She's really not so spoiled when you get to know her, but it still wouldn't mean anything... I mean, it's you I love. It would just be an arrangement...."

"Is that what you brought me up here for?" She was on her feet.

"No, of course not!" He threw a handful of sand hard against the blanket. "Forget I ever said it. I'm not marrying anybody. I was a shmuck to bring it up."

She was standing, legs spread, facing him with the sun behind her head, radiating spokes like an avenging angel. "But you wouldn't have brought it up unless you wanted to. I don't believe anything you say. You've never given me anything but shit!" She grabbed the pearls from him and, naked, ran down toward the water.

"Hey, wait!" he hollered, hopping on one foot as he pulled on his wool bathing trunks.

But before he got to her, she flung the pearls out as far as she could, the sun glinting off them before they plopped into the dark swell of a wave as it broke. The wind was beating at her face and her crying was blown away to sea.

He waded out, scrabbling about with his hands in the rolling foam.

"You son of a bitch," she screamed at him.

He grabbed her arm, shaking her. "What did you do that for? You know what they cost?"

"Is that all you think about, you dirty"—she tried to think of what would hurt him the most—"you dirty . . ."

"Jew?" he yelled back. And though she denied it, his eyes were cold points, looking at her. "Ma always said they get around to that in the end."

She insisted on going back to the city immediately. On the endless ride back, he tried to apologize, saying he wasn't going to marry Miriam. It was just an idea, but he saw it was wrong and he was a bastard to even bring it up. She said she was sorry too—she shouldn't have thrown away the pearls, she'd regret it the rest of her life.

But when they got back to Perry Street in the middle of the night, deathly tired from the drive up and back and no sleep, she said she needed a little time to get herself together and asked him if he would mind staying at his own place.

"You're sure you're not still holding it against me?" His eyes were sad and searching.

"Sure."

Under the streetlamp she watched him get back into the car. She hadn't noticed before his new sports clothes, the plus fours, the jaunty cap. At the wheel of the expensive sports car, he shifted gears expertly and roared off down the empty street.

She packed the next morning—it was Sunday—and got a cab to take her trunk to the boat.

Around noon the phone rang for ten minutes. She didn't answer. She knew it was him. But when it rang again half an hour later, she was afraid he'd come by—he had his own key—and she didn't want that. She left a note for him to have the telephone, gas, and electricity turned off, and to avoid any chance of seeing him, spent Sunday night in a hotel before catching the boat the next morning.

1927

IT WAS WITH A MIXTURE OF FEAR AND ELATION THAT Eugene Endicott stood at the ship's railing and tried to make out the New York skyline in the cold fog that shrouded it as if symbolic of his uncertain reception. He hoped America had changed during his years abroad. The two things that gave him confidence were the letter in his pocket from the publisher accepting his novel, and his sister Polly's promise to meet him.

His mother had died in Paris in 1922. It had been a tranquil death. She had slipped away without a word as he and Polly were at her bedside in the American Hospital at Neuilly. In death, her face had the translucent elegance of an ivory carving. They had laid her to rest in the American Cemetery with its old chestnut trees heavy in the Parisian drizzle.

He would always thank God that his mother had shown him in his darkest time that his writing would be his salvation. And he had applied himself to it since her death, to the exclusion of almost everything else. In her last days they had long talks about the novel he had started to write—the story of a group of expatriates like himself whom America had broken and forced into exile.

But no matter how well his writing went in Paris, he didn't feel at home there. New York was never far from his mind. He had been driven out, defeated and humiliated, holding on to an old woman's skirts. But when *Tortured Souls* was taken by the publishing firm of Boni and Liveright it had seemed to him the sign he was waiting for—it was time to return to the country where he was born, where his roots and traditions, so necessary to a writer, were.

He had cabled Polly his arrival time from the ship. His sister was his only real family now. After the death of his mother six years before, she had stayed on for a few months in Paris. At that time, neither of them had the least idea about how to handle the legal problems of his mother's estate. Polly's friend, Hymie Liebman, had come to the rescue. In a letter of condolence he had offered to take care of all the details for them. Subsequently, Hymie had gotten them a mortgage on the family home and invested the money in the booming stockmarket. This and the rest of their mother's estate gave both Polly and Eugene a modest income.

When their mother's will was settled, Polly's share had been enough for her to open a small art gallery in the Village. When she was still in Paris she had spent a lot of time making the rounds of the art galleries, studying up on all the schools of modern French painting from Cubism to Surrealism. Some of it reminded her of the kind of art Larry Mathews and other painters she knew at home were now doing. It was the art of the future, she told Eugene, but no one was taking it seriously yet in America, and it was going to be her job to make them swallow it.

After her return to New York, she regularly sent him clippings of the reviews of the shows in her new gallery. The critics jeered and she wasn't finding many buyers, but her gallery had already become a focus of the avant-garde art world in the city.

Polly wasn't at the pier to meet him. After he got through customs, he looked for her everywhere beyond the barrier where the flashily dressed crowd waited to greet the arrivals. The noisy shed was almost identical to the one he had disembarked into from the troopship nearly ten years before, and he now felt himself a stranger just like then. The baggage handlers wheeling great stacks of luggage jostled him as he carried his bags through passport control and out into the street in front of the pier. He was trying to find a free cab amidst the welter of vehicles coming and going, when Polly leaned out of a cab window calling his name.

He breathed a sigh of relief, but the bleached blonde he saw stepping out of the taxi with her narrow skirt above her knees and wearing too much makeup in the raw daylight didn't look much like the sister he had last seen in Paris a few years before.

"I bet you're ready to kill me," she cried, pecking him on the cheek. "I know I promised to meet you. I really meant to, but I got so involved in hanging the show it completely slipped my mind." She stepped back to take a look at him, raising a penciled eyebrow. "My God, a beret—and a mustache too! Don't *you* look like a fugitive from the Left Bank."

The artificially bright manner was jarring enough, but to ruin everything completely, she poked her head back into the cab and called, "Don't just sit there, darling. Get out and say hello to my big brother."

A husky fellow who looked like a prizefighter in a leather jacket and paint-spattered denims slid out grinning sheepishly. "Hey, Polly's big brother," he said, going along with her fib and extending his arm.

Gene mumbled something. The boyfriend wasn't more than twenty-five. No wonder she was trying to make herself sound younger.

"Gene, you're going to be amazed when you see Jock's work at the gallery. He's going to knock the critics on their asses. He's the best surrealist painter in America." She looked at the muscle-bound kid proudly, as if he were a prize possession.

As the driver strapped his luggage onto the rack, Polly pulled Eugene into the cab beside her, directing her prizefighter boyfriend to the jump seat facing them. "I'm simply desolate," she told Eugene in a voice that cut through the noise of the shifting gears as they set off, "but I'm going to have to drop you off at the house alone. The critics are coming and I have to get Jock back to the gallery in time. You only have to see him"—she ran a hand appreciatively over his thigh—"to realize how talented he is."

The boob's sheepish grin again. It was sickening.

The cab made its way down to the Village, bouncing over the cobblestones, past the waterfront warehouses and tenements, but her chatter didn't let up for a minute. Eugene had only heard her sound so hysterical once before. It was shortly after their mother's death in Paris when a friend sent her the clipping from the *Times* about Hymie Liebman's wedding to the Lauterbach heiress. He knew she had thrown Hymie over, but he had been repelled at her tone as she read him, mockingly, about the extravagant wedding on Long Island's north shore—the guest list that included Guggenheims, Lehmans, and even a Rothschild, the month-long honeymoon cruise to South America, the house in Larchmont a gift of the bride's father, and the bridegroom's plan to open offices in the Lauterbach Building. "Look at that shit-eating grin," she had said with a laugh that grated on his nerves even then, holding out the picture of Hymie with his bride. "He's pulled off the biggest business deal of his life."

And now as they turned into the maze of familiar Village streets where he had grown up, that he hadn't seen in years, she refused to shut up and the same strident voice blocked out anything he might feel but irritation.

While the driver unstrapped his suitcases in front of the house, Eugene's one thought was to get into his own room and shut the door. But she even loused that up. She called after him through the cab window that she had forgotten to tell him, he couldn't stay in his old room, she was using the whole top floor for storage up there. "You'll have to take the room next to mine, okay?" Without even noticing his chagrin, she turned back to the muscle-bound boob with her as the cab drove off.

Only the outside of the house was the way he remembered it. Throughout the entire parlor floor the wallpaper and woodwork had been painted over dead white, and the front room had nothing in it but stark, tubular-steel chairs around a mirror-topped coffee table.

Polly had taken over their mother's old room on the second floor and it was a mess, with her clothes draped over everything. A silk stocking dangled from a ceiling fixture. Even if he had wanted to, he couldn't move right into the bedroom next to hers. Two full suitcases were open on the unmade bed and a pair of trousers hung over a chair. She must have people staying there and was so dizzy she forgot. And just as she said, the whole upper floor where his old room was was chockablock with family furniture from downstairs. It wasn't much of a welcome. Glumly, he carried his suitcases down to the dining room in the basement to sleep on the daybed in the corner, wishing he had never come home.

It seemed to him those first days back with Polly that she was constantly bringing artists or hangers-on home from the gallery. And more people would drop in, and someone inevitably put jazz on the Victrola, turned up loud. He never seemed to be alone with her. She was always talking to someone he didn't know, waving a cocktail glass in her hand, in perpetual motion.

Even when he moved into the extra bedroom after her friends relinquished it, he couldn't get away from the noise of the partying downstairs. And when finally that was over, there was no way of not hearing through the wall between their bedrooms her wild transports with Jock. And within a week there was a new "Jock," this one also with muscles and introduced by Polly as "the best Dadaist this side of the Atlantic."

Though the house had been left to both of them and she had written him that she wanted him to come back and share it, he ought to have realized that she had had it to herself a long time and he couldn't expect her to adapt to his quieter way of life. And he certainly was never going to accustom himself to hers.

He had to find somewhere else to live and he went out to look. In the years he had been away, the Village had changed—for the worse. Many blocks were scarcely recognizable. On Greenwich Avenue, the old Jefferson Market had finally been torn down and was being replaced by a monolithic women's prison overshadowing the once-elegant clock tower of the old courthouse, now forlorn-looking with its windows boarded up. A whole section had been torn away in the south Village as well, to make way for traffic ramps leading to the entrance of the new Holland Tunnel under the Hudson. On the main streets, sidewalk salesman in berets hawked cheap paintings of gauzily draped lovers kissing in the moonlight and galleons under full sail, and tour buses rumbled down the narrow side streets with megaphones blaring nonsense about "artists and bohemians," while the tourists aboard gaped.

The noise level seemed to have risen everywhere. Undaunted, he turned in wherever there was a For Rent sign. He looked at all kinds of rooms and cold-water flats, but even when they were tolerable always there seemed to be noise coming from somewhere—from other apartments, from the courtyard, or from speakeasies right below, as if nonstop parties were all anyone had time for, with frenzied jazz and floors shaking from the Charleston and the Black Bottom. New York was supposed to have one hundred thousand speakeasies and it seemed to him as he walked the streets looking for a place to live that at least half of them were in the Village.

At his wit's end, he stopped into the drugstore on Sheridan

Square where he used to have breakfast years before, hoping to run into a familiar face, someone who might steer him to a decent place to live. Once there had been a bulletin board where people put up notices of neighborhood rentals. But the bulletin board was gone, the counter where he used to have breakfast was torn out, and even the druggist was a stranger.

He returned home discouraged that evening, dreading to find the usual party going on. But for once the house was quiet and Polly was in her room, sitting at her vanity table painting her nails. Delighted at being alone with her, he said he had seen Hymie Liebman's name in the paper that day. He knew she saw him occasionally when she went up to his office to get her dividend checks, since he was still handling their affairs.

But at mention of his name she jumped, almost spilling her nail polish. "What's it say about him?"

He told her Hymie was a member of an investors' group that was erecting a luxury apartment building on Beekman Place.

"Is that all?" She turned back to her nails. He was always on the business page, she said. It was such a bore. Was she ever glad she had finished with him. "Thank God I'm not his hausfrau stuck up in Larchmont. I hear he keeps her pregnant from one year to the next." She laughed harshly and reaching to rummage for something in her bag, knocked it to the floor.

He was gathering up the contents for her when he came upon the picture. It was a snapshot of a boy in a scout uniform, and no one had to tell him it was his son, Seth.

He hadn't had the nerve to ask Polly about him. He knew that she corresponded with his ex-wife, but guilty as he felt about the son he had never seen, he preferred not thinking about it. Now, seeing the picture of the boy with Patrick's Irish grin, Eugene was filled with a confusion of feelings. Polly started to tell him what news she had of the Harrises, when up the stairs came a couple of loud friends who had barged in as usual without ringing, and she jumped up, her abrasive self once again, screaming for them to meet her famous brother who was having a novel published, and did they want a drink.

He fled the house, out into the night. As he walked toward Washington Square Park, barkers tried to pull him into strip joints and drag shows. Everywhere people filled the streets, looking for what the papers were calling "Sodom on the Hudson." The speaks were packed and even louder and more unruly than during the day. The bar where he once had worked,

86 Barrow, had been a speak catering to the literary crowd, now it was jammed with a hard-drinking bunch in paper hats and tin horns. This new Village he had come back to seemed as tawdry and commercial as a carnival midway.

Then, a block from the square where it was already quieter, he heard the piano and the woman's husky voice singing "Someone to Watch over Me." It was coming from a small, unpretentious bar called Blue Notes.

Something about the voice drew him inside, and he was at the bar and ordering a drink before he realized that there were only men there and they were homosexuals. He always avoided such places and he was about to leave, when he recognized the singer accompanying herself at the piano—a woman about his own age with the doll-like features fat girls often have. She was a friend of Polly's and her name was Stella Banks. He had met her at the house once or twice. They had only exchanged a couple of words and he had dismissed her as just another one of Polly's fast set.

In a full yellow gown with filmy sleeves that did little to disguise her plump arms, she was giving herself completely to the sentiment of the lyric, as she belted out the song to the rapt patrons around the bar. Nobody was talking or even lifting a glass. Against his will Eugene fell under the spell of the song. He had hardly had a moment of peace since his return from France. Beyond any limitations in her voice, beyond the simpleminded lyrics, something came through that gave him courage—something that said that in spite of endless defeats, you could go on. He could have listened forever, not to have to come back to reality.

When she finished the song, he joined the group of admirers around the piano and waited his turn to compliment her.

"Don't tell me. You're Polly's little brother," she cried, jumping up and giving him a quick hug. "Eugene, the party pooper."

He was momentarily flustered as the others laughed.

"Forgive me," she said to him, "I can't help playing to the house." And linking her arm through his, led him away to a small table in a corner and ordered drinks. "Don't worry," she said, opening a compact and dabbing at her nose with a powder puff, "I'm not hustling. The drinks are on my tab." She snapped the compact shut. "I didn't embarrass you, did I, calling you a party pooper?" Up close, under the exaggerated, showgirl makeup, her eyes were understanding.

Eugene admitted maybe she had just a little.

"I thought so. I can spot a sensitive ego when I see it. I ought to keep my big mouth shut." She waved away a couple of young men from the bar who had come over, wanting to buy her a drink. "They're sweet, but I'm not going to listen to their troubles tonight. I'm giving my full attention to you."

They sat together until time for her next set. She told him that she had sung in a variety of little clubs around the Village. She had been at Blue Notes for nearly a year, longer than anywhere else, and had developed a following. He told her about Paris and his book that was about to be published. They couldn't begin to tell each other everything they had to say. At her next break—after a set including the torch song. "The Man That Got Away" that brought tears to the eyes of more than one patron, followed by lively "Button Up Your Overcoat"—she came back to Eugene and they went on talking.

She laughed when he confessed that he was going crazy staying with Polly. "She's a terror, all right. You have about as much chance getting any writing done there as if you set up your typewriter in Grand Central Station."

But she had a solution. She lived in an old building on Weehawken Street where the rents were cheap. It was a quiet block over by the Christopher Street ferry. An old man on her floor had just died and they hadn't cleaned his junk out yet. Two perfectly good rooms, and she'd love to have him as a neighbor.

It turned out to be a cold-water flat, four flights up with the john in the hall and a high-legged bathtub in the kitchen. It was still a mess, but it was next door to Stella and there wasn't a speakeasy on the block.

He gave the janitor a month's rent, and he and Stella spent a week cleaning out the piles of stuff left by the old man. They ripped up the rotten layers of linoleum that successive tenants had covered the floors with, and after they put a fresh layer of paint over everything, the last traces of musty smell were gone.

There was only an ancient iron kitchen stove to heat the place with, but when he had stuffed the worst gaps in the window frames with newspaper and puttied the chinks in the panes, it was as cozy as central heating. Stella showed him how to put a pan of water in the oven to cut the dryness in the air. It was luxury compared to the chilly little maid's room he had lived in in Paris, eight flights up under a mansard roof, where he had done his writing in the winter and most of the rest of the year wearing all his sweaters and coats, with only a smelly alcohol burner for heat.

He moved over some furniture from Perry Street, and the janitor brought him up an old folding iron bed from the cellar. Stella sewed bright patchwork curtains for the windows out of her bag of remnants—she had to make her own clothes because she couldn't get dressy-enough gowns for her act in her size. They went on expeditions together, searching in rummage sales for whatever else he needed.

Polly, wearing a cloche hat with a feather, surveyed the apartment skeptically as she perched on the table next to his Remington typewriter. "It beats me why you think this is better than having the whole third floor at home. I told you I was going to have it cleaned out." She slipped another cigarette into an ebony holder and lit it with the stub of the previous one. "I've been trying to get Stella to move out of this dump for years, but if you two want to do your *la vie bohème* thing, okay." She tossed a long knitted scarf over her shoulder and sailed out, wishing him lots of luck.

But it suited Eugene perfectly, and the next morning when he was having breakfast with Stella, the mailman brought up a package for him, the first piece of mail in his new home. It was the galleys of his novel to correct.

In Paris, when he had gotten the letter from Boni and Liveright, the publishers of Sherwood Anderson and Willa Cather, accepting *Tortured Souls* for publication, he had been so exhilarated that he went to the Select, his regular café, and blew the remains of his quarterly dividend check on treating everyone to drinks, including the old *garçon* and the *patron*. Recognition as a writer was oxygen to his suffocated ego. It was going to be his passport back to respectability. Ever since his mother had picked him up out of the gutter and taken him off to Paris, he had given himself over to his writing with a singleminded passion. If his life had led him down devious paths that brought him scorn and ridicule, the publication of the novel was going to redeem him. Just the writing of it had done a lot to heal his psychological wounds. The theme of the book was exile, after a man's descent into degradation, but the ending promised rebirth through art—and now it seemed to be coming true.

And always in the back of his mind had been the prayer that something would make him worthy of the son he had never seen, who was growing up in the midwest without knowing him. Once the book was in print and he was a published author, his son Seth would be able to think of him as something more than an outcast.

But when the proof sheets of *Tortured Souls* were spread out on his desk for him to go over, and he actually saw his words set up in print for the first time, he squirmed, imagining the world's ridicule when it came out. What had seemed to him in manuscript a serious book, now looked embarrassing. He had an impulse to send a telegram to the publishers saying that he had changed his mind, and catch the first boat back to Europe and anonymity.

Through the wall he could hear Stella at her upright piano working out an arrangement for a medley of Gershwin songs. He didn't like to interrupt her, but he felt so panicky he hoped she would forgive him for tapping on the wall to let her know he wanted to get together.

He told her what was bothering him as they sprawled in her sagging, overstuffed armchairs. Stella was comfortably dowdy in a chenille robe, with spit curls set with hairpins peeping out from a hairnet on each side of her face. He couldn't bear to go on correcting those damn proofs, he said. He couldn't even stand to look at them. Everything was rotten since he had come back—the Village, his sister, and now his book.

"I know what you're going through, sweetie. Believe me, I get it too whenever I go into a new club. First-night frazzle, I call it."

"It seems so ridiculously personal," he said. "Even if it's fiction, everyone will know it's about me."

Stella shook her head. "The book is marvelous. I read it and loved it and the world will too. But if you're nervous about the exposure, why don't you use a pseudonym? Lots of writers do. You could be . . ." She considered, toying with the strap of her wristwatch. "You could be Elgin . . . Elgin St. John. Doesn't that sound like someone from the Main Line—went to Yale, and lives in the country somewhere raising horses?"

He couldn't help laughing. "It's a little theatrical, isn't it?"

"What's wrong with that?"

"I don't know . . . maybe it's not so bad."

"Good!" She jumped up and kissed him on the cheek. "You're Elgin St. John. And I'll help you correct the proofs myself. It'll go faster that way, and I won't let you think about it until the raves are coming in.

"As to your sister," she said later on, when they had moved over to the kitchen table, "it's all a front with her. Don't let all that brittleness fool you. The gallery world is tough, especially when you're trying to push modern art on a bunch of old fogies. She's got to act that way to make them listen."

He stirred the coffee she handed him, glad to get off the subject of his book and talk about Polly. "You're probably right," he said. "I've felt so suffocated by her since I've been back, I haven't been able to stop and think about why she's like this. It's just that I wish she was like she used to be. She was so much easier to take when she was going with Hymie." He told Stella he had run into him a few days before and heard a little bit about the breakup. Hymie was coming out from lunch at the White Horse Tavern on Hudson Street and they had had a beer together. The only thing Hymie wanted to talk about was Polly. He never saw her any more, he said to Eugene, except when he made her come up to his office on business, and then she never let him take her out to lunch or even stayed long enough to talk about old times. "I'll never get over that sister of yours, Gene. She really threw me a curve when she walked out on me."

Stella poured them more coffee and said Hymie was such a doll she would have tumbled for him herself if he had whistled. "But don't forget, sweetie, he's a salesman and he's always going to put himself in the best light. The truth is, he dumped Polly." And she told him the story of Hymie's mercenary courtship of Miriam Lauterbach, and how it hurt Polly to be offered the role of back-street mistress.

So that's what explained her transformation—part of it at least. The misery she was going through in Paris had not only been over their mother's death as he had assumed, but over losing Hymie. "I'm actually relieved to find this out about her," he told Stella, "even though I'm sorry it's from being unhappy."

"Oh, you don't have to feel sorry for her. It's just her way of looking after herself—the same as I do myself."

"You're nothing like her." Eugene laughed. "You're the most loveable person I know."

"And I'm beautiful, and the original 'It' girl besides." She stuck her lips out, imitating Clara Bow's cupid mouth. "Don't be fooled by my act," she said more seriously. "It's just an example of the fat girl compensating with a laugh-a-minute personality. Polly's lucky—I never had a great love. Men lay me and leave me, it's the story of my life. Polly may be going from pillar to post with a new man every week, but it's just a device she hopes will keep her from being hurt again. She chooses to have brief affairs. I'm forced to take what I get or get nothing. So I take the men who come down to the Village looking for an easy lay, most of them married or just passing through, because that's what's available." She sighed exaggeratedly and slurped her coffee.

"The Village has changed," he said gloomily.

"It's not easy for you here, is it?" she said, looking up quickly.

"I didn't expect it to be." Until now he hadn't opened up to her about himself, but he didn't want to keep it back any more and he went on to tell how it had begun in the cellar and ended with him being driven out of the country. "Well, not exactly ended," he said, grinning, "but I try to hold off as long as I can. What you get when you pick someone up is a lottery, and even when you want to, you never see them again."

Stella laughed, and seeing the ridiculousness of their whole sexual predicament, he laughed along with her.

"We're a real combo, you and me, sweetie," she said, crossing her legs and beginning to repaint her lips. "Love ought to be easy and nice, and everyone for the asking—if there were a kind God in the sky. Instead we stumble around like cripples searching for it."

"But you have your singing. That must make up for a lot."

"I don't deny it." She blotted her full lips on a tissue. "The boys at Blue Notes, I couldn't keep going without them. They save my life. The same as Polly's gallery saves hers. And talking of galleries..." She got up and retied her robe over her ample breasts. "Come on, Elgin St. John, we have your galleys to correct."

As he read the proofs aloud to her, correcting the printer's errors and making minor textual changes, it didn't sound so bad. In fact, it sounded as good as it had during his moments of wildest elation when he was writing it. It made all the difference having her there.

They were finished in a week and he sent the galleys back

to the publishers—the novel would be out in a couple of months, but Stella wouldn't hear of him waiting around for that and got him started writing another. Whenever his confidence flagged, she sat him down and made him talk through his writer's block.

Usually in the evenings, he walked over to Blue Notes to meet her when she finished her stint at one in the morning. On the way home together, they had fun speculating, when a man passed them, about which of them he would give the eye to. On her nights off they went to concerts, and in the afternoons matinees of Broadway plays. Along with everyone else in the Village, they went to rallies in Union Square to save Sacco and Vanzetti from the electric chair. More often, they didn't go anywhere, but stayed in their dilapidated little building by the river, and over a bottle of wine they sat up half the night telling each other their life stories. Inevitably, she made him see the funny side of all the things that had tormented him.

He never got tired of hearing her hilarious description of how she was a homely fat girl in high school, never being asked out and having to content herself with her pretty girlfriend's stories of their dates—until she went to music school and fell in with a crowd of gay boys, and never sat home alone again.

Polly was giving Larry Mathews his first one-man show, and Eugene and Stella went to the opening together. The gallery, on Greenwich Avenue, had been a spaghetti maker's shop before Polly took it over. It had a crude painting of a peacock on the window and Polly had painted the words "Peacock Gallery" above it in bright letters that stood out vividly against the green tangle of tropical plants left from the previous tenant. She hardly changed anything in the place, except for giving it all a coat of white paint, including a pasta-making machine that stood there like a strange cubist sculpture. She even left up the noodle drying racks at the rear and pinned watercolors and drawings to them like clothes on a line.

Larry Mathews's unframed canvases on the walls looked almost like paintings of tangled strands of multicolored spaghetti. He had long before given up his Iowa cornfields, which he now looked on as his student work. In front of one of the canvases, Polly, in a coral dress with no waist and a dipping hemline, was waving a long cigarette holder as she explained the painting to a bespectacled man. "It's like modern music.

It embodies all the harsh, jangling colors of the machine age . . . American to its fingertips. . . ."

"Look at her," Stella said to Eugene. "Isn't she something?"

He had to admit it. This art she was showing had no support from any recognized authority. In fact, the magazines were full of cartoons ridiculing it. If she seemed aggressive, how else to get people to accept modern art? Stella was right—she had to shove it down their throats.

Stella ran up to throw her arms around Larry Mathews who was grinning bashfully at all the unaccustomed attention. He was wearing a whipcord suit and polka-dot tie, and balancing self-consciously on the balls of his feet. "I always knew you'd hang at the Met someday, lover," she cried.

As people came up to congratulate him, many of them declaring that his work was so *original*, it did not escape Eugene's notice that others, behind his back, were raising their eyebrows at the bizarre canvases.

One of the paintings, at least, had been sold. It had a red star next to it. But Stella told him that Polly had bought it herself, and to keep it a secret. She was letting Larry think that some collector had bought it, because of his ferocious pride. "My God, do I remember his pride," she said between clenched teeth with mock anguish.

She turned away to greet two of her young men from the Blue Notes bar, and he was about to look for the coffee—many of the people around him had cups in their hands—when a familiar voice spoke to him.

"I bet you don't remember me, Gene." A round-faced man in a waiter's jacket handed him a coffee cup.

"Dominic!" He pumped the hand of his quiet relative whom he hadn't seen since Mario's funeral. "You haven't changed a bit." But he *had* changed. His hair was thinning and he had a paunch and looked middle-aged, though he was two years younger than Eugene. Eugene hardly knew what to say. He had left the country without a word of good-bye to the Alfanos, but he had been in so much trouble then. "You have a couple of sons now, I understand." It sounded to Eugene like something a stranger would say, but Dominic didn't seem to notice anything, and told him that his son Steve was six now and Frankie was four and a half, and he and Rosalie were about to move out to Bellmore, Long Island, where he was buying a little restaurant. He was going to sell the family place on Carmine Street and get out of the nightlife business.

Eugene said he'd come by soon and see Rosalie and the boys, taking a sip of the coffee—which turned out not to be coffee at all.

Dominic smiled at his surprise. "It's my grandma's dago red. Polly asked for it special, but I thought we ought to disguise it a little just in case a cop walked by and looked in the window."

"It's very good wine."

"Polly told me about your book being published. I always knew you'd do something important."

"Thanks, Dom, that means a lot to me."

It was Polly who interrupted—suddenly the old Polly again, slipping an arm around the waist of each of them. "I'm glad you two have reintroduced yourselves. We were all a family once, remember?"

They looked at one another, feeling as close as they had when they were children, as the people in the gallery chattered away around them with their coffee cups of wine, until Dominic moved off to fill empty cups from the silver pot.

"This came today," Polly said, handing Eugene an envelope. "I almost forgot to give it to you." She was watching him curiously.

It had a Cincinnati postmark. It was from his twelve-year-old son, Seth, whom he had never dared to communicate with—and it was addressed to him.

THE BOCCE HAD CHANGED WITH THE TIMES. MIRRORS AND painted panels simulating marble covered the old bucolic paintings on the walls and columns. The bocce court in back had been floored over and more tables jammed in. In the rosy glow of the modern lamps it looked warm and intimate, though when the doors were briefly opened in the dawn light to let out the smoke and stale air, the varnish over the artificial marble was yellow and the tables and chairs battered looking.

Dominic dragged out the garbage cans to the curb, but instead of going back inside to get out of the bitter cold of the February dawn, he stayed on in front of the Bocce in his maitre d' jacket and soiled apron, not caring about the cold, looking down deserted Carmine Street. Finally, he could think of no more chores to do.

Rosalie hadn't come back. It had been hours—Was it possible that she wasn't going to?

She hadn't given any indication she was going to leave him—and certainly not the way she had done it. He knew he had enraged her by putting down the money for the lunchroom out on Long Island, but his cousin Filippo and his uncles had all said that if he took the step, Rosalie would not be able to do anything about it—she would have no choice but to go along with it.

Getting out of here was the only thing he had been living for—moving somewhere decent to raise his boys, a place where Rosalie would stop thinking of herself as a hostess and settle down to being a wife and mother. He hated the Bocce and what it was doing to her. Here he was paying off the Mafia and the cops, playing along with the stinking system his father had given his life to stay clear of. Even if it did bring in a good living—more than they could ever have made with just the restaurant—it still made him feel a traitor to his father.

Worst of all was what it had done to his wife. She hardly paid attention to the kids, Stefano and Franco, leaving them to his grandmother who was too old now to take proper care of them, so they were running wild in the streets. She hadn't gotten pregnant since Frankie was born five years ago, and he sometimes suspected she might be doing something to prevent it. Maybe that's why she had gained so much weight.

She had long before defied him and had her hair bobbed and insisted on wearing skimpy dresses that showed only too clearly how she was going to fat. It looked cheap the way she used so much makeup, and heavy powder always seemed to be sprinkled on the collars of her dress. He knew the customers liked her, yet it disgusted him to see her carrying on the way she did, sometimes stopping to take a drink with them, and with a few drinks in her, talking back to him with a filthy mouth like he wasn't her husband.

His grandmother was always complaining to him that Rosalie was shirking her duties as wife and mother, and though he agreed with the old woman, Rosalie was still his wife and he had to put up a show of defending her. She was an American, he told the old woman, and didn't she know women here didn't have to hide away in the house like they did in the old country? His grandmother had never understood American life—she had been over here fifty years and still couldn't speak English.

"When I have time to learn English? I too busy taking care of my own kids, then when your poor mama die, you—and now your kids because your wife won't. What do I need English for? I'm not a *puttana*."

Rosalie was always telling him that she had to be friendly with the customers because he didn't know how to. It was good for business, she said. Besides, she liked people, even if he didn't.

But it was more than just being too friendly with the customers. He had to fire a couple of bouncers for getting too chummy with her, and once even the bartender.

And now this, he thought, as he stood on the cold sidewalk in the thin jacket, rubbing his arms and stamping his feet, wondering where she was.

The lunchroom in the old house on Long Island with gas pumps in front was exactly the kind of place he had wanted for years. It was on the highway on the South Shore, within driving distance of the city where families could come for Sunday dinner. The water was nearby, and it was a healthy, law-abiding, and peaceful place where Frankie and Steve could grow up honest men. Rosalie would come to see how much better life was there for all of them.

The elderly couple who owned the lunch counter were retiring, and the price was low enough for him to buy it outright. He had taken his wife out to see it on the Long Island Rail Road, explaining to her how he saw them fixing up the lunchroom—which he agreed didn't look like so much now—into a real Italian restaurant. And there was plenty of room in the house above it for them all to live. There were other Italians living out in Bellmore, family people who had already left New York. He had explained to her that as soon as summer came all the trees would be green and full. They'd have a backyard with grass and fruit trees and a rock garden—just like in magazine pictures. But she hadn't even tried to see what he had in mind and couldn't wait to get back to Carmine Street.

That was when he had decided to go ahead and buy it anyway. It was the only way to make her come around. But last night when he told her he had done it, instead of throwing the fit he was waiting for she hadn't said a word. She just finished fixing her hair, got up, and went down to The Bocce as she did every night. That had worried him. Whenever they disagreed, she always let him have it about his never doing anything to make her happy.

He should have known something was wrong when she started carrying on more brazenly than usual with a big blond guy from out of town who had been coming in for several nights in a row, Rosalie laughing coarsely as he whispered to her. He had put up with her flirting with the customers for years, knowing there wasn't much he could do about it, but last night she had let herself go even further, once even putting a hand on the customer's shoulder as she laughed. Filippo, who never said anything, had come up to him once at the espresso machine to tell him that maybe he ought to do something, she was making a spectacle of herself.

But Captain Dennis Yates had come in with another cop for the weekly payoff and he had had to turn his attention to them. Ordinarily, he liked listening to the bluff Irishman. They were related by marriage through the Endicotts, and besides, he was grateful to him—payoffs or no payoffs, Dennis was the main reason the Bocce had never been raided. The one time the Feds had come around, Dennis had warned him in time so that they were able to get the liquor hidden away, lowered into the cellar through a trapdoor, and when the law showed up everyone was innocently eating spaghetti and drinking seltzer.

After he had given the envelope to Dennis and they talked for a while, he noticed that Rosalie was no longer with the man at his table. She wasn't anywhere around. At first he thought she must have gone upstairs to the apartment for a minute as she sometimes did, but customers started piling in and he found himself doing everything at once. He kept watching for her through the side door from the hall. Finally, he got Filippo to take over and started to go up and get her, relieved to see her customer paying his check.

His grandmother was sitting at the kitchen table. She always stayed up after she put the boys to bed, listening to the Italian language broadcast on the radio and often dropping off to sleep in her chair. When he shouted at her where was Rosalie, his *nonna,* her ear to the speaker, shouted back she didn't know, Rosalie had come up and grabbed her coat, scooped some things out of a drawer, and left.

He ran back down to the street and there she was, halfway down the block, leaning into the open window of a car talking with some guy. Dominic shouted her name and began to run toward her. She screamed when she saw him coming, jumped into the car, and it roared off down the block.

It was that customer she had been flirting around with the last few nights, the big blond American out-of-towner, and the last thing he saw in the red glow of the taillight was a Florida license plate.

Finally he had gone back into the speak. But busy as he was, he kept watching the front door every time it opened. She was pulling a joke, getting the guy to drive her around the block to scare him. But the hours passed and she didn't return. It crossed his mind that she might have sneaked back up to the apartment through the hall entrance. He ran upstairs again. But she wasn't there.

It was just after dawn that Rosalie Alfano returned—on foot. She was wearing only a light coat—she hadn't been expecting to come home at all. But she wasn't feeling the bitter cold. She dreaded having to face up to what she had done this way, but there was nowhere else to go.

Last night she had been so mad at her husband when he told her he had actually bought that piece of shit property out in the middle of nowhere and expected that she was going to go live there with him. If she ever did move out of the neighborhood, it would certainly not be out in the sticks to some filling station–diner. Maybe some roadhouse-type place in Sheepshead Bay or Coney Island might be okay, someplace that would attract big spenders, be lively, exciting. That was what she needed to put up with her dull husband.

And when she heard he had actually bought the lunch counter with the filling pumps in front without a word to her, she had gone crazy—that was the only way she could explain it, as she walked through the chill early-morning streets toward home.

It was a nightmare in the hotel room in Newark. That wasn't what she wanted. When she had been kidding around with the guy, rubbing Dominic's face in it to get even, it wasn't that she really fell for his line about taking her off to Miami Beach, where he was in the hotel business, and showing her a good time. That was the place for a full-breasted woman like her, so full of life, he said. All she knew was that he had made her feel like somebody, feel desirable—and she had gotten reckless. But she never would have gotten into his car if Dominic hadn't come out just then and yelled for her like a dog to come back.

Tears filled her eyes, partly from the early morning cold as she turned into a gust on Bleecker Street, and partly from fear, knowing what she was going back to.

She had tried to get out of the car, but the man had only laughed and told her to pipe down, hadn't she told him she wanted a good time? Then, in the hotel in Jersey, drunk and slobbering, he had come at her. She had fought him off—he had never actually gotten all the way. He had started beating her and her screams brought the night clerk and the police had come and she had escaped. Somehow she had gotten herself to the ferry back to Manhattan.

In the eyes of God, as well as the world's, she was just as guilty as if she had gone through with it. And she had to admit that in her fury at her husband the night before, part of her had wanted that man. Now her life was over. She was coming back only to take her punishment. She had once seen a movie where all the men of a village were stoning an adultress to death in the marketplace, as the other woman huddled behind them in the doorway—and she knew that was what she deserved.

Dominic watched her coming from the front of the Bocce. As soon as he saw her, he realized he had known she would come back, but certainly not bruised and battered like this. He kept his eyes turned away—even after what she had done, to look at her directly in her humiliation seemed an additional violation.

She passed him without a word and turned into the building. He followed her up the stairs, automatically stepping lightly in the sleeping building, knowing what he had to do—what every husband would do in the circumstances, what his father would have done. He was glad his father was dead, would never have to see this.

But instead of rage, he felt only desolation for the years of their loveless marriage, for her always looking at him with contempt as if she thought him worthless, for her never smiling at him as she smiled at the customers.

Inside the kitchen, she waited with her back to him, her head drooping. *La Nonna* was not up yet to start the fire and for the first time he felt the chill. He saw that the green enamel paint on the walls, only recently applied, was already beginning to peel, not hiding the swollen places in the old plaster underneath. A roach ran down the wall and disappeared under the open edge of the linoleum on the floor.

"I didn't do nothing," she said in a flat voice looking away.

He couldn't speak.

She turned her bruised face to him. "I know what it looks like, but I didn't do nothing. I swear it."

He knew he ought to hit her. He wanted to. He even raised his arm, but couldn't.

"Go ahead!" she cried out. "I got it coming!"

Still he hesitated.

"What are you waiting for?" she yelled. "Hit me, for the love of God, hit me!"

The old grandmother opened the door, the two little boys clutching her nightdress, their eyes saucers.

Rosalie went on taunting him to hit her, the children were screaming, and the old woman kept croaking darkly, "Kill her! Kill the *puttana*, Domenico!"

They were all at him at once—the old lady like a witch, the boys orphans like he was, and most of all, the woman who was supposed to be his wife, drawn up to the size of a howling fury, whom he could never satisfy, who made demands on him he could never meet, who had done this thing that the heavens cried out for her to be punished for.

It was too much for him. He sat down on a kitchen chair and put his head in his hands. Why couldn't they all shut up? He couldn't hit her even if she had done it. That wasn't why he was so unhappy. It was because the way he had set up his life had been shattered. It was all he had—the only thing he cared about. If only there were someone to tell him what to do.

Rosalie saw that he was not going to beat her and her fear evaporated. With different eyes she looked at the man she was married to slumped before her. He had always been dull, but now she had total contempt for him. She didn't have to be ashamed of herself, whatever had happened. She was still a wife, and that was a lot more important than being a man's whore in Miami Beach, running after will-o'-the-wisp schoolgirl dreams of God knew what. None of that meant anything and she had been a fool to think it did.

She looked at her husband weeping, at the old lady in the doorway cursing at her with her gums, and at her boys whimpering because their father was weak and their mother had never paid attention to them in her stupid hopes for romance. She had misunderstood everything about marriage. Now that she saw how weak men were—and all men were weak, not just her husband but drunken loudmouth salesmen who promised the world as well—it began to be clear to her how powerful and satisfying the role of wife could be. What a sap she had been, waiting for his smiles and approval. He was waiting for her to take charge of his life. They all were. The strong woman was at the center of everything.

She told the old woman to shut up and light the stove, took

off her coat and pushed back her hair. She picked up both of her crying children, wiped their noses, and sat them down at the table. Ordering them to stop their bawling, she peeled them each a banana.

When he saw that she was taking charge, Dominic got up and wiped his face. "I better go down and get ready to open up," he said. "It's Filippo's day off." But he stood at the door as if waiting for permission.

"Maybe you better," she said.

"Will you be down later on?"

"When I get the boys off to school."

He disappeared down the stairs and she washed her face at the sink, moving the feeble old woman out of the way, to fix the kids' breakfast herself. She knew that, bad as things might be, there would be no more talk about moving out to Bellmore, or anywhere else for that matter—not unless she said so.

EUGENE'S SON HAD WRITTEN HIM THAT HE HAD HEARD HE was back from France, and hoped that someday they could meet. Seth went to junior high school now and was in the science club, and his stepfather took him fishing a lot, he said.

The letter set up an even worse confusion of feelings in Eugene about the boy. On Stella's advice, he wrote back to his son a friendly but noncommittal note, and at the same time wrote to his ex-wife asking how she felt about his coming out to meet Seth. Clare let him know by return mail that she was in favor of the boy meeting his real father, but for a number of reasons she thought it wiser that Eugene not come out there. She had a better idea. She and Toby and Seth were about to take an automobile trip through New England and would stop off for a day in New York, staying overnight at the Brevoort Hotel near Washington Square.

The night before their arrival, Eugene was so jumpy he didn't think he could go through with it. What did he have to offer his son after all this time?

"Uh-uh, sweetie, that's not what's wrong," Stella said. "But you have nothing to worry about. There are boys at the club who are fathers too, just like you, and I can assure you it doesn't rub off on the children."

"Am I that transparent?"

"You forget I'm an expert on the subject—I have been since I was a pimply-faced teenager at music school. All the sons turn out straight as an arrow. It must be some kind of natural law."

Eugene said he wouldn't know what to talk about when they were face to face.

"Give him a present. That will start things off."

With her along to bolster him, he went to Wanamaker's department store, but toys were ridiculous for a twelve-year-old and clothes weren't any better solution—he had hated gifts of clothes when he was twelve, they were always wrong. In the sports department, he settled on a fishing reel.

The Brevoort, on lower Fifth Avenue, was no longer the center of elegant international bohemia that it once had been when people like Caruso stayed there, but even if its sidewalk café attracted a somewhat raffish artistic clientele, it was still the best hotel in the Village. Mabel Dodge—who had held her "evenings" across the street and once had seemed the most important thing in Eugene's life—had long since moved on to Taos, New Mexico. As he stepped through the ornate doorway into the Brevoort lobby, his stomach in a knot, he remembered Mabel's advice not to hold back from the adventure of life. This was an adventure all right, a terrifying one.

When he got up to the Harrises' suite, Seth was not there. The middle-aged woman with crimped hair and corseted figure who greeted him hardly resembled the pale, brainy girl with coiled braids he had once been married to.

"You look as young as ever, Eugene," Clare said, handing him a sherry. "How do you keep from getting older like the rest of us?"

Her eyes were scrutinizing him as if she expected to see something else showing.

Toby was out with Seth, she explained, but they'd be back any minute, and meanwhile she was going to enjoy having him all to herself.

It occurred to him that she had planned it this way to make sure that he wasn't a freak before exposing him to Seth.

She had tried to do her best bringing up her son, she said. He was a happy boy and Toby Harris was a good stepfather. She didn't want Eugene to think there was anything wrong with Seth, but there naturally had to be some trauma when a father disappears—she knew that from her reading. Even though she lived out in the Midwest, she told him, she had kept up with the latest psychological theories and had come to the conclusion that it would be healthier for Seth to confront his feelings for his real father before any trouble developed later on. So when Polly had written her that Eugene was home again, she had made Seth write the letter to him for his own good.

"You mean it wasn't his idea to see me?"

"Well, I didn't mean that." Her hand primped at her marcelled hair. "I think he's much too busy with his own life to consciously think of it one way or the other." She told him about the very comfortable life she and Toby were providing for Seth and their other children in Cincinnati. Toby had the Pontiac franchise for the southern Ohio area and Seth had every material advantage, while she saw to it that important things like books and good music were not neglected in his education either.

But as she prattled on, all Eugene kept thinking was that the letter was her doing and the boy had no interest in seeing him and that it was a mistake to have come.

A door slammed, and he heard voices in the adjoining room.

"They're back," Clare said.

The door opened, but instead of Seth, a fat, middle-aged man rushed over and began pumping his hand and slapping him on the back. It was Toby Harris. "You old son of a gun, Gene! It's been a coon's age!" He noticed Eugene's eye on the door. "Seth had to go take a leak. He had three orangeades at some little stand on Eighth Street. I hardly recognize it around here any more. It's really changed." He sprawled in a chair. "I guess we've all changed. You'll have to tell me about your war experiences. Goddam it, my flat feet kept me in the Quartermaster Corps at Fargo, North Dakota." He held out his hand and Clare put a drink into it. "I do envy you guys who saw action. Seth is a real bug on the war."

A toilet flushed somewhere and Eugene waited, but nobody appeared.

"Hey, Seth, what are you doing?" Toby called.

A boy with curly, dark hair in knickers stood in the doorway, looking uncomfortable.

"Come in, dear, and meet Gene," Clare said in a fake mothers'-club voice, as she got up to rummage for her bag among some department store boxes on the table. "I've got to dash down to the lobby to see about theater tickets for tonight.

It's our only chance, we're leaving in the morning for Boston." She touched her husband's shoulder. "Why don't you come with me?" Toby, as if by prearranged signal, drained his glass and followed her out.

The boy still hadn't moved from the doorway, red-faced, looking at the floor.

Eugene was just as awkward and got up to refill his glass. "Want some sherry?" he said stupidly, then corrected himself, "no, of course you don't. There's seems to be a lot of stuff to drink here. Can I get you something else?" He looked at the bottles to see if there was anything suitable.

"No, thanks," the boy said.

"Too much orangeade, huh?" Eugene's voice was unsteady.

Not a muscle moved in that face set against him, something in the expression reminded Eugene of his own father.

"Too bad you've got only one day here." Eugene talked faster, sounding more false to himself with every word. "That's not much time for sight-seeing. I've lived here all my life but I've still never been to the Statue of Liberty, can you beat that?"

"You don't have to put on any act for me," the boy said.

Eugene's uneasy smile dropped as the boy faced him. Yes, like his father.

"I know what this is all about. My mother got this big idea in her head and expected me to go along with it."

Eugene sat down on the arm of a chair, nonplussed by the boy's bluntness. He took a deep breath. "And there was never a reason why you should. But when I got your letter, I had a loony idea that this might work out. I should have known that you couldn't possibly want anything to do with me. I've never so much as tried to get in touch with you—oh, once maybe, but that doesn't count. . . ."

He almost imagined there was a sneer on the boy's face, like a prosecutor, and he babbled on out of guilt. "I could try to excuse myself by saying it had something to do with all I went through when your mother and I broke up—that's always supposed to be some kind of alibi. And then there was the war, that's a real clincher. Four years in the trenches—no man's expected to come back from that with his marbles intact, is he? A psychiatrist would exonerate me on that one alone. . . ."

The boy was still not letting him off the hook with his prosecutor stare.

"But how could anyone fall for that crap. I don't. To tell

you the truth—I won't give you any phony excuses—I'm a real louse. I haven't even thought about you that much. I've been too busy thinking about myself."

Eugene got up to go, apologizing for having put him through all this, and was about to tell him to forget the whole thing, when Seth said, "I told my mother this was crazy. You're not my father, Toby is. Who cares about before?"

Eugene was confused. All that psychology of Clare's, those prosecutor looks, or at least how he had interpreted them. . . .

"I'd really like to hear about what happened to you in the war, though. Dad told me you went through the worst of it at Chateau Thierry—that is, if you don't mind."

"Well, no," Eugene said, recovering, "not if you really want to hear . . . I'd like to tell you about it."

And as his son sat across from him in the big armchair, leaning forward with elbows on his knees, looking so much like the young Patrick in an old photograph, he told him how he was in the ambulance corps, then when America had come into the war he had transferred to the A.E.F. where a touch of mustard gas had left his vocal cords paralyzed for six months, and the bombardment that hadn't let up except for Christmas Eve, when the Americans and the German troops had sung Christmas carols across to each other before the shells started again.

And afterward, Eugene heard about the boy's life in Ohio—the big Victorian house they lived in on a hill, about his half brother and sisters, a vacation they had taken the previous year to Yellowstone National Park, and his plan to go to the University of Ohio at Columbus and major in mechanical engineering.

Eugene hurried back to announce to Stella how well it had gone, but since she wasn't there, he went over to Perry Street to Polly. For once, he was the one to monopolize the conversation, overcome by his reunion with the boy. He looked so much like their father in that old faded photograph, he told her, and how Seth came down in the elevator with him and said good-bye on the street, promising to write him all about the science museum at M.I.T. in Boston. "And I've got you to thank for all this," he said to his sister.

"What are you talking about?" she said, concentrating on painting a coat of purple varnish on her long fingernails. "I had nothing to do with it."

"You can't kid me. I know you twisted Clare's arm to get her to give in."

She smiled, blowing on her nails. "Well, wasn't it about time after twelve years that you two got a look at each other?"

✦✦✦✦✦✦✦

EUGENE ENDICOTT'S FIRST NOVEL APPEARED LATER ON IN the spring under the pseudonym of Elgin St. John. The cover was maroon and the title *Tortured Souls* in flowing green script. He gave copies to Stella, Polly, and other friends, and sent one to Clare who wrote back saying he must write a special inscription for Seth when he came out to visit. Polly gave him a small dinner at Chumley's restaurant, but there was no party thrown by the publisher, and his editor over lunch only said that they'd be waiting for the new novel he had begun.

After the first week, walking past bookshop windows to see if his book was displayed along with Sinclair Lewis ceased to be a novelty. Only a few mentions of it appeared in the press. On the day of publication the *Times* listed it under "New Fiction," and in the *Telegram*'s fictional roundup, the reviewer dismissed it, saying that while it had some first-rate passages, he was fed up with one more novel about self-pity in the so-called Lost Generation. It was quickly apparent that it was not going to earn Eugene more than his modest advance.

He was having trouble settling down to his writing again when a literary agent got in touch with him and told him that as a play *Tortured Souls* had real possibilities and she'd like to handle it if he built it around the book's one dramatic situation—the expatriate hero's involvement with a married woman who gives him back his self-respect.

Eugene had had big ideas about what would happen when *Tortured Souls* came out, but though he was disappointed at the lack of acclaim, the book actually was sitting there on the shelf, proof that he could do it, and in his mind's eye he saw the shelf filled with his Collected Works. Meanwhile, he had the play to fill him with hope. The agent's conviction that it would be a salable property set him to work immediately.

But no sooner was he back at the typewriter than the first heat wave of the summer descended, and even with the windows in his room wide open and the door ajar, not a breath moved in from the hot pavements. The city was blanketed in a stagnant air mass. The river half a block away might have been made of molten glass—only the stink of the pig farms from the Jersey flats wafted over it. And Sacco and Vanzetti were on Death Row facing execution.

He tried to get started by telling himself that writers must have always written in the heat of the city, like Melville, who worked at the custom's shed just a few blocks to the north. But sitting in his shorts, the sweat trickling down his face and dripping onto the sheet of paper in the typewriter with "Act One" typed on it, his mind refused to care about the problems of the artist as a young neurotic on the leafy avenues of Paris.

One evening in the middle of June, instead of working he sat there wishing Stella were free, but she was with a date on the other side of the wall. It was a dull family man from Valley Stream she saw once in a while who took her out to dinner, then came back to her place for an obligatory tumble. Her bed knocked against the wall in mechanical repetition and he imagined all that flesh of Stella's bathed in sweat on the soaking sheet, and her bored and putting up with it.

"You're absolutely right, sweetie," she said next day when they sat together on the end of a nearby pier hoping for a breeze. She wore a big straw sunshade hat and a flowered wraparound, and had made them a thermos of lemonade spiked with gin. But even out over the river, the heat seemed to be reflected off the glassy surface of the water where an occasional used condom floated by unromantically among the debris. "He's a perfectly nice little man, but, poor darling, adultery is just not in his line. I think I'm the only girl who's ever really come across for him in the twenty years he's been married. I try to give him other ideas, but all he does is pump away like I'm his filling station. It's better than nothing of course, and he's hardly the first man who's used me as a filling station, but in this heat sex takes a lot out of you, and if I'm going to give out so much I'd like something more for my money."

Stella was glum because Blue Notes was closing down for the summer. With the heat, most of the clientele moved off to cooler places like Provincetown and Atlantic City. "I guess I'll have to get a job in a hash house to pay the rent. The only thing that might make it bearable is a real love affair, but I'm thirty-nine, sweetie, and Prince Charming hasn't come along yet, so I'm not getting my hopes up."

Eugene said if he was jerk enough still to be waiting for Prince Charming it wasn't bothering him so much any more. He had been nervous about it, coming home, considering what had happened before, but she was the perfect antidote. Besides, there was nothing like throwing yourself into your work to take your mind off your frustrations. He laughed. "It's very puritan I guess, like taking long walks or hot baths to overcome temptation. At least, I'm not getting into trouble these days."

"Aren't we nearly perfect saints?" she said, pouring out the last bit of spiked lemonade. "We sound like St. Francis and St. Theresa justifying why we're not having any fun."

Eugene finally gave up trying to work at all until the heat broke, and they tried to cool off by trips to Coney Island, but the long subway ride and the sweltering multitudes packed tight together on the sand was not much help. They tried to feel nonexistent breezes riding on the upper deck of Fifth Avenue buses, or pretend they weren't so bad off lying on the drying grass in Washington Square, hearing the pitiful dribble of the fountain.

One afternoon they didn't go out. They lay around giggling and snacking on potato salad on her bed in front of the window, she trying to keep cool in an old Chinese kimono, he in a pair of walking shorts and undershirt. They got into a playful squabble when he tried to force her to eat the last mouthful of potato salad and he found himself lying on top of her, a position that had never occurred to him. Before he realized it, things had gone further than play. He hadn't been with a woman since Clare. He had been a kid then and hadn't felt the slightest impulse since.

Stella caught his uncertainty. "It's okay, sweetie. Why don't we just hold each other. It's so comfy—two waifs in the storm."

And it happened—not perfectly, but comfy, as she said. And afterward, when he tried to apologize, she told him that it was a lot better than her married men banging away at her. "And my God, you kissed me after you came! And you're not even getting dressed now, saying you've got to catch a train!"

"Maybe I'd better catch a train," he said with a nervous giggle.

"Don't think that this is going to change anything between us. A friendly fuck doesn't have to mean anything more, just another game to play when we're bored."

He was relieved. "You mean I'm not your Prince Charming?" he said with a smile.

"I wouldn't dream of trying to cast you in that role, sweetie. I don't want to convert anybody. I'd rather stay friends." And she kissed his sweaty forehead as she got up to go to the sink.

The heat wave continued. Stella couldn't rouse herself to go look for a job any more than he could sit at the typewriter. It didn't cool off enough to sleep until about four in the morning and most of the time it was easier to stay on over at her place and sleep there, and not as lonely. He wasn't as clumsy the next time they reached for each other.

They weren't in love. Neither of them had any illusions. Stella had slept with other men like him and he wasn't the dumb kid he was when he was married to Clare. They were settling for what was possible, and it felt grown up. His whole being breathed a sigh of relief that he had escaped out of that land of fantasy where in the shadows beautiful strangers turned into assassins.

On the last day in June, Stella was sponging herself off in the washtub in her kitchen while they listened to the cries of street urchins diving off the pier and wished they could join them, when he said why didn't they go to Provincetown? She ought to be able to find some kind of summer job there, and he might actually get at his play if he could stop having to mop off the sweat.

On the day that the whole city was cheering Charles Lindbergh with a ticker-tape parade up Broadway, they slipped off and took the bus to Cape Cod. In the little fishing village they found a housekeeping room for themselves on Commercial Street in a house whose split-cedar shingles had curled with age and salt air and turned to silver. They had to share the bath with the other roomers, and the fuses blew whenever they tried to change a twenty-five watt bulb for one bright enough to read by. But a cool breeze always wafted in the open windows from the bay, and from Eugene's worktable he looked out at the pier in back where the fishing boats unloaded their catch each day to be trundled across to the processing shed.

He had no trouble getting down to work adapting his novel as a play, and Stella found a job at a lunch counter from eight to three. When she got off work, he left his typewriter and they took their rented bicycles and rode out to the beach. Sometimes they stayed on after dark and grilled hot dogs over a fire and Stella sang her songs to him.

For Eugene, living with Stella was perfect because it didn't have to be anything it wasn't. They weren't newlyweds filled with expectations of never-never bliss—Stella was hardly the young, inexperienced Clare with opinions of how things ought to be. She was the ideal solution. In the fall when they went back to the city, they were going to put in a connecting door between their rooms to make one big apartment. It would be a real home for both of them, a home for Seth to come visit them in.

But the returning fishing fleet was always breaking into his reverie over the typewriter. He began to look forward to it each day sometimes getting up, when he heard the screeching of the gulls, to lean out and watch the boats coming in through the breakwater, chugging across the bay. He could make out the fishermen, mostly of Portuguese descent, colorful in their sweaters and dungarees, lounging on the deck, and one young fisherman in particular in a ribbed maroon pullover, always the first to leap off to catch the lines and secure them to the pilings.

And one day Stella told him to go buy a fish for them to grill on the beach. He walked over to the pier where the boats had just tied up. The fish were being unloaded and he could have asked any of the fishermen, but he delayed. He had almost given up when he saw the young man in the maroon pullover coming out of the hold of his boat holding a large striped bass by the gills.

"Any chance of you selling me that one?" Eugene asked. The fish was far too big, but he didn't care.

"Cost you a dollar." The kid grinned. "Striped bass don't come cheap."

As he got out his money, the fisherman squatted on the edge of the dock, slit the belly of the fish and pulled out the guts to throw to the gulls who flapped up, practically seizing them out of his hands with rapacious beaks. He wrapped it in an old newspaper, and Eugene, wanting to go on talking and not able to think of anything better, asked him where was the best place to buy shellfish.

The young man told him that if crabs were to his taste he could get him some himself. He went crabbing most every evening during the season at the mouth of Sconset Creek that emptied into the bay just outside town. It was a good place to dig for clams, too.

Eugene asked if he could come along and dig for clams himself, and the kid said he'd be glad to show him how and where.

The sun was going down across the bay the next evening as he bicycled out along the dirt road looking for the creek. He had begged off going with Stella to have drinks with two of her fans from the club they had run into on the beach. Along the way he had to stop at two saltbox cottages to ask directions, but finally he came to the bridge in the gathering shadows where the creek emptied into the bay, and heard the sound of flowing water beneath.

He parked his bicycle and leaned over the wooden rail, peering through the twilight. Along the banks on the other side of the creek were thick bushes and reeds filled with night insects, but no one was there. He was disappointed. The fisherman must have finished his crabbing already and gone home—or worse, had never come. He was about to get back on his bike when he heard a splash underneath the bridge.

"Hello?" he called out tentatively.

"Down here!" came the friendly voice from the dark. "The big ones are out tonight all right." He was standing in the water under the bridge in rubber boots, using a flashlight to spot the crabs as they scuttled away from shelter, and scooping them up with a net. A gunnysack on the bank was already full, a moving heap.

It was hard to make him out in the dark. Eugene really didn't get a good look at him until they were seated on the bank with a small bonfire in front of them and the young fisherman was showing him the best way to roast crabs.

His name was Manuel, but everyone called him Manny. He was twenty-two. His brothers and sisters were all married, but he still lived with his mother. He was halfway engaged to a local girl—the families had been pushing it for years—but he was in no hurry. He had never been farther off than Boston in his life, but he had the notion that he didn't want to be a fisherman forever, though he hadn't told anyone yet since everyone in his family, from way back in Portugal, had always been fishermen and he had worked on his brother's trawler since grade school. But there were other things he wanted to do. He liked to read. He had read all of Jack London and he had read Melville about the white whale. He was impressed when Eugene told him he was a published writer, and said he'd sure be pleased to have him come out crabbing with him again.

Eugene rode home under the great sweep of stars, the wavelets washing on the gravel shore, the lights of the little fishing town strung out ahead along the bay. And when he got back Stella was there and he told her about Manny. She was glad for him, and over the next nights encouraged him to go crabbing again. She had plenty to do working on her songs, she said, and had any number of friends from the club who wanted to go out with her.

But after a month of it, in mid-August, she told him that she had decided to go back to town early after all. She wanted to look for some new songs for the fall and it would be easier for her to work them out without his being there to distract her.

He said there was no reason for her to leave.

"Uh-uh, sweetie. Stay on and have me always here to remind you you're not free as a bird, just as we always agreed?"

"I'm just like all your other men," Eugene said ruefully.

She put her arms around him. "I'll never put you in that category, I swear."

He saw her off on the bus, but neither of them mentioned anything about when he was returning, or if he was going to at all.

All kinds of people showed up at Polly's parties after her gallery openings, the last years of the twenties—artists and would-be artists, and Village personalities like the baroness with the shaved head who painted each side of her face a different color and hung sardine cans from her breasts, masquerading as the spirit of Dadaism, and the best-selling novelist and poet, Maxwell Bodenheim, who was always being pursued by girl poets and their irate fathers, making headlines when the tabloids needed something spicy. Even Jimmy Walker, the city's fun-loving mayor—a Villager himself, living only a few blocks away on St. Lukes Place—sometimes dropped by. The mayor told Polly he didn't give a damn about art—he never set foot in a gallery, hers or anyone else's—but he came for her bathtub gin and the chance that one of the artist models would take her clothes off, which invariably happened.

No matter how late these bashes went on or how boisterous they got, the neighbors seldom complained, because several speaks had opened on hitherto quiet Perry Street, and cars jammed the neighborhood into the wee hours. When they did call the police, nothing happened since the captain of the Sixth Precinct was Polly's cousin, Dennis Yates.

Sometimes, if one of her openings had attracted a wealthy collector, he would take them all up to Harlem to the Cotton

Club, or even to one of the notorious drag balls where Park Avenue socialites as well as Villagers danced with the exotically bedecked Harlemites.

More often, they went on to a club in the Village. After her big Futurism show, she and her friends ended up at a dive called the Bunny Hug on Third Street under the el. They only went to the place because the man Polly was currently going with was a part-time bouncer there and they wouldn't have to pay the cover. But from the way they were being clipped for their drinks, she suspected her boyfriend was getting a cut. His paintings weren't as impressive as the muscles under his shirt, and in soberer moments she had to admit that she had let his physique affect her judgment. The only times she let her critical acumen be swayed were for the man of the moment. Otherwise, she was hardheaded about what she showed at her gallery.

The drinks at the Bunny Hug were flagrantly watered, and the entertainment a broken-down comic with stale routines that were funny only to the drunks who wanted an excuse to stamp their feet. Her boyfriend was looking more asinine to her by the minute as he leaned over to a girl at an adjacent table, boozily assuring her that he could get her paintings into a gallery if she was nice to him. Polly tried to talk with Stella Banks who was at her table, but when she heard her boyfriend tell the girl that he had the owner of the Peacock eating out of his hand, she slugged down her drink, stood up—the long fringes of her black silk dress shaking—and called him a no-good bastard. She didn't want to see him or any of his idiot paintings again.

The scene got uglier. The muscular boyfriend yelled back that he wouldn't show his pictures at her cheesy gallery if she paid him—everyone knew about the junk she showed, and all she ever wanted him for was his big meat. He shook off the club's bouncer, grabbed the floozy at the next table and left.

"Let him go," Stella said, as Polly tried to get by her chair to follow. "He's a worthless son of a bitch. You're well rid of him."

"You bet your life I am," she said with a bitter laugh. "There's plenty more where he came from," and, black fringes shimmying, she tottered out to the powder room.

The "powder room" was only a single toilet, and the door was locked. She waited outside in the dank hallway, furious at herself for having built up that punk's ego when she should have told him right off to dump his canvases and get a job housepainting. What really galled her, though she didn't want to admit it, was that he had walked out with a girl his own age—half her age.

"Don't let it get you down, Pol." Hymie Liebman was there in the hallway, how she didn't know, but his arms were around her. He had been across the room with a party, he said, and he had seen it all.

Humiliation and self-pity washed over her and she began to cry. Hymie held her until she could get herself together, then said he would take her home. They could slip out the back and she wouldn't have to say good-bye to anybody.

Their cab zigzagged through the crowded nightlife streets. Still not sure where he had come from or even where she was, she held tightly to his arm in the back seat. It was as if the years since their breakup had never been.

Her living room was a mess of spilled drinks and overflowing ashtrays from the party earlier in the evening, and Hymie took her up to her room. As he poured them drinks from a bottle questionably labeled Gilbey's, she complained that he never came to any of her shows. "The critics won't pay any attention because I'm not on Fifty-seventh Street, but no matter what it looked like tonight, I believe in the kind of thing I'm doing."

He said he was sorry he had never been around, but he assured her he always kept track of her. It was just that the demand for office space was so great now, business took up all his time. He hardly even saw his family. "But those critics, they don't know their asses. You're a damn gutsy little dame and I'm proud of you."

"The same old soft soap," she said, smiling. "Tell me more."

He grinned back. "You never fell for it, did you? Would you believe me if I said I've stayed away because I was afraid of what it might lead to? I'm still a sucker for freckles and turned-up *goyish* noses."

They made love, and afterward, perfectly content, she told him she wanted to take back everything she said that time on the beach. She had been such a sap then. She was ready to take him on any terms, back street, back stairs, behind the barn, whatever he wanted—they could work it out.

He looked away and said that might not be so easy now.

But why shouldn't it be, she said, raising herself to look at him. It was wonderful what they had together, wasn't it, just like always?

He reached for his pants and said sure it was, but he had a family now. It made a difference, even if it wasn't the same with his wife as with her.

Why did he let this happen then, she asked, sitting up abruptly. Did he think that fellow tonight meant anything to her? Did he think any of the men she had been putting up with did? She hadn't cared for anyone since he left her.

"That's not true, Pol," he said as he tucked in his shirttail. "Your life is all different too. We both got our feet on the ground now."

"You may have. You think this brassy front I put on is real? If I let it go for a minute, I'd crack up. You can't walk out, not again."

"Pol, don't," he said, buckling his pants. "You think I want to leave either?"

"Then don't!" She jumped out of bed naked, and thrust the phone at him. "She can get along without you for once. Call her. Tell her the car broke down."

He backed off. "I can't. Miriam's pregnant again. She's going through a bad time. It wouldn't be fair."

"Fair?" She tried to stop him from putting on his jacket. "She has you every night, is that fair? If you go now, I'm afraid what will happen."

He moved her firmly aside and started for the door. "I'm sorry, Pol."

"No!" She sank down and grabbed at his legs, but he extricated himself and went down the stairs, leaving her hysterical on the floor.

She didn't stay in that night. She went out to a speakeasy and got drunk all over again. The next afternoon when she failed to show up at the gallery, Larry Mathews went to her house to look for her and found her passed out on the sofa, still wearing her clothes from the night before. He helped her get herself together.

"What would I do without you?" she said, trying to laugh it off as she made up her face. "That jock painter I've been wasting my time with wasn't worth going on a bender over." She splashed some gin into the orange juice he had fixed for her.

"I saw Hymie at the club, Polly," he said, taking the bottle from her.

Her puffy eyes that the makeup couldn't cover watched him

put the bottle away. "I guess I don't have to tell you what happened then?"

"No."

"Don't worry, I've gotten that man out of my system once and for all," she said, drinking off her spiked orange juice with a grimace.

But she hadn't. Although she went to the gallery, and even thanked Larry for looking after her, that night she made a round of the speaks again, and again the gallery didn't open. This time he found her passed out in her slip on the floor.

She started going out drinking every night, and no matter how much he tried to get her to see what she was doing, she wouldn't listen. At first, he stayed with her at the bars as long as he could take it, watching helplessly as she belted them down. He had never seen her falling apart this way. She had always been the strong one, the one he could rely on, and suddenly it was all reversed.

The only thing he could finally do was to go out in a cab in the early hours of the morning and check all the speaks she frequented until he found her and she was ready to let herself be taken home.

"Why are you doing this?" she said angrily one morning when he was helping her into a cab. "Why don't you just let me go to hell like I want to?"

"Maybe because I think you're worth it."

"You innocent kid."

"Pretty big kid by now, aren't I?"

"You'll always be a kid to me," she said, settling back in the cab and switching to a boozy nostalgia, "the kid who came into the Teaspoon and told me all about Toulouse-Lautrec, remember?"

"I'll never forget." It was almost a moment of sanity in a sea of madness.

By the time he got her home she appeared to have sobered up a little, and he told her he was scared and asked her what he should do—he wanted to help her but he didn't know how. He was nearly crying.

She put her fingers to his lips. "You can help me by dancing with me," she said and, refusing to listen to anything else, wound up the victrola. With her arms around his neck and pressing up against him, she insisted on stumbling through a fox-trot. "You can go as far as you like. I'm not very hard to get any more."

"It's late," he said, trying to work her toward the stairs. "Don't you want to open the gallery tomorrow?"

"Good boy," she said. "Good, good Larry. Everybody's so good— except me."

She didn't open the gallery next day. He couldn't get her up at all. And after that the gallery seldom opened. When she woke up, she flailed out at him if he even suggested she go, and yelled at him to get out of the house. Or, she locked the door to him and he knew she was drinking at home.

Finally there came a night when Larry couldn't find her, though he hit all her favorite haunts. She had let herself be taken to a saloon over on the Bowery that featured a Gay Nineties floor show for slumming uptowners. At the bar, titillated tourists had the opportunity to rub elbows with bums invited in off Skid Row by the management.

A bum was cadging a drink from Polly who was on a barstool trying to figure out where she was, her beaded bag open on the bar in front of her. She fished out the change for him, and when he had his boilermaker he put his arm around her, said she was a real nice tootsie, and called some pals over to join the party.

LARRY WAS WAITING BACK AT THE HOUSE WHEN THE TELEphone rang at dawn. The bartender had got her number from her bag and told him to come and get her. Larry found her, her stockings loose, passed out in a booth at the rear, where a number of the regulars were slumbering in the sawdust and vomit.

It was the next afternoon before she woke up, still in her rumpled clothes—she had been so out of her head he hadn't been able to undress her. Her lipstick was smeared across her face and on to the pillow.

He was sitting beside her bed, wondering if he ought to call a doctor, but when he saw that she was awake he came alive and rushed down to get her some coffee.

Ashen without her makeup, she crawled back into bed after cleaning herself up and changing into a nightgown, looking as if she were in the throes of a long illness. She took the coffee with shaking hands and told him she didn't remember anything about the night before—and didn't want to. "But I can guess how it was for you. I don't know why you go on doing this." She couldn't meet his eyes. "How I must disgust you."

"You don't. I love you."

She asked him what he was talking about. He should have left her in whatever sewer he had found her.

None of that mattered, he said. He understood what it was like not to have a hope in hell.

"I wish there was something I could do," she said, "to make up for what I'm putting you through."

"There is," he said. "Marry me."

She tried to laugh it off until she saw that he was serious. "Don't kid me. I'm just a drunk."

"You're not just a drunk to me," he said. "I know what it's all about." She had no one who understood her like he did, he argued. He had always loved her. But even if she didn't feel the same about him, they could make it work. It would give them both the stability they needed. They weren't kids any more. He was tired of drifting through life with women he didn't care about, and he thought she felt the same way about her men. Would she be willing to take the chance?

She listened and began to believe. A drunk had to believe in something, and if it was only a straw he was offering her, she was going to clutch at it.

Once she had made up her mind, she couldn't wait. Still hung over, her head splitting, she got out of bed and dressed, insisting he call Grand Central Station to get the train schedule to the first town in Connecticut where they could find a justice of the peace who would marry them without any waiting period.

On the train she didn't stop talking the whole way, beginning to plan their future. Larry could get a job as a draftsman, doing architectural drawing—maybe on the Rockefeller Center complex that was going to transform the whole midtown area. They might even move out of the city to one of those places where married people lived, like . . . it was on the tip of her tongue to say "Larchmont" but she said "White Plains" instead. She'd give up the gallery and devote herself to being a housewife and, ignoring the fact that she was forty years old, she talked about the children they would have. Larry might even become a builder like those German Bauhaus architects who believed that art should put itself at the service of industry. Life would be transformed for both of them. She could never express how grateful she was to him.

When they got to Stamford, he bought her a bouquet at a florist in the station—the first violets of the year—before they got a cab to take them to the nearest justice of the peace.

They had to wait for the judge to finish marrying another couple, and, getting nervous, it was on her mind to say maybe it might not be a bad idea to have a drink before the ceremony. But just then the other couple came out, and they were called in.

When the judge got to the part about the ring, they didn't have one, and he brought out a tray of rings he had for sale. Larry picked one out and, holding her still-shaking hand, tried to slip it on, but it didn't fit and he had to try three more before he found one that did.

She was still nervous and would have liked to stop off to celebrate—even a little ginger ale. After all, they weren't going on a honeymoon cruise around South America. But Larry insisted on them getting back to the station and she made a joke about him being such an eager bridegroom.

She was suddenly exhausted on the train going back, and when they got home, her headache was so bad she had to go right to bed. Larry brought her bicarb of soda and tomato juice spiked with tabasco sauce, before lying down beside her and holding her in his arms until she got to sleep.

She felt better the next day. Larry was still solicitous and came with her to the gallery. She couldn't stand the show she had on the walls, a nightmare surrealist that had been left up for weeks. What she wanted was big, bright abstractions like Larry's, and she made him help her take down the show and get out all his paintings from the storage racks and hang them again.

That night, though her stomach was still queasy, they went out for a wedding supper—just the two of them. She didn't want to see anybody from their world just yet. She kept up a flow of talk about the new life they were starting, and though she was able to eat most of her chicken marengo and wild rice—no wine, of course, Larry the old stick-in-the-mud was adamant—she couldn't keep anything down and threw up in the ladies' room. But she wasn't in the least interested in going home to that empty house after dinner and dragged him to the Loew's Sheridan to see Al Jolson in *The Jazz Singer*. As soon as the lights went down, in spite of the novelty of hearing a live voice from the screen she promptly dropped off to sleep on his shoulder.

Then, when they got home, with the emptiness of the house like her own emptiness, she was in a panic and clung to him fiercely, begging him to respond to her the way she remembered from that night on Washington Square arch, when he had pressed up against her with all his boyish ardor. She was desperate to feel married, to feel safe.

But though she did everything she could, she failed to arouse him, and, embarrassed, he started apologizing. The trouble was that he really loved her, he said—unlike the other women in his life. She was the only family he had ever had.

Dear Larry, even with tattooed arms like a sailor, still putting her on a pedestal. It was all right, she said, holding him protectively in her turn. It didn't mean anything. They had been like brother and sister until now. It wasn't easy to see each other in this new way. There was no rush. They were married. They had their whole life.

But the next night was the same, and with her demons coming closer, it was harder to be sympathetic. She was irritated by his excuses about wanting her more than anyone else in the world and having dreamed of her for so long. Lying awake, she mulled over the problem, and told herself that honeymoon impotence was common but temporary, and the worst thing she could do was to push.

He needed to get back to his painting, she decided, and the next day she made him go to his studio while she was at the gallery. It was the spring of 1929, and she needed time to work on a show she had been planning that was to be a roundup of the decade.

Without him there to watch her, she kept a bottle in her desk. She didn't go too far, just a nip now and then to keep the panic away. She had her drinking under control. She knew where it could lead.

But no matter how patient she was, Larry's repeated failures became her failure. His anguish and apologies only made things worse, and her tippling became more necessary. She kept another bottle in the clothes hamper in the bathroom for the nights.

One night, after the usual fiasco, she suggested that a drink might help him, and just because she was on the wagon didn't mean that he had to be on it too. He didn't say anything when she brought in the bottle and poured him a shot. He drank it straight off and she poured him another, this time pouring herself one too. She ought to have thought of this before, she said. One drink made her feel like Cleopatra, how about him? He laughed and said it made him feel like Antony. But though there was a flicker of the old ardor, it ended in the usual way.

In a flash, the shreds of her patience snapped and she lashed out at him that he had tricked her when she was down and would have fallen for any baloney—who the hell was he to think he could help anybody? As he lay across the bed, his arm with the ridiculous tattoos covering his face against her onslaught, she spat out that she despised him and she was going to get a real man and have a real honeymoon for herself.

She stormed out of the house, unclear about anything except to find someone, something, anything. . . . But the liquor she drank expecting to get some music going in her head only played back the hideous scene in the bedroom. It was Larry she had said those things to. He was her friend, her dearest friend. She didn't want to hurt him. She had castrated him. She was going to get down on her knees and beg, Larry, Larry, Larry, I didn't mean it, forgive me. Forget what I said. It's all right. Everything's all right. Tell me about Toulouse-Lautrec again, how you found his book in the library that time, how he changed your life.

But when she got back to the house, he was not in the bedroom. There was only the mussed-up bed, his clothes on a chair, the whiskey bottle turned over on the rug with a puddle around it.

The faucet was running in the sink in the bathroom. She pushed open the door calling his name, expecting to see him washing up, turning around with his friendly smile, forgiving her.

But he wasn't at the sink. He was hanging by a belt from the water pipe on the ceiling, his body still swaying from kicking away the stool, his unseeing eyes open and staring at her in accusation—and, like a cruel irony, sticking out through the gap of his pajama fly, the proof of the manhood she had ridiculed.

EUGENE CAME DOWN TO NEW YORK TO TAKE HIS SISTER back with him to Provincetown where he was still living. It was nearly a month before the tourist season on the Cape began, and the fishing port, which later on would be bursting not only with the influx of summer people but with whole ferry loads down from Boston for the day, offered the isolation he hoped would be good for her.

In the nearly two years since first going up there with Stella, he had moved out of the rooming house on Commercial Street to a fisherman's shack on the bay that belonged to Manny Silva's family. It had been fixed up for rental to summer people—Manny had done all the work on it himself, shingling it and putting in a kitchen and bathroom—and when Eugene needed a place to live, he had rented it to him.

Eugene gave Polly the bedroom that opened on to a wooden porch, sunny in the morning and shady in the afternoon. Except for the few times when they were kept indoors by the lashing of a late spring squall, she would lie outside for hours in a beach chair while he revised his play at a weathered table where he could keep an eye on her.

The first weeks, she lay around most of the time hardly responding at all, not even looking at him. Beyond the clatter of his typewriter, the only sounds were the distant putt-putt of a motorboat in the bay and the cries of the gulls. Although her eyes were closed and she wasn't making a sound, from the trembling of her body he knew that she was crying. Sometimes it seemed to him that she cried that way for hours. He tried to comfort her, but she only turned away. He saw to it that she ate something every day, he was with her all the time—there was nothing else that he could do. His friend, Manny, stopped by to bring whatever provisions they needed from the town.

After a while he got her to go on walks along the bay and tried to interest her in shells and driftwood he picked up. Sometimes a dog from the town joined them. The dogs always took to her, and once when a friendly little mongrel was leaping up, trying to lick her face, she bent over and clutched it in her arms.

Another time, they came upon an abandoned dock of a boathouse that had long ago washed away in a storm. He gave her a hand up, and they walked out to the end where they sat on the rough silvered planks, letting their feet dangle above the shallow water, and watched schools of minnows flash by in the sun. It was there, after a long peaceful silence, that she said out of the blue, "Isn't it funny, Gene, I always thought that of the two of us, you were the unhappy one."

It was the first time she had made a real comment about anything since she had been there. She was coming alive. But much as he wanted to tell her that things wouldn't always be so bad, he knew it was too soon for that. So he simply said that things had worked out pretty well for him up here, and ambiguously added he was glad she had noticed.

She looked at him affectionately. "I think Manny's awfully nice. You don't have to send him away so fast when he brings the groceries, just because of me."

So while he had thought she was isolated by her grief, she had understood about his friendship with the young fisherman. . . . He started telling her about Manny, at first so as to have something to talk about with her, something to take her outside herself, and then because he wanted to. He hadn't had a chance to talk about it to anyone before, and he was surprised how it poured out of him.

It had been a kind of healing, he said. Until Manny, he had never believed it possible to find someone he could feel so close to, a real friend. The age difference didn't mean anything—in many ways Eugene felt himself the younger one. Manny approached life with a physical joy that was an education for Eugene. And he had a mind that had developed without any outside stimulation. It was a miracle that anyone who grew up here could have escaped the narrow small-town outlook. All on his own, he had accumulated a vast knowledge of the natural world, and he had never even finished high school. Eugene often considered what his young friend might be capable of if he were to have a real education. Of course, Manny only scoffed when he brought up the idea of his going to college. He still worked on the fishing boat, participated in all the family events, and went on seeing his fiancée regularly, even taking her to the movies every Saturday night. The amazing thing, Eugene told Polly, was that Manny saw nothing out of the ordinary in their friendship and would have been surprised if Eugene were to bring up the subject at all—there was nothing to talk about. And as far as the world knew, Manny was just his landlord.

Polly wouldn't hear of them leaving Manny out after that, and from then on, whenever he wasn't off with the fishing fleet, they became a threesome. Manny thought up all kinds of excursions. One day he rowed around in a skiff and took them out on the bay to fish for mullet with balls of dough on tiny hooks, explaining to Polly they were vegetarian fish with little mouths.

Another time he came by in an old jalopy belonging to an uncle and they drove down the cape to Wellfleet to see a Buster Keaton movie. After bringing over fish from the day's catch, he often stayed for dinner and showed them how to make his grandmother's fish stew with lots of garlic and chunks of bread soaking in the sauce. And once after dinner, with Manny mending a casting net on the floor, Eugene read aloud the play he had adapted from his novel. He was calling it *The Weak and the Strong,* which Polly agreed sounded more up-to-date than *Tortured Souls*. Eugene's agent had already sold an option on it to the Greenwich Village Playhouse on Sheridan Square and a tryout was scheduled for that winter.

"If you like," he said to Polly, "maybe I can get you a juicy role in it."

She laughed. "I gave all that up long ago. I have a gallery to run, have you forgotten?"

"Of course, I haven't," he said offhandedly, but he could have thrown his arms around her. Until now, she hadn't mentioned having any life to go back to.

By August, when the town was full of summer people, she was confident enough to hang on to the packed little trolley that went along the length of the town's main street out to the beach. She even enjoyed going with Eugene and Manny to the plays at the Provincetown Theater on the wharf.

One day at the end of summer, they took a picnic basket to the beach, but the wind was too strong and blew sand in their eyes. Manny, who knew the whole tip of the cape like the back of his hand, led them to a secluded inland area where there were cranberry bogs among the dunes. He found a sheltered hollow in the sand above a pond with redwing blackbirds whistling in the reeds.

After they had gathered driftwood for a fire, Manny rolled up his dungarees and went down to the pond to dig for shellfish for chowder. Eugene was trying to get some dry reeds burning to ignite the damp wood, and Polly, slicing vegetables into an old pot, said that she wished their parents could have known Manny.

Eugene said he was just as glad their father at least never would. "We never exactly saw eye to eye, if you remember."

These last days, brother and sister had been talking a lot about their growing up on Perry Street. It seemed to be the subject Polly was most comfortable with. It was so long ago, there was no pain in it.

"Oh, papa wasn't as much of an ogre as you think," she said, "and mother was hardly the innocent one of the two."

"Come on, she was okay."

She turned from the pot. "Do you realize that she went to Vassar, but never even considered the idea that I might also go? The subject never even came up."

"I never thought of that."

"What a circus it was, that house," she said, sprinkling in salt, "you taking her side all the time and me taking his."

"They had a real death grip on each other," he said.

"And with us two brats egging them on. Doesn't it give you the creeps, them sharing the same bed all those years when they hardly spoke to each other?" She giggled. "Do you think they actually ever got together—you know what I mean—that way. . . ."

"Nope," he said, "only the four times—Alice, Jack, and you and me."

They were laughing when Manny came back up from the

pond with his burlap sack full of clams and crayfish, and something in his hand for her.

"Don't be scared, it's a present," he said, squatting down beside her with a gleam in his eye and holding out his fist.

"Will it hurt?"

"Uh-uh. Open your hand." He was teasing her. "But be careful, don't let it get away."

She closed her eyes and held out her hand.

Into it he placed something cold and wet, and when she looked it was a green frog, its belly pulsing against her palm, its eyes yellow jewels. She shrieked, and the frog leaped out of her hand and down the slope, hopping into the pond.

They all laughed and Manny began opening the clams with a knife and Eugene silently thanked him for doing so much to bring Polly back to the world.

POLLY RETURNED TO THE CITY AFTER LABOR DAY TO REOPEN the Peacock Gallery. She didn't have to face being in the house alone because Stella Banks was living there. Stella had come up to spend a few days with them on the Cape, and when Polly heard that she wanted to get out of Weehawken Street because the neighborhood was getting too rough, she invited her to move into the Perry Street house, which had plenty of room for the both of them.

There was no question of Polly going back to the bottle or the old life of parties and speakeasies. She had nothing to run away from any longer. The vision in the bathroom had divided her life like a cleaver into a before and an after.

Everything before it was dream. The other deaths—her mother's, her grandfather's, Mario's, gruesome as it had been, even her father's—had scarcely touched her like this. She knew now that until Larry's death she had been in some state of unreality, living out childhood fantasies of escape. But his death had been like a jangling alarm clock jolting her awake and there was no more escape from pain and guilt. She was paying for that dreamlike innocence she had clung to until now.

The one part of her she had left to give would be devoted to the gallery. Her work, at least, would never cause pain to anybody. She threw herself into assembling her Art of the

Twenties show that she had begun work on in the spring. It was to be a survey of all the avant-garde movements American art had embraced since the war. During this period, hers had been the only gallery in the city to show such controversial art by native-born artists. Since she originally expected to have the whole summer to work on the show, she had to put in long hours to meet her October opening date, and she was relieved not to have time to think of anything else.

The news of the show had gotten around and she was astonished at the number of artists, working in the most original styles, who brought their work in for her to look at. She also made the rounds of Village studios to see sculpture and canvases too large to bring in. Then there was framing to supervise—she had to keep a sharp eye out to be sure they gave her the simple frames she wanted.

She was making an unbelievable amount of money from the stock market, so she didn't stint on the cost of the catalog, even to a full-color reproduction on the cover of a Picasso-like African mask. If she was right that Art of the Twenties was going to have, in its own way, the impact of the Armory Show back in 1913, the catalog would become a collector's item. She wrote the introduction herself, and included not only prints of some of the works in the show, but manifestos by the artists and photographs of them as well.

She was timing her opening to coincide with the opening of the city's first permanent museum of modern art, which was to occupy a converted brownstone on West Fifty-fourth Street and was getting all the publicity.

"That place is just a rich bitches' plaything," Stella fumed, as she helped her write out invitations. "What the hell do the papers think you've been doing down here? They treat Villagers as a bunch of nuts and bolts, whatever we do."

Polly reminded her that she and the new museum were not competitors. The museum was going to specialize in European art rather than American as she did. "It always takes critics a hell of a lot longer to appreciate what's homegrown," she told Stella, "but this is going to be one show they won't be able to overlook."

But if she expected Art of the Twenties to knock the art world on its ear, it never had a chance. On October 29, ever after known as Black Thursday, the bottom fell out of the stock market, and two days later the gathering that took place at the

Peacock Gallery was more like a wake than an art opening. In the middle of things, two homegrown Bolshies wandered in and said out loud that the art on the walls was a symptom of the decadence of the capitalist system that had finally collapsed under its own rotteness, and good riddance to bad rubbish.

Stella told Polly they were just crackpots, but with the news papers and radio blaring about bank failures, mass layoffs, and tycoons jumping out of windows, it seemed to Polly a fitting epitaph. The canvases in the show that had looked so revolutionary to her before had a hollow look, tinselly, superficial as the boom times that were now bust. She remembered with an oddly amused detachment Hymie's New Year's toast at the start of the decade. They were going on a roller coaster ride to hell and back, he prophesied then. Well, the part about the roller coaster into hell wasn't wrong at least, but that's where the ride ended.

Along with everyone else's, her stocks were wiped out. The gallery became a luxury she could no longer support, and she had to let it go. She couldn't even pay the framing and printing bills she had run up for the show. Her quandary was simply how to survive herself, with a house heavily mortgaged and no way to keep up the payments, not to speak of the taxes.

With the bank threatening to foreclose, she swallowed her pride and went up to Hymie's office to see if he could find her a buyer for the house so she could rescue something out of the debacle.

But it was impossible to get in to see him. The secretary turned a stone face to her pleas. She had strict orders to admit no one. Couldn't Miss Endicott comprehend what a businessman like Mr. Liebman had to deal with? He was working around the clock trying to pick up the pieces.

Polly waited anyway, and an hour later he came out talking a blue streak to a bunch of worried-looking associates. But when he saw her he stopped, mumbled something to them about finishing their business later, and hurried over to her. She started to tell him what was wrong, but he said, "Wait a minute," and to the secretary's chagrin, told her he was taking Miss Endicott down to the Bocce for lunch.

What had happened to the market was a lousy stinking shame, he told her in the cab going downtown, but it couldn't last long. Corny as it sounded, he was still hanging on to the idea that this was America, land of opportunity and all that. He had just about lost his shirt himself, though he had hopes he might be able to rescue his shirttail. Everyone he knew was in the same boat.

The Bocce was nearly deserted. Although it was the height of the lunch hour, business had dropped off. Since the Crash, uptowners, long the Bocce's mainstay, were not coming down to the Village. But Dominic's normally glum face lit up as it always did when he saw Polly. Rosalie gave her a barely perceptible nod from behind the cash register, but Polly wasn't in any mood to care.

At their table, as Hymie broke chunks off a loaf of Italian bread, smearing them with butter, Polly said she didn't mind losing the gallery, it was having to sell the house that bothered her. It had been in the family for nearly a century. But she and Eugene had talked it over on the phone and both had agreed there seemed to be no way out of it.

"I don't want to let you down hard, Pol, but you couldn't find a buyer for that old house now. No one has the money. Anyway, the mortgage is bigger than the house is worth."

"But what can I do? I haven't a cent."

Dominic arrived with plates of spaghetti, and Hymie set to twirling the long strands around his fork. "I wish there was something I could suggest. If there was any chance to get the bank to delay the mortgage payments . . . there's going to have to be a moratorium on foreclosures, or everyone will be out on the street." He told her about the fix he and Miriam were in over his father-in-law's house out in Oyster Bay—forty rooms, it really was a white elephant—there was no selling it either now. The only possibility was to tear it down and cut up the estate into lots, but the neighbors weren't going to like that. He was just about to take a mouthful of spaghetti when he put down his fork. "Wait a minute, how does this strike you? Maybe I could get the bank to hold off if we made the house an income-producing property."

"But who's going to rent it now?" she said. "And besides, where would I live?"

"You don't get me. You could stay on. We'll cut it up into rooms for rent. It'll be a rooming house. The whole world's looking for a cheap place to stay." He explained how it would work, as she did her best to take it in. He was sure he could get her a second mortgage to pay for converting the house into furnished rooms. That way it would generate enough income to take care of her and pay the bank too. He stopped, seeing her brows knitted together. "You don't think much of my idea, do you? I wish to hell there was something better I could offer. Forgive me for being blunt, but you don't have a pot to piss in. Even to raise this much capital for you wouldn't be easy."

"Was I looking unhappy?" Polly said, breaking into a smile. "Actually I was just thinking it's not a bad idea at all. Running a rooming house might be fun." But she confessed she didn't have the remotest idea how to go about it.

Fired up by her approval, he said she had nothing to worry about there—he'd handle the whole thing himself. He'd round up the workmen—they'd be happy to have the job.

She listened to him elaborating his plans for partitions, washbasins, secondhand beds, thinking how she could never hold any rancor against him for long. With all she had gone through over him, he always came through for her.

Over coffee—after the preliminary details had been settled—she mentioned seeing Miriam's picture on the society page, proud of herself for being able to talk about something casually that once would have killed her. But she wanted him to know that she had gotten past all that.

He told her he hadn't been home in a week, he was so busy trying to untangle the mess his business was in. He'd barely had two hours sleep since this thing happened. But she had never seen him looking better— clearly he was flourishing on the challenge of the crisis. When he pulled out a gold watch on a chain across his vest, she saw his impatience to get back into the thick of things and said she didn't want to take up any more of his time.

He told her he always had time for her, and out on the street he even offered to walk her home, for old time's sake, but she countered that she didn't quite feel up to the temptation. His eyes gleaming mischievously at her, he said that probably it was just as well.

Before he kissed her on the cheek and got into a cab, he told her to keep her chin up and he'd send a man down on Monday to get things started.

She walked back home in an altogether more hopeful frame of mind than before, even passing the stacks of newspapers with their headlines about new financial disaster, just thrown off delivery trucks. Already the streets of the Village seemed quieter, more deserted, even grimier. Some stray tourists called to her from a car and asked her where Greenwich Village was. A prematurely cold wind was blowing leaves and litter down the street and she wrapped her alpaca coat with its luxurious beaver collar more snugly around her—it was the last expensive present she would be able to buy herself for a while, but what did it matter?

In a store window with a for rent sign in it at the corner of Christopher and Bleecker, she caught her reflection and stopped short. She hadn't taken a real look at herself in ages. Was that ravaged woman under the burgundy cloche hat actually her? Could it just be age that had done that to her face? She was only forty-one.

1937

As far as the outside world knew, the great bohemian era of the Village appeared to be over. More than ever the lament was heard "the Village is not what it was," but this time even a lot of Villagers themselves sadly believed that it might be true—so many of their friends had left and the old haunts gone out of business. In the artist hangouts that remained they went on reminiscing about the glorious time before the Crash—the artist balls, the party on top of the Washington Square arch, the openings at the Peacock, that wild-eyed playwright O'Neill winning two Pulitzer Prizes. It had all receded into mythology.

Those who stayed on had a far harder time keeping their heads above water, or justifying to themselves what they were doing in front of their easels and typewriters, when panhandlers and the unemployed filled the streets of the Village just like everywhere else. Not that young people still weren't drifting in from all over, attracted by the old reputation, even if they seemed to put their energies as much into political causes as the arts. But they were much less visible, and it almost seemed as if the neighborhood belonged to the Irish and Italian residents again.

ROSALIE ALFANO, A HOOVER APRON AROUND HER LUMPY BODY, her hair stringy from a grown-out permanent, was sweeping the sidewalk in front of the Endicott house. Her fifteen-year-old son, Frankie, sitting on the stoop, was rolling his shirt-sleeves up over his skinny arms, admiring incipient biceps.

Rosalie stopped her sweeping to glare at a woman from down the block walking a fat little dog. "Look at her, she's letting it crap right on the sidewalk," she announced loud enough for the woman to hear, as Frankie snickered. "It's people like that make this street a pigsty."

The woman, like everyone else on the block, had heard Rosalie's loud mouth before and jerked the leash of the dog that was still sniffing at something on the sidewalk, dragging it away.

"They think I like coming out here six times a day to clean up after them?" Rosalie muttered, half to herself, as she began to raise a cloud of dust on the same patch of sidewalk in front of the house she had been sweeping for the past half hour. Actually, she preferred being outdoors to being shut up in the kitchen all day with Dominic where they made ravioli to order for restaurants.

"You scared the hell out of her, ma," Frankie said from the stoop. "She's running away like she's got a poker up her ass."

Rosalie turned on him. "You shut your filthy mouth. You can talk profanity with the bums you go around with, but you respect your mother, you hear me?"

Rosalie's life had not improved during the years of the Depression, but whenever she complained, Dominic said they were lucky to have a roof over their heads and enough to eat. Let him be satisfied with that, she never would. At least when they had owned the Bocce she was still part of the world, even at the end when they were hardly making out. But after the repeal of Prohibition in 1933, a little bar like that couldn't survive, with the old Bocce crowd able to get liquor anywhere, and even when they had tried serving food again, the neighborhood people couldn't afford to eat out any more. Finally, the city marshal had sealed the place for unpaid debts. Things had gotten to the point that they were about to be evicted from their flat, when the Endicott relatives offered them the basement floor of their house to live in until they got on their feet again. Even with the old grandmother dead, Rosalie and Dominic and the two boys—almost men now—hardly had room to breathe, all jammed in together in two rooms.

She hated taking charity from Dominic's high-and-mighty relatives, and the two of them worked day and night making the ravioli for a restaurant supplier on Grand Street so they could save up enough to start another place of their own and get out of here. But even working like dogs, after three years they were still just barely keeping their heads above water. It was the loneliness of the life that got her, the endless rolling out of the thin sheets of pasta dough, mixing the ricotta filling, and then separating the bulging raviolis with the perforated cutting wheel, with the boys helping out packing and delivering. From here, the life of the speak seemed like a paradise she had lost forever.

She hated living on Perry Street away from her own neighborhood, on a street of private houses where people didn't get to know each other, not to speak of the bums who lived upstairs in the furnished rooms. It wasn't good for the boys. Her oldest, Steve, who was sixteen, didn't have any friends and didn't seem to want them. He was too serious—like his father—too studious. Whenever he wasn't working or going to school, he was alone with his books. No good for the eyes. And Frankie, having to go blocks away to hang out with boys their own kind, and she didn't know what he was up to most of the time.

Steve came out of the basement kitchen door and up the

steps to the street, carrying a stack of flat boxes of ravioli for delivery to the supplier on Grand Street. He was taller than his younger brother, light-haired, and already filled out. As he opened the iron gate in the fence with one hand, he balanced the boxes in the other.

"How many times I got to tell you don't carry it that way?" she snapped, not caring that she was being unreasonable. "You drop it and we got ravioli all over the goddam street."

"I got it all under control, ma," Steve said. "Nothing to worry about." He tied the boxes on the rear carryall of his bicycle leaning against the iron railing, and wheeled it into the street before slinging his leg over it and pedaling away.

Rosalie knew perfectly well that Steve wouldn't drop the ravioli. She didn't know why he always irritated her. He worked hard and got high marks and everybody praised him. Not like her younger son who was always getting notes from school and being left back.

"What you looking at, big eyes?" she said to Frankie, taking a swipe at him that he easily ducked. "You ought to be more like your brother, that's all I got to say. You wouldn't get into so much trouble."

"I'm not looking at nothing. What you hitting on me for?" Frankie went on combing his thick dark hair, training in the sleek pompadour at the front.

He was her favorite. His cocky attitude—the way he wasn't afraid of life, wasn't afraid of anything—was exactly her own. He wasn't going to settle for making ravioli all his life like his father, not this one. He took after her, he didn't think it was a crime to want to have some fun once in a while.

Sometimes when they were all at the table in the crowded kitchen, Dominic bent over his plate never talking, never interested in anything, she could tell from the way Frankie looked at his father that he shared her contempt for him. But she enjoyed being hard on the kid to see how he fought back. It was like a game between them. He was the only one with balls in the family.

"Don't you have anything to do but run that comb through your hair?" She was about to send him down to help in the kitchen when at the top of the stoop the front door opened and one of the roomers came out. Mother and son watched as a girl with her long hair pulled back tight ran down the steps, barely giving them a glance. It was Norma, the modern dancer who lived on the top floor where Manny Silva and a refugee professor named Weiss also had rooms.

Rosalie glowered after the girl walking away down the street in her haunchy dancer's stride, swinging a canvas satchel holding her leotards and dance slippers. "Doesn't she think she's the cat's meow? You can bet your life she's on her way to see a man somewhere."

"She's got a man right upstairs," Frankie said, trying to sound nonchalant as he watched the movement of the girl's buttocks.

Rosalie gave him one of her looks. "How do you know? You been hanging around up there again?" The dancer claimed Frankie had been bothering her, and Eugene and Polly Endicott both had made a stink to Dominic about it—as if they had any right to complain about anyone else's morals.

Frankie leaned back with his elbows on the step. "Didn't have to. I was coming home last night and the colored guy's window was open on the second floor and I saw her in there with him."

Rosalie gave him her full attention. "Go on! You trying to kid me? They hate each other's guts." A few nights before, the whole house had been awakened when the black saxophonist, who lived directly beneath the dancer, stormed up to bang on her door because of her practicing her dancing all night over his head. Rosalie had trooped upstairs in her bathrobe along with everyone else. The musician was yelling through the door that if she didn't stop that thumping and playing her victrola while he was trying to get some sleep, he was going to break every record she owned over her head.

The dancer had opened her door, just as mad as he was, and told him she wasn't going to stop for him or anyone else, and what about his saxophone when she was trying to sleep. Then she slammed the door in his face.

"I seen her in there with him, ma," Frankie said, enjoying his mother's disbelief. "They finally pulled the shade down, but I saw the shadow of the two of them kissing."

As much as the news outraged her, and though she knew she should slap him for snooping, still she saw the lust in her son's eyes, and it held her. "The dirty tramp," she said, her cheeks on fire. "It's hard enough bringing up my kids decent with all the nuts living in this house, and now it's not only a nuthouse, it's a whorehouse." She couldn't help going on in a manner that would excite him further. "A dirty whorehouse!"

She turned, ready to announce it to the whole neighborhood, but stopped short. Coming up the block was Polly Endicott, walking with a shabbily dressed, balding man.

She was not about to give that one another chance to lord it over her—Dominic and the ravioli were easier to take than that—and she opened the gate and started back down to the kitchen, snapping at Frankie to come on and get the orders packed.

Frankie lounged back on the steps and said he'd be in in a minute.

She took a step toward him, a hand raised. "Now, I said."

Reluctantly he got up and slouched down after her.

"Isn't she a snake in the grass?" Polly said to her artist friend, Paul Miller, as she closed the front door behind them. "Did you see her sneaking away so she wouldn't have to say hello to me?"

Paul, in his old tweed suit with elbow patches, was enjoying the handwritten notices tacked up in the front hall requesting tenants to keep it down if they wanted to talk all night, not to smash the furniture if they got worked up, tenants' friends not allowed to use the bathtub, and one in bold print, RENT DUE EVERY FRIDAY, NO EXCUSES.

"I don't blame her for being scared of you," he said, following her down the hall. "You sound like a pretty tough landlady."

"I'm nowhere near as tough as I ought to be on her." She unlocked the door to her room at the back. "She still makes me mad," she said, pulling off her tam and ducking to arrange her hair in the mirror. She didn't lighten it any more, the gray in it naturally toned down the red she once hated. "I'd like to give her the boot."

"Then why don't you?"

She was rummaging in a drawer for the key to the empty room upstairs he had asked to see. "I wish it were that simple. She's a relative. Anyway, it's her husband who's my . . . oh, it's too complicated."

Polly lived in her father's old study with the bay window looking over the backyard. It had been partitioned off from the parlor where Eugene was living. When the tenants' rooms had been furnished with secondhand beds and dressers, she had jammed as many of the old family things as she could into her room, and still leave room for a bed.

"I can't figure you out," Paul Miller said, examining an antique Tiffany lamp she had saved. "You've got Italian relatives in the basement, you tell me your Irish father dug sewers, and you have to rent rooms—yet you're a gold-plated bourgeois."

"Don't try to fit me into any of your lefty pigeonholes," she said as she led him upstairs, letting him see the bathroom before unlocking the door of the vacant room at the rear.

She had discovered quickly enough after the house was converted to furnished that she would have to get a job. She couldn't live off the rents alone, not with all the bills—mortgage, taxes, gas and electric and the rest. Moreover, a lot of the tenants were unreliable. She never knew how long they'd stay, in spite of her being so easy on the rent. They often moved out without notice, not to speak of several who had disappeared owing weeks of back rent.

After a series of temporary jobs, she had been hired because of her gallery experience to work in the Village office of the W.P.A. Federal Arts Project, which Roosevelt set up to provide work for unemployed artists.

It was there she had met Paul Miller who brought his artwork in one day to try to qualify for the program. She had been on tbe selection committee. The subject matter of his paintings—noble workers, smokestacks, and social themes—wasn't much to her taste, but he was a competent painter and she saw it was the kind of thing that would do for the murals they were assigning artists to paint in public buildings around the city.

"Ow, it gives me a headache," Paul said, as they stood in the room to let, looking at the zigzag orange and purple stripes painted over the walls and ceiling by the previous tenant, who had skipped out at the first call of the robins, leaving the washbasin filthy and the gas hot plate encrusted with food.

"I guess I shouldn't have let you see it this way," she said, picking up a sticky peanut butter jar from the dresser and dropping it into the wastebasket. "My brother and his friend will be cleaning it up and repainting this weekend, but I can tell you're not very excited. They really wreck the rooms sometimes."

Paul threw up the window and, looking out over the yard where the trees were flowering, inhaled deeply. "Did I say I didn't want it?" he said, turning around.

"You mean you'll take it?"

"Sure. Where I'm living on the Lower East Side I look out on concrete and garbage cans."

She smiled and flicked a lamp on and off to see if it was working. "Maybe you'll stop painting garbage cans and paint something beautiful here. A great poet wrote in this room once." She looked at him impishly.

"Who?"

"Me. Didn't I tell you that I once had a book of poems published? I paid for it myself. It's still mildewing down in the cellar somewhere."

"You mean this was your room once?"

She sat on the windowsill and told him about growing up in the house, the way her parents had wrangled on the other side of the wall, and how her brother Eugene had come back from Provincetown after the Crash wiped out their income—and how curious that after all these years Eugene and she and their nephew Dominic were forced by circumstances to live together.

"Boy, you've really got it tough," he said, teasing her. "You each have your own room and plenty to eat and a nice backyard to look at."

"Oh, Paul, do I have to stand in a breadline to please you? You're always spouting your party line."

He unrolled the mattress folded over on the bed and lay back with his head propped up on his hands. "Listen, Miss Capitalist," he had a twinkle in his eye, "I've gone through a lot for my 'line,' as you call it. I didn't give it up for my wife and I'm not giving it up for you, even if it bores you."

"Wife! I thought you were married to the class struggle," she said, smiling. In his shabby tweeds with papers bulging from the pockets, she had never thought of him with a wife. It was precisely because he was such an unromantic figure that she felt so comfortable with him and had let their friendship develop. The men she had been attracted to had always been dynamic. Paul had a gentleness that put him in a safe category.

She asked him about his marriage. He said it was a dull story, but she pushed and heard for the first time about his life after the war during the Red Scare. He had been active with the Wobblies, a radical labor organization. When he had been branded an anarchist and kicked out of his job as a high school art teacher in New Jersey, his wife had left him and got a court order preventing him from seeing their children.

"Where are your children now?" she asked, absorbed.

"No more of your questions," he said, swinging his legs off the bed and sitting up. "I'm late for my meeting."

She had always admired his quiet idealism, but she had never suspected he could stand going through what he did. He was a far more complex man than she knew. "I'm impressed," she said simply.

"Well, if you're so impressed, why don't you come with me to the meeting then?"

She made a face. "I hate politics."

"You're for Spain, aren't you?"

"Of course. Isn't everyone?"

"That's what the meeting's for—to raise money for the Loyalists. And if you're bored, let me take you out afterward for a bite."

He gave her a very winning smile.

In 1937, the Spanish Civil War was the most important cause in the Village since Sacco-Vanzetti. At the subway stops at West Fourth Street and Christopher Street, and all around Washington Square where people came to see the outdoor art show that spring, volunteers were shaking canisters as they called out for contributions for his Abraham Lincoln Brigade.

Paul took her to a meeting of the fund-raising committee in a back room at Romany Marie's. There were a dozen people around a table at the restaurant, representing all kinds of political groups who were united under the name of the Village Coalition for a Democratic Spain, on the issue of helping the Spanish republicans in their fight against Franco. Polly knew a woman there from the New Deal Democrats and someone else from the League of Nations Association, and she felt at home as she listened to the various suggestions being thrown out on how to raise money.

Though everyone was sincere, she didn't think too much of the ideas proposed—street-corner speakers, writing letters to prominent people, getting actors to make appeals at fund-raising dinners—and when they had all but decided to hold a hootenanny with fiddlers and square dancing, she couldn't keep her mouth shut any longer and said she didn't think a hootenanny was right at all.

What was wrong with folk music, Paul asked. It was wholesome and progressive.

Nothing was wrong with it, she said—if you were a hillbilly. But since it was the Village, she thought they ought to do something a little more sophisticated.

Like what, for instance?

Well, she improvised, what about a ball—an arts ball? People could invent their own costumes. It would be like the old days. It would be reviving a tradition.

Before she knew it, she was put in charge of the dance, though she protested that she hadn't meant to put herself forward at all and wasn't even a member of the committee.

Paul Miller raised his arm and made a motion, and by unanimous vote, she was acclaimed an honorary member on the spot.

"Paul, you're outrageous! I never would have gone with you if I knew I'd get into all this," she said later, as they sat at a delicatessen on Eighth street over their corned beef sandwiches and egg creams.

"I did it on purpose," he said with his twinkle. "Now I can sneak some of my ideas into the entertainment. Maybe we can do an agitprop theater piece to show how the boss class exploits the workers."

"Oh, no you don't," she said, "we're going to have fun."

She was already full of ideas. There would be posters plastered all over the Village announcing the art students' ball, with nude models, artists, costumes, entertainment. It would be a revival of the great days of the Village that everybody always talked about. And best of all, nobody would have to feel guilty, in spite of the hard times, because it was all in a good cause.

After Manuel Silva finished his classes at C.C.N.Y.—it was usually nine or ten in the evening by then—he worked all night at an outdoor wholesale produce market. When he graduated he would be qualified to teach general science in high school, but that was still at least a year off, maybe two. Going to college in the evenings was a lot looser than during the day—he could take as much time as he needed, getting a degree.

It was hard to make his family on Cape Cod understand what he was aiming at. Fishing or maybe a factory job was all they knew. Nobody went to college up in Provincetown, except occasionally a son from one of the better families off to Boston University or a daughter to Marymount. His family had even discouraged him from finishing high school—what did he need it for? He had had to make up the missing credits the first year he was in New York before he could enroll at City College.

The Depression had hit Provincetown like a fall hurricane that broke the boats from their moorings and washed them away to sea. The radio kept saying the hard times were only temporary, and for a while, after Eugene had to go back to New York, Manny and his brother had tried to continue with the fishing boat. But as the Depression continued into the early thirties, the processing plants closed down and hardly any summer people showed up for rentals. They had finally dumped their fish back into the sea and given up the boat and his brother had gotten a county job on the roads.

It was then that Manny got the idea of going on with his education. Fishing wasn't to be counted on, but teachers were always needed. Gene said he could stay with him while he completed high school in New York and worked his way through college. Manny didn't have to worry about running out on his family—they would never starve, with the sea to live off and their vegetable garden, and in the years he had been in New York, he always got back for Christmas and other holidays, hitchhiking if he was short of cash for the bus.

His fiancée was getting a little tired of waiting. She was nearly twenty-four and didn't see why they couldn't get married if they both worked. But he came from a family of seafaring men who didn't let women tell them what to do. A lot of the men went off on long voyages and got married years later when they had saved up a nest egg. Even if his fiancée wasn't happy about it, he could only see settling down to start a family when he had his degree and a steady job. He loved kids and he couldn't imagine not having a lot of them someday. Kids liked him too. Everybody liked him, he was lucky that way.

His greatest piece of luck was meeting Eugene in Provincetown that summer. It had changed his life. He was improving himself, living with the Endicotts. There was a lot to learn from Gene and Polly, and even from the other tenants—there were always all kinds of artists and writers living in the house, and even a refugee professor from Germany had just moved in across from him next to the dancer and told him all about the Nazis taking over. The rest of his family felt uncomfortable around educated people and were always kidding him about becoming a brain when he went home.

City College, where he went, was on the fringes of Harlem and sometimes, carrying his gym bag with his books and work clothes, he would walk down to 125th Street and have a beer at a bar next to the Apollo Theater before taking the long subway ride downtown to work. He liked the colorful life of Harlem and never got tired of the diversity the city offered.

The produce market he worked in was below Canal Street in an area of warehouses with loading platforms where fruits and vegetables for the city were tucked in from the farms during the night. He helped unload the trucks along with several hundred other men who stood around fires blazing in oil drums, waiting to be called. Later, there was more work loading the pickup trucks and station wagons of the buyers from restaurants and food markets who came to get the day's provisions—crates of lettuce, oranges, tomatoes. You could make enough to live on if you were called out regularly, and he always was because he was strong and cheerful and got along with everybody. Then, there was the extra bonus of food from broken crates, that didn't always get broken accidentally.

But even while waiting around to be called, he liked the bull sessions over the burning barrels, as they tossed in pieces of crates to keep the fires going. Most of the men were drifters who had lost their regular jobs years before and left families behind all over the country. They might be college professors, executives who had fallen on hard times, even jailbirds—and a lot of them were alcoholics. Because of the Depression they had all ended up on Skid Row.

He was always telling Gene about them and even got him to come down and listen in. Gene found the market interesting in a literary way. He saw everything as material for his writing. Manny always kidded him about it, but he was flattered that the hero of Gene's new play was a lot like him, and it was even set in a produce market, though he was nowhere near as good-looking as that guy in the play. There was a chance it was going to be put on. A group in the Village was interested in it—Gene knew the director, whose name was Dubinsky, from the twenties when he was going to do his first play, *The Weak and the Strong,* that he had written in Provincetown. But then the stock market collapsed and that had been the end of that.

Manny felt he was getting more of an education at the market than from his classes. He liked the way his life was divided up, using his brains at school and his muscles on the trucks. Ever since he was a kid he had worked on boats, scraping down hulls, hauling in nets, fixing engines. Now, spending his nights lifting crates of fruit and vegetables kept him in shape. Not only did the fresh smell of corn and celery remind him of the country he missed, but there was a whole world of good-natured roughhousing, and he and other men sometimes wrestled with each other just for the fun of it. They had plenty of time between jobs in the long night hours to catch thirty winks stretched out on flattened cardboard cartons behind the crates or to go off for a beer together.

After a hard night's work it always felt good getting home to Perry Street at dawn with the city still asleep and the air fresh and the light clear, and his gym bag full of food he had snitched from the market. He looked forward to breakfast with Gene and then up to sleep in his little room at the top of the house that he kept shipshape, like the cabin of a boat.

Coming back to the house, he checked to see if any windowpanes were cracked. He didn't like the messy look of underwear hung to dry in the windows or the bottles of milk and food the tenants kept out on their windowsills. But he liked the life of the rooming house, with all the running up and down stairs, the loud conversations on the telephone in the hall, the hubbub of radios in different rooms. He sat in on long discussions over what was wrong with the country and about endless schemes for making money. Some of the tenants brought in women, and Gene joked that none of them stayed in their own rooms.

From the top of the stoop he could lean over the railing and tap with his key against the nearest front window before going in. That was to wake Gene up. After another tattoo on Gene's door, his friend would come yawning to let him in, tying on his bathrobe. Then Manuel opened up the gym bag, took out the eggs, oranges, and bruised bananas, and made them breakfast. Gene liked his banana omelets that Manny called "Portugee tortillas."

Gene worked days at the uptown office of Polly's old friend Hymie Liebman. His job was to put together the real estate catalogs and dream up flowery descriptions of the properties for sale—to snare the suckers, he said, in a difficult market. Even though Gene griped about it all the time, it was the first job that made any use of his talents after a few years of running an elevator, taking inventory for a paint store, and typing bills in a bookkeeping office.

Because of their different hours they hardly saw each other during the week, except for breakfast. But on weekends they got together and had time to do repair work around the house. Gene had never done this kind of work before. He had had to show him everything, from how to put a new plug on a lamp cord or tar over a leak in the roof, to unstopping the toilet with a wire snake when a tenant tried to flush down a sanitary napkin in spite of the notice saying not to.

With the two of them working together, the house was in a lot better shape than when he had come down from Provincetown to find the furniture falling apart and half the windows broken. Gene said he felt a lot better about the house now than ever before. It was something like a person when you took care of them. Manny could understand that, like the way he felt about the boat when he had to burn off the old paint and sand down the hull.

He never got over how different Gene was from him, the way he talked, the way he handled people, even the way he ate his breakfast. Manny always wolfed his down after working in the open air all night—he sometimes felt a little crude next to Gene. His friend had something that it took more than a college education to get. He could see Gene as best man at his wedding, godfather to his children. When he said he wanted to be best man at Gene's wedding too, Gene kidded that he had been through all that, and now his writing would have to be enough.

It was Friday, and on his way out after breakfast Manuel reminded Eugene that the next day they had to paint the room on the floor above for the new tenant Polly had found at work.

He started upstairs to his own room feeling pleasantly sleepy. The house still had that early morning quiet, except for the racket Rosalie Alfano made, getting breakfast for her family in the kitchen below. He couldn't get used to the way everyone in the house slept so late. In Provincetown, by this time the boats were already far out in the bay.

On the second floor the bathroom door was locked, but a woman yelled she would be right out. He recognized the voice of Norma Lucas, the dancer whose room was across from his upstairs. There had been a stormy time in the house for a while before she and the colored sax player below her had settled their noise fight and gotten together.

With a sound of flushing water the door opened. "Oh, it's you!" Norma said, coming out in a cloud of feminine cologne.

"Who'd you think it was," he said, "Frankie?" He knew how the fifteen-year-old Alfano boy drove her crazy, and liked to tease her.

"Thank God it's not," she said, tying the sash of her flimsy robe in a way that showed off her figure. "He looks at me like I don't wear any underpants."

"Well, do you?"

"That's for you to find out," she said over her shoulder as she went upstairs, doing everything but bumps and grinds.

Norma was something. She was always hollering that nobody ever took her seriously as an artist. It wasn't her morals—

though Rosalie Alfano had plenty to say on that subject to the whole neighborhood—but she was just a natural-born sexpot and no man was going to let her alone.

He shut the door of his room and threw open the window to the morning air. A blue jay in the backyard was squawking at a squirrel running through the branches. There was that special scent given off by the sun on new leaves.

When he first moved down to New York he felt cut off from nature—it seemed all concrete and asphalt. But since then he had started appreciating these little Greenwich Village backyards with their plants and trees. Though it was the outcroppings of rock in Central Park that really gave an idea of what the island had once looked like. He had done a term paper in botany comparing the adaptation of the plant life in the city to the flora of the sand dunes of Cape Cod. He got a good grade for that one, though he had only done average in his other courses. There was too much going on in the city to study as much as he should—he was content to get by.

After taking off his sweaty work clothes, he threw himself down on his bed in his shorts and dropped off to sleep. He never had any trouble sleeping, or waking up either for that matter. He had an inner alarm that would get him up in time to study for a math final that evening.

He thought at first his own snoring had awakened him, but as he came to he heard voices in the hall outside—Norma yelling at someone and a male voice protesting. He went and looked out.

It was Frankie Alfano, and the dancer, in a black leotard, was letting him have it.

"This kid is driving me out of my mind," she said when she saw Manuel.

He asked what was wrong. According to Norma, while she was doing her exercises in her room, she heard something outside her keyhole. She yanked her door open and Frankie practically fell on his face.

"She's full of baloney!" Frankie held his ground, a tough little street kid with a teenage pompadour and ragged corduroys rolled up at the cuffs.

Manny couldn't blame him for whanging off over the bosomy dancer in her tights. All you thought about at that age was pussy.

"Okay, what were you doing up here then?" said Norma, not letting up on him.

There was a phone call for the new guy, Frankie said.

"The new guy! Professor Weiss you mean? You know damn well he's away at work, you slimy little pervert!"

"And you're a whore!"

"Hey!" Manuel put on his robe and came out into the hall. "That's no way to talk."

"Oh, yeah? What do you know about it?"

Manuel put a hand on the defiant shoulder. "One thing I know is you don't talk to girls like that."

The kid shook him off. "You're full of shit. You're a fairy!"

It was unreal. Norma's mouth fell open in astonishment. Manny reached out and grabbed the kid by the shirtfront. "What was that?"

"You heard me," said Frankie, not quite tough enough to keep a tremor out of his voice.

"Say it," Manuel repeated, gripping him tighter. As the accusation sank in, he felt something boiling up.

"Maybe we all ought to cool down," Norma said, but Manuel paid no attention.

"You little bastard!" he said, and began hitting the boy back and forth across the face with his free hand. "Who the hell you think you're talking to? You wouldn't know how to put your dick in a woman if you had the chance." It wasn't the boy in front of him he was punishing. It was something nameless, unclear, threatening from the periphery of his consciousness and he had to beat it back.

"Stop!" Norma was screaming, as she tried to protect the frightened boy who was holding his arm in front of his face to ward off the blows. "Stop, Manny!"

Manuel came to and saw the frightened, cowering punk in front of him and let him go. "Oh, Jesus," he said.

"Beat it, Frankie," Norma said gently. "You're not hurt."

"He's crazy," the boy said and escaped down the stairs.

"Are you all right?" she asked Manuel, who was leaning his forehead against the wall with his back to her.

"I wanted to kill him," he said, aghast at himself.

"He deserved it," she said. But Manny suspected she was as stunned as he was.

"I never hit a kid before. I hate people who beat up kids. It's like hitting a woman."

She came over and made him turn around to face her. "It's all right. He knew where he was hitting you." She stroked his face maternally. "You're just a man, that's all. Any man would have felt the same way. Why don't you go get some sleep?"

He tried to, but he lay on his bed listening to the noise of the traffic from the avenue, the yelling in the backyard, a telephone ringing. He hated losing control like that. Frankie didn't deserve it. The kid didn't even know what he was saying. He called everyone names.

He twisted himself in the sheet until he was so uncomfortable he got up, threw on his clothes and went downstairs. In the kitchen, Dominic told him Frankie was out on a delivery, so he went outside to sit on the stoop to wait.

Frankie looked at him warily as he rode up on his bike.

"You don't have to worry," Manuel said, standing up. "I want to apologize."

"What for?" Frankie said, leaning the bike against the iron railing but keeping his distance.

It made him sick to see the boy's fear of him. "I guess I lost my head. I'm sorry. I didn't mean to hurt you."

"You didn't hurt me." He was still over by his bike.

"Then why don't you come here and shake?"

"Forget it," Frankie said, going to open the gate leading down to the kitchen.

"No, I mean it. I want to make up," he said, keeping his hand out.

Frankie, still watching him warily, reached over and gave a quick shake and then dashed down the steps to the kitchen.

But the handshake Manny thought would settle it left him dissatisfied.

THE ARTS BALL IN JUNE TO RAISE MONEY FOR THE Spanish Social Loyalists was the biggest event in the Village since the Depression had laid its pall over the euphoric twenties. It took place at Webster Hall on East Eleventh Street—the owner was a fervent supporter of Spain himself.

Polly's instinct that Villagers were ready for a good time again—as long as it was coupled with a worthy cause—proved right. The crowd packed the place, dancing under a great banner proclaiming LONG LIVE THE SPANISH REPUBLIC to the music of a swing band on the stage at one end. The colored saxophonist who lived above Eugene had put the band together from a group of his out-of-work friends. There was a steady traffic between the tables around the perimeter of the dance floor and the long bar set up along one side, where Dominic Alfano, a cummerbund around his middle, supervised the volunteer bartenders.

Times might be hard, but Villagers had turned their talents to good advantage, concocting costumes of whatever came to hand—old clothes, papier-mâché and paint, even out of newspapers with headlines showing. It being the Village, artists' models with surrealistically painted bodies were everywhere, and men in loin cloths, men dressed as women, and women as men.

Eugene, as a poet of the 1860s, danced with the saxophonist's girlfriend, Norma Lucas, who was impersonating Marlene Dietrich in a tuxedo and high-heeled shoes. Out of the corner of his eye he watched Manny cavorting with a series of scantily clad girls who couldn't get enough of him in his fisherman's dungarees and blue-and-white-striped pullover and a gold earring that Eugene had suggested for a pirate touch. Some men, defying the law, were dancing together, and Eugene had a fleeting impulse himself to cut in and dance with Manny.

Later on, after a centaur with a papier-mâché erection that kept getting in everybody's way cut in and danced Norma off, Eugene was leaving the crowded bar with a drink when a bass voice called, "Gene baby, wait up!"

A six-foot Shirley Temple with five o'clock shadow pushed up to him and told him he had some news. Under the ringlets and dress it was his director friend, Dubinsky, who had all but given the go-ahead on a production of Eugene's new play about the wholesale vegetable market where Manny worked. Dubinsky had a new theater group that was putting on plays at the Cherry Lane Theater in the Village.

"Good news? Are you going to do my play?" Gene said, rescuing his drink as someone bumped him. He had had no luck with his writing for years and, deciding finally to change his style to fit in with the realism the times demanded, had worked up a raw drama of drifters and laborers.

"Not the new one. I'm talking about your old play, *The Weak and the Strong*. We're going to give it another chance."

"You're kidding! Isn't it a little dated—exiles in Paris and all that?"

"Not if we give it a different slant." As Eugene gulped his drink, Dubinsky said they were going to do his play like Chekhov's *Cherry Orchard*, which also took place in a decadent society about to collapse. They would be rehearsing evenings over the summer, and he hoped Eugene would sit in and give him his ideas all the way through.

Eugene saw his play about the wholesale produce market drop into the ocean without a regret. *The Weak and the Strong* had been written from his heart, but when its production had been canceled he had put it in a drawer, never considering that the Depression would give it a meaning it hadn't had in its own time. Dubinsky was smart enough to see that, and now—after so long with nothing to look forward to—he felt like a writer again.

He went looking for Manny Silva to tell him. A slowly rotating mirrored ball on the ceiling reflected from its facets colored lights, playing over the crowd of dancers on the floor. He found him on the other side of the dance floor in close conversation with a Pocahontas leaning voluptuously against a pillar. He tried to break in, but all Manny had to say when he heard was, "That's swell, Gene," and turned back to his Indian maiden, whose breasts were splendidly displayed in a fringed leather bra.

Eugene moved off to look for Polly, telling himself that Manny was younger than he, after all, and had a right to enjoy himself. But his friend's lack of enthusiasm made the news about the play seem less important.

At ten o'clock, Polly came out on the stage to announce the entertainment. She was done up as a Greene Street madam of the Gay Nineties in an old purple satin dress of her mother's, jet pendants at her ears and ostrich plumes in her hair. After the usual screeching from the loudspeakers as she adjusted the microphone, she introduced Jules Garfinkle, a young actor from the Group Theater who was going to read a poem by the martyred Spanish poet, Federico García Lorca.

After speaking of the need for solidarity with the Spanish people, Garfinkle read the famous poem about the bullfighter's death in the arena, with its ominous refrain, *"At five in the afternoon."* The crowd cheered, understanding at once that Spain was the bullfighter and the bull that gored him to death was Franco's Falangist army. Before the applause for the poem subsided, on came a group of flamenco dancers, castanets clicking and shoes tapping.

With the audience all but ready to lay down their lives for Spain, Paul Miller seized the microphone to appeal for donations. The band took up the rhythmic beat of Ravel's *Bolero* as he exhorted the crowd to empty their pockets, and Norma, in an elaborate evening dress and elbow-length gloves, appeared on the stage behind him with a hand provocatively on one hip.

"Five bucks!" a man shouted from the front as Polly had arranged for him to do, and Norma unpeeled one of her gloves, swinging it professionally to the rhythm of the drums before tossing it out to him. The audience caught on with a roar of laughter, and the pledges came in loud and clear as Norma peeled off ever more intimate items of her clothing against the hypnotic beat of the music in the background. She took off her bra for fifty dollars. Her panties went for seventy-five. The crowd was tumultuous as the bidding started for her G-string.

* * *

Behind the bar, Dominic was splashing out Seagram's 7 into a row of highball glasses, humming along to the insistent beat of the music and keeping one eye on the doings on the stage. He didn't judge people like that girl—they were a different world from him—any more than he judged other people's politics. His wife Rosalie thought he was crazy for volunteering to work the bar for Polly and getting mixed up with this kind of people. Who cared what was going on over there in Spain, she said. The American government wasn't taking sides, so why should they? Except for the president of the United States, Mussolini was the only one that knew what he was doing, according to her.

She had tried to stop him from taking on the responsibility of ordering the liquor from his old supplier. The lefties were a bunch of bums who would never pay him back, she said. And then where would they be, saddled with a debt they could never pay no matter how much ravioli they sold, and they'd end up with their arms broken besides.

But Dominic wasn't worried about that. Rosalie would never understand that Polly and Eugene were his family. They had taken them in when he and Rosalie and the boys were about to be thrown out on the street, and he would never forget it.

He was running short of seltzer. He looked around for his younger son Frankie, who was supposed to be helping out, bringing supplies from the storeroom backstage. But he had sneaked away again. Dominic had already caught him finishing off the remains of somebody's drink. Rosalie let him get away with everything.

He wasn't close to either of his sons, but at least Steve—who was helping with ticket sales at the door—was no worry to anyone. Steve was more like him. Though only a year older than his brother, he took things seriously.

The *Bolero* was building toward its dissonant climax. Dominic caught sight of Frankie up near the stage, gaping at the almost-naked girl who was keeping time to the music, her breasts shaking, as Paul Miller over the loudspeaker encouraged the crowd to higher bidding. He was holding out for one hundred dollars for the G-string, but eager as everyone was to see the sequined patch yanked off, nobody had that kind of money, and to the *Bolero*'s final beats, the dancer, still wearing her G-string, ran off the stage throwing kisses.

Between acts the bar was busier. But when a men's chorus

came on to sing songs of the Abraham Lincoln Brigade, Dominic had a chance to go back to get the seltzer himself.

He was about to pick up a crate when he heard the screams from inside the dancer's dressing room and rushed in. At first he couldn't believe what he was seeing. Norma, in bra and panties, was shrieking, trying to hold off an attacker. It was Frankie, and his knickers were down as he grappled with her. "Lemme," he begged, "lemme do it!"

Dominic grabbed his son by the hair and pulled his head back until the boy cried out from pain.

The girl backed away, white-faced and shaking. "The crazy kid, he's mad," she said, grabbing her clothes and running from the room.

Dominic held Frankie's arms pinioned behind his back as the adolescent kicked and howled.

"What's it to her? She puts out for niggers, why not for me?"

Frankie was totally drunk, Dominic could smell it. "Shut up!" he said, shaking him hard. "Shut up," until the boy finally stopped his tantrum and began to cry like a child.

Dominic let him go and sank onto a chair. "You animal. Why? . . ."

His son turned his back and fastened his pants, still crying. "They call me a punk. They think I can't . . ."

". . . an animal," repeated Dominic, his voice shaking. "You're out of control . . ."

"You can talk," the boy said, turning on him in a fury. "Ma says you're just a fucking ravioli maker!"

Outside, the chorus was singing some anthem from the banks of the Ebro.

Dominic shook his head over and over, exhausted, saying, "You did what you just did, and you talk that way to your father?"

But Frankie had bent over and was puking in the corner.

"Norma?" The voice of the black saxophonist called from the hall. "Oh, Dom, is Norma around?" Then seeing what was going on, he said, "Sorry," and withdrew.

"He didn't mean to do it," Dominic said inconsequentially, but the musician was gone.

When the boy was finished being sick, Dominic told him to wash up at the basin and then come help him. Still wet-eyed and sullen, Frankie followed his father outside and hoisted a crate of seltzer onto his shoulder.

* * *

The band was playing "Night and Day," and Polly was dancing with Paul Miller on the crowded floor. The entertainment was over. It had gone much better than they had expected. Young Steve, who was keeping close track of the receipts at the door, said they had raised more than five hundred dollars, including the donations, and that wasn't figuring in the profits from the drinks.

"I'd never guess a man with all your principles could approve of dancing," Polly said lightly. She had removed the ostrich feathers from her hair so as not to appear taller than he.

"You mean dancing is the opiate of the people?" He laughed. "Even lefties believe in having a good time—sometimes."

"I believe in having a good time all the time," she said. But the truth was that she hadn't allowed herself to dance in years. It made her vaguely uneasy to have someone's arms around her again, feeling the heat of another body after so long. But her Gay Nineties ball dress was made for dancing and she let herself be swept away with the nostalgic tune.

When they were back at their table, Paul Miller said, "Ever since my wife left me I haven't had a personal life. I thought I didn't want one—now I'm not so sure." His hand touched hers as if by accident as he brushed away some pretzel crumbs on the tablecloth.

The touch was more disturbing to her than if he had grabbed her hand. She liked him and she valued his friendship. She didn't want to have to hurt him. She said he knew all that was behind her, didn't he?

"I know I'm not the pot of gold at the end of any woman's rainbow." The shabby middle-aged man smiled deprecatingly.

She told him not to be foolish, it had nothing to do with him. "Things have happened to me, that's all." She tried to make a joke of it. "I have a past."

He was no angel himself, he said. He didn't care how many lovers she had had, if that's what she was worried about. Or if she got drunk once in a while—so did he.

The room was shaking with several hundred people doing the rumba. Some men in the middle of the floor had found a blanket somewhere and were tossing a wildly shrieking, naked girl into the air. Couples at the tables were necking.

Polly took a deep breath. "Paul, there's no possibility of anything between us." And then she told him that she had killed a man. When he didn't say anything, she went on in a rush.

"Oh, not with a gun, I didn't need a gun—that would have been kinder."

She had never mentioned Larry Mathews to anyone, not even that first summer with Eugene in Provincetown. She had never intended to talk about it—never wanted to, never thought herself able to—but now, in this bacchanalian atmosphere where nobody was holding anything back, with this kindly man who didn't judge her, it was possible to tell the story. It even felt right.

"I'm sorry," he said when she was finished.

They sat quietly together with the costumed dancers swirling around them.

It was when the competition for the best costume was going on that there was a disturbance at the door.

"What is it?" Polly said, trying to see over the heads.

Paul stood up on his chair. "Somebody's making trouble."

The people at the front were pushed aside as a band of beefy men broke into the room, yelling, "Commie queers!" and began overturning tables. The music stopped. Pandemonium broke out. People were yelling and screaming, trying to get out of the way of the goons attacking in all directions.

"The money!" Polly cried, remembering Steve at the door.

"Fascist bastards!" Costumed men were rallying and fighting back. In the middle of the melee, police whistles shrilled and cops charged into the hall as if they'd been waiting just outside for an excuse.

"The money!" Polly said again, as bottles flew in every direction.

"I'm getting you out of here!" Paul cried, hustling her toward the alley door.

She had a last glimpse of Eugene ducking a chair and Manny wading in on the attacker with his fists, before she and Paul fell out into the crowd outside that had been attracted by the noise and shattering of glass. Paddy wagons were lined up, sirens screamed, and a newspaper photographer was already on the scene snapping his flashbulb.

In the Alfano's basement kitchen Polly sat with Paul Miller and Dominic over coffee. She was too weary to care about Rosalie being there. She felt closer to Dominic tonight than she had in a long time. They had run into him outside Webster Hall as they helplessly watched the police loading nearly naked girls and men in drag into paddy wagons to be hauled off to night court and charged with public indecency.

They had gone directly to the Coalition office to see if by some miracle anybody had rescued the receipts, but nobody knew anything about it.

Although it was after one in the morning, Rosalie had gotten up and come out in her housecoat and was eyeing them sourly from the sink where she was occupying herself cleaning spinach for the next day's pasta. Eugene and Manny had escaped with a few bruises, and Norma—who had been picked up briefly—had been released. Frankie had already gone to bed, but his brother Steve still hadn't shown up and they were worried.

"You'd expect this kind of thing in Nazi Germany," Paul said. "Those cops are workingmen too. They should be on our side."

Polly, whose finger was examining a rip in the skirt of her costume, asked Dom to try again to remember when he had last seen Steve. Dom thought he had caught a glimpse of him around the stage, but so much had happened he was all mixed up and he couldn't be sure.

"I told you you were a sucker to get mixed up in it," his wife muttered into the sink as she shook water out of the spinach. "Now we're in hock up to our necks over all that liquor you signed for."

Dominic said not to bring that up now. Polly tried to get in that she'd find some way to pay for it, but Rosalie ignored her, keeping on at her husband. "They just want to use people like you. I read in the *News* that it's the Commies behind all that Spanish business."

"Mrs. Alfano, I don't think it's quite as simple as the *News* makes out," Paul tried to explain. "All kinds of people are upset over what's happening there and are trying to work together to do something about it."

"Why collect money for them? There are plenty of poor slobs here in our own country."

Paul tried again. "But if Spain falls to fascism—"

Polly put a hand on his arm. "Don't bother, Paul."

"Nobody wants to hear the rotten truth," Rosalie said at the sink. "That's it, isn't it?"

"I didn't say that," Polly said patiently. "We're all upset—it's been exhausting." She got to her feet. "I think maybe we should go upstairs, Paul."

Rosalie turned around and looked at her directly. "Go on,

have a good night's sleep. Who gives a damn about us? Thanks to you, we're bankrupt, and one of my boys is out there—maybe beaten up—and you ought to have seen the way Frankie was acting when he came in." She was building up a head of steam.

"She didn't have nothing to do with it," Dominic said to his wife. "Why don't you lay off?"

"Lay off?" Rosalie sneered. "You'd like that, wouldn't you? I been keeping my trap shut for three and a half years, cooped up in this basement—oh, so grateful we are to be here, and all thanks to your generous relatives." She looked Polly's fancy Gay Nineties dress up and down and pretended to spit.

"Come on, Paul," Polly said, as she gathered her skirts to go.

Rosalie was back at her spinach again, chopping it up on a board. ". . . us working our tails off down here, with a houseful of chiselers upstairs living off the government, and we're supposed to kiss her ass and say thank you for taking us in out of the gutter."

There was no stopping her, though Dominic kept trying to interrupt.

"I know you don't care for me, Rosalie," Polly said at the door. "These are hard times, but we've got to make the best of it."

"Best of it? The best of what?" Her knife went at the spinach faster, chopping it to bits. "It's easy for you to talk, with a regular paycheck, and raking in all that dough from those bums upstairs—whores and fairies, all of them."

Polly turned pale, hating the woman's fat evil behind at the sink as her vicious chopping continued. "You are full of shit," she said.

Rosalie threw the knife into the sink, her face triumphant. "Ah, so we're off our high horse," she crowed. "Now the Queen of the May is down here in the mud with the rest of us. The truth hurts, doesn't it?"

"You're vile!" Polly's voice was shaking. "You're so filled with hate, you're . . ."

Paul tried to restrain her.

She shook off his hand, already carried away. "You think I like having you here, you fat sow? You think I like seeing your ugly face blabbing to the whole street every time I go out?"

Rosalie leaned back against the sink, from the blast of the unexpected attack.

"I'd throw you out right now if it weren't for Dom. You could go crawling right back to the gutter where you belong." Polly stopped, breathing hard, amazed at what was coming out of her.

Rosalie's bluster was gone. Nobody had ever talked back to her like this, not on her own terms. Feeling the other woman's contempt, she wilted and put her hand over her mouth, as self-pitying sobs broke out. "They hate me here . . . everybody hates me." Tears smeared her contorted face. "I got no place to go. I'm trapped." With her arm she swept the chopped spinach off the board, scattering it across the floor, and wailed. Dominic tried clumsily to comfort her, telling her they didn't have to leave, but she cracked him across the face. "Get away from me! What kind of a life have I got? I want to be happy." She laid her head down on the bare table and cried.

Polly was sick over having blown up at the unhappy woman and tried to apologize.

While Dom was hovering around his wife, making gestures to Polly that it would be all right, the gate on the sidewalk outside opened and they heard footsteps. Rosalie lifted her tear-swollen face, curiosity distracting her from her misery, as her son Steve came in looking like the perfect student with his book bag and cap. He cast a quick look at his mother who gave one last burst of sobs for the new audience.

"Don't worry, ma. I'm okay." He hung up his jacket and tossed a copy of the early edition of the *Mirror* on the table with the headline COPS BUST RED BALL.

"Where you been all this time?" Dominic asked angrily. "We got back hours ago."

"Don't ride me, pop. I had a lot of trouble getting away. I didn't want those goons to get me, so I had to lie low." He pulled open the flap of his book bag and dumped the contents out onto the table—the receipts of the dance.

As a jubilant Paul Miller questioned him about it, Steve told them he had been counting the take in the back when the trouble began and he had managed to hide under the stage, waiting until the cops had cleared the hall and finished questioning the employees. With all the exits under police guard, he eventually shinnied through a window and got out over the roof.

SETH HARRIS LAY AWAKE IN HIS UPPER BERTH IN THE PULLman car in anticipation of seeing his father again. The train was getting into Penn Station first thing in the morning.

He and his wife Barbara, who was in the lower berth, were taking a belated honeymoon to New York, and he thought the sleeping car porter had a wicked gleam in his eye as he showed them to their separate berths. Seth had met Barbara after moving to Cleveland to take a job in a department store. Seth was in a training program to become a buyer. He had once had ideas of becoming an engineer, but with his stepfather, Toby Harris, losing the auto dealership, he couldn't go on to college—and he didn't want to stay in Cincinnati and sell cars. Whatever the economic situation was for some people, with a new wife he was nuts over and a job, he himself didn't have anything to worry about.

He and Barbara had gotten married several months before and had been saving for this trip ever since. Lulled by the train wheels rolling across upstate New York, he let his mind drift ahead. They had ten days to spend in Manhattan and were going to stay with his father and his aunt Polly so there was no hotel room to pay for.

Since their first meeting at the Brevoort Hotel when he was a kid, he had only seen his real father a couple of times, the last being at his high school graduation when Eugene had made the trip out to Cincinnati. He liked Eugene, even if their personalities were very different—he himself wasn't anywhere near as quiet as his father. At his graduation, Eugene had remarked that Seth had the same outgoing personality as his grandfather Patrick. One thing he was sure of, he liked having a good time. He had been popular in school and had a lot of success with girls, who went for him and he for them.

But he had never met a girl like Barbara. Before he knew her she had been a prom queen. He liked that about her. In high school he had always pictured a prom queen as he jacked off. He didn't go for the girls his mother tried to push him on to, girls with four eyes and books under their arms.

Barbara was only going to keep her job another year or so until they had saved enough to move into their own house and start a family, instead of the apartment they were living in now in a decayed old Victorian mansion on Euclid Avenue. He was looking forward to children—they were the next best thing in marriage to making love.

The motion of the train rocked him in his berth and he thought of his wife's terrific breasts in the berth below. The sheet covering him rose like a tent. He and Barbara had actually gone all the way before they got married. She had the same devil in her that he did and since they had gotten married, life had been one long happy screw.

"Hey," he whispered down through the curtains to the berth below, "you still awake?"

"What do you think?" his new wife whispered back, showing her mind was on the same thing.

He laughed, and peeking into the aisle to be sure the porter was not around, he slipped down through the curtains into her berth. "Be quiet, dopey." His giggling wife was snuggling up against him recklessly.

"But I want to play." She groped for the drawstring of his pajamas.

He let his feelings overcome him, holding her, the cutest little thing in the whole world, as the train whistle hooted through the night.

His father let them have his front room on the first floor, where they could look out the windows at the street and watch the Greenwich Village characters going by. It was only a few blocks away from Sheridan Square with its clubs and bars and coffeeshops that stayed open all night. Nobody ever seemed to go to sleep in New York.

Gene was temporarily staying in one of the small rooms on the top floor that belonged to a friend of his who worked nights unloading trucks and slept days, he said, so they could use the bed in rotation.

Before going off to their jobs the first morning, Eugene and Polly had breakfast with them in the Alfano kitchen. Polly explained that Dominic and Rosalie had started serving cheap meals to the roomers to make extra money, so they could eat there. It always struck him funny that Eugene and Polly were actually Dominic's uncle and aunt, though they were all about the same age, and Dominic was his cousin though he was old enough to be Seth's father.

Seth got to know the Alfanos for the first time. The older boy, Steve, was a bit of a grind, but Frankie was quite a wise guy, and it tickled Seth to see the way the skinny kid looked Barbara up and down. Seth couldn't blame him—she was the perfect sweater girl. It was what he liked about her himself.

But his favorite was Rosalie. They took to each other right off. They had the same sense of humor. When she asked him what he liked to eat—canned pork and beans, maybe?—he threw back, "No, pasta fogioul."

"Come on, you're kidding me," she said. "It's got to be something like apple pie."

"I'm not kidding," he said, "my favorite is spaghetti and meatballs."

Rosalie was fat and had to be on the far side of forty, but she kidded around with him whenever he ran into her on the stoop. She was always out there with her broom. He could hear her through the front windows yelling to the whole neighborhood how the country was going down the drain. She couldn't pile his plate high enough when they ate in her kitchen, and wouldn't take any money from him. The trip east would have been worth it just to get to know her. Though when he talked to his aunt about how terrific she was, Polly said dryly that she had never seen Rosalie take to anyone so fast and it must be because he was so good-looking.

This was the real Greenwich Village he had heard about, running into all the characters in the rooming house. There was the sax player, a terrific guy who told him right off that anytime they wanted he could get them in free to Eddie Condon's, the jazz club in the Village where he was playing. They went to see the modern dancer from upstairs rehearsing with her company in a peculiar work where all the dancers made movements like the different parts of a machine. It was called *Assembly Line*. Barbara liked it better than he did and signed up to take a class herself. She said it would be good for her figure.

Paul Miller, a friend of his aunt's, was a bug on unions and said Seth was being exploited at the department store. Seth didn't take any of it seriously and joked that he was hoping to become one of the bosses himself someday. Another tenant in the house was a refugee from Germany who lectured at the New School for Social Research, which was full of refugee teachers. He and Paul Miller didn't believe in capitalism and were always talking together about setting things up in some pie-in-the-sky idealistic way. Every time he went up to the bathroom, he heard the two of them arguing about the Spanish Civil War in Paul's room. Everybody in the Village seemed nuts on that subject—you never heard about it in Cleveland.

Paul never talked about women, it was all politics. Though Seth couldn't fail to notice from the way Paul looked at his Aunt Polly that he went for her. Barbara, with her feminine intuition, said that if he did he was out of luck, Polly was a gold-plated virgin.

It was a pity, he thought, to be fifty and an old maid. She had missed so much in life. He had only known her from a few brief meetings and letters and birthday gifts, but now she was coming alive to him as a remarkably interesting person.

The professor was German, the Alfanos Italian, the sax player black, and Manny Silva—whose room Eugene was using while he was off to his night job—was Portuguese. It was just like the Village was supposed to be.

Gene said he had hoped to spend a lot of time with them and show them around, but a play of his was being put on and he had to go to rehearsals every night. It was opening at the end of the week and he and Barbara would be able to see it.

Seth wasn't particularly interested in going to rehearsals, but it would be a way of spending a little more time with Gene. They had never been together much. Gene was totally different from his other father at home, not an easygoing, hale-fellow-well-met like Toby. His writer father had a way of taking things seriously that made Seth curious to know everything about him. His life had followed none of the conventions—living in Europe, not tying himself down to regular jobs, having a novel published. There were gaps Seth was anxious to fill in—the women in his father's life, for instance. Gene was foxy about it, but now that he was grown up they could talk man to man.

The first chance he had, he asked Gene about Stella Banks, whom Gene had brought out to Cincinnati with him for his high school graduation. He had assumed she was his father's girlfriend then—there didn't seem to be anyone else around now. When Gene told him Stella would be at the opening of his play, he guessed they were still carrying on long distance. Stella had a job with the Internal Revenue Service in Philadelphia. When her club work had given out, she had taken a civil service exam and turned out to be a whiz at figures.

He had thought at the time Gene and Stella came out to Cincinnati that it was super-sophisticated of his father to bring along his mistress, though now, thinking back, he couldn't get over how innocent he had been. Hell, he knew some men at the store who had mistresses, but the difference was, in Cleveland you had to keep it quiet. Crazy as he was about Barbara, he could imagine wanting some variety himself someday.

Before going uptown to the midnight stage show at the Roxy, he and Barbara stopped off at the ramshackle little theater called the Cherry Lane in the crook of Barrow Street. Seth had taken a look at the script of *The Weak and the Strong*. It was about the Lost Generation, and he suspected it was based on Gene's life in Paris, years ago. He didn't see why the characters had to talk about their agonies so much and it was hard to concentrate on it.

But sitting on the dilapidated seats in the empty theater with the bare bulbs of the work lights on the stage and hearing the actors saying the lines, the play made more sense. It wasn't nearly so morbid—parts of it were even funny. It was amazing how the director, a bald-headed man named Dubinsky, got the actors to sound so real by making them remember similar moments in their own lives. Gene whispered to him it was called the Stanislavski Method.

Though she didn't want to, he talked Barbara into stopping by the rehearsal again with him the next night before they went on to hear the sax player at Eddie Condon's. He was curious to see how the director and the actors would do the rest of the play. This time he asked Eugene more questions about the Method. When his father told Dubinsky how interested Seth was in what was going on, the director asked him if he'd like to fill in during the remaining rehearsals in the small part the director was going to play himself. It would be a big help to have someone else walk through the role, Dubinsky said, and leave him free to direct. It would only take an hour or two for the next few evenings before the play opened.

Seth agreed to do it more as a joke than anything else, but it turned out to be a lot more fun than he expected. Not only being on the stage and saying your lines to the other actors, but listening to them answer as though they meant it, which made the situation seem real instead of make-believe. For minutes at a time he even felt like the character in the play. Everybody, including Dubinsky himself, told him how good he was and no one could believe he had never been on a stage before.

Barbara was bored stiff having to sit in the darkened theater all by herself, waiting for him to get through. But he made it up to her when they went home at night and he made love like a Trojan. She had to admit that being in the play had put extra lead in his pencil.

He was doing so well in the role that Dubinsky told him that he would be happy to turn it over to him, if he would stay on in New York for the run of the play. Much as he was tempted, he didn't want to lose his job in Cleveland.

But even if he didn't play the role, the opening of *The Weak and the Strong* the Saturday night before they had to leave was the biggest night of the trip for him anyway. As the audience poured into the theater, at least half of them seemed to know his father. Gene's boss Hymie Liebman, and his wife, both in evening clothes as they shook his hand, were in sharp contrast to the rest of the crowd. Most of them looked to Seth like they had escaped either from Skid Row or some carnival, but Polly, sitting next to him, seemed tickled pink. "Isn't it marvelous," she kept saying, "the whole Village has turned out."

He looked again. They were mostly around his own age. Theatrically made-up girls and long-haired men with books and magazines under their arms were carrying on discussions from row to row.

Stella Banks got there just in time. In a flashy cape that didn't do much to camouflage her plumpness, she was just as he remembered her from his high school graduation. When the lights signaled everyone to take their seats, she popped into the empty place beside his father in the front row and gave him and Manny Silva a quick hug and kiss before the curtain went up.

The play made a hit with the audience that clapped after

every big scene. Seth wished he were up there. He was ready to throw up Cleveland and job, if it weren't for Barbara, and take over his role again. And when the cast came out afterward for curtain calls, the audience wouldn't let them go. It looked like a terrific success. Yes, Polly said, if the critics had bothered to come—she indicated the empty seats on the aisle—but she was sure word-of-mouth publicity would do just as well.

Seth was so enthusiastic he could have hugged his father as a lot of other people were doing. Stella, dragging Manny Silva after her, told Gene his play was such a relief after all that "ghastly social realism" she was forced to sit through all the time. Hymie Liebman's wife said she had laughed and cried.

The director held a party for the cast afterward at his apartment on Eighth Street, the main street of the Village, with nightclubs and bars and the Saturday night crowd hooting it up right below the windows. Seth could imagine how Eugene felt as the center of attention. He and Stella were really cute the way they carried on, their arms around each other, making no bones to anyone how they felt about each other. It was easy to see Stella had been in show business herself.

The director came over to thank him for filling in at rehearsals, and when Seth told him how exciting the whole experience had been, Dubinsky suggested he look into the community theater out in Cleveland. It was a good one, he said, and he might also enjoy reading Stanislavsky on acting. As Dubinsky talked about the growing importance of regional theater, Seth watched Barbara dancing with one good-looking guy after the other. Gene came up at one point and, seeing his concern, laughed and said he had nothing to worry about.

Seth noticed Manny Silva now and then, drinking in a corner by himself. He looked out of place and sullen and wasn't talking to anyone. It was when Gene was with a group of the actors joking about flubbed lines and missed cues that Manny Silva broke in and said good-night. Gene followed him to the door, trying to talk him into staying, though Seth didn't see why he bothered, Silva just didn't fit in.

"You don't have to work tonight," he heard his father saying. "I thought you were taking the night off."

Stella Banks was talking loudly, trying to cover up the exchange at the door, but no one was listening to her.

Then things got ugly. "What do you need me here for?" Manny Silva erupted drunkenly. "Don't you have enough admirers?" Manny's eyes were glaring at Seth as he said it, but he couldn't imagine why.

He didn't hear what Gene said then, but the pleading in his father's voice made him feel sick. Barbara looked at him quizzically, but Seth couldn't meet her eye. He hadn't realized his father had been drinking so much.

Whatever he said, it seemed to drive Manny Silva berserk. "Get your tentacles off me!" he shouted, shaking off Eugene's arm. "I'm not your fucking wife!" And he slammed out the door.

Stella went right over to slip her arm through Eugene's. "Don't mind him, darling, he's just drunk," she said in the embarrassed silence. "Come on, it's time for the champagne."

Champagne was brought out and his father seemed to come around again, even apologizing with a joke for interrupting everyone's fun. But Seth couldn't look at him as he raised his glass with everyone else.

What had happened was a shocker. Things weren't quite the way he thought they were. Stella came up to him—and later, Polly too—trying to suggest that Eugene had some kind of father-son relationship with Manny, that Eugene had been impressed by Manny's ability when he was living in Provincetown and had encouraged him to come to the city to finish his education. Naturally, since Manny had come to depend on Eugene so much, it had upset him seeing a real son displace him.

Seth pretended to go along with it, but he knew it was window dressing. He wondered what his mother would say if she knew. He wondered if she already knew.

"Sorry about the little scene," his father said to him when everyone was getting ready to leave.

"The guy was drunk, that's all," Seth said, doing his best to sound natural.

"Try to forget it," Eugene said. "I wouldn't want it to spoil anything." Then, as if reconsidering, he added, "No, maybe we ought to talk about it—it's important. Let's go out to breakfast tomorrow, just the two of us."

They fell silent as they walked down to the street together, letting the women follow when they finished repairing their makeup.

Seth was in a quandary. It was all more complicated than he had thought, this mysterious father at the periphery of his life. He was glad they were going to have a talk tomorrow morning, and at the same time, he didn't know if he wanted to talk it over with him, his feelings were in such confusion.

Eighth Street was packed with the Saturday night crowd and it was a moment before they saw the fracas down the block on the other side. Stella said she thought it was at the Main Street and hurried on ahead. As they followed her, Polly told him it was a gay bar and it was always being raided.

From across the street, they watched with the crowd at the curb, as the police were hustling out the customers.

"What are they going to do to them?" Barbara asked. Eugene pulled her by the arm and said there was nothing to see, but Barbara held back. An obstreperous customer was being dragged out of the bar, putting up a fight against four cops trying to hold him.

The onlookers seemed transfixed at the sight of one of the customers actually resisting and spitting out drunken obscenities under the flailing clubs.

"It's Manny!" Stella cried.

Eugene shoved through the crowd and jumped out between the parked cars, heading across the street at a run.

"Don't, Gene!" Polly screamed.

With a squealing of brakes, the delivery truck struck him. Stella shrieked. Barbara threw herself against Seth, sobbing, "No . . . no . . . no. . . ."

"I know I haven't been burning the midnight oil lately, Gene, but I'm going to go to summer session, and I'll have my degree by next fall."

Manny Silva was at Eugene's bedside in a private room at St. Vincent's Hospital after the emergency operation. With Manny's head haloed against the sun pouring in through the window, to Eugene he was the same boy who had held up the fish for him to buy at the dock ten years before.

It was several days after the accident—Eugene wasn't sure how many—but he was able to receive a few visitors. Manny had some bruises left over from his scuffle with the police and had paid a fine for disorderly conduct, but otherwise was okay. He couldn't stop telling Eugene how sorry he was. He knew it was his fault, the way he had been acting lately. He kept promising to make it all up to him as soon as Gene was on his feet again. Eugene smiled as best he could and said it might be a week or two before that happened.

He didn't feel anything from the neck down and his body

was covered with casts and bandages. He listened remotely as Manny talked on about how they would get away from the city and he would get a job as a high school biology teacher and Eugene would be able to do his writing, the way they had planned.

Eugene said he wouldn't mind that at all, wondering if his words were audible. It felt good to see Manny so full of life and optimism, his callused hand resting on the plaster cast around his chest.

Manny asked him again if he could forgive him—as if there was anything to forgive.

When the nurse said it was time to go, Manny put on a blustery act, saying he expected to see Gene sitting up the next day or he'd pull him up himself. But as the friend who had filled the great gap in his life turned to leave, Eugene saw that his eyes were full of tears.

Eugene Endicott died in the night. Among his other injuries, his spine had been crushed—there had been little hope from the beginning. A funeral service was held at St. Luke's Church, although neither he nor his sister had been there since Sunday School as children.

Before Polly took Seth to the station to see him and his young wife off to Cleveland, her nephew asked for something of his father's as a remembrance, and she gave him a watch fob Eugene had always treasured, that had been handed down from their Uncle Claude.

A week later, with Paul Miller's help, she was cleaning out her brother's room—his clothes and most of his things had already been disposed of. As she went over his manuscripts and put them into a carton, they were talking about Manuel Silva, who, the morning after the funeral, had packed his duffel bag to catch a freight train heading west—with no timetable and no destination. He had seemed so broken up. She was sorry he had gone off without giving her a chance to help him as once he had helped her.

Paul, who was clearing off the mantelpiece and bookshelves, said she didn't have to worry about him. He had given Manny a list of contacts around the country.

"I hope not your Wobbly friends," she scolded him gently. "The boy's not interested in organizing unions."

He smiled. "I'm not trying to convert him. I thought he might need a free meal now and then."

As she went on sorting the manuscripts—so many more unfinished than finished—she thought about all the people that had been uprooted by the Depression, living in Hoovervilles, riding the rails around the country, looking for something, they didn't know what. Everything had fallen apart. People had to go on as best they could.

In her hands were the pages of the last novel her brother had begun. She dropped it into the carton with all the rest. She would read it—someday. She sighed. "Isn't it strange, Paul, how every member of my family is buried in some different place? Papa is over at St. Mary's in Queens, mother's in Paris, and now Gene's up at the cemetery in Westchester. It's as if we were all just waiting to get as far away from one another as possible. I wonder where I'll end up. Probably unclaimed at the morgue." She bit her lip, trying to smile.

Paul picked up the old-fashioned ormolu clock from the mantelpiece to wrap in last Sunday's *Times* that Eugene never had a chance to read. "Not if I have anything to say about it, you won't."

"Do you realize if Gene had died a year ago before I met you, I'd be completely alone now? I wouldn't have a friend in the world." She looked at him gratefully.

Paul opened the clock face and moved the hands to twelve, shaking it to see if it worked before wrapping it up. "I'm glad you finally recognized that."

She got up and went to kiss him on the forehead. "I do, and I've never given you a chance."

When the parlor room was anonymous again, ready for the next tenant to come along, Paul carried the carton of Eugene's papers into her room and shoved it under the bed.

"You know, if you and I are going to start keeping company," she said, as she ran water into the percolator, "we've got to do something about our names. Polly and Paul, it's like the Bobbsey twins. People will howl."

"Keeping company?" He straightened up and looked around at her.

She set the percolator down on the hot plate. "Well, won't they?" She turned to meet his eyes.

"They'll just have to get used to it," he said, and went over and embraced her tenderly.

1941

WHEN THE ATTACK ON PEARL HARBOR CAME, THE political controversies of the Depression evaporated, as patriotic fervor swept over Greenwich Village—not many had a sympathetic ear for the die-hard pacifists. Artists who had never known anything but paintbrush and canvas found themselves struggling to master the intricacies of assembling a rifle, bossed about by master sergeants from Iowa and Texas. Frank Alfano was among the first to enlist—in the Marine Corps—and his mother, after getting hysterical, gave him a big send-off party, and hung a star proudly in her window. His brother Steve, who was studying business administration on a scholarship at New York University on Washington Square, didn't go in until he graduated two years later.

As the hordes of GIs poured into the city on leave and weekend passes from nearby military bases, the Village hadn't been so lively since the twenties. Some of the faces seen regularly every weekend belonged to boys lucky enough to wangle cushy assignments at posts like the Brooklyn Navy Yard, the recruiting station in Times Square, or in the mammoth complex of the Whitehall Street headquarters.

The Village was the one part of town where prostitutes were put out of business by the competition of local girls, unencumbered by conventional morality. They couldn't do enough for the wholesome boys from the hometowns they themselves had once deserted. If lonely GIs didn't end up with any of them, they could always get temporary consolation from sympathetic civilians glad to buy them drinks and listen to their troubles and even offer them a berth for the night.

Polly helped to set up the U.S.O. at the busiest corner in the Village, Sixth Avenue and Eighth Street, where thousands of military men came for a last fling before shipping out, disgorged by the new Independent subway line—the old elevated that Patrick Endicott helped to build having at last been torn down. Polly spent all her time at the U.S.O., hardly taking a day off, and though she was the age of their mothers, the boys quickly learned that nothing fazed her—whatever they asked for—and they could talk to her about anything. With her easy sophistication, her savvy and her frankness, she wasn't like any woman they knew back home. Sometimes she took them on tours of the Village, showing them historic sites and landmarks, never failing to point out coffeehouses and nightspots they might want to visit later.

Paradoxically, in spite of the congestion of the streets and the bursting bars and restaurants at night, apartments and rooms went begging as the local boys were drafted. Most of Polly's tenants left, as the war effort sucked them up and the unemployment of the Depression was a thing of the past. Paul Miller was directing an arts and crafts program at a military hospital in Maryland, and when he and Polly occasionally corresponded, it was as old friends, nothing more.

The German refugee from the top floor was giving anti-Nazi indoctrination lectures in a P.O.W. camp in Texas. Norma Lucas had put aside her modern dancing and was kicking up her legs in the chorus of U.S.O. shows from the Aleutians to the Philippines. The black sax player who had briefly been Norma's boyfriend held out at first—he was not joining in any war as long as there were Jim Crow laws, and he especially wouldn't fight against another colored race, the Japanese. He was also bitter about the harassment he was getting from white southern GIs who expected him to step off the sidewalk and say "Yassuh" when they passed. Rosalie, the mother of a marine already in the Pacific, had to be restrained from smashing his head in with a frying pan when he talked like that.

But with the loss of Guadalcanal, even he enlisted, and after basic training in a segregated unit, a postcard arrived saying he was in officers' candidate school. It went up on Rosalie's bulletin board where she kept the letters from all her boys and her map of the war zones.

The war was Rosalie's great period. Instead of her litany of complaints while she swept the sidewalk, she endlessly recited to the neighborhood the military exploits of her sons. Then she surprised everyone by getting herself a pair of overalls, tucking her hair into a snood, and going off to a job in a war plant in Long Island City. She wouldn't tell anyone what she did—it was "a military secret."

Her husband Dominic also got a war job, at the Brooklyn Navy Yard, but what he took most seriously was his patrolling a four-block area around Perry Street at night as an air-raid warden. He was scrupulous about seeing that people drew their blackout curtains, as if a single chink of light would bring the Messerschmitts over.

But if the tenants were gone, Polly kept the house full of GIs from the U.S.O. who needed a free place to stay, and the Alfanos made sure they got plenty to eat. Though Rosalie loved the houseful of boisterous young men who slapped her behind and called her Mama Mia, she wasn't so happy when she found out that they were sneaking in their dates and practically never slept alone. Once she even followed a sailor and his girl upstairs and pounded on the door, screaming that this was not a whorehouse and they were abusing the privilege, but Polly came up and told her to mind her own business, there was a war on, wasn't there? Rosalie glared at her and went back downstairs and thereafter pretended not to know. On the stoop she continued to proclaim to the neighbors or anyone else who passed that she couldn't stand people who weren't giving everything they had to the war effort. She had two sons in the war, one fighting to take the Solomon Islands from the Japs and the other a second lieutenant with Patton as an interrogator in the invasion of Sicily.

Seth wrote Polly that he was on the staff of *Stars and Stripes* in London, though because of his experience at the Cleveland Playhouse, he had hoped to be assigned to Special Services and do camp shows. He still wanted to be an actor. His wife Barbara had opposed the whole idea, but the marriage was on the rocks—she had sent him a "Dear John" letter. He wasn't broken up about it—it had been over for a long time. He had met an English girl, and they had seen John Gielgud play *Hamlet* at the Old Vic. He was thinking of not returning to Cleveland when he got out, but trying his luck on Broadway.

One night at the U.S.O., a serviceman stopped by Polly's desk, where she was working on the week's schedule of the volunteer hostesses, to ask her for a dance. Without looking up, she told him she was busy, why not ask one of the girls? He didn't want to do that, he said, he had a yen for her. She looked up at the handsome, dark-haired man in Coast Guard uniform. It was Manny Silva.

They talked until he had to catch his train at midnight. He had just been home on leave in Provincetown where he had married his fiancée, and was working on his remaining college credits by correspondence at his base in Puerto Rico.

Amidst all the reports of men killed and missing in action—Norma Lucas wrote from Guam the news that her old boyfriend, the sax player, had gone down in a Flying Fortress over Berlin—the Alfanos got a telephone call from the Bethesda Naval Hospital. It was their son, Frank, who had been wounded in the retaking of Okinawa. Nothing could stop Rosalie and Dominic from fighting their way through the crowds at Penn Station to board a train for Washington, standing up all the way.

With a Silver Star pinned to the cast that covered half his torso, they found Frankie basking in the fuss everybody was making over him, giving a detailed description of how he had wiped out a machine gun nest, single-handed. It was hard for him to listen to the letter Dominic read aloud from Steve, telling about the retaking of their grandmother Angelina's village outside Naples where everyone was named Alfano.

In June of '44, Seth covered the Normandy invasion for *Stars and Stripes*, and in August sent a picture postcard of the Eiffel Tower to Polly. When Steve Alfano helped complete the liberation of Italy, he went on to Germany, and in the spring of '45 shook hands with the Russians at the meeting on the Elbe.

1945

It was open house on Perry Street on V-J Day to celebrate the end of the war. Polly had invited a lot of the GIs from the U.S.O. and they were spilling out into the street. The Alfanos were serving up spaghetti as an endless parade trooped down the stairs to the kitchen. There were cases of beer and gallons of wine, and the music of Tommy Dorsey blasted out the windows from the radio, interspersed with news bulletins.

Seth, still in uniform, was dancing almost in place in the packed hallway with a blonde and trying to decide if he wanted to make out with her. He would have preferred to be with his girlfriend in London, but that affair had ended when her husband arrived back from a P.O.W. camp in Singapore. Seth was staying in his aunt's house on temporary leave, waiting to be discharged.

His cousin Frank, the war hero, was being made a great fuss over by Rosalie and everyone else. He was strutting around with his Silver Star prominently displayed on his uniform as if he had won the war all by himself. The only mistake America was making, Frank was telling everyone, was not to finish the job and clean up the Russkies while we were at it.

Steve was there too, sporting a chestful of campaign ribbons that showed he had been in major battles from North Africa to Germany, but as far as his mother was concerned, it was only Frank who existed.

Steve had laughed when Seth suggested that his brother was hogging the spotlight. "Let him have his moment. I may be the quiet type, but I get mine, too." Steve had plans to go in with several fellow officers to start an electronics business in New Jersey. He didn't know much about the technology himself—he was going to handle the administrative end—but his partners had learned everything about radar from the war, and had the idea of manufacturing component parts for radio and television sets.

When Seth was cut in on and he saw his blonde lay her head just as happily on somebody else's shoulder, he pushed his way to the punch bowl set up in Polly's room. Frankie, with two fingers above his mouth like a mustache, was giving an imitation of Hitler making a speech. Seth thought that if he were still writing for *Stars and Stripes*, Frank would make a good subject for a story about a returning war hero, handsome as they come, fatuous and self-satisfied. Even the girl hanging on his arm was perfect. Not bad looking but obviously still in her teens and trying to look older—and totally taken in by the handsome show-off. They might both be a little simple-minded, but they certainly made a good-looking couple.

His aunt Polly refilled his glass. "For a returning hero," she said, "you don't look so happy. You're supposed to be having a ball."

"You mean like that?" He nodded toward Frank who was now jitterbugging with his teenage girlfriend to a Glenn Miller tune with an admiring circle around them. He gave a wry smile and told Polly she didn't look so happy herself.

Rosalie was shrieking with laughter as she carried on with a group of soldiers nearby.

It wasn't that she was unhappy, Polly said, but now that the whole thing was over, she was letting herself feel how tired she was for the first time in years. She was going up to the Cape to spend some time with Manny Silva and his wife. It would be a real rest. Did he remember Manny?

"How could I ever forget."

They were both silent a minute. People were filling their glasses at the punch bowl.

"What about Paul Miller?" Seth asked. "Is he still in the picture?"

She laughed. "Oh my heavens, no. That ended before the

war." But she had just heard from him. He had married again and was becoming a scenic artist in a television studio on the Coast. "Can you imagine a lefty like him starting a commercial career? I think the war must have shaken up a lot of his old ideas."

"Well, I'm just sorry it wasn't you he ended up with."

"You're sweet." She pinched his cheek. "But love and marriage is not what I need any more. I had enough of all that business. It's your turn now."

Seth had come out on the stoop with his punch to join the crowd for a breath of air. It was late afternoon and celebration parties were going on everywhere. The street was full of people drifting from one house to another. On the sidewalk below, the indefatigable Frank still cavorted for his admiring audience. When a car full of out-of-towners went by, he shouted, "What are you looking at, you fucking rubberneckers?" He swaggered to the curb. "Want to see something? I'll show you something!" He grabbed his crotch. "Here's a souvenir of Greenwich Village to take back with you to the boondocks!" And he made pelvic thrusts at them, to the delight of his buddies.

"Wasn't that crass?"

It was Frank's girl, standing next to Seth on the stoop, more annoyed than embarrassed. Although she was very young, close up she was remarkably attractive, with lively dark eyes and an already womanly body—a more intelligent girl than he would have guessed his simple-minded cousin could attract. "It's his way of having a good time," Seth said. "That's what we're all trying to do today, isn't it?"

"I suppose so," she said. "He really is pretty sweet."

Seth asked if she had known Frank long, and she told him they had just met outside the U.S.O. on Sixth Avenue. She had pretended to be one of the volunteers there. She laughed. "I don't know why I told him that. I guess I didn't want to admit I came down from the Bronx with a girlfriend to pick up a soldier."

Seth looked at her to see if she was trying to shock him, but she betrayed no self-consciousness as she watched Frank hug his mother who had come out to let everyone know, in case they missed the fact, that he was her son. She was just a kid, but her boldness attracted him.

"There's nothing wrong with liking soldiers," he told her.

"But it's already passé, isn't it?"

Frank came up and grabbed her arm. "Hey, is this hide-and-seek, Susan? Don't give me a hard time. I'm just a love-starved returning marine, remember? You got to do your part." He pulled her chin toward him and kissed her on the mouth.

So Susan was her name, Seth thought, watching Frank lead her down the steps into the middle of his group. If he had met her when he was eighteen, even twenty, before Barbara, how he could have gone for someone with her intelligence, her New York brashness. A pity Frank had to be her GI experience. He was too much of a clod for her. Seth drank off his punch and went looking for his blonde.

From Susan's reading of D. H. Lawrence, Frank seemed the basic male. He was the epitome of the "dark forces," like in the smuggled copy of *Lady Chatterley's Lover* passed around at the High School of Music and Art. A real woman didn't want an intellectual man. She was also fascinated by Wilhelm Reich, and she believed in the ultimate importance of the orgasm, and with practice she was determined to achieve it, as well as everything else she put her mind to. At Music and Art she had been a brilliant student, but according to Lawrence and Reich, that was the wrong direction. She had to get out of her mind and more into her body.

She knew she was too much for the grandmother she lived with up on the Grand Concourse. She longed to get an apartment for herself, share it with a girlfriend maybe, but at sixteen she was too young. She had just graduated from high school and was going to Hunter College in the fall. Unless a miracle occurred, she would have to continue commuting from home on the subway for another four years.

As night came on, she and Frank left the party at Polly's house and he took her on a round of clubs in the neighborhood. Every place was packed, the streets were wild, the jubilation never ending. The bars were full of girls as young as she was—nobody was asking for IDs tonight. She knew the Village. She had been coming down here with her friends ever since going to Music and Art, but they went to jazz clubs, and Frank only wanted to go to the dumbest tourist spots.

He was such a perfect proletarian. That, of course, was what made him just right—there had never been any barriers to his fulfilling his animal nature from the start, while she was just starting to experiment clumsily. According to him, he had been doing it since he was ten. With both his arms around her on the crowded dance floor, he was nuzzling her with every part of his body, his hands cupping her buttocks—it was like being with a completely healthy animal.

The Village had always meant sex to her, and tonight more than ever, with couples making love in doorways, and behind every window she imagined people copulating in every position she had seen in a marriage manual passed around at school. It wasn't Rome burning exactly, but it was just as historic an occasion, and people were commemorating it in the best way possible—with their sexuality. She was determined to be a part of it. She would never tell her grandmother, but someday she might tell her grandchildren about how she had spent the day the Second World War ended—and about the man like the gamekeeper she had chosen to spend it with.

With more drinks in him, her GI was getting sloppier in his attentions, and she was beginning to feel sexy herself. They ended up back at the Perry Street house where the party was still going on. But waving off his friends, he led her upstairs to an empty room. On the way up she saw his cousin from Cleveland necking with a blonde girl in the corner.

But lovemaking with this instinctual primitive did not come up to the heights of ecstasy or the cosmic fulfillment she read about. If only he wouldn't open his mouth. He sounded so inane with his "You got a gorgeous pair of knockers, baby," or "It's so juicy down here."

But there she went being mental again. As his body crushed her, she tried to imagine she was Lady Chatterley with the gamekeeper. He was sweating like a pig and she couldn't help thinking that thank God he had on a rubber.

After he dropped off to sleep for a few minutes, he was at it again. It wasn't so bad and she thought she had an orgasm this time, but she wished she could at least talk to him.

He held on to her afterward and said how crazy he was about her. He had big plans. He had his pick of jobs—with his Silver Star everybody wanted him, all the big shots in the Village. He'd make lots of money and give his girl anything she wanted. "Now I'm really going to show you what a man can do," he said, but before he started in again she slipped away and started putting on her bra.

"Hey, where you going?" he said, "Wasn't it great?"

She said sure it was, but her grandmother would kill her if she wasn't home by twelve and explained about the long subway ride home to the Bronx.

As she left, she looked back at him lying there, the most visually perfect specimen of a man she had ever seen. But, she thought regretfully, if only he had a brain to match.

"Frank's got so many girls throwing themselves at him, he doesn't even notice I'm not there any more," Susan Schlesinger was saying to Seth at a table inside the Riviera Café. On such a beautiful October day it was a shame, he thought, that there weren't outdoor cafés to sit at, like in Europe.

He had hardly recognized Susan when she spoke to him outside on Sheridan Square, without lipstick, only heavily made-up eyes. It was the style from the Existentialist cafés of the Left Bank.

He was out of the Army. He had already been to see his parents in Ohio and come back in time to register for acting classes with Lee Strasberg, the leading teacher of the Stanislavski Method.

"Frank was quite an education. He got me over my fixation on D. H. Lawrence," Susan said, smiling.

With her straight hair cut in new bangs and the makeup emphasizing the pale skin and dark eyes, he liked her looks even better. He had to remind himself than even if she looked so much older than she was, even worldly, he mustn't think of her as a woman—she wasn't. She was only sixteen.

She told him she had just started Hunter College and he told her his hopes for Broadway, and about his marriage that had broken up during the war.

"You're a real WASP," she said, "and you look the part perfectly."

"How?" He laughed. She was a kid, but she was the first woman since his girlfriend in England who was fun to be with, who was not just a quick lay.

"Well," she said, studying him as if she were analyzing a painting for an art criticism class, "your short nose, your proper tweed jacket—my God, how smooth, how professorial, and you can't be more than . . ." She waited.

"Twenty-seven," he fibbed, then smiled. "No, thirty."

"It's all right," she said. "I lie about my age too—the other way. And your manner, the way you act, so perfectly polite, so agreeable—not letting it all out, like people I know."

"Bland, you mean?"

"Not exactly," she said, enjoying their game as much as he was, "but I suppose over the long haul it might get that way."

"Well, you're wrong," he said, his elbows on the table, leaning closer toward her. "I'm not a real WASP at all. I've got an Irish grandfather, and I'm not so agreeable—I've got perverted impulses."

"Oh, good. What are they?" She laughed.

She was perfect New York—cool, nervy, smart. She was lovely. "For one, I wish to hell you weren't sixteen years old so I could make love to you."

She blushed like the kid she was. "Don't worry. I've been taking care of myself for a long time." She told him about being raised by a grandmother who hardly spoke English and who didn't know what she did.

He still held back. "But I'm thirty—and divorced, to boot."

"You told me you were glad that your marriage was over—you were too young to know what you were doing."

"I was older than you are."

"You think I'm going to tell my grandmother and get the police on you?"

"But it's crazy," he said, taking her hand.

"Now you sound like a movie, conforming to the Hays office code."

He argued what did she want him for, he wasn't any war hero. He hadn't seen action at all, he had spent the war at a desk mostly. He didn't even have a Good Conduct medal.

She said, as they got up to go, not to be jealous. But she asked him please not to take her to his aunt's house, if that's what he had in mind. She'd rather not run into Frank Alfano.

They didn't go back to Perry Street, but they made love that afternoon. This time, it wasn't a cosmic orgasm for her either, but what a relief to be with someone intelligent, and afterward they went out for hamburgers and walked through the Village streets half the night, talking about orgone boxes and Jean-Paul Sartre and Seth's hopes of getting into a Broadway show, discovering all the things they had in common.

And he met her after her classes at Hunter the next day and rode up with her to the Bronx where she introduced him to her grandmother who was horrified, not that she might get married at sixteen—the old lady had been fourteen when she got married in Russia and thought girls ought to get married when they were ripe—but that he was a *goy*, that's what put her off. But Susan explained that he wasn't the usual *goy*—he had a mind—and with a wink at Seth she invented a Jewish grandfather for him, leaving out that he was going to be an actor and she would have to get a job to help him out, and if it was taking a chance, she was willing to gamble, and besides, she couldn't stand living up on the Grand Concourse any longer. Seth already had a little apartment lined up in the Village, not Perry Street, and she didn't want to go to Hunter any more, anyway.

Grandma eventually came around, but for her sake they had the ceremony at the temple social room.

Polly came up for it and stood with a lump in her throat as the traditional canopy was raised over the bridal couple, Seth in a top hat—the groom's head had to be covered—and Susan with a crown of pearls over her wedding veil, before the rabbi. Then, the ceremonial breaking of the wineglass, and the merry dancing afterward to a three-piece band, folk dances interspersed with waltzes.

Polly hadn't felt the pain of Hymie for years—the wedding that never was—until Seth, after the obligatory waltz with his bride, danced with her to the applause of the wedding guests sitting around the decorated hall.

"There are tears in your eyes, Polly dear," he said, whirling her around as others joined them on the floor.

"Why shouldn't there be? I'm at my nephew's wedding. I'm so happy for you."

"I think you're hiding something."

"How the hell do you know?" she said with a little tearful smile.

"Gene told me all about you and Hymie Liebman."

"Now you've done it, you son of a gun." She laid her head against his chest and cried softly as they danced on, the grandmother happily clapping in time at the bridal table.

On a platform erected in front of the Church of St. Anthony, the South Village chapter of the American Legion was honoring Italian-American war heroes of the community. But the crowd passing by wasn't much interested any more in the inflated patriotism of the speeches. People wanted to forget about all that. It was the fair they had come for, and the strolling crowd on the blocked-off street looked indifferently at the veterans being introduced at the microphone, wearing decorations on their rumpled uniforms with nonregulation ducktail haircuts, and here and there a pair of plaid socks showing above civilian shoes. When they saw there was no entertainment, just speeches, they turned away and headed for the sound of a band farther on, stopping to buy sausage-and-pepper hero sandwiches and orange popsicles from the booths that lined the street.

It was hot up on the platform, and Frank Alfano loosened the collar and tie of his Marine suntans, once tailored in San Diego by a Mexican girl he was banging at the time—the uniform was too small for him already. He had drunk too many beers, the speeches were too long, and he had had his moment at the mike.

He felt like taking off. It wasn't as much fun playing the hero as it used to be. Two years ago in the postwar euphoria he was welcome everywhere—everybody bought him drinks, made him feel good. He was still ready for action, but there was no more action, no more excitement. He couldn't wait until the blowhards at the microphone finished their gab and they'd all go back to the bar, even if he had to put up with their old stories about the First World War.

His eyes drifted over the passing crowd, looking at the girls in their summer dresses, some with bare shoulders, a bare midriff here and there. The dark-haired beauty whom he was following with his eyes turned her face and it was Susan Schlesinger. She was Susan Harris now, married to his cousin Seth, and they were walking along licking paper cups of Italian ices.

He swung himself off under the railing at the side of the platform, calling their names as he pushed through people to get to them. They were glad to see him, and Susan smiled that smile that had first attracted him outside the U.S.O., as he explained why he was in his old uniform and not his civvies.

He had only seen them a couple of times since they had gotten married. He knew they lived over here in the south Village somewhere. He wondered if maybe they hadn't been around to Perry Street much because she was embarrassed to run into him again. He didn't feel that way—that was all past. They were family now, he wanted to be friends.

When Seth heard from him that he had left the platform just to catch up with them, he insisted that they all go back for the rest of the ceremony, but Frank said it was just about over, and anyway the legionnaires would never miss him. He got between them and took their arms and asked them where they had been hiding so long, as they walked on looking at the various booths. Seth said he and Susan were busy as hell these days. He was going to drama school and had an evening job, and Susan worked for an architectural magazine all day and took classes at the New School nights.

They couldn't kid him—he knew what kept them so busy. He envied Seth having a girl as pretty as Susan, though he doubted that Seth was able to keep her happy in the sack, not after she had seen what a real man could do. But she had class. Next to her, the bimbos he was screwing now were pigs.

But he didn't want to think of her that way, she was his cousin's wife—that was good enough for him.

He insisted they come with him right away and let him buy them an Italian dinner. It would be a delayed wedding present. But Seth said he had to work that evening. So he said, then they'd have to let him buy them a drink—they were all family now, wasn't that right? Susan smiled back her beautiful smile at him and said of course they'd have a drink with him, but it would have to be a short one.

He took them into a local bar where they all knew him. "Did your husband tell you what kind of crazy family you got yourself into?" he asked Susan as they got a table. She didn't just have dago relatives like him, but half the Sixth Precinct was relatives too.

He dropped a couple of nickels into the jukebox to liven up the place. The Andrews Sisters came on with "Boogie Woogie Bugle Boy from Company B." "What'll you have?" he asked them, snapping his fingers to the beat. It was natural to be a little stiff with each other, but they would all loosen up with a few drinks in them. "Whiskey sour, sidecar, gin fizz, you name it, it's on me."

Seth said beer for him and Susan asked for a Pepsi, but Frank said this was a celebration, wasn't it? And he called for three Tom Collinses.

It made him feel good to be with family. Sometimes it seemed like he hardly had a family any more since coming home from the war, with his brother Steve moving out to Verona, New Jersey, when he got married, and even his mother talking Steve all the time nowadays and making him feel like a bum.

Waiting for the drinks, they talked about the art gallery their aunt was opening on Waverly Place. She was calling it the Peacock, like the gallery she used to have years ago. Frank didn't know anything about art, but his mother thought she was going to lose her shirt, and said the one business you couldn't lose on in the Village was a bar—but his mother was always talking about the good old days at the Bocce. Did they know about the time his family owned a speakeasy? He could tell them a lot of stories about that. He wiped the sweat from under his loosened collar. There were wet patches under his arms where his tight shirt bound him.

Susan said it must have been hot sitting up on that platform. She was damn right, he said. It was no fun being looked over like he was a horse.

But wasn't it nice getting the recognition? she said. His parents must have gotten a kick out of it.

He told her they hadn't come. They were in Verona at his brother's, where they were going ape now that Steve's wife was expecting their first grandchild. He didn't blame them—everybody was getting tired of hearing about the war anyway. Sure the war was over, but he thought it was chickenshit for the country to forget the guys who won it for them. "We were gung ho to go on and clean up the Russkies, but they didn't let us. They're all pinkos down there in Washington. You hear what McCarthy says?"

But what were they talking about that for? He raised the glass the bartender set down in front of him and toasted the newlyweds who smiled at each other and leaned closer.

It made him feel more left out than ever. "You know, my brother's doing great," he said. "Want to hear how he did it? He and two drinking buddies from the officers' club got together to start up this electronics business. You get in with the right contacts, you got it made. You don't have a chance if you're just a dumb marine like me."

Susan said he wasn't a dumb marine, he had a Silver Star. And Seth said he had heard that he was selling used cars at the big lot on Houston Street.

"Oh, that," Frank said. All the offers he had and just his lousy luck to choose that one. He had put four months into it, but the boss turned out to be a shit. The boss had it in for guys who had been in the war because he had stayed out—flat feet, draft dodger—and kept riding him until he had to leave. Another job, selling insurance, fell through because people weren't putting money into insurance—they were buying things, now that stuff was available again. The boss had wasted him on penny-ante contacts, so it wasn't his fault his sales quota was piss-poor. They were all a bunch of bums trying to cash in on his war-hero reputation, but he wasn't going to play along with that any more. His brother wanted him to go into electronics with him, and he had just about made up his mind to do it.

Though Seth said they really ought to be going, he told them to sit down and ordered another round of drinks, and went on about how Steve had married a girl who was a college graduate over in Jersey. She even had her own white Buick convertible. They were living in a garden apartment now, but they had made a down payment on a split-level in Montclair. The electronics field was booming. He was going to start out in the service department of his brother's company, but that was only to pick up the basics and then the sky was the limit.

There was a fortune to be made in television and he was getting in on the ground floor.

"Let's drink to that," Seth said, and Susan picked up her glass.

"Nah, let's drink to all of us," Frank said, feeling warm with them. "We're going to see a lot of each other from now on."

Leaning against Seth's shoulder, Susan asked him if any girl had caught him yet.

"You know me, dames keep trying, but Franco knows how to fight them off."

They all laughed, but he was thinking if he ran into someone like Susan now, he might be ready to settle down. He called for another round of drinks, but Seth was getting up, saying he was already late for his job, they'd certainly have to do this again sometime. Seth even tried to pay, but Frank wouldn't hear of it, slapping his money on the bar and calling for the bartender to hurry up with the change so he could catch up with them going out the door.

"Wait up!" he called after them. "I'll walk you."

He took Susan's arm and steered them through the street fair crowd where a bunch of kids was running around with colored pinwheels. At a booth of Neapolitan specialties, he insisted on buying her a bag of greasy crullers called *zeppole*.

Outside their building a few blocks away, Frank held on to Seth's hand after shaking it and said now that they had gotten together, he wanted to take them out to a club on Third Street where one of his buddies worked. They'd get a kick out of it, real floor show, people came from all over to see it, he'd make sure they had a good time, everything they wanted. He wanted to set a date right then, but Seth said maybe they'd better let him know because they were so tied up. Frank said he'd call them, what was their number? They all searched for a pencil but nobody had one. Never mind, he said, he'd get it from Information and call them first thing next week to make a date.

"Next week," he said, shaking Seth's hand again. "It really meant a lot to run into you." Then he put out his hand to Susan who was looking at the ground as if she was embarrassed, but she looked up quickly and smiled and, before following Seth inside, kissed him on the cheek.

He stood there a moment after they had gone in, sweaty in his old uniform that was too small for him, a bad taste in his mouth from all the drinks, but it was too early to go back to the house. Nobody was home anyway. He decided to take the D train to Coney Island. He'd have a snooze on the beach, and then hang around the boardwalk and pick up a girl.

1951

POLLY STUDIED THE WALL OF ABSTRACT EXPRESSIONIST paintings in their simple strip frames. She had hung the show that afternoon for tonight's opening, and with the people about to arrive, she kicked herself for letting her assistant talk her into putting the big, vacuous Rothko in the middle. It trivialized that whole side of the gallery devoted to abstracts.

She looked out the window to see if her assistant was coming back with the wine and cups he had gone to buy for the opening. A student at Parsons School of Design, he tried to tyrannize her with his automatic putdown of anything *Art News* wasn't raving about. Seeing the coast was clear, she took the Rothko down and rescued the handsome Jackson Pollock that he had hung in a corner and put it up where the Rothko had been. Immediately the wall was right. It brought into focus the whole abstract expressionist movement.

But then she started to worry about the paintings on the other side of the room—the realist painters from the thirties, in their conventional frames. Would they be overshadowed, look old-fashioned? She didn't want that. She liked them as well. That was the whole point of the show and why she was calling it Dialogue. Later in the evening, after people had had a chance to look at the pictures, she was holding an informal discussion between the two factions, realists and abstractionists, and there were stacks of folding chairs waiting to be set up, so that everybody could sit down and have it out.

Frederick, her assistant, came back with gallon jugs of wine and the cups, huffing and puffing as if she were a slave driver making him carry blocks of stone up the pyramids. She sent him back to her cubbyhole office to retype the price list, instructing him to add a hundred dollars to everything and two hundred to the Pollock, and began to arrange the wine and cups herself.

She wondered if she should have at least bought some pretzels, but she had never tried to compete with the big galleries uptown where champagne and canapes were served by waiters at the openings. Not only couldn't she afford such things—her revived Peacock was turning out to be no more profitable than her first gallery—but one thing she had learned from her long experience in the art world was that what brought people in was controversy, especially if it got written up in the papers. And she had spread the word that reporters as well as a lot of the critics were coming—and they would be, if her old contacts meant anything.

Frederick came to tell her there was a phone call from her nephew. She finished uncorking the last wine bottle and told him to stack the pile of mimeographed announcements by the door next to the guest book, noticing with satisfaction his raised eyebrow as he spotted the replacement of the Rothko with the Pollock. She had her own way of paying him back for tyrannizing over her in his fussy, narrow-legged Bloomingdale's suit.

Seth told her over the phone that an audition had come up and he couldn't make the opening. An evening audition. That had to be for another of his paltry little productions, probably in some church social hall. She'd have to go to it, he always expected her to come. God knew, his wife Susan wasn't so devoted.

She got up to look in the mirror, tucking in a few wisps of her gray hair that had come undone from the topknot she wore it in. At sixty-three, for the first time in her life she liked her looks in her dirndl dress and sandals, and not bothering with makeup any more or dying her hair. She hooked on her dangling mobile earrings that her old friend, Alexander Calder, had given her. They were a good luck charm. She wore them to every one of her openings, and never failed to sell at least one painting.

If only her nephew could have a little luck in the theater. Ever since he moved to New York it had been nothing but acting classes, semi-amateur productions, and temporary office jobs, with Susan having to work full-time to support them both. No wonder she always had that resentful undertone in her voice, as if she thought she wasn't getting her chance to fulfill herself and that Seth wasn't supporting her as a husband should. But then, what did she want to get married so young for?

Polly couldn't understand why they stayed on in that horrid, cold-water flat, in the south Village, but Susan had put her foot down against moving in when the Perry Street house had been remodeled into studio apartments a few years before—she didn't want to live with Seth in one room without a door to close between them, she said. Maybe they did fight a lot, but the studios were perfect for a young couple. If they were small, each had a modern bathroom and kitchenette. She herself had never been so comfortable as she was in her snug studio, transformed out of her father's old study.

Hymie had persuaded her after the war to modernize the interior of the house. Young professionals would jump at the chance to move down to the Village to live in historic houses like hers, he said, as long as they had all the conveniences. What's more, the remodeling had freed the house from rent control, and it was profitable again.

She had made it perfectly clear to Seth that if he did the janitor work, which would take up no time at all with the new oil burner, she could arrange with Liebman Associates for him and Susan to have one of the basement apartments at a nominal rent. It would have been particularly convenient because at the time of the renovation, the Alfanos had moved to New Jersey. Their son, Steve, whose electronics firm was prospering, had set them up in a little restaurant where they could be near their grandchildren. Things were good for all the Alfanos—except for Frank. He had trained as a technician, but he had no aptitude for it, and though Steve had tried to fit him in elsewhere in the company, he had quit in a huff and moved out to Phoenix and gotten married there. They didn't hear from him much, but Dominic had told her that things weren't going well.

People were beginning to arrive and she could already tell from the buzz in the gallery that it had been an inspiration to dramatize the feud between the two opposing camps in the art world, and that her Dialogue show was going to make a splash.

* * *

It was a bigger crowd than she usually got at her openings. She was talking to the art critic who was going to act as moderator at the symposium later on, when she noticed the woman whose mink coat stood out among the Villagey crowd. As far as she could tell without her glasses, she had never seen the woman in the gallery before. Probably a culture-vulture from the Upper East Side who had taken an art appreciation course. She was holding a pair of glasses before her in one hand as she studied the Pollock. Polly could almost hear the voice of the instructor telling the class to feel the rhythms in the splatters of paint, and not to look for subject matter.

It was only later when the woman moved closer and came into focus that she saw, with a shock, it was Miriam Liebman. Polly hadn't seen her in years. Miriam had to be fifty now, but in the classic black dress from Bergdorf's and her expensive coiffure, she looked ten years younger. They only had time to exchange a word or two because the symposium was about to start and people were setting up chairs for themselves around the room or settling down on the floor.

The discussion began better than she could have hoped for. The moderator hadn't even finished making his introductory remarks before an artist she knew from the W.P.A. Arts Project jumped up and denounced the abstract expressionists for throwing over traditions that went back to Leonardo. Then a young painter in button-down shirt, jacket, and jeans hit back, calling the realists "leftovers from the thirties," and declared what the abstract artists were doing was "art that belonged to the American century." The war was on, and accusations flew back and forth across the room, the moderator throwing up his hands and letting it take its own course.

Polly sympathized with the realists, who were fighting to survive against the new wave of abstract art that was getting all the attention. It had become a situation like the cold war, where no coexistence seemed possible. Though she remembered well enough back in the Depression when the social realists had been equally as ruthless in suppressing the avant-garde work of the twenties.

She caught sight of Miriam Liebman leaning forward, absolutely enthralled by the goings-on. From the way she looked, life with Hymie must have certainly been fulfilling—anyway, if you could afford reducing farms and Elizabeth Arden. Miriam, her symbol of the woman who had everything, had always made her feel so inadequate, from the first time Hymie had brought her to the house.

The shouting of a wild-haired woman painter brought her back. Action painting was "infantile self-therapy, throwing paint at the canvas," and "art had to express the higher aspirations of the people." Others were standing up, yelling back and forth, nobody listening to what anyone else had to say, almost on the verge of blows. Polly's assistant was sending her alarmed looks with his eyebrows, but she sat back pleased as punch, as words like "reactionary," "decadent," "philistine," "fascist," "fellow travelers," "McCarthyite hack," flew through the air. But what an irony it was that her artists could sound so much like those ridiculous politicians in Washington labeling everybody in sight a subversive!

When the meeting finally broke up, people were too agitated to leave and stayed around arguing. Polly moved from one group to another thinking how healthy it was, how American, that such an evening could take place. It almost justified her existence that she was the one who had set it up. It was the Village as she loved it, a center of controversy.

Miriam Liebman came up to her on her way out and gushed that it was the most exciting art event she had attended in years and the show itself was a triumph.

There was a write-up the next morning on the art page of both the *Tribune* and the *Times*, and the gallery was busy that afternoon as people came in to look at what the fuss was all about. Nobody bought, of course—the realist painters were going out of fashion and the abstract expressionists too expensive, but she had never measured success by sales.

She was exhilarated. She let Frederick handle inquiries out front and went back to her cubbyhole office to fire off a sharp letter to the *Times*, criticizing their version of the symposium, which championed the abstractionists. "Isn't there room in the world for both kinds of art?" she was writing, when Frederick looked in and said in an excited whisper that there was a woman asking to speak with her and she was wearing an emerald the size of a doorknob.

When Polly went out, it was Miriam Liebman in a Chanel suit, looking as expensive as the night before.

"I couldn't sleep a wink thinking about that Pollock," Miriam said, as Polly led her into the office, "and I've decided to buy it." She sat down and without a flicker wrote out a check for seven hundred and fifty dollars. She didn't know what Hymie would think of the painting, but she was going to hang it in the living room anyway, and if it demolished her other pictures, she was willing to take the chance, and in any case it would be a conversation piece. She had been going to the art lectures at the Cedar Street Tavern given by that young poet, Frank O'Hara, and even taken classes from Hans Hofmann, though of course she was just an amateur, but it was the discussion last night that had finally got her to take the leap and start a modern collection. "You know, buying this painting feels like the most daring thing I've ever done. You live so adventurously, can you understand what I mean?" She smiled warmly and handed over the check.

Polly had made a big sale and it was cause for celebration, but more than that she was surprised to learn how "the woman who had everything" saw her. Adventurous. Who would have thought it! She got out a bottle of cognac and, complimenting Miriam on her good taste in choosing the Pollock, poured a bit into two glasses, only pretending to join in the toast herself—she had been careful about alcohol ever since Larry Mathews.

Miriam went on to say how glad she was that she finally was having a chance to get together with her. She had always been so interested in Polly's life, which she only knew about in bits and pieces. Polly was an independent woman who used her mind, while Miriam felt herself to be in the role of a china doll, protected from the realities of life and never able to think for herself. "But when was the last time we saw each other?" she asked.

"It was at my brother's play at the Cherry Lane," Polly said, liking her better. "I'll never forget how your evening dress stood out in that shabby theater."

"It did? The truth is I was totally miserable that night. I had just become pregnant again and I was sick as a dog. But I loved the play."

Polly was saying what a pity it was that the play had been withdrawn so quickly after her brother's death, when her assistant came in, clearly dying of curiosity to know what was going on, and when she told him to put a red star on the Jackson Pollock, he nearly dropped his bracelets.

"I live such a hopelessly conventional life, compared to you," Miriam said, her eyes following the departing figure interestedly.

Looking at the emerald on Miriam's hand that had made such an impression on Frederick, Polly smiled and asked if that didn't make up a little for the conventionality of it all?

Miriam laughed and agreed it was vulgar, but it was Hymie's gift for their twenty-fifth wedding anniversary. "He does everything in a big way. He even threw a party with a tent on the lawn and Duke Ellington's band, and I couldn't stop him." Their house was far too big for them, she said, now that their daughter was married and their older son at Harvard. But they were planning to move back into the city once their thirteen-year-old son was bar mitzvahed. It was hard to believe how traditional her husband was underneath it all, she said confidingly.

Polly remembered the night on the boat when Hymie had used the word "traditional" as his excuse for not marrying her, and she said dryly that she knew all about it.

Miriam caught her tone and smiled. "Of course, you do. I was never taken in by that story you were just his secretary."

"You weren't?" Polly felt herself on the point of blushing. How naive to have assumed Miriam was completely in the dark.

Miriam sipped her cognac. "I've sometimes thought if he had married you instead of me, it might have been better."

"I once would have agreed with you," Polly said, surprised by the woman's generosity. "But you were the only woman who could have kept him."

"I'm afraid he was never meant to be monogamous," Miriam said, and went on to confess that though he had always been attentive to her and a good father to the children, for years she had known she was sharing him with other women. It had almost broken up their marriage. She was in such despair over the infidelities, she had even tried an affair of her own to pay him back, but it had led to a nervous breakdown and she had gone through a long stretch of analysis. When she finished therapy not long before, she decided to leave him, but he had cried and begged her to stay, and she understood that he couldn't live without the solidity of the home she made for him. "What a masochist I used to be, but analysis cured me of that. Anyway"—and she looked at the twenty-fifth anniversary emerald on her finger—"Hymie made me a vow and everything's all right again."

Polly suppressed a feeling of skepticism, remembering how easily she had fallen for his promises herself and what they were worth. But she said nothing, and instead told Miriam about her own years of jealousy, and how stupidly self-destructive she had been because of it.

"I'm so sorry," Miriam said, placing a hand on her arm. "I wish we could have been friends through it all."

Polly smiled. "I'm not sure I was ready for it, until now."

They said good-bye out on the sidewalk, and Polly watched the handsome, immaculately dressed woman get into her limousine as the chauffeur held the door, disappearing back into her sheltered, elegant life.

There was a smell of burning leaves in the crisp air, someone cleaning up a courtyard. Joining hands with Miriam at last had completed the circle. It was absurd that she had held on to any rancor toward her or Hymie or anything that had happened. It was so much better to be beyond the turmoil of youth. This was the age she always should have been, with passions and crises behind her.

Before going back inside, she stopped to buy an afternoon paper for the art reviews. On the front page, below the usual scare headline of McCarthy's latest bombastic accusation, her old friend Paul Miller's name was listed among a group of people in television called to testify before the House Un-American Activities Committee.

HER FIRST THOUGHT WHEN SHE GOT THE SUBPOENA WAS THAT it had to be a mistake. Her name was being confused with someone else. F.B.I. agents had been snooping around the Village for months questioning people, but nobody had questioned her and why would they? She had nothing to do with politics. Besides, neither she nor her friends spied for foreign governments or conspired to overthrow the government. Even Paul Miller, who was a homegrown leftist, had never had the least interest in anything like that.

She had talked to him when he came through the city on his way to testify in Washington. The same quietly determined man he had always been, he said he had made up his mind not to cooperate with the witch-hunters in any way, no matter how intimidating they were. He was going to take the Fifth—stand on his constitutional rights not to testify against himself—even if it made him look guilty as hell.

But later, watching him being interrogated on television, her heart had gone out to him, seeing the strain in his face from holding back his anger when they badgered him and made ugly innuendos about his radical past and his associates. She called him at his hotel afterward to tell him she understood what he had gone through and that he had been magnificent. The only thing that had held him together during the ordeal, he said, was concern for his new family—his two children were the joy of his old age.

But when she studied the legal document that ordered her to appear before the House Un-American Activities Committee, she decided that she had better talk to a lawyer about it, and when she thought it over, she remembered that there was a lawyer in the family—on the Yates side. Dennis Yates had a son, Timothy, who was with a law firm down by City Hall. There were Yateses all over the place, but she had never paid much attention to that side of the family. Timothy was running for City Council—if he had any political connections at all, he might be able to get her off.

Timothy said of course he would help her, sitting her down in his modern office overlooking Foley Square.

He wasn't the least like the other Yateses. In his Brooks Brothers suit and Ivy League haircut, he might have been an ex-Harvard debater, though she had a vague memory of him winning a title as a wrestler at Fordham.

Her confidence in him was short-lived. When she insisted the subpoena had to be a mistake, he made a quick call to the Senate Office Building in Washington to check on it, then told her there was no doubt about it, she would have to appear.

"Well, I don't have the slightest intention of going," she said crossly. But then he had the nerve to tell her it wouldn't be wise not to cooperate, and she couldn't believe her ears when he parroted McCarthy's line that subversives had infiltrated every branch of the government, and that the country was ripe for a takeover if they didn't clean them out. He went on to say that if she answered the committee's questions fully and without hedging, she had nothing to worry about.

She got up and told him she'd do nothing of the kind, and she was surprised that anyone as bright as he seemed to be would go along with this witch-hunt. If it was just to get himself elected to the City Council, it was cynical, she said, and she would manage very well without him.

She was breathing hard as she left, but she still had two weeks before she was scheduled to appear, so there was plenty of time to find another lawyer.

It snowed in the night, and the next day at the gallery, after sending Frederick out to shovel off the sidewalk so he wouldn't listen in, she phoned the American Civil Liberties Union, but their lawyers were swamped with civil rights cases as it was and couldn't take her on. She was just starting to call Paul Miller in Los Angeles to recommend her a lawyer, when she heard the roar of a sports car pulling up out front and saw, of all people, Hymie Liebman getting out of a red MG with wire wheels, turning back to kiss the cheek of the attractive girl in the driver's seat who was the image of the young Miriam. He *would* buy his daughter a car like that.

Frederick held his snow shovel in midair, agog not only at the English sports car driving off, but at Hymie's expensive appearance in his homburg and topcoat with velvet collar as he strode into the gallery.

"I hope you know what I'm giving up for you, Pol," Hymie said, taking off his hat. His bald head and gray sideburns only made his mischievous dark eyes stand out more. "I've canceled appointments worth a bundle, but Miriam says I've got to see this show. Who's the artist, did she say?"

"Nobody you ever heard of," Polly lifted her cheek for him to kiss, "and you're a hero for coming. Miriam tells me how you hate the Pollock."

He went over and wrinkled his forehead at a canvas of an enormous cow skull with a desert landscape seen through the eye sockets.

"Well, what do you think?"

He smiled the old wicked smile. "You're right, I'm a dumb shmuck when it comes to modern art." He put an arm around her. "I'd rather look at you."

"Suppose I fix us some coffee instead?"

"I've got a better idea," he said. "How about coming for a walk?"

"In the snow?"

"Let's enjoy it before it turns to dog shit."

She laughed. "I'm supposed to be running a gallery."

"Can't junior outside mind the store?" He waved in Frederick whose nose was practically glued to the window.

Hardly giving her time to get into her snow things, tie a kerchief under her chin, or even advise Frederick not to spend the whole time on the phone, he led the way out the door, before she caught up with him and took his arm.

In the midst of her anxiety over the subpoena, Hymie's showing up out of the blue was just what she needed to get her mind off it. She was grateful to Miriam for sending him down, whatever the reason. Out in the icy air, their footsteps crunching through the untrampled snow, she felt lighthearted, as if they were off again on one of the old larks he used to cook up out of nothing. All the parked cars and fire hydrants were wearing snow hats, and dogs were frisking in the white fluff they couldn't understand, and lifting their legs and making yellow holes in it.

As they walked into Washington Square along an uncleared path, it was almost too much like a Grandma Moses scene in the middle of the city, with the sun glinting off icicles hanging from the branches of trees outlined with snow, and children bellywopping on sleds, their scarves colorful against the black-and-white landscape.

Hymie scooped up some snow. "What's this I hear about your commie past catching up with you?" He threw a snowball at the mottled trunk of a venerable sycamore.

"How did you know about that?"

He grinned. "Joe McCarthy tells me everything. Don't you know I'm a big shot?"

"The whole thing's ridiculous," she said, remembering that her name had been listed that day in the paper. But it was buried in the back pages and she was surprised anyone would notice it. "I can't imagine why they called me."

"You are one naive dame. No wonder you never made a cent." It was plain as the Jewish nose on his face, he said, why her name was on the list. The name of the game was to name names and somebody had named her.

"Why would anyone name me?"

"You've spent your life with oddballs in Greenwich Village, so what do you expect?"

If someone had named her as a subversive she couldn't imagine who it was, but she was annoyed with his flippancy and told him so. She let go of his arm and immediately slipped on an icy patch.

He steadied her and said he wasn't trying to be funny. "I know this is serious, Pol, and that's why I'm getting you the best lawyer in the business to see you through it."

To her surprise, she felt a tremendous sense of relief. He had always been there when she needed him. Why hadn't she gone to him in the first place and saved herself all that worry? With her arm tucked firmly into his again, they walked in the direction of New York University, ahead of the rapidly lengthening shadows of the apartment buildings behind them.

Just as she had guessed, he told her that when Miriam showed him her name in the paper at breakfast, he thought right off of coming down to see if he could help her out, for old times' sake. To tell the truth, he said, he didn't know whether she had ever been a commie or not—not that he gave a damn, and he didn't think those shmucks in Washington did either. They were just out to hog the headlines like all politicians.

She told him that she had been too surprised by the subpoena to be able to think straight. There was so much paranoia on both sides, and he was an island of sanity.

He laughed with the old boyishness and suggested that they go warm up at the Chock Full O' Nuts on the corner.

It was extraordinary that here they were, together again after all these years, she thought, sitting at the formica counter, his shoulder touching hers as he liberally spread mustard on his hot dog.

She breathed in the steam from the cup of coffee in her cold hands. "I think your daughter's lovely," she said, remembering the girl at the wheel of the MG.

He was chewing his hot dog blissfully.

"You should have brought her into the gallery. I'd love to meet her."

He looked at her, a gleam of wickedness in his eye as he licked mustard off his fingers. "Who says she's my daughter?"

With a flush, she realized her naiveté again. Poor Miriam with her emerald. He was back to his old tricks.

Whatever she expected to feel at the hearing in Washington—indignation, fear, humiliation—she felt nothing. The massive government buildings, the officialdom engulfing her from the antechamber to the hearing room with its cameras, staged chaos, scare tactics—it was hard to believe any of it was real. And she felt most unreal of all, as if she were watching it on television.

She listened to them questioning her about her involvement with the W.P.A. Arts Project . . . fund-raising for the Spanish Loyalists . . . signing petitions of all kinds, way back to Sacco-Vanzetti . . . and repeatedly asking the names of her friends. Whatever they said, she looked at them blankly, even when they called the Peacock Gallery a hotbed of subversion. She did what her lawyer advised her to do, each time repeating the odious words, "I refuse to answer on the grounds of my Fifth Amendment right against self-incrimination."

She still felt nothing as she and the lawyer made their way

through the crowd out to a taxi, newspapermen throwing questions at them and bulbs snapping.

It was on the train returning to New York that she came back to life, the consciousness of what she had been through flooding over her. She was furious and humiliated to have been treated so cheaply—used, violated in front of the whole country, before millions. And most of all, she felt alone. She longed for someone to talk to, someone who might understand how she felt, who could help her sort it out. Not Hymie—he would only try to distract her.

There was nobody—except for Paul Miller out in Los Angeles who had gone through it and also taken the Fifth just as she had, and everyone assumed he was guilty, just as they would her. Nobody understood that not answering anything was the only way to avoid smearing people you knew.

As soon as she got home, she placed a long distance call to the television studio where Paul worked. When the receptionist didn't recognize his name, she thought for a moment the worst had happened and that he had lost his job like so many others. She remembered to tell the receptionist that he was a set designer on *The Sid Caesar Show*, and would she please check again.

There was a long wait, and then Paul's familiar voice came on. "I know how you feel, Polly, but it's over and they can't hurt you any more. You're lucky about one thing, you work for yourself and can't lose your job."

She told him how relieved she was to get through to him, she was afraid he might have been blacklisted.

"It was touch and go for a while, but my lawyer says I'm okay." His voice changed. "What was so wrong with what we did back then, Polly? It was the Depression. I thought we were the good guys. They twist everything you do, and just when I was in the union, doing sets, here where I wanted to be—you'd love my kids, Polly—they tried to ruin it all. . . ." He broke off and asked her if she thought she heard a clicking on the line.

"I don't hear anything."

"I got to go, Polly," he said fast. "I got to get back to the set. . . ."

"Wait, Paul!" She tried to hold him. She wanted to go on talking. She made a joke about the two of them being "uncooperative witnesses."

But he didn't laugh. He wasn't even listening. "I just want you to know, Polly," he said, almost in a whisper, "they got all the power, I just want you to know. . . ."

After he hung up, she puzzled over what she first took to be his lack of sympathy, his erratic talk, the incompleted sentences. Everybody knew about witnesses who took the Fifth, but afterward—behind closed doors—decided to "cooperate" to save their skins, their careers, their families. She wondered, sadly, if it were possible that the man she used to tease about his fuzzy-headed plans to reform the world might have been the one to turn her in.

In the years after the war, Seth tried to get somewhere as an actor, but nothing happened. In fact, as the fifties began, he had hardly progressed beyond the productions in church halls, except for a few TV commercials and summer stock, while his wife Susan was rising rapidly at her architectural magazine from editorial assistant to becoming one of the editors herself. By twenty-five, she was already one of the top writers in her field, while Seth, nearing forty and with gray in his hair, saw his hopes for success in the theater fading.

Since Susan was making a good salary they were no longer strapped for money, even though Seth covered his own expenses with part-time office jobs. They moved from their walk-up on Sullivan Street to a smart three-room apartment on West Tenth, Susan paying for it. She demanded a decent level of comfort for herself, she said, even if he was content to live on nothing. Seth hated the new apartment and the newly acquired flair for interior decoration his clever wife brought home from the job. Everyone was impressed with her. He had married her when she was barely seventeen and he was fifteen years older, and already she had outdistanced him. Susan avoided talking about his bleak acting prospects, but he could tell by the tightness of her otherwise beautiful face whenever the subject of theater came up that she had stopped believing he was ever going to get anywhere.

He quit his part-time office job and went to work as a desk clerk at a shabby hotel nearby just off Washington Square. The hours were flexible, and the manager let him get away for casting calls and auditions. The only problem was that being turned down year after year was written all over his face, and he started to shrink from making the rounds and putting on an animation for the casting directors he didn't feel. He sometimes pretended he had an audition to go to just to impress the hotel manager, but it was worse having to kill time at Forty-second street movies. His job as desk clerk had been only a means to an end when he took it, but after he moved with Susan to the new apartment, his job became the place where he felt more at home, where he didn't feel accusing eyes watching him, impossible demands being made.

The hotel began to be the center of his world, as his acting hopes faded. On the outside, it still looked a respectable place. Its ornate, carved-granite facade and the striped awning from the entrance to the curb gave tourists the idea that it must be a charming little place to stay in the middle of the Village. Yet they no sooner came in to inquire about a room than Seth saw them take in the linoleum floor of the lobby, the prominent Coke machine, the pipe in the ceiling where the chandelier had been. And usually there was at least one resident staring at a crack in the wall, lost in a heroin stupor. The hotel was full of the deranged and the aged, many of them artists who had long given up.

Whenever he did go to try out for a part, the competition all seemed to be younger than he was, more aggressive, more talented. He showered and shaved and doused himself in after-shave lotion, but he still felt the smell of the hotel's clientele clinging to him, its reek of failure. Yet back on duty at the front desk, it was the same smell of failure, otherwise so repulsive, that began to fascinate him. The world he came from was middle-class and respectable, and if people had depraved habits, it didn't show. But in the hotel everything was in the open and it couldn't be more sordid. He came to believe that he belonged to this, more than to Susan's world of upwardly mobile, young professionals.

If he was not allowed to be part of the world of professional theater, then here was a theater of the lower depths that didn't reject him. And he—the room clerk—was at the center, not just a spectator but a participant, studying the undisguised behavior of the cast of characters for the time when he would portray them on stage.

When he and Susan were talking to each other and when their hours at home coincided, he told her about the residents of the hotel—like the scraggly-haired Beat poet who gave poetry readings in his room, ranting about his generation going insane from drugs and an insane society, to the accompaniment of a jazz clarinet. The audience bundled in heavy winter coats listened glassy-eyed, calling "go, go" to the verbal riffs that filled the room along with the marijuana smoke.

The hotel switchboard always lit up with tenants complaining about noise or heat or the plumbing and it was Seth's job to go up to check. Some of the calls were from women. He didn't tell Susan about the women. He once got called upstairs by a woman resident whose room, facing an airshaft, was stacked with her dusty oil paintings, and when he got there she was lying naked on her bed, her old sagging body hopeful. He felt sick to see her there like that, the last shreds of her dignity gone, but he couldn't forget how she looked, and the next time a woman called him to check on a leaky faucet, not much younger but in a kimono that hid her used flesh, he stayed on five minutes, almost against his will, doing what she wanted. After that, there were always women of all ages and descriptions who were ready for quick sex in their rooms.

He found he didn't want to make love to Susan any more. When he did, usually after a fight over something trivial, he was sure he smelled the presence of another man on her—men from the magazine, from the world of martini lunches at uptown restaurants she was now a part of.

One warm day when the front doors of the hotel were open to the street where sightseers were looking at the paintings lined up against the sidewalk railings in the annual Washington Square outdoor art show, a chambermaid came down to get him. That night when Susan came home from the magazine, looking cool and immaculate as always, he told her every sordid detail of what had happened. He had gone upstairs and had opened the door of the third-floor room—it smelled of stale booze—and had seen the old bum, once a famous poet in the twenties, lying on the bed with his girlfriend snoring beside him. But the poet was not snoring. He was covered with blood and his eyes were open. One of their alcoholic cronies had stabbed him to death. There was a stab wound just below the eye tattooed around his navel.

"Stop," Susan shrieked at him, covering her ears. "What's the matter with you anyway? You sound like you enjoy this whole disgusting mess you're in. You're sick!"

But it was incredible, he said. Didn't she see the dramatic possibilities in it? The man had been a great artist—Polly had known him and said women had killed themselves over him. Then the world turns its back and he destroys himself. What a play it would make! He'd give anything to do the role..

He would never play anything, she said with bitterness. He was a failure like his father, and she wanted out.

When he asked what she meant, she said she was leaving him, that's what she meant. She then packed a bag and told him that when she came back the next day, she didn't want him there. It was her apartment.

His flimsy defenses began to crack. Maybe their marriage hadn't been going too well, but if they broke up, there was only the sordid life of the hotel. He got scared. "We could start over. We'll go to Hollywood where I can get work as an extra. I know some people out there. They'll get me in. I don't need Broadway."

But she only laughed at him—an ugly laugh—and told him he could go to Hollywood if he liked, to a nuthouse for all she cared, but she was sick to death of all his fantasies of what he was never going to do.

She left, and he began to shake uncontrollably. The fantasy of the theater had been dying for a long time, now she had demolished it— only her presence had kept him from falling apart. Terrified by the void opening up around him, he rushed out to look for her, to beg her to come back and put him together again.

But he didn't find her. Instead, a policeman found him walking barefoot up Eighth Avenue at four in the morning, raging to the world at the top of his voice that he never had a chance, that it wasn't fair, and blubbering like a baby. And when the policeman didn't smell liquor on his breath, he sent him to Bellevue.

They kept him there in a ward with bars on the windows and attendants who administered sedatives every time he became conscious and started to cry.

* * *

They were going to send him upstate, commit him to another institution. He heard them talking about it, a doctor and a couple of attendants at the foot of his bed, though he kept his eyes shut, pretending to be asleep.

His mind was immediately clear. He stole a dime out of the bedside drawer of the patient next to him and called his aunt on a public phone and told her where he was.

Then he was in a quiet room in St. Vincent's Hospital, the tumult of his emotions over as he lay there listlessly, watching the traffic below on Seventh Avenue.

Polly sat beside him. She came every day, bringing him tidbits to tempt him to eat—cottage cheese and ice cream and pieces of fruit. She was looking older, tired, though she spoke brightly about his being discharged soon and coming to stay with her. Trying her best to be cheerful, but he wasn't fooled. Life wasn't so easy for her any more, not since the harassment in Washington. The art critics had stopped coming down to her gallery after the papers printed the story. Her best painters had moved uptown to better galleries. The painters she showed now were getting old like she was and their work was out of fashion, and nobody came to the openings but relatives and friends.

"It's been a while since I've been connected to the theater," she was saying brightly, as her hand fiddled with the ceramic beads around her neck, "but I know the man who runs the Provincetown Theater on MacDougal Street. Of course, it's not the same theater I was with—that was torn down—but still, if there was something for you, it could be a showcase."

"Polly, please," he said, annoyed at her nervous fingering of the clunky beads. "I'm not an actor any more, can't you see? An actor acts." He had resolved not to unburden himself on anyone, yet her attempts to cheer him up got on his nerves. "I'm a failure, a complete failure—just like Gene was. Like father, like son."

"What are you saying?" she burst out with a vehemence that surprised him. "Gene was no failure. You may think of yourself as a failure if you want, but Gene wasn't, and don't you ever say that again. Gene was a talented writer, and his tragedy was only that he was cut down in his prime. Don't you remember his play?"

"*The Weak and the Strong?* I loved it once because it brought me to the theater, but it would be pretty dated stuff today."

"That's not true. It's still a fine play. I'll show you."

She brought the old manuscript to him the next day. She

had kept it in a box under her bed with all his father's other writings. Seth was impressed by her fierce loyalty and pretended to go along with her, scanning the opening pages as she sat there watching. But as half-remembered lines jumped up at him, he began to read it more seriously. The excitement of the production at the Cherry Lane all those years ago came back. The play was not just a nostalgia piece. He started reading it out loud, and Polly came over to sit beside him on the bed and they read it together, Seth stopping to call her attention to ideas in the play that were still pertinent, to the poetic use of language, to the sharp delineation of the leading character—the exile who was coming back from the dead.

"What a role!" he said, when they finished. "I'd give anything to have played it. I mean, there are some dated references, the title's all wrong, but it's powerful."

"I told you," she said.

"It's got some of the quality of *Streetcar*. I think it could almost go today. Of course, it would take an intelligent director, and the actor in the lead would have to have the experience to know how to bring it off."

"You could do it." She had stopped fingering her beads.

"I almost think I could. The guy ought to be played by someone my age."

"Then why don't you put it on yourself?"

He loved the way she always bounced back. She was indomitable. "My dear aunt, you're forgetting a few little things such as producer and money, theater and money, director and money."

Polly didn't see why they should be such obstacles. Back in the days when she was working for the Provincetown, they hadn't waited for Broadway to come along and offer them anything. They did it all themselves, putting together everything on a shoestring. "They ignored us for a while, but we got them to pay attention at last. We gave them O'Neill."

It was a different situation then, he said. New York had been a simpler place. People could get together and put things on without much money. There wasn't any possibility of theater in the Village nowadays, not real theater. It was all Broadway and that took big money and contacts, and he was finally ready to admit that there was no place for him in any of it.

"Never mind all that pessimism," she said. If she could get some money together, wouldn't it be possible to put on the play, at least for a short run?

He knew well enough she was only encouraging him this way because she wanted him to be well again, but how full of energy she was all of a sudden, sitting up in her chair, her animation making her look years younger than her mid-sixties, like he remembered her after the war when the Peacock was going great guns and she was in the thick of the art world. She must have seen his look, because she repeated, "But maybe I can get the money."

And she did. She came back the next day to say she had it. She had gone to Hymie Liebman. He and his wife were living in a penthouse atop a high-rise building on Greenwich Avenue he had put up. Much too elaborately furnished for her taste, she said, with a garden on the terrace and a spectacular view of the Hudson—it belonged on the Upper East Side, not the Village, but never mind, the Pollock still looked good.

Hymie had scotched her idea of taking out another mortgage on the Perry Street house—it was mortgaged to the hilt already. And as far as his sinking money into some play to be put on in the Village *or* on Broadway, she must have more wires loose than he already thought.

But his wife Miriam had thought the play a wonderful idea and it would give her something to do. She was going to put up the money herself, and she and Polly would co-produce it.

"You must be crazy," Seth said admiringly. But Polly brought Miriam to the hospital to meet him, and they read the play again, and he immediately saw how to make the necessary changes to bring it up-to-date—a new title to start with, then move it up from after the First World War to Paris in the late forties. And when Seth left the hospital, he showed the play to an out-of-work director he knew and they got a cast together. Polly's friend at the Provincetown Playhouse rented it to them for three weeks between scheduled productions, and Seth went to work.

Under the title *Night Falls with the Sound of Guitars,* the play opened on a September night in 1955, eighteen years after its abortive run in the Depression. As before, no critics showed up, but Villagers came, attracted by the title, and told their friends. The audiences were sparse until a critic from one of the uptown papers came the second week and reviewed it favorably. The next night the *Times* and the *Tribune* came. Their reviews were even better, and people who did not ordinarily go to the Village came down to see it.

At the end of the three weeks the run was extended, the

manager of the theater having canceled the play that was to follow it.

Several Broadway producers had already shown interest in Seth, when a scout for a movie studio saw the play and got him to test for the lead role in a film version of O'Neill's *The Iceman Cometh*. The part was made for him, a middle-aged man in a phantasmagorical world of derelicts and dreamers. When he was signed for the part, his picture appeared on the movie page of the *Times* over the caption, "An Actor's Life Begins at 40."

1975

THROUGH THE OPEN WINDOWS OF THE FRONT APARTMENT, a radio was blaring out minute-by-minute coverage of the helicopter retreat from the roof of the embassy in Saigon. Sitting in his usual place on top of one of the garbage cans on the sidewalk where he could keep an eye on the whole of Perry Street, Frank Alfano, the super, chewed on his toothpick impatiently. Hadn't he been saying for years to drop the bomb on them? If they had listened to him, this never would have happened. "Hey, doll, turn it down," he yelled over his shoulder to the girl who lived in the apartment. "Do we have to have our noses rubbed in it?"

But she did not turn it down. She was probably too deep in her art-work or too stoned to hear anything except a phone call from one of her hippie boyfriends. It was like one of them was coming in the door while the last one was going out the window. He was always telling her that if she'd ever seen him in his marine uniform with his Silver Star, she'd go for him like all of them used to. Regretfully, he rubbed a thick hand over his thinning hair and shifted his heavy body. He was sweaty in his work clothes. The sun was hot for May.

The sanitation truck was coming down the street and he got up and started lugging the garbage cans over to the curb. He was the only super on the block who thought about making it easier for the sanitation guys, but he knew what it was like. He had once had a job carting trash himself, among all the other jobs. That was before the car-wash place where he was working caused him all the trouble. He had tried to explain that he had only borrowed that money from the cash register to pay the bills his last wife had stuck him with when she walked out.

Polly was the only one who had written him back when he was doing time in the road camp out west. He hadn't gotten a single line from his brother—him and his fat-assed wife out in Jersey, too busy living it up on all their millions from the electronics business. When he got out, Polly had arranged for him to have the job of superintendent of the Perry Street house, which included an apartment in the basement, and sent him a bus ticket home.

This last year, since her broken hip, she wasn't as strong as she used to be, and he was glad he was able to look after her to pay her back a little for all she had done for him. She was the only one he cared about. It made him sick to think she was going away.

The garbage truck stopped in front of the house and the grinder churned as a sanitation worker dumped the garbage into it. But instead of tossing Frank the empty cans to catch as usual, he slid them over noisily on the pavement.

"What'sa matter, too much pussy last night?" Frank kidded him, as he pulled the cans on to the sidewalk.

"I don't get to sit around on my *tokus* like you, Frank," the young sanitation worker kidded back as he jumped onto the running board of the truck starting down the street.

Frank gave a gravelly chuckle and assembled his empty cans back in place by the iron gate, replacing the lids attached by chains to the railing, before he settled down again with his toothpick. In the wake of the garbage pickup, empty garbage cans and lids littered the sidewalks up and down the block.

With the war news still blasting from the front apartment, it was a moment before he heard the wavering voice calling him. It was his aunt, who had come out on the stoop to ask him to help her with something. She'd been going through her things for weeks, sorting and disposing, getting ready to leave for California to live with Seth.

He scolded her as he got up. "You're supposed to be takin it easy. Everything's done. You got a long trip ahead of you tonight."

"I've found a whole carton of things I overlooked," Polly

said. She pulled her cardigan around her as she turned back into the house.

Frank's bad knee throbbed as he hurried up the stoop to follow her in. It was hard to believe she had broken her hip the winter before, the way she walked so briskly ahead of him back to her door, though her ankles were bone thin and her white hair wispy. Under her sweater she could hardly weigh more than ninety pounds.

Behind her glasses her eyes still flickered with the old gaiety as she turned to him and said, "Seth will be here before we know it. I've got so much to do yet."

"Aw, you got plenty of time," he said in a voice made even more gravelly by his concern over her departure. "Why don't you just take it easy?"

His aunt had spent six weeks in a nursing home until her hip healed, and that was what led her to her decision to move out to her nephew's, Seth Harris, in California. Frank was no good with words and couldn't make her understand that he would take care of her when she needed it, he'd do everything for her. But she was stubborn as a mule. She had told him she didn't want to wake up and find herself in a nursing home again, and just because she was as old as the hills—she was eighty-seven, a ridiculous age for anyone to be, she said—was no reason she couldn't try someplace new.

In her room, she directed him to pull out a carton from under the daybed she slept on. "I was sweeping out just now when I came upon it. God knows what's in it."

Feeling his bad knee throb, he got down on the floor and pulled out the dusty carton and set it over on the seat of the bay window. Even with the windows open onto the backyard where the ailanthus trees were in new leaf for another spring and a lilac bush had managed to bloom, he still smelled cat in the room. She had two of them, and a cat carrier was waiting to go beside her suitcases. The cats were hiding, Polly told him, sensing something was afoot. He hated to see her apartment with all the pictures down, leaving faded patches on the walls, and most of the furniture gone. The place already looked abandoned and so small he wondered how she had ever crammed so much into it. Cartons filled with junk she was leaving behind were stacked by the door. She had made him promise to put them all out at least a day before the garbage pickup. They were the kinds of odds and ends that Villagers would enjoy going through, she said.

She had already given away all kinds of things to her special friends in the building, the man-crazy artist chick in the front apartment, and a long-haired kid who lived upstairs and came in at all hours of the night. Those two sometimes took her out to the theater and art galleries, but it was Frank who did the heavy stuff for her like cleaning and shopping when the weather was bad.

Polly was running a dustrag over the top of the carton. "I do hope none of this is anything I want to keep. There's not another inch of space in my luggage." She folded back the cardboard flaps.

"Can I help you with that?" Frank stood by feeling helpless and awkward, as he always did around his indomitable little aunt. He couldn't stand to see her going off forever. He swallowed, afraid he might break down and bawl.

She pulled an old book from the carton and her eyes lit up behind her glasses. "I wondered where this had gone!"

He waited a little while longer, but when she failed to respond to him in her preoccupation, he felt too upset to hang around and went out.

Polly sat down in the bay window, caressing the old copy of *Tortured Souls*. Its magenta cover was faded, but the shiny green lettering still reflected the light. She had put it away at the time of Eugene's death.

She held it up and smelled the fine-quality paper and admired the handsomeness of the typeface. The ink Gene had used writing an inscription to her on the flyleaf was faded too, although once it had been a daring violet—the color had seemed so appropriate in that long ego era. They had all tried to be so sophisticated then.

> Polly dearest, here is the first of my achievements, *at last*, but nothing I write in the future, and let's hope there'll be a shelf of them, will ever come more from the heart. Love, Gene.

She smiled, remembering. Of course she had to take it with her. She went over to put it in an open suitcase, but it was jammed. On the very top lay a poster of Timothy Yates for mayor that she wanted to show to Seth's family. Her lawyer-nephew's face was pasted up all over town. Although they often didn't agree politically, she was sorry she was going to miss the excitement of the election. She'd have to repack the whole bag to get Gene's book in somehow without bending the poster.

Rummaging through the contents of the carton again, she came across a handful of theater programs for *Night Falls with the Sound of Guitars*. Once, years after, José Quintero had confessed to her that it was that production that gave him the idea of starting his Circle in the Square Theater, because it had shown him that audiences and critics were ready to come down to the Village again for a serious play. But the birth of Off-Broadway had not been her motive in mounting that production—it was to save Seth, and it had accomplished its purpose. She had always been thankful. It had given him his chance at Hollywood, though he hadn't become a movie star after all. It was just at that time that the old studio system was falling apart, and *Iceman* had never been released.

But the move out there had been a good thing for him. He had become a producer in a company making TV commercials, and his second wife was less trouble for him than mentally restless Susan Schlesinger had been. Seth didn't need anyone with that kind of brain. He had married just the right woman for him, one of those tanned, perfectly groomed Southern California women who was satisfied with domesticity.

He had never really belonged in New York. He had a vulnerability about him, lacking a certain tough resourcefulness of the Villagers she knew, like the young tenant from the front apartment who was always coming in to talk about her men and the various therapies she was in. The girl managed to find all kinds of free-lance jobs to support her painting—posing for art classes, decorating local shop windows, silk-screening rock-music posters. Like they'd done back in her time.

Her other special friend in the house, who lived above her, was just as inventive. He was one of the young men who had stood up to the police at the raid on the Stonewall Tavern, and didn't let anyone tell him how to run his life. He did street theater, worked as a waiter, and even sold handmade jewelry on the sidewalks. Sometimes, if he saw a light under her door when he got home in the wee hours—and it was usually around dawn—he would stop by and share his pastrami sandwich and coffee from an all-night deli. He wore his long hair in a headband and a gold wire in one earlobe and always made her feel gay on her insomniac nights with his flamboyant banter and talk about his nocturnal adventures. It was all so different for him than it had been for Gene. That was one way the world had improved at least.

She started throwing a lot of inconsequential souvenirs from the carton into a box of trash. Until now, she could never have imagined living anywhere else but the Village. She didn't really want to go to California all that much, but she was hoping the little bungalow in the backyard of Seth's house in Santa Monica would make more sense for her at her age. She'd still be independent, but he and his wife would be there to help her if she needed them. And there were no steps to climb, no risk of her breaking another hip on the ice, no danger of another nursing home. It might be deader than a doornail out there, but there was sun and this old house was always chilly, even on a warm day like this. She'd never felt the chill until the last few years. That sunshine would feel good, even if her mind did turn into a vegetable.

She cheered up when she found in the box a postcard with Zoran's illegible scrawl, written in 1940. The mad Hungarian cook from the teashop had had a great success on the coast as a cult leader. The picture on the card showed an odd circular structure in pink stucco with neon over the door spelling out "Temple of Divine Love," built for him by his adoring followers. If he were still out there, he'd be able to keep her blood perking all right, but he had been dead for years. She had gone to look him up once on a trip out west. That was after she had visited Hymie and Miriam in Arizona where they had retired after Hymie's stroke. The pink stucco temple had been turned into a supermarket.

She sighed, and leaned the postcard against the window frame. Everyone she had known seemed to be dead now—all her contemporaries, friends in the Village, in the New York art world, in the theater. She seemed to have outlived everybody, lived so many lifetimes. It had been a complete lifetime in itself since giving up on the gallery, after that mindless Pop Art came in, ruining everything, and even the collectors who were her mainstay wanted to throw their money away on it. Well, she hoped they had learned their lesson. Most of that junk must have been relegated to their basements by now.

After she had to close the gallery came the period of black voter registration in the South and she had gone on a Freedom Ride. And then there was the anti-war movement and she was busy with read-ins, talk-ins, and teach-ins. She had been eighty at the time and one of the newspapers had written her up as the little old lady who wouldn't quit. Thank God the country was out of that mess at last. She didn't intend to stay idle in California either.

Beneath the jumble of odds and ends at the very bottom of the carton, she found a peeling, leather-bound portfolio. It was a book her grandfather had printed back in the eighties, *The Legend of Greenwich Village*. She got it out of the box and opened it in her lap. She'd forgotten how striking the old lithographs were. An artist friend of her grandfather's, Albert Cogswell, had done them. Her mother had always described him as "a bearded, homegrown Rousseau," with bushy hair as red as her own. She remembered having seen an old photograph of him and his kindly face had stayed in her mind.

Her two cats came out from under the bed and set up a racket beside their bowls. She had forgotten all about them. What was she doing sitting here musing like an addlebrained old bag? She'd better feed them right now, since they'd be cooped up in their carryall on the plane for hours, and she had all kinds of things left to do before Seth got here. Every time she looked at the clock, it seemed she had less time.

But when she got everything done she could think of, there were still hours to go. She thought of going for a walk to take a last look around, but there was the front stoop up and down, and she didn't want to tire herself out before the plane. She sat down in an armchair in the bay window, picking up *The Legend of Greenwich Village* again, intending to study Cogswell's litho technique in the good north light. But the book was soon forgotten on her lap, and she found herself looking out on the small sooty backyard that never got quite enough sun to flourish. All the extravagant flowers and greenery of the California lotus land she was going to would never mean anything compared to this. Her eyes lingered on the scrubby ailanthus trees, their twisted trunks etched against the sharp sunlight on the brickwork of the opposite houses. No matter how many seasons she had watched the miracle of the delicate green clusters of new leaves through this very window, they never failed to fill her with joy.

And that was where Frank found her when he came to bring her a container of coffee—huddled lifeless in her chair, the portfolio of her unknown father's fallen to the floor.

After the ambulance had taken her away, the police hung around a few more minutes to finish filling out some forms.

Her friend, the girl in the front apartment, wasn't there—she was delivering a commercial art job in the garment center. And the long-haired young man who brought her pastrami sandwiches had stayed out all night and wasn't back yet either. Two other tenants exchanged words by the newel post at the foot of the stairs about what a nice person she had been and how lucky it was she had gone so quickly and without any pain, but they hadn't known her very well and they had to get back to their own work. The cats, spooked by all the confusion, had gone back into hiding behind the waiting suitcases and the cartons of thrown-out junk and didn't come out again until the tramping of strange feet ceased.

To keep himself busy as he waited for Seth to arrive from the plane, Frank swept the steps and the front walk. He swore automatically as he went over to pick up a soda can that someone had dropped around one of the young trees the city had recently planted up and down the block. Finally, taking a rumpled handkerchief from a back pocket, he mopped his brow and sat down to wait in his usual place on the lid of one of the garbage cans in front of the house.

The late afternoon sun had gone behind the row of houses across the way and cast a shadow that was a relief from the day's glare, as he kept watch on the nearly deserted street. A rock group could be heard rehearsing somewhere down the block. In one of the neighboring houses, a soprano practiced scales. A typewriter was clacking away.

The late sun lit the upper windows of the old Endicott house with a harsh fire, but as Frank waited below in the deepening shadow, the sun's glare above him gradually changed to a softer orange, a light that shimmered on the glass, that gave the illusion in the shimmering of things that weren't there. For a moment, at one of the windows of the old master bedroom on the second floor, it almost appeared that a woman in a nightdress looked out with wild eyes and tangled hair.